PEREGRINE:

The Ceremony of Powers

Book I of the Peregrine Series

CAROLE DI TOSTI

Peregrine: The Ceremony of Powers
Published: January 2021
Printed in the United States of America
ISBN: 978-1-7359752-0-7

This book was published by A Priori Publishing.

For Dakota, Dom, Dylan

ACKNOWLEDGEMENTS

After I completed my first novel, *Peregrine: The Ceremony of Powers*, I continued to publish articles in various blogs. I did freelance work for which I was paid, contributed to *Technorati.com* and *Blogcritics.org* where I concentrated on theater and film criticism in earnest. *Peregrine: The Ceremony of Powers* sat percolating, while I published in other genres and outlets. I was undecided about the future of *Peregrine*. Should I look for an agent, submit to small presses, or something else?

It was a two-week residency at the Tyrone Guthrie Centre in Annaghmakerrig, in Ireland that provided the grist for my decision. As I worked on a film review and interviewed the artists and writers in residence for a feature article I intended to publish, I spoke with authors who had self-published or obtained agents. They were thrilled about the results they achieved. Our discussions gave me the inspiration to follow their lead.

I am forever grateful to the Tyrone Guthrie Centre and the nation of Ireland for its support of artists in all areas. The warm staff at Tyrone Guthrie did their utmost to provide a place where creativity flourished. The residents' encouragement and advice helped me get *Peregrine: The Ceremony of Powers* published. The Tyrone Guthrie Centre continues to be a wellspring for Irish and international artists who work to find their voices and evolve their expression in a place that appreciates individuality and uniqueness.

The young may die, but the old must."
—Henry Wadsworth Longfellow

"What lies behind us and what lies before us
are tiny matters compared to what lies
within us."
—Ralph Waldo Emerson

CONTENTS

THE CRYPT

Chapter One

THE ATMOSPHERE IN THE CRYPT was an eerie presence, invisible yet palpable. Peregrine Randolf lifted her arms, stretching her palms into the grey-black shadows. She read the air with her fingertips. Oppressive, heavy like a fog, it swirled and seeped, oozing cold and damp. She lowered her arms and faced the sliver of moonlight reflected in a thin, pale, blue strip outlining the massive, heavy, oak and bronze banded door. To deceive intruders she had left it open a crack and that tiny moonbeam was the only light they could work by until the ceremony.

She had turned up the ancient ceiling light moments before. Sounding like a hundred insects simultaneously immolated by a bug zapper, it crackled and sizzled, then flared out. Peering through the grey-blackness for another switch, she had seen none. Hardly seemed like a coincidence, this bad beginning for a momentous occasion. A stirring chill gripped Peregrine, encircling her shoulders. She shook it off. There were worse places to be than this crypt, waiting for Fen and Mocha. There were worse places to be while waiting to change one's life. And there were worse places to die.

Peregrine untangled herself from the straps and lowered her backpack, filled with tools and artifacts to the concrete floor, where they settled and clanged into their own disorganized heap. The care-worn pack that had solidly lain across her lean back muscles was burdensome. From where the cab dropped her off by the parking lot, she had carried it all that distance up and down the labyrinthine paths of Old Calvary Cemetery in Queens, New York to her family's mausoleum. She needed a rest. The contents would be safe on the concrete floor which appeared dry. She had wrapped the delicate phylacteries in bubble wrap before she put them in the pack, so the long trek wouldn't damage them. If the arcane, ancestral items remained unused for a while longer, so be it. For a very long time, no relative had employed these artifacts in the way that she, Fen and Mocha would employ them. What were a few more minutes?

Days before her Aunt Rachel died, she had shown Peregrine the forbidden relics passed down to sisters Madeline and Rachel from their Black Nobility ancestors. Aunt Rachel had promised that Peregrine would be able to activate their supernatural powers when she was of age, and the conditions were appropriate in the ancestral mausoleum. Well, Peregrine had forced the time. Unable to confide in Madeline, her mother, or ask her permission fearing she wouldn't understand, Peregrine had snatched the antiquities from the safe in the hidden room in Madeline's closet. She would be the first of her generation to anoint herself with the oil, the first to wear the priest's garments and amulets, the first to utter the ancient words from the journal and invoke the powers. Mocha and Fen would assist her.

That is if Fen and Mo ever got there. Peregrine sighed. Some things never changed, no matter how momentous the occasion or how serious the undertaking. Mocha would probably be late. She was always late. And Fen was probably tied up with Manny, though he had said that Flavia had promised to watch his brother. Poor Manny. Poor Fen. Fen, the younger, responsible for Manny, the older.

Peregrine bent down and felt for the side pocket of the pack. Her eyes had become accustomed to the dimness illuminated by the shard of moonlight. Even so, she couldn't make out the details, only vast generalities through the shadows and blackness. She pulled out a pack of gum and stood up quickly, tearing at the wrapper to deliver herself a slice. Peppermint. She had stopped smoking a month ago, but every time she felt anxious or nervous, the cravings overwhelmed her. Gum was an unsatisfactory if workable substitute, though she was tempted to try her mother's stash of nicotine patches. But they didn't work for her mom who was a rainy-day smoker. They probably wouldn't work for her either. It was better to end it in an extreme act- quit cold turkey. Peregrine believed in doing the extreme. Like tonight.

Someone pounded on the unwieldy, wooden door, startling Peregrine. It wasn't the signal she had worked out with Fen and Mocha. Peregrine's initial relief churned into anxiety. Convolutions of fear snatched her logic like a whirlwind snatching roof shingles. If it wasn't Fen or Mocha, who was it? The gangs who raided tombs for corpses, jewels and valuable carved stone statues? The police? She shouldn't be here. No one should be here. It was past midnight!

The pounding resumed, booming echoes in the crypt. In a desperate panic, unable to see through the grey-black mountains of darkness, she sidled two steps to the right and stumbled over the back-pack. Stupid. She regained her balance and breathed deeply. With fresh determination, she ignored the bellowing thumps at the door, bent down and grasped the sides of the pack to center herself in the disorienting dark. Ripping open the top flap, she reached inside and grabbed the crowbar. Raising herself, she swung away from the pack and leaped toward the splinter of moonlight with the implement in her left hand.

It had to be the night raiders. She must be the first to attack. Adrenaline rushed through her limbs as she jumped to the door to compel the resistant mass of oak and bronze. She inserted the crowbar in the tiny opening, and with all her strength and determination, hurled back the massive block of oak. "Stand back. I'm armed."

"What the hell?" Thrown off balance, Mocha fell to her knees on the dusty, grey concrete floor. "Damn you, girl! Mocha hissed. "Can't you see it's me?" She lightly lifted herself up from her sprawl and brushed off her hands.

Relief cooled the fires in Peregrine's blood. Her beautiful friend had finally arrived. "Sorry," Peregrine grinned and hugged Mocha. Both stood in blue moonlight on the door's threshold. Their casting shadows merged with the darkness inside the crypt.

"The signal was supposed to be four, three, four," Peregrine chided.

"You should have seen your face." Mocha laughed. "In all the years I've known you, I've never seen you so frightened. Remember, we agreed to pound ten times, then stop, then ten times more?"

Peregrine was sheepish. "Yeah. Well, I don't know what happened. It was dark. I was alone." Peregrine realized what happened and said, "My imagination distracted me. It was hard to keep focused. It's a creepy place."

Mocha lightened her friend's mood with a familiar repartee. "You're as necessary as a condom in a fertility clinic."

"As oil on a fire."

"As drought to a farmer."

"As Cialis to a stallion."

Peregrine broke away from her friend. She peered around the right corner column, one of four that held up the intricate and ornately carved stone frieze. Scanning the length of the building, she checked for interlopers. "I thought you were the police."

"Not me, girl. One is enough in the family. Perish the thought." Mocha gripped the door with both hands and motioned for Peregrine to help her. Together, they grunted and pushed until the oak and bronze slab was a hair's width away from its housing. The light evaporated except for a pale blue crease edging the doorjamb, where the door was open. The tall, slim, brown- haired, twenty-four year old and her curvy, light skinned, hazel-eyed friend of the same age retreated from the warmth of the summer night and paced deeper into the cool shadows of the large, main room of the dead house.

"You're sure no one followed you?"

"They're coming, the vampires and the ghouls and the haunts." Mocha stretched out her arms like the mummy in the Boris Karloff film. Haltingly, with infirm gait, she shuffled and dragged herself to Peregrine, clasped her neck with both hands and rocked her back and forth, growling incoherently.

Peregrine shook free, laughing. "You can't frighten me. I'm ready to face whatever happens. I prayed for strength."

Mocha released her friend's neck and chided her. "Yeah? Why ask me a question like that? Like I said when we planned this night, we can't operate in fear. Fear destroys faith. Fear is living destruction. Faith is living creation. It materializes goals. Now turn on the lights, so I can get situated while we wait for Fen."

"Burned out," said Peregrine sardonically, "like your lame rap about fear."

"And we're supposed to make preparations with no light? You've been drinking absinthe again and are dither headed." Mocha snorted.

She was referring to the time they had gone to an upper east side New York party, where bottles of the liqueur, illegal at the time, had been passed around. As Mocha watched, a posh, dreamy-looking older man extended his manicured hand to offer her stunning friend a brandy snifter. Despite Mocha's vociferous warnings, Peregrine smiled and took the elegant glass, batting her eyelashes at him, as he gave a generous pour of the green magic. With a chic pose, she guzzled it down between three deep, swift hits on a rope of hash, then hallucinated skulls. Peregrine spent the rest of the evening like a clown, spread eagled on an antique settee. She had passed out with her mouth opened, loudly sucking in and snorting out air with drool foaming on her lips. The next day, Peregrine woke up at Mocha's, mortally hung over and enraged at herself, swearing she would never be so stupid again.

"Yes. It's become my passion in life to paint the perfect skull, while I'm unconscious." Impatient, she said, "Did you bring the candles?" Peregrine didn't remember seeing anything in Mocha's hands when her friend fell forward on the concrete.

"In my back pockets. Flashlights would have worked here, but you are such a traditionalist. It has to be the ancient way. Can't we open the door, so we at least can see?"

Mocha stood near the back-pack and tried to tune her eyesight to a more comfortable precision.

"No. The gangs could be alerted. And then what? We'd be at their mercy. No thanks." The thought of mixing it up with the ruthless crypt gangs made her headachy. She changed the subject. "Fen is bringing that old oil lamp to locate the names on the wall of drawers. Once we find the coffins of the healer and the prophet, we'll begin the ceremony with the sanctified candles. They're not meant to be used for frivolous purposes. And you know that the laws of the ceremony instruct that nothing modern, like electricity, is to be used."

"Yeah. Right. I forgot that seeing is frivolous." Mocha bowed ironically, "Yes, Madam High Priestess." She hesitated. "Are you sure you've told me everything about this place?"

"I told you what my Aunt Rachel knew, which wasn't very much. The place could be booby-trapped, rigged against intruders, a killing field for the uninitiated."

"How encouraging. Your words inspire me." Mocha's sarcasm morphed into a Peregrine imitation. "You can't frighten me. I'm ready for whatever happens. I prayed for strength."

Peregrine smiled. She was grateful her friend had finally arrived. The long wait in the dark crypt had capsized her emotions into the fright zone.

She would not have been able to stay there a minute more without being overwhelmed. Now, if only Fen would show up, she would return to her calm state, and they could begin.

Both of the young women took hesitant steps into the tomb's dark heart in the center of the main room. They were aware of the soft sound of their echoing pace and the musty smell of ancient air and dampness and mold, though there was no evidence of water, only the moisture in the ambient atmosphere. They listened, then ceased their shuffling. Pleasant silence. Unnerving silence. Something was wrong. They were enveloped in a blackness that was too black, too dense. Peregrine spun around to locate the lighted outline of the door. Total darkness. The door had shut completely against them. "Oh, God."

Confused by the sudden blackness, Mocha turned and saw the problem. "We left it open. You saw the latch didn't click." Mocha was apoplectic. "It was stuck. The wind must have blown it shut."

"What wind? There's not even a breeze. It's as breezeless as a vacuum." Peregrine groaned aloud. She hated the darkness. As far back as she could remember, she always slept with the small desk lamp lit in her bedroom. As a three-year old, she had bawled and fussed if her mother intentionally forgot to turn it on as she was readied for bed. Peregrine searched her left pocket for the ornate bronze key to the crypt door, then her right pocket. "And it would take a hurricane to push that heavy door shut." She steeled her nerves and thrust away the growing fear that crept up her throat. "Anyway, it doesn't matter how it closed. We have to deal." She tried to sound confident.

"Use your key, and it'll pop open," Mocha said feeling guilty, though she refused to believe she was responsible for this current wrinkle in their plans.

Blind in the darkness, footfalls scraping the concrete, arms and hands outstretched, seeking the door's rough surface, Peregrine scuttled forward. She grappled through her pockets and the waist of her jeans. "Don't get mad. I can't find the key." Peregrine tried to calm her own inner hysteria.

"What?" Mocha shouted crazily. "Damn you, girl. Don't play me like that. Come on open it."

With a measured voice, Peregrine spoke each syllable separately. "I cannot find the key." Then she said rapidly to get it out, "I left it outside, I think."

Mocha knew her friend was upset, but she was more upset. Her anger spilled, flowing over her victim. "You think? You think? Christ, Peregrine. All right. Review what you did. What did you do first?"

Out of habit, Peregrine closed her eyes to visualize her movements, though the darkness was black enough to serve as shut eyelids. In her imagination, she replayed the previous hour. "After I turned the lock and heard the click, there was a rustling in the hedges on the side of the crypt. I got scared. I didn't want to be seen, and I thought it might be the police or gangs, so I moved fast. I didn't have the strength to open the door. It was stuck. I used the crowbar as a lever to pry it open and quickly got inside. I left it open a hair's breadth for you."

"Think," said Mocha, teasing the vision from her friend's mind. "Did you put the key in your pocket or leave it outside?"

Peregrine considered, paused and reconsidered. She detoured around Mocha's question. "You know, I don't think you can use a key from the inside to get out. I think you have to open the door another way from the inside. Check if you don't believe me. It's a bronze door, lined and fortified with solid oak and bronze strips from within. No keyhole. Must have cost a fortune." Peregrine babbled to calm her nerves. "But you know, the family is incredibly rich. Their wealth extends back to European nobility and banking houses for twenty generations. Black Nobility. My Aunt Rachel said the crypt was used for ceremonial rituals and other purposes, in addition to being a resting place for our ancestors. I mean the mausoleum is custom made, no expense spared. You can see that, can't you?"

"No, actually, I can't see a bloody thing." Mocha was exasperated by Peregrine's empty ramblings, which she had heard countless times. She sidled next to her friend and asked the question again. "Did you put the key in your pocket or leave it outside?"

"My mind's a blank. I was in such a hurry I did it unconsciously. I can't remember."

Together they searched for a keyhole. There wasn't any.

Peregrine sighed. "You see, it doesn't matter if I left it outside. We couldn't use it in here anyway. Damn, I hope I can find it. I have to return it to my mom's safe with the other relics. She will be so pissed if she finds out I took it."

"I know." Mocha raised her eyebrows. "You aren't supposed to touch any of this or even be here until you're twenty-five, can't handle the responsibility. Ummmm. Hmmmm."

"Two words are what I have for you. Shut up!" She popped the "p" emphasizing its plosive sound. Peregrine felt for the seam where the door met the wall in the hope of using her fingers to press it away from the jamb if possible. The door was secured. In mindless frustration, she pounded and slapped at the wood with open palms. Mocha joined with her fists. Their thumping marauded the silence.

"It won't budge." Mocha stepped back, reorienting her breathing.

"Help me look for a handle or door knob." Inching her fingers and palms along the grooves of wood and metal, Peregrine searched for a crack, a seam, a pull, a chain, a rope, a switch, a button, anything. Mocha took her turn, retracing Peregrine's movements. The door was impassive and solid-a silent, unsolvable mystery, as if it had never been opened and they were in a hermetically sealed chamber.

"No handle, no knob, nothing. Now what?" Peregrine wailed. "If we can't open it from the inside, Fen will have to find the key and open it from the outside."

"And if Fen can't find the key?" Mocha's voice was low and dry, as if she had swallowed cotton.

"Then he'll have to get help, and there'll be no ceremony." Peregrine paused, "If he comes." She was beginning to think something had happened. He never let them down. "And if he doesn't come, we are so absolutely screwed. I don't want to think about it." Standing with her back to the door, she bent her right knee and backward kicked the door, hitting it with fury.

Mocha shook her head to reject Peregrine's words, but they gnawed at her like starving rats seeking flesh. "No! We did not just get slapped with a one-way ticket to Hell. No, no, no. Let me think." Mocha breathed deeply to stave off the panic assaulting her rationality. "The crowbar."

"Damn." Peregrine shook her head. "To use it, the door must be unlocked. Even with it open, I wrecked two nails and skinned my fingers with that bloody crowbar."

"Fine." Mocha's annoyance pierced the air. "I'll do it. Where is it?"

"Back-pack."

Bending downward, groping in anticipation toward the floor, Mocha slowly crept in the direction where she last remembered seeing the bulging, black cloth. After a few minutes, she felt the rough mound and opened the side flaps, then top, feeling the bubble wrapped items, the metal cross, the stake, but no crowbar. "It's not here."

"Oh, yeah." Peregrine shook her head in delayed remembrance. "I took it to defend myself against the night crawlers, you. It's by the door."

Mocha wrestled with the darkness until she reached the wall. There, she dropped on all fours, and with the palms of her hands, scanned the cold concrete for the missing implements. "Where by the door?"

"Near the door seal?"

Mocha splayed her fingers along the threshold and the floor around the wooden seal. Her fingertips were eyes that saw all. Nothing. Just powdery concrete dust and grains of what probably was the soil that they had carried in on the souls of their Nikes. And spider webs. "Ugh." Mocha screamed, "Aieeee."

"What?" Peregrine waded in the dark toward her friend's voice. She stopped at Mocha's reply.

"A spider. I hate spiders."

"Did you find it?"

"No. Are you sure you dropped it inside the door?" Mocha's tone was dry ice.

"Or did you leave it outside?"

"No, No, it can't be." Peregrine agonized. "Check again."

More minutes passed. Peregrine's thoughts were droning flies. Where was Fen? It must be 1:30 AM by now. She had been there almost two hours.

"It's not here." Mocha stood up. "You want to try?"

"I didn't leave it outside."

"And I didn't shut the door."

"Oh, this is just great. Chillin' in the tomb. What could be better?" Peregrine's mouth tasted like bitter, brackish water.

"We have to light the candles." Mocha insisted.

"The candles!" The shock in Peregrine's voice was visible, though Mocha couldn't see her.

"Well, let's just stay here and do nothing. Take out your phone, and we'll listen to music. I got it!" Mocha snapped her thumb and middle finger. "Let's text Fen and tell him to bring another crowbar."

"We agreed to leave everything at home, except what was needed," Peregrine reminded. "Unless you sneaked your cell?" she asked hopefully.

"No, the one time I didn't." Mocha shook her head and leaned against the door. "I must be prophetic. I knew something would happen. I knew not having any tech was dangerous, that we'd get jammed. I told you we were crazy not to!"

"If you use technology, you are walled in by the present with no access to the past. You can't fuse the present with the past. That destroys all hope of releasing the magic. To connect with the ancients, you follow the ancient laws. So, leave Drake and Nicki Minaj home for once." Peregrine's frustration now overflowed with passion. "If we can't follow simple instructions, how will we deal when things get really dangerous? You have to set up the conditions for this to work. Otherwise, all the sacrifices we made to get here will be for nothing. No one knows this better than you." Peregrine paced back and forth in the darkness. "Do I have to remind you of Billy?

Mocha said nothing. The import of Peregrine's words reminded her of the scene by her brother's bedside the previous night and her mother's desolation, "You have to prepare yourself, Mocha. You know what hospice means."

Mocha deep knee bent her body gracefully to the crypt floor and sat cross-legged, her arms hugging her knees. She rested her back against the indifferent door, peering into the dark for Peregrine.

"Stop moving back and forth. You're distracting me. I can't think."

"Well, I just sat down. I'm sitting against the wall of the dead," said Peregrine in surprise.

"Very funny. You should be on *Social Medium*." Mocha was growing even more frustrated. They would have to wait for Fen to rescue them and then return another night to enact the ceremony. Billy might not have another night.

"I'm sitting down. What are you talking about?"

"I can hear you scuttling like a crab. Are you trying to scare me? It won't work." Mocha's voice dripped bile. "Stop fooling around. We have to get out of here. Think."

"Mocha, I'm not moving. Now, you're scaring me."

Mocha had never acted afraid in front of Peregrine. She was not about to begin.

"I'm coming over there to slap you silly." Mocha jumped to her feet and cocked her head to one side, acutely attentive to Peregrine's movements.

Hissing, clicking, humming, thudding. In the darkness, she imagined thousands of maggots writhing, and huge tropical bugs feeding. Fear enveloped her. She tried to recover the courage that had taken her to the crypt at midnight, but panic swamped her breaths. Her intake of air shallowed. Her muscles tightened with cramp. She backed into the door.

"Peregrine, cut it out!" Mocha called. "Peregrine, cut it out!" her voice mocked back at her.

Emptiness greater than a vacuum.

Humans gain comfort by altering perceptions to accommodate each other, combining distinctions to create a compatible sphere of similarities. Each woman tried to adjust her senses to the other's reality, with no success. They became disconnected from time and space. Mocha could no more understand where she was in relation to Peregrine than Peregrine could to Mocha. Confusion reigned. It birthed every kind of error of discernment in the women's imagination. The dam of reason broke beneath the weight of insanity. Terror sluiced through their veins, searing its information in the channels of their minds.

Mocha pressed her body so hard against the door, the metal ridges bored into her back. The thudding, hissing sounds intensified, echoing in upon themselves. "Hsssssss, shsssss, sssss, shssss, click, click, click." There was a rapid rotation of sounds. "Shsss, ssss, click, shhhhhh, hssss, click, click, click." They pealed out and swallowed the vacuum of silence, intensifying, augmenting. Mammoth bugs with huge pincers clicked toward her neck to decapitate her. "Get the hell away from me. Away,

away." She tried to wiggle her torso and shake tentacles coiling up her arms. Chills shuddered nerve endings in electrified waves. Her skin vibrated with panic and disgust. The hairs rose up on her head. Worms slimed, biting through her jeans to attack her legs. "Peregrine, Peregrine…"

Mocha sobbed. Her cries smothered into gobbling and gurgling sounds. A foul-tasting, slippery, coarse, hairy tentacle forced open her tight, grimacing lips. Slicing pincers pierced and dragged down her tongue. The tentacle expanded and stuffed itself into her mouth. More pincers encircled her throat and pressed hard to crush her windpipe. She screamed in pain but no sound came out. The stinking, wriggling tentacle snaked down her esophagus. She was being eaten from inside out. Consumed, Mocha's legs crumpled under her and she collapsed to the floor, unconscious. The creature swelled and blew up, straining her inner membranes to their limits. Hungry, it undulated its maw downward into her belly to feed.

Chapter Two

PEREGRINE SAT, HEARING NOTHING, seeing nothing. But she sensed a dynamic change, though she was blinded by darkness and deafened by silence. Like a mother ewe intuiting a predator stalking her baby lambs though it is below the radar, Peregrine feared for Mocha's life.

Outside, the pleasant, warm, summer night wrapped its comforting arms around the perimeter of Calvary Cemetery. Inside the mausoleum, an unfathomable cold fanned the room. It flumed upward in engulfing clouds and mingled with the dark and silence, creating a thick wall between Peregrine and Mocha that heightened to the outer reaches of the earth's atmosphere. Mocha's spirit had flown far from Peregrine. She was as distant as a star.

"Mocha, why are you playing me like this?" Peregrine screamed. She importuned, commanded, ordered, chided and fussed at her friend, then surrendered to exhaustion. "Mocha? Mocha?" Her throat raw with screaming, Peregrine whispered her friend's name while she groveled on hands and knees, sweeping the area by the door where she had been. When she was unsuccessful scoping around the corners and the seams connecting the floor and walls, she rested, sitting cross-legged for fifteen minutes. Then she resumed on all fours, like a crab, filtering the dust and dirt particles between her claw-hands, scuffing her knees as she swathed the room's center and traced circumferences within the burial chamber's walls. Nothing. Not even her back-pack. The stillness contemptuously answered with emptiness graver than a vacuum.

Now, Peregrine experienced the darkness of fear. It was a cold presence, crouching next to her as she sat on the cool concrete near the wall of the entombed, and hugged her knees for warmth. She waited again for the knowledge of intuition. It eluded her. Instead, the darkness leaped, coursed up her legs, pulled at her stomach, raised the tiny fleece hairs on the nape of her neck, then flew zigzagging against logic into her mind, like a bat on the prowl. She heard it pulse in her breaths as they rasped and evanesced in the dead air. She was confronting the worst of her fears, the terror of being isolated, alone, utterly alone. Multiple ancillary childhood horrors of the dark, of monsters, of ghouls and witches beat at her like locusts' wings. Her mind gyrated. There was no one but herself and the darkness of the vacuum. And the things in her pack, the water, food, precious artifacts and magic spells which could have saved her were gone, all gone, along with her best friend. Trapped in this damn crypt with no means of escape, she had no sustenance until rescue which might be days away.

No one but Fen and Beach Comber knew where she was. What if Fen never came, if something happened to him? What if Beach Comber didn't get back from his trip in time to find out from her mother she hadn't come home? She would be here with only the dead for companionship. Starvation would overtake her. No! Dehydration! Her mind smashed into the gruesome reality. Seven days. She had seven days before unquenchable thirst strangled her.

Peregrine shuddered. She would go insane before she died of thirst or starved to death. She would drive herself mad, so she wouldn't think about what was happening. Or she would force a heart attack. She would work herself into frenzy, imagine a horrific nightmare world and frighten herself to death. She would not die of thirst. She knew what happened, the agonizing, "raging fever of the throat," the thick and foul-tasting saliva, the unswallowable lump in the throat and the prune tongue, clinging to the teeth in the "cotton-mouth" phase of dehydration. And as her thirst intensified to voraciously consume her waking moments, her tongue would harden into a "senseless weight," a foreign member in her mouth. There would be severe pains in the head and neck and hearing impairments and hallucinations. The tongue would swell and grow until it slowly protruded from her disappearing leathery lips. Her nose would wither and shrink in her discolored face, the nostril linings blackening, as her tortured kidneys moment by moment squeezed out every last drop of precious liquid, until they shut her down to a comatose state, the prelude before death mummified her.

Last year, she had read a description of the phases of dehydration in Nathaniel Philbrick's, *In the Heart of the Sea,* a description which included a museum director's account of a prospector's experiences dehydrating in the Arizona desert over a seven-day period. The morbidity of it had fascinated her. Horrified, she realized that probability measured against chance that she would be charting the phases of her own dehydration. There was no fascination now, only panic.

"Calm, I must remain calm," she agonized. "I can't help myself unless I am calm, collected, composed, calm, collected, composed." She repeated the phrase until she believed it. "I must think of something I can do. One can always do something. All is not lost. Today, I am alive." She comforted herself with the present. Thoughts of the inevitability of her future paralyzed her.

In the passion of her fears, Peregrine's awareness of her surroundings in the dark grew more acute. The temperature was dropping. She could feel the coolness intensifying. Goose- bumps trailed her bare arms. Her tailored cotton shirt was an inadequate protection against the buffeting atmosphere. Starting from her upper arms, she unrolled the long sleeves to her wrists and buttoned the cuffs. She felt warmer. But because of her lack of sleep the previous night, the penetrating air sapped her strength, and the tightening atmosphere rendered her to a morbid passivity. Mind did not supplant matter. The sense depriving void deceived her. She haphazardly wedded her intelligence to illusion. Her ability to think logically fluctuated between clarity and opaqueness. She craved sleep, wanted to lie down, to curl up in a fetal position and rest like those around her. She knew it would be perilous to fall asleep in this cold. Yet she ached for sleep. Her body longed to sleep like the dead around her.

From her slouching position, Peregrine tiredly slid back on her behind until she reached the wall of drawers where the ancient ones lay. Exhausted, she dragged her legs to the side. With one luxurious, flowing execration, she released herself to the heaviness of her need which pulled her to the floor. There, she lay stretched out on her right side. In her drowsiness, she felt warmth. She sighed. She had been awake for twenty-four hours. This entire struggle for what? She, Fen and Mocha had failed in every conceivable way. They had been separated from each other on this night when they especially needed to be together in the supporting powers of agreement. What arrogance to believe they could change their destiny through spiritual magic! They couldn't even get it together for ten minutes in this bloody crypt!

The angry fears that had dogged her emotions dissipated into hopeless vacuity. Her emotional emptiness reflected the emptiness of her surroundings. What did it matter after all? Alone, she couldn't carry out the ritual by herself and not without the ceremonial artifacts that had disappeared along with her back-pack. It was pointless to resist. In quiet resignation, Peregrine surrendered to unconsciousness and the darkness of oblivion until the steady rise and fall of her labored breath were the only sounds in the mausoleum. And Peregrine slept the profound sleep of the dead.

The hours drew out. The sun rose shining into a hazy, somnambulant day, a blazing day that neither Peregrine nor Mocha saw. Neither did they see the sunset or the transit of the Dog Star across the blue-black heavens to the next sunrise and sunset of the second day. Corporeal reality had been swallowed up; the natural elements that govern all living creatures and the circle of time…seconds, minutes, hours bore no impact on their consciousness. They were suspended beyond such quaint human notions of a time and space continuum.

If Peregrine's outward form registered stasis, her dream state was a hive of charged activity. Her unconscious churned as thoughts tumbled over each other. She must rise out of this black hole. Find out what happened to Mocha. Look for Fen. But the tomb held in the night. And night extinguished her will and threatened her mortal soul.

She must resist with all her strength. Get out. Leave. She struggled to open her eyes, to wake up paralyzed arms and legs. She shook herself. Immobility. She moaned. Her tongue was thick. No words formed. She would cry out, rouse herself to consciousness. Scream. She opened her mouth, but as she forced the air out of her lungs and propelled it out her throat, no sound emerged. An impossibility. Her ancestors' machinations to thwart intruders to the crypt had succeeded. She had fallen prey to their devices and stratagems. How to find a way out of their enchanted pit?

On she slept, like the dead. And her dreams unraveled into phantasms and spiraled out of control. In them Peregrine awakened to darkness. She raised herself up from her supine position. Intermittently touching the wall of entombments, she gingerly inched forward, like a tightrope walker. Ahead was pitch dark. If she moved faster, she might fall into an abyss or stumble and break her shin on a marble impediment. As she forged into the mouth of the black cavern, with her right hand, she felt cool marble indentations, the engraved names of the deceased. In a world absent of color, the tomb's wall of drawers steadied her journey into another realm.

Uncanny transformation! She was Mocha. She blinked Mocha's eyes. Her inner reactions were Mocha's. She knew the depth of Mocha's despair against the darkness. She struggled against the huge creature. She became paralyzed by hissing and clicking sounds that bounced off the nerve endings of her inner ear. Fear electrified her body. The scraping, shuffling movements neared. She cringed against the phenomena's hot breath and her impending doom.

In the midst of being devoured, her spirit delivered her. She plunged the shaking fingers of her left hand in her jeans pocket and pulled out a candle. And simultaneously with her right hand, she fumbled for the matches in her other pocket. She'd immolate the monster in a blaze of devouring flames. Its howling destruction would light her way out of this dead house.

Through her identification with Mocha, Peregrine's reason intruded into the dream. Mocha must not light the candle but must succumb to the creature. The candles were sanctified for one purpose only. And that purpose was not to banish fear. The True Elect faced their fears, extinguished them with faith. Faith would destroy the creature. Mocha's terror, her absence of faith and her inability to yield were a selfish indulgence. It would destroy her brother and chain Manny to the darkness of a world he did not understand. It would freeze out Beach Comber and her, Peregrine, from a world they rightfully belonged to. She, Peregrine would succumb to the beast rather than waste the candles. She would sacrifice her life rather than destroy other's lives. Would Mocha do such a thing to her own brother?

The answer was swift. She would. In the unfolding dream, once again Peregrine morphed into her friend, yet retained the strand of her own conscience. With fingers stiffened in a paroxysm of guilt, Mocha opened the match-book and ripped out a match. A stench of rotten flesh filled her nostrils. Waves of hot, putrid air blew her hair back and burned her face. She cried out and dropped the match. Her neck snapped back, and hairy tentacles grasped her scalp. Seething foam and spray filled her nostrils and ears. She ripped out another match, scraping it along the flint edge. The entire matchbook caught. The air vibrated. She saw, as if through cellophane, black of smoke puffed up in a cloud above her head, then vanished. Her mind brought her senses back to her body. Flames nipped at her fingers. Her nails were on fire, the matchbook having burned through. Mocha flung the flaming cardboard to the ground, then quickly bent down and held the candle to the dying embers. Luckily, the wick caught before she was pitched again into the darkness. The fragrance of the white candle suffused the air. With pleasure, she inhaled its essence.

In the deepness of her sleep, Peregrine scented the candle. She was herself again. But the dream continued and became noxious. She was infuriated at Mocha's wastrel act, could not shake off the consequences. The sacred flames diffused the monster's power. But Mocha had corrupted their future since the candle was now unusable for the ceremony. Their future was dire. Their way to the Ancient of Days was blocked.

In her dreaming state, Peregrine's anger boiled into rage. She cried aloud, "Mocha, how could you ruin everything? You bitch!" Violence underscored Peregrine's epithet and this violence broke the stillness of the tomb. Hearing her own voice, Peregrine stirred from the death sleep into consciousness. She opened her eyes and blinked at the darkness. Then, she forgot the dream that saved her.

Chapter Three

BEACH COMBER RAN HIS FINGERS through his sun-bleached hair. He always did this out of nervousness. It was the way to relax his nerves. He needed to remain calm. His friends were in trouble and if anything happened to them, he would be in trouble, too. It would set him back for years. He couldn't mentally or physically function without them. They were his meds, for God's sake, like the Effexor his mother took for her depression. Along with his surfer dudes, Fen, Mocha and Peregrine were the closest to him on the planet. No one else mattered more, not even Sylvia, his mom.

The police had been to the Hamilton's and the Randolf's homes, and missing persons' reports had been filed. Mocha and Peregrine hadn't returned since Thursday evening, three days ago. Ms. Randolf was on sedatives. Ms. Hamilton, already overcome with her son in hospice, now had one lousier ordeal to contend with. Beach Comber didn't know where she got the strength.

No mention had been made about Fen who was supposed to meet Mocha and Peregrine at the crypt. He had tried to contact Fen and Fen's mom, but no one returned his calls and messages. Fen lived by himself. Occasionally, he took time off between acting jobs and dropped off the planet to resurface glamorously days later with exotic, jaw-dropping adventures to tell, all perfectly and enviously true. Beach Comber didn't know if Fen was with Mocha and Peregrine. He would have to find them to find Fen or not find him. With Fen, the situation was tricky, especially if he did not want to be found.

Beach Comber turned the black '57 T-Bird left down Willow Park Lane. He had gone to Google Maps and had gotten directions to a few cemeteries. He just couldn't remember where Fen, Mocha and Peregrine were going, but that made sense. He was still a bit lagged from his seven-hour trip.

He couldn't tell Ms. Hamilton or Mrs. Randolf about their daughters' plans. He didn't know them well enough to swear them to secrecy. He doubted they would keep the secret since they believed their daughters' lives were in jeopardy. In the Hamilton/Randolf corner of the universe, everyone must behave with equipoise, everything regular, like the Winslow Homer painting in Peregrine's living room. Telling the police was a part of going through regular channels.

Initially, Beach Comber was ready to throw down because he had a very bad feeling when Ms. Randolf told him that they had gone missing. But common sense took over, and he stopped himself. If he told, he knew what would happen. Assuming they were found where they said they would be, arrests would surely follow, then negative publicity and prying questions that were unanswerable.

He could see it in his mind's eye. Mocha, Fen and Peregrine emerging from the Queens County lockup, surrounded by yelping reporters, snapping their questions like canines and the photographers, slaves-in-tow, spinning images of sticky hype, all-together-now, jousting for position and sparring like a Renaissance fair.

"Just what were you young women and this man doing at the dead of night in a crypt? Is this a sexual tryst?"

"Are you necrophiliacs?"

"Were you committing some lurid sex ritual?"

"Are you Satanists? Wicca enthusiasts? A last days evangelical cult?" all said in the same tonal equation.

"Are you living dead initiates?"

"The Isis and Osiris offspring?"

"Members of the Enlightened Eighteen?"

"The two young women and one man apprehended for grave robbing at Trinity Hills Cemetery are thought to be the ringleaders of the notorious gangs that have been marauding the cemeteries these past months, vandalizing and destroying graves, searching for buried jewelry and valuables. More at 6:00 PM."

Beach Comber laughed out loud. It was no coincidence he had booked his flight one hour after Fen told him their plan. He was thankful he had seen that something like this was going to happen and left before he was caught up in the craziness. Too bad he had not come back sooner before the missing reports had been filed, before Ms. Randolf and Ms. Hamilton went frantic. Then no one would have been missing. He would have found and rescued Peregrine and Mocha.

Stopped at the light, Beach Comber glanced at the directions again. Two more turns and he would be at the cemetery. Now, it was too late, and the police were involved. There was no one he could trust except his Dudes, but they were incommunicado. If anything happened to him, no one would be catching his back. He'd be alone.

He turned right and passed the shopping center, then looked for the single lane road which paralleled the cemetery and led to the final left turn into the gateway. He wryly considered that another reason he couldn't tell was Ms. Randolf. Never mind the arrests or the negative publicity. After she found out that Peregrine had stolen the priceless family heirlooms and used them for healing and magic spells, the police would be called again. To arrest Ms. Randolf for Peregrine's murder.

Better if he worked on his own to avoid a myriad of problems. But what if they weren't at the cemetery, and he didn't find them? He couldn't think of that now. Things had obviously gone wrong and for good reason. They had been tampering with something they didn't really understand, something that didn't want to be understood.

When Peregrine and Mocha asked him to be a part of the ancient ritual, he arranged the trip to the Republic of Suriname, so he wouldn't have to say "no" to them. If they wanted to go to the cemetery and raise the dead, that was fine. Live and let live, but not with his life. Surfers weren't into the paranormal anyway. He had no frame of reference for desperate actions and the ends justifying the means. None of that made sense. For him, there was only the pull of the wave, the sun and the sand and surfing the beaches of the world. He carelessly ran his fingers through his hair. Chrissakes, sometimes he was amazed that they were his friends at all. They were so different from him.

He had come to the end of Decatur Street and made a left onto Peace Lane which curved around to the mammoth, black gates of Trinity Hills. Beach Comber looked beyond the elaborate wrought iron to the rolling, lush, green terrain, peppered with square and pyramid shaped headstones, obelisks, saintly and angelic figures of concrete and marble, luxurious mausoleums, concrete dead houses, trees, bushes and the attendant flowers, showing the care for the beloved. A peaceful, undulating, if not artificial landscape. Beach Comber smiled. It was in the middle of the day. No one appeared to be around, no funerals, no visitors to graves, not even the caretaker and his associates.

He headed the T-Bird into the forty-slot parking area and grabbed the freesias that he had remembered to purchase from the green grocer to appear purposeful. He carefully got out of the car and quietly shut the door. Squinting in the bright sunlight, he surveyed the immediate area. The gates were open and probably would stay open until 5:00 PM, so he had plenty of time to try mausoleum doors and look for any clues near the crypt that Mocha and Peregrine had entered. He could even get to the other cemetery, Calvary, before dark if this place was a washout. God, don't let it be a washout, he thought. Let me find them. He couldn't see himself thrashing around at night in a graveyard.

His shoes crunched upon the grey gravel pathway that snaked under the high gates, and his heart grew heavy with the sound which bit into his soul like an alarm that pierced the air with somber warning. This was the last place he wanted to be and the last activity he wanted to do. The thing he had greatly troubled himself to avoid by traveling to another continent now sneered back at him with fateful malice, "What you seek to avoid, you cannot escape."

Trinity Hills without the mausoleums and headstones, was a lush, beautiful park. But as he trudged off the path and onto the grass, he disregarded the showy display of the flowers and prettily situated bushes and hedges which carried no peace or rest for him. He felt so alone, so responsible. Time was running out. Tomorrow would be the fifth day Fen, Peregrine and Mocha had gone missing. The longer they were gone, the less the likelihood they would return on their own. Something had definitely happened. Sucks for him that he was their last, best hope.

Chapter Four

PEREGRINE PROPPED HERSELF UP on her left elbow and dispelled filmy confusion from her mind. She sat up trying to accustom her eyes to the tarry atmosphere and orient herself to the dullness of the black void. Where was she? Her head was pounding, and the penetrating cold irritated her. She could see nothing, not even her own body, as she stretched out her legs on the frigid, concrete floor. Was she alive? She wasn't even visible to herself. Did she exist at all? Disembodied mind!

With spurts and starts, she jarred her imagination to precision and reviewed the chronology. In this way, she fired memories of the neoclassical structure, its columns, and beautifully ornamented frieze with the name JOHNSON thickly inscribed just below it. She pictured the heavy, rusted, old crowbar that she sneaked from the garden shed and the pick that reminded her of those cartoon pictures of Death grinning crazily with his sickle--razor sharp, dangerous, jauntily loped over his shoulder.

She recalled prying open the solid, cumbersome oak and bronze door. It eerily creaked as she swung it open, as if sounding an alarm to the inhabitants that intruders were entering. She remembered waiting for Fen and Mocha and craving a cigarette and Mocha crash-falling into the crypt. Images flashed in the darkness. From her imagination, she teased each picture and the feelings they evoked, all these and more. But then she came to a chasm and there was no moving forward. Why was she here? Why had they come to this place? Why would they want to be here at night, risking their lives?

It came to her in a slow, rolling cloud. The ceremony to save Billy and Manny and find her father. And with remembrance of the foiled plans and Mocha's disappearance, a cavernous sorrow filled Peregrine. In a surge of denial, she clawed down hope from the heavens and allowed its sweet uplift to flood her soul. Mocha was there after all. "Mocha?" she cried out in anticipation. Rising to a standing position, hands outstretched, her chin lifted, she pealed her voice like a bell to thrust back the oblique vacuum. "Mocha, you are there, aren't you? Mocha, answer me!" she commanded despite her growing doubts. "If you can, groan or whisper or scratch your fingers. Anything." After a long pause, she joked, "Yo, hottie!!! Get down. It's freezin' in here!" Useless. Crying out to an empty room.

She sighed in remembrance. "So, nothing has changed." Her voice was hollow like the darkness, but hearing her own humanity, however humbled, comforted her. Strengthened, she stove off the unnerving silence and crushing loneliness.

In the somber, dense and grave atmosphere, Peregrine was acutely aware of change. Time had abandoned her. Today was the refuse of how many days passed with the dead? It was impossible to tell in such utter light deprivation. If her intense thirst was any indication, she had been in the crypt two, maybe three days. She craved water, wished the damp concrete would yield a few kind drops she could lap with her tongue. How long had she passed out? She had rested, but paradoxically, the cold had drained the benefits. Now once again, she must battle the lethargy that had enveloped and dumped her into the sleep of oblivion. She badly wanted to sleep and forget. Weird. Were seductive, unseen forces drawing her like Sirens to a death sleep? Well, this time she must elude them. It was a miracle she was awake. She wouldn't get a second chance.

Rationality, stirred up after her uneasy rest, clarified her thoughts and swamped her insect fears. She was calm and purposeful. And the tomb was not an oven which prevented a more rapid dehydration. But the saliva in her mouth tasted acrid and thick, and her cotton mouth whipped her to frantically search for droplets of moisture.

Crawling on hands and knees in the ebony atmosphere, Peregrine painstakingly retraced her movements across the floor, stowing in the back of her mind her failed search for Mocha and the back-pack. Gingerly, she fingered every scrap of dusty, concrete. Each inch of the icy flooring yielded nothing. Not even a dirty puddle of water. She leaned back on her haunches. She had to think, to get herself out of this mess. Along with the chilled air, her thirst and gnawing hunger would eventually dull her will. As time elapsed, she would weaken until death's progression incapacitated her mind and emotions, to say nothing of her physical body.

She must not let her anxiety intensify. She got to her feet and paced a small area. Emotional pain was easier to take than physical pain. She was inured to it since her teenage years, the mental sorrow and emotional torment. Yes, hellish hurts, death, loss, soured loves. Those she could endure. But she had no courage for physical pain--she who refused to get in the dentist's chair unless he promised he would give her the triple whammy: sweet air, anesthetic for her gums (so she wouldn't feel the needles) and Novocain and this just for a tiny filling.

She stood transfixed. She remembered her grim thoughts before passing out: unbearable fears of dying alone; her yearning to bring on death quickly by forcing a heart attack and imaginings of death's stealthy, creeping mortification of her beauty and youth, as it slowly siphoned off her life energy. Brutal images of death's appearance in her body haunted her. The loveliness of her face spiked in a grimace, laughing hideously; her skin, mummified, stretched super-taut; the skull breaking through its desiccated, papery sheaf and her eyes bulging, unable to close, all tears dried up, a desert staring unceasingly into fearful eternity. Ugly, ugly, horrible.

Peregrine shuddered. The inevitability was a few days away. Could she do it? Commit suicide? No. Now that the final decision encroached, she realized she had no taste or imagination for suicide. Self-inducing a heart attack was difficult. How to go about it and not fail? At the last minute before her heart seized up, she would anticipate and instinctively fight because aggression was the inexorable response of youth. No young person naturally sought death, regardless of how much they wanted to escape pain. Wanting death was an artificial state. Crack-heads overexposed to numbing drugs confused emotional oblivion with comfort. Youthful suicide was an oxymoron. Perhaps it made sense, for someone else, but not for her. She would go out raging against the darkness, like the Dylan Thomas poem; do something to free herself while she still had the strength. She would not perish in this crypt, the living mummy withering from life to death in a searing emotional and physical torment.

Peregrine closed her eyes and screamed, "Damn me for dithering around." The sound bounced off the crypt walls, then trailed off in dim memory. She had no time to lose. She would pull open the drawers in the walls and search the coffins, rifle the bodies for anything, implements, objects she might be able to use to pry open the door. People were buried with all sorts of stuff for weird, symbolic reasons. Who knows what she might find? Hell, if necessary, she would shred the coffin innards, ransack and pull apart corpses, grab femurs and tibias and skulls to bash down the door, blotting out all fears of contagion and retribution from the dead for disturbing their peace. She would do anything to live. Her aggressiveness soothed her nerves and renewed her vitality. Anyone would do the same in her position.

To work. Sightless, with arms outstretched, she shuffled through the darkness over to the nearest corpse wall, locating the indentations of engraved names she had stumbled upon earlier in her wanderings. With her left cheek and both palms pressed flat against the frigid marble entombments, she slowly moved with mincing steps, right foot, left foot. Rapidly and deftly checking up and down, high and low, her fingers were eyes that saw all. She used her limbs like the arms of a compass, circling wide arcs to happen upon the metal or stone handle pulls that she imagined were used to gain access to the coffins. So far there were none, but on she went. The wall was endless. Unknown names long forgotten passed beneath her fingers. A phrase drummed in her mind. "The dead bury the dead. The dead bury the dead."

Her right foot bumped up against a corner merging in a right angle with the next set of marble drawers. If the room was, as the mausoleum appeared from the outside, a rectangle, at least three of the walls held the drawers, Peregrine surmised. She didn't remember seeing any on the same side as the door. The significance of this escaped her, as she plodded on, boring into the dark and cold, unaware of the tick of time and her thirst, which she suppressed below the threshold of consciousness.

Nothing. Maybe there was only one handle for each wall, or maybe there was a recessed button, situated between the engraved names. Adjusting her modus operandi, she pushed in each letter of each name. Her arms and back ached, but she slowly continued around the room, determined not to give up but to investigate the area within her reach. As she went, she took in a long breath in a rise of expectation, then exhaled it in short bursts, barely aware of the extreme tension in her muscles as her fingers and arms stiffened with anxiety and cramp. With each step, each exacting movement, each exasperated fingering, she gave up success and swallowed the ashes of extinguished hope. Silently, she prayed that if there was only one handle for each wall, it be at shoulder height. The ceiling was about seven feet above her, and there was no way she could reach that far up over her head since she had nothing to stand on. Even if she could get up there, she doubted she would have the strength to open the heavy coffins while maintaining her equilibrium from such an angle.

Her mind broke off its thoughts. Underneath the fingers of her right hand, she felt striations of coarse wood and thick, ice-like metal bands. The door! She had come full circle. She couldn't believe it. Every inch of foul stone and concrete within the range of her fingertips yielded nothing. Once again, the tomb had drowned her expectations.

So, there was no way to get to the coffins. The three walls were just that, huge slabs of marble with names carved into them. The coffins must be somewhere else, not in the wall. Behind the wall? She had never imagined anything like this, but then she had no experience with custom-made burial sites and the deviousness of her ancestors. There must be a mechanism to raise or lower the marble or slide it aside or swing it out. Where could it be?

Another thought plagued her. What if the coffins were buried underneath the floor, like those she had seen in the Vatican or St. Mark's Church in Venice? No. Designs and outlines of figures would be etched into the concrete flooring, indicating the burial places. Her knees, hands, behind and the soles of her feet knew every inch of the area. It was smooth and flat with no burial carvings or art. So, the likeliest place for the coffins was behind the name entombments.

"Think, Peregrine, think," the words echoed in her mind softly. The only place she hadn't searched was the wall on the same side as the door. Pushing aside the dense, black atmosphere with outstretched arms and extended fingers, Peregrine nudged her way to the door. Feeling the familiarity of the wood, she bent down and traced the door seam along the floor, following it to the left corner, then stretching upward, following the door's outline and the section of wall to the right and left of the door, once again, searching for a handle, pull, buttons, switches, levers, anything. Nothing. No means of escape. The same as earlier when she and Mocha combed the area repeatedly.

Peregrine relaxed her arms to her sides and turned around with her back to the unyielding, monolithic exit. A groan escaped her lips. Obviously, she was missing something. Maybe her thirst and the chilling conditions had so overwhelmed her senses, she couldn't accurately gauge reality. No. Her fingers had carefully blanketed all the walls to a dead end. OK, she resolved. Get over it. Change course. Do something else. But what?

As she sighed in resignation, her bodily needs, thirst, hunger, cold and the pressing force in her bladder rushed forward and flooded her will. She sagged against their weight, reeling. Her legs caved in and she collapsed on the concrete. At the fall she urinated, feeling the hot liquid seep through her jeans and silk underwear. Though exhausted, to avoid re-soaking herself, she quickly lifted herself up from the floor, away from the steaming puddle. Standing, Peregrine sidled to the left. For support, she steadied her back and head against the door and rested.

This new weakening struck her as an unforeseen extravagance. She had peed on herself like a kid. Damn it to hell. The last time she peed herself was when she was two-years-old. She had fallen down the stairs and when her cousin picked her up to soothe her, she rewarded him with hot, yellow liquid. Peregrine laughed and spoke aloud, "Like the saying goes …die young." She wouldn't be leaving a good-looking corpse, but one stinking and rotted to the core.

Self-pity washed over her in resignation, the worse kind of mental and physical breakdown. After her initial search for Mocha, she had relieved herself in a corner of the mausoleum, farthest away from the door, and had made sure to avoid the spot in her travels around the room. But now it was obvious she was breaking down in her habits, no longer able to control her bodily functions. So, this was how it was going to happen. Her body would deteriorate by degrees, ratcheting to greater levels of distress, until it reached its limit and she became comatose and tumbled down into Death's abyss. Whatever. "I don't care," she screamed to the tarry cold. But she did care, and her concern was symbolized by her body's urgings and her inability to fulfill them. Her thirst and hunger had blossomed evilly, and the biting atmosphere assaulted her nerves with rivers of fiery pain.

The temperature drop was unfathomable, an anomaly considering the month of the year, June. Unless! Suppose her ancestors had devised a security system against interlopers, a system that locked the door, imprisoned the marauder and lowered the temperature to freezing? Preposterous, someone could be killed. Precisely! Someone could be killed, a macabre recompense for trespassers and grave robbers. For a small sum of money, corpses easily could be disposed of. Bodies were always turning up in the East River. Such a security system, if gruesome, left the tomb inviolate. Murderously clever.

Peregrine's thoughts leap-frogged. She had trailed her aunt's opaque stories of her Black Nobility relations right to this icy, central room of the crypt to uncover a truth. Her ancestors were Machiavellian amoralists, and the current European crop of relations with all its extensions probably mirrored their progenitors' traits and behaviors. Certain things were beginning to make sense, like her mother's silence about the European family and her exile from them, like her Aunt Rachel's fear of the mausoleum and the promise she compelled Peregrine to make: to wait to perform the ceremony with her mother.

When she stole the relics, she knew she might be opening the door to a world of trouble, but the risk-reward ratio seemed worth it. Her mother appeared to be denying her entrance to a world of privilege, power and familial community. Desperately, she wanted in, and the ceremony seemed the way. But she hadn't hedged her bets. She was an intruder in the wrong place at the wrong time. She would suffer an intruder's reward unless she was rescued or found a way out. If Madeline's secrecy was a curse, then she, Peregrine, was surely suffering from its effects. And now she must deal alone, in the freezing night of the tomb, without water and food.

No! It couldn't be. She was imagining things. There was no security system. She must remain calm, though the darkness seemed to whisper, *"Soon, too soon. Gone, all gone."*

An hour passed, then another. The sun plummeted. A full moon unobscured by clouds rose over Peregrine's fourth evening in the tomb. Above the cemetery, the stars danced their twinkling parade.

Peregrine removed the long violet, silk scarf she wore as a sash around her waist and put it around her neck. She felt it dangling limply to her knees. She was grateful she had worn this for fashion instead of a leather belt. She would be able to layer it against her skin to keep her core temperature higher. She unzipped her jeans. With fumbling fingers shaking from the cold, she numbly grappled to unbutton the shirt's center buttons and cuffs. She jerked up a few inches of the cotton material to allow herself enough maneuvering room to peel off each sleeve and get out of the shoulders while securing the shirttails inside her jeans.

"Hot damn! It's bloody cold," she chattered through gritted teeth, abruptly breaking the stillness. "Get motivated, come on faster," she encouraged herself. Her shivering multiplied into shaking. Between tremors of pain from the blazing cold, she peeled off the shirtsleeves letting them fall about her waist. "Oh, God," she groaned aloud. The glacial air hovered and bit into her bare flesh. The exposure of her arms and chest to the infernal atmosphere menaced her to abandon her intentions. Her movements became gross and thick.

Pulling the scarf from around her neck, she clumsily grasped its flimsy ends then slowly wound it tightly around the top of her head and over both shoulders, using any overflow to circle her torso. With her shuddering right hand, she pressed the scarf securely against her chest. She slipped on the left sleeve and shirt over her left shoulder. The cold fell away from her left arm. She was grateful for the immediate warmth. With her quaking left hand, she attempted to press the scarf securely to her chest. Her hand faltered. She ended up rubbing it against the silk to accommodate her shuddering and hold the material. Her hand tremored furiously, and the silk slid away from her chest. Again, she tried and again. Eventually, she managed to hold the scarf using her left upper arm as she bumbled her useless right hand and arm into the shirt sleeve and over her shoulder.

The ordeal was worth it. The scarf felt snug against her body. With frenzied fingers she worked at the center buttons and cuffs. She crossed her arms and placed her hands underneath her armpits to warm them. As she stomped her feet in a crazy rhythm, she felt the blight of cold fading. She knew her scarf layering would reprieve her from the hibernal air, for a time. As her hands warmed, she removed them from underneath her armpits and violently rubbed and hit her upper body, shoulders and torso. Painstakingly, she fumbled as she fastened the three top buttons in their havens to seal off her body from the piercing, cruel air. Her trembling fled away and then stopped altogether.

Peregrine sat, leaning her back against the wooden section of the door for warmth. Occasionally, she rocked sideways while vigorously massaging her arms with rough kneading and slapping. She hugged her upper torso and pounded her sides with her fists. She grabbed her knees and rolled up into a ball, then released her grip and stretched her arms upward and her legs outward. Regularly, she shifted her position, bending and stretching her legs, then sliding them apart and together rapidly against the floor in a scissors-like motion. She banged her Nikes together to the rhythm of her favorite tunes. When she tired, she folded her legs underneath her body and sat on them, grateful for their heat. After she rested a few moments, again she began her light physical stimulation, sustaining a vital and regular movement. She was careful not to overexert herself and break into a sweat, counterproductive in this ice box. The lethargy, which had threatened to return, she had kept at bay with the circulation exercises learned in yoga class. She was clear-headed and as she moved, she deliberated.

In the blackness of the tomb, there were no distractions. Because of the gradual diminution of her normal body processes in the frigid atmosphere, Peregrine's five senses became dislodged from their comfort zones, and eventually, her isolation and the environmental conditions disarranged her apprehension of reality. This disassembling elevated her consciousness to a profound state. Like unruly students, her past and future had been expelled. She dwelt in the present moment, and revelation upon compounding revelation drove in on her. A harbinger of insanity? Perhaps. Unlike those who suppress prophetic awareness or thwart it by indulging their senses through an intensification of hedonistic delight, Peregrine accepted her state because she had no other options.

In another time and place, she might have sought sensation through the high or low arts, forbidden acts, athleticism or the isolation from live human interaction in the mind grabs of digital gadgets, which appear to extend human connectivity to self and others. But the utter and complete darkness, her thirst and the nefarious atmosphere obliterated her imagination. She could not sensationalize herself to greater levels of distraction, nullify her soul or thwart her ability to navigate incorporeal realms. She was forced into an acute state of being, where she was in touch with a full range of human capabilities.

Like many distracted in the hyper culture, she had been cut off from self, buried in a flesh crypt. Now, enveloped as she was by the mausoleum's darkness, cold, death and absence of sensual delight, she was forced to acknowledge and confront her soul's entombment. The encounter shattered her former state. She emerged with spiritual awareness and power. This previously unacknowledged human capacity flooded Peregrine's being.

When Peregrine confronted this metaphor and her soul's grave shattered, illumination burned in her with an intense flame. Esoteric, arcane discernment arose in her mind like a ghost in the ethers. She had floated into the supernatural playground of shamans, Native American medicine men, mystics, prophets, saints and martyrs.

In the last hour, Peregrine, had entered and left the incorporeal realms, though she was unaware of what was happening because there was no one to guide her. She thought she was lunatic. Now, she fully immersed herself, embracing the mystical knowledge that enabled her to flow with the music of the earth and the wisdom of supernatural foolishness and faith. This was not the survival instinct. Some of the greatest survivalists had been experts who, negotiating extreme environments, have themselves died though they "knew better." It was not the revelation that comes to every human being aware that death approaches. Receiving a revelation and knowing what to do with it are two separate conditions. Not everyone knows what to do when death nears. How each individual responds and confronts death is as varied as each human being is unique. The choice between life and death dwells in each human consciousness and each soul. But who really chooses when death is imminent? It is the riddle of the ages.

Prophesy had risen up to speak to Peregrine's soul from the Eternal Spirit. In confronting the tomb in herself, she had broken its hold over her natural senses. She had become deaf to hear and blind to see with the eye of faith. Now she listened, like one of the powerful remnant who travels beyond the bounds of religion, magic and occultism to the nether worlds of spirit, where Death can be commanded if you only know how. The most advanced do know such mysteries.

Though she was herself, she also was a supernatural vessel, able to navigate corporeal and incorporeal worlds in a Truth of absolutes. She knew that Death was, above all else, a spirit and not a condition or state of being. And she discerned that the Angel of Death had a different purpose, to come for you when the Great Compromise was achieved and the end was a new beginning. Knowing this distinction, though her knowing was beyond any ability to articulate it, made all the difference between life and death. Like many in such a situation, Peregrine recognized the extreme danger of the double threats of hypothermia and dehydration. But her recently awakened mystical sensibilities gave her the confidence to choose the only perfect way of escaping Death's Kingdom because she knew the difference between the spirit of Death which could be commanded and the Angel of Death which could not. In the darkness and the malevolence, Peregrine commanded. She commanded silently in her Spirit, and she commanded with force and power.

Spiritual wisdom took control of her mind. A well-spring of information penetrated her remembrance and cast down her desperate situation. She recalled reading stories of individuals lost in the desert who used the moisture from their urine to slake their thirst. In his sojourns to beaches around the world, Beach Comber told her of holy men in India who drank their own urine for its beneficial effects. Were such stories myths? In her college bio class, she learned that urine was a by-product of blood filtration by the kidneys and it contained what was taken in by the host which could make it toxic if excessive metals or chemicals or drugs were ingested. Fluoride, chlorine, antibiotics, pharmaceuticals, preservatives and dyes couldn't produce the benefits the holy men were looking for, could they? And surely, she had ingested particles of this stuff just before she had entered the crypt. She had recently gotten over a urinary tract infection using a powerful antibiotic. Just how toxic was her urine? If she drank it, would it poison her and produce a death more painful during the agonizing hours before the coma that was inexorably coming her way?

Peregrine threw off her doubts. Faith and peace settled in her spirit. Her thirst was overwhelming. Soon it would drive her to madness so that she wouldn't be able to help herself. She understood how people got dysentery from drinking water that they knew was polluted and yet, drank anyway. They were dying for a drink. Stupid cliché was true. And because they drank, they grew more helpless with cramps and diarrhea until they died, unless there was medical intervention. And what were her chances of that? No, she must help herself. Wherever Mocha had gone, she was probably struggling to stay alive herself, and Peregrine knew deep in her spirit that Fen wasn't coming. She must survive on her own.

Peregrine sifted through the folklore. Urine wasn't dirty. It was sterile in the body. But hers had changed chemical composition and for hours had been exposed to the air, probably becoming bacteriologic. But she must have something to drink to quell the flames in her throat and the growing enervation of her body, signs of her desperate condition. She decided. Drinking her own urine was unnatural, but it would add hours to her shortened life, and her unbearable thirst would be quenched. She gave herself excellent odds: a fifty-fifty chance. Either the chemical composition of her urine would hasten her death, or it would benefit her disastrous condition and stave off dehydration. Doing nothing would be worse.

As she thought about these things, the icy atmosphere made her blood recoil and sink deeper into her core, leaving her fingers dangerously exposed to the death grip of glacial air. The blood in her fingers was becoming an ice flow. Soon it would stop flowing altogether and her flesh would blacken. With a ferocity she never would have believed herself capable of, Peregrine smashed her dead fingers and banged them against her thighs, until they tortured her. The soaked jeans had not dried from the heat of her body core. Instead, the hibernal atmosphere carried the chilling wetness to the denser area of her body, speeding her toward hypothermia. The slow thought collided with her dulling wits. "How cold is it anyway?" She knew the temperature was dropping to the forties. How long would she survive when it went below freezing?

Peregrine palmed the floor, locating the urine puddle. Within moments its surface might be firm and smooth to the touch, layers of ice skimming over it, the more dangerous for drinking, though less distasteful. She could not wait for it to ice. She must use her energy in her remaining minutes to find a way into the coffins.

She eased herself into a reclining position, then turned over on her stomach. Using her hands to center herself over the urine, she lowered herself until her lips contacted the cold liquid. This way she could salvage every drop of moisture instead of scooping it into her hands where some of it might spill onto her clothing and be lost. Slowly and gently, she extended her tongue downward until she made contact. Fearful of the taste, she quickly dipped her tongue into the wet, receiving a few drops of moisture. It wasn't enough. The fires in her throat raged intensely. Disregarding the contents, Peregrine leaned forward on her arms and like a cat, lapped noisily three times then swallowed in great gulps, trying to place the liquid on the back of her tongue, where the taste buds were the least sensate. Surprisingly, she welcomed the cooling drops. The moisture soothed her thick, parched tongue and refreshed her cotton mouth as it trickled down her throat. But the residue on her tongue was acrid, and she raised her head and waited for a moment for the resolve to either continue drinking or heave the contents from her stomach. Finally, her feverish throat and inner craving for water won out. This is like water, is water, she repeated to herself, and believed.

Again, she lowered her head and extended her lips, lower this time, immersing them in the liquid. She slurped and lapped whole gulps, greedily dispatching the urine, finding the taste intolerable but the idea of liquid heavenly. Again, she retreated and waited for nausea. It never came. She lowered her head and lips to the puddle a third time and sucked up the acerbic fluid as quickly as she could, pushing away thoughts of revulsion, concentrating on the coolness and the quenching of her thirst. The more she clung to the belief that it was water, the easier it was to drink. She was thankful there was no light. If she had seen the yellow color, she might have gagged and vomited, dehydrating herself further.

She consumed the reviving liquid until she finished the entire puddle. Lowering her face to the floor, her palms on either side of her, she lapped any remaining moisture until she fingered the area, finding it bone dry.

Not fully gleaning what her source of strength was, Peregrine lifted her head upward and grinned in self-satisfaction. She was astounded at her courage and resourcefulness. The residue of urine left a taste in her mouth that was bloody awful. She coughed and hacked. She wished that she had a stick of gum or piece of candy.

Peregrine rolled herself onto her back, faced upward and peered into the interminable blackness. Though she couldn't see, it comforted her to know that the darkness ended beyond the walls of the tomb, that the ceiling above her stemmed this void of light, heat, beauty. She sat up and slid herself into a position with her back to the door, the warmest place in the crypt. She started her cycle of circulation exercises once more and waited for any ill effects of what she had done to come upon her. With the waiting came the doubts that whipped her mind and nullified her faith. Maybe she had committed suicide after all!

Chapter Five

MOCHA BREATHED DEEPLY. Her closed eyelids fluttered, evidence of rapid eye movements. She watched interplaying images. Pastel sunset colors floated like immense ribbon bands about her, undulating in waves and spirals that in slow motion elongated then compacted, like the bellows of a gigantic accordion. Melodies, fluid and sonorous wove tapestries of sound in a joyous accompaniment to the cyclical visual undulations, elongations and compressions of variegated pinks, peaches, yellows, mauves, violets and oranges sweeping around her.

In complete stillness she lay, contented, pleasured by the breathtaking visual and aural magnificence of her surroundings. Her face in a peaceful repose smiled with sustained satisfaction, a satisfaction unlike any that human experience could elicit, whether it be sexual pleasure, romantic love, familial love or the self-satisfaction one experiences achieving the pinnacles of wealth and power. Beyond joy, beyond the gratification of a life completely justified and vindicated, Mocha knew, without evidence or proof that glory was a substance that transcended corporeality and the whirling earth that carried her through space. And she was swimming in it, like a dolphin leaping and frolicking exuberantly in a water paradise.

Unaware of light summer evening breezes or the heat of the sun, Mocha received air into her lungs and exhaled it, carried on regular bodily functions, expelled waste and urine and remained in a homeostatic state, though her blood pressure had dropped considerably and the oxygen in her blood had decreased. But her brain waves pulsed in a powerful and regular rhythm. She was neither asleep nor awake, though she remained aware, and functioned in a universe not like our own and indescribable in any human language.

In the twenty-first century, the dark ages of enlightened science, the realm of the mind is a vast, unexplained, little-understood land. Mocha was a conundrum, an anomaly, outside the world of science and medicine, and there was no reasonable explanation for her condition.

Chapter Six

H ELL AND DAMN!" Beach Comber muttered under his breath, falling over a tiny cream-colored headstone, obviously an infant's. Give him sand and waves. He rocked them with the power and grace that came from years of experience, practice, athleticism, innate dexterity. On land, he bumbled and shuffled his feet like an Alzheimer's patient, always embarrassing himself by tripping over stuff that his visual radar never picked off. The motion of a wave was easy. He did it blind, riding the sensations and flows of the ocean currents and rhythms. On the wave crest he never looked down. He drove, pushed, skidded, twisted and rode the slide into pure momentum, all the better with his eyes closed which he had done countless times. Watching and looking always screwed him up.

Like now. He had been wandering around Trinity Hills looking for signs of Mocha and Peregrine for hours. So far, he had tripped over three baby headstones and nearly sprained his wrist saving himself in a fall in which he nearly put out his eye on a metal name marker. And he had come up with nothing.

Beach Comber jumped to his feet and rearranged the overturned headstone, so it lay flat as before. Frustrated, he pulled out a pack of Guyanese cigarettes from his jeans pocket, grabbed two and put one behind his ear for later. As he returned the pack to his pocket, he took out the gold lighter Rebecca had given him, lit the cigarette and put the lighter back. These actions were an enjoyable ritual, more enjoyable than the act of smoking, which messed up his lungs and impaired his athleticism, at times setting him into a coughing frenzy the surfers ripped him about. But Rebecca's gift meant a lot and was why he still carried cigarettes around with him and occasionally smoked.

Beach Comber sauntered over to a large, grey, marble tombstone with the name LOTHAN and sat on its top edge. He tried to relax into the unusual flavor of the cigarette and soothe his thoughts, assuming a California calm to encourage the pragmatism of which he was capable and which the situation demanded. As he smoked, he looked at the sun slipping below the horizon. Dusk was falling, and the gates were closed. He could not easily climb over the metal fence topped with three ropes of barbed wire, which in some places appeared lower because of the rolling terrain. At its highest it looked to be about eight feet.

The height wasn't the problem. He was conditioned by survival training. He could climb like a mountain goat and support his body weight with his superior upper arm strength. But he had no intention of scraping and tearing his flesh and risking blood poisoning from the barbed wire. Scylla or Charybdis? Spend the night in the cemetery terrorized by his imagination and every fearful sound, mouse squeak, squirrel shriek and owl cry? Or shred and bloody his sun- soaked, expertly sculpted body on the rusty wire? He'd decide later.

He snuffed out the cigarette against the headstone, then brushed away the ashes as best he could, but the soot seeped in, leaving a black mark on the grey marble. Unconsciously, he let the butt fall out of his hand. He hadn't counted on being there so long and not finding Mocha and Peregrine, which upset him. Damn! He didn't want to be at Trinity or any cemetery after dark, but he promised himself he would see it through until he found them. He had to suck it up and get on with it.

There was one portion of the cemetery he had not checked. Situated to the most westward area, down a steep slope and obscured by a thicket of trees and bushes, stood a number of older-looking mausoleums, ornately decorated in an architectural style similar to buildings he remembered seeing in Paris. He had traversed the length and width of the Hills, scoping out all of the concrete houses except for these isolated by their distance and the surrounding landscape. He now loped westward toward the glowing, pink-mauve and deep yellow-orange sky. Though he was not religious, more agnostic than anything else, he rubbed the silver St. Christopher medal and tiny gold menorah, both gifts, and prayed for a miracle.

Fifteen minutes later, after another two cigarettes, the latter more anxiously smoked than the former, Beach Comber arrived at the site. The sun's back glow left a dark blue sky while casting the trees, bushes and tombs in the deepest shades of black. The larger the object, the darker it appeared against the deep blue. Shadows were everywhere, and the cemetery had lost the more pleasant and benign aspect it had held for him in the gleaming daylight. Now the inhospitable tombstones and rustling leaves and branches projected an eerie balefulness. Behind every large headstone, he imagined ghouls and grinning gargoyle-faced demons waiting to slash him with their bony fingers as he passed by.

Not a stranger to death's grim adventures on his travels to the more exotic coastlines of Southeast Asia, Beach Comber had brushed up against the dead and dying, had managed to be victorious in his marathon race with the Master of Life. He knew the abject fears of outrunning tsunami bearing down on him in Thailand, of clawing and tearing up the side of a building to reach the roof, just as the crashing, swirling floods swept by him, carrying off his beloved Rebecca, whom he had never been able to find while picking his way through debris, mud and noisome stench of rotting corpses. He had known the terror and force of hurricanes while at sea, He horrored over the swell of huge rollers that threatened to swamp the cargo ship he had traveled on, and would have if not for the brilliance of the captain's navigation through the treacherous and mammoth waves.

But these fears were different. The unseen world that existed just beyond the reach of materiality terrified him. You couldn't see danger coming like you could in the natural world. You couldn't hear it or feel this other reality, but it was there all the same, and there was some deficiency in the human character, some pathetic crack in the human psyche, not to be able to deal with it, not to be able to comfortably navigate the great ocean of other worldliness. Centuries of institutional beliefs and knowledge systems and not one of them adequate to definitively prove where Rebecca was now. Thoughts of her which normally comforted him only made him more distraught and alone in this creepy place. Beach Comber hated uncertainty, and so he hated his spooky fears and the shadows and his growing discomfort because he couldn't control the unseen circumstances to stop that rustling in the hedges near the mammoth black mausoleum looming in front of him.

Beach Comber hesitated in his tracks, then became immobilized to suppress his panic. Stiffly, he tilted his head toward the shusssshing, clicking sounds. He couldn't make out whether the shusssshing was the light breeze of the evening or an animal in the undergrowth. Or something else, something unnatural. The thickness of the black shrubbery and the moonlight shadows of the trees and towering crypt foiled his ability to see what was there. It disoriented him and confounded his hearing.

"No," he thought. It was his imagination that scared him. "Yes," he whispered. There was something there. He heard it, became transfixed. And now that something treaded heavily, breaking twigs and crushing them underfoot. Beach Comber's hearing became acute. He heard the magnification of footfalls echoing toward him but saw no one in front of him or from the sides of his peripheral vision. Confused, he swiveled around. In the instant before receiving the blow to the back of his neck, he discerned a towering, dark figure, outlined in the color of lightening upraise its arm and bring it crashing down upon his head.

Chapter Seven

S ARDONIC LAUGHTER, HIGH-THROATED and hysterical, bounced off the walls of the vault. In riffs and waves, it pealed in the dead air, ceased for a few minutes, then low-throated, began again and rose in pitch, sustained by deep diaphragmatic breaths. The laughter sounded like that of a patient just admitted to a psych ward, after removal of the straight jacket, after the initial psycho-tropic injection wore off, and before the determination was made to increase the dosage or modulate it through a medication cocktail.

Her back against the door, she sat in her usual place, chortling and guffawing. Alone, light deprived, struggling against dehydration, hypothermia, starvation, Peregrine laughed. She laughed to go mad and bring herself another awakening of intense revelation. And she laughed to keep from going mad out of horror that she was totally wacked out, bonkers, loco weed, manic, schizophrenic, Looney Tunes, crazy.

The situation had reduced to an extreme contradiction of her desires and actions. She was afraid to sleep because she knew it would be the last sleep she would ever have on earth, and yet she desperately coveted sleep for the healthful rest it would bring her traumatized mind and body. When she stood up to pace the floor to stimulate her legs and feet which were going numb from the glacial temperature, she yearned to sit right back down again because the blood rushing from her core to her extremities stabbed her legs with excruciating pain and ached her feet so severely, she could barely take a step.

The urine which had revived her and satiated her thirst, initially, now stimulated her urgings for liquid. If she could pee again to appease her thirst, she would, but like a bear in hibernation, all waste elimination had ceased. And so, she laughed, guffawed, cackled and chortled until she could bear it no longer. Funniest of all were her fears of death by dehydration in seven days. She screamed with howling, deep-throated, belly-aching laughter. Hours! She'd be dead in hours if she could last that long. For hypothermia had begun its creep. She had wanted a painless death, and she had been granted her wish. Her hands and feet were numb, and this pleasurable sensation would gradually move up her legs, her arms and eventually embrace her thighs, her head and down her neck, until death's gelid fingers softly molested her waist, shoulders, bosom and chest. A heart attack after all.

Peregrine grew silent, stymied in an agony of indecision and an agony of self-pity. Should she continue to endure this raw, brutal, violent and humiliating torture of fighting for her life? Or just float in the exquisite absence of feeling and freeze to death? She pushed a thought into her dull, thick mind. Maybe she was being unrealistic. Maybe her situation wasn't that grave. If she did nothing, she might still be rescued. If she lost consciousness, that wouldn't be the end of it. She would become comatose. But if they found her, she could be revived if she wasn't too far gone. Doctors had brought people back, missing toes and fingers to frostbite, even limbs. Yet, they had revived and lived productive lives. So could she…if they found her in time. Maybe Fen was on his way to her. Certainly by now, Beach Comber would be back and would have gone to her mother's and found out they were missing. He would come for her and Mocha. Be there any minute.

It was too much to hope for. Beach Comber wouldn't remember where the ritual was to be held. He didn't even want to hear about it when Mocha carefully explained everything to him. Made up an excuse and left early that night, though they had prepared his favorite Indian dishes. And Fen? He would have come. He never let them down. But something must have happened to him or his family. Unlucky for her and Mocha, it happened when they needed him the most.

Finally, Peregrine curled up in a fetal position, broke down and wept. "Oh God, don't let me die in this place." She lifted her impassive hands up to her face and covered her eyes, but she couldn't feel her forehead or her cheeks or hands, though her brain said her fingers rested there. She cried until the hopelessness drained out like a festering wound. Then she was still. By now, she knew how to merge with the silence of the tomb as if she wasn't even there.

"Change direction. Do something. Don't despair," she yelled. "Never despair." She straightened out her legs and rolled over, propping herself up on her elbows and whispered, "Beach Comber, Beach Comber, Beach Comber," into her cupped hands, like a prayer, the moist, warm breath unannounced and unappreciated by her indifferent palms. Because she could do nothing else, she rolled over on her back, then rolled again on her stomach and rolled over and over again and again, past the door, until her body was perpendicular to the wall adjacent to the door. She rolled over again, repeating, "Beach Comber, Beach Comber, Beach Comber," into her palms because it was silly and ridiculous, and it made her momentarily happy.

Again, she rolled over, faster this time and louder, "Beach Comber, Beach Comber, Beach Comber." She underestimated the ferocity of her exertions. Hot torment sliced through her feet and hands, like a knife cutting meat. Wretched, she moaned aloud in misery. Her hands and feet were coming to life again. They burned and mortally lacerated her numbed bliss.

OK, she had started it. This was the last time she would go through this wicked process of rejuvenating her extremities. She beat her dead hands against her thighs and banged her heels against the concrete. She sat up, wrenched her body right and left, and in a sitting position, slid herself parallel to the wall, moving farther away from the door in an attempt to stem the spasms and pangs as blood rushed to the outer depths of her body.

Peregrine twisted her torso and stretched her arms upward. A searing pain smashed her side. Peregrine screamed in pain. "Oh God, I've ruptured my intestine." Simultaneously, cacophonous chords of metal grating against metal echoed throughout the mausoleum with frightening amplitude. As the pangs in her side subsided, the harsh metallic soundings diminished.

Peregrine was confounded for a moment. Had her agony caused the harsh and intense loudness? What had happened? Using her left arm as her eyes, she gingerly moved her elbow near the wall. Her upper arm bumped against a metal rod and cross piece that she traced with her lower arm since her paralyzed hands could feel nothing. The rod extended outward in the room. That was what she had smashed into, and that was what had caused her pain.

Her mind and heart raced. Was this the lever that opened the door? With rapturous hope, in a frenzy of excitement, Peregrine jiggled the rod with her lifeless palms. She heard the metal scour and scrape, though she had no way to see or feel the impact of her exertions. With force, she toggled the lever from side to side with her arms. It resisted her. Probably rusted. Exasperated she fell on the rod with the entire weight of her torso, pushing it to the left as far as it would go.

Discordant grindings filled the tomb, deafening her. It was the equivalent of fingernails on a chalk-board, amplified to the highest volume. Peregrine was thoughtful. Or maybe it was heavy stone dragged against stone, the kind of sound made when a massive marble wall is being propelled away from its mooring.

Chapter Eight

B EACH COMBER INHALED THE PLEASANT SMELLS of fragrant grass and fecund earth moistened by early morning dew. He had a crushing headache, like he had been roaring drunk the previous evening, hung over from too much gin and vodka. Only he didn't drink, hadn't had a hangover in years. Alcohol was poison, worse than cigarettes. He carefully lifted his head an inch from the grass, and recalled, ruefully, the sledgehammer blow. On his head, he appreciated the sunrise, edging from its horizon point in the east into the azure blue of a magnificent day. He did not appreciate the abysmal ache that ran across the back of his neck and pummeled the crown of his head.

Man, he didn't see the trap coming. Distract you in front to clobber you from behind. But who got him? He couldn't remember. Whomever it was had walloped him. For what reason? He was trespassing. Beach Comber touched the back of his neck, felt swollen flesh, a long, lateral, massive welt. But they didn't have to hit him so hard. He had been ready to run like a mouse. A few more minutes of shaking tree branches, and the dude could have had the graveyard to himself.

Beach Comber shook his head and massaged the back of his neck where the welt had grown like a thick tree root. Gradually, he was recovering. He glanced at his watch. It was 6:17 AM. Unconscious all night. He lifted himself from the soft turf slowly, moving from a crawl position, his left knee bent, pushing upward until he stood. He rolled his head from side to side. The pain was intense. He would have to go home, ice his head and neck and rest. He checked the right back pocket of his jeans for his cigarettes and lighter. Everything was there. In his left back pocket, he grasped his car keys. His leather wallet with driver's license and debit card was missing. His fingers scrambled deeper inside. His iPhone was gone. It made sense, but damn, what a blasted inconvenience. He needed to leave right away to straighten out his affairs before the thieves, probably the cemetery gangs, used his license and debit card. For

Chrissakes, what more did they need to put a hole in his credit rating? He wondered why they didn't take his car keys and car. The custom-made silver keys held the T-Bird logo and the car was unmistakably his. The only one in the lot. Weird.

Beach Comber decided to look around. Maybe, the stuff fell out of his pocket during the assault. He examined the immediate area and backtracked a two-hundred-yard circumference, thinking his attacker might have quickly riffled the wallet for the money and cards and then tossed it. No such luck. He chided himself. He should have left the phone in the car. He knew he wouldn't need it. Stupid. Mocha had told him they couldn't bring anything modern into the tomb, so he couldn't call them to find out where they were. That much he remembered. He massaged the back of his neck, which ached like the devil. He hoped he didn't have a concussion, but intuited that he did.

Beach Comber turned and slowly walked toward the dead house, which looked macabre with its stark, grey, concrete, neoclassical design, striking in the illuminating sun. He wanted to check the bushes and under the trees to see if his wallet or the phone might have been thrown there. Then he thought of his presence in the cemetery, too early for visitors. He looked for the flowers that he should have dropped where he had fallen. They, too, were gone. As Beach Comber scoured the bushes, he considered that people were guilty of all manner of strange things. They left his custom restored car, silver keys and the gold cigarette lighter, but took his wallet, with documents that would be reported immediately, locked iPhone and the flowers. Go figure. Then he remembered the fifty-dollar bill tucked in the side panel of his wallet. All gone.

He idled down the slope of the ravine over which the back of the sepulcher presided. He wanted to investigate behind the crypt, at the farthest corner, where the fence abutted a forest of pine and scrub brush that continued westward beyond Trinity Hills. It was an isolated place, hidden from all other cemetery views, an excellent place to dump his stuff. Probably no one ever went back there, not even the cemetery caretakers since the acidic pine needles eliminated any need for manicuring the grass.

He found it incredible that the situation had gone from bad to worse. The women were still missing. He had been prevented from investigating Calvary Cemetery on Queens Boulevard after his visit to Trinity Hills last night. Now there would be a further delay. He would be too preoccupied with his own troubles to concentrate on the urgency of finding his friends. He vowed to drive to Calvary after he had a Starbucks, called his bank, took care of his license and called Mocha's and Peregrine's moms to see if they had returned.

As he rounded the corner of the mausoleum, Beach Comber nearly collapsed in amazement. Mocha lay stretched out on a soft bed of rust-brown pine needles. He had found one of them at least. Ignoring the misery in his neck, he ran to her. Her appearance was normal. Her hair was disheveled, but her shirt and jeans had no marks on them. Her eyes were closed, and her head was slumped on her right shoulder.

"Mocha, Mocha," he called loudly as he dropped next to her on the pine needle bed. She didn't stir to the sound of his voice. In fact, she didn't move. And the way her head was positioned frightened him. Had her neck been broken? He knew he shouldn't touch her. Staring intently, looking for any signs of wakefulness or recognition that she heard him, he bent over her face and gently called, "Mocha, Mocha." She was listless, vacant. He grabbed both of her shoulders and despite his misgivings shook them lightly with tenderness, careful not to lift her head from the support of the ground.

Her light, coffee-colored skin was ashen, and she didn't appear to be breathing. She was unconscious. Taking her right hand, he felt for a pulse in her wrist which was cool to the touch. Then he cupped his fingers to the right side of her neck. If there were beats, he couldn't find them. He was terrified that she was dying in front of him, and he was helpless to do anything, afraid even to give mouth to mouth. What if he injured her further? But he had to get her to a hospital immediately.

Then he thought of Peregrine. He had completely forgotten about her. Convulsed with panic and frustration, he stood up and looked around the ravine and pine grove. No one else was there. He foraged around the other side of the crypt, checking the bushes and landscaping, thinking he missed something, but he was right the first time. There was no one.

Unless Peregrine was inside. Beach Comber went to the solid, bronze metal door and boldly pounded with both fists. "Peregrine, are you there? Peregrine?" Silence. Not ready to give up, Beach Comber yelled louder and pummeled harder. "Peregrine, shout to me. It's Beach Comber.

Scream, yell. Are you inside?" He massaged his aching neck, as he waited for any noise from within. There was nothing. Maybe she wasn't inside. Maybe she had gone for help. If she was inside, he feared she was unconscious and couldn't hear him. He would come back for her.

His head throbbed, his neck ached. Nevertheless, he ran down the ravine to the pine grove and Mocha, who was unchanged. She appeared to be asleep. He reminded himself, so did the dead. He bent down on both knees and cautiously raised her to a sitting position. Her head jerked backward, limp, like a broken doll. He gently held her head with his left hand as he cradled her upper body close to his chest. In the crook of his right arm, he eased back her head safely while sliding his left arm under her knees.

Normally, light as a moonbeam, Mocha was dead weight, unable to help him or hold herself up. As he struggled to rise, he found he could lift her by placing his left knee solidly underneath her behind, while standing up with his right leg. She weighed a ton for such a slight woman. He didn't know how he was going to carry her the length of the cemetery to the gates or how he would get her over the steel fence. And he didn't know if it mattered since it was probably too late, anyway.

Chapter Nine

PEREGRINE GAPED WITH OPEN-MOUTHED astonishment and repeatedly blinked her eyes, disbelieving the view which emerged from the darkness. Accustomed to sense deprivation, her eyes teared as she gazed upon the glowing ceiling lights of a separate vault of entombments, ensconced, secreted, behind the huge cream-colored marble wall which evidently had collapsed into the floor after she threw herself on the mechanical lever. She had felt the seams in the concrete by the wall of drawers but never guessed their purpose. Peregrine breathed a great sigh of relief. One infernal element had been conquered, the darkness. Now, to deal with the others.

She quickly surveyed her surroundings in the diffused light that seeped into each corner of the room, making the blackness grey. The large area appeared to house two other walls of entombments also with name carvings of the deceased. Only the wall against which she leaned was unblemished. To her far left in this wall was the impassive, oak door. Next to her, was the mechanical lever. But Peregrine sensed that the room was a canard of illusions and magic. If the walls began to close in on her and squashed her like a bug, she would not have been surprised.

Spiritually, she discerned that nothing in this crypt was what it seemed. From the outside, the sepulcher was monolithic, at least three stories high. Though this room was huge, its rectangular shape and nine-foot ceiling belied the massive form of the outer structure. She imagined there were other mechanical buttons or rods which opened onto secret passageways and corridors. But she had no time to investigate in the gelid atmosphere. Hypothermia was squeezing out her life blood with its icy tentacles.

Peregrine slowly pushed her left palm down on the floor, then her right, carefully, because both were frozen senseless without the continual pounding and smashing against her thighs. She looked at her fingers to gauge whether she had succeeded in willing their extension. The lifeless lumps outstretched. Palms down, knees pressed into the concrete, she rested on all fours for a moment before she raised herself up and stood on spongy legs and ice-block feet. Only one thought filled her mind. Escape the freeze. The temperature must now be plummeting toward twenty degrees Fahrenheit.

With renewed determination, she robotically clomped toward the drawers in the wall to her left. About twenty-five were visible, stacked in horizontal and vertical rows. They reminded her of the dead stacked in the ancient catacombs of Rome and Paris, burial grounds that extended in elaborate, multi-layered stone labyrinths and underground passageways.

Peregrine came to a shoulder level drawer she guessed would be accessible to her evaporating arm strength. On the front, above a metal handle, was the picture of a beautiful woman who had lived and died over a century before. She was dressed in sumptuous clothing accessorized with jewels, what looked to be diamond and pearl necklaces and bracelets with matching earrings. Hesitating, Peregrine wondered if time had desiccated and mortified the body into a horrific, ghoulish and disgusting corpse or whether the remains were just bones. She could deal with skeletons, had clowned around with Lady Matilda in her high school Bio class, waltzing with the spare, light skeleton while friends took videos with their cell phones. But what if the corpse was rotting flesh?

She considered moving on to the drawer of one more recently interred. But she was freezing to death. Now was not the time to be fussy. She only prayed she had the power in her hands and arms to grasp the handle and pull out the drawer. Regardless, she would have to deal with the ghoulish contents.

Peregrine commanded her useless fingers to circle the large handle. Using both hands, with all her strength, she yanked back the burial drawer. It slipped toward her a few inches with a screeching noise, as if the occupant protested the undignified disturbance. She yanked again. This time her exertion exposed one third of the closed, copper-colored coffin. Not enough. Excruciating pain in her fingers. They were savagely avenging themselves for interrupting their frozen sleep. She beat her hands against her chest with ferocious abandon to alleviate the ache and cramp and decided to go on despite it. Again, she curled her fingers around the handle, one by one mentally infusing each with power. With determination, she yanked the drawer a third time. As if in empathy, it relented and bounded outward, exposing three quarters of the coffin. Now there was enough room to lift up the top half of the bi-sectioned lid.

She moved around to the right. On this side of the coffin was a decorative gilded lock. Mysteriously and illogically dangling from one arm of the lock on a red ribbon was a delicate, gold, filigree, skeleton-shaped key. Peregrine tried to lift the lid with the palms of her hands, but it resisted, stupidly locked.

Now the simple task of holding the key and turning it in the lock became Herculean. The Arctic air had ravaged her fine motor skills. Peregrine grasped the key only to see it slip away from her index finger and thumb and clink against the copper as it swung on its red leash. She tried again with the same result. And again! Stubborn, Pavlovian, hypnotically spurred on by defeat. After ten minutes, repeated fruitless attempts brought frustration and fogged up her mind in confusion and panic. She was going to die of the cold before she could get warm in the snug death bed.

The atmosphere was crystalline; her jeans' crotch was solid ice. All feeling in her feet had slipped away, though she stomped and pounded them repeatedly. The hibernal air gripped her legs, sluicing higher, and the brutal numbness iced up her arms. She craved sleep, and thought to recline on the floor to get her strength back, revive and then tackle the lock and key. But somewhere in her fog-shrouded mind, a distant bell sounded the warning. The freeze was embracing her core. With the last shred of her consciousness, she dumbly stuffed her hands under her arm pits to cozen out any bit of motion there. It worked. After a minute there was an explosion of sensation. A thousand stabbing knife tips pricked her fingers. Her sleepy brain awakened. Red hot flames ignited her cramped hands and arms, and the resurrected pyres mobilized her fingers.

Now she was able to hold the key long enough to place it in the keyhole. And after a few tries, she was able to force the key deep into the lock. During these attempts, Peregrine returned her dead hands to her armpits to invoke the flaming wrath of freezing flesh. And the miserable immolation enabled her crippled fingers to turn the key. She sighed in relief when the lock released with a little click. She removed the key and slipped the crimson satin strip over her wrist. As the flames in her fingers died away and the numbness resurrected, she unhooked the lock. It slipped from her lifeless grasp and dropped to the floor, bouncing twice with delicate, silvery pings.

Peregrine panted with fear. She couldn't hold back frostbite. The room was a glacier. She must warm herself in the next few minutes or join the sleeping dead. Now was not the time to be squeamish about the corpse in the coffin. She was dying. She mollified her imagination and tried to inure herself to Death's hideous handiwork. She had seen dead bodies at a wake: her Aunt Rachel, Mocha's grandmother, others. This was a wake. No more, no less.

Palming the coffin lid's metal rim, she slowly raised the door into Death's Kingdom. Rushing away from their captivity, mephitic odors that had combined and rebounded for over a century pounced upon their nearest victim. Ach! Ugh. Whew!!!

Peregrine reeled backward, her arms gyrating like windmills. She tripped and kicked the lock across the floor as her feet scraped back from the rotten and stinking cocoon. Repulsive!

Coughing and gagging, Peregrine spun away from the corpse and tried to shake off the skunk scent. The violence of her flailing movements vibrated the air, and the precariously balanced lid banged shut with a startling thump. Peregrine jerked up in surprise. She arched her back, then bent over double with both hands on her abdomen. Her empty stomach lurched, revolted by the malodorous insult to living, whole flesh. If she threw up, she felt she wouldn't be able to stop herself until every drop of liquid had been purged from her horrified stomach. But she couldn't sustain the loss of any more bodily fluid.

Bile vomit rose. She swallowed and took in small breaths through her mouth, but the acerbic liquid heaved to the threshold of her throat, threatening to rush over her tongue and out her mouth. In labor to keep the glut down, she bent over to the ground and increased her breaths. Revulsion and fear were starving her sanity. She swallowed the acid liquids spilling into her burning throat. She pushed them back down her esophagus into her stomach and fought to calm herself by gulping in air through her mouth until she regained focus. Breathing deeply, she felt the earthquake was over. She straightened up. How would she be able to use the coffin if the stench and idea was so odious?

Peregrine swiveled around toward the closed copper box, readying herself to face the ordeal. This time she held her breath and averted her face to the left. Clumsily fumbling at the lip of the metallic lid, she flung it back to its furthest extension, where it remained open as in a viewing. The putrid air released its corrupted molecules. Peregrine ran to the farthest corner of the entombment wall. With her face to the corner like a punished child, she fiercely flailed her gross arms, smacked her mortal hands against her hips and stomped obtuse feet, waiting some moments to aerate the coffin. "I've got to deal," she muttered to herself. She had to adjust to the baleful smell. She could wait no longer. The ice flow in her blood was drifting in waves to her core.

Panting and breathing through her mouth, Peregrine walked back to the coffin. Facing the body, but refusing to focus her vision directly on it, she imagined the woman in the coffin was her Aunt Rachel transplanted to this crypt. The image soothed her. She stared at the yards of plush, creamy satin and delicate lace and fringe lining the lid. Continuing her rapid tiny pants, she edged forward and stood in front of Death and steadied herself. She continued breathing through her mouth and relied on her peripheral vision. Mentally instructing her lifeless fingers to grasp the lace and satin bodice of the dress worn by the dead woman, she pulled and dragged the torso over the lip of the metal box then rested, fiercely exhaling and yelping in air. Her fingers and palms burned as if she had touched the fires of hell in a satanic revival.

The body was heavier than Peregrine had imagined, and though she avoided looking closely, the embalming fluid, or whatever was used in the 1800s as a preservative, had worked a miracle. Remarkably, the woman was recognizable and looked like her picture. Peregrine rapidly subtracted the years of birth and death; the age in no way correlated with the woman's appearance. Strange. As the coffin aired, she became inured to the stench and found she could tolerate her flaming fingers as they became intimate with death.

To work. She must hurry while she had the strength. Breathing through her mouth, Peregrine plunged her burning hands under the body unable to feel the satin and lace white burial garments and luxurious bed of death. She grappled, twisted and wrestled with the corpse, as she contorted it into a manageable position to lift it to the floor. In a ludicrous struggle, that was more like a female wrestling match than an attempt to pick up a passive figure, she tugged the head, torso, behind and right leg half over the burial case. This leverage enabled her to hug the upper half of the body, pick it up and, with a rapid twist, flip the other leg out of the metal box. She then let go, allowing the woman to drop rudely onto the crypt floor in an angled heap, parallel to the drawer wall. "Sorry?" she said guiltily, then joked, "You need to stop eating those fatty lunches." Bending over the still lovely woman, Peregrine straightened out the woman's legs and crossed her arms at the wrist in a position of solemnity. "Forgive me. But I need to borrow your resting place," she said, to mitigate the macabre weirdness she felt.

Peregrine stood momentarily with her aching arms crossed and fiery hands under her armpits, gazing at the sleeping woman. Still inhaling and exhaling the rank, crystallized air through her mouth, she said a prayer of thankfulness that it was not hot. The reeking miasma would have been hyperbolic, and she would have died of dehydration by now. Her agonized movements had brought life back into her tortured hands and fingers, which she could move more easily, though her feet were still glacial. She was like Frankenstein clumping around on antic platform shoes. Maybe she'd only lose a few toes to frostbite, that is if someone rescued her, or she figured how to open the door.

Again, she turned to the copper death box. Propping both hands on the edge, she boosted the upper part of her body inside with her legs hanging outside. Like a seesaw she rocked her legs in space and pressed her face into the coffin bed, moving her body forward, trying not to breathe through her nose. After she had inched herself in farther, she curled her body sideways until she pulled both her legs in the fetid, but warming, bed. She lay in this fetal position and accustomed herself to the odor, then gathered the stamina to slide her legs and feet into the closed section of the casket. She panted and gulped air into her mouth and turned over on her back and stretched her legs, looking upward at the grey fleur-de-lies carved mausoleum ceiling. For the first time, she began to feel warmth, as the cramping and mobility of her fingers increased.

Amazingly, she fit, as if the burial bed had been made for her. She didn't dare close the upper lid against the freezing air for fear of locking herself inside the coffin. If her claustrophobia didn't kill her, the stink would. She laughed. How her attitude had changed since her first night in the tomb. Then she was thinking of ways to commit suicide. Now, she was struggling to hope herself into the next minute.

Peregrine rubbed her hands against the satin and lace, intensifying the flames in her fingers. Then she undulated them, like a pianist practicing scales to lessen their clumsiness. When her fingers gained flexibility and strength, she tore out huge pieces of material from the lid and sides, shredding and ripping the lacy, satiny, creamy white padding underneath. Loosely, she insulated her entire body, stuffing whole wads of cloth and padding down by her feet, making sure to leave no area uncovered, not even her face which she veiled like a bride's with lace. Though she still breathed through her mouth, she found the putrescence had diminished, or it so clung to her she had become the reek. No matter. She was in a paradise of luxurious warmth, packed like Royal Dalton in yards of posh satin and lace. As her torso, neck and legs warmed, she sank prickly hands deep in the burial bed underneath her bottom and held pieces of padding in her fists, opening and closing them, opening and closing them.

Gradually, the fires died down to tolerable embers. But her feet were in hell. She thought about removing her sneakers and taking off her socks. She knew her feet were swollen and brutally restricted though she had loosened the shoestrings three times. But then she might never get her shoes on again, and she needed her shoes to accomplish the second part of her plan. No, she thought, that's not it. She was terrified that her feet were turning black with frostbite. But she refused to think about that now. She would try to get warm. Her core temperature

would increase so that the blood would get to her feet…eventually. She prayed that the tell-tale aching and burning would come to her toes sooner rather than later.

While Peregrine reveled in the warmth, her mind playfully wandered to distract herself from the irredeemability of her situation. She imagined that from afar and with myopathy, she looked like a huge mound of whipped cream that roiled underneath when she shifted her position. She smelled worse than a slaughter-house, more noisome than an overflowing cesspool. She reeked like a decaying animal ready for the sanitation maggots to collect the garbage. All her cravings for hamburgers and French fries and pizza had vanished. Occasionally, she napped, but struggled to catch herself from falling into the deep sleep from which she would not wake.

In this way, Peregrine passed an hour, floating in and out of consciousness until she became aware that something was wrong. Her body felt toasty. If she remained under the loose pack much longer, she would be sweating. But near her feet, there was a monstrous cold rising up, as if from the deepest section of the drawer, in the recesses behind the casket wall. She mused this was why she probably couldn't heat her feet like she could the rest of her body. And it probably was an explanation why the crypt was a glacier. Beyond these thoughts, she did not venture how or why.

Peregrine figured that maybe six or 8 hours had passed since the time she drank her urine up to this very moment. Maybe she had been in the tomb four days, and today was the fifth. Maybe not. Impossible to tell, even in the light. Without a window or watch to calculate the days she had spent there, Peregrine equated her former state of darkness and her current state of light as equal backdrops to her interminable captivity, each minute a chore to get through. Now that she had satiated her compulsion for heat, like Tantalus, she became fixated on thirst. How many more days could she hold out against dehydration before she went into a coma?

She wasn't going to wait to find out. Peregrine sat up in the coffin, pushing away her toasty blanket. She had lain there doing nothing long enough. Carefully, turning to her right side, she pulled her left leg then her right out of the bottom section of the burial box. She curled her knees to her chest, and grabbing them, swung her legs up and over the side. Leaning back on her arms with her palms as flat as possible on the shredded coffin innards, Peregrine lifted her behind up on the side rim, and though the metal dug into her, she slowly worked her way to a sitting position, then jumped to the floor.

Easier to get out than in, she mused. Turning back to the warm sanctuary, she reached into the box and riffled through the material, selecting various sections and shredding them for functionality. She chose five lace pieces to wrap around her head, tying each like a kerchief. She made four capes of the heavier satin lining and fastened each loosely around her shoulders. She ripped more fabric from the casket and with it, fastened pieces around her torso, tucking them into the waist of her jeans.

She chose large sections of padding, dumped them on the floor and bent over, removing each of her shoelaces. Sitting on the hibernal concrete flooring, she arranged a large piece, so it covered her entire right shoe from the sole to the ankle, then fastened it securely around her ankle with one shoelace. Haphazardly, she tried to do the same with her left shoe, but because the piece wasn't big enough; she could only wrap the sole of her shoe. Better than nothing, she thought.

What to do about her hands? Peregrine scoured the demolished box for padding. She gloved her left hand, making it into a mitten, wrapping it round and round with satin, like a thick present, and securing it with a torn strip of lace around her wrist, stuffing its tail underneath the binding. The right mitten was harder, but she fumbled until her hand was snug. Eventually, she knew, the freezing temperature would pierce through, but she felt comfortable for now.

She looked at the device on the opposite side of the wall which had saved her from hypothermia. Warm enough, she could investigate it. Leaving the coffin's upper lid open and the corpse where she lay sleeping, Peregrine padded over to the metal rod that had released the monolithic slab into the floor, exposing the inner vault. She was frantic for water and realized she had only hours left before her strength to get herself out of this place would fail.

She must open the door or find another way. Peregrine assumed from the complexity of the pseudo wall that had disappeared into the floor, there had to be alternate entrances and exits to this custom-made mausoleum. The crypt was luxurious with costly marble and granite walls and bronze appointments, and the casket she raided was more like a plush bridal bed than practical resting site for a woman who would never feel or see its beauty. This place must have cost a fortune, she thought, remembering what her mom had told her about the family and the trust funds and foundations into perpetuity. The generational wealthy were eccentric and secretive and fantastical monument builders. Her mom had told her countless stories of the upper classes' machinations to defy death. Hell, they had conquered aging with surgery, medicines, elixirs, therapies. Anything was possible for them. And why not? Through privilege and entitlement, their money bought access to the most advanced treatments, inventions, information, developments and technologies that the masses could never afford and never knew existed. Peregrine related these thoughts to the task at hand. The elaborate entrance/exit was probably for show, a public funeral. Most likely, the family left the crypt through one of a number of secret exits to secure a rapid and discrete retreat.

Peregrine crossed the floor and poised herself in front of the iron lever that had lowered the wall. Examining it quickly, she noted that it worked mechanically, probably with pulleys. So much for advanced technology. But the place was like the hall of mirrors in the fun-house. Distortion and transformation warped reality. Anything was possible. She searched the area, lightly fingering the wall space, then stamped the flooring. There was no other instrument, implement, button or switch visible. She looked for seams in the concrete. There didn't appear to be any. Illusion and prestidigitation. She knew she was making a crucial mistake, missing something, but she lacked the imagination and energy to think what. Maybe you had to have a remote to move back the other walls or open the door, she smiled to herself.

She returned to the lever because her thirst was straining her patience and the frigid atmosphere was sniping at her hands and feet reminding her to hurry. She hesitated to pull it for fear of the result. If the lever only moved one wall up and down and did nothing else, the doom bell would toll, and the countdown on her life that had been halted by her temporary solutions would continue. She would have to endure each tortuous second, minute, hour until she was rescued or became comatose. She stretched her arms up and out to gain flexibility, then tugged and patted down her hand-made gloves to improve their gripping power. She said another little prayer, then wrenched the lever back toward the wall, figuring that if she moved it to the right, the opposite from her initial movement earlier, the wall would resurface from the floor. She heard a creak, then silence. Nothing happened. "Why does everything have to be so hard in this place?" she proclaimed to the ceiling and her silent companions, who couldn't have been more in agreement if they had the inclination to express it.

This was her last chance. She had no other choice but to stand behind the iron rod and push it outward into the room. In dread, she circled the lever, positioning herself to exact the greatest momentum forward. She gripped the cold metal with the makeshift gloved hands and pushed. It budged with a scraping sound, then halted. She saw no corresponding outward manifestation anywhere in the dead house. Probably was rusted, but at least the direction forward seemed right. She spread her legs and leaned into the metal, and this time she placed her right hand higher than her left and grasped the rod firmly, though the gloves made her grip uneven. Peregrine counted backward, infusing herself with faith. "Three, Two, One," she screamed mightily with an exhalation from her diaphragm in a volume that surprised her. Then she threw her entire weight forward onto her hands.

Shrieking! Startled, she jumped back, pulling her hands from the lever as if it were red hot iron. The high-pitched wails stopped. The situation was familiar, but her dull wits couldn't remember specifics. She shuddered. Evil flowers bloomed in her imagination. These were wheeling, terrible screams, like someone being impaled on a spike. A demon, one of the familiar spirits of the dead, was coming for her soul. She turned to her right with eyes half-closed. She expected a sneering skeleton would float over her shoulder, whipping a scythe in the air to take off her head!

Peregrine gasped. To her right about ten feet away between where she stood and the door, a section of the floor had dropped away. "Thank you, God!" With exuberance Peregrine, bundled in her cream puff grave clothes, vamped an Egyptian walk toward the square pit in the floor from which warmth rose upward into the mausoleum and from which stairs crept downward to the basement, and, she prayed, to an exit.

Chapter Ten

S WEATY AND EXHAUSTED, Beach Comber stood in front of the black iron and gold spiked gates of Trinity Hills, grunting under Mocha's one hundred and six pounds of weight. He had carried her in his arms for a mile or more, over hills and around tombs and graves, praying he would not blunder into a hole or stumble over a child's headstone, dangerously crashing both of them to the ground. He had rested twice for fear of dropping her, but he forced himself to go on because Mocha's breathing was barely perceptible, and her pulse was a butterfly's breath.

As he raced-walked to the gates and the parking lot, doubts battered him with each step. Weren't you supposed to carry comatose people on a stretcher? What if he was injuring her with all these jolting movements? What if her back or neck had been broken? You were supposed to keep the person as still as possible, give them fluids and cover them with a blanket. At least, that's what he had seen on medical shows, but his mind was a blank screen about such things. He had become so muddle-headed and mental, at one point during the brief time he had rested, he had lain Mocha down on the ground and absently reached for his iPhone to call 911, settling his fears once and for all. The moment he felt his empty pocket and remembered it had been stolen, he chided himself for being so stupid, then considered that he, too, probably needed medical attention and had suffered a concussion.

The realization provoked him to gently pick up Mocha and continue his arduous journey back to the parking lot. But the turmoil within his mind gained momentum: should he leave her and go for help or stay with her? He didn't want to abandon Mocha, who was defenseless and vulnerable to the marauders who might still be lurking around, while he raced back all that distance to his car, then climbed the fence, drove to a working phone, bummed change off someone, called 911 and met the ambulance at the gates a half hour later. Then he would waste more precious time calling the caretaker to open the gates if the ambulance arrived before 9:00 AM, which was highly doubtful. The option seemed too complicated and dilatory. He felt he could be at The Parkside Medical Center within the hour. So here he was with a pounding migraine, carrying her back to the car by the most direct route in the cemetery labyrinth to get her to the ER before the caretaker arrived. This way, he would avoid having to respond to questions he couldn't answer, like: "What were you doing locked in Trinity Hills all night?"

Mocha and Peregrine had insisted on Fen and Beach Comber's secrecy. Their oath was a fervent commitment to the arcane ceremonial rites. They agreed if something terrible happened to any of them, they, themselves, would bear the consequences, even death. For the magic power to be heralded in, the oath was a vital bond with the realm of the supernatural, even if the stakes were life and death.

Beach Comber realized that they had painted themselves into a corner. He spoke aloud his bitterness. "For Chrissakes!" He couldn't call 911, regardless of what he might like to do. Police involvement would ruin Mocha. Her cousin in the department would show up and want to know everything. He would be compelled to answer out of guilt and familial pressure, destroying his friends' chances to save lives, the purpose of the ceremonial ritual. They were exchanging their lives for others; that was the sacrifice. If they got into trouble, the terms were fixed. No help was to be called; they must deal and survive or perish.

He was between a rock and a hard place. This vow of secrecy was destroying them. Throughout his laborious rescue, carrying Mocha past stone crucifixes and stately granite monuments, the nagging suspicion that he was harming her with each step ate up his mind and distressed him into a morass of guilt. And he never went mental, except for Rebecca. He sighed. He had lost one woman to a hell storm of horror. He couldn't live with the guilt of losing another.

Weighed down by her heaviness, Beach Comber, cradled Mocha in his arms, nestling her head against his chest in the 6:20 AM sunlight. He looked at the lowest section of the gates which were shaped like an upward facing bracket and topped with one curling spiral of barbed wire rope. He was in a quandary. If he waited for the opening at 9:00 AM and drove to the hospital, it would be two hours later. Mocha needed attention now. It was obvious she was in shock. On the other hand, how was he to climb over the gates holding her and risking her further injury with all the jarring and banging? Additionally, both of them would be sliced by the wire. There was less barbed wire on the gates, but they were higher, about ten feet, while the fence was eight feet topped by three, spiraling, barbed wire ropes. Either way, it looked hopeless. He had better wait for the caretaker.

Racked with doubts, he reviewed the 911 scenario once more. If he climbed over alone, drove to a phone, called and drove back? No. By the time he got to a phone and the ambulance arrived, and they got her to the ER, it would be about 9:00 AM, maybe later, given the rush hour traffic. Still hopeless. He wished he could avoid the ER altogether, take her to a doctor friend. The ER would be problematic since he and Mocha had no identification. Mocha's pockets were empty, and she had no purse with her, probably stolen along with his wallet and the other stuff. So, he would have to give all the details to hospital personnel before they called Ms. Hamilton. The situation was unusual, and Mocha couldn't corroborate his story. Ms. Hamilton would be grateful he had found her, but Mocha's cousin would be on duty. Even if he was off-duty, he was law enforcement. He and his buddies would be protective of Mocha. Beach Comber would be questioned and scrutinized by police, whether he called 911 or not. What other choices did he have? In a daze, he was incapable of making a cogent decision.

Beach Comber looked down at Mocha's face. Her head dangled backward; her skin was paler than before. He had to do something immediately and couldn't waste any more precious time. An idea came to him. He could climb over the fence and check his car trunk to see if he had anything in it he could use to either pull the gates open with his car or pull her up and over the gates. In slow motion, Beach Comber knelt, using his right knee to steady Mocha as he bent down, then gently sat her on the grass to the side of the gravel pathway, closely holding her head with his arm until she was securely positioned. With steady hands, he carefully cradled her torso and head to the ground and straightened her legs, then he leaped to his feet from his kneeling position. She looked asleep, comfortable.

Beach Comber pulled his Polo shirt over his head and arms and placed it between his teeth, gritting into a forced smile. He spun around from Mocha, ran five steps and then leaped onto the vertical iron bars of the gates, like a tiger jumping on its prey. With muscles rippling, he scrambled up the metal like a monkey, using the power in his legs and arms to lift himself up the ten feet until he neared the top of the gilded, iron, curved bracket and spiraling barbed wire rope. Gripping an iron cross bar with his stronger right hand, he removed the shirt from his mouth with his left hand and quickly flipped it over the menacing wire, elongating the shirt as far as it would go. He gingerly held the T-shirt and didn't think about the barbs lurking underneath. The flimsy material afforded little protection from the tiny spikes which dug into his left hand, jabbing like an ice pick. Wincing and groaning with pain, he grabbed the other end of the shirt covering the metal pricks with his right hand. He vaulted himself up, straddling atop the wire, split in half with his chest and head above, legs below. The jagged points peppered and pierced the flesh on his abdomen. Impaled by the thick needle points, he tried to gently and slowly dislodge himself. But with each tearing movement, he left flesh on the pricks and bloody pock marks on his skin as he pulled the metal away. Instead of easing his pain, he was intensifying it. He should have waited for the caretaker.

Holding himself still, Beach Comber precariously balanced on the strength of his arms and deliberated. If he threw himself off the gates, he would have broken bones and might not be able to walk. Not an option. If he attempted to unpin himself from the torturing wire, his body weight would force his abdomen deeper into the barbs as he wriggled to free himself, like a butterfly whose struggle against the tortuous pin abetted its destruction. His arms were tiring as he poised like a see-saw atop the harsh, wire rope. He sighed and imagined that this was like a waxing, or burn treatment, the faster the better.

With rapid, precise intention, he pressed into the piercing wire, bending it down to the top of the gilded bracket which intensified his misery, as the curve of iron dug into his abdomen. Leaning his torso forward in a horizontal position, quickly he threw his left leg over the curved iron and spiraling barbs which tore at his jeans and scratched his legs. All the while, he unstuck his hands to adjust and tighten his grip to balance himself. He was in a semi-reclining position with his legs straddling each side of the gate, his bare chest forced into the piercing barbs and wrought iron.

As his 160 pounds bent the taut wire downward, the barbs bit into his chest, and the unyielding iron pressed him. Beach Comber writhed and groaned. He fought to free himself, like a great fish fighting an angler. Painfully, he adjusted his grip, managing to hold firmly to the wire and top of the curved iron bracket, elbows bent over opposite sides of the gate. Crying out, he pulled out more torso flesh from the metal and quickly threw the right leg over the wire and the curved iron bracket. The barbs hissed against his jeans and resisted his movement. He held on with all his arm strength, letting gravity drag his long legs toward the earth. His white-knuckled, tortured grip stopped his body's downward plunge, and he momentarily hung with legs dangling over the front of the gates, like a string puppet, his shoes four feet from the ground. Then he released his hold on the wire and curved, gilded iron, gashing the flesh on his hands, bloodying them, and tearing the shirt as he dragged it off the prongs. He fell to the earth, landing in a tuck and roll, breaking the momentum of his fall and diminishing any potential damage to his feet and ankles.

Beach Comber sat up from his rolled position, feeling for sprains. He glanced down at his burning torso, which was covered in bloody holes and scratches from the wiry piercing. His hands were shredded with jagged tears as if an alcoholic, blind, neophyte surgeon had been butchering him during gross anatomy class. Other than the fact that he looked a bloody mess and didn't think he could hold the wheel of his car or anything else without screaming, he seemed to be OK. He put the shirt over his head, using his knuckles, and eased it down over his bleeding torso. It pained him to cup his palms. The shirt was tight because the bloody stripes were swelling. Like a man who had been whipped with a cat of nine tales, the tight shirt pressured his wounds, which bled through the yellow and white Ralph Lauren. The ER doctor would probably have to cut the shirt off him. Since it was tattered, it was no loss. He smiled ruefully. He had a new respect for the efficacy of rusty barbed wire and tried to remember when he had his last tetanus shot.

Scrambling to his feet, he ran to the T-Bird, giving it a quick glance. The thugs who had stolen from him did not mess up his car. He carefully removed the keys from his pocket and opened the trunk. He remembered he had nylon cord and a few old surf leg ropes. Maybe he could tie them together if he could tolerate the searing pain in his hands while he manipulated his fingers. Trying not to open the wounds further, he rummaged through the trunk and found the cord and leg ropes under a bag of clothes and piles of assorted rubble. The nylon cord wasn't long enough, even if he tied it to the surf leg ropes which weren't strong and would probably snap in half. How to get around the barbed wire and height of the gates? The gulf that separated him from Mocha seemed wider than the Grand Canyon. He looked at his watch. 7:00 AM. Again, he considered. Should he wait? Then he remembered Mocha's paleness, her shallow breaths. It wasn't an option. And there was a way.

Beach Comber unlocked the door of his car, got in, and tried to relax in the custom black leather upholstery. Thank God his back was uncut, but the excruciating gashes on his torso and shredded hands were weakening him. He needed water. He realized he had nothing to eat or drink since yesterday, which could account for his dizziness and disorientation. Then, too, he had been hit over the head, making it harder to concentrate on a viable course of action. Beach Comber grasped the custom seat belt between his thumb and forefinger and pulled. His hand strength had dissipated, and he had to struggle with both hands to put it on and straighten out the shoulder strap. Now, could he put his palms on the wheel without breaking open his wounds? He breathed deeply and using the leverage from his knuckles, turned the key in the ignition. The engine purred from the recent tune-up. He put his knuckles inside the steering wheel, turned it and peeled a backward curve out of the parking space. Using the outside of his hands, wrists and knuckles, he maneuvered the car forward and drove to the entrance, looking for the area where he had left Mocha stretched out in a sunny position on the soft grass.

She was far enough away. Still using his knuckles and trying not to crunch his palms, sluicing his wounds to blood flow, he turned onto the gravel path in front of the entrance and drove up to the gates slowly. He gauged their distance and assessed the large, black, square locking device and the seam between the gates as they closed in together. He put his T-Bird in reverse and slowly moved back about twenty-five feet, as far back as he could go. He decided to take her to the closest emergency room. Then Beach Comber floored the gas pedal and gunned the T-Bird from zero to sixty, heading straight for the ten-foot iron gates of Trinity Hills.

Chapter Eleven

I N THE DIM LIGHT THAT WEAKENED with each step away from its source over her left shoulder, Peregrine edged her body sideways along the narrow passageway, questioning whether she should continue. The tunnel had been carved out of the earth. Its flooring, walls and ceiling still retained a composite of tamped down earthen material interspersed with a detritus of rock, pebbles, broken field stone and varying pieces of concrete. The walls and ceiling had been reinforced with occasional wooden beams, field stones and a smattering of concrete blocks, none of which was wired for lights. The whole affair reminded her of a crude mine shaft sloppily thrown together. She feared that colliding with the rough construction might trigger a cave in. So she sidled thinly, holding in her breath, tensely restricting all movements to a delicate, rigid formality, no swinging of the arms or hands or any extraneous and casual motion. Thankfully, it was warmer underground than above in the dead house, or her chattering teeth and shivering limbs would have sent her careening into the walls, rocking the shaft to pieces and smothering her with stones and dirt.

For illumination, she was using the light that splayed down the wooden steps, trickling into the passageway from the upstairs. But in a few more feet, she would be pitched in darkness once more, unable to see the decreasing pigeonhole of light as an anchor. This cringing thought and the suspicion that she had stumbled upon an unused and useless portion of the vault that led nowhere and wasted her precious time and energy nearly egged her to stop, carefully turn around, go back up the stairs, look for another exit and finding none, wait for Fen or the coma, whichever came first.

But she had not wanted to give up so easily and was driven by the realization that there was no water upstairs. Yet, there might be some ahead, if not an exit. So, she adjusted her feet and began tiny crab-like steps, plunging her right hand into the increasing darkness and brushing it lightly against the wall in front of her for balance and direction. She continued this way until she struck a regular rhythm, then proceeded down the now dark and spooky corridor of earth, stone and rock, mincing sideways, as if she were on the ledge of a building or walking a tightrope. All light extinguished, she was an intimate of the darkness once more.

Peregrine had dropped her ragged, cloth, head and body armor and the padding from around her hands and feet and left it in a chaotic, twisted mound at the bottom of the stairs. A visitor to the scene would recognize the fatal materials and well imagine that they were the random work of an insane, homeless person who had haphazardly snuck inside the tomb, mangled a corpse's sleeping quarters and used the cloth shreds for the exact purpose that Peregrine had. She would have put the coffin guts and the cadaver back in the casket, but instead, she encouraged herself to keep searching for an exit and water since her strength would soon leave her, and she would collapse immobilized.

She vowed that if she found a way out, she would return in the next week to straighten out the vault, place the decedent back in the casket and crank the wall back to its proper place, so that everything appeared untouched. She had to return anyway for the key, the only one of its kind, which had been given to her mom on her thirtieth birthday, the year she received her trust fund payments, and the year Peregrine was born, twenty-four years ago. Peregrine felt assured she would find the lost key by the boxwood hedge near the entranceway. She pictured herself dropping it there to manage the door and forgetting to pick it up as she scrambled for cover inside the tomb.

Thinking about the key, Peregrine became distracted. When her fingers fell upon a rough, unbroken and gnarly stone or concrete slab, she couldn't tell which, she nearly passed it and then realized what it might be. A door or entrance. Stopping, she gently ran her fingers where the cool slab met the earth to the extreme right. She alternated positions, slipping her fingers over the extreme leftmost edge. She fingered the stone as it rose to an unreachable height over her head and traced it down to the floor. There was no knob or handle, where she imagined one might be, nor was it anywhere else on the door. Peregrine pushed with all her might; first, the left side of the slab. Then, she felt the right edge to see if the door had swiveled outward. It hadn't. She did the same with the other side. The result was the same. If this large monolithic stone was an entrance to a room or passageway, she was barred from it. Another mystery of the mausoleum remained unsolved. Again, she had missed the architect's sleight of hand. She decided to continue her sidling and mincing down the black tunnel, shrugging off the depression that tore at the exhilaration she had experienced a minute ago.

Peregrine extended her right hand, brushing the wall to her right in her regular movement sideways. She was unprepared for what happened next. Instead of the wall, she touched empty space. At the same time, her hand encountered dead air and her right foot dropped downward into nothingness. She lost her balance and careened to the right. With fingertips and nails, she grabbed and grappled the wall to save herself. She skimmed the dirt and scraped stones but could not grasp hold to recoup her balance. As her right foot plunged downward, downward in space, her body and arms cart-wheeled, and she tumbled, free falling in the darkness until she smashed her right leg and side into a bank of loose rocks. The momentum of her fall slid her over into a spin down a bumpy decline that twirled her careening and bumping walls until she plopped in a miry pit where she rolled into a full and body aching stop. Her arms and legs were entangled like a pile of twisted sticks. The terrifying fall had knocked the air from her lungs. She couldn't catch her breath. Rasping and gasping, she forgot how to breathe easily. She lay recumbent in the wet earth and concentrated on her chest. She hollowly sucked in huge gulps of air. As the oxygen in her lungs regenerated her, she moderated her panic and set into a pace of regular breaths. It was then they started, the crucifying aches. Slowly, she untangled herself.

A shutter closed down her mind. Now I've done it, she thought. I've broken something. I'll never get out of here. Shooting pains ripped up her right leg and arm. Her left ankle throbbed. The stones had flayed her skin through the long-sleeved shirt, torn above and below the elbow. Dirt and bacteria were in the wounds, and all along her upper arm, scrapes and cuts burned. The putrid odor of rank, musty flesh, dried urine and body perspiration she had carried like an honor badge of survival. Strangely proud, she was able to bear up under the malodorous scent. But now she was bruised, cut up and covered in muck, a humiliating blow to her ego. After all her clever ingenuity and success, she had been outdone by her own stupid carelessness in not anticipating the treachery of her surroundings to avert an accident.

Using her left arm to maneuver, Peregrine slowly raised herself to rest on her left elbow. She leaned forward hunching over until she sat with her left leg crossed toward her right which she straightened with misery. She paused a few moments, thankful she couldn't see the extent of her injuries in the darkness. First, kneading her right leg up and down with her hands, then manipulating her left leg, she searched for protruding bones. She found none. The throbbing in her ankle had lessened to a droning ache. She gently patted the bones along her foot and ankle bone but was unable to gauge the amount of swelling. The ache seemed to be subsiding. She might be able to put weight on her foot. But every time she attempted to bend her right leg, a piercing sword stabbed through her knee, radiating arcs of pain down her leg. She had wrenched it or maybe had torn tissue or tendons in the fall.

Peregrine put her hands on her face and cursed. Remembering they were covered with mud, she peeled out a long and hysterical laugh. The only part of her body that was not streaked with the gooey mess, she had now obliged to make filthy as well. "Oh, God!" Her broad laugh melted into a sigh. What an ass! She put the palm of her hand in the sludge, poking for a drier area when a thought sprang up. Water. This might be a well, the tunnel a section of old, crumbling aqueduct. The cravings in her body swamped her rationality and tossed it into a dusty corner of her mind.

Straightening her left leg and sliding it away from her right, Peregrine created a wide V with her long legs. She rolled up both her shirt sleeves and leaned over, clawing the mud between her legs, digging with fierce fingers and ragged, overgrown nails. She scooped up fistfuls of the cool, mushy, slimy clay which she slapped around the border of the hole she now furiously excavated. She rested for a moment, rolling up each shirt sleeve carefully, trying not to further tear the right one. Peregrine's mouth tasted like cotton. Her tongue was caked and swollen. Her lips were chapped and cracked and felt like they were bleeding. Her throat was a lump, and she couldn't remember the last time her mouth felt moist. All saliva had been drained hours ago. She desperately needed water. Knowing it might be close, she could think of nothing else.

Determined to put her full force and concentration behind her search, despite the miserable agony when she jarred her legs, she removed squishy mud clumps, enlarging and deepening the hole. Sloshy ooze filled the excavation, a sure sign of water. But the pounding in her right knee galled her. Taking care with her ankle, she crossed her left leg under her right and leaned on her left elbow stretching her body forward, so she was closer to the dig. She reached in her right hand, repeatedly sliding up liquid goop and mounding it on the growing bank in front of her. As she patiently labored, the ooze liquefied into a deepening puddle. She prayed it was water and not something else. For better access, Peregrine stretched out lengthwise on her left side, straightening her left leg so it was parallel to and underneath her right. Then she turned over on her stomach and edged over her handiwork. With her right arm, she reached downward while securing her left arm on the top of the mound of wet earth, balancing herself from falling in head first for a mud bath.

"Damn this darkness," she repeated for the hundredth time. Only then, she realized that even if she could see, and the liquid was water, her eyes couldn't perceive microscopically. Neither with sight nor in her current state of blindness, could she discern whether or not the water was potable. Still in the dark.

"Always in the dark and dark days ahead," she muttered aloud to herself. She stretched her arm downward, extending it until she immersed her hand in the liquid which she brought up to her face and smelled, sniffing for any telltale chemicals or putrid, decaying odor or fecal scent. There was none. She licked a little from her palm. It seemed OK, had an earthen taste like the dirt on a potato. But the coolness! Delicious, heavenly to her parched throat and thick, rough tongue. She moistened her cracked dry lips with the residue on her palm and basked in the luxury of the moisture!

Now what to do. Conundrum. She was like an inhabitant of Dante's Inferno, who had succumbed to temptation and in death, had received the sentence of eternal damnation in one of the nine circles of Hell. Seduced by her thirst to dig for water, she had miraculously discovered water but of dubious purity. Pick your punishment, Peregrine! The torment of unquenchable thirst or the aching pangs of dysentery, both ushers of death. Life was hell!

She should have tried to climb out of the pit instead of flirting with her temptation like an addict. Now she desperately wanted a drink. Her thirst whetted by her senses of touch and taste that deceived her to believe this cool, liquid beauty wasn't the origin of diarrhea and dehydration.

"I'll just take a little. A little can't harm me," she said aloud to justify her decision. Peregrine reached once again into her roughly hewn well and cupped her palm to fill it with the earthy water. Dripping with heaven, she raised her palm to her lips and greedily slurped. In orgasmic delirium, it washed over her tongue to the back of the throat. Water had never tasted so wet. As she gargled and rolled it around, she let the coolness play in her mouth and savored the moment. Then she spat it out to the left of the well and kept on spitting until she was sure the last drop was gone from her mouth. The wetness was like a refreshing mountain spring, but the clay aftertaste was troublesome. If she dug deeper, she doubted the water would be clarified. Again, she reached down. Again, she drew up water and slurped it up with pleasure. Desperately, she wanted to swallow. She let a little slip down the back of her throat, then hesitated with the rest of the gulp which she spewed out on the mud mound. She did this three times, each time pushing herself to the brink of the luxurious, sensual engorging, allowing a trickle to pass down her throat, spitting out the rest.

Unlike the inhabitants of the Inferno, Peregrine's imagination was deep and wide like the sea, and like the sea, confounded by unpredictable winds that frolicked and raged upon it. With illogical and convoluted thinking, she feared the consequences of what would happen if she drank quantities of the contaminated water: stomach cramping, diarrhea, nausea and vomiting. This she feared more than death. For in her derangement, she had already confronted the Spirit of Death and rebuked it. Her ego would not countenance such a trifle as getting sick from polluted water because she was too thirsty to control herself. Yielding to brainwashing by Western Nations' "First World Status," prompted more by the depravity of her condition than any bigotry in her heart, she disassociated from her own "Third World cravings" for dirty water. Unlike "them," she had control over her own destiny and would "not drink the water." The skewed attitude discouraged her from sloshing more in her mouth, even though the tiny action reinvigorated her.

"I can do this. I can rise above my physical needs. My spirit is stronger than my body," Peregrine repeated the tenant of Eastern mysticism, a philosophy embraced by "Third World Countries" for millennia. She was a sublime hypocrite. But survival has an integrity of its own, understood by those who, deprived of the necessaries of life, must grip life's waning vestiges, minute by minute, using any means at their disposal.

Strangely, like a vacation, the water torture had diverted Peregrine's attention, giving her a respite from her wretched knee and drilling ankle. Now, as she focused on standing and scrambling up the incline without incurring the wrathful agony of her leg and drumming ankle, her unquenchable craving for water subsided. In profound simplicity, the mind cannot multi-task its locus of control over pain. One misery subsides, another dominates.

To situate herself and stand up freely, Peregrine found she needed more room since she had used the area in front of her to bank the clay from the deep hole she was too enervated to fill in. Sitting with both legs straightened, her left leg over the hole, she placed her palms down in the mud behind her. Carefully, noting any changes in the terrain which felt to be level, she scooted backward on her behind, using her hands in a reverse walk, twisting first to the left and then the right, until she had scrambled herself back about ten feet. She was amazed that the muddy pit was so large, but then she had no visual comprehension of distance and could only imagine it based upon her sense of touch and hearing which were distorted by the darkness. By sit-walking backward on her behind and using her hands, she had moved with relative freedom from pain. She was only subject to an occasional fiery jolt if she lulled herself into believing all hurt had vanished and grew careless in not keeping her leg straight. She vowed her hands and backside would be the new means of travel out from this cave or catacomb or whatever it was. She was only sorry she had not kept the coffin padding to save her hands from the pressure of rubbing against small pebbles and stones which pricked and scraped. Maybe she would wear her shoes on her hands since she was moving sufficiently by slumming on her behind.

Peregrine ran her hands over the ground to her left and right. She was out of the pit finally, though she was not aware of having moved up a slope, unless of course it was very gradual and happened as she preoccupied herself with dodging the hammer to her knee. She felt behind her. More passageway, roomier. She couldn't discern any walls in her immediate area. She must keep on going. She was fairly comfortable scrambling on her backside. To have to return up the incline would take energy she didn't have, a senseless chore leading to a dead end. She decided to go in the opposite direction from the incline, though scrambling on the earthen floor she was vulnerable. She prayed no rats or poisonous snakes were thirsty or hungry.

"Oh Lord, no," she said aloud. The creatures were probably on their way to the watering trough. Peregrine sighed. It was becoming her main expression of exasperation. She shouldn't have been lazy. She should have pushed the clay back in her excavation.

In the black of the cave, as her imagination roiled with ugly faces of rats and snakes baring ferocious fangs, she cringed backward, hand by hand, expecting each second to be hideously gnashed with rat bites. She stopped suddenly and rolled down the sleeves of her shirt. This would give the rat muddied cloth to bite through instead of flesh. She took off her sneakers and slipped each hand in the toe section for protection. The creatures could bite through her socks or jeans but with greater difficulty. And by that time, she would grab them by the necks and squeeze the life from their wriggling, writhing bodies. Plopping backward with the sneakers on her hands, her movements became clumsy, and she discovered she had to slide the Nikes against the earth to gain any pace or speed.

"Ayieeeeeee," Peregrine screamed. She scuttled sideways like a crab, losing both of her sneakers and paining her ankle and knee with slicing jabs. "Oh, God. What?" She sat still for a full two minutes, listening with all her senses pinned to the point behind and to the right where she had bumped into something, a creature.

All was still. Maybe the thing was listening and watching, waiting for her to make a move. Utterly distressed, she sat immobilized and quickly considered her next course of action. She had to go back up the incline in the other direction. The creature was lurking there in the tunnel, blocking her path. Could she go around it? She had lost her direction and wasn't sure where it was in her scrambling mania not to be savaged.

Then she remembered her sneakers. Where did they fall off? Behind her by the thing. She had to get up. As much as it pained her, she couldn't just sit there and wait for a stealth attack. If she was upright, maybe she could kick or stomp the thing with her good leg. If she found her sneakers, she could go on the offensive. Again, she listened, her hearing acute. Silence, except for her restricted, panicky breaths. *OK, just do it.* She urged herself to stand, fearful of the coming wretchedness in her right knee, the gnashing of teeth from the malevolent creature.

Peregrine folded her left knee outward, bringing her left foot to her inner right thigh. She listened and waited. No response to her movement. She leaned forward and rocked herself up, balancing on her left knee while keeping her right leg straight in front, her fists clenched to punch and jab in defense. She waited in the awkward position as moments slid by. Her breathing steadied. She grew bolder. Maybe it could only watch her. She felt stronger. Her ankle was at a low tonal ache, and her right leg only throbbed if she joggled it too much. She must move quickly. With fingers spread wide to gain every ounce of strength, she placed both hands on the ground and pushed up, using her thigh muscles and the toes of her left foot. But she underestimated the injury in her ankle, which screamed in revolt, as she placed her full weight down on her left foot. Wracked by pain, Peregrine began a grotesque balancing act. She must remain standing and not collapse under the torture, falling on the ground, subjecting herself to the power of the thing. She shifted her weight to her right leg, lifting her left foot off the ground.

"Ahhh! Owww!" Peregrine groaned. Nerve endings frazzled with stress, blew flames into the pain centers of her mind. She moaned like a madwoman, felt her ankle would burst and gush blood. She shifted her weight, tiptoeing her left foot on the ground, to balance the weight on her right leg. "Damn and hell!" Her knee was skewered by an electrical prod.

Why stand? Sit, sit! The agony had distracted her, clouded her intention. She remembered. She couldn't sit. There was that creature, listening and waiting to lunge.

She slid her right foot a step. Her knee hammered and thudded. She sucked in breath and quickly lurched forward two excruciating steps. She needed a support to lean against. She stretched her arms out in front. Where had the walls gone? There used to be walls. She shook her head in confusion and stiffened her body against the anarchy and rebellion rising in her ankle and knee. She shuffled an inch, then waited for the hot iron to strike. It never did. Her leg collapsed under her, throwing her against the thing she had worked so hard to escape.

The absent walls closed in on her. Peregrine fainted. Her brain seized up and shook itself out. Moments later, refreshed, it recovered, and she awakened. She came to with her arms lying over a body with her face pressed against it. Pulling herself into the present, she sniffed, and smelled a faintly recognizable smell. The creature? Peregrine pushed with the little strength she had in her arms and panicked, shoved it away. Its insides clanged in muffled protest, like someone striking horseshoes to ring the pole in a successful pass. Familiar sounds. Her frenzy stilled. She knew that metallic ringing, and it wasn't made by anything alive. She slapped and smacked the ground for the thing she craved. Yes, there it was. With feverish fingers, she grasped her back-pack and dragged it near her.

Peregrine hugged "the body" overjoyed, ebullient, the happiest twenty-four year old on the planet. How had it gotten there? No matter. She received it like manna from heaven and sobbed in utter happiness, no longer feeling alone and trapped. When she shoved it, it felt full. She prayed that nothing had been removed. Peregrine ripped open the top flaps and plunged her hands inside. The stake, the large, heavy, metal cross, the translations and journal. But there was no pick, no crowbar and no key. There wasn't an explanation for the missing pick. She must have left the crowbar and key outside, after all. The small, bubble wrapped ceremonials were there. Thank God! They were priceless. At some point she could still enact the ceremony. All was not lost.

"Yes," Peregrine cried in triumph. She opened the side flaps and found the protective linen sack with the priest's outfit and the oranges and pomegranates. She would eat the fruit, replacing it for their future ceremony, if she ever found her way out of the cavern. But her chances had greatly increased now that she had found her pack. No negative thinking! There would be a ceremony, and it would be successful! She would make sure, she vowed, believing her efforts in the mausoleum had secured the prize.

With vitality, she spun the pack around to the other side flap. She had saved the best for last. In fearful hesitation, almost afraid to trust her good fortune, doubt slithered up in her mind. What if it wasn't there? She could wait no longer. She ripped open the flap and pulled out the large, unopened bottle of Evian. Peregrine threw back her head and laughed with pure delight. She had looked death in the face; she had earned the right to laugh at him. And she laughed because she knew, she was sure that she would make it out of the tunnel alive.

Trembling with anticipation, Peregrine swizzled off the cap and put the bottle to her cracked, bleeding lips and took a long, long drink of celebration. All the foul tastes in her mouth from the urine, clay and effects of dehydration evanesced. The cooling liquid flowed over her tongue like a balm, soothing all her wounds and drying all her tears. Her throat trembled to receive, like a baby bird, frantic and crying for sustenance. Water, limpid and reviving. Water that was brilliant and sublime and luscious, the freshest and purest water she had ever tasted. The more she drank, the more she thirsted. As she gulped widely, she considered stopping, though it seemed like she could never have enough. Then her arm, as if in an independent movement from her mouth and bodily cravings, pulled the bottle away. Not too fast. Conserve. Don't overdo it. There are three oranges, three pomegranates. Eat them instead.

Peregrine riffled the pack and took out an orange. She reveled in peeling it, enjoying the sensual pleasure of plunging her thumb into the plump rind; hearing the reassuring soft scrunch into the white inner coating; feeling the sizzle of moisture popping up the pungent, sweet, zinging fragrance and spilling it out into the darkness, suffusing the catacomb with the remembrance of sunshine. Peregrine took two larger pieces of the rind and rubbed the white part along her hands to disinfect them as best she could, then threw them on the ground. She selected three other pieces to massage her neck and across her chest, giving herself a luxurious bath, which released an explosion of natural oils and flavorful smells that drowned out her putrid, malodorous body scent and whetted her appetite. Before touching the fruit, she thought about using some of her precious water to rinse her hands, but she reconsidered. She couldn't waste it for washing, and without soap, it would be useless anyway. She dismissed thoughts of bacteria and sectioned off dripping pieces. She ate sumptuously, intentionally spilling the juice on her pants to mask her putrescence with the daylight fragrance.

The orange was magnificent. If the water had cleansed her palate, the orange sanctified it. She was whole again. She chewed slowly to savor all the captured life force the tree had nurtured in this miraculous fruit. She thought that she had never known the sweet beauty of an orange. But how could she appreciate such complex simplicity? Did she even appreciate that she was alive before the ordeal in this sepulcher? Silently, inwardly, Peregrine praised the glory of her life, and all of her aches and pains fled away. She finished the orange in peace. It was enough.

For the moment, her fiery trials were over. Peregrine relaxed and settled herself in calm. She took another swig of water from the bottle to wash down the orange's nectar which rekindled her thirst. Its juice covered her hands, but she embraced the sticky coating, where once she would have wiped it off in annoyance. She returned the bottle to the back-pack, thinking she might want a pomegranate, when she heard the plastic scrape against something else in the bottom of the compartment. Taking the bottle out again and placing it between her legs, Peregrine swiveled her hand around in the bottom of the sack. Her fingers closed around paper and cardboard and toothpick-like sticks. She couldn't believe her good fortune. The matches. She had forgotten they were loose in her pack and had brought them to light the candles as a backup if Mocha forgot. Too bad she didn't have the candles, but Peregrine dismissed the complaint. Her outlook had changed. She was ecstatic, grateful for all she had received this day. The matches were another miraculous gift.

Peregrine counted. Five wooden matches for the ritual and the pack of matches she had gotten when she purchased her last cigarettes. Combined, they couldn't provide a sustaining light to take her twenty feet down the passageway.

Peregrine lit a match from the pack to locate her sneakers. Stretching her right arm forward, she moved the match right and left while the blue-yellow flame fiercely devoured the cardboard. She saw her Nikes scattered five feet apart from each other to her left. The flame climbed downward and bit into her fingertips. She dropped the match and the darkness swirled in around her as it went out. She tried to imprint the details of the catacomb on her imagination in the fifteen second glow, but the darkness overpowered the tiny illumination, preventing her from properly discerning the size and location of her cell of captivity. She needed sustained light, more forcefully brilliant than all of the matches burning together to find her way out of this labyrinth. She put the matches in her right jeans pocket.

Peregrine lightly patted her ankle, then her knee. Both were swollen. Using her hands she pushed and slid her behind across the ground and palmed it for each sneaker. As she squeezed her Nike onto her left foot, her ankle scolded her for the foolish act and she left the shoe off. She did manage with slow motion care to gently bend her knee and get her right sneaker on without too much hellish aggravation.

"God, I do despise pain," Peregrine mugged in a posh British accent. As long as she kept her leg straight, she could stand on it and take halting steps, albeit like the mummy in the film of the same name. Anyway, she felt fitter and revitalized and if she could locate the wall, she would use it as a crutch. It had to be near. Without the support of walls, the catacomb would be wholly unstable, so they must be behind her and to her right since in front of her was the pit and the incline and narrow passageway leading to the stairs and floor above.

On her behind, Peregrine inched back to her pack and placed the left sneaker in one of the compartments. She thought intently about how she could use the matches and keep a flame lit. There was a way, but she must not compromise the value of the relics nor waste them; otherwise, the ceremony could never take place. Reaching into the middle section of the back-pack, she took out the bubble wrapped antiquities and dislodged the adhesive tape that encircled the bundle and kept it secure. She placed the parcel on the ground in front of her and lifted up the leaves of the wrapping, uncovering the items. Though the darkness was like a blindfold, when she touched them, she recognized each. They were all there intact. With shaking hands she picked up the small clay pottery. It was a small, clay cruse of oil, allegedly 1500 years old. She separated it from the other equally antique and priceless items which had been handed down through the centuries from ancestor to ancestor and finally fell into her mom's care. One day, they would be hers. She placed the cruse safely on the ground near her left knee. Whether its powerful healing anointing had been passed down according to family legend, Peregrine's generation had not yet realized.

Now, she worked quickly. She pulled away the scarf from her head, unbuttoned her shirt, pulled it out of her jeans and peeled it off. By now, the mud had dried and stiffened the shirt which she hoped would not be a problem. She gently laid it across her right thigh. She unwound the scarf from her torso and placed it on top of the shirt, then unhooked her bra and dropped it across her left thigh. Then she picked up the scarf and wrapping it around her bosom, exposing her slender midriff, she tied the ends in the front to hold it. Because she had found a solution to the problem of light, the darkness no longer abused her. She was a creature of the night and underworld, able to deftly use her fingers and hands to move the nearby objects in her kingdom and remember where she had positioned them.

With her right hand, Peregrine dragged her back-pack near her right thigh. Careful not to disarrange the relics and cruse of oil in front of her, she slowly reached in and took out the large metal cross and the iron spike. She pushed the pack away and placed both items near her right thigh. Because of its shape and two-foot length, she decided to use the cross first. She took her shirt and ripped it at the bottom seam, then tore off a long strip and wrapped it around the bottom of the cross three times, tying the ends in a double knot. This was the handle. She took the remainder of the shirt and wrapped it around the three limbs of the cross. Slipping each bra strap on the horizontal cross plate and bunching up the shirttails toward the top of the cross, she securely tied the cloth to the metal with her bra. She jiggled and tugged at her contraption, but the cloth stayed firmly wound.

Peregrine angled the cross on her outside right thigh, placing the handle on the ground. She felt for the cruse of oil inside her left thigh. Removing the stopper, she picked up the cross and drizzled oil on the top, where the cloth was heaviest. She knew there was still enough oil in the cruse for the future ritual. She lay the anointed cross to her left on the ground, freeing both hands. She returned the stopper to the cruse, rewrapped it with the other relics in the bubble wrap and secured it. Then stretching over to her right, she carefully placed the ceremonial parcel in her backpack. She went through each flap, taking inventory. Everything was there, most importantly the bottle of water. She twisted off the cap and took a small, fleeting drink and put the cap back and returned the bottle to the pack. Over a quarter of the water must be gone; the bottle felt light.

Peregrine lifted the sack, heavier for her weakness, slipped each arm into the straps and centered it against her back. She stuck the handle of the cross in the top compartment, keeping the cloth head outside. It would be difficult, but she must stand. Using the iron spike, which she plugged into the ground in front of her, she lifted herself to a kneeling position, her left knee on the ground, her right leg straightened in front of her. Pushing all her weight down on the metal spike with her hands, she leveraged her body upward, groaning as she shifted her weight to the left leg and foot. She nearly collapsed again, but in counterbalance, gritting her teeth, she pushed the rod into the ground, holding tightly with her hands, hopping, and shifting her weight off her left foot to her right without bending her knee too much. She found she could hunch over and lean on the spike, taking a good deal of weight off her left ankle, relieving the driving, pounding pain from the swelling tissues.

It took her about fifteen minutes but pleasant amazement struck. Bent over, tightly grasping the iron rod, she now stood on her right leg. Trembling, she lifted her left foot from the floor. She was unsteady. With care, she put her left foot down for balance. She could remain stationary and was not in great agony, but could she move? And where was a convenient wall?

She was afraid to light the cross torch because she might lose her balance and fall, burning herself horribly. The flames would eat through the silk in a flash and fueled by the oil, engulf her flesh in a molten char. No, she needed to lean against a wall to balance herself, then she could light the torch. Without a light, she didn't know where the tunnel continued, only that she was in a large room. Peregrine considered sitting down again and lighting the cross, but how would she get up quickly? By the time she did, the torch might fall over and be snuffed out by the damp earth since she would have to sink the makeshift handle into the unstable ground while she stood.

She took out three of the wooden matches and the matchbook from her right pocket. Holding the rod between her thighs and placing more weight on her left foot, which antagonized her for it, she struck the wooden matches against the matchbook flint strip, then returned the matchbook to her pocket. The three wooden sticks flared a greater illumination, and she saw she was in a fairly large circular room with four dark holes encroaching toward her, the passageways, leading away from the center like spokes in a wheel. The closest was to her right, the direction she had been taking. Then the flames ate her fingers, and she threw the matches down. Though plunged in darkness, Peregrine's mental image of the room's layout remained bright in her imagination. If she kept going to her right, she would bump into a wall.

Rendered a hunchback by the stake converted into a short cane, Peregrine, like a malformed creature spawned from a macabre scientist's laboratory, made her way with a grotesque hop and shuffle to the wall. Once the torch was lit, she would have to endure the pain of her left ankle because with the cane, she needed both hands; and this bent position ached her back muscles and cramped her right leg. Also, she wouldn't be able to hold up the torch, use her iron cane and hobble, hop shuffle, which would slow her down even more. Her only other option was to sit on the ground again, which was no option if there were obstacles ahead.

Peregrine sighed in relief. Thankfully, she had bumped her left shoulder into the corner of the tunnel, and not her head. Leaning her left side against the wall, she breathed deeply and thought about drinking water, then resolved against it, already feeling a slight urge to urinate, which she had to hold off as long as possible. She couldn't squat easily, would be forced to soak herself through her jeans once more. So, thoughts of drinking put her off. If her thirst became acute, she would quench it by eating an orange.

Peregrine turned her back to the wall, straightened up and leaned against the bulging pack. With her right hand, she reached behind and inside the top flap, retrieving the wrapped cross, which she held between her thighs. She placed the iron rod she had used as a cane in the same compartment that she had placed the cross. Peregrine removed only the matchbook from her right pocket. She would conserve the two remaining wooden matches. Not wanting to immolate her face, she quickly struck a match and held it out in front of her, placing the book between her teeth. With her left hand she grabbed the torch from between her thighs and held it out in front to the wavering flicker just as the yellow match flames blistered her fingers and went out. Though it had dried, the oil-soaked cloth burst into flames with an explosion of hissing, devouring light. The radiance translated her from the darkness of being a night creature into an artificial light. Until she could comfortably adjust her sight to the brilliant oranges and yellows, Peregrine shut her eyes and turned her face away. This was a new world.

Now she could see her surroundings, spooky, with tall shadows cast by the dancing flames of the torch. The room was actually smaller than she anticipated, and there were five separate tunnels, counting the one she had fallen down. She noted her excavated well and how the pit sloped gradually upward around its circumference, an oblivious detail in her agonizing travels across the room. She looked up. The ceiling was concrete, stone and earth. Each of the passageways was actually arched with field stone and mortar and reinforced with concrete. Peregrine thought she might be under a section of the crypt but wasn't sure. In front of one of the passageways was a carved, stone, female statue with printing underneath in Latin that she couldn't make out in the shadows. She wondered if she should take that passageway. Did the carving signal the way out?

There was a twenty-five percent chance it did. But the passageway was directly across the other side of the room. At her worm pace, it would take fifteen minutes to get there. Considering that there was a twenty-five percent chance each of the four passageways lead to an exit, she turned to the nearest one to her right. She had to conserve her strength for whatever lay beyond. This way was as good as the others, she prayed.

Peregrine began her laborious hop, shuffle, hop and shuffle. For support, with her left hand, she gripped the uneven field stones in the wall. With her right hand, she held aloft the flaming cross and penetrated deeper into the catacomb.

A RUN OF BAD LUCK

Chapter Twelve

F ennelly Girardo crept into the sedge grass and beach plum bushes that wandered up the dunes and back down again in front of the eight-chimney, grey, cedar-shingled mansion that overlooked taupe-colored sand and the crashing waves of the Atlantic Ocean. The beach, fronting the length of the palatial residence, was one of the more exclusive and secluded in the Southampton Township. Fen was exhausted, and he had to take a leak. The dense, exuberant foliage was the only place he could relieve himself. There, he would be invisible to evening beach strollers and hidden from servants who occasionally peered out the floor-to-ceiling windows that blazed with light from the second floor of the luxurious estate house.

There were two portable toilets where he had parked his '97 Mercedes convertible SKL on Ginn Lane in the parking lot between the two private beach clubs, but that was about one mile away. He couldn't risk leaving now that there was apparent activity in the stately building which gave out a greater illumination than the full moon in the 11:00 PM sky. Was the residence lit up as an offshore signal for a surreptitious pick-up or landing? He glanced at the waters of the Atlantic on the calm, summer night. No boat skimmed the vicinity. No yacht lights shined out from the rolling dark waters. There was only the milky surf which was brightened by silvery moonlight, shimmering a ribbon path on the black sea, then threading out to an oblique fade, where the deep purple-black sky and undulating waters merged into an indistinguishable horizon wall of black.

Fen relieved himself, then hurried back to his sentry post. He had left his surveillance only a few times, going to his car to raid his stash of bottled Evian and energy bars, lugging quantities of both back to his hideout near the estate, where he had camped out for two days and nights. He was legally parked, and no one would break into his Mercedes, which melded with the upper-class neighborhood, as did he. But he was worried servants from the residence would see him and call the Southampton police. If they forced him to leave, he had a plan. He would park his car in the Chase Bank parking lot and hire a cab to drop him off a mile east of the mansion. From there, he would walk westward along the shoreline until he reached the three-acre estate, where he would continue his watch for any sign of Manny. Fortunately, he had managed to keep out of sight of the windows, setting up an umbrella, beach chair and blanket with his food and water at the corner of the weathered cedar fence of a neighboring estate. With his binoculars, he was able to peruse the heliport, the driveway, the gatehouse, the five-car garage and most of the activity on the mansion grounds.

In the last two days, no one had come or gone from the shorefront villa. He had spoken to a man over the security intercom, who refused to open the gates. When he had visited with detectives Allan and Dietz from the Queens DA's office, he told them he saw no family members, only male servants in highly stylized dress and the Johnstone family's security team who fronted for the Johnstones with a grace unusual for the lugs typically hired for such positions.

Liam, the head butler, had given them a tour of the thirty-odd elaborately decorated rooms, including the walk-in closets and the Carrera marble and slate bathrooms that were the size of Fen's Manhattan apartment. In a cool tone, the head servant casually mentioned that the family was vacationing at their summer villa in Lake Maggiore, Italy, until September when they returned to New York. The tour seemed thorough. The butler threw back the door to each room with an open-handed flourish compounding the certitude of Manny's absence and Fen's mistaken assumptions. The only wrinkle in the collar of Liam's magnificent apparel of veracity creased when Fen asked the pretentious servant about the conspicuously nonexistent wine cellar. The butler coughed and assured him the water table didn't allow for such appointments. In his heart, Fen didn't believe a family of such wealth would forego them.

Afterwards, at Starbucks, Fen tried to persuade Allan and Dietz to visit the county clerk's office to investigate the property records and architect's plans for incongruities in room sizes and layouts which might contradict the floor plan they had circuited. But the detectives were called back to Queens on a homicide, so their investigation into Manny's disappearance had to be postponed. They had protested that they didn't have the manpower to spare for surveillance. Had the Southampton police's assertions that the Johnstones were above reproach convinced Dietz and Allan to be less aggressive about searching for clues at the estate? Fen was afraid this was the case, especially since the police agreed that they would keep their radar tuned for clues related to the case. He felt they wouldn't.

Most egregiously, the detectives and police had shined their spotlight on Fen's story, attempting to shake him from his conclusions like a terrier shaking a rat to the death. In his chase on the Cross Island Parkway and LIE, might he have mistaken one limo for another? After all, he only had the first two numbers of the license plate and could easily have followed the wrong car. They emphasized the black Lincoln's lack of distinguishing features. There were hundreds of limos servicing clients to the Hamptons, Manhattan and Westchester. Stressed, desperate and overcome with guilt at losing his brother, Fen easily could have missed a turn and headed in the wrong direction, say east, when the car he should have been following turned west for Manhattan or north for the Throgs Neck Bridge. After all, the limo had a two-mile lead until Fen caught it in his sights. Making mistakes in a high-speed chase were probable even for professional law enforcement.

Allan directed his attention to Fen's brother's need for constant supervision because of his wandering problem. An adult of twenty-six who had the mind of a ten year old, Manny was like an aging senior citizen who left his house to go shopping and forgot how to get home. Despite Fen's instructions not to, Manny obviously had wandered from the car and willingly allowed himself to be picked up by the men in the limo. They had probably taken him to a hospital or shelter since Manny wouldn't go home until his mother returned from her business trip. The detectives suggested Fen check area hospitals and get back to them in a few days if Manny was still missing.

Allan's logic left Fen confused, even willing to make concessions. Maybe, he had mistaken the license plate and the car. Maybe Manny had been rescued by good Samaritans. Maybe right now, he was in a Queens's hospital or developmental center. True, Manny didn't know Fen's city address and phone number, and because he didn't know how to contact his younger brother, perhaps that was why Fen hadn't heard from him.

Despite making these concessions, Fen's soul was in crisis and his head was spinning like he had downed Tequila shots. Though he couldn't convince Allan otherwise, Fen knew the detective was wrong. He had seen what had happened. He was a credible eyewitness. Two men forced Manny into a limo. He would recognize those men anywhere. Just because the limo ended up in the driveway of a Southampton estate didn't alter the fact that they had kidnapped his brother. As he reviewed the events in his mind, he ordered his thoughts and felt a quietude flow over his emotions. He must take authority over the investigation by taking authority over any fears and doubts about what he had seen.

When the detectives left, he had driven back to Ginn Lane, parked the Mercedes at the Beach Club and walked the hundred feet to the hot sand, where he watched the beach goers relaxing in their chairs under umbrellas or stretched out on striped towels, assimilating the full blast of the three o'clock June sun. Their serenity and luxurious indulgence on this weekday somehow reminded him of a time when he was not shackled with hellish guilt. Eventually, he was able to free his intellect from Allan's attempts to brainwash him.

Perhaps he underestimated the man's sycophancy toward wealth and power. He recalled Dietz and Allan's reactions during Liam's tour of the mansion. They were like impoverished street urchins out of a Dickens novel, starry eyed over the sumptuous splendor of the villa. As they apprised the three-thousand-square-foot living room, and equivalent family room, two-story library, elaborate music room, solarium, dining hall and ballroom, Dietz's and Allan's mouths opened, like a great fish catching flies. Their middle-class upbringing cowered in the dark corners of economic humiliation, dwarfed by the vast ostentation of riches. Fen recognized their self-loathing. It was the curious illness of the middle class when confronted with elaborate wealth. With less dignity than field slaves, the detectives had bowed and scraped, obsequious in their emotional deference, obeisant in their mental intimidation. Fen noted all this and more, even his own discomfort when after seeing the expansive game room that contained a billiard table, fencing studio and bowling alley, Dietz and Allan, turned with enthusiasm to the butler and asked him technical questions about the pin setting machine. Yes. This had been the turning point in their cursory and unofficial investigation. By the time the butler served coffee from the silver urn, both detectives were genuflecting like priests before the Pope, and all the pointed questions they had assured Fen they would ask had been swallowed with the refreshments. Over Fen's objection, they disregarded the garage storage area and the gate-house which Liam claimed hadn't been used in years. The butler had cleverly used his position and the grandeur of the estate to deflect their will and thwart a search of the areas where Manny might have been imprisoned. When Fen became insistent, the deferential Allan took Fen aside and told him to shut it. They had the situation under control.

Liam had won the first round. Fen had been pinned like an insect under Allan's arrogant and searing disputation of his integrity. With the detectives' middle-class values laid bare, Fen decided to manipulate their weaknesses as Liam had. After Allan had flayed his heart open on the drive to his car, Fen treated the detectives to Starbucks and casually shared personal details about his acting career while waiting to pay for their orders. The detectives had recognized him from episodes of *Law and Order* and *Criminal Minds*. Fen torched their obvious admiration, dropping celebrity names like a tree shedding ripe fruit. They were drawn in and agreed to sit and finish their iced coffees, while Fen peeled off information about famous actors he had worked with or knew. It never failed. Celebrity and wealth, like twin idolatries, drew humanity to worship at their baleful altars. As a come-on, Fen provided a contact, an agent who placed detectives as consultants on crime shows. Both men were grateful. Their salary wasn't commensurate with the overwhelming grind of the DA's office. When they shook hands and parted, the men agreed to take his calls. The investigation was in frozen suspension, hanging by a brittle thread over a glacial crevice whose yawning mouth threatened to swallow it whole.

Fen dismissed his indignation at being forced to curry favor with the detectives. Ingratiation and quid pro quo were the way of the world. Liam had snowed Allan and Dietz, playing on their foiled ambitions while turning the clues to ice. If Fen's pride disintegrated like grass in the desert sun, he didn't care. Manny's life was at stake, and the investigation must be kept alive with promises of jobs and passes to his film shoots.

A day later, Fen's self-doubts vanished. After he contacted surrounding shelters and hospitals and affirmed that Manny was still missing, he dropped the information in their laps, blowing fire to melt Allan's logic in a cryptic phone conversation with Allan's colleague. Relenting, Dietz agreed to access all property records related to the Johnstone residence and continue the investigation for a few days. But he insisted that they needed a chain of evidence linking the limo, the men who kidnapped Manny and the Southampton estate, or Fen's lead would stay cold. Without probable cause, they could never obtain a search warrant to investigate the gate-house and storage areas. Though he didn't know how, Fen promised he would get sufficient proof.

The days had merged into one another rapidly, unfolding a blank canvas. Fen counted. It had been six days since Manny had been kidnapped at the cemetery and five since he had filed a missing person's report. Four since he toured the estate with Dietz and Allan. Three days ago, he had visited his mother and told her the heartbreaking news, after she had returned from her trip, the same day Fen phoned hospitals and developmental centers and affirmed Manny's disappearance with the detectives. With his mom he had tried to minimize his blame, telling her he had left Manny in the car for just five minutes when he returned to see two men force his brother into a black limo and speed away. He assured her that no one could have exerted themselves more during his two-hour chase which eventually ended in the driveway of the heavily guarded, palatial residence with automatic iron gates, iron fence, hedge rows, security cameras and gatekeeper's house, an estate like Fort Knox. He told her the only missing element was a military presence, Hummers in camouflage, like in the film *Godzilla*, his first SAG role as a kid.

As Fen repeated the details of Liam's tour to his mother, he realized what he must do. Over her objections, he packed up his gear and supplies and returned to Southampton, late in the evening of that productive third day. When he arrived and set up camp, the estate was dark except for lights in one room on the second floor. And they were on the entire night.

The next two days, he had lived on the beach and kept watch for any sign of Manny. But nothing had happened, and he had nothing to report to the detectives since he had made his promise to get proof. The place looked deserted except for this evening, with every window of the mansion illuminated and the servants occasionally standing in the back light by the window in the far-left corner of the second floor. Any moment Fen expected to see Manny peering out at the ocean in the fullness of the moonlit night.

Fen tuned his ears like radar for betraying sounds, of car engines revving or doors slamming or footfalls on the gravel pathways. There was a profound silence, except for the waves playing on the sloping sand, calmer than usual because there was little wind. All seemed still, very still. Too still.

The exclusive beach had thinned out at dusk, but occasionally a couple strolled past and some waved at him. Earlier, a few locals stopped to talk. He had told them he was an actor researching a part in an upcoming film, white lies since it wasn't a beach film, and it was a small part that required little research. Like Hollywood sycophants, they fawned and fussed over him, invited him for dinner or coffee with the usual pathetic idolatry because he fit the playbill and happened to be very photogenic and athletic, a golden boy. The third most important idolatry after celebrity and money was natural good looks. He could give a rat's ass about his physical endowments except they opened many doors for him, often ones he would never walk through since he was mostly straight, with one extraordinary exception with a producer who gave him his career when he was fifteen. That was the last time, though he had many gay and lesbian friends. Being sub rosa LGBT was often a prerequisite for getting a variety of choice parts. But only the gay actors who had established themselves for decades like Sir Ian McKellen, could with ease maintain a fabulous career. Eventually, things would change. But for now, year of our Lord 2011, in a recovering economy, gender equality was still a struggle in the U.S.

Because Fen's story carried the seeds of truth, because his appearance looked upper class, his umbrella, towels and clothing were appropriate for the neighborhood and he sounded like a Yale Drama School grad, no one, as yet, reported him to the police or thought he was homeless scum mucking up the neighborhood, usurping their right to their ocean front paradise. He knew if he lived there beyond a week, even he would overstay his welcome, yet, if he accepted the invitations he had received to be a house guest after he was done with his research, he knew he could stay as long as he liked. So, Fen was friendly with everyone he met and he took down names and numbers and gave out his. Networking with the locals could produce information about Manny.

A tumult of guilty thoughts overtook Fen as he stared out at the play of dark and white water crashing along the shoreline. Five minutes. Fen was not with Manny for five minutes. If Manny left the car or was threatened or cajoled out of it, he had no way of knowing. Five minutes. In those crucial minutes, he had been looking for Peregrine's family mausoleum, and when he realized he was on the wrong avenue of the cemetery and remembered he had forgotten to take the lantern with him, he went back to the car. That's when he saw the shadowy men pushing Manny into the sleek, black Lincoln. Five minutes. If only he could redeem those five minutes. He would have his life back and Manny's and his mom's, whose pitying sobs at her eldest son's disappearance, pierced his heart with each remembrance. Five minutes and a lifetime of guilt.

He took his binoculars out of the canvas sack and peered through them for the one hundredth time since dusk. Nothing had changed. He looked at his watch, 11:30 PM. If only something would happen to give him the evidence he needed. But he had already decided that whatever was necessary to do, he would do it to recover Manny. He was determined, even if it meant sacrificing his own life, which technically had begun already.

For six days, he had been consumed with nothing else, not his career, his finances, nor his friends Mocha and Peregrine, who ironically had gone missing, too. Because he had taken an oath of silence about the crypt and the ceremony, he couldn't tell Ms. Randolf or Ms. Hamilton where he thought they might be. He was counting on Beach Comber, who had returned from his trip two days ago, to look for them. He had probably found them by now. Thankfully, at least one of them was free while he was stuck here, waiting for clues, text messaging and phoning everyone and not able to do a damn thing anywhere.

The time was certainly out of joint with this lousy run of bad luck. A bunch of text messages from his agent regarding a few auditions he couldn't get to in Jersey, Manny in Southampton, Mocha and Peregrine in Queens, his mother in Levittown, Long Island. Talk about being drawn and quartered with frustration. He hated passivity, and now he was forced into it by the situation, ever reminded about it by his agent who understood but was afraid he would lose the film gig if he didn't get back into the city tomorrow for the shoot.

The producer and director had been adamant about the strict schedule. Since he had little clout, he couldn't take it or leave it. If he left it, word would get around, and he would be out of work for months. His American Academy of Dramatic Arts teacher had told him, "Professional actors who are serious and disciplined work for life. If you just want to be famous, string up a bunch of nude videos and put them on YouTube."

Fen would have to drive back into the city at the latest by tomorrow noon, since his call was around 3:00 PM, arranged by his agent in a quid pro quo of some kind with the producer. He looked wistfully at the heliport at the edge of the estate grounds. Too bad they were enemies. Otherwise, he would charm them into giving him a forty-five-minute helicopter ride to Manhattan. It would sure beat the three-hour drive back on the LIE going seventy-five miles an hour. Thank God for the old Mercedes. The cops left him alone.

Fen's mobile buzzed, a text message from one of the locals, the wife of a couple he met earlier, checking to see how he was doing, if he was still there. Fen quickly answered with short hand "2 late 2 b or not 2 b" and a sleeping smiley face with a "CU 2 MRO." Blast. He didn't want to be compelled to message half the night. He almost regretted giving out his number, but knew he had to for Manny's sake. Fen decided to check the rest of his messages. Beach Comber hadn't replied to any which was strange, and Ms. Hamilton and Ms. Randolph hadn't answered his latest texts either.

A slight breeze was picking up. He took his US Open Tennis Polo sweats out of the canvas bag. As he stood up, he hunched over while he stepped into the pants, taking a glance around to see if anyone was on the grounds near the neighbor's enclosure. There was no one. He sat on the blanket, facing the ocean, and finished putting on the pants and zipping up the matching jacket. He had to be patient. His efforts would not go unrewarded. Manny was an innocent and didn't God surround innocents and the fatherless with His loving care and the protection of his angels? You didn't muck with the innocent with impunity.

Three was his lucky number. That meant that on his third day living on the beach, something would happen to break the case wide open with clues. He must not be discouraged. If it meant that he had to stay out in Southampton and not make the shoot, then so be it. Manny was the priority. The sting of guilt he felt from his mother's accusations and judgmental tone would never be out of his mind until Manny was safely with them again. Then he'd deal with his conscience about leaving Manny for five minutes.

Fen picked up his binoculars from the blanket and looked once more behind him to his right, focusing one by one on each of the lighted windows of the stately residence. Blazing brilliantly for what reason? The grounds, too were lit, everything except the heliport lights were on. He reclined on the blanket and rubbed his eyes, reviewing in his mind the conversation between himself, the detectives and the Southampton police. They had questioned his judgment. He was persuasive in his response and still they doubted him about the car. "I am right. No one can convince me otherwise, no matter how convenient it is for them. The truth is the truth," he muttered. When he spoke it aloud, he believed it fervently, remembering how the men pushed Manny into the limo, recalling the high-speed chase on the LIE, remembering the limo turning into the security gates that quickly closed after entry. That was the answer. He must not forget. He must remember, encourage himself, be confident and not fall into a depression.

In the next few hours, Fen repeated his movements, surveying the estate with his binoculars, looking out over the ocean and checking his messages. His battery was running low. He decided not to use the phone for the rest of the night, and prayed that if something happened, he had enough juice to capture the evidence with stills. He didn't think he had enough power to get 60 seconds of video, but maybe that might be all he needed.

He would have to go back to the car at sunrise and among other tasks, recharge the iPhone and use the porta-potties. He didn't dare leave his post for more than a half hour. If he took the road which eventually curved into Ginn Lane, he could sprint there, refresh himself, get supplies, charge the phone and be back with a few minutes to spare. The only problem was he needed a few hours to charge, so he would have to leave it there and then go back for it, the earliest at 9:30 AM. Unless he brought his car to the area, but there was nowhere to park, and he could be towed if he parked on the road in front of the mansion, or worse, his car would be recognized, and the police would come looking for him on the beach, the only place he obviously could be. So that meant, for three hours, he would be in the dead zone. What if something happened? The way his luck was running, it probably would, and he would be screwed, again. Luck was everything.

He thought about the ceremony which would have guaranteed a change in his luck and so many positive things for him and his mother and Manny, a reversal of their fortunes. Now that, too, was on hold. He wondered how Mocha and Peregrine had managed without him, and if they went missing before or after the rituals, or if they were even able to get through them without incident. Well, something obviously had happened, and he wouldn't find out until tomorrow when he recharged his phone. Beach Comber would have answered him by then.

Fen tried to close his eyes and take a nap. He was overtired but too overwrought to rest, so he opened them and looked at the stars blanketing the skyscape and wished upon Orion's Belt and the Big and Little Dipper, wishes about Manny and his mom. The full moon, high in the sky, was whiter and smaller than it had been earlier, and its footsteps reflected with a fainter cast on the ocean and beyond, where the black horizon line was indistinguishable from the Atlantic.

He was looking for the North Star when he heard a rumbling sound coming from the west and saw a spotlight flashing on the dark water. It was a black helicopter. Fen panicked, scrambled up from the blanket and swiftly covered the distance between it and the beach plum bushes. He clambered in amongst the leaves and thorny branches, then covered his mouth with his fist to stifle a reaction to the painful burning he felt on his legs and arms as the long thorns bit through his jacket and pants. *"Jeez.,"* he thought as he picked the fabric away from the clingy prickles. He should have put on his white jeans instead of this flimsy, trendy bullshit. But with his dark tan and this dark blue outfit, he blended with the night. He was grateful when the helicopter spotlight flashed to the eastern dunes and dense hedges, which bordered the other area of the estate. The pilot was distracted by the thicket which obviously made the best hideout for anyone canvassing the estate from the beach. That was why Fen selected this position by the neighbor's fence and tried to look like a wayward beach bum camping out. The thicket was the first place security would look for spies and trespassers.

From his uncomfortable view, Fen watched the helicopter gradually sink, raising up sand and blowing stray twigs as it jerked and settled, whining to a halt on the blacktop facing the residence to the left of the dense thicket. Damn! He had left his binoculars and iPhone on the blanket. He would wait until the pilot went inside, get them and then crawl back to the covert of flowering beach plums and video the activity. He noticed that the heliport lights had never been turned on. That was probably why they fired up all the mansion's lights. Tricky landing, but it was a clear night, so by training the spotlight on the helipad, a superior pilot easily could manage it.

As Fen was making this deduction, the pilot jumped out from the left side of the helicopter and strode over to a casually dressed Liam who had emerged through sliding glass doors and waited on the patio. Fen watched them shake hands, then vanish behind the glass into the mansion. A shadowy figure moved in the copter. The activity in the cockpit nearly prevented Fen from dashing to his blanket for the phone. But because he needed it to collect crucial evidence, he had to risk being seen. He crawled out from the bushes, cursing with every prick and snare of the thorns and slithered in the sand like a lizard, hoping the co-pilot was looking out to the eastern darkness of the thicket and not to his left on the beach, where Fen had set his course.

Fen lunged onto the blanket. Kneeling then sitting on his heels, he threaded the binocular straps over his head and pocketed his iPhone. Then he snaked on his belly back to the beach plums, curled his body around so that he could crunch his head and knees into his chest and wriggled backwards into the bushes while cursing under his breath against the pricks. He would have to add his first aid kit to the other stuff he must bring back from his car at sunrise.

Fen's heart dropped. As he pushed deeper into the stubborn branches he heard loud, masculine voices. He couldn't make out the language. It certainly wasn't English, too many rolling Rs. They had discovered him and were coming. Fen would play them off. He peeked his head from under a branch smothered in pinks grayed by the night. Thankfully, it wasn't about him. Peering through the lenses, he watched Liam on the patio, directing two of the security team who were dressed in black. They were carrying someone on a stretcher who Fen couldn't see because a sheet was over the body, and the head was turned away. He didn't recognize the security men who looked tall and buff. The individual on the stretcher looked to be of a moderate weight and height, like Manny. He saw little else. The men were crossing the lawn and moving to the right side of the helicopter. Fen took out his iPhone, framed the scene, adjusted the zoom and pressed for video.

The men were walking around the nose of the helicopter and continued to the right. His view was blocked, but he could see intermittently through the pilot's open door. The other man in the copter struggled to pull up the stretcher, as one member of the security team negotiated the weight of the patient while the other jumped inside the copter and helped his colleague lift and situate the stretcher, so it was out of the way of the pilot and co-pilot. Suddenly, Fen's view went black. He had stopped recording. He shook the device and clicked it off and on. Dead battery. He clicked it off and returned it to his pocket, then lifted the binoculars from his chest and looked through them. He wondered if he had successfully videoed the security team carrying the man on the stretcher. Whoever the patient was, and from the heaviness it looked like a male. In their rush and struggle to get him onboard, Fen saw the patient's arm dangle from the stretcher. And that arm was clothed with a light weight, green material, the same color and fabric of the windbreaker that Manny had worn the night of his abduction.

Inwardly, Fen was ecstatic. He had the proof. He had outsmarted the bastards. Even if he didn't get the arm with the jacket on video, he had seen it hanging off the stretcher in all its green glory. Manny probably had been drugged for easier transport. It was a chain of evidence, and a videotape was irrefutable. Why had the helicopter come in the middle of the night? He glanced at his watch. It was almost 3:30 AM. There would be no witnesses, as they secreted Manny away with impunity.

Seconds later, Fen's joy converted to panic. He couldn't sit back passively and watch them take Manny. He must stop them. But how? He was outnumbered. He didn't have a gun to threaten them. Each member of the steroid-buff security team carried a firearm. And the helicopter would take off in a few minutes.

The chance to do something was leaking away. He must act. But action was foolhardy without resources. If he ran to the copter, leaped in and tried to rescue Manny, the security team would rip him like lions bringing down an antelope. Better if he waited and watched without their knowledge. Justice would be served with this latest evidence on video. If he tried to intervene in some other way, what would he discover that he didn't know already? That the body on the stretcher was Manny? If he confronted them with their kidnapping, would they let him live to tell the police? Two of his mother's sons would be missing instead of one. Fen felt his adrenalin silt into reasoned restraint.

As he gazed through the binoculars, Fen memorized every detail of activity. The pilot jumped onboard, and security man jumped off. He conned their looks, their expressions. Liam who had been supervising the getaway went inside through the sliding doors again. The remaining security team, who had conversed with Liam, waited on the patio, presumably to watch the copter's takeoff. Fen had videoed Liam, security, the pilot and the patient's arm. He had made sure the date was on the video. With his testimony about the jacket and the video, the detectives had probable cause for a search warrant. Fen considered. But what was the point of a search now that they were removing their prime witness and victim? They would sweep evidence from the place where they had held Manny. The search would be moot, and he would be back to square one, Liam's lies versus his truth. But the video did reveal a chain of evidence linking Manny with the estate. Maybe it was enough for the detectives to arrest and hold Liam for questioning. They could squeeze him until he spilled where they had taken Manny.

Fen strained his neck and torso up above the cover of the bushes. Through the binoculars, he saw the pilot adjusting the instruments for takeoff. He couldn't see Manny. The "patient" was deep in the guts of the copter, which furiously revved its blades, raising a small cloud of dust that had remained from the first landing. Fen watched transfixed, his emotions in turmoil. The copter droned upward from the manicured grounds, like a gigantic, malevolent dragonfly and in mid-air, turned its heading toward his hiding place. Fen plunged to the bottom of the bushes, where the wood grew out of the sand, nearly putting his eye out on a thorny barb. He hoped that the flowers and leaves thoroughly camouflaged him. White light trickled down through the branches and delicate flowers as the helicopter blared its spotlight directly over his position, then bumbled, humming over a small stretch of beach. Its buzzing slowly faded over the white breakers and undulating black water into the blue-black night sky. Forgetting his need for stealth, Fen quickly rose from his crouching position and tore his arms free from the thorny defenses. Through his binoculars, he watched the black insect with its piercing light spiral away westward down the coast, bearing its priceless cargo. He flashed his binoculars toward the mansion. The security team had disappeared.

A thought occurred to him as he pointed the binoculars back to the retreating helicopter. If the copter hugged the coastline, he could follow it driving his car down the other side of Ginn Lane which paralleled the oceanfront for miles. Though the idea had little merit, his passive voyeurism ambushed him. He needed to take action. He plucked his sweatpants from the complaining woody barbs and flew to the blanket, where he quickly fumbled on his sneakers. He would leave the rest of his stuff there and come back for it.

Through this mist of frenetic activity, Fen's mind tried to get his attention. There was something wrong. Something sounded wrong. Instead of a steadily fading drone, there was a misfire and another misfire and sputtering sounds. An ancient Model-T Ford had taken flight and was making loud, coughing noises in the sky to the west. He looked up in the direction of the whirring dragonfly and its tell-tale white light skimming through the night sky. Time became compressed and crushed inward. In that split-second gaze into eternity, he saw a single flare out, spiking upward, a luminous, white hot arc. A half-second later into his mind came an ear-splitting explosion. Somersaulting fireballs combining tongues of yellow, orange, red, black and white flames violently torqued, bursting through the static blue-black curtain of night. Fen grabbed his binoculars from around his neck and lifted them to the western sky. Odd-shaped black fragments and yellow orange droplets sprayed the dark sea. Yellow, luminous scarves of fire catapulted through the night, zigzagging crazily in a free fall until they plopped into the brine, sizzling and hissing into thin, rising smoke columns or landing intact, fiery floats riding the undulations of oily, shimmering, silvery, wet darkness.

As burning, dry tongues thirstily licked the salt waves, Fen tried to hold onto watery hope. He was beyond shock. *Weird*, he thought. Flaming surf. Incongruous paradox. Death.

Gradually, the Southampton locals emerged from their estates and mansions and palatial havens of security and comfort. Some recognized the lone figure dressed in expensive Polo sweats, and they joined him. Uncommunicative, Fen answered their questions with one-word responses. While they waited for the Southampton Volunteer Fire Department, they scanned the waters for survivors in the remnants of flaming wreckage that had once carried his wonderful, beautiful brother.

Chapter Thirteen

In the darkness, Mocha screamed, a high-pitched wail, a scream that sounded like a lost child crying for its mother or the keening of a wild, trapped animal, sensing its own imminent death. Beach Comber tried to comfort Mocha, but his mouth was gagged, and he couldn't breathe. He had all he could do to force the air into his lungs. He moved his head from side to side to break the bonds in his mouth, but he was immobile, his upper torso in a long canal. Mocha screamed louder. With fury, he struggled to reach out to her and, tell her it was OK. She should stop her screams because they hurt his ears, and he couldn't think with all the noise. And then he opened his mouth and forced the air through his lungs, and he discovered that he was screaming with her. He screamed for all the injustice in the world, and for what had happened to Mocha and to him, the Beach Comber. Then he was unconscious once more.

Hours later, Beach Comber awakened for a few moments, captivated by the wilderness of white surrounding him in the small, dimly lit room. The gag had been removed from his mouth, and he could move his upper body sideways, no longer enclosed by the canal. But he had a crashing headache and his arm seemed pinned to the blanket by a long, thin, clear tube extending from his wrist, above his white gloved hand. In the low light, he barely could make out a pole and pouches attached to his arm by clear, external veins. He lifted his unencumbered hand to his face. It was awash in a white, filmy sash. He looked down at his chest and saw a shroud enfolded him. He was bathed in white, a monster unrecognizable to himself. He leaned back onto the softness and closed his eyes.

By the next day, Beach Comber had regained full consciousness, benefiting from the extended rest and medicines in his IVs. Gradually, he understood his hospital surroundings, but he couldn't remember how he got there, only that Mocha was screaming, and he had tried to calm her. Later, he realized her screams were the ambulance siren. His own screams had occurred in his head since an oxygen mask had been placed over his nose and mouth.

His mind gripped events and images but couldn't hold them, and they drifted, echoes in a shrouding mist. This upset him because he had an identity, but he wasn't sure what it was; and there was no one around to remind him. So, all he cared about was sleep. Then his mother and brother arrived. He knew them and remembered. Beach Comber shook the apes from the various neural branches of his cortex and cleared a path through the underbrush of temporary amnesia, but he still didn't remember the accident. His brother had left for Wall Street, leaving his mom to fill in the details.

Sitting on a hospital chair across from him, she explained his situation with animation and marked contrast to the sterile environs. "When the caretaker arrived, he found you bleeding and unconscious, and your T-Bird smashed through the cemetery gates which were off their hinges, flat on the ground. Luckily, the gates just missed crushing Deidre. That caretaker was insufferable. He cared more about the funeral then your injuries. He was put out because there was a procession that morning, and they had to tow your car and remove the gates. That's when they found Deidre."

Sylvia Reynolds tried to be reassuring and calm, like the doctor had suggested; but the idea that more of her son's trust fund would be eaten up by a lawsuit from Deidre's family galled her. She intended to get the best personal injury and criminal defense lawyers in Manhattan. She patted her handbag which held the date book containing the names of four recommended attorneys and their firms.

Beach Comber smiled at his mom who was fashionably dressed in heels and a color coordinated, slim fitting, Ralph Lauren suit with matching Fendi handbag. The materialism that he usually found annoying now charmed him. Happy to recognize her, she looked especially lovely to him this morning. He now remembered that she was always a knockout. The slim and petite, green-eyed, honey blonde would still be turning heads in her seventies afforded by her high-end lifestyle, surgeries and her third husband who was in Arbitrage. He let her rattle on about her distress when she and his step-brother had visited yesterday, the solicitous doctors and nurses, and her annoyance that the private hospital room wasn't up to her standards. He was glad to hear her voice and remain in a silent daze to mask that he couldn't readily gather his thoughts.

"You had no identification on you. EMS took your license plate number, and the police ran it through DMV. I got the call yesterday and rushed here. I told them your medical history, and they put you on painkillers, and antibiotics and a mild sedative and gave you a tetanus shot. Your lacerations on your torso and arms are going to heal quickly. But they're concerned about the concussions. They're afraid that your brain might swell because you have a bump on the back of your head and here," Sylvia gestured, "above your forehead, probably from the crash." You had two concussions. Second impact syndrome is what Dr. Patel calls it. This can be very dangerous. So, you'll be here for a few days, and the MRI and CAT scan will show any serious injuries, if there is edema or hemorrhaging, if the neck was injured from whiplash and is pressing on the spinal cord. If not, you can go home. And then we have to watch for post-concussion syndrome, if the headaches, nausea, confusion and memory loss continue or grow worse in the next few weeks."

Beach Comber was depressed. He didn't remember hitting the cemetery gates. He wasn't even sure why or how he drove into them, unless he lost control of the car for some reason. But he remembered that Mocha was in trouble and he wanted to help her.

"How is Mocha? Did they bring her here?"

"Deidre is in intensive care. She is unconscious. So, they are keeping her stable and her family is around her praying in tongues, mind you, and talking to her constantly, trying to awaken her. I spoke to Ms. Hamilton, and she wants to speak to you as soon as possible." Sylvia looked at him, then looked away annoyed, but she caught herself. "It is obvious to me that you found her, but the Hamilton family is pressuring Ms. Hamilton to question you. I think they are going to litigate, but I have the names of a few excellent attorneys. Now, Paul, do you remember what happened?"

Beach Comber winced and turned his head to look out the window next to his bed, but the blinds were closed. Whenever his mother called him by his given name he was reduced to the pampered ten-year-old who had lain in bed for months because of a heart ailment. His mind was gradually clearing. Probably the sedative had worn off. He remembered that he, Peregrine and Mocha had sworn an oath, so he couldn't tell her anything. "Mom, I just don't remember," he lied. Before he spoke to anyone, he would have to concoct a plausible story, but he would have to synchronize it with Mocha's condition and pepper it with just enough facts to satisfy the others and Mocha's detective cousin and cop uncle.

"Well, today, I have an appointment with one of the attorneys. I've spoken with the corporation that owns the cemetery, and your insurance company, and they will settle. I called the towing repair service. I'm afraid your T-Bird is totaled, but I told them you would still want the car repaired and wanted to check it out yourself, as you had friends in the business." Sylvia had run out of breath.

"You know they want the car for its parts or for themselves. It's historic." Beach Comber snorted. "I figure it withstood the impact without too much damage if it was able to bring the gates down." Beach Comber didn't want to give too much away. A thought flashed up a memory. He had floored it and glanced down just before he smashed through the black iron. The speed gauge had registered sixty miles an hour. He didn't think he had crushed the engine. Anyway, whatever it cost, he and some buddies would repair it. They had restored cars in worse shape. "Why lawyers?"

"Deidre's cousin, the Queens Detective Mr. Matthews, thinks you assaulted her. They think she was raped, then hit over the head. Her throat is raw, as if something huge was jammed down it to suffocate her. And when that didn't kill her, she was hit over the head and left for dead. Thank God she is strong, or as Ms. Hamilton would say, 'protected by God's angels, Psalm 91.'" Sylvia fluttered her eyes in mockery and disgust, while Beach Comber said nothing. It was too much to take in.

After a few minutes of silence, Sylvia stood up and paced, wringing her hands. "I knew I wasn't a good mother, that I spoiled and privileged you, the best private schools." Sylvia's tone tended toward an inner questioning. "Yes, we interrupted your education when we went on business trips, but you had tutors. And when you didn't finish college, I said, 'he can always go back and be a perpetual student if he likes. He has his trust fund.'" But I never thought our indulgence would make you a criminal."

Her voice already in a crescendo, augmented to eruption. With objectifying wonder Beach Comber went deaf, saw her tongue through gritting teeth flick out words he didn't register and saw her mouth a black hole, encircled by Este Lauder's Silver Rose, the latest summer, lipstick shade. His headache was intensifying, but he allowed the river of hatred to seek its own level. There was no stopping this shrill termagant. He remained calm, continued his silence and watched as if separated from her by a glass wall.

"You have never liked any of my husbands, and you resented me for never allowing you to know your father who abandoned us. But I thought that the money would answer all that. The men I chose to marry were kind and generous and accepted you as their responsibility. I knew that one day you would be able to understand that a man who gives his family everything must be appreciated and loved. And a man who doesn't support his family sufficiently isn't fit to populate the planet. Poverty destroys a man's character. It's naive to think otherwise. You have to carve out your destiny with your own two hands. If you can't make something of the life handed to you, then you shouldn't be allowed to live it."

Beach Comber inwardly cringed at his mother's rosy confabulation. After Sylvia closed in with her silk-tipped fingernails and heavily, moisturized hands, dramatically illustrating "carving out destiny" with clenching, grasping fingers, her anger subsided. Shaken by her negativity, Beach Comber's memory clarified another fifteen degrees. Sylvia had always credited herself for marrying "good men." But in her harangue, she had forgotten to mention she had divorced two of them, the first for fondling him instead of her.

He had never known his biological dad, a professional athlete. She refused to speak about him beyond that general job description. He sensed that in appearance and athleticism he was a mirror image of his father, but he didn't even know the man's name. He had been adopted by "good" husband number one when he was three. After Sylvia's divorce, she and Beach Comber had received very generous settlements, in exchange for not pressing charges and avoiding a messy public trial, which, regardless of the jury's verdict of guilt or innocence would have ruined Jack Carver and diminished his assets. At eighteen, Beach Comber gained control of his own trust fund. The millions could be rescinded at any time if Beach Comber decided to hold Carver to account for his pederasty. Beach Comber's silence was the alchemy that purified Jack Carver from taint and granted him the power to maneuver freely in the business world.

Beach Comber groaned as remembrance of his identity returned. After the divorce, Sylvia had encouraged him to keep Jack's prestigious surname. To Beach Comber, the quid pro quo was a lurid reminder of the luxury of cowardice. As therapy for his broken emotions and craven masochism, he could indulge every whim, and Carver could indulge his lust for boys with impunity. Beach Comber remembered what he tried to forget daily, and he also remembered that this was the year he had resolved to change his life of hypocrisy and cowardice. In fact, that was one of the many reasons why Peregrine, Fen and Mocha had gone to the crypt, to help Beach Comber achieve this resolve. He had asked them to proxy for him during the ceremony.

"Mother, why would I rape Mocha?" He resumed the discussion with annoyance and felt better for letting his anger erupt. Sylvia's complete absence of logic subdued his patience. "We have been semi-involved for a while but more importantly, she's a close friend. I will submit to DNA testing, and that will prove I wasn't with her. How could I? I just got back from the trip. When I learned Peregrine and Mocha were missing, I went to look for them and rescued her."

"From a cemetery of all places. How did you know she was there?"

Beach Comber cut her off. "Please don't ask me anything else. I have a bad headache. My vision is blurred, and I need to close my eyes and rest. When I sit up, I am nauseous and dizzy." Beach Comber remembered Sylvia's list of symptoms and now used them to his advantage. Actually, he felt much better except for the persistent headache and thought he would get himself released by tomorrow if he could manipulate his mother not to interfere.

"Don't you have to get ready for your appointment with the attorney in Manhattan soon?" He needed a break from Sylvia and wanted to talk to the doctor to arrange for his release, probably over Sylvia's objections. For Christsakes, he was twenty-seven and could sign himself out of the hospital. The CAT scan and MRI results would be given to him in two hours. Barring any dangerous findings, after he signed out, he would hire a cab to take him back to Trinity Hills in the morning and look for Peregrine or investigate Calvary Cemetery if she wasn't at Trinity Hills. He'd search all day if necessary. But first he would have the driver take him to his bank to get more cash and straighten out the problem with his license and phone.

Now Sylvia was set on a task. She came over to her frail boy of ten-years-old and kissed him on the cheek. She sat on the edge of the hospital bed and motioned to the bandages. "How did your hands get so cut up?"

He ignored her lapse into logic. "Mom, could you call the repair shop and have Solly tow the car to Bill's? You should have the number in your book since you used them to restore the Mercedes. And you have my apartment keys. Could you have Benson go there and get some clothes and a change of underwear? I don't get the no underwear thing here. I feel vulnerable, a bare-assed bum."

"You are not destitute. You have a private room for goodness sakes." Sylvia was typically exasperated. "Before I forget, I ordered your meals from Jordan's Vegetarian, so they should be here with lunch. I made sure the doctor checked off on it. You can have soup and seven grain toast and by tomorrow, some real food since there was no internal damage, just a little bruising, thanks to my encouraging you to install those very expensive air bags. But you must drink plenty of liquid because you were dehydrated. I ordered three different drinks fortified with vitamins from Jordan's juice bar."

He smiled. "Mom, you are a treasure, despite all your faults."

Sylvia rolled her eyes. "Make sure you get the male nurse, Robert, to help you go to the bathroom since you are still unstable on your feet. You don't want to fall and hit your head."

Would she never leave? "I am going to ask for that adorable, cute nurse who was just in a moment ago checking my IV. My ass is safer with her than with Robert." He moderated the joke just to the edge of offensiveness. Then he remembered. "Oh, one more thing. I seem to have lost my wallet and iPhone. I think someone saw the accident and stole them from me while I was unconscious."

"The caretaker." Sylvia's eyes narrowed. "A smarmy deceiver."

Beach Comber dismissed her. "It could have been anyone. What I need is to contact DMV and my bank. Tell Benson to bring my laptop. I'll do everything online, including closing down my phone service." Beach Comber broached the next subject with care. "Do you have any cash?"

"Why do you need cash? It might be stolen here."

"In this private room? It's always good to have cash. Cash is king." He used her beloved maxim.

Sylvia looked at him with curiosity. Had the concussions converted him to her thinking? She reached in her handbag and handed him three twenties. As she readied herself to leave, she spoke with emphasis. "You should speak to Ms. Hamilton. I'll leave word for her to stop down after lunch." She looked at her watch. "How about at 2:00 PM? Jordan's should be here shortly."

Her parting words distressed him. "Let's make it 3:00 PM, today. No, mom actually, tomorrow afternoon at 3:00 PM. I need to rest. It's impossible to sleep at night with the hospital noise and disturbances. I'm exhausted, and I can't do polite conversation, yet. Just tell Ms. Hamilton I hope Mocha is recuperating. When I found her she was unconscious. Other than that, she didn't look injured, no bruises or cuts anywhere." Beach Comber decided to put off speaking to Ms. Hamilton, especially if her relative suspected him of assault and rape.

Sylvia nodded, blew him a kiss and left. There was nothing like impending doom to spur one on to health. With the medications and IVs and Sylvia's departure, Beach Comber revived. He felt back to normal. In the next few hours, after lunch, he could convince the doctor he was well enough to remove the IVs and insinuate that he should be released tomorrow. If they refused, he'd take matters into his own hands. Tomorrow morning, after Jordan's came with his breakfast, he'd get dressed, quickly eat, and sneak out if the doctor didn't sign his release. They were so busy, but he had a private room, so, they wouldn't notice. He'd get to a phone and call a cab. Too bad he couldn't have either Benson or his mom's chauffeur take him but he couldn't risk their involvement. Then he'd go back to the cemetery and look for Peregrine. In the back of his mind, he knew it appeared like he was avoiding Ms. Hamilton. If he couldn't convince the doctor to sign him out and he just left, from the doctor's point of view, it was foolhardy high jinx, reflecting the sensibility of a daredevil surfer. From a detective's point of view, it was tantamount to culpability. Ms. Hamilton and Sylvia? They'd understand after he found Peregrine.

Beach Comber looked up at the IV which would soon have to be changed and then stared at the modern art print on the wall. He thought with cogent intellect about his assessment of the gates two days ago. He had been right that the gates could be smashed open, wrong about the speed needed to do it. Forty miles an hour would have been sufficient. The strikes he had received from the man of lightning had completely misdirected his usually accurate judgment of such things. But for the assault, he would have been better able to sustain the impact of the crash and the inflating air bags. The ephemeral monster's blows had landed him here with a busted head. They had caused him to sack his car and threatened to immeasurably complicate his life with a lousy run of bad luck.

Chapter Fourteen

H ours ago, Peregrine had finished the last of her food, a pomegranate. She had consumed all the oranges and the last of her water perhaps three days ago. But she was so deranged, she was incapable of calculating with any accuracy the full transit of an hour, let alone a day. For all she knew, she could have consumed her food in three days or one day.

As the torchlight cast obscene and eerie shadows on the walls immediately behind and in front of her, the darkness beckoned in the distant passageway, but she leaned against the wall and rested to calculate her mileage. She had begun to count off her paces and synchronize them by counting off seconds in the hope of approximating rough miles and crude hours. The calculations took her mind off her body's complaints, the perpetual thirst, the aches, the loneliness and growing terror that she was lost and would never get out of this mole hole.

Her disorientation in time and her dislocation in space and direction frustrated her to the edge of hopelessness and gave rise to errors of estimation and judgment. Convinced she was shuffling right, a passageway might circle to the right for a while then gradually list by degrees to the left, then suddenly double back to the direction from which she had come in some great cosmic joke. These convolutions in the maze of passageways taught her to mistrust her own feelings of certitude. Was she making an error of estimation or of judgment? One could be recalibrated. The other, evidence of her devolving condition, could not and would continue to devolve.

Three times, she had come to a circular room, like the first one at the beginning of the hellish journey, but different. From each of the three rooms, four passageways led into the darkness, like four spokes emerging from the center of a wheel. She marked the wall of the room with a symbol before entering the selected tunnel. With her iron spike, she scratched a circle the first time, then a cross. And after searching the largest of the rooms, she decided upon the smallest tunnel and before entering, carved a triangle on the wall perpendicular to the passage. She never saw the marks again and so assumed she was not doubling back on herself. However, without a compass, she had no way of knowing if she was making an error of judgment or estimation or if she was correct. She feared that an aerial cross section of the labyrinth would reveal she was indeed a cog in a wheel, traveling up and down the spokes, never making any linear progress, until she eventually hobbled into the final circle of the outermost rim, where she would go round and round like a niggling rodent until she was dead. The image provoked her to laugh and then weep in frustration. Every emotion a human could experience, she thought she had experienced in the crypt. But her range of emotions had intensified since she had come to this demonic, twisted, underground puzzle.

Peregrine switched the torch from one hand to the other and reaching out with her hand to grab the wall, hop limped to the opposite side of the passage. Grasping a section of mortar and stone, she steadied herself and mummy walked counting aloud, "2582, 2583, 2584..." Added to her present physical and emotional miseries was her self-doubt and intellectual torpor. "Shall I go out of my mind with boredom?" she asked the walls, then sighed. The mediocrity of sameness: mile upon mile of stone, concrete, mortar, dirt, unvarying and architecturally logical. Surely, this was a man-made structure built for utility, the unequal of Nature's infinitely varied creations, unparalleled in stasis. Whoever had built this labyrinth knew he was going nowhere, and he clobbered the travelers of his passageways with the manifestation of his understanding.

As she shuffle-hopped and counted her steps by rote, she tried to keep her mind active to stave her downward mental spiral. In her most recent fantasy, she was a beautiful Naiad stalked by a seducing wizard who wanted her for himself. One day, this ugly and hump-backed sorcerer had lured her to a magical and refreshing, crystalline underground river, where she played and brought lovers, and became so addicted that she forgot the sunlight and flowers and the serene, azure skies and vibrant bucolic greens of the lush paradise above ground that surrounded her river home. In malice, because she spurned him, the wizard drew up a potent spell, preventing her escape and causing her magical fairyland to dry up, replacing it with dung-colored earth and inanimate, cruel stones and cement, materials that would never procreate or regenerate themselves.

And with a second spell, he fabricated the Moloch tunnels which had the power to sense the desires of immortal creatures. And when the immortals sought to escape to the bright, sun-filled, airy world above, the Moloch tunnels would immediately generate passage upon passage to thwart them. Every time the Naiad came near to an escape hatch, the Moloch tunnels would sense it and fabricate a labyrinth that doubled-back on itself in twists and turns and with such convolutions that the Naiad became hopelessly lost. The wizard had doubly triumphed over the Naiad; first, she grew to despise herself for being duped into a lifestyle which was a living death; and second, he kept her for himself, for no one wanted to join her in the underground dung heap.

"The end," Peregrine shouted, then muttered under her breath. "Well, at least I'm not going mental. Ha, ha, ha, ha." She tried not to laugh with bitterness. And she thought, my prince may come and lift the curse of this labyrinth. In her fantasy, her prince was gorgeous, and he rather looked like Fen. But how would Fen find her here? It was an impossibility. He would be looking for her in the crypt.

"Five thousand two hundred and eighty..." Another crude mile in her journey of a billion hopes. She rested her shoulder against the wall. "Well, things could be worse." She thought of jobs she would loathe having: a bank teller, a bean counter, a file clerk, Maybe not. Well, this was better than the crypt. She was grateful a freeze wasn't peeling apart her will. And she would not die of hypothermia. The tunnels were comfortable, perhaps ten degrees cooler than above ground. She had eaten and drunk, and her body functions seemed to be intact. She had another few days until she was in a dehydration coma, maybe. And she still had light, though soon she would be darkness's intimate friend once more, like the description in the song.

Peregrine switched the torch to her other hand and did her shuffle step to the opposite wall, her hand reaching out to steady herself against it. The torch burned a dull flame as it ate up the oil and her jeans which she had twisted around the head of the cross. She was so sick of the phrase "searching for the light at the end of the tunnel." She swore if she got out alive, she would personally kill anyone who dared say it to her.

After her first torch had devoured her bra and shirt infused with oil, the burning cross had flared out, and the darkness had flooded in. She had been amazed at how long the anointed material had burned. Damning herself for leaving the casket cloths behind, she considered burning the ancient robes of the high priests still in her back-pack, but decided to burn her jeans instead. She must conserve the bulky, silk robes which were priceless and irreplaceable. They were a necessary condition of the ceremony, which would lack efficacy without them. Her jeans were sufficient fuel. They were dense and would burn a long time if she anointed them with a few drops of oil. The remaining half cruse she would keep for the ceremony.

Peregrine remembered she had laughed so hard at the vision of herself as the "bride of the living dead." She had bent over and collapsed on the ground until the fit of mirth ended. The joy had strengthened her, and it was then that she had decided to take her second long nap and sleep while she still wore her jeans, so she could stretch her legs on the ground without feeling the insects through the tough cloth. In the impenetrable darkness, she had been able to rest some hours with the compact soil as her mattress, the wall her pillow and the spiders and various insects her bedfellows.

After she woke up, refreshed, she had maneuvered out of her jeans, repulsed by the cool earth on her backside and underneath her legs. Once more, she had reached into her backpack and retrieved the matches and oil. She had poured ten drops into the palm of her right hand and smeared her jeans with the wetness until her hand was dry. Turning her jeans upside down, she had pulled the waist and hips over the crossbars and secured the cloth by tying the legs of her jeans around the top of the cross. She had slipped each strap of the pack, first under the right then left arm, and aligned it against her spine. Firmly, she had stuck the torch in the soil floor of the cave and lit it easily from her sitting position. She envisioned crawling creatures being squashed beneath her as she knelt and holding onto the wall, painstakingly lifted herself. Then once more, she had limped forward, holding the torch in her left hand, like the celebrated statue's mocking inversion: she was the tired, the poor and the nearly naked, yearning to be free.

That was days ago. She had become accustomed to hobbling in her underwear, the silk scarf and bikini briefs the only items between herself and the cave's crawling inhabitants. If she ever escaped from her dungeon, her state of undress would be an enticement to the unscrupulous. On the other hand, her skin itched from the accumulated dirt and the odiferous corpse. Red scratch marks streaked it, and dry patches dotted it here and there, where her nails had dug in to relieve the maddening tickle. She was as fetid as a cesspool, septic as a tarn. Her hair was matted with tangles and knots. If anyone wanted to be romantic or affectionate, she would open her arms wide and grin exposing her un-brushed, filmy teeth and smack her lips with smooching sounds and walk toward them like a robotic, underworld creature crying, "Kiss me, kiss me." Their lust wouldn't hang around and neither would they--all thoughts of sex made unappetizing by her stench and aggressiveness.

If anyone wanted to follow her trail and overtake her, it would be easy, for she made no rapid progress. Each mile that she counted off with disabled steps took all of her concentration. She moved with a grotesque cadence, at times putting weight on her ankle. Because she had taken long rests and occasionally slept, the ankle swelling subsided, though her knee ache had not. The miles, where she counted off paces were strewn with seeds from the pomegranates after she had drained them of their nourishing juice. Before that, she had tossed onto her trail the orange pits. As she dragged herself up and down the passageways, she scoured the ground for the seeds. Finding none, she convinced herself she wasn't retracing her steps. After she had eaten the oranges, she stuffed the peels down the scarf, saving them for their moisture and fragrance, for the last ration of water was gone, and she knew she must ration the pomegranates.

Every now and then, she would eat one of the peels to moisten her throat and regenerate herself with the vibrancy of citrus aromas. Then the peels were gone and the pomegranates, too. Now nothing was left to eat or drink; she had checked her pack a hundred times. After living in the luxury of water and food, to have to bear the intensifying agony of dehydration once again seemed an infernal injustice, as if mocking Death grinned down at her from his imperial height and sneered, "You overcame me once. Can you do it again?"

Along with injustice, indignity, too, was her special acquaintance, as brutishness slowly infiltrated her external appearance, attitude and personal attributes. Once, serenely feminine, proud of her beauty and meticulous in her dress, conduct and hygiene, she no longer cared or paid any attention to how she looked and smelled. She had become inured to the mephitic odor of her body and had no compunction about adding to its noisomeness. Not having bathed in days, and having resurrected her bodily functions with the intake of food and water, Peregrine relieved herself whenever she pleased, and it pleased her more often than not. She allowed the residue of waste to cake and dry on her person, because she dared not pollute her hands and fingers with additional bacteria that would make her sick, since she had used her fingers so prodigiously with the oranges and pomegranates. These conditions had whittled her ego to a fine thread of humility, and her assertive nature had been diluted by the floods of anarchic circumstance. She was a rubber band, and some unseen actor, whom she dared not name God, brutally stretched her mentality and being, reminding her that humankind was a subordinate species and its mortality was as fragile as the gossamer of fairy wings.

As Peregrine struggled down the cave length, she hopped to the other side of the passageway and switched the torch to her left hand, holding the wall with her right. When her arm tired, she hopped back to the left side. She moved this way, from side to side, switching hands and trying to keep alert as she bumped down the length of the curving tunnel. "3478, 3479, 3480…" she droned aloud the nullifying routine.

The shadows deepened and the blackness in the distance crept nearer and nearer. Jolted out of her lethargy, Peregrine saw that the flame flickered dangerously low. It would be out in minutes. She had a few matches left in the matchbook and the two wooden ones, but there was nothing left to burn except the priests' robes and her socks, inadequate, insubstantial fuel, but better than nothing.

She stopped. Grasping a protruding field stone from the wall, she bent down nearly double and averting her face from the glowing trickle of the last tiny flame, spiked the earth two times with the bottom of the dying cross, searching for a firm place to secure it. On the third try, she found an area in front of her, which seemed appropriate. Letting go of the wall, with both hands, she twisted the metal down, down until the cross stood upright in the soil. Using the wall to balance, with most of her weight on her right leg, she straightened herself, and with her left hand, removed the straps of her back-pack from her left shoulder. It would be easier to get to the floor without it, and she needed the oil. Sitting there, she would remove her socks and sneakers, put her sneakers back on, then douse the socks with oil droplets and light them. She had conquered so much, the revulsion she felt sitting bare-legged on the ground, the possibility of spiders and insects crawling on her, was inconsequential.

She turned her back to the wall and leaned against it, securing the pack with the pressure of her weight. Using her right hand, she disentangled herself from the right shoulder strap and lowered the bag to the ground. Her ankle ached. She bent over the pack to retrieve the iron spike to help her raise and lower herself to the ground. Then, the wavering red embers expelled their last dying exhalation and gave her up to the darkness. But she was not alone.

Chapter Fifteen

The darkness and moisture were always a problem in the catacombs. The light wands, supposedly guaranteed to last an hour, petered out in fifteen minutes, making it imperative that the batteries for the flashlights be restocked often. But they never were and that caused problems. It slowed down their work, forcing the men to use one flashlight between three of them, like now, if they were lucky and the remaining juice didn't drain.

Seals made a mental note to pick up more supplies and stash them safely in the O'Conner crypt. There, he could get them at will, and he and his fire-team would never be disadvantaged again by the other squads who appeared disorganized, but who probably intentioned inconvenience. The squads weren't supposed to compete. It was contractual. But unofficially, they sabotaged each other's business when the opportunity presented itself, like not replacing or restocking supplies, overlapping their schedules and sneakily swapping inferior products for quality. Experienced and organized, Seals ran a tight ship, so The Hallows never screwed up. But then he had been in business for years and was second in seniority after Quinn who had started the company. Experience had taught him how to get along with his men to get the most out of them.

Not so for Quinn and his Gits, and Tiny Tim and the Prue. In the last year, their situation had become dicey with the recent young hires who were lazy. They cut corners to make the money fast, opening the door to mistakes, which could rain down hell on the entire operation. And they were superstitious and easily scared, which was anathema in this line of employment that required nerves of steel and a sound mind to work in the dead of night, when every noise conjured up images of the ghoulish dead coming to eat them alive. The Gits and Prue never worked during new moon cycles. Both teams avoided various cemetery divisions and were loath to use certain crypts that might be conveniently located near major worksites. This forced the crews to use selective, but inconveniently located, mausoleums which oftentimes lengthened the squads' work hours. But since Quinn and Tiny Tim had to retire workers and find replacements, the latest round of recruits was the best they could find and they put up with cheek to maintain the steady haul of product.

Seals was fortunate in his crew of older, conservative, socially-established fellows. They were mostly atheists, like him, pragmatic men who disdained superstition. They were immune to moon cycles and went everywhere in the cemetery with few exceptions. However, there were two crypts in the entire burial grounds which were rumored to be supernaturally cursed. One of the Prue, who had been missing for a week, had turned up in the O'Conner crypt dead from a heart attack. Six months later, another from the same team had been found dead near the hedges of the Johnson mausoleum. One of his hands had been severed clean off and was lying next to his face, his eyes staring upward in shock. That was two months ago. Replacements had been found, but Tiny Tim was as shaky as a sheep. Even Seals' hardy, prosaic fire-team was loath to enter the black granite, two story O'Conner dead house after dark. As for the phantasmagorical Johnson mausoleum, all the squads tried to avoid the place even in the daytime. Something about the atmosphere; it was too dark, too dense, too weird. Only when there was a special haul did they make an exception, but this was infrequent.

Distracted by thoughts of the mausoleum, Seals hit gravity when the flashlight beam leading him and his men, Salmon and Kippers, dimmed to a red-orange fade.

"Do either of you have a lighter or matches?" Seals turned to Salmon who vanished as the darkness fell on them.

"Yeah." Kippers reached in his pocket for his butane lighter and flicked it on. "I'll break out ahead." Fantastic shadows leaped up in the meager light as Kippers squeezed between Salmon and Seals at the front.

"We're near the old drain pipe. We better surface there and get more supplies at the Blake mausoleum. We don't want to be stuck down here in the black when the lighter blows."

Heavy with tension, the three men lumbered through the earth-works. They despised their victimization by the selfishness of youth and loathed being preyed upon by nascent fears, threatening to rise up from their unconscious: of beasts, of ghosts, of bogeymen, of the things in the dark. The wavering flame from the lighter was small comfort and barely sufficient illumination for them to make their rapid exit out of the labyrinth. They had to hurry. They had work to do before sunrise, and someone had put them behind for the scheduled pickup. If they were late, there would be hell to pay.

Chapter Sixteen

S o, Deidre should have regained consciousness by now? And you can't say conclusively why she hasn't?" Frustration and helplessness sounded in Ms. Hamilton's tone. She was a first mate struggling to sound the leagues of water depth. But as Dr. Song hesitated, Ms. Hamilton correctly surmised that the waters were shallow, and the vessel was about to crash on the reef of uncertainty.

"Well, as I mentioned when I discussed the Cranial CT, I mean the CAT scan and MRI results with you, we found no clot, no hemorrhaging, no edema, no tumor, no aneurism, no mass effect or midline shift, nothing abnormal that would clearly indicate TBI. We performed the cerebral angiography and SPECT which confirmed the same results. We are looking for other causation and additional symptoms that may take a day or a week to manifest clearly. Diagnosis is rather an art, and the patient is the artist we must analyze. Initially, because she was dehydrated and in neurogenic shock when she came in and because of the initial examination and blood tests, we thought we were dealing with a moderate TBI, ah, traumatic brain injury.

The neurologist subtly had laid down this track yesterday, and now he drove the train over it. But Ms. Hamilton was ready for him. "She had received a blunt trauma to the head, you said. And you stated that oxygen may have been cut off to her brain when she was being asphyxiated, possibly resulting in brain damage. Her symptoms simulated this. Are you changing this opinion, again? You've already changed it once."

Dr. Song was noncommittal and elusive. "Well, on closer examination, the swollen bump on her head has gone down and is unrelated to any internal brain injury. We will need to closely watch her in the next week to understand the extent of trauma, if any. Now, you know the results. The tests have come back, and her brain waves appear to be normal. As for her condition, we are surprised that she has not regained consciousness."

"Well, what could be causing this if it's not what you first thought? When I call her name, she doesn't open her eyes, though she turns her head from side to side and seems disoriented and confused. I know she hears me when I speak to her or pray, but she isn't coming out of this to the next level. She doesn't recognize me or respond to conversation."

Dr. Song shrugged his shoulders. "On the Modified Glasgow Coma Scale, a scale we use to measure the extent of her condition, her score is improving. She localizes to pain. She opens her eyes in reaction to pain. She has said some words, though not conversationally. And she has awakened, but goes right back under. We need to gather more information. So we have to wait until she returns to us, or something shows up as we do more tests."

"Doctor, I'm afraid that's not good enough. Is there material that I can read beyond what you gave me? I want to understand my daughter's condition, and I feel like I'm foundering."

The neurologist recognized Ms. Hamilton's piercing stare as one of general mistrust and suspicion that came with such an opaque diagnosis. He modified his level of dispassion and objectivity to warmth. "Of course, I will prepare additional material for you that we give to the family when TBI occurs, and I will also go over what to expect as your daughter recovers. You'll be glad to hear that because she is stabilized and has been breathing on her own, we will be moving her to a sub-acute unit of the hospital. And also, I need to tell you we are going to put in a gastrointestinal feeding tube if she doesn't regain consciousness today. She should have more nutrition than the liquids and vitamins she is now receiving along with the medication to prevent blood clotting. And also, because we want her throat to heal more rapidly."

"And the contusions at the back of her neck, I mean throat?" Ms. Hamilton intended to keep Dr. Song as long as she could, hoping that her nephew, homicide Detective Reginald Matthews, would return in time to question him further about Deidre's assault wounds. "Any idea what could have made them?"

"There are also lacerations and very tiny, what look to be, puncture holes. Unusual instrument that caused it," the neurologist shook his head. "And the individual or individuals who did this to her went to a lot of trouble in its use. There are simpler and more effective ways to dispatch someone."

The situation had drained Ms. Hamilton and emptied her of emotion. She found it incredible that Beach Comber could have done this to Deidre after his kindnesses to the family and his close friendship with her daughter. "Well, thank you. I will continue to talk to her and make sure someone will be with her at all times," she spoke in a monotone.

After the doctor left, Ms. Hamilton phoned the loft and spoke to the nurse about Billy and then she called Third and Thirty-ninth, where she spent her twelve-hour days. She and Deidre held positions at a Madison Avenue marketing agency. She was vice-president of the division that specialized in generating accounts with rising black entrepreneurs. Because she had just finished opening an account, she was able to take a few days off. Though her colleagues were sympathetic, her workload, left undone, whispered like a sinister troll in Geiger's ear. He was a martinet, prototype of the "Boss" in the film, *Office Space*. Her performance review would suffer if she stayed with Deidre. If she was not careful, these events would stifle her chances of angling toward a partnership in the agency, unless she could "inadvertently" get Geiger sacked. Thank God, the agency granted that Deidre would receive disability insurance, though she had not been injured on the job.

After the calls, Ms. Hamilton checked her messages and texted replies. She remembered Deidre's secrecy the previous Saturday. Mother and daughter were very close, but Deidre had been abrupt, distant when she asked about Deidre's plans for the weekend. Of all weekends to absent herself from the family. Elizabeth's anger had spilled out at her daughter, a torrent unleashed by a summer thunderstorm. Didn't Deidre understand how Elizabeth felt about Billy's first days in hospice? Didn't Deidre know her mother needed her there when the nurse came to review the procedures? As Deidre had slipped out the door like the serpent she was, Elizabeth vowed she would never forget this egregious cruelty.

Now, Elizabeth regretted her vengeful attitude. Perhaps her anger, spilling out in hot, poisonous blooms, somehow manifested Deidre's assault and attendant condition. Had her rage opened the door for the evil that had tried to snuff out her daughter's life? She blamed herself for not working through it. The guilt eviscerated her. Daily, she enacted the dual roles of female Promethean counterpart and tormenting raptors.

She only received succor by kneeling on the threshold of her family's Pentecostalism, which she did now, quietly praying in tongues, her head on her hands that rested on the white blanket covering Deidre's slim body. Dry of words, and the emotions behind words, the holy language she had been anointed to as a child rolled off her tongue mellifluously and was a great comfort to her, where valium and anti-depressant cocktails were not. She craved acute consciousness and hyper-reality, not the absence from it in the delusional pain-killing state of anti-anxiety meds. Pain was life. It was inescapable. Dealing with the pain brought joy and happiness, not the other way around. So, she found that prayer brought the morbid dose of reality into focus. Contrary to stereotypic cultural fanaticism that labeled such things as wacko or puerile, it gave her the courage to confront reality and envision hope. As she whispered the divine language, her soul filled with peace and she was able to still her mind. The anxiety and stress that had accelerated the mental simmer into a boil, slowly leveled to a calm.

Detective Matthews walked past the nurse's station in the center of the intensive care unit and stood inside the curtain edge, gazing at his beautiful and amazing aunt. He didn't know how she kept it together. If not for her faith, she would have taken to alcohol or drugs or put a bullet through her head. Yet, there she was, sitting next to Deidre's bed, praying and at peace and looking like she stepped out of a successful business women's fashion magazine. He hated to disturb her, but he must. He pushed aside the curtain cocoon, looking at Deidre who appeared to be sleeping. When he quietly tiptoed to the opposite side of the bed, Deidre mumbled something to him which he couldn't understand, but she didn't open her eyes. Aunt Elizabeth raised her head and when she saw him, settled her prayers and smiled, sitting up straight in her chair.

"Sorry, Aunt Elizabeth. I know you were praying, but I had to see you. How is she? Any change?"

"Dr. Song is surprised she hasn't awakened yet. Everything appears to be normal, except she won't come back to us." Elizabeth's calm broke open into waves of anger, which crashed in and overwhelmed her once more. "I have been kept in the dark. Twice they have changed their opinion about what is causing this coma-like state." Ms. Hamilton stood up and took on the role of the forceful executive. "I have asked for another neurologist to examine her and for more information and resources. And Reggie, I will take her out of this hospital if they can't give me a proper diagnosis or if the doctors contradict each other." She looked around to see if anyone else heard her. She placed a finger to her lips and gestured for Reggie to speak in whispers.

"Aunt Elizabeth, doctors rarely contradict each other if they are working out of the same hospital. That only happens on *House*. I think you should move her once she is stabilized to a hospital that specializes in trauma care, maybe one in Manhattan or Nassau County. I have a few friends checking for the names of top neurosurgeons and neurologists in the area and the hospitals they are affiliated with. We'll contact them."

"We'll transfer her tomorrow, because they've stabilized her and are going to move her out of this unit."

The detective changed the subject. "Aunt Elizabeth, there is another reason why I'm here. Remember I was going to question Paul Carver today at 3:00 PM because you wanted to talk to Deidre and pray with friends who are coming around that time?"

"Well, I spoke to his mother, and we rescheduled the time. I was planning to see him later, around 7:00 PM. Did I tell you what he told his mother about finding Deidre?" Elizabeth went back to the chair and sat down crossing her legs in a relaxed position.

Reggie knew that his aunt liked the surfer. She would not be a willing ally in his intention to press charges against the hedonistic, amoral Adonis. "No." He was about to say, "astonish me," but held his tongue and sucked the roof of his mouth, instead. He sat on the edge of Mocha's bed and smoothed out the coverlet with his right hand.

"She was unconscious. And he checked to see if she had any injuries, and she didn't. No cuts or bruises." Elizabeth loved her nephew, but she was not going to encourage any investigation of Beach Comber. She had already made a mistake with her vow of anger against her daughter, which she sorely regretted. She wanted no more regrets, least of all with a friend of her daughter's who found her and saved her life.

"Aunt Elizabeth, I'm sure he's a wonderful person, but we don't know what happened. We only have his word that he found her, and we can't even corroborate that with the cemetery caretaker or EMS. They are the ones who saw her by the flattened gates."

"But why else would he drive his car into the gates. He couldn't get to her any other way."

"For all we know, he intentionally drove into the gates to make it look like he was trying to save her after he raped her, and it went wrong, and she was dying. Very convenient. It's a great way to get everyone's sympathy. He gets a concussion totaling his car to save her." Reggie gestured with his left fist to emphasize the benefits of the accident. "Aunt Elizabeth, all I am asking is for you to keep an open mind." His tone was sharp and insistent. She frustrated him. Sometimes her Christian faith's adherence to the tenet of "giving the benefit of the doubt to people" got in the way of reality.

"You know I will, but you must do the same." Elizabeth rearranged the covers around Mocha's chest.

"I'm trying to, but it seems that Deidre's angel has a few black, flight feathers amongst his white wings." Irony suited the situation, so he let the telling comparison fly to its mark, noticing with inner satisfaction as the comment reverberated. His Aunt looked distressed and hurt.

"Whatever you want to tell me about Beach Comber, please be direct about it. Circumlocution is a bad beginning for a truthful account."

"I had an appointment to talk to him this afternoon? Well, he's gone. Vanished."

"What? His mother told me he's still under observation because he received two concussions. It seems he was hit over the head and then had the accident, so he has to be very careful of brain injury. He has to receive bed rest for a few more days."

"Tell him that." Reggie was indignant. "I looked all over for him. He's not here. And the doctor didn't authorize any release, so he left without telling anyone. The sly fox snuck out. Now, why is that?"

Elizabeth Hamilton struggled against Reggie's implication, stuck like a moth pinned to a child's science project. She smiled at her nephew. "You are so egocentric." She tried to sound playful, but her tone didn't mask her upset. "It's not all about you. He is probably in the hospital. If he left, he will be back. Why don't you come back? Be there when I talk to him around 7:00 PM this evening." She stood up.

"Aunt, I bet you box tickets to the next Mets game that he won't be here tonight." Reggie was in his element. He reached over the bed and held out his hand to slap an agreement to the bet.

"You know I prefer the Yankees, so you'll owe me tickets to the Yankees game. And I will win. He'll meet me. He said he would."

"No, Aunt Elizabeth, his mom said he would. You know what this appears like? Criminal Justice 101."

Elizabeth shook her head. "No."

"Culpability. Flight is tantamount to guilt. If he's innocent, he has no need to fear me and no need to run."

"Doesn't he, nephew? You've already convicted him." The pale rage that prayer had placated once again seethed in her chest and staggered her breaths. She tried to remain calm, knew she was visibly disturbed. Reggie meant well, but he could be toxic. Why did she foolishly allow him to steal her peace? Now, she was taking flight to preserve calm.

"See you at 7:00 PM." She picked up her handbag and slipped past the curtain. As she walked away, she turned her head toward Reggie and smiled, tossing the comment over her shoulder like a high-flying ball, "Better come with those box seats to the Yankees game."

Chapter Seventeen

D o you know when he'll be back?" Madeline Randolf looked at the painted green, yellow and red hummingbirds and purple wisteria on the kitchen clock. The dial registered 3:30 PM. How was she ever going to angle a new lead in the investigation if Matthews never responded to his text messages and phone calls?

"He's out of the office for the rest of the afternoon. He's in the field," the voice sounded dry, bored.

"Is that why he is not answering his mobile?" Madeline Randolf mingled a smidge of annoyance with a smattering of frustration.

"I'm not aware of the order in which he answers his cell phone calls." The voice towed the line and had no intention of flipping it overboard into helpfulness.

"Is Detective Phillips in? He is also investigating my daughter's disappearance."

"Hold on please." The voice came to life with a task, finding the detective who was in another section of the department.

Madeline knew if she persisted, she could surreptitiously slide them in any position she wanted. If she couldn't get hold of Matthews, she would try his partner who also worked on the case. Amongst friends and colleagues who worked at the nonprofit organization of which she was president, her tenacity was legend. She was sure her officiousness by now had been the subject of conversation at the coffee machine in the missing persons division of the Queens DA's office. But time was a factor. Her daughter was in dire trouble, and she had to work quickly.

"This is Detective Phillips, Ms. Randolf. How are you?"

He sounded interested, but this was customary. She ignored his stupid question. How would any mother be if her daughter had gone missing for a week? "Yes, Detective. I've been in touch with Ms. Hamilton who tells me that Beach Comber, ah, Paul Carver, found Deidre Hamilton at Trinity Hills Cemetery. I was wondering if you or Detective Matthews followed up on that information yet. Did you search the cemetery for Peregrine? She was with Deidre. Did you find her or any of her clothing or other clues?"

"Our men are there now with blood hounds, Ms. Randolph. And so far, no one has called me with any information. But we will let you know the first we hear of something."

"If you don't find anything, are you planning to search any other Queens cemeteries?" There, she had done it.

"I'm not sure what the next step will be. We are hoping to uncover clues by the entrance where Deidre was found."

Madeline was upset by the shallowness of the law enforcement's assumption that whoever assaulted Deidre dropped her off at the entrance. She couldn't press her case unless they progressed deeper into the cemetery. "Aren't they going to check the entire cemetery, check the more remote areas?"

"Well, they will go on any leads they find. That is why they plan to interview Paul Carver this evening. The three o'clock meeting was postponed. We understand he is recovering from head injuries. He should be able to tell us more, but he does have amnesia."

Madeline was prickly. "When is the interview with Paul Carver? I would like to be there and ask him some questions." She would stay after the detectives left and determine if he was well enough to go with her to Calvary.

"Well, Ms. Randolf, I think Detective Matthews prefers to interview Paul Carver alone."

"Well, you have no objection to my visiting him as a private citizen, do you?" Madeline realized Beach Comber wouldn't be able to go. He would be tailed by the paparazzi who wanted to sensationalize the story and make him a hero, then two months later shade him with villainy.

"Of course not. I'll get in touch with Detective Matthews and get back to you."

How astonishing that he can contact Matthews, and I am rolled over like an empty can of cat food, Madeline thought but said with wryness, "If you call me on my cell phone, I will be sure to pick up. You have the number. And please call me immediately if anything new materializes."

When she received the news about Beach Comber and Mocha, Madeline was happy but envious that Peregrine was not with them. She was in shock over her daughter's disappearance. With her lawyer spokesperson who handled the obtrusive media, the investigating detectives and Ms. Hamilton, she exchanged pertinent information and gradually received the details of Mocha's rescue, assault and rape.

With the flurry of activity, she hadn't had a moment to rest and quietly process the information. But at night in bed in a dream sleep, the significance of where Mocha had been found jolted her awake, and a rush of images nudged her to her Eastlake salon chair. There, she meditated, cobbling together a nostalgic mélange of forgotten discussions and heartbreaks. As these swarmed her like bees, in a transient moment of lucidity, she had thought, Trinity Hills? The central family mausoleum is in Old Calvary.

Terror had gripped her. She had scrambled out of the chair and opened the door to her closet, nervously fumbling for the light switch. Inside, she had walked the lengthy and cavernous space, ignoring four double racks of her designer clothing, shoes and handbags until she had come to the very back of the closet, which was a disguised faux wall painted as an optical illusion, a black bull's-eye spiral that appeared to be rotating inward and outward. She had extended her hand at waist level and pressed the center dot.

The wall slid open to reveal the closet paneling, stained in dark walnut finish with thin striations of lighter teakwood running in a vertical pattern between every five walnut panels. Madeline had pressed the first and third strips of teakwood until she heard a click. Then she had pressed the seventh and ninth teakwood panels. She listened for the tell-tale whirring as the walnut between the first and ninth teakwood striations opened inward like swinging doors to reveal a secret room made of fragrant cedar.

She and her sister had the room built when they first bought and refurbished the upstairs of the old Tudor House in Forest Hills Gardens the year after Peregrine was born. The idea was to store their expensive cashmere and vicuna coats, sweaters and other outfits in a protected place. Other valuables were secreted there as well. Only she and Rachel knew the chamber existed, as did the old craftsman, long dead, who had built it.

Rachel had died two years ago. No one else knew about the hiding place. Certainly not Peregrine, for Madeline had not told her.

Madeline had entered the small room, which was six square feet, and had switched on the dangling overhead bulb. Recently, she had been in the room maybe twice, once to place her sister's Cartier jewelry in the safe. Madeline planned to give the jewelry to Peregrine on her twenty-fifth birthday. If Peregrine was alive when they found her, she would give it to her in celebration, she thought absently. Madeline preferred to keep her most precious jewels in the safe and her lesser jewelry in the safety deposit box since she was afraid she could be robbed going in and out of the bank. This safe was fireproof and waterproof, could only be opened with explosives, she had been told. She hoped never to discover the truth of the warranty. An iron column extending upward from the basement through the first and second floor reinforced the area where the safe rested.

Madeline had remembered the combination, but she also kept the numbers in an unpretentious gold locket that she wore around her neck. She had opened the locket and checked to see if the paper with the numbers was there. It was. At three o'clock the previous night, Madeline had kneeled with anticipation before the safe and twisted the dial left and right five times until the door with a heavy whoosh swung open. She had quickly inventoried the gold and jewelry. All was there. But the relics, the cross of the crusades and the broken Templar sword that resembled a stake and the Randolf journal with notes from the *Book of Shadows,* were not. Nor were the other relics. Madeline had collapsed onto her back and put her hands to her face in panic and remorse.

Someone had discovered the secret room. Someone had finagled the combination. Someone had taken the candles and the High Priest's garment. And Madeline knew that someone was Peregrine.

She sat cross-legged in front of the safe to see what, if any, books were missing. She counted. The valuable first editions of the occult and witchcraft books were tucked securely in their protective cases on the shelf. But two English translations had vanished. *Chazar Shamanism* and *Necromancy*. Other sacred and religious books were there. The *Geneva Bible*, thank God, was sitting on the shelf in its protective cover and a secret first edition of the *Tyndale Bible*, one of a very few in the world, was there also in its high-tech shield against moisture and air. The protective cases of the *Book of the Tarot* and the Tarot cards were shoved in a corner on the floor underneath the shelves.

There was one more place that she had to search to verify what Peregrine probably had planned for months, the scheme that had backfired, or she wouldn't have gone missing and Mocha wouldn't be in a coma. Madeline had pulled out the small, rectangular, mahogany strong box from a lower shelf reachable from her seated position. She felt underneath the shelf for the key hook. If any of these precious and arcane antiques were missing, it meant that Peregrine had gone to the Johnson mausoleum.

Madeline had held her breath and said a prayer when she turned the silver key in the silver lock and forced up the mahogany lid. The strongbox was empty. The cruse of Nard oil, the silver pentagram amulet, the Templar ring and the small, silver unicorn with attached chain were gone, all of them powerless unless used in the crypt or its multiple extensions. And the key to the mausoleum was missing, the final proof. She knew that Peregrine had ventured into Calvary to enact the Black Nobility's Ceremony of Powers, the ceremony first enacted by emperor ancestors of ancient Rome and later ancestor emperors of the Holy Roman Empire.

Drained, Madeline held her head in her hands and wept. She had underestimated her daughter. She had perceived their differences in character, behavior and attitude, yet never recognized that they were the same in ambition and desire. If Madeline had conned her daughter's nature, she would have turned the items over to a museum instead of secreting them in an insecure safe in their home. As she wiped her eyes with shaking fingers, Madeline considered Peregrine's desperate act. She was once as desperate as her daughter. She had invoked the Powers to keep a man and make her life with him. And she had later taken the ancient ceremonial artifacts because they were rightfully hers, the only remains of a dispossessed legacy that ruthless and cunning family members had sought to deprive her of through disinheritance and abandonment.

Peregrine had pushed the envelope and bested her mother for what purpose? Unfathomable, dangerous behavior. Madeline had never indulged her appetite for the supernatural after that first time, fearful of the consequences, the addiction to the Powers. For generations, members of her wealthy family had embraced transcending to the alternate realities, believing that they, the Neri, the Black Guelphs or Black Nobility, and only they had the right to rule the world as descendants of Roman Caesars, the Emperor Justinian. As a child she had witnessed the baleful consequences of her family's supernatural obsessions, and she had chosen not to take up the mantle. But for that one time, she had kept her promise to herself. And she had suffered miserably for it, sacrificing her love, her destiny, her blood ties. But she told herself it was worth it. At least her daughter was safe. Now, her self-deception tormented her.

Madeline groaned inwardly. It was in their historical blood, unpurged, unpurified. Like her ancestors, Peregrine had stolen for the power to transcend and rule in her life. Thwarting all her mother's efforts, she unconsciously, psychically, would expand the family's destiny, though she little understood her identity or theirs, a neophyte, ignorant of their history; a child, unwittingly charging back along the same footpaths their nefarious clan had walked. The Powers destroyed her ancestors as they craved higher realms of transcendence, governmental authority and wealth. The Powers would destroy her daughter.

Madeline sat on the floor in front of the safe until 5:00 AM, thinking preposterous thoughts, in Sisyphean agony, burdened with her theft and its unfolding karma. Were the generational sins of the mother to be repeated upon her daughter like a devolving House of Atreus? She had considered contacting estranged family members to return the antiquities, but hard truths prevented reconciliation. Once her European family discovered that she was the thief, for they believed another was responsible, the results would be much worse than the ones she now faced with Peregrine's disappearance. Refusing to recognize any right to rule except their own, her family knew no boundaries between states of life and death. They obeyed their own system of justice, incorporeal and infinite. They scorned natural law and laughed at the quaint arrogance of modern science. Once they knew, there was no where on earth or under it that she could hide. And Peregrine would be theirs.

Regardless of what happened now, she was forced to trudge up the mountain of life without respite, weighted and blighted with guilt, responsible for her daughter's soul death. Stumbling with despair, she must acknowledge she could not expatriate Peregrine from the expanding universe of maledictions. Tasting the forbidden fruit of transcendence addicted one for eternity. If alive, Peregrine was an addict. Madeline refused to believe that Peregrine had died in the crypt.

If her daughter was returned to her, she would expose herself, filter out the occult poison Rachel had injected into Peregrine with her alluring stories. Unlike Rachel, she would divulge the gore and malice. "If they find Peregrine…" Madeline had sworn a vow on the *Geneva Bible*, though she was agnostic.

Narrowing her mind to face a hard reflection, Madeline accepted that the police would never find Peregrine at Trinity Hills. She had returned the strong box to the lower shelf of the safe and closed the heavy, steel door. Torment had stifled sleep. As she had secured the hidden closet and trotted past the clothing racks into her bedroom, she mulled over the options. Somehow, she must skew the investigation to include Old Calvary, and she must remain uninvolved, couldn't let the police know that Peregrine was at the family crypt, illegally trespassing with the intention of enacting a ritualistic, feast of magic.

With the police came publicity, the end of civil rights, the right to privacy and personal choice. There was a groundswell of interest about Mocha and Beach Comber's heroic rescue and about Peregrine's disappearance. And why not? The players were visually stunning, young, photogenic, ripe carcasses for the vulture paparazzi and baboon press. Both she and Ms. Hamilton had declined interviews, appointing family spokespersons. That was all she needed, to have her face plastered all over the media outlets and internet sites, where someone would be sure to recognize her, make inquiries and contact her European family.

The sharks were circling. News crews had camped out at the Hamilton's and the hospital. Reporters had forgotten about her for the moment. Once the scent of a story was in the air, the feeding frenzy would become a bacchanalian orgy. Avoidance of photographers and reporters was tantamount to an admission of guilt or worse, a surety that scandalous behavior lurked beneath the surface of respectability. Evasion stimulated rapacious inquiries until friends, acquaintances and relatives were eviscerated and bloodied. Eventually, whether you were permeable or reticent, after the baboons gobbled your sinew and muscle, they vanished, their fat, bulimic bellies full while your life's peace and integrity became refuse of teaming maggots. The next day, the sordid creatures vomited up your unrecognizable flesh in newsprint or virtually. The purge readied them for their next gorge. Madeline sighed. What explanation could she give about Peregrine's behavior that wasn't lurid and sensational? Now, she understood why the European branch of the family had burial grounds and sepulchers sequestered away on their great and private estates. Much easier to enact their rituals without fear of interruption, censorship or robbery from newshounds, blood-hounds, prying eyes or criminal gangs.

Not possible for her American relatives. New York enacted the Rural Cemetery Act in 1847. Because of the cholera epidemic and sparse land in churchyards designated for burial grounds, Queens County, with its vacant hectares of farm country, emerged as cemetery heaven. Calvary Cemetery opened its welcoming gates to the abundant dead in 1848, around the time Madeline's family ensconced itself in New York City's town houses during the Civil War, and later, in Fifth Avenue mansions during the Gilded Age. Wealthy family members flitted to and from dinners, balls and galas and orbited like moths around the city's lights, the unscrupulous rich, the railroad and oil barons, the land magnates and others of the grand fifty, who had made the list of Manhattan's wealthiest socially prominent.

Because there was no extra land to be had for a private burial repository anywhere on Fifth Avenue, many of the newly rich housed their eternity-minded relations in Westchester or Long Island cemeteries. Her family's appetite for furtive rituals required a dark arts arena that was sufficiently macabre, amply spacious and accoutered, and appropriately secluded. Accessible to the ferry and a Victoria coach ride of long duration, Queens Boulevard on Long Island was the most direct route to access their nocturnal family gatherings after an overnight stay in an area inn. Thus, when the largest, most elaborate mausoleum at Old Calvary was completed, the family celebrated with a rousing Chazar shamanistic initiation. And for the next five generations, her family peacefully entombed relatives and paid off the local constabulary and councilmen to secure privileged access to the dead house, where they could enact their dark rituals sub rosa, thumbing their upturned noses at the unsuspecting and naïve trustees who owned and operated the Catholic cemetery.

But then, both the European and American "Johnsons," their Anglican alias, hated papists, believed them to be the most hypocritical of the ecclesiastical tribes, much more reptilian than the Pharisees and

Scribes of Jesus's day, who were lambs by comparison. It was a constant source of gleeful, near Satanic merriment that the pagan, dualistic Mother Church now offered sanctified ground as a holy burial site for those progeny, who used Calvary Cemetery to revel in the arcane ceremonies for which their ancient ancestors had been burned at the stake and exiled, while the Church ransomed their rich lands, leaving the remaining heirs destitute.

It was another source of sardonic pleasure, which the papists had sought to destroy, but perversely they had strengthened. For the "Johnson" European ancestors staunchly and covertly observed, refined and shaped their arcane knowledge into a working spiritualism. This spiritualism encouraged them to increase their riches. And in the shadow of the most wicked, grasping and arrogant ecclesiastical or Mother Church's predators, their ancestors thrived. Eventually, the family's vast holdings and influence enabled them to assist behind the scenes with The Reformation and the translation into the common tongue of the New Testament, which had been selfishly horded for centuries by the richest institution in the world.

No small coincidence that when the Bible scriptures were restored to the meek lower and middle classes, they prospered and became wealthy and indeed, inherited the earth. The Mother Church had actively understood scriptural prosperity and feasted on that truth daily, while starving their subjects of the Bread of Life. And they burned at the stake those audacious underlings who expected and sought more than the crumbs the papists threw them. And when the Protestants grew strong on that Word, they got revenge and burned papists or heretics at the stake in a turn around. One bestial institution devoured the other in like behaviors as the true tenets of the Word never filtered down to purify ecclesiastical souls of either institutional branch of faith.

But the oppressor was being worn down. The "Johnsons" had been instrumental, if not active, invisible participants, in fomenting continual upheavals against Mystery Babylon, the Church of Rome. The battles still raged to the present day. Strategies on both sides were more covert, complex, attuned to the politics of the modern world and globalization. But the malice was the same, despite the fact that they of the Black

Nobility and the Pope of the Catholic Church were Guelphs and on the same side in their struggle against the Ghibellines.

Exhausted by these meditations that she had long denied herself, Madeline fell on her bed and wept again. She cried for who she was and what Peregrine had become. If her daughter was alive, she would explain the significance of the artifacts and the Ceremony of Powers. If necessary, she would sacrifice herself. She would reconcile with the family and return the baleful antiquities. Perhaps, Peregrine could be saved with the truth. With this new determination, Madeline's torment ceased, and a fresh resolve filled her spirit. She would continue to eschew her American family and their internecine struggles with the Europeans who believed them to be twisted by cultural idolatries and misanthropies. She would remain neutral. Madeline leaned back on the bed pillows and closed her eyes. She would do this for her daughter who might still be alive and had everything to live for. Madeline's life was over.

When Madeline had awakened in the morning, she resolved to get someone to Calvary to search for Peregrine. First, using the power of suggestion, she would encourage the detectives to widen their investigation to include some of the other Queens cemeteries, for instance, Calvary. Second, she would enlist Beach Comber's help, if he was stable and the doctors had released him. Then she remembered that along with his aide came the paparazzi who would stalk him wherever he went. Beach Comber would be a liability.

She thought of Fen. He had texted her and called her land line and cell, but she had been so overwhelmed with the police, her spokesperson, the media and her friends, she had forgotten to call him back. She was thankful she didn't have job responsibilities like Elizabeth Hamilton and could rely solely on her trust fund and investments to support herself and educate Peregrine. Otherwise she would have been hospitalized with stress-related anxiety and forced to go on medical leave. In the last week, she could barely organize her plans for each day.

Madeline called and texted Fen. But that was hours ago. It was now 4:00 PM. Maryann Linden, a publicity agent who her lawyer hired to navigate the media outlets, was scheduled for an interview at the hospital around 5:00 PM. Madeline went to the latticed window, shaded with curtains now drawn, and looked into the street. Forest Gardens Hills with its beautifully landscaped, park-like, tree-lined streets was designed by Frederick Law Olmsted Jr. Its Tudor, Brick Tudor, and Georgian-style mansions, English-style Inn and courtyard of brick cobblestones was home to the former US Open's West Side Tennis Club and was the oldest, planned, private enclave in the US. Even in the early 1970s, restrictive covenants forbid mansion sales to Jews, Blacks and working-class people.

From its creation in the early 1900s to the present, street parking was prohibited to non-residents of the community. Without a permit to park your car, you could expect a boot, tow and heavy fine. An unsuspecting, foreign journalist caught up in the frenzy of photographing her house parked his car without a permit. It was booted and ticketed after one-half hour. Swift punishment considering the NYPD ticket squad sometimes looked the other way on ordinary New York City streets. The journalist was stuck without a car, had to walk to an undesirable area of Queens to retrieve it and pay hundreds to remove the boot. But this secluded privacy, insured by narrow-winding streets was an integral part of Ebenezer Howard's Garden City Movement, to prevent raucous through traffic. It was a thoughtful element to provide luxurious living in one of the most high-priced communities in the borough of Queens

Word had gotten around, so now the media outlets had parking permits for the Gardens. There was a TV van across the street and a Honda Accord behind it with license plate NYP. They might follow her if she went to Calvary. At this point, Madeline was willing to try anything. Perhaps she could lose them in the traffic on Austin Street. With luck, she might find a parking spot and go shopping. Her stalkers would be forced to go into one of the paid lots. By that point, she would be out of the shop and on her way down Queens Boulevard, where she could lose them amongst scores of traffic lights. She knew the area blindfolded. Maybe they didn't. It was worth a try.

Missing for eight days, Peregrine was alive or dead somewhere in Calvary or at the Johnson mausoleum. Obviously, something had happened during the ceremony. The time was off. Peregrine wasn't twenty-five, the age of accountability for the Ceremony of Powers. And she and Mocha hadn't been with an elder magus to instruct them on the ways of the mysteries and the other realms. Probably, the crypt rejected them as intruders, and that could only mean disaster, their own fears materializing to destroy them, like being attacked by one's own immune system. Peregrine wasn't even at the first level of initiation. She didn't have the arcane sensibility to navigate the mystical networks between physical and metaphysical strings of reality. She herself had only been instructed to the third level, a neophyte who could only remember opaque glimpses into a hated past. How would the mausoleum react to her?

Madeline couldn't worry about it. She would confront the realms as they came upon her and try to make the best of a horrible situation. She must find Peregrine before it was too late. She took a bottle of Evian out of the refrigerator and picked up her Louis Vuitton bag, then let herself out the back door and locked it.

Chapter Eighteen

After the helicopter exploded in the night sky, Fen, Southamptonites and Summer renters congregated west of the villa along the beachfront adjacent to the back of the Dune Church, which was parallel to the location where the helicopter had disintegrated over the ocean. Fen wandered slowly to the top of the ancient, sloping, sand walls, layered with wild dune grass, blue-white in the pre-dawn sky. The dunes protected the stained-glass windows and auburn-and-rust colored church clapboards from the pounding Atlantic storms and high tides. From Fen's position on the crest, he gazed at the square nineteenth century spire that was blacker than the lightening sky. He looked from this height downward on the church's one-story, cross shaped structure that appeared lonely against the distant background of shining, friendly streetlights on Ginn Lane.

Then he turned to face the Atlantic, closing his eyes before they settled on the flickering flames scattered like vibrant flora on a dark prairie sea. He would wander the rest of his life haunted by visions of the bursting wall of fire and the horrific physical torments of Manny's last seconds of consciousness. He opened his eyes and stared at the sea which would be forever tainted by frozen and twisted emotions.

For the rest of his life, time would be marked by Manny's murder. Days and weeks would be categorized as happening before Manny's murder and after Manny's murder: BMM, AMM. Visions of the explosion already drowned his every attempt at peace and forced him to relive the event again and again unexpectedly, when random and painful memories seized up from the bank of his unconscious, triggered by the most benign things, a green windbreaker, waves breaking, a beach. At the sight of them, his body would ache, longing for Manny. How would he tell his mother that his brother had been atomized, his particles cast to the wind that now blew up whitecaps and trumpeted this new and terrible day, the first without Manny? Fen slid, stepping with large and long strides, back down the soft, white hill to the flat beach, marking a trail of tears where his huge footprints marred the timeless sands of the dune. He weaved in and out among the subdued onlookers, closing himself off from them, in shock, staring and staring with eyes mirrored over, seeing inward, weeping inward.

With solemn patience, those on the beach awaited the police and fire department and the forty-seven-foot motor lifeboat launched from the Coast Guard Station on Shinnecock Inlet. With a healthy recognition of the preciousness and precariousness of life, all attention to status, wealth and class, which normally would have held sway over the various individuals in the crowd, appropriately dissolved. Small clusters of people mingled and exchanged theories and discussed what they had seen and heard, and shared their fears and concerns about their own fragile mortality. Each sought reassurance that their lives had some smatch of meaning. And as if to prove it, a few residents brought out coffee, biscotti, low-fat muffins, buttered bagels and donuts and shared their bounty as they ministered solace and comfort to each other, staving off the violent and mysterious event that they little understood and that ran counter to the peaceful existence of their earthly paradise.

A vivacious, attractive middle aged woman with a tray of coffee and bagels dressed in a flowing gauze sarong saw Fen standing alone. She smiled, came up to him and offered him coffee and a bagel from her diminishing supply.

"Such a terrible tragedy. It brings to mind another terrible tragedy, TWA Flight 800 off Moriches Inlet which is farther west. So many lives lost. Thank God with this one there must have been only one or two passengers on board."

As Fen took the Styrofoam cup and a bagel, he nearly interjected there were three, but he restrained himself, tuning his perceptions to the timbre of the social atmosphere. He mumbled an assent between slurps of coffee and bites of fresh buttered bagel. He imagined for the people who lived on the beach in the summer, there was no shortage of fresh bagels and breads. They probably threw hour's old baked goods to the seagulls and terns.

"Very unusual for a helicopter to be flying at this time of night."

Jolted by the statement, Fen came to life. He tolerated conversation if it related to anomalies surrounding the incident. Watching the fiery wreckage splatter the briny waters, he had sworn that the only task remaining for his life was vengeance, justice for his brother's death. So, his intelligence gathering begun two days ago would continue with redirected focus. Fishing for information, he introduced himself, mentioned his work as an actor and briefly charmed Mrs. Alicia Gold with tales of his overnight research on the beaches of Southampton.

"So you were sleeping on the beach? Oh, look." Ms. Goldman motioned with the tray, indicating the dark, slim figures grouped at the water's edge. As she and Fen observed their actions, other onlookers came up and helped themselves to the food and noted the ensuing water drama.

Three bold, young men in wet suits, legs leaping over crashing waves, pulled a dinghy into the water. The wet suits were necessary for the Atlantic was always cold the end of June, despite a week of hot and humid days. In the distance, Fen could see that two other men also in wet suits had gotten in kayaks and were skimming the waves, heading for the crash site. Both volunteer teams were searching for survivors and investigating the burning fires, orange and yellow funereal blossoms that floated about one-quarter mile out from the shoreline. Their flashlights splayed like beacons of hope across the dark, watery graveyard.

"What a terrible experience for you." Alicia intoned with empathy. "You were enjoying a pleasant sleep on the beach, and you awoke to a horrific nightmare." Alicia cued in a few others standing around. "He was on the beach at the time of the accident, saw the explosion, an eyewitness."

"Yeah, like the play *Life is a Dream* by Calderon de la Barca. Only that play is a comedy, and no one here is laughing."

"What did you see?" One of the stragglers at Alicia's tray queried in a matter of fact voice.

"A Universal Studios' special effects explosion with mayhem, blood and death thrown in for my good pleasure." Fen's sardonic humor cut off further questions from the woman in white who looked confused at his cavalier attitude. The straggler's older partner in matching outfit sauntered off toward the water's edge to follow the exertions of the volunteers in the water. Fen tried to be objective. "Totally unexpected, totally horrific and totally indescribable."

The woman nodded in response and munched lightly on half a shared bagel.

"And the noise. It is still reverberating in my ears." Alicia shook her head.

"Yeah. I'll never get over this. Never." Fen felt wobbly in the knees then recovered himself. He hoped Alicia's bounty would extend to information, and in his sweeping glance, he included the woman in white linen who looked ready to join her partner. "Since your neighbors put in the helicopter pad, have they flown at all hours of the night like tonight?"

"I haven't seen them use the helicopter during the summer," she added as she gracefully slipped away from them and moved to watch the swimmers.

"Mr. Johnstone has the helicopter fly him into Manhattan sometimes during the day, but as far as we know, he returns early evening. But I believe there are ordinances against flying after certain hours in Southampton Township, too disruptive and noisy unless they fly out over the Atlantic."

"Well, I guess that's that," a nearby onlooker chimed in.

Washing ashore with the waves and debris, like Charon's helpers, the provident volunteers skidded their kayaks on the beach, then leaped ashore, dragging them along the sand away from tumultuous breakers. Fen thought to himself, but how could there be any survivors? The devastation had pulverized and wedded the hapless victims' molecules with those of their transportation vehicle and transmogrified both into a grotesque, new substance of melted flesh, plastic, fat, foam, blood, metal, feces, steel, bone, hair, residues of oil, kerosene and machine parts that the watchers on the beach took into their lungs and exhaled in a rare, if unconscious, fit of Shakespearean humility.

"We rarely see the Johnstones, only briefly in the summer and the fall. The children have governesses and are home schooled. Quite traditional, like old-fashioned upper-class British families," Alicia mused.

"So, you know the Johnstones are not at the villa at present? They are in Europe."

"No, I didn't. But whoever is taking care of the estate, the house manager or servants would know of the town's noise ordinances. So perhaps it was an emergency, and that's why they sent for a helicopter." Alicia seemed impatient to get out from under their conversation to work the crowd, demonstrate she was making a difference in the face of this home-grown cataclysm.

"If it was an emergency, wouldn't they medevac the patient?" Fen tried to think logically in order to remind himself of murderous Liam's insidious and surreptitious behavior.

"The police and fire department are here." Notes of reassurance sounded in Alicia's voice, as if to say now all would be properly disposed of, and they could go back to their happy and productive lives. "I rather wonder what took them so long."

"Have you or the neighbors ever been inside the mansion? It's quite beautiful."

"Actually, no. I've never been invited and the family stays by themselves when they are here. Coming, darling." Alicia gave a relief-filled smile. "My husband is waving to me. So nice to meet you." She shook her head. "But under such dreadful circumstances. Next time we meet, surely, it will be more pleasant." Alicia was the perfect upper-class hostess working the spacious outdoor room of beachfront.

As she delicately picked her way across the sand, the crowd swelled, milling in a frenzied chaos, like goldfish during a feeding. They knotted up and swarmed the officers to give statements and heighten the drama. By now, the police boat and Coast Guard motor lifeboat had rapidly advanced to the patchwork of fires still flaring and consuming the fuel slicks and helicopter refuse. With spotlights blazing in the dawn, both trolled the waters for human remains, body parts and clues, occasionally picking up items and dropping them into white containers. Fen watched the increased activity, as if he were in caught in a Salvador Dali oil canvass or posing atop a huge and buoyant boulder levitating in the azure skies of a Rene Magritte painting. Events were spiraling out of control, and the distance grew between the truth of what he had seen and the interpretation and testimony of others who would be heard.

He wasn't sure whether he should only talk to Detectives Dietz and Allan or whether he also should give information to the local yahoos for the sake of continuity. The more he repeated the same details, the more credible a witness he would be. But he knew from experience that law enforcement, local, state and federal, despite the supposed transformations since 911, often worked at cross purposes. They were jealous of their hard-won information and hoarded it like treasure, each division wanting to receive the rewards and credit for breaking a case. Because local police disputed his allegations about the Johnstone's and their hired help's involvement in Manny's disappearance, he was loathe to give any information to the officers. What was the point? They worked at the behest of the upper classes, received favors that took many forms, from restaurant vouchers to game tickets and more. Besides, he would have to align Manny's disappearance with his nocturnal surveillance of the villa and allegations of murder or negligent homicide. He lacked the faith that they would follow up his leads. It would be like blowing incense up their asses, and they'd just fart in his face.

No. He would call the Queens' DA's office at 8:00 AM and tell the detectives who knew his case best. He'd meet them, show them the tape, if it was viable, and they would have another visit with Liam and bring in the local cops. If the law enforcement investigations were inconclusive, he would hire a private investigator. Unfortunately, investigators were expensive, and his family didn't have money. He'd have to work something out.

Fen meandered while he drank his coffee and chewed bagel remnants. A female acquaintance, Marina Eberhard, whom he had met earlier in the week, grabbed his arm, nearly spilling his coffee. She apologized and excitedly launched into a riff that the helicopter had been sabotaged. Fen listened glumly. He wondered aloud if the National Transportation Safety Board had jurisdiction over the matter. If they did, there was a better chance for the truth to come out in an extensive investigation. That might depend upon the influence of the Johnstones, whose powerful tentacles might reach to personnel in federal agencies or even the White House.

Fen asked his comely acquaintance, who stood before him in a combination bikini nightie robe, "Do you know if the Johnstones charted their helicopters or had one of their own?"

"I'm not sure. I think they own one and sometimes charter. They keep the one they own at the Manhattan heliport when they are away."

"This one was probably chartered then." Fen finished his bagel. He hoped the media outlets would have this information. He would use his contacts in the industry. If they didn't know, he would call some of the charters, first the Southampton Heliport, then Gabreski Airport in West

Hampton and the East Hampton and Montauk Airports. Hell, he would check any other airports on the East End of Long Island. He hoped the helicopter wasn't borrowed from another estate.

The moon had fled away, and now the sun's arc broke the eastern horizon with blazing orange glory, bringing joy to the forty or so beach people who ahhhhhed in appreciative worship of the showering rays that they were alive. Fen recognized the same policeman who had accompanied him and the detectives to the Johnstone estate. He and another cop were taking statements and personal information from the dwindling crowd. The police and fire departments had closed off the beach for about one-half mile west and east of the accident sight, putting up white barricades, signs and the telltale yellow crime scene investigation tape as other investigators combed the shoreline for pieces of helicopter and other detritus the waves carried in. The police and Coast Guard boats were still crisscrossing each other's wakes, as the incoming tide slowly blotted out the fire plumes, returning the ocean to its eternal movements, regular as the rhythms of the human heart. The crowd gradually dispersed to resume their weekday lives, and two pockets of locals and visitors waited for the next heightened state of activity.

Emotionally wrought like a damp rag that had been twisted tightly to drain moisture atoms, Fen sat away from the shore where the dunes, as if to mimic the ocean patterns, undulated in a series of peaks, valleys and ridges. He found that he couldn't leave. He had willed himself to get up, get his blanket, umbrella and clothes and go to his mom's and from there, contact Dietz and Allan. But he was powerless, inert.

Transfixed, he sat watching the activity that was a grotesque side show. The center ring main attraction had finished. The ring-master was getting ready to introduce him as the final act. He had reversed his position about not giving his eyewitness account to the local police. His innocent brother had been the victim of negligent homicide. Though it was his word against Liam's and the other servants, and Fen had little proof, he had to speak out, create controversy, stir the pot, stimulate a ground swell of interest at the location where Manny's life ended, Southampton. If Liam and his bums had created the intrigue, he would uncover it as intrigue. If they continued to lie, as they had already, he would reaffirm that they lied, raising guilt and their fear of detection. This was the only way he could strengthen his resolve to press on, the only way he would be able to live again. Eventually, he would bring the truth to light, the proof following.

Another individual stood talking with the officers who looked like they were ready to pack up and leave. He got to his feet and brushed the sand from his pants, then began his slow walk over to them, affirming to himself his importance to the investigation. After all, he had watched the helicopter take off. Except for him, the beach had been deserted. That made him a valuable eyewitness. He knew he'd make an impression. He had saved the best testimony for last.

Chapter Nineteen

Police cars everywhere! Then he realized he was jumpy and had exaggerated the number. Actually, there were only four inside the entrance of Trinity Hills Cemetery sans iron gates which had yet to be replaced. Deep within the first division of headstones, Beach Comber noted two police officers with blood hounds. Nearing the second division were another two officers with German shepherds. Men and dogs fanned out in a line progressing away from the entrance, in the opposite direction from the mausoleum where he had found Mocha.

"Shall I wait for you here?" Amazingly, the dark-haired driver who appeared to be one of a million immigrants who barely spoke English had understood him. He spoke intelligibly, albeit with a thick accent.

"I don't think they are allowing anyone to enter." Beach Comber referred to the blue and white NYPD car blocking half of the entrance with a white barricade angled in to let only one car pass at a time. Two officers stood outside manning the area and drinking from Dunkin Donuts cups. Beach Comber assumed the police were filtering visitors to the grave-sites during their search for clues or Peregrine. He turned his face away from the window, not wanting to be identified. "Let's drive around to the other side of the cemetery by the apartments. It's on Fiftieth Street. If you wait for me there in the parking lot, I will make it worthwhile." Familiar with the area, the driver continued down Horace Harding Boulevard and then made a right onto Main Street.

As the car pulled away from the cemetery, Beach Comber looked out the back window, making sure they had not been noticed and that paparazzi had not followed them. The officers were talking to each other and didn't appear interested in the cab, whose driver and passengers could have been rubbernecking and seeing nothing of interest, got bored and left. The cemetery, after all, had been the focal point of news coverage since he and Mocha had been brought to the hospital.

Sylvia, like Ms. Randolf and Ms. Hamilton, had appointed a spokesperson to handle the media. Nevertheless, he had nearly been found out by clever journalists who nosed around posing as relatives of other patients during visiting hours and who had pounced when family arrived. *New York Post* journalists circled Sylvia and Ms. Hamilton like hawks as the two women talked to each other. They dived into their midst when a nurse approached Ms. Hamilton about Mocha. Sylvia didn't mind, but Ms. Hamilton became disturbed by their probing questions about Mocha's condition. She turned her back on them, leaving without a response. Sylvia didn't take Ms. Hamilton's cue, as she should have. Whether out of naiveté or knowing, she indicated Beach Comber's room and after answering a few more questions, rushed away to her attorney appointment.

Just before Beach Comber was about to leave for the cemetery, the officious print reporter, eager for an exclusive, poked his annoying face into the room and addressed him as Paul Carver. Because Beach Comber had slicked his hair back and styled it with gel for a sexier Latin look, he was able to play the arrogant know-it-all, introducing himself as Matthew Carver, Paul's brother. Hiding his bandaged hands under his arm pits, he mentioned that he was leaving. The reporter could wait there for Paul who the attendants would be bringing back from MRI central in ten minutes. He motioned for him to take a can of coke from the room's fridge, which Sylvia had rented and stocked with various organic drinks for him and other drinks for visitors. Thirsty for the coke, the reporter was preoccupied hunting for it in the fridge. Satisfied about his artful duplicity with the reporter, he walked out of the room with the casual insouciance of a brother, tossing a sideways glance over his shoulder to ensure that the bastard wasn't following him.

Beach Comber slipped unnoticed into a maintenance closet, where staff kept sheets, blankets, towels, trays, cups, mops, sponges, cleaning agents and other supplies. He waited for five minutes. No one knocked on the door and pulled him out. The nurses' station was at the other end of the hallway, and the overworked staff disregarded anyone with whom they were not industriously involved. Inside, dangling on the handle of a mop, he discovered a ripe-smelling, blue shirt with a maintenance tag stitched onto the lapel. He threaded his arms through the sweat- stained, blue material that draped over his clean polo shirt, protecting his bandaged torso. He buttoned it up to the neck and tucked the tails into his black pants. Unwinding the loose bandages on his hands, leaving the white gauze patches that covered his palms, he stuffed the bloodied strips behind the bottom metal shelf that was loaded with cleaning supplies. He intended to keep his palms pressed together, so no one noticed the telltale clues that he was a patient. He slung his back-pack of clothing, water and necessary supplies over his left shoulder. To appear busy, he grabbed some blankets, which he carried out of the closet, past other patient rooms and finally dumped on a rolling metal cart at the end of the hall. He walked out the exit door and down the two flights of stairs to the first floor.

So far so good. Keeping his palms close to his thighs, with casual confidence, he sauntered unmolested through the automatic entrance/exit sliding doors, past a photographer who scrutinized everyone going in and out, but didn't suspect a maintenance man whose greased back hair looked darker and more ethnic than Beach Comber usually wore it. Once again Sylvia had pulled through for him by giving him her mobile, which he had used to call the cab. Beach Comber climbed into the waiting vehicle, and they sped away.

The driver pulled into the run down, dreary, 1950's garden apartments converted into co-operatives that typically dotted the middle-class areas of Queens. Beach Comber directed him to the back of the parking lot which abutted the extensive lands of Trinity Hills. Here, the barbed wire fence was only four feet from the ground, and he could either vault it, standing on his back- pack, or use the wire cutters along with the sturdy, oversized workman's gloves that Benson, his mother's house manager and jack of all trades, had brought with changes of clothing, shoes and toiletries. From this location, he could easily navigate to the mausoleum and search for Peregrine with impunity and freedom from the police officers and their dogs. Beach Comber told the driver to turn off the motor and wait until he returned, even if he was delayed until after the cemetery closed at 5:00 PM. He had taken out a wad of twenties and fifties to prove to the skeptical driver that he had enough cash for the fare. They exchanged mobile numbers, and he asked the man to assist him.

Beach Comber looked around outside the cab, making sure no one was in the immediate vicinity of the parking lot, and quickly got out with the driver in tow. He strode confidently to the fence as he put on the gloves, threw the backpack on the ground near the lowest section of fence, stood on it and gauged the necessary movements. He decided not to use the wire cutters. Instead, he joggled the fence, wincing as his hands grasped the barbed wire and pulled it down. He probably would open a few cuts that were now stinging him, but he would get patched up when he went back to the hospital. Not to worry. His body was full of antibiotics. He launched himself upward, maneuvering first one leg over nearly touching the ground, and then the other. He had vaulted the piercing barbed cruelty in less than half a minute. He smiled, remembering the ordeal he had faced a few days ago, glad that his memory was returning.

The driver picked up the back pack from the ground, lifted it up and handed it to him over the metal ropes. Beach Comber thanked him and pretended to fumble with the pack as he slung both straps over his left shoulder. From his peripheral vision, he watched as the driver got into the cab and looked back at him, bored, in waiting mode. Beach Comber gave a thumbs-up sign, then turned around and headed out into the land of the dead, trying to remember the placement of the mausoleum in relation to the apartments and the main entrance, which was east of his present location. Once he recognized familiar headstones, like the towering angel statues and the section of baby headstones that he tripped over almost a week ago, he would be able to recall the pathway to the mausoleum.

Circling to the left and zigzagging in and out on the patches of grass between metal markers and small and large slabs of granite, three-foot headstones and tall monuments, Beach Comber jogged, attempting to cover the ground to the crypt quickly. Far away in the distance, he could hear the blood hounds keening the scent, their cries frenzied and predatory as they whipped their masters, driving them in the chase, man and dog one creature, expectant, hungry. They must not find him, at least not before he found Peregrine.

He could care less if they arrested him for alleged rape or some other trumped-up charge that Matthews manufactured to lay on him. If he had to suffer those fools for Peregrine to be found safe and alive, it was worth it. But he had to find her. She had been missing since the previous Friday the twenty-ninth, and four days had passed since he had found Mocha. He would have found her on Saturday, but the lightening man had brained him. But then it was dark, and he was unconscious; and he didn't know if

Mocha had been carried there for him to find on Sunday or if she had been there since Friday night. When she woke from the coma and if she remembered, they would be able to piece together the missing details. Maybe.

Frustration and annoyance blotted out Beach Comber's normal good nature. The death house was farther than he had anticipated, and he was unsure of the correctness of the path he traveled because the direction from the entrance was in the reverse of his current position. Confusing. He believed he recognized the angel monuments, but every deceased aunt and uncle, father and mother appeared to favor angels. There were too many similar monuments. Angels with wings arched upward and downward. Angels with wings unfurled. Six-foot, white, marble pyramid monuments with angels flying atop the pinnacle and humble, four-foot granite, angel statues standing on rectangular blocks, blowing horns, announcing the good news--all beautiful, all similar--probably because he had reached this division, 14 F, around dusk, over a week ago. It looked familiar, so he decided to continue.

He contemplated that he had been imbued with a weird, superhuman strength to have carried Mocha so far and under physically stressful conditions. Was it three miles or more he had carried his lovely burden? Or was it now three miles or more he was traveling to find the dead house, which confined another lovely burden, Peregrine? He would be so glad when all of this was over, and he was free of the responsibility of her life.

Winded from his slow jog, Beach Comber stopped and bent over with his hands on his thighs to catch his breath. From the apartments, one couldn't sight the mausoleum, and when he turned around, he could still see the depressing two-storied, red, brick buildings in the great distance he had come. He believed that the ravine that led into the most secluded area of the cemetery was beyond a copse of trees to his left, westward. Somewhere to his right and east were the officers and dogs, though their inhuman cries, which he still heard, seemed not to be advancing. He looked at his watch. It was nearing five-thirty. Maybe the cops were leaving. He considered returning to the cab, then decided against it. He would make it to the crypt and back, would be there within the hour, if he was right about the direction. As long as he was back to the hospital by 7:00 PM, the time he had scheduled to speak to the Hamiltons, everything would be fine. He could talk his way out of anything. Now, he must do this. Peregrine was out there amongst the dead, and he owed it to their close friendship to bring her back alive.

Refreshed from his momentary respite, Beach Comber jogged along the sterile landscape, vowing that unlike this self-absorbed Egyptian crowd, his body would be cremated, his ashes spread over his beloved ocean. His remains wouldn't take up space and waste good land. He'd be dead; what would it matter the color of the coffin, the luxuriousness of the appointments, the elaborateness of the vault? He wouldn't be able to appreciate it. Money was better spent on the living. But one never knew. At an ancient age, one might feel differently and like his grandfather, become a sentimentalist, a romantic, build a monument to himself that graveyard buffs would enjoy viewing. Weren't graveyards an outdoor, natural historical museum, after all? He mused, maybe when the earth's population exceeded thirty billion, the land starved governments of the earth would confiscate cemetery land, passing land use laws against cemeteries and environmental laws against carbon emissions from crematoriums, putting undertakers and mortuaries out of business. All corpses could be dumped into active volcanoes for incineration meltdowns in superheated lava flows or chucked into the ocean as fish food.

He had reached the copse of trees and the ravine, where he rested from his run. He removed a bottle of water from his pack and drank heavily. Off in the far distance, looking small and grey and sheltered by bushes and trees against an azure sky stood the striking crypt. He shifted his back-pack, thankful that the lacerations were on his chest and lower abdomen, and trudged toward the mausoleum, occasionally drinking from the water bottle. He took out his mother's phone from his left jeans pocket and called the cab driver. All was well. No one had come to ask any questions, and there were no suspicious cops darkly lurking in the area.

As he walked down the hill into the tree-sequestered valley, thinking how he might break into the mausoleum with the crowbar he had brought in his back-pack, he became aware of the silence. Except for his footsteps on the grass and soft, moist earth, he heard nothing except his inner thoughts. The air was unfettered by any breeze, and the leaves were motionless in the bushes and trees. It was unlike his first visit, where in the darkness, the rustlings had unnerved him, and the palpable sense of otherworldliness had overwrought his imagination, making him a believer in supernatural beings. No harbinger of movement was anywhere. The police had probably left by now. It was almost six, and the hounds' moaning cries had faded to the present stillness. He felt relief. He had secretly feared a chase and believed the shepherds could outrun him in his enervated state.

As he neared the crypt, he found he could recall the events of that unfortunate evening clearly. The medications and his athleticism and prior physical stamina and youth, like the doctor told Sylvia they would, had helped him through a tenuous period. Someone older or less fit would not have come through half as well. Raising his age and diminishing his physical condition, they might not have survived.

The direction he walked in faced the back of the crypt. He scoped the ground for any signs of Peregrine, and he scanned the area for his stolen iPhone and wallet, which he doubted would be recovered. In the daylight, all was manifest and benign looking, even pleasant. The gray granite mausoleum looked beautiful with rainbow-colored, stained glass windows of lambs and the Madonna and child. He had been anxious about once more confronting the lightening man, but his fears were dwarfed by the radiance and solitude of his surroundings. He stood at the back of the crypt, which rose up just shy of two stories, and he marveled how his fright had distorted his perception of its size. It was rather smallish, eight-feet wide, he thought, certainly smaller in the daytime.

There was no sign of Peregrine or anything unusual for the crypt's placement and its musical accompaniment of solemn stillness. He would have to go around to the entrance and hammer the door. Perhaps Peregrine would hear him and answer. He prayed that the door would easily open and that he wouldn't have to crowbar his way in, an action that would be interpreted as vandalism.

Beach Comber sauntered with his head down, scanning the ground as he proceeded along the length of the right side of the crypt. All his instincts kicked in at once, and he sensed a breath of movement. He jerked his head up in rapid fire and saw something black and glistening edge out from the corner front of the crypt.

It was the nose tip of a German shepherd's snout. "Shit!" The word exploded from his mouth as he spun around to bolt and got four steps off in a leap. Behind him, he heard deep- throated snarling and growling. Turning his head slightly, from his peripheral vision, he saw two shepherds swinging in an arc on his left, galloping toward him. They yelped, and with jaw- snapping barks, prodded and called one to the other to rapidly close the distance. He imagined their hot breath upon his heels, the hounds of hell coming to drag him to the Torments, a prison lock-up. But he could outrun them. He was faster than they.

Beach Comber felt the adrenaline pump through his lower leg muscles. He smashed his feet into ground-grinding forward sprints, jumping over smaller gravestones, dodging large ones, a jackrabbit bobbing and racing. But his physical state, redirected toward filtering powerful medications, and his immune system laboring for recovery, crashed. He faltered and sputtered and ran slow-motion, underwater, heavy-limbed. Voracious, livid, keening the weakness of their prey, the shepherds bounded raggedly, forelegs and hind legs churning up a turf wake, with tongues panting foam and spit toward victory. Ancient traits boiled in their canine blood, the song of the wolf pack howling. They were machines in their precision and calculation, attacking together. One tugged at his pant leg, then lunged and bit his left calf. Beach Comber cringed and gasped in pain, thrashing his legs forward as the dog incredibly held on and snapped to gnaw his leg. The other shepherd leaped upon his back and with all its forward momentum used gravity to slam Beach Comber to the ground.

He landed on all fours. Yowling with surprise, the dogs skidded and slid away from him smacking into the ground and rolling on either side of Beach Comber, their energy diffused. Scrambling to his feet, he crouched facing them, ready to kick their snouts. The shepherds lunged to their feet, barked and circled around and bounded back and forth, blocking his attempts to run. In unison, they flashed dripping teeth and with low, growling menace, asserted their dominance, taught muscled, staring, ready to maul if he breathed. Exhausted from keeping pace, two officers loped up from behind. Coordinating their positions, one ran to Beach Comber's left, the other to his right. The dogs and men had snuffed his escape.

"We were waiting for you. What took you so long?" the heavier officer panted sarcastically as he assisted his colleague, roughly pulling Beach Comber's arms together.

The other officer cuffed Beach Comber's hands behind his back. "Let's go down to the precinct. We'd like to ask you a few questions!"

Chapter Twenty

E lizabeth Hamilton leaned over her daughter's bedside and gently touched Deidre's forehead with her right hand. She was thankful that the wounds at the back of her throat were healing quickly, and the color had been restored to her cheeks. She had asked for a second opinion from another neurosurgeon, Dr. Liu, and he was energetic and positive, the antithesis of the reserved, laconic Dr. Song. He told her that physically, Deidre was healing and had made excellent progress. But he offered no solution to the mystery why she had not maintained consciousness. He suggested that each individual's situation was different. If the brain had been injured and this had not shown up on any test results, it probably would show up in a week, and this could be the reason why she had not yet awakened. He stuck to the proverbial maxim they had to "take each day at a time." But he assured Elizabeth Hamilton that they were fortunate that Deidre had responded exceptionally well to treatment, was off the respirator and had awakened briefly. He assured her that she would be with them very soon.

After Elizabeth said goodbye to her nephew earlier that day, she returned home to check up on the nurse and her son who was no better, but no worse. Even though he was considered to be formally in hospice, she violated the rules and took control, giving him whatever he could take by mouth. Taking the cue from her son, after she returned to the hospital, she tried the technique with Deidre and had a breakthrough in the evening meal at 5:00 PM, with the cooperation of Dr. Liu who had ordered up the food specially. Through trial and error, she found Mocha accepted liquids through a straw, drinking carrot juice donated by Sylvia, Paul Carver's mother, and Mocha's favorite Gatorade. She even accepted soft foods like Jell-O, ice cream and pureed spinach from a spoon, though by comparison it seemed turtles could race across a road ten times faster than Deidre could finish a teaspoon of spinach. Elizabeth had the patience to introduce the spoon, placing it between Mocha's lips, stimulating the tip of her tongue and then Deidre, sensing the food, tasted it and savored it, letting it melt in her mouth. She still swallowed with difficulty. It took Elizabeth over a half hour to work with her to finish most of the spinach and Jell-O, and fifteen minutes to down all of the vanilla ice cream, but Dr. Liu was very encouraged and insisted her tremendous progress eating and drinking would speed her recovery. He added they might not have to place her on a feeding tube if she continued improving.

As Elizabeth waited for Reggie and her meeting with Paul Carver, she watched her daughter, scouring her face and behavior for signs, differences in her reactions to stimuli. Deidre slept fitfully, turning her head from side to side, moaning. At times, she spoke aloud full sentences, as if she was talking to someone and the person annoyed her; but though the thoughts seemed coherent in themselves, Elizabeth couldn't relate them to anything in Deidre's external environment. Her daughter's internal existence was richly populated with people and events, and she was an integral participant in this world. But how did one connect her inner experiences with external consciousness to communicate with others? Deidre did not open her eyes or respond to Elizabeth when she asked her to describe what she saw. Elizabeth believed Deidre understood her, but she revealed no tangible sign of this comprehension. The disconnect between them was still profound.

Elizabeth believed that her daughter encountered the supernatural in this state, and that she was struggling against forces and powers which intended to keep her in a limbo of darkness. Yet, there were times Elizabeth noticed that Deidre smiled, and her countenance reflected peace. Her features relaxed, as though she related to other beings who gave her peace. At these moments, Elizabeth thought Deidre received divine revelation and supernatural infusions of beauty, love and wellness. These beliefs reinforced Elizabeth's faith that her prayers were effectual, and the healing power of God was gradually restoring her daughter. The mother intuited that the struggle was Deidre's personal assertion to gain authority over her own body and the world's evils. And she was her daughter's spiritual guide and protector, warring with her against dark powers that fought to bury Deidre alive in an insensate tomb.

But there was no one with whom Elizabeth could share her beliefs. Science simply had no system to apprehend the spiritual realm. All she could do was offer a translation of Deidre's dreamlike, spiritual state, grounding it with her behavioral reality: her facial expressions, comments, hand movements, the fluttering of her eyelids and the pressure of her grip. From these cues, she knew her daughter was in touch with other dimensions that no words could describe because language had not been developed for it. No nouns or verbs had been agreed upon by cultural consensus because what her daughter saw was rare, weird, unique, in the realm of the prophets, mystics and saints. It was madness, and it was divine. Since empiricism eradicated faith, deeming magic, fantasy and prophets as schizophrenics, how could she explain?

Elizabeth believed that Deidre had the courage to see what others from the dawn of time would have sold their souls and all their possessions to see and yet could not see. Only the gifted, the elect, had faith, saw visions and dreamed dreams that came to pass. Only the courageous could overthrow all the carnal, worldly institutions of learning to embrace faith, which required the ability to believe without seeing. Faith: "the substance of things hoped for, the evidence of things not seen." Because Deidre was her child, Elizabeth believed she passed her faith gene to her daughter. She believed that they were the elect, the anointed to receive divine wisdom and supernatural power. But in receiving such grace, ultimately mother and daughter would at times feel very alone, as Elizabeth did now. All of these thoughts Elizabeth shared with no one, not even her spiritually-minded friends.

Even before the doctors encouraged Elizabeth to talk to Deidre to relocate her in time and space, she spoke to her daughter whenever she was in her presence. She intuited that Deidre heard her voice as she floated in the ethers, with one part of her being in the material world, the other in the preternatural. Perhaps, it was her inability to decide which realm she preferred that had caused this condition which Elizabeth believed was more like a state of hibernation than a coma.

Now, heartened by the doctor's news, Elizabeth spoke to her daughter with encouragement. "Deidre, you can see into the spirit. Remember, everything you see, so we will break the death chains that bind Billy." She gripped her daughter's hand, and Deidre grasped hers firmly in response.

"God has not given us a spirit of fear, but power, love and a sound mind. You have wisdom. You know how to come back to me."

Elizabeth recalled the story of the daughter who was in a coma, whose mother remained at her bedside day and night praying. The family was Catholic. The daughter had manifested the stigmata, and others had been healed. The family believed that in the daughter's suspension between dimensions of reality, she was used in the unction of healing. But Elizabeth knew Deidre's calling was not as ambitious. If Deidre had any divine healing to invoke, Elizabeth felt it would be through Deidre's active prayers and conscious laying on of hands, not as a passive and unconscious vessel of mercy.

"Billy misses you. I know he wants you to pray with him. I tell him you'll be coming to visit any day. I tell him that you are speaking to God about him, that the angels are protecting you and him from harm." Elizabeth put her head down and wept openly in intercession for her children.

Aunt Elizabeth is heading for a nervous breakdown, Detective Reggie Matthews thought as he watched the mother's interactions with the daughter from the doorway of Deidre's new room assignment. His aunt demonstrated all the signs of mental collapse. True, with both children in severely debilitated physical states, these flights of fantasy were a respite from the horrors of dealing. But the woman was losing all sense of proportion. Her hold on reality was disappearing. He had had enough.

"Aunt Elizabeth," Reggie loudly interjected. His was the sane voice in this increasingly pathetic drama.

"I didn't hear you come in." Elizabeth reached for a tissue in her handbag on the floor by the table. She dabbed the tears from her eyes.

"No. You had more important things to attend to." He knew he sounded annoyed, but he felt justified. "Any sign of Paul Carver?"

"Nephew, it's not 7:00 PM!"

"You're right, it's 7:30."

"I lost track of the time." Elizabeth humbly admitted.

"Don't worry about the time. In fact, you won't need to worry about questioning your family friend. Did you bring the tickets?" A smile played across Reggie's lips.

"You haven't won, yet. He might be late." Elizabeth got up from the chair and poured herself a glass of water from the pitcher on the tray table by the foot of the hospital bed, then drank it down.

"He's not coming, Aunt Elizabeth." Reggie paused for effect, enjoying the look of surprise on his aunt's face. Her assurance that Paul Carver was a friend angered him. He knew the truth. The world was brutal and harsh. She often accused him of being too pessimistic. Well, he clung to his cynicism. It sheltered him from those who would beat him down. He had trusted no one but his family. They had betrayed him when his mother died, except for Aunt Elizabeth. But she would betray him, too, if circumstances forced her to choose between him and her faith. Blood was not thicker than water.

"If he's not coming, then you probably detained him to get your tickets." Elizabeth laughed. "Well, I'll buy them for you, but tell me how you did it." She wagged her head in the chiding confidence of correctly assessing her nephew.

He couldn't be angry with her. "Well, he was brought in for questioning after policemen found him at the crime scene probably to sweep the area and destroy evidence. His lawyer is with him."

"Arrested?"

Reggie smiled. "He fled from the police. Clues were found linking him to the assault. We found his footprints and confirmed a match with his sneakers. Investigators located the matted grass near the crypt, where a struggle took place when he assaulted her."

Reggie sat down on the bed and motioned for Elizabeth to sit in the chair next to him. "According to medical reports and pictures, it seems that they had oral sex. He flipped out and stuffed some sort of implement down her throat. When she collapsed, he panicked and fled, then went back to revive her. When he couldn't, he carried her to the entrance. We found his prints on her leather belt. Investigators are looking for the implement he used or the rock, whatever it was."

Elizabeth was quiet. Her nephew was swaying her with his arguments. Now, she faced the additional strain of possible criminal proceedings along with the civil action she would commence against Carver. She would have to call the Manhattan personal injury lawyer that her friend insisted she retain.

"Did you call the doctor I recommended?"

"Yes, it worked out he has a patient he is attending to here, so he said he would come by. I expect him tomorrow morning."

"Why don't you go home and get some sleep?"

"I will, but I might stay over since he's coming early in the morning. I've decided to take another week off from work to get Billy adjusted. And Deidre needs me. No one will take the time or has the patience to feed her like I do. My presence is vital to her recovery, and there's no one else. Her closest friends are either missing, or in jail."

"What about her actor friend?"

"Can't get in touch with him. It's strange, really. I'm her only support, except for you. And other family is..." Elizabeth trailed off, her voice tinged with misery.

"Yeah. I wouldn't mention them in front of me either. I think we're the only black family without family." Reggie snorted.

"There is family, but we're estranged. You have your father's clan, which in deference to my sister, I can't be close to."

"Yes, well, neither can I. So I guess, for now, it's just us." Reggie leaned over from his seated position on the bed and hugged his aunt. "You know, I am here for you."

She put her arms around him, and her chest filled with emotion. "Thank God. You've been a great help to me, Reggie."

They ended their embrace, and Reggie stood up. "Well, I've got to head down to the precinct to interview Carver. I'll keep you posted. If he's arrested, the media outlets are going to be like a firestorm consuming all in their path. I dread it."

Elizabeth laughed. "Sure. I'd really dread publicity that would boost my career and soften the landing for a political job, too."

"Once the press light's on, it stays on, spotlighting the glittering and grimy aspects of your life. Who needs it?"

"Apparently, you do." Elizabeth smiled. She stood up and escorted him to the elevator.

Later that evening, after an extra cot had been placed in the private hospital room and Elizabeth had returned from her second visit to Billy, she lay down on the cot and rested, reflecting on the day's events. She was disturbed from her reverie by Deidre's restive movements. The lights had been set to dim, but from her position on the cot, she saw Deidre batting the air with her hands.

"No, stop! You can't put this around my neck. I've done nothing." Deidre sat up, opened her eyes and staring through the picture of a child playing on the beach, opened her mouth and threw back her head. "Ahhhhhh." Her bloodcurdling scream pierced the hospital silence.

In shock, Elizabeth jumped off the cot and ran to the bed. Sitting on the edge, she put her arms around her wild-eyed daughter and hugged her for comfort. Deidre struggled to free herself from her mother's grasp, then went limp in her arms, her head flying back and her mouth gaping open. Elizabeth prayed in tongues in a fierce audible whisper. She gently placed Deidre back on the pillow, where she moaned and tossed her head back and forth.

Mrs. Ball, one of the night-duty nurses, peeked in at the door, then entered and strode authoritatively to the bed and pulled on the light chord. The patient was moaning and tossing her head from side to side.

Elizabeth stopped praying and explained. "She was dreaming... nightmares. She screamed something and touched her neck. Then she sat up and opened her eyes and stared right through me, like to give me the chills. I hugged her. She pulled away. Then she was unconscious again."

Both women gazed at Deidre who had settled into the covers and was peaceful.

"Why won't she stay awake?" Elizabeth was sorrowful complaint.

"It's hard to say." The nurse checked the IVs, making sure Deidre had not pulled them out. She cursorily examined the young woman not sure what she was looking for. Then she pointed underneath her chin. "What's this?" There were red ridges encircling the young woman's neck. It was as if she had worn a rocker's dog collar, but the studs had faced inward and the metal had scraped and chaffed her, leaving red marks.

"They weren't there earlier." Elizabeth was frightened. "This makes no sense. She was suffocated from within, not strangled." Elizabeth feared they would blame her for the bruises. She had been the only one in the room, and there were no witnesses.

"There was nothing for her to tangle herself in. I'll be right back. I have to write this up."

Elizabeth watched her leave, eyes wide with panic. Then she turned back to her daughter who rested calmly with her eyes closed, both of her arms at her sides. The red marks were a flag that something had happened internally, whether physically or psychically. Elizabeth quietly prayed for strength and for answers, as she waited for the nurse to return, which she did, shortly, clipboard in hand and another colleague in tow, who examined her daughter's neck.

"Do you remember what she said?" the second nurse asked as Ball stood ready to write.

Elizabeth repeated the story. "This actually was the most animated I've seen her. I expected her to get out of bed. That's why I rushed over and put my arms around her to comfort her and make sure she didn't."

"Well her catheter's full. She must have been afraid. I've never heard such a scream. For a moment, I thought I was back on the psych ward." The second nurse tried for humor, but she was the only one that smiled.

"I'm going to get Dr. Delacroix, the doctor on call, and have him speak to you. I think she may need a stronger sedative. We don't want her getting out of bed and collapsing since she's not stable on her feet. She is liable to injure herself or pull out her IVs and catheter. Maybe he can tell us more about the bruises around her neck." Elizabeth heard a suspicious lilting of Ball's voice and sensed she was assigning the blame for the marks on her.

"Did you want to say something to me?" Hot, Elizabeth stood up and squared off, envisioning a target on the bridge of the woman's nose, where a bullet hole should be.

Nurse Ball gave her a wry look, ignored her and left the room, followed by the other nurse.

The B word formed on Elizabeth's lips. She sighed and shook her head, dragging the chair that had been placed in the corner back to the bedside. As if she would harm her daughter. Suspicion and distrust were the coin of the realm. Why should things be different in this place? She considered. If she hadn't been resting on the cot, she would have missed Deidre opening her eyes, missed knowing of her dream terrors. What other behaviors had she missed because she couldn't be there twenty-four-seven? What had staff missed because of changing shifts and lousy nurse to patient ratios? It wasn't as if Deidre was able to ring the buzzer for help. Blast it! Elizabeth decided. After she conferred with the doctor tomorrow morning, she would have Deidre transferred to Mercy Hospital. Their staffing situation was better.

An attendant quietly entered the room, smiled at Elizabeth and emptied the catheter, then left. She was alone with Deidre once more. Elizabeth leaned over her daughter who appeared to be sleeping peacefully. She examined her neck. The angry red marks had deepened. Elizabeth was confused. Her faith could support many things, but stigmata were not of her faith. Should she believe that this manifestation was for the benefit of healing another person? There was nothing similar to this in her evangelical experience or her knowledge of the Old or New Testament, though she spent a number of minutes recalling scriptures that recounted frightening examples of demonic possession. She didn't believe her daughter was possessed, but she did believe that Deidre was at war with the powers of darkness. But that was completely spiritual and wouldn't manifest on her body. Or would it? She wished she had read Deepak Chopra on the mind, body connection.

Whenever Elizabeth was confused, she prayed in tongues which she now did, and soon she was at peace. Deidre was still. Elizabeth called her name. Nothing. Twenty minutes ago, her daughter was reactive and screaming for help. Now a chasm separated them once more. Elizabeth ached for her. Tirelessly, she had talked to her with no response, had shared what each day was like. Then she thought that maybe Deidre wasn't very interested, and what could her response be anyway? "Ma. You think you had a lousy day? Let me tell you about mine!" OK. She would discuss a subject Deidre knew nothing about because it was a secret.

Her Great Gran Elizabeth had told her some of the family history when she was a child. Great Gran had said that on Elizabeth's twelfth birthday, she would reveal the secret story. Her Great Gran made her swear to tell no one or something bad would happen. Her great- grandmother hesitated to tell her for fear of some dire result. Elizabeth had kept her word, but her Great Gran never got the chance to tell the secret story because she had died before Elizabeth's twelfth birthday.

When Elizabeth had asked her mother and grandmother whether they knew the covert history, both affirmed that there were no family secrets. Her mother claimed that their great- grandmother was senile and couldn't remember, so she fantasized about the past. But Elizabeth had believed that she was not a crazy, senile old woman. When both her grandmother and mother were killed in a car accident her freshman year of college, the maternal family history had died with them. Alienated from other maternal family members as a child, by the time she was old enough to care about her heritage and reconcile with family, all of the old timers had passed. The current generation were strangers.

Elizabeth related the events of the recent past to Deidre, the car accident, and the family estrangement over the inheritance. These facts, which Deidre had never heard before, she now experienced through the dark glass of unconsciousness. And for Elizabeth, unburdening her soul was the pathway to clarity. The distant past of her girlhood with her great-grandmother held the most pleasant memories. It comforted her to return to Great gran's kitchen in the Harlem townhouse, where Great Gran would pull out hot, fresh baked biscuits or corn bread from the old gas range oven. And as she taught her great grand-daughter to lightly dollop just enough butter or molasses to melt on the hot, sweet, loving goodness, they would eat and Great gran would share the secret stories. The greatest of these she now told Deidre.

"We are the direct descendants of Alexander Hamilton, Deidre. I am the seventh, and you are the eighth generation. Our ancestor was William Hamilton, Alexander Hamilton's mulatto child. He lived from 1773 to 1836, but his father Alexander never publicly acknowledged him. He was a free black carpenter who lived in New York City and was a leader in the black community. He worked to abolish slavery in New York in the 1820s. He co-founded black societies and promoted education and self-help for blacks and actively opposed the American Colonization Society, which President Lincoln supported for a time. Their idea was to deport all African Americans to a colony outside the United States. But William Hamilton would have none of it, and neither would his friends and acquaintances. Our ancestor Hamilton was a well- known journalist. He was an eloquent speaker and exceptional writer like his father. He produced male and female heirs. We are descended from his son, Thomas. Thomas and his brother Robert were editors and publishers." Elizabeth's eyes grew huge and bright as she remembered each detail Great Gran told her and whispered it softly in Deidre's left ear.

"Oh, Deidre, my Great Gran Elizabeth was so proud of being a descendant of Alexander Hamilton. She refused to take her husband's name because she wanted us to know our heritage was from one of the greatest, most noble and brilliant of the founding fathers. And Great gran saw to it that grandmother and mother never took their husband's names either. It was in Great gran's will that the women who came after Great Gran would always be known by their maiden names or suffer disinheritance of her land, the Harlem house, and the black folk art. Since Grandmother Roberta had no use for her husband who had left her anyway, she kept the name of Hamilton.

"But this was a source of terrible discord in the family. Both of the grandaunts, Great Gran's other daughters who had married, sued the estate to get around the will, keep their married names and get the property. The estate ran out of money with all the legal fees and lawyer's squabbles and feuding and hell raisin'. To this day, that side of the family doesn't know the secret, doesn't know why Great Gran made that condition in her will. They thought she was senile. They never imagined there was a reason why she wanted them to take her word on faith and go by the name of Hamilton.

"But then Great Gran always thought the other daughters were dull. 'Dull as blades rusting in the rain,' she used to say. Even Grandmother Roberta, her youngest child, was skeptical, and she so discredited the story in her heart, she didn't tell my mom. But Great Gran did entrust me with the truth. And maybe she would have told some of her great grandchildren, but she died before she could. Now only you and I know part of the story and the others don't know any of it.

"There were only a few mementos that were left from Great Gran's estate. Mom and Grandmother passed them to me after they were killed in the accident, and I will pass them to you. Nothing else remains but the name of Hamilton. Mom refused to give it up after she married because it was a sore point with the family. She didn't even hyphenate it with her married name. And I won't give it up either. So, you see, we are claiming our right to our spiritual and intellectual heritage, though our own family members despise us for it. And even if they knew the truth, it wouldn't matter to them. They care more about riches than things of the spirit. They embody the worst of the American Dream. The grandaunts only sued to prevent Grandmother and Mom from inheriting. Their husbands were well-off, doctors in business together. They didn't need Harlem property, which wasn't worth much in 1960, or a series of crude paintings and folk art. Of course, today, the inheritance would be worth millions."

Elizabeth touched Deidre's cheek. "You are born of greatness. This magnificent man's nature is in our blood, and we are never to allow others to make us lose respect for who we are. There is a memento that has been passed down from Alexander Hamilton who gave it to ancestor William's mother, and it is in the safety deposit box. When you awaken and fully recover, I will take you there and show it to you. Though we don't know the entire story, which was lost to us when Great Gran died, there must be others who know it. One day, I am going to trace our genealogical records and have DNA testing and discover the rest of our family story." Drained, Elizabeth looked closely at Deidre who seemed to be at peace, the spiritual wrestling over for the moment. Then Elizabeth dropped her head on folded arms, pressed them on top of the blanket and fell asleep.

Five minutes later, footsteps awakened her. A light-skinned black man dressed in doctor's garb had slipped into the room and was staring at her when she lifted her head and turned toward him. Shaking herself awake, Elizabeth stood up and shook Dr. Delacroix's hand in introduction, then explained Deidre's behavior as he examined her daughter and looked closely at her neck.

"Ms. Hamilton, I have reviewed Deidre's charts, blood work, the imaging and her test results. But the sudden appearance of these marks around her neck defies all medical science, unless they were put there by you?" As he said the last four words, Dr. Delacroix abruptly lifted himself from the sleeping patient and whirled around to stare directly into Elizabeth's eyes. His expression was deadpan.

"Yes, doctor, I abused my daughter. I tried to stop her screams because I was, I was..." Elizabeth stammered. Was the irony and sarcasm lost on this man who seemed as dull as her relatives who would deem such humor beneath them?

"Yes, well, you have small, delicate hands, and you wear two rings on the inner fingers of each hand." He continued with precision. "Your fingernails are fill-ins, most likely silk-wrapped? All these would have made marks, though I doubt you would have gotten both hands entirely around her neck as the redness shows. Aside from the fact that anyone can see you are a loving mother, it is obvious you are not responsible for these." He smiled. He had been kidding her. "The question remains. Who or what is responsible?

"Is it an allergic reaction? Could some chemical have caused this?"

"Not likely. It is a mark more like that which occurs from the chafing of some instrument. The marks are unbroken, like those one would receive from wearing a collar of some kind. An allergic reaction to a chemical would raise welts or hives in a random series and most likely she would be scratching herself, tormented by itching. No. If these occurred, attendant upon her nightmare and flailing in the air with her fists, I think it may be one of two things, both of which are beyond my power."

"So, you won't give her a sedative?"

"She is already sedated. I do not think we should raise the dose because of the other medication she is on to prevent any swelling of her brain. And if this is psychophysiological, sedation won't help. It might even exacerbate the problem and make her dependent on the medication. This is not my field. I will recommend that a psychiatrist see her tomorrow and give a diagnosis, though it will not be easy in her present state."

"We may not be here. I am thinking of transferring her to another hospital that might be more suited to dealing with her condition." Elizabeth hesitated to tell him about her plans, but she felt honesty would harvest anything the doctor might be holding back from sharing with her.

"Well, regardless of your decision, tomorrow we will have more evidence. The marks might disappear by morning. They may have been brought on by her own hypnosuggestion caused by the stress of her nightmare, if indeed that is what upset her."

"What else could it have been?"

"Ms. Hamilton, where do individuals go in her state? Do they dream? Or are they in oblivion until they wake, if they wake? Can they remember anything they experienced? To what extent can family members influence the recovery of their loved ones through prayer? Ms. Hamilton, we have progressed very far in the science of the brain, but that does not mean there are not tremendous gaps in our knowledge. In fact, what we don't know is greater than what we do know. I am afraid what is manifested here is anecdotal, with no conclusive causal explanation. I'll leave the name of an excellent psychiatrist, and by morning, you can make your decision." Dr. Delacroix moved to leave the room.

"What do you think personally? Nothing shows up on any of the tests. Everything appears normal. The injuries to the back of the throat, such rapid healing. She is taking food and drink by mouth. Of course, she is very slow about it, but she is doing it. The two neurosurgeons that are familiar with her case think that with all the accumulated documentation, tests, charts, physical examinations, she should have been fully awake by now. What do you think?" Elizabeth knew she sounded desperate, was desperate. She wanted to affirm her faith that Deidre had been healed, but strangely was too afraid to believe her prayers had been answered, panicked that something terrible would happen like it had with Billy.

"Ms. Hamilton you must have patience. Whatever they told you was based upon the evidence gathered. We are doing everything we can. But with this situation, as the doctors told you, there is uncertainty. A wait-and-see approach seems inadequate, but it's the best that medicine has at this time. Now, you don't have to accept our word for it, by all means transfer her. But you must admit, she has made tremendous progress." Dr. Delacroix smiled. "We must remain positive." He took both her hands in his and gave her right hand an encouraging pat.

Elizabeth allowed herself a small smile. "Thank you. I am usually positive, but I think I am just exhausted and stressed. I probably need a sedative."

"If you like, I can prescribe a very mild one, which will calm you, so you can sleep."

"No. It's OK. I hate to take any medication, prefer naturopathy and organics."

"I understand. It's unfortunate that hospitals exclusively practice allopathy. But the field is beginning to open up, and I am sure in time, the best of both will be practiced."

"You are very kind." Again Dr. Delacroix turned to leave the room, but Elizabeth's question held him back. "Doctor, you said there were two things."

"I don't follow you."

"You said both things were beyond your power to help her and one was psychosomatic."

"Psychophysiological. Yes, the mind forcing the body to receive its mark. For that, you will talk to the psychiatrist."

"What was the other thing that was beyond your power to help?"

Dr. Delacroix laughed. "Well, are you trying to back me in a corner? No, the two things were in the answer I gave you. I am not a psychiatrist, who is more familiar with such things that are psychophysiological."

"You are holding something back." Elizabeth smiled and tried not to sound threatening. "I intuited you to mean something else. I am a woman of faith. There is nothing you can tell me that I will find silly."

"Well, this has brought to mind an experience that I had when I practiced medicine early in my career in the Caribbean, Haiti, and then in Louisiana near New Orleans, deep in Bayou country. In both areas, the residents and our clients were Catholics, Christians."

"Well, I am not Catholic. I am, I guess you would say, the closest to being Pentecostal, praying in tongues, baptism of the Holy Spirit, the nine gifts, healing, a word of wisdom; like that but without the politics, the red and blue states and all that, which is just rhetoric and manipulation by politicos. So, if there are Catholics who practice these things, then I guess I am Catholic. I don't know what words and labels mean any more, doctor, except that politicians often use them to alienate people from loving each other. And that duck will not quack at my door."

"Well, then, I guess you might say that these were people of great faith. They believed in the supernatural. Some believed in Voodoo which is a religion steeped in Catholicism. In Haiti, it is said eighty percent believe in Catholicism, twenty percent in Protestantism but one hundred percent believe in Voodoo. In New York City, it is said that over one million people practice Voodoo."

"It is steeped in occult practices, root working, Santeria. I know educated people at my job who practice the black arts to get ahead in their careers."

"Well, many years ago, as I was saying, similar marks appeared on a young girl who had a high fever. I was called in, as was a Voodoo cleric. I brought down the fever, and after the cleric's ceremony, the red marks disappeared."

"What are you suggesting, Dr. Delacroix, that someone has cast a spell...worked roots on Deidre?" Elizabeth laughed. "Should I call in a priest of Santeria or Voodoo cleric?"

"To put it more succinctly, I will take a quote from Shakespeare's *Hamlet*, 'There are more things in heaven and earth that are dreamt of in your philosophy.'" He paused for dramatic effect. From the look of puzzlement on Ms. Hamilton's face, she had no idea where he was heading. "Science, of course, is today's operative word, so the quote could be modernized to, 'there are more things in heaven and earth that are dreamt of in medical science.' We offer the most advanced knowledge of the day. In Shakespeare's time, the equivalent was philosophy. The rational man studied philosophy, Ms. Hamilton."

"Meaning?"

"It is as you will, Ms. Hamilton. There are more things in heaven and earth than we can possibly dream of in medicine. We must keep an open mind. I will leave the name and number of the psychiatrist at the nurses' station. Have a good evening, and try to get some rest."

Elizabeth allowed Dr. Delacroix to abruptly and finally leave the room without further questions. In his circuitous response, Elizabeth felt she received the validation for all her beliefs, her faith in God to overcome and her fear that Mocha had tampered with occult mystery religions. What he had given her was one hundred times better than a sedative. She lay down on the cot and slept the soundest sleep she experienced since Deidre had gone missing.

Chapter Twenty-One

The more she considered it, the more Madeline believed with her whole being that Peregrine was lost at Calvary. To visit the family crypt and hunt for her there, she had concocted a clever plan to slip the reporters waiting in front of her house. With tires squealing in protest, she had plowed out of her driveway and turned left onto Continental Avenue, then made another left heading west on Austin Street with the news truck close on her tail. For them, the trouble began when she eagle-eyed a parking space eastbound on Austin. She stopped in front of it. It was on the opposite street side. She let the cars behind her pass, including the news, then she swung her Mercedes around in a quick U-turn on Austin and headed east. Victoriously, she double parked by the spot to prevent an approaching SUV from stealing what she had claimed. As she had crammed into the rare space in front of Sparkles, she noted the white van which, following her lead, raced down Austin, then did a U-turn.

She was getting out of her car, when she saw the van pass her, then turn down 71st Avenue, hungry for an opening that would allow them stalking rights to all her movements. It was a stupid mistake. They would be stuck at two stop lights, as they drove the three blocks down the Queens Boulevard service road. Then, they would have to make two right turns before they could get back on Austin to head west two blocks, then wait through one stop light to check if her car was still there, which it wouldn't be. She was back in her car and heading west on Burns, then cutting over to Queens Boulevard through side streets, while the news truck probably was just turning west onto Austin looking for her car.

Madeline had traveled at a clip down Queens Boulevard toward Calvary Cemetery, gliding through yellow caution lights which was atypical. A year ago, unable to stop as the yellow turned to red, a waiting cop had pealed out of 108th Street. With sirens blaring, he scared her over to the right lane of Queens Boulevard, where they clogged traffic, while the cop wrote out the ticket. She remembered she felt like screaming, as he got out of the blue and white, smiled and handed her the yellow sheet with the $200.00 fine, fulfilling his quota for the month. After that, she stopped at yellow lights. But today, she removed caution and slid through red lights to get to the cemetery by 4:00 PM, which she did and without the companionship of the press or the police.

Madeline had driven through the gates of Calvary, unviewed by gatekeepers or caretakers. She parked at the spaces designated for the Old Cemetery division. She walked to the Johnson mausoleum, which was as intensely macabre and eerie as she remembered it, with its neoclassical style and massive, granite, rising six stories to the top of the domed roof. Stained glass windows arched rich hues of color among the folds and angles of reddish brown stone. The largest mausoleum in the cemetery, larger than most Levitt houses and cape cods thrown up to colonize the suburbs after World War II, the ornate, elaborate structure was built during the Gilded Age, when tycoons indulged their opulent, architectural whimsies. The mausoleum exemplified Blake's assertion: "The road to excess leads to the palace of wisdom." Madeline remained convinced that only the darker tenants of wisdom related to her family's crypts, which were, indeed, excessive structures.

Madeline craned her neck upward. The transfixed angels, perched on the portico roof, their wings extended eternally, anticipated the call to Rapture. Their task was to lift the building heavenward, aided by cherubim. Birds and other beings, some, whose grotesque forms perched on a ledge encircling the dome, recorded time until the august event. Though she hadn't visited since childhood, the crypt remained fresh in her imagination. If she had artistic talent, she would have drawn it from memory. Such was the iconic, phantasmagorical vitality of the Johnson family's, death-house creation.

Madeline climbed to the top step of the portico and looked at the bronze door, weathered green by atmosphere. Without the key, it would be impossible for her to enter. She lacked the strength to pry it open, even if she used the tools that she always carried in the trunk of her car.

"Peregrine, are you there? Peregrine! Call out if you are inside." Madeline pounded on the door with both fists, hearing the booms resound on the inside of the crypt, and the silence when she ceased.

"Peregrine, Peregrine Randolph. It's Mom. Can you hear me? I know you are in there. I looked in the box and saw the key was missing. Peregrine." She raised her voice and shouted into the seam between the door and the stone. Nothing. Rough images of her daughter lying on the cold, concrete floor of the vault crowded out her confidence and belief in her daughter's self-reliance and resilience.

"Peregrine. Please come to the door. Don't give up. It's Mom. Make a sound. Peregrine?" Madeline pleaded.

She waited and listened for five minutes, then trotted left around the corner to the first and lowest of the stained glass windows. She lifted herself, as close to ballet point as she could muster, and peered inside. Through the vibrant crimsons, blues and greens, she noted a tiny chapel the size of a small closet that was closed off from the main rooms of the crypt. She saw only an altar, above which hovered Christ, holding a lamb. She lowered herself and continued around the left side of the mausoleum. She picked her way on the ledge of grass, careful not to slip and fall, for the tomb grew out of a thick concrete platform, which precipitously dropped four feet to a gravel path. Landscaped with grass and crowded with bushes, which discouraged foot traffic, the narrow ledge on which she gingerly walked, encircled the structure and added to its imposing and impregnable aspect.

As she made her way to the back of the building, Madeline recalled her mother scolding her when, as a child, she had skipped along the footpath, now overgrown. Because the sepulcher had been built on a hillside, the drop was even greater at the back, perhaps seven feet. Madeline stood and looked out over the drop at the distant headstones, obelisks and monuments of Old Calvary. If the content were not so gruesome, it was a beautiful panorama of white, grey, black and graphite-sculptured stone, with varying shades of green foliage like a park on a summer afternoon. Madeline turned toward the back of the building. In stark contrast to the entrance, and with imbalance and asymmetry, the fourth story just below the huge dome was uninterrupted, undistinguished, brownish-red granite. The absence of stained glass windows and architectural accoutrements and refinements gave credence to the idea that the builder and architect either raced to meet a burial deadline or ran out of money. Knowing her family as she did, there was probably another reason for the stark simplicity. Madeline walked along the edge of the drop and looked down. She expected to see Peregrine lying dead, neck broken, a limp heap that smashed bushes struggled to hold up. But there was no one, no clues, nothing.

In discouragement, looking downward, searching for any remnants of her daughter, Madeline followed the course around the other side, back to the front of the building. So many days had passed. With an absence of proof that her daughter was alive, fear and panic crept into Madeline's mind, like a pestilence taking over a town, sector by sector, house by house. Cruel imaginings spun and unraveled like an ancient horror movie. Peregrine was inside the tomb, rotting like one of the corpses, struck down by panic, hunger, dehydration, her last moments tortured and baleful. She had prayed for death to come swiftly, but instead, she had lingered in consciousness, lying in excrement, too weak to scream or cry, drying into a skeleton. Madeline believed that Peregrine was in tremendous emotional and physical pain, aware she was dying, incapable of staving off the descending void. Did she think, 'Why didn't her mother rescue her?' Or worse, did she die of humiliation and resignation, alone in the darkness, no angels, no faith, no God to comfort her?

Clouds of misery dismantled Madeline's grip on her emotions. She had betrayed herself by bowing to fears, that her execrable relations would avenge her devious theft. Fear of discovery, and revenge on her own life had swallowed up Peregrine's. She would have to live with the guilt of killing Peregrine for eternity, a soiled, ignoble twenty-first century Medea. Madeline wanted to die. Let the family come for her. Her life was over. Peregrine was dead.

She crumpled, falling onto the steps of the crypt, sobbing at her selfishness and cowardice. Like the slimy creature she was, she crawled up to the top and across the portico, where she huddled against the door and rolled herself into a ball. She stayed there, until the emotional fit passed and she surrendered to pragmatism and cold rationality. She would go home, pour herself a stiff drink and contact the police. She had a lot of explaining to do, but she promised herself she wouldn't lie. The police would break down the door and find Peregrine, take her to the morgue, do an autopsy. There would be an inquest and so many questions. How could she answer them truthfully? She would be forced to explain her family history. Would they believe her? It was like a story posted on a conspiracy website. On the other hand, they just might believe the weirdness of her upper class childhood. It would justify their middle class values and affirm that the love of money, indeed, was the root of all evil.

Though fascinated by them, the middle class neither understood nor tolerated what they saw as the queer machinations of the ruling upper classes, in the United States, what was referred to as old wealth. Led by press spin, moralistic, self-righteous media mavens, whenever they could, championed lopping off moneyed heads, so that they could ingloriously plunk them on the pikes of middle class rectitude and censure. As the hypocrites ignobly thrust up these to ignominious, public display, the masses jeered their approval. And the vulture media gouged out and gorged on once omnipotent and gold-filled eyes. If a few wealthy elites were brought low to the shameful perdition of middle class scorn, their sacrifice freed their peers to reap another century of wealth and power accumulation. These would be able to live above the law: engage in double-dealing and political buy-outs, manipulate financial markets and conduct internecine battles for world domination, effected by war machines that were oiled by the blood of middle and lower class youth. That was the modus operandi of both her American and European families and their cronies, and the political sheep they owned and manipulated in their respective barnyard countries.

Was she to be the next sacrifice, head on a media pike, tabloid exclusives ripping apart her substance? She was already someone the press painted as upper class, living in an exclusive neighborhood. Once she contacted the police, she would be subject to tight scrutiny. An elite prize, she might even be charged. This untenable situation with Peregrine had already morphed Madeline's life into that of a defenseless creature, hunted by media jackals, who waited for her to weaken and collapse, so they could chew her flesh and suck on her marrow. The phone call to the detectives would be the fatal blow, and her public confession would be the dinner chime calling birds of prey and hyenas to feed on the seamy and hellish carrion of Peregrine's death. Madeline laughed aloud with bitterness. What did she have to fear from her European family? They wouldn't seek physical vengeance. It would be too swift and merciful a punishment. Her public pillorying and digital decapitation would be a living death, much more just, with her identity forever sullied.

The gloom of the cemetery settled into her spirit. Depression took her in its arms. She didn't want to go home and face herself. One evil always led to another, even in defense of a good cause. She should never have taken the heirlooms, never have sold the painting, even though it was the road to freedom. She should have relied on her own talents and intelligence to lift her from that morass she had left behind in Europe. Madeline raised herself from her sitting position and dusted off her hands. She had to go make the call. As she stood and turned to take the first step off the portico, she spotted a glint of metal on the ground near the landscaping of juniper bushes. She raced to the bottom of the brown granite stairway and moved into the hedges, where she thought she saw the metal. But the bushes created obscuring shadows. She had to crawl on her hands and knees and sift the earth for the metallic object. Finally, her fingers grasped something cold, hard and slim. With a faint heart, she looked in the palm of her hand to see the key to the mausoleum. It was the key which Peregrine had secreted from the strong box.

Muttering thankful praises, Madeline leaped to her feet and scrambled up the stairs to the bronze door. Her hands shook, as she turned the key in the lock, and pushed hard on the door, which was stuck, and required her forceful grunting to move it even an inch. Eventually, she pounded it open and slipped inside. To be safe, she wedged her large, full, Louis Vuitton bag in the entranceway, so the door wouldn't swing shut and lock her in.

Moving beyond, she saw the crypt's innards were black shadows. Madeline found the light switch and flicked it, illuminating the main room which she remembered seeing, when as a child, she had attended the funeral of a distant relative. The room was the same as her sibilant memories. While the reverend prayed, they had clustered around a casket that was placed in a drawer on the other side of the room, near a narrow hallway entrance. She and her mother had been staying with American relatives on her first visit to the United States and New York City, when the ancestor died and they attended the burial at the magnificent tomb.

She breathed a sigh of relief. Nothing in the room had changed; there were three massive walls of drawers where the dead slept. Thank God,

Peregrine was not, as she had imagined, moldering on the cold, concrete floor. But that didn't mean that worms weren't feasting on her daughter elsewhere in the mausoleum. She must search every room, corner and hallway, until she found Peregrine, alive or dead.

Madeline was unfamiliar with the layout of the burial site, but her sister had told her it was elaborate, mammoth and labyrinthine, like a convoluted puzzle. Madeline looked toward the entrance door, which was still ajar, her bag blocking closure. She hesitated. Was Peregrine in another area of the building? She ran back to her bag, removed her cell phone and quickly dialed her lawyer friend. She had a signal. His number was ringing. She stopped the call. Carrying the phone with her, she walked away from the entrance to the furthest extension of the entombments.

Madeline remembered that as a child, she had slipped away from the others to play during the cleric's eulogy. She had discovered a doorway at the farthest end of the southern wall of drawers. This led into a spooky, narrow hallway. But she didn't get very far because her mother discovered she was missing and had come after her, grabbing her hand and scolding her in an embarrassing scene, as she pushed her out into the main room to rejoin the others. Later, during the final closing of the metal drawer, when her mother was distracted by the ceremony, Madeline sneaked back to the hallway, hoping to continue her search. She remembered her shock. It was as if the door had melted into the wall, and there was no way she could discern its outline, because there was no seam, no knob. Nothing indicated that a door had even existed in that spot. Once again, her mother had come to retrieve her, but this time she wore a smile on her face, a private acknowledgement that her daughter had been hoodwinked by one of the secrets of the crypt. Madeline, in her young years, felt the first sting of being played the fool, as if an older child had designed a fabulous playhouse, tempted her into seeing its delights, then slammed the door in her face, because she was too young to experience them.

Madeline went to the far corner of the most westward side of the crypt. She bent down and felt along the seam where the main wall merged with the westernmost outer wall and the floor. At the juncture of the walls and the floor, there was a small, black button which she pressed. A latch clicked. Suddenly, the door's outlines, once invisible, appeared. During her only visit to the family crypt in Italy, she had seen her uncle gain access to the inner chambers of that mausoleum by pressing such a mechanism.

Madeline knew relatives had taught her mother to navigate the various family tombs. But she had never been initiated into the mysteries, because of her exile from her family before the age ceremony. Living incognito in the United States, she had renounced her heritage. Her life had been consumed with her husband, his death, the parenting of her child, and the tremendous effort it required to remain one step ahead of her family, before they discovered her whereabouts. She never imagined that she would be drawn by Peregrine's foolhardiness into this crypt to push open a door to a hallway she had not traversed in thirty-nine years.

The passage was shorter than she remembered but more strange and creepy, because she was there alone. Slowly, Madeline followed it in the darkness. She stumbled into another room. There, she found and flicked on a wall light switch. This chamber appeared a bit smaller than the main room, but resembled the other's shape and function. There were body drawers against three of the walls. She breathed a small sigh. Again, there was no sign of Peregrine.

Madeline shouted hollowly and senselessly into the entombments to quiet her nerves. "Peregrine? Peregrine?" All was desolate.

She proceeded along the southern wall to the easternmost end where there was the dark opening into another narrow hallway. She turned and glanced around the room she was leaving. Its layout was in the reverse of the previous burial site, the hallways on opposite ends of each other, like in a maze. She entered the dim passage, whose outer wall, she imagined, was the eastern outer wall of the crypt. And if this guesswork was accurate, she thought that beyond the inside wall of the passage, were the drawers holding the corpses. She pictured the crypt in cross-section, like a square layer cake slice on a plate, alternating layers of corpse wall icing and viewing-space cake, joined by alternating halls at the easternmost and westernmost ends of the crypt. This was her experience of the mausoleum, but it might not be its true reality. Her family was known to enjoy artifices that confounded the senses and blurred boundaries between fact and fiction. They were magicians and, she reminded herself, the crypts were their masterpieces of creation and deception.

She emerged from the passage into another room of the dead, indistinguishable from the two previous burial halls. After she found the light switch and turned it on, she trudged past the entombments and entered the slim passage at the westernmost extension of the mausoleum. Now, the corpses beyond the wall passage in this layer of the cake would be to her left. She drove deeper inward. Was the progression of layers supposed to be symbolic? How? She knew she was missing something. If she had blueprints or a map, she could visually read where she was, and sense the overall pattern and design to discern how the crypt impacted the sensibilities of the adherents who wandered there. If she had time, she would examine the names and dates carved in the marble. She checked her watch. She must hurry to search for Peregrine on this level. If she didn't find her down here, she must scope the upper floors and complete this before dusk. She knew her family well enough to understand the mausoleum's paradigm would shift after dark, and she would be at the mercy of their Mephistophelian connivance.

Madeline entered and exited room after room, hallway after hallway. She found each to be arranged in a patterned, serpentine rectangularity. She saw no clues or evidence of living humanity. If Peregrine had been there, she had left long ago. This thought relieved and disturbed her. Were her assumptions about her daughter going to the crypt mistaken? No, she reasoned. She was her mother's daughter, but an innocent.

"Peregrine? It's Mom. Where are you?" she whispered in the silence. She had come to a circular, metal stairs in the middle of what appeared to be the antechamber to the last room, before she reached the back wall of the crypt's first floor. She assumed the stairs led to the second and third stories, and that the upper floors extended into the dome, which she supposed was empty space. She reminded herself not to trust her vision, because of her family's mischievousness and the wanton architectural duplicities. Since the layout of the building intentionally obfuscated, from floor to floor and room to room, there was no way she could see into the dome, unless she made her way up there. There was no way she could anticipate, from one room to the next, what she would find. She decided to put the stairs on hold, until she investigated the last room, the seventh, presumably at the back of the crypt.

Madeline held onto the right wall in the narrow hallway, moving slowly in the deepening shadows. The longer hallway opened up into a massive room. Fumbling inanely for a light switch, she realized there was none. With her acuity greatly impaired, she could see only the blackest darkness staring back at her from far corners. In the great dimness, she made out a number of statues situated at right angles to each other in a geometrical pattern. The figures filled the large room. Whether their subject was her notable ancestors, gods or goddesses, she could not discern. In the absence of light, they were the deepest black. The most interesting room was the most obscured and inaccessible.

The hell with the room, she thought. "Peregrine, are you here? Peregrine!" she screamed loudly, attempting to pierce the darkness with her presence. The room swallowed the sound. Once more, there was utter desolation. She would go upstairs. If Peregrine wasn't there, Madeline would return home. It was nearing the cemetery's closing time. In an hour, the natural light would recede, and the tides would revert to the powers of darkness.

When she reached the stairs, she glanced at her watch. She had ten minutes. She must hurry. Madeline athletically bridged two steps at a time up the circular and narrow metal stairway, which spiraled into a short second floor landing. This branched off into a massive room and adjoining chambers. Again, there was no light switch. But artificial illumination wasn't needed, because light came in from the stained glass window of the Madonna and Child. Madeline thought it the most beautiful and magnificent of the windows, but then, it was the only window she had been able to see, as it was meant to be seen, with the drooping, western light shining radiantly onto the crimsons, yellows, greens, blues and vermilions. Drawers were interspersed in the walls on three sides. It seemed, that the wall without drawers, alternated from room to room in a confusing and perhaps meaningful order. But she had no time to divine what it was. She did recognize that the second floor appeared to be less expansive than the first. Again, she called for her daughter. The silence rebounded eerily.

Conscious of the time, Madeline scoured the second floor, grateful that the rooms without stained glass windows had operable artificial lights and no Peregrine. She climbed the stairs to the third floor. With the exception of one room brilliantly illuminated by a stained glass window depicting St. Paul's vision of Christ on the road to Damascus, the other rooms boasted unassuming candelabra that shined dimly but provided enough light for her to rapidly advance. She moved through the various rooms with cursory interest, noting that the arrangement on each floor was different. Yet, the serpentine pattern that moved the adherent from room to hallway to room was the same. Except for the initial door into the maze, she had encountered no locked entrances. It was as if the crypt had been rigged to welcome her and allow her freedom of movement through the maze. This made her suspicious. She trudged in wary anticipation, expecting trap doors to open suddenly and walls to collapse in on her.

From the outside, it was impossible to discern the inside layouts and their floor differences, a clever feat, perhaps ordered by the patriarch of the family back in Europe in the nineteenth century. Externally, the tomb was a facsimile of one of the mausoleums she had seen on the family estate in France. She had never been inside that one, though she had been inside others. Along with this one, she had visited enough crypts for ten lifetimes.

Branches of her European and American family held ceremonies twice a year in the crypts. As a teenager, she had participated for five years, then had renounced their traditions, embracing the unseemly pleasures of her generation, and the prosaic adventures of youth, rebelling to discover "forbidden delights." But years of living had sealed the truth of the cliché, "There is nothing new under the sun." In hindsight, she was forced to admit that the "forbidden delights" she had sought as a teenager, were tame by comparison. The exceptional, arcane and antiquarian culture of her upper class family were unparalleled to youthful "flights of fantasy."

It was an irony that Peregrine had embraced what Madeline had rebelled against. Apparently, Peregrine believed, like her family, like old New Orleans' families, and those families of Mexico, China and the Far East. For them, ancestral connections were integral to the thriving prosperity of the current generation. The living and the dead were together with no separation between the states or conditions of being. It all was a continuum of spirit. Though she had tried to protect her daughter from the dangers of this theoretical system, her sister had betrayed her trust. Surreptitiously, Rachel had acquainted Peregrine with the more glamorous aspects of it. Sadly, neither of the sisters had given Peregrine what she needed, a complete understanding of her place in her history and culture.

If they had, such an understanding would have equipped Peregrine, to resist with circumspection, the lurid manipulations of relatives into the unpredictable and volatile arena of spiritualism, magic and the occult.

In the last room of the third floor maze, which Madeline presumed was two stories above the room with the statues, she spied another circular stairway. This one was narrower than the one that had brought her to this level. Standing on the bottom rung, and looking upward into the darkness, she could barely make out upper floor landings, and what she thought might be the dome much higher up. Was this where her daughter had gone? Was this where her daughter had possibly fallen and injured herself? She called out with frustration. She wouldn't waste her breath. Her daughter obviously couldn't answer.

As Madeline raced up the stairway toward the dome room, progressing deeper and deeper into the crown of darkness, she mulled over her relationship with Peregrine. Her love for her child had been founded upon deception. Now, the lies had rebounded to strike her with fierce blows: Peregrine's theft, Peregrine's compulsion to embrace the family's occult practices. Betrayal had brought her daughter to this place. It was the same behavior which had caused Madeline to leave Europe in exile. She had rejected her family's most noxious elements. Hypocritically, she had mirrored them in parenting her daughter. A light went off in her soul to expose her own self-betrayal and self-deception. Despicable! If Peregrine died as a result of this fraud, there would be no forgiveness.

Madeline sighed. She took in gulps of air, as she paused on the landing of the final set of stairs to the dome room. She looked up into arched space. Complete darkness. She glanced down to the third floor and groaned. Preoccupied in thought, she was plunging helter-skelter into the dome, without having investigated the rooms on the lower fourth and fifth floors. Now, she would be forced to go back down each flight and investigate.

Madeline trod down to the fourth floor, cursing herself for her lack of focus. From the tight, narrow landing, she tramped under the small arch that led into a hallway, which she imagined would open into a larger space. Guided by the residual light from the stairwell, she passed her right hand over the left and right walls near the archway. No switches. She must investigate without benefit of lights or stained glass windows.

The darkness distressed her. Should she use her cell for light? She considered. Ten minutes had passed. She wouldn't be able to leave the cemetery through the gates. She would have to call her friends to retrieve her. She mustn't waste the battery, which she hadn't charged before she left for the cemetery. Madeline was isolated. Her cell was her only connection to the world. So, she must scull the darkness without benefit of lights. She headed into the shadows and pitch, inching forward with care, and then calling out for her daughter in each of the rooms. Scouring the floor for Peregrine, and hearing and discovering nothing, she left the area, and rambled with uncertainty up the metal stairs and through the rooms on the fifth floor. All was a blind.

The atmosphere of the chambers on the fourth and fifth levels was close and smelled of ancient mustiness and damp. Did these areas contain coffins, drawers, storage or something else? The dark prevented disclosure. To channel through, Madeline had kicked and scraped the flooring with her shoes. And she jumped and slid across boards with outstretched hands, readying her equilibrium to trip across whatever might be in her path in the trench of this eerie void. She screamed for her daughter again and again. Each time she expelled her lungs, the echoing vacuum responded with a familiar hollowness. No one is here, Madeline. Welcome to oblivion.

She sensed that there was rampant symbolism on the fourth and fifth levels, a macabre deception, probably undetectable even in the light. Only the inner circle of family would be privileged to access such knowledge. It was at this juncture, that Madeleine realized the full extent of the problem. Peregrine could be hidden anywhere in the tomb, lying unconscious behind walls or secret passageways, locked in crypt drawers, or trapped in some other confabulation of the burial site, unable to respond to her calls. Perhaps Madeline's search was useless after all, and invariably, she would have to enlist the help of squads of police and their canine units to find Peregrine on this site. Exposed to public scrutiny, she would be carrion for the vulture media, preyed upon by her European family, after they discovered her whereabouts. Disturbed by her selfishness, she stumbled back to stairwell five through the sour odor, pitch and damp. She had to find her daughter. Time was running out. She needed help.

In the leaden light, Madeline paused. Why continue? Peregrine was probably not in the dome room. On the other hand, could she risk not going upstairs on the outside chance she was? She must go on. If she discovered nothing, then she would elicit the help of Detective Matthews, with the caveat that there must be no publicity.

Madeline shuffled up the sixth flight which extended beyond into the blackness of space. She could see nothing; she could sense nothing. But she continued step after step in an eternity of darkness, white fear gripping the metal hand rails, as she plodded upward, cursing her family's Machiavellianism in devising such a thwarting structure. Lifting her foot, where she believed the next step should be, she fell. She slammed onto the plank flooring of the crypt's piece de resistance, the dome room. As she rolled onto her back to settle her nerves, she stared absently. From the lingering illumination, fading up the stairwell, she caught a two second glimpse of the ceiling curvature. It vanished, as the darkness of the vaulted dome and inaccessible space descended. Madeline felt the torpid oppression. She turned over and crawled on her knees, sweeping her right arm from left to right in an arc in front of her, as she progressed, unsighted. To substantiate its solidity, with her fists, she pummeled the floor, testing the planking for weakness, fearing it would give way, and she would plunge downward to broken bones on the fifth floor concrete.

Though she had managed to find her way, however inefficiently, eliminating room by room, and floor by floor any clues of Peregrine's manifest presence, this negation of light stymied her. She had been stupid not to bring a lighter or matches. Upending her former confidence, the wall of blackness, yes, that was the right description, appalled her. Frightful pictures of ghouls and demons crept into her mind and prodded her to make a quick survey and retreat.

"Peregrine?" Silence rudely answered. Assuming nothing, Madeline slithered on her belly like a snake. She inched across the rough wood, calling for her daughter with an uninterrupted mournfulness. Sometimes, she lifted herself upright on her knees to wrestle the air and wildly scrape the darkness with outstretched fingers. Other times, she sat and slid forward on her behind, her heels kicking the floor as she anticipated the crack and splinter of wood, her hands and feet dumbly ocular. In this way, she progressed until she palmed the smooth, curved, rising wall of the dome. She sighed, relieved. She had tested the planking and discovered its solidity. Now, she had her assurance that she could stand and cross the floor without falling through it.

Madeline leaned against the wall for support and raised herself up. To encounter any obstructions that might be in her path, she sidled and wind milled arms and legs; she peppered her movements with alternating kicks, to make her sure way across the wooden boards. She headed in what she believed was a north-south direction, perpendicular to her initial path. As she kicked her right foot outward, shooting pains radiated from her toe to her ankle and up her leg. Hobbled by the misery, her legs buckled; her arms flew up, and she fell sideways on top of a lump. She discovered, that she was embracing a bundle of putrid, rank clothes covered with bits of earthen matter. Madeline screamed in shock and jolted to a sitting position. She scrambled backwards like a crab. It was a body. Peregrine's body: a moldering, bundle of rags. She had found her daughter rotting on the rough, wooden tablet of the dome room. Or was it?

"Bloody hell, bollocks and blast. No, no, no! Not Peregrine!" She shook her head forcefully. "You're not Peregrine!" The repudiation encouraged her. The pitchy air had closed down all sight. With tears flooding her cheeks, Madeline crawled on weak knees to the odiferous pile and lightly palmed it, groaning and whimpering in disgust. Her daughter had become an unsanctified, stinking corpse. A dull, feverish sickness ripped through the core of her being, and she wept, long, deep, mournful cries that blanketed this highest of chambers in the tomb. Shuddering and quivering, Madeline lay on the floor, until her moans dissolved into the oblivion. Then, she was quiet, deadened. She forced her mind to take over and redirect her zombie emotions. *"Calm down, Madeline. Stay calm and think."* She wouldn't have to do an extensive examination to know if this was Peregrine. Even in the immobile blackness, with her sense of touch, she would recognize the familiar, the stunning, perfectly featured face and long hair.

Madeline raised herself to a kneeling position. To her left, she surmised, were her daughter's legs. So, Madeline moved to the right and lightly patted the body upward from the waist. She ignored the wriggling movement of feasting bugs underneath the cloth and searched for Peregrine's straight, thick hair. She fumbled around the shoulders into the curve of the neck, struggling with her revulsion and disbelief at the overpowering stench of rot and seething worms. Her fingers circled around a hard, cold stump and jellied mass. It took her a moment to register. Peregrine's head had been decapitated. Madeline fainted, falling forward on the mangled and decomposing body.

Ten minutes later, a few stray maggots crawling on her hands and face, jarred her fogged-in unconsciousness. In her nostrils the smelling salts of foul, fetid flesh revived her. And the welding arc of revelation reminded what her head pillowed on. She lurched upward and vomited. She had never thrown up so forcefully; not when she was drunk, not when she was sick. She had never experienced this projectile vomiting of her lunch and whatever contents were left in her stomach. It was a full five minutes, before she realized that her dry heaves croaked and rasped, breaking the silence. Then, her stomach convulsions stopped. Dehydrated, she was too enervated to continue. Madeline lay back on her elbows in exhaustion. She breathed deeply through her mouth to avoid the noisome reek of her own filth, Peregrine's putrefying flesh and the miasma of fear and helplessness.

Her daughter's anomalous corpse lay beside her in this house of corpses. She was beyond wretchedness in a whirlpool of despair. Her mind groped for the facts to connect the dots. There was the empty strong box, its contents stolen. There was the key by the crypt entrance. Her daughter had been missing for days and here, was the evidence of her whereabouts. Most likely, the gangs who often marauded the cemeteries, had found her. Peregrine had probably stumbled upon their activities. Madeline prayed her daughter had died quickly, and that they had not raped her; that she didn't suffer the torment of knowing her life was ebbing away, while others watched in leering pleasure, or worse, that she had been left to die alone. After they killed her, they had decapitated her to prevent her timely identification. It was a cruel blasphemy; before her time, her daughter's beautiful, stately body had been reduced to the mutilated repast of maggots.

Having confronted the worst, Madeline considered another possibility. Maybe this wasn't Peregrine. Maybe her daughter had escaped and was wandering elsewhere in the huge cemetery. The only way to prove this was to be intimate with the corpse, search it for any revealing marks.

Her body quivered. How could she bring herself to touch this mutilated thing, discover it was Peregrine, and inhabit the violation of her lovely daughter? She couldn't. She would go back downstairs and return tomorrow, with a flashlight and Bill's security team. Madeline crawled on her knees away from the body, and lifted herself up on wobbly legs. She couldn't face Peregrine's identification here, in the dark, alone.

The dome room was a hutch of tar. Outside, shadows deepened the night. She deliberated. The stairways would be unnavigable without the stained glass window light. By the time she called him, it would take an hour for Bill to arrive with his team and a rope ladder to get her over the barbed wire fence. She couldn't stay a moment longer. She wanted to run, to hang truth from the top of the dome, and be done with this place forever. But could she bear the uncertainty of not knowing if this was Peregrine? And if it was? How could she leave her daughter in this ghoulish, unhallowed state? What kind of mother was she? How could she rest, as long as her daughter's remains groaned to right this infamy? Peregrine's headless corpse would haunt her every waking minute. Inaction, even for a day, would revile her. And if it wasn't Peregrine? She must stay to find out. She must overcome her impulse to flee. She was here now. She must do today, what she might not have the chance to do tomorrow.

Madeline bellowed a low-throated cry that rose in pitch to a scream. She dropped to her knees and crept in the direction of the corpse. Finding it, she manipulated deft fingers away from the stump of spinal cord and bone, where the neck had been severed, and the blood had congealed into slippery, cool pulp. Her touch slid against cloth, some cotton fabric, maybe the tailored shirt Peregrine wore the last night she saw her. Underneath, the maggots writhed, devouring her daughter's failed flesh. The putrid smell revolted her. Bile churned in her throat. This couldn't be Peregrine. "Peregrine wouldn't die this way," she whispered to the seething remains. Death's refutation restored her courage. Freezing her mind away from the vibrating cloth, her fingers stumbled down to the verge of the chest. Her guts dry heaved. She gagged. She would get through this, she would. Numbing her imagination, she distanced herself from her surroundings, then lightly tapped the flesh pile. There were breasts. It was Peregrine. The abyss swallowed her. Madeline let out a wail. "God, please, no!" She was drowning in a purgatory of woe. A bleak revelation threw her a spare rescue line, and her spirit grasped dull hope. It still might not be her daughter. She had gleaned the sex, not the identity.

She could tell by the length of the body. With the intention of measuring with an arm stretch, she situated herself to face the corpse, but her right knee encountered wet cold. Her imagination exploded with images. Blood pooling from another freshly killed corpse? She would go out of her mind in this dead house. With each attempt at closure, another door opened into Death's kingdom.

A thought niggled. The wet could be hers. She stuffed her hand under her knee then brought her palm to her face and sniffed. Benign goopy vomit. Anxieties shifted. Her frazzled mind had sacrificed reason to heart guilt. She must limber her feelings which were as taut as suspension cables. If she snapped, the flow of courage would whip and coil, then fling outward in an apocalyptic devastation. And she was on the brink of snapping.

Push diaphragm out and hold, then pull diaphragm in and close. Repeat. The yoga exercise succeeded, and she concentrated. She and Peregrine were not the same size. She was two inches shorter than Peregrine's five foot nine inch frame and one size larger, an eight. Madeline inhaled and held her breath, while sighted hands scanned the rippling, noisome bundle that might be Peregrine. She poked both index fingers into the girth of the woman's waist. She was slender. Peregrine, too, was slender. Madeline exhaled, gagged and gulped air like an oxygen-starved fish, then held her breath. It was a misery to go on. She didn't want the truth; knew in her heart Peregrine had been murdered and decapitated, buried, then exhumed, and dragged to this desolate place, where no one would think to look for her.

Madeline exhaled a great breath, sucked in the putrid air and held it in her lungs. She focused her mind, then remembered. Peregrine always wore a ring on the middle finger of her right hand, given to her by a former boyfriend, who had died in a car accident. The emerald setting was unusual, the stones arranged like a hibiscus, symbolic of Peregrine's beauty. Madeline slowly grasped the right arm at the elbow and squeezed it gently moving to the wrist. Her stomach pitched, but she forced herself to brush away the hustle and flow of worms as her avid fingers inched downward toward the ring. Madeline grasped for the fingers. Instead, she held sharp splinter points and cold jelly. Bone protruded where the hand had been, and blood had flowed and congealed. Despair. She felt for the left arm and plunged her hands downward to the wrist. Splintered bone and oozy blood mash. She dropped the arm, recoiling and pushed herself backward, sliming her pants in the filth of her stomach contents. The murder was premeditated; the killers stealthy and clever. There would be no identification of the body. Forgetting the bad air, she swore under her breath at them and prayed that Peregrine had put up a fight before they had overwhelmed her.

Madeline edged toward her daughter. On the shirtwaist she wiped her hands of the throw up and bits of congealed blood. She would never forget the sensation of the vibrating frenzy of rapacious worms underneath the earth-dusted cloth. Nor would she forget this rank, mephitic smell of death. It had corrupted her blouse and jeans. It was in her hair, on her arms and neck, under her fingernails, on her entire person and presence. Even if she burned her clothes, took baths and showers, and had a masseuse rub her skin with scented lavender unguents, the stench would live in her nostrils. The malodorous powers of evil had fouled her being, because they had consumed the fragrant blossom of innocence that had once been Peregrine.

Kneeling, Madeline sat back on her heels, allowing her thoughts to dissolve into the mundane. She tried to close off all feeling and return to objectivity. The killers were professionals. They had left their handiwork to rot on the little trafficked attic of an ancient and desolate tomb. There was a greater probability of someone discovering a body dumped in the river than finding it in a crypt where cadavers were naturally kept. Perfect crime. Unless. Unless, someone serendipitously stumbled upon the body, as she had. But odds were still in the killers' favor. Identification would be difficult, even if there were revealing and recognizable birthmarks, scars, marks or tattoos, that is, if forensic investigators got to the body before the maggots had finished dining. DNA evidence would be computer matched against information supplied by families of missing women, a sifting through thousands of records. There might be a resolution to a missing person's case, though the killers might never be found and punished.

How would her family react, if they knew their place of ceremony had been desecrated in this way? But the Europeans would not find out. She would tell no one of her discovery, especially if she could prove conclusively this representative of mutilated womanhood was her beloved daughter. She had kept Peregrine's whereabouts hidden from them, after she moved from California to New York. Now, Peregrine would remain hidden from them for eternity.

Madeline sighed. All these inner ramblings had brought her no closer to the truth. She decided to lie next to the body to judge its height. Since she had twice smeared herself with vomit, she carefully raised herself up and stumbled in the dark to the other side. When Peregrine was a teenager, mother and daughter would stand next to each other, measuring who was taller. She remembered that Peregrine had exceeded her own height, first by one inch, then by two. On the day of a final measurement, they celebrated Peregrine's rite of passage. Her only child equated height with stature and success. She believed that in her maturity, she would best her parent. With tears flooding her eyes, Madeline lay next to Peregrine's left side. It was agony that the daughter only had exceeded her mother in death.

Breathing through her mouth, Madeline touched Peregrine's shoulder then scooted her own body upward so she was parallel, shoulder to shoulder with her daughter. She sat up and bent forward checking the position of their knees. Hers were lower. Was she imaging it? Was she taller by more than two inches? She hesitated, then decided to gauge the distance using the legs. Swallowing with difficulty, she felt for the calves, then ankles, expecting to discover another splinter of sharp bone as she had with the hands. Amazing! The bare feet had not been lopped off. She continued her journey downward, flinging away maggots that writhed for a dominant position, gorging at their flesh table. Her fingers fumbled for the toes. They had been chopped off. Her stomach lurched in revulsion, and she jerked her hands away from the exposed mess of stump and cold jelly, her investigation halted. Once again, she performed yoga breathing exercises. After a few minutes, she recouped and coached herself, "I can do this. I can do this." She calculated, and measured her own knees and legs in comparison. Adding an inch for the missing toes and a foot for the head, the woman was shorter, much shorter. Could it be? She had so determined that the woman was Peregrine, she couldn't believe that it wasn't.

Absent concrete evidence, Madeline thought of variables which could account for the disparity in height. Peregrine did have a long neck. Perhaps the body wasn't straight. Madeline scrambled on all fours and made sure the corpse was lined up on its back, the knees uncurled. From lightly brushing the bundle so as not to feel the gorging maggots underneath, and running her hands gently up and down the dead woman, she concluded the body was straight. .

Could it be? Her mental paroxysms ceased. Her mind clarified. Peregrine was taller than she. This wasn't her daughter. Her heart leaped with praise. Her happiness strengthened her spirits. Overjoyed, she jumped up from her kneeling position and stood over the dead woman, thanking her. She vowed to the woman, somewhere in the realms of spirit, that she would notify the police so that she would have a proper burial. Perhaps with DNA testing, her identity would become known. But as Madeline turned to navigate the darkness on her journey to the stairway, she regretted her promise. Peregrine was her priority. Until she found her daughter, nothing else would occupy her soul.

Placing the ordeal behind her, Madeline turned to confront another: leaving the mausoleum and cemetery without mishap, without discovery by predatory gangs.

As she slowly waded through the darkness to the thin, cool railing of the stairwell, fear descended like enveloping thunderheads. She placed her right foot on the top step, listening to the scrape of her shoe pinging the two, flat, metal rungs segregated by airy space. How could she not plunge into the bottomless abyss that dropped five stories, even if she gripped the railing with both hands? Looking below her, she saw the blackness of space. She was suspended in air, only secured by two metal slats and her quivering grip on the handrails. Her alienation in this insensible vacuum made her dizzy and unsteady. Her anxiety mounted. She felt she must scream, throttle herself, topple forward, release the dragon of suspense, fail, somersault to the bottom and break her neck!

Madeline staggered and tripped down four steps and could endure no more of her heart's compulsion to catapult into gravity's pit. Quaking, she sat on the very next step, put her head between her knees and breathed. The blood rushed to the still point. Momentarily, she revived.

Her reactions were natural. Horror had overwrought her psyche. She found a dead woman's rotting and decapitated body in her family's mausoleum. How inappropriately appropriate! Then, there was the stunning relief, happiness, amazement that the corpse wasn't Peregrine's. Her emotions had boiled over like the headwaters of three flooding torrents gushing into a small inlet. She was a tortured prisoner freed from her captors, but still traumatized. The physical manifestation, she rationalized, was the compulsion to throw herself down the stairwell and end the intense pendulum swings of feeling.

She needed time to decompress, yet had no time. She must escape the mausoleum, but was frozen, stuck, immobilized by icy fright, her behind clinging to the outer edge of sanity on two thin metal strips. Madeline concentrated on her breathing, in and out, in and out, windy, profound breaths. This soothed; her panic slid away. She returned to solid ground. Peregrine was still alive.

The hopeful thought anchored her will. Holding tightly with clenched, icicle fingers to the stairway rail, and snorting breaths through her mouth like a horse, she descended step by agonizing step on her behind, until she arrived on the fifth floor landing, where she stood up and moved three paces backward to lean against the archway wall. The earth resumed its twenty-three degree tilt, rhythmic lung waves calmed, and she relaxed, no longer darkness-fraught.

She was ready to descend. She sat on the floor and inched forward feeling the flooring, until she kicked the stairway railing. Gripping the metal prongs tightly with both hands, she scooted on her behind to the top step. Her compulsion to throw herself into the abyss returned. She panted like she was giving birth and threw back ice balls of fright. What she had done once, she could do again. Pounding her legs with her fists, to loosen the twisted chords of muscle, first, she lowered her right foot to the second top step, then extended her left foot to the same step, inhaling and exhaling like a bellows to stabilize her vertigo. Squeezing her eyes shut, clenching the metal, she flopped on her behind to the next step, then the next. She was making progress. She opened her eyes, but the darkness wound her head like a top, and she yearned to plummet forward, end the compulsion and the fear of falling away into nothingness. Closing her eyes, she rested, throwing her head's cumbersome weight between her knees. When the spinning stopped, she lifted it up and practiced breathing rhythms; hearing the soothing crescendo and decrescendo of air in the quietude, as she waited for clearance which eventually came, albeit slowly. Madeline slid down the bumpy decline, eyes closed into the lower depths of pitch.

The stench of vomit and putrescence of rotting corpse filled her nostrils. The headless, dead woman was stalking her, reminding her of her promise. She realized the stink contributed to her nausea. Her world was spiraling out of control. She must determine to balance herself, balance her realities and redirect her imagination away from the encompassing blackness. She bounced with taut, fear-grip down each step to the fifth level, halting when vertiginous anxieties intensified. Then, she resumed her thumping pace when the tides of darkness ebbed. As she bumped down the stairway through the abyss, she thought of reaching the third floor and the lights. The encouragement distracted her from her need to jump. But visions of the headless woman still haunted. And distress that her bag holding the door open had given way, and locked her in the crypt, dogged her progress. At least she had her mobile. She was grateful that she had overcome temptation and not wasted the battery for the menu screen's miniscule amount of light.

Madeline wrestled in the ebb and flow of vertigo and anxiety, until she reached the third floor landing. She glanced at the luminous dial on her watch. It had taken her two hours to plop down three flights. Lifting herself from her seated position on the last step, she ranged out into the warren of rooms, disoriented by the necessity of reversing her pathway. How had she journeyed through this maze to the stairway at the opposite end of the crypt? Confusion tagged alongside dizziness. She paused a moment, switching in her mind the left pattern to the right. Then, she began the circuitous backtracking through the rooms that were slinking east and west. She gradually adjusted to the labyrinth, in the exact reverse of her former progressions. Though the candelabra on the walls shone less forcefully than she remembered, after tottering in the darkness upstairs, she was thankful for the soft halo of comforting, if dimming light.

Madeline entered the last section on the third floor. Yes. She was where she should be. She noted the familiar window, St. Paul's Vision of

Christ. But its staining hues startled her. The sunset-filtered shadows of dusk had deepened. The colors in the panes vibrated wildly. They were alive and deepening, reminding her that she was alone at night in the cemetery.

Fear shrouded her mind and hurried her down the stairs to the second floor, past each weirdly situated room arranged in the left arm of the building, over to the westward section of rectangular rooms, then twisting back like a serpent, down the short hallway to what she thought was the largest room with the stained glass window of the Madonna and Child. If she was right about the layout, she would enter the great room here. She was mistaken. She didn't see her favorite stained glass window. The lights, burning their last had snuffed out, sinking her into oblique, ebony despair.

Blackness, blackness everywhere and not a light to think, she mused, paralleling the rhythm of the Coleridge poem, "Rhyme of the Ancient Mariner." Now she would be forced to use her cell to track the light switch. As she clicked on her mobile, notes of John Coltrane sliced through the eeriness and relaxed her. She switched screens to the menu page which beamed brightest. The light barely radiated out six inches, but it comforted her. In the grayness, she spied the wall with the drawers and moved to it, tracing it with her left hand until she came to the corner seam where walls joined. Then she proceeded along the rectangular room to more drawers which she traced until the black entrance to the hallway loomed beyond. There she discovered the switch and jiggled it.

Nothing happened. Burned-out bulbs, a short, snapped wires. Did it matter? She was so sick of the darkness! Madeline followed the tiny illumination from the cell under the arching hallway into the last room on the second floor. Though she sensed her bearings, the silence and stark emptiness unnerved her. The massive room of drawers on three sides devoured the tiny light, and shadows pressed, as if the walls were converging inward to crush her to death.

Her fears of the dead woman, the compressing walls and the tomb's malevolence spurred her to a rapid exit. Brushing the wall with her left hand, guided by the phone in her right, she paced quickly around the room until she reached the archway of the hall. She bumbled through it, a shuttered pressure cooker, stifling her desire to scream. She was ejected from the belly of darkness to the second floor landing, which was bathed in graphite. She prayed the lights in the first floor rooms were on. Clicking off her cell phone to save the battery, she lifted her right foot to launch this final effort, but once again, her equilibrium upended, and she tottered precariously on the top step, her stomach pitching and rolling like a foundering boat in a vortex. She felt the urgency to leap, to suspend her anxiety by embracing the inevitable submergence into the death pit. Her shaking fingers wrapped like claws around the metal railing, and she stopped her plummet into the ebony tarn.

Terror, sickness, mutilation, death, pressed her. She sat on the landing for a long while, resting her heavy head of affliction on her knees. Negotiate the descent on her backside, or stay there until the morning light infused the mausoleum with clarifying illumination from the windows? She must get home. What if the police called with information about Peregrine? Repeating the familiar pattern, bum, right step, left step, bum, right step, left step, she thrust her quivering body in declension. She slid the remaining four steps, bruising her calves on the edge of the metal rungs as she crumpled on the floor grateful to lean against the sharp, bottom riser and feel it digging into her back.

With stiff, creaking limbs, she raised herself up from the concrete flooring and brushed herself off. She stretched her arms upward, and then bent to touch her toes. A planet had been created and destroyed; but she had reached the first floor in one piece, she realized, to experience a leaden hued void. The candelabra had given up the ghost. The absence of light on this floor was as unsettling as in the dome room and on the stairs. She sighed. She should have switched off the lights to save them, before she ascended to the upper floors. Hindsight is an exact science. Murphy's Law I, or was it Murphy's Law II?

Madeline ached physically and spiritually. Conflicting impulses of hyperactivity and exhaustion cascaded through her body. Foremost, she wanted a scalding shower and apple martini. She was desperate to finish her search for Peregrine. She believed the family crypt held many secrets, but none of them would lead to her daughter who, most probably, had left days ago with Mocha.

She clicked on her cell and turned to the right. Moving into the hallway and beyond to the serpentine and rectangular room arrangement, she was confident that she could wend her way back more easily. In reverse order, after the stairway, was the macabre invisible room. Madeline brushed the wall for support, as the cell allowed her to inch into the short arched hallway, which spilled out into the massive room of statues. She glanced around. At this hour the statues had melted into the black atmosphere and were one. Gliding calmly, steadying herself by lightly touching the wall with her right hand, she was carefully tracing its extension, when she realized her mistake. The invisible room at the back of the crypt was separate and unconnected to the warren of rooms, a cul-de-sac. At the stairwell, she should have gone to the left, and retraced her steps backward through the serpentine layout of rectangles. She turned to leave but thought better of it. She must exhaust her search of all the rooms in the mausoleum. This was the only one she had not investigated.

Madeline spun around and switched her cell from her left hand to her right, leaving her left free to guide her against the wall of the dead. Preoccupied with her search, it didn't register that the light from the cell was reflecting something. When she held out the phone toward the center, at a right angle to her body, she thought she saw a twinkle in the darkness. She sensed moving molecules. In the leaden atmosphere, a black statue breathed out its being. Madeline's body released a spasm of terror. She could feel her urine flow into the panic, but she managed to hold it in and spoke aloud in pretense of not noticing anything.

"Oh damn. What is wrong with this thing?" Her voice wavered uncontrollably in a spell of fear. She turned to bolt, but her legs rooted to the concrete: paralyzed stalks. She panted terror: her breaths short, rapid bursts. There was a clumping sound. A stone leg had been pulled up with exertion and set down hard. A statue vibrated.

"Ahhhhhhhh." Her milky fear curdled. Compelling her body forward, she sprang with huge leaps, like a leopard, away from the room's center to its outer edges. She hurdled her body forward, blindly and with abandon, then collided against the wall of drawers and bounced backward. Inuring herself to the pain and shock of the impact, she recovered her balance and continued, hurtling through the flumes of darkness toward the archway. Looming ahead was the opposite wall that led to the large hall. She crashed into it and knocked herself backward. Somehow, she held her balance and didn't sprawl out on the floor, where she imagined the outstretched claw-nails of the stone figure would grab her and drag her into invisible darkness then flay her flesh to her bones.

Ignoring the shooting pains along her arms and elbow, she stumbled into the ebony, densely-atmospheric hallway. She blundered through it into the second room. There, she paused and listened to the faint death of her echoing steps. She heard nothing else. Loosening her heavy grip on her cell, she raised it in front of her like a compass and focused the tiny light guide. She recognized the area, more drawers. She tracked the wall lightly with her left hand, then raced its extension, careening right, through the arch. She bumped against the sides of the long, gloomy hallway then burst with thumping paces into another room of drawers. She smashed her back a glancing blow, and bounced off the uneven wall of carved names. Her mouth was a cavern sucking up the air, laboring, as if on a mountain top devoid of oxygen. She halted and bent double, her breaths rasped hollowly. She wheezed, unable to fill her lungs. Dizzy. Hyperventilating. She repeated the mantra. *Calm, stay calm.* She breathed from her diaphragm and placated her irrationality. *You're not being followed. Stone statues don't move.*

Five seconds later, her feet pounded concrete. She ran sightless against the walls of the dead, smashing her arms when she miscalculated her speed or closeness and ignoring the clanging pain. She believed she had reached the last bloody arch of the last bloody hallway. Slowing her pace, she jogged the short distance to what she hoped was the main chamber where she first began the grotesque journey into the dead landscape. She halted to peer through the fuscous soup. The mammoth room was Stygian. From where she imagined the door would be, lurked a deep abyss. Had she made a mistake in the warren of rooms? Confused, she forgot the reason for her panic flight. She held out the phone in front of her to gauge the distance from the wall. She couldn't discern it in the outer darkness. This meant she was on the westward side of the building and the last room was on the eastern side. If she crossed the center she would reach the arch and hallway to the entrance.

Quickening her pace to a fast walk, she navigated with arms spread wide, her right hand holding the phone. Lunging forward she anticipated it would take about forty steps to reach the opposite wall of the dead, and the last arch. Fifteen, twenty, twenty-five. Madeline stared at a figure, immersed in Night which stood eight paces away. It came in silence, arms open to catch her. Madeline screamed and dodged to her left. She flicked off the phone, extinguishing the target light. Racing with the madness of fear, she bashed into the wall of drawers. An explosion of pain launched a rocket of stars and knocked her to the ground. She was nearly senseless, her emotions in a tumult, but she didn't moan or cry out. She held back all turmoil, allowing the murky atmosphere of pitch to obscure her location. The figure crept closer to her below the radar of sound. As silent as a spider, she furtively got up, located the wall with her left hand and then raced forward, feet pounding, as she grappled in the air for the invisible archway which she knew was directly ahead, maybe ten paces. She felt the sharp corner, grasped it with her left hand, and swung her body into the hallway gaining momentum for her rush down the tyrannous passage. Fingers clenched her blouse and tore it. The stone figure was upon her.

Extending her hands outward to balance herself between the narrow passage walls, she leaped and lurched through the arch which opened onto a massive room. There was the crypt's entrance, the door flung wide open fifty feet away. There was her Louis Vuitton bag on the opposite side of where she left it, the slant, and indigo-gray light from the opening, emanating from the dusky cemetery. She raced with heart-pounding, stomping strides. She must get to the door and beyond, before the throbbing pace of the runner behind, overcame her and wreaked damage on her being, fulfilling his violent, havoc of intention.

Madeline zig-zagged, twisting and writhing away from the creature's clenching grasp. She leaped to the door and grabbed the handles of her bag, swinging it heavily in front of her and into a man, waiting on the portico of the mausoleum. Pummeling his groin with the bag, the momentum of her run sent him and herself roiling down the steps of the entrance. When they ceased their tumble, Madeline landed, sprawled on top of a man who appeared to be in his thirties with staring blue eyes. His attractive Aryan face filled with terror, then his eyes rolled back into his head and closed. She had knocked him unconscious; or rather the step on which he hit his head had flattened him. She labored to get up as the penumbral figure inside the crypt popped out the door, morphing into a dark haired man with wild eyes. Eyeing her, he jumped down the concrete steps of the crypt. Adrenalin pumping, she screamed and scrambled off the

Aryan. As the wild man lunged to grab her throat, she screamed a warrior's victory cry. She swung the bag smashing him on the side of his head and knocking him to the ground. Her violence fueled her. Madeline darted to the right side of the mausoleum and leaped over the hedges toward the interior of Calvary Cemetery.

Nerves and muscle fibers tormented by pain, her lungs screaming for air, she caved. She couldn't last another full minute. She raced to a grove of trees and bushes that she hoped would obscure her momentarily from her crazed pursuer. On the edge of the woodland grove was a series of one storied mausoleums, built into a hillside and landscaped with rioting, ill-shaped evergreen bushes, box hedges and hollies. She ran to a building which offered overhanging, ill-kempt shrubbery and slowed her run. Stopping, gasping furiously for air, she crouched down. The hunter was nowhere in her sight lines. She prayed she wasn't in his. Between two large and scratchy bushes, she pushed herself amongst the pine scented needles, trying not to poke out her eyes. Sitting on the ground she prodded, arranged and pulled branches around her body and stuffed her handbag behind her. The greenery in the dark was a camouflage. As the nighttime shadows deepened, she grabbed her knees, curled up into an invisible ball and waited.

Chapter Twenty-Two

B last, blast, blast!" Fen pounded his fist on the steering wheel of his Mercedes and unconsciously pressed the gas pedal to the floor. The speed gauge jumped to eighty-five. "You lying devil, I've got you. I've got you. You're mine. You messed with the wrong person." The gauge notched to ninety and kept rising.

"Achoo." Fen sneezed. He had been without sleep for thirty-six hours, and had caught a cold from the stress of his overnight on the beach when the helicopter exploded. Preoccupied by reaching for a tissue in the packet on the passenger seat, he lightened his foot on the gas pedal and the gauge plummeted. He blew his nose loudly in a futile attempt to stem the flood of nasal liquid infirmity. To the policeman in the patrol car waiting one half mile up the road, it appeared that the speeder was reigning in his illegal impulses and doing obeisance to authority at seventy miles per hour, so he affixed his radar gun on another target. Fen escaped one indignity, in his life of mounting indignities: the speeding ticket.

"Hell and damnation!" Clear mucus continued to flow out of Fen's nose. That was his last tissue. He glanced to his right. There were no cars in the right lane of the two-lane Sunrise Highway heading westward toward Wading River. No one was watching, so he used the back of his shirt sleeve to dry his nose. "Sucks for me." He had to go to a drugstore for cold medicine and more tissues. The incredible stress of the last twenty- four hours had eroded his immunity, ushering in a headache, fever and chest congestion. He was a mess, everything was a mess.

"Bastard, son of a bastard!" In fury Fen increased the pressure on the gas pedal, realized it and decreased his speed. He should just pull over, rant and rave and get it out of his system. That way, he wouldn't kill himself or anyone else or provoke the police to arrest him. He was swinging, punching, killing mad. When he was in this state, he needed to get alone by himself and work it out, because he was insane around people, violent, vengeful. He needed a drink. Too bad there weren't any pubs on

Long Island like the pubs one found in Australia or Canada. There, a guy could get a couple of beers and lay it all out on the table, come out swinging, and the fellows would pitch in, calm you down, give you some support and sympathy. Here, you'd be thrown in jail. No sympathy. The American system was hypocritically unrelenting. The rule of law was the rich got all the law and the poor got screwed.

"You will be sorry. You lying devil. Liar, liar!" Fen jerked at the steering wheel pulling into it, shaking and tossing his body forward and backward. "God give me justice!" He got into the right lane without signaling, then swung onto the Wading River exit at 50 miles an hour, nearly losing the turn. He stood on the brake pedal, slowing the car to 10 miles above the exit speed which was more manageable, and finally came to a stop at the light. He was breathing heavily and surprised that tears of rage flowed freely. He made a right and drove one quarter of a mile to a shopping center, where he pulled into a space hidden away from the other cars and turned off the engine. Hands on the steering wheel, head on his hands, he sobbed until there were no more tears and his face was drenched in clear liquid, from his eyes and dripping nose.

Liam and the others were getting away with murder. So far the Suffolk County DA had done nothing because Liam had contradicted everything Fen had said, and police were holding hands while they made decisions whether to let the Feds handle the entire investigation.

As he listened to Liam's lies, Fen thought he was schizoid, thought that he had fantasized the helicopter landing and taking off from the estate heliport. The servant didn't even attempt to obfuscate the truth or intersperse it with falsehoods. He baldly denied everything. Plausible deniability, it was known to be in intelligence circles. The helicopter? A ghost. Never landed. Never took off. No one at the mansion saw it. No one heard any helicopter pass by the estate. Mr. Johnstone's helicopter was in Manhattan, and when the family returned, it would be brought to Southampton. No other helicopter was allowed to land there. Yes, he and the servants heard a noise, but the size of the compound buffered any sounds over the ocean. By the time the staff got up to check, police cars were on the beach. They assumed everything was under control and went back to bed. In discretion and in keeping with the wishes of the family, they stayed inside not wishing to be part of the media circus of onlookers and general "free-for all" that in recent years was sinking the gracious dignity of Southampton into cannon fodder for scandal sheets like *The Enquirer* and *The New York Post*.

Bullshit! Fen believed Liam stayed inside because he had planted the bomb on the helicopter himself and knew the inexorable outcome down to the second!

On the beach that morning, Fen had stayed until the last person was interviewed, making sure to avoid the Southampton police. After introducing himself, he had told his story to two policemen from East Hampton who had been called in to help with the crowds and take down statements. Two hours later around 9:30 AM, he had persuaded the officers of the truth of his account by having Queens Detectives Dietz and Allan verify his identity in a phone conversation with them. Then Fen, Sergeant Vreeland and Officer Finlay rode in through the iron gates up the long gravel drive of the magnificent estate to question Liam and the other servants about the explosion.

Initially, Fen regretted that the officers insisted upon taking him to question Liam. He thought perhaps it would have been better to just file a complaint and let the police deal with him at the station. But when he saw the servant's reactions, Fen knew they had made the right decision. At the door, upon recognition, Liam had glared surprise to see Fen with the officers, though he immediately recouped from his anger and was politeness and servitude. Maybe if he dropped off Liam in a Bronx alley where a few of his "get down" actor friends lived, they could teach him the Bronx's version of Miss Manners.

During the questioning, Liam remained calm and maintained the story that the helicopter did not land or take off from the estate. When the officers questioned each of the servants alone, their responses, to a man, supported Liam's testimony. He had rehearsed them well. Fen had had enough. The last to leave, he stepped to the threshold of the elaborate and heavy double doors, then whirled around to confront the murderer.

"Damn you for being a liar and for getting the others to lie."

"I'm sure I do not know what you mean, sir."

"I was here, on the beach. I saw the copter land at this heliport, saw the stretcher. I saw everything!" Fen screamed.

Liam's face was impassive, a vacant eyed Venetian mask. "We were asleep. You saw nothing. There was nothing to see."

"You psycho. You had Manny blown up!" Fen lunged at Liam. Grabbing the lapels of the butler's uniform, he brought Liam's face inches away from his. They were both the same height, though Fen's build was wiry and muscular, the older man's filled out, on the verge of beefy.

Fen's lips were an inch away from Liam's. He made a lightening move to kiss him, as Liam jerked his head backward. Fen threw both arms around the butler who struggled in fury to escape. Fen held him, clenching him tighter by curling his right foot around Liam's left, drawing him in tightly, chest to chest, abdomen to abdomen, their bodies clenched like lovers in an embrace of loathing. Fen grinned and with quiet malevolence hissed in Liam's ear just above a whisper. "I ought to kill you right here. If they put me in Attica it would be worth it to hear you whimper as I drain the life out of you."

As he menaced the immobilized butler, Vreeland and Finlay ran through the open double doors and tugged at Fen's arms, pulling him away from Liam. Fen let them, but his fingers held on to the silly uniform and he ripped the lapels before they completely dragged him away. He snarled in a growl that rose to a crescendo in a high pitched scream. "You killed an innocent, an innocent, who never harmed a soul. Cretin! You burned him alive, you twisted, sick…maniac! You aren't even human."

Liam recovered his balance and brushed off his outfit as if to remove the stench of the middle classes from his person. As Liam escorted the men out a second time, an officer was on each side of Fen who considered. Liam was remarkably self-possessed and cool in response to his frontal assault.

They had made it to the cedar porch when, like a choral refrain, Liam said in measured tones, "Gentlemen, I cannot say it has been a pleasure." Fen broke free and whirled around to look at the cobra in a butlers' uniform. Liam looked above Fen's head at a spider web. "No offense taken at your impropriety, sir."

Incensed, Fen leaped to strangle the reptile, but the servant was careful to slam the double doors as Fen's hands rose up to pulverize him. His fists smashed the heavy, white wood, ripping the skin off his right hand and bloodying his knuckles. Fen manipulated the bones in his hand

and wrist. Slicing pains shot out; he had sprained his hand against the impassive door.

Sergeant Vreeland put his arm around Fen's shoulder, guiding him down the red and tan brick walkway, gilded on each side with blue fescue and other ornamental grasses. He walked him to the white pebbled driveway, where they had parked the police vehicle. "You'll be lucky if he doesn't press charges for assault and battery, and then sign out an order of protection. You just threatened him in front of two credible witnesses. Pray that he doesn't trip down a flight of stairs and charge you with attempted murder."

"Give the guy a wide berth for the next few weeks, until we have something more conclusive," said Finlay. "Let his daily routine set in. He'll forget you assaulted him."

"Assault? I'm in love with the guy. I can't get close enough." Fen dropped the sarcasm. "I want to press charges against him and the entire staff."

Vreeland was direct. "There isn't enough evidence for probable cause. Did you see Liam place a bomb on board the helicopter? It could have been an accident."

"Then why is he lying about the helicopter taking off and landing from the heliport?"

"Wait a day. Let's see what other evidence turns up. Southampton police have to share everything they've collected with the Feds and Detectives Dietz and Allan, who will be contacting you. The investigation and report may take months or we could get some major breaks. We don't know yet. So far, no one we talked to saw what you saw. No one was on the beach at the time, or if they were, they haven't come forward. We don't know what statements the Southampton police took. There might be corroborating testimony. Someone might have seen the helicopter leave from the pad. We'll do background checks on the servants and Liam. That's why we took down everyone's information. If any are illegals, we can squeeze them."

"If I press charges, it's my word against theirs."

"You can do what you want, but there has to be probable cause that Liam or anyone killed Manny, if that was Manny on the stretcher. What if he is lying about the helicopter? He could be lying for a hundred different reasons. It doesn't prove that he put a bomb on it or sabotaged it to kill Manny. We don't know the reason why he's lying.

Vreeland seemed skeptical. "Say the DA has enough to arrest Liam and the servants and arraign them on murder charges. The Grand Jury has to bring in an indictment. Unfortunately, juries are somewhat less open to eyewitness testimony since Barry Scheck's book and movie and his Innocence Project. You know the organization that uses DNA testing to help acquit innocent men who, through faulty eyewitness testimony, are wrongly accused of murder. And Grand Juries have been spoiled by *CSI, Law and Order* and other crime shows. They think that criminals leave a lot of evidence and that forensic criminalists will be able to use their highly sophisticated technological instruments to link it with the perps. Not true. Sometimes there's just eyewitness testimony, no murder weapon, no body, no prints, no motive, nothing. The jurors think the police and detectives are incompetent and that they overlooked or destroyed evidence. Then the DA's credibility is on the line. He's reluctant because there's one witness and that's it. He needs more evidence. Oftentimes, he can make a better case with a lot of circumstantial evidence, than with one eye witness. I can't tell you how many alleged murderers have been acquitted because there was one witness, whose credibility the defense destroyed, since there was little or no material evidence. This has been especially so in New York."

Finlay spoke up, diverting the subject to another topic. "If we can prove the second crime, we've proven the first. With the explosion there is an official investigation, more resources, more statements, more evidence to sift through, which will help. Was the explosion an accident, foul play, negligence, terrorism? Can any of the debris picked up at the scene identify Manny? Now, you gave us identifying marks, jewelry he wore and stuff like that already. Don't forget to give Dietz and Allan the dental records, just in case they find something in the ocean or something washes up on the beach. With such evidence there is a greater likelihood the Grand Jury could bring down an indictment. But whose? Evidence has to suggest the connection between Liam and the explosion. At this point, we have nothing linking Liam and the others to the kidnapping or the explosion, except your eyewitness account. But by all means, press charges. Liam and the others may get nervous and make mistakes, giving us more leads."

Finlay drove Fen to his car which was still in the parking lot of the Beach Club on Ginn Lane. "You could always bring a civil suit for negligent homicide or wrongful death. Less evidence is required. It would help if you could get corroboration from another eyewitness, proof that Manny was on the stretcher and not someone else who wore a similar jacket."

"I'll get my lawyer on this today. It would be worth it to give Liam grief and get the publicity hounds up his butt. With reporters snooping around, they might be able to turn up other eyewitnesses." Fen began to feel a sliver of hope.

"Anything's possible with the media. They also bring the nuts out of the woodwork." They had stopped by his car and had turned the engine off and lowered the windows in the heat. Vreeland gave his advice. "You need to really think about the logic of this. If Liam lied, that means there's massive collusion on the other end. He couldn't just lie without all the players on board. Someone is out fifteen to twenty million on a helicopter...the insurance company...the owners. They aren't likely to take a loss unless it was worth it...the risk reward ratio, knowing there would be investigations by the Feds, the insurance company, and the DA."

"Liam lied to hide the truth."

"Against a twenty million loss? Why kidnap your brother anyway? You don't even know if the kidnappers, who you didn't see at the estate, are in collusion with Liam." Vreeland played devil's advocate.

"I saw two men dressed up in suits put Manny in the car, and I followed them to Southampton."

"At night, in a near high speed chase? You need other proof."

"The explosion is the proof. His windbreaker is the proof."

"It was nighttime, and you were how many yards away?"

"Don't forget I had high powered binoculars."

Vreeland shot back words that now echoed in Fen's mind and infuriated him because of their truth. "But you didn't see your brother's face. You just saw a windbreaker which appeared to be like the one he wore, but could have been different."

Fen made no reply.

Finlay interjected. "Too bad there wasn't enough light for the phone camera to photograph the helicopter. If you knew the type of helicopter, we could trace its origination and from that trace ownership."

"I can recognize it anywhere." Fen was positive. He thought of something. "Aren't helicopters supposed to file a flight plan?"

"Flying to a public airport, of course. Private helicopters and helipads operate differently. The flight plans may be unknown. And anything is possible. Look what happened on 9/11! That will be the first thing we'll be checking. Terrorism." Vreeland spoke quietly but forcefully.

Finlay was encouraging. "Look. We'll work on angles and leads from our end. We're working with Dietz and Allan and all law enforcement on this. We're a united front sharing information with each other. Anything you can do to help, we'd appreciate."

"OK, I'll do my best." Fen thought he might go online and check the manufacturers' websites first. Fen opened the backseat door and got out of the cruiser. He leaned into the right opened window and was gracious. "You guys have been tremendous, more helpful than your Southampton bros. Can I count on you if I call from time to time to check out how the investigation's going?"

"Work through Dietz and Allan. They'll keep you up to date." Vreeland looked up at him impatient to leave because of the heat in the car. Finlay turned on the engine and the air conditioner.

As the car swung away, Fen waved goodbye feeling discouraged. They didn't arrest Liam and his fellow rodents and bring them down to the station for questioning. They weren't aggressive enough. They should have gotten a search warrant for the house. That's what he would have done if an eyewitness had produced an account like he had. But what did he know. He was not law enforcement, never would be.

In the shopping center parking lot, as he retraced the events in his mind, calm returned. Opening the glove compartment, he rummaged inside, found a package of tissues in the back corner and took a few out. He dried his face and blew his nose. Physically, he felt better. Finlay, the younger of the two officers, empathized with him. He would work through him to get information about the case. Fen started the engine. Emotionally spent, he returned to stability. Objectively, he considered Liam's supercilious, British demeanor. The more he thought about him without the butler's outfit, the more he doubted the man was indeed a butler. Too arrogant.

Fen turned left out of the shopping center and headed for Sunrise Highway westbound. He checked his phone which was still charging. Using Bluetooth, he called his lawyer's firm in Garden City, making a rare appointment to see him that evening. Next he phoned Dietz and Allan, but they were in the field. No matter. After conferring with his lawyer, he would go to the DA's office to file charges for kidnapping against Liam and the servants, something he should have done five days ago, instead of being persuaded to wait for more evidence.

In retrospect, the detectives had been wrong. As time progressed, events would become more muddled and disconnected. The material evidence, his eyewitness account, would grow more insignificant and opaque, until finally Kafkaesque, the police would minimize it, perhaps redefining his brother's kidnapping and murder as a mistake and accident. With their logic, they were transforming a compelling drama into a benign theatrical. The spin was frighteningly modern.

Later that evening, around ten o'clock back in his Manhattan apartment, after he had showered and eaten Chinese take-out, he called his mother and lied to her about Manny who, she reminded him, had now been missing for over a week. He couldn't bring himself to tell her about the explosion. He knew that what he was doing was cowardly and selfish, but she would hate him as the fatal messenger. He wanted to offset her loathing for as long as he could, until he had the courage to sustain it and counter it with love. He couldn't face Manny's death, her hatred of him, and his own guilt, until he had been sufficiently distracted by his life's routines, at least for a day.

Fen contacted Sam, his agent and agreed to be at work on the set tomorrow morning. His call was 6:00 AM. He had lost another audition for a film, and Sam was furious until he told him about the explosion. Because it was a private helicopter and involved few deaths and little information, Sam had missed the twenty-second bite on news channels. All about making money, his agent had the audacity to tell him his adventure would make a great movie. He had to remind the ass there was a difference between fiction, even if it was based on the truth, and the real experience which was tantamount to a hell beyond what anyone could attempt to imagine. He had no desire to relive the dredging up of raw, bleeding emotions in the telling of it. Sam didn't hear a word he screamed, and just said goodbye after Fen had spewed his outrage. He pictured the wheels turning in Sam's steel-trap mind to get publicity for him out of this mess.

By twelve, Fen made it through his mountain of text messages and emails and called his closest friends or their parents. Like a permanent Friday the thirteenth, nightmarish bad luck plumed like toxic water in the lake of their lives. Mocha was still unconscious, though off the respirator, according to Ms. Randolph, whose nephew had persuaded the DA to press charges against Beach Comber. Beach Comber arrested? Fen had laughed bitterly at the inanity of his friend's arrest for sexually assaulting Mocha, whom The Comber had tried to help. But the police had probable cause, words Fen had come to hate. The evidence was circumstantial and there were no eyewitnesses that he had saved her life, only that she had been injured, and his fingerprints were all over her and her stuff. As usual the injustice system functioned smoothly to bring the innocent to jail, while the guilty went free.

Having made his one call to Sylvia, Beach Comber couldn't phone out or use his cell. Sylvia was livid that the jailers had confiscated her mobile from her son and refused to give it back to her. She had been exhausted from a flurry of activity getting another phone and then meeting with a top defense attorney, who practiced in Queens and knew the idiosyncrasies of its judicial system. The attorney, Michael Van Allan, told her Beach Comber probably would be arraigned in the afternoon, within the twenty-four hours after he had been arrested. Fen silently laughed when he thought to himself that it wasn't the first time Beach Comber sat in jail, even though the arrests didn't count because they took place in other countries.

Sylvia kept nothing back from Fen, whom she treated as family. After Van Allen interviewed her and made some phone calls to various friends in the DA's office, he warned her of the worst case scenario. She would have to contact a bail bondsman. The judge most likely would set a high bail because of any or all of the following: the nature of the crime, the circumstantial evidence, Beach Comber's extensive travel history, his surfer lifestyle, his disguised escape from the hospital, his flight from police at the cemetery, his lies of omission, and his money which gave him the mobility to easily leave the shores of the US and live in a country with no extradition, like the ones he had already visited on surfing vacations: the Maldives, Vietnam.

Fen had asked how the judge knew so much about Beach Comber. Sylvia's reply was apoplectic. In addition to what was emphasized on the news outlets, Ms. Hamilton had supplied details about Beach Comber's life to her nephew who turned the information over to the DA. For Sylvia, this was the cruelest injustice. The friend he had tried to help was being used to destroy him. Sylvia had declared war on the Hamiltons, especially Reggie.

The only mitigating factor, Sylvia said, was that Beach Comber had no priors. Van Allen would aggressively argue this and the fine points about Beach Comber's character, like his charitable work for the Ocean Conservancy, Riverkeeper, Clearwater, and The Tsunami Relief Fund. His college education and other sterling attributes would be emphasized. However, just in case, the attorney already worked out the arrangement with the bail bondsman so that Beach Comber could be out of jail, the bail set and money given to the court right after his arraignment, if all went smoothly. Van Allen also had warned her that it was no secret that the relative of the victim, who was a detective in the DA's office, was out for Paul Carver's blood. Van Allen was going to lodge a complaint against Ms. Hamilton's nephew, Detective Matthews, because of his conflict-of-interest on the case. Van Allen assured Sylvia that when he was finished with him, Matthews would be so far from the case he'd be working vice in Far Rockaway's projects, the Outer Mongolia of Queens. Sylvia had invited Fen to the arraignment with her and the lawyer, but Fen declined because of his early morning call. He promised to contact him the next evening if Beach Comber was out on bail.

Fen's final call, his third to her that evening, had been to Madeline Randolph. Again, she didn't pick up on the land line. He had heard from Ms. Hamilton that Peregrine was still missing. He checked for any texts he might have received from Madeline. There was only one. Earlier in the afternoon she had messaged him that she was going to Old Calvary, where she believed Peregrine was at the family mausoleum; it was the crypt where Fen was supposed to have met the women for the ceremony. He was amazed that Madeline knew this when Peregrine had sworn everyone to secrecy. He decided to try both her land line and cell one more time just before he went to bed.

After Fen removed his jeans and shirt, he went into the bathroom and brushed his teeth. He looked in the mirror. He looked like hell: dark circles under his eyes, paler and thinner. Good thing he didn't have any close ups. His ill appearance fit in with the character, a streetwise punk whose arms and back were filled with tattoos. The make-up, mostly tattoo transferences, would take about two hours. He would sleep in the chair throughout the application. He didn't have a lot of lines, only a choreographed fight sequence which could be rough.

He left the bathroom and took his cell off the night table and phoned Madeline. He listened as it rang continuously. There was the possibility that Peregrine was still at Old Calvary. If so she had been there eight days. What could have happened? He put the phone down after he left Madeline a brief message.

As he got under the coverlet, he thought of the irony that he was the only one of his close friends who was sleeping at home in his own bed that evening. He had been so preoccupied with his inner hell, it was a comfort to worry about others and forget his problems. Tomorrow evening, if Beach Comber was out on bail and Peregrine was still missing, the two of them would visit the mausoleum at Old Calvary, following Madeline's phone lead. That is if he remembered the name of the family's mausoleum which was different from Randolf, probably because it was her maternal family's crypt.

Fen lay in bed going through the letters of the alphabet, sounding out last names. Sliding from wakefulness, he drowsily considered that he would have to ask Peregrine the name instead of going through all this trouble of staying up before a shoot. It wasn't until he was in the twilight of sleep that he remembered the family name was similar to the bastard estate owners, the Johnstones. Distracted, he drifted off at 1:30 AM, determined to haunt the Johnstones until he received justice for Manny's murder.

Chapter Twenty-Three

The torrential rains flooded the streets as rivers of mud, excrement and garbage swept up any loose items that their owners had left unattended. Boxes and crates of foodstuffs surged along with the occasional smaller creature, stray dog or cat that struggled to keep afloat in the onrush of water. She stood in the doorway of a building, well situated on higher ground and waited for the storm to subside. These tropics were unlike the environment of her childhood in her country village. There, the rains came not as wrathfully, nor ended as abruptly. Everyone could more easily prepare. Always forgetful of the fury of the downpours, in St. Croix, no one readied themselves as they should for the rains, though the rhythms of weather were familiar. But then the desire for escape made one forgetful, escape from the oppressive atmosphere that knew no class or quality of people and escape from other things. All suffered under the torment of the heavy, burning heat and moisture, thick air, stifling to the lungs. The atmosphere resisted each movement one took, creating a universal indolence, so everyone walked and worked in slow motion.

Eventually, the deluge stopped and islands were emerging from the receding waters that evaporated to replenish the humid, fetid air they would take into their lungs. Her gown already muddied would now be splattered with filth, but she must jump quickly from island to island even slosh ankle deep in the muck until she reached the docks. Soon they would discover her absence, and the distance she must put between herself and them must be ample enough for a delay of fifteen minutes. As the sun peeked out from the drifting, gunmetal,-flecked clouds, she breathed a great sigh, then leaped to the emerging mound of light brown, sandy earth. She landed firmly on both feet.

Mocha awakened from her sleep and stared at the white ceiling then glanced around the sterile room, noting the long, darkened light fixture above her head, the plastic orange chair in the corner, the door opened barely a crack to halt the light or let it in, the night stand next to her bed, the tray stand to her right and the woman sleeping in the cot underneath the picture of the little girl playing in the sand on the beach. She was like that little girl, digging shovelfuls of sand, suspended in time before she filled her red bucket; before she carried her prize to the shoreline where waves kissed the beach; before she upended the packed rampart of the dirty grey sand castle. Her mind, arrested from all anxiety and fear, wandered into the notion that she was in a hospital, and she was being cared for by the woman stretched in sleep on the cot and the people beyond the door. Their care was unnecessary. She felt comfortable and secure, but her throat burned and was dry when she swallowed. She needed water.

Mocha sat up stealthily, not wanting to disturb the lady on the cot. There was a tube in each arm attached to a plastic bag filled with clear liquid. They were IVs. She slowly and gently pulled each out and turned off the monitor for each to stop its crazy blinking. She gave her attention to the bed. Rails were up on both sides. She rolled back the blankets and sheet with care then tried to scoot to the foot of the bed but found herself encumbered by white padded sleeves on her legs and another tube which after further investigation she realized was attached to a plastic bag on the side railing. She knew the padding was supposed to stimulate and invigorate her muscles and the plastic bag was attached to a catheter that was supposed to help her pee. But she didn't know how she recognized these things for sick people; and she was shocked that they were attached to her, because she wasn't sick and she shouldn't be in this place.

Annoyed, Mocha tugged slowly at the tubing and felt discomfort, but continued until the tube came out, spilling a few drops of urine on the bed sheet. No matter, she dangled the tube end over the side railing next to the bag of her urine which she decided she would empty later. She intended to get as far away from the appearance of illness as possible. She removed the padding on her legs, then scrambled to the foot of the bed on all fours, negotiating her dizziness. Her confidence returned. She slowly climbed over the edge but immediately sat to regain her bearings. When she felt stable she stood on her feet grabbing the bed railing for support. She felt better. She had been in bed too long and needed to move. She tiptoed three steps to a nearby tray stand and poured water from a plastic pitcher into a glass. As she stood there and drank greedily, she was surprised that the cooling liquid felt silky and soft when she swallowed. But then she had imagined the burning was caused because she breathed through her mouth as she slept.

After she poured herself another glass and drank heartily, holding the railing, she tiptoed to the left side of the bed and unhooked the catheter. Her equilibrium was restored completely; she walked quietly to the bathroom where she drained the bag of its contents in the toilet and threw the plastic holder into the garbage can. She sat on the toilet and relieved herself, then quietly and slowly tiptoed back to the bed. She wasn't sleepy. She was very hungry.

The clock radio on the nightstand registered 2:00 AM. Rather than wait, she decided to ask the nurses if they could get her something. She craved toast and eggs and tea. Could they get it for her, she wondered? The floor was cold. She tiptoed around the bed then dropped on all fours looking under it for slippers or shoes. There were none. No matter. Mocha stood over the woman who was still sleeping and took in her face and form with a sweeping glance. The woman, who looked to be in her forties, slept with her mouth open, and she breathed heavily, as if having so succumbed to the sorrows of life, it tortured her to take in breaths and expel them. Mocha pitied her, but hunger pangs surpassed her emotions. On wobbly legs she walked to the door, drawing it back just enough to slip through without throwing more light into the room.

The bright lights were outrageous. She rubbed her eyes and blinked many times, steadying herself against the wall with her right hand before she felt the glare had softened. There was little activity on the floor. She noticed the bank of desks and large counter at the end of the hall. Confidence returned as she walked with strength and purpose to the nurses' station.

"Hi. Is there any way I can get something to eat? I'd like some toast and some scrambled eggs, and tea. A proper English breakfast. But without the beans."

The heavy set black woman looked up from her paperwork. Perplexed she fixed her eyes on Mocha's. In recognition she jumped up, shocked. "Honey, what are you doing out of bed? You pulled out your IVs and catheter? She rushed around the corner of the counter with her arms outstretched to cradle Mocha who she imagined would fall, striking another concussion into the gnarly ridges of her brain. "Come on let's get back to your room. Easy, you are not well." She looked her up and down.

"I got rid of those tubes. I don't need them anymore. I'm perfectly well." Mocha was not going to allow this cow to define how she felt. She shrugged out of the woman's tender grasp. "Please allow me to continue on my own. I assure you, I am very well and I feel wonderful, only hungry. And if you please, if you would be so kind as to fetch me the breakfast I requested?"

Mrs. Reba Grant was from Jamaica and she found this young black woman's British accent annoying. Was this upstart trying to be better than she? The Hamilton mother was not from the Islands or the UK and didn't speak with an accent. Where did this woman get off passing herself off like someone from the upper classes? Reba Grant dragged over a folded wheel chair that was leaning against a nearby wall and opened it, motioning for Mocha to sit. "Please, Miss Hamilton, take a seat. I will bring you back to the room and get your breakfast. The doctor has to sign off on your menu. It is wonderful that you have regained consciousness, but we must take these things slowly. We don't want to make you sick again."

Mocha felt the blood rise in her temples. Not want to make her sick? The oppressive heifer was like an emetic. How dare this hulk distrust her own assessment of her wellness, and take on a condescending tone like she was an ignorant, ungrateful child? Mocha became insistent. Looking at the nurse unabashedly with power she quietly spoke. "When people speak, you rarely listen. That is a grave fault indeed. What did you do when teachers instructed you in your nursing coursework, or when your parents corrected you? If you listened with your whole heart the learning was easy. If you did not quiet your mind, you could not hear and the learning was hard. We both know how it went for you." Mocha saw that she had gotten the cow's attention. "Thank you. I need no help with walking, only help with breakfast. But if you have something else to do, I will arrange to get it myself." She turned on her heel and stalked barefoot in defiance back to her room.

Stunned by the verbal slap, Nurse Grant realized for a full three seconds that she hadn't moved the wheel chair or her mouth which had dropped in surprise and now, gaped open, a black hole, as she panted to control herself from lunging at the skinny bitch and going upside her head with a smack. But the uppity cow wasn't worth getting fired over, especially one who wasn't "all that." She went back to her desk and pressed the phone extension button for the doctor on call

Mocha slipped through the door and tiptoed over to a chest of drawers that doubled for a night table. She opened each drawer looking for clothing to wear. The drawers were empty. She checked the narrow room closet with the same result. Quietly moving to the foot of the bed, she climbed back into it, sitting on top of the covers. She waited growing more and more impatient with her situation. She decided to force the issue and pulled the light chain igniting the florescent bulb into a distinctive, dull hum.

The woman in the cot stirred. Heavy with sleep, her eyelids fluttered, then opened gradually, as she adjusted to her unusual sleeping arrangements. Elizabeth Hamilton turned her head to the right, then yelped in joyful surprise. She rubbed her eyes, not sure if she was dreaming. There was her daughter sitting up straight, staring wild-eyed at her, no, staring through her, studying her as if she were a creature to be examined. Elizabeth leaped from the cot and ran to the bed reaching over the metal railings to hug her daughter.

"Deidre. Thank God. God is good. You're up, at last." Elizabeth encircled her arms around her daughter who seemed wafer thin and delicate. She wept. "God works miracles. Yes He does. He does."

Mocha felt embarrassed with such carryings on. The woman was practically lunatic, so public and openly unashamed of her faith. "It's quite all right, I assure you. Please don't trouble yourself." She patted the woman's shoulders and disentangled herself from the smothering grasp. "If you can help me push the railings down, you may sit here with me on the bed." Mocha patted the coverlet on the edge of her bed to the right.

Elizabeth took the remote off the nightstand and pressed the application for the guard rails as Mocha shuffled pillows and pushed herself back toward the headboard to sit comfortably cross legged.

"I requested that the nurse bring breakfast, as I am very hungry. I wonder. Could you see about it?

Sitting on the bed, giving her daughter a deep, penetrating look, Elizabeth asked the question to which she already knew the answer.

"Do you know me?"

"Yes." Mocha assured the woman. "You are my permanent caregiver."

"Your mother, Elizabeth Hamilton."

"Yes, my mother."

"Why are you speaking with a British accent?"

"This is the way I speak." Mocha was offended. "Why bother about it?"

Elizabeth blinked in surprise and smiled. "Normally, you don't speak like that. I am amazed that you have the accent right."

"And I am amazed that such an insignificant detail as the way that I speak should astound you. If I spoke with a Spanish or Italian accent, it would be as immaterial. I am still me." Mocha sniffed.

"Well, that's true. And, you are awake and conscious." She put her arm around Deidre once more and hugged her. "We were so worried. The doctor felt you should have awakened when you were breathing on your own and he took you off the respirator."

"There is no need to fuss. Truly, I am well and ready to get on with it." Mocha was cool, direct.

Elizabeth didn't press her. How did amnesiacs respond after waking from a coma? As she conned Deidre's reactions and behavior, she grew fearful that the head injury had erased her exuberant, loving daughter and redrawn a strange, cold mannequin. How long would this go on? Elizabeth got off the edge of the bed and went to the door. Before walking to the nurses' station, she turned to Deidre who stared at her with huge black eyes. "I'll check about your breakfast."

Mocha felt trapped, pinioned in a glass case, like an exotic species of butterfly. She was sure the woman, her mother, had lied, and left to confer with that heifer about her condition. It was pointless. She was as she was, and nothing could change that. Annoyed, Mocha jumped off the bed and pushed open the door striding through it and down to the nurses' station where she knew her mother would be standing. She was right. Her mother was leaning over the counter whispering intently to the fat beast, their heads together in a conspiratorial conference. Mocha hastened her stride adjusting her hearing for telltale snippets of conversation.

Nurse Grant saw her, jumped from her chair and circled the counter to face her. This bitch would not get the best of her. She was solicitous.

"Now honey, you should be in bed. The doctor will be here shortly to examine you, and then we'll see about breakfast. Ms. Hamilton, could you take Deidre back to the room?"

"Please do not patronize me. I am an adult." She turned to her mother, "Do you know where my clothes are, my shoes and underwear? I am feeling very well and I am anxious to leave as soon as possible. As my breakfast is not here," she looked with disdain at the sniveling Jamaican cow, "I will have to do for myself."

Elizabeth felt rage rise to her throat. She lifted her hand to strike the face which looked even more photogenic in its gauntness, then put her hand down. Deidre was sick, probably brain damaged. She turned away from her daughter. "I'm sorry," she said to Nurse Grant who gave two quick little nods of assent acknowledging the situation. "Deidre is adjusting to...life." She smiled.

"No, I don't have to make an adjustment. You are the ones adjusting to me because I speak my mind. You feel you have to signal to each other like sneaky rats, speak around me, ignore my questions like I don't exist? I assure you, I see you plainly. You think I'm mental? Ha, ha." She laughed. "I feel wonderful but you would have me sick again. And, I am strange? Look to yourselves, ladies. Look to your selves. Your humanity is showing and it is not a pretty sight!"

Mocha felt transformed, happy. She felt free to speak her feelings, to hold nothing back. She quickly bowed to her mother and the nurse, one hand on her stomach and the other extended outward. She lifted her head from the suppliant position and looked up at them. "Feel free to discuss me. I give you leave. But be careful of your words. Though you are deaf, you are not hard of hearing, and your own heart condemns you." She stood erect, turned and left for the room.

Elizabeth shook her head then turned to Nurse Grant and said in ironic deadpan, "Comic philosopher." Elizabeth rolled her eyes upward then back to the nurse. "Could you please get her something to eat? I think she has very low blood sugar. And when will the doctor be here?"

Nurse Grant heard the panic behind the humor in Ms. Hamilton's voice and saw the misery in her eyes. "I know this is not easy for you, but if you can be patient. I'll see what I can do." She patted Elizabeth's hand. "If you don't want to face your daughter, just sit here with us for a few minutes until the doctor arrives. I'll have an assistant take her some orange juice."

"Thank you…anything." Elizabeth raised and dropped her hands in resignation. "I can't catch a break. I was beside myself when she was in the coma, couldn't wait for her to be out of it. She came out of it and wouldn't remain awake. Now, this! Not that I wish her back in that state, but I don't recognize her. I brought her up to respect her elders. She was always polite and sweet." Elizabeth felt uncomfortable, not wanting to confide in this stranger, though she felt compelled to explain herself. "I'm sorry she was so rude to you. It was uncalled for."

"I don't think she understands her situation, Ms. Hamilton. Oftentimes, people are very upset and confused being in a hospital and they overreact. Until their sensorium clears, it's like a psychosis. The doctor knows. He will explain things to her. Maybe he'll suggest counseling. Sometimes it's recommended after injuries such as hers."

Elizabeth sat in the chair behind the white counter in the nurse's station. She was overtired, stressed, and not thinking clearly herself. Maybe she was overreacting to Deidre because she was emotionally drained and physically exhausted. She had barely slept two hours and Deidre had slept for days.

Inside the room, Mocha sat on the edge of the bed and thought. She had combed the room once more looking for her clothes. Walking around naked, wearing only a hospital shirt diminished her dignity and institutionalized her identity. She would receive the respect she deserved. But not here, where they expected you to passively grovel in gratitude as they shoved their guinea pig into a medicated cage and were shocked if healed, she revolted against the padded bars. Spying her mother's clothing, draped over the orange chair, Mocha picked up the blouse and held it against her body. Loose fitting, not her size, but near enough. Too bad there was no underwear. She removed the gown and quickly pulled on the blouse and buttoned it. She grabbed the slacks and hurriedly stepped into the left then right leg and drew them up to her waist. Intently preoccupied, her back to the door, she did not notice Elizabeth glaring at her from the opening.

"What are you doing?"

Mocha jerked around as she zipped up the pants. She sighed. "You are not blind, though you lack vision. You know what I'm doing."

Elizabeth strode over to her daughter and pushed her down in the chair. Off balance from dressing, Deidre sat abruptly then tried to get up. Elizabeth shoved her down, and gently put her hands on Deidre's shoulders, keeping her down. "Please listen to me, Mocha," she referred to her daughter by the loathsome nickname Deidre used with her friends. "Please."

Mocha struggled against her, but Elizabeth had the advantage, so she became passive. Words were more effective anyway, if said with power. "I told you I was hungry. I told you I am well. But something is not clicking up here." Mocha pointed to her head. "You're not getting it. So you backed me into a corner, giving me no choice but to take your clothes. I'm sorry. But would you have sent for mine if I had asked? No you would keep me here."

Elizabeth screamed "Mocha, you have been severely injured, You are not acting rationally. I am sure you have amnesia."

Mocha screamed back with a lower toned pitch. "I remember everything about my life. The only thing I don't remember is how I got here."

Both women stared at each other in silence, not giving in to look away. Mocha took in her mother's drained and downcast appearance. Once again, she felt pity for this woman whose grief cast an oppressive shadow. Mocha settled back in the chair resuming a stern calm and continued to study her adversary.

Elizabeth straightened up, removed her hands from Mocha's shoulders, turned away from her daughter, and sat on the bed. "Mocha, I promise you, we will leave after the doctor comes and they do more tests. This is for your safety. It is just to make sure there are no blood clots and no brain swelling. But you are vastly improved. It's miraculous."

"Will you be capable of keeping your promises, if others around you try to persuade you not to?"

"I will, Mocha, if I am convinced you will not be hurt."

"How easy it is to decide for others, even though you do not have the right. I cannot be held here against my will. I will not be held here, nor will they treat me without my consent."

Elizabeth felt herself grow cold inside. Her little girl was slipping through her fingers like water. She didn't know if she would be able to restore their closeness again, but she must try by regaining Mocha's trust. But what if she jeopardized her daughter's life in the process? It had happened with her son. She would not let it happen with her daughter. Elizabeth removed herself from her desolation, the eye of the hurricane. "Well, you have to stay until they release you. And the doctor must examine you before that happens. The hospital doesn't want to be held accountable, if something goes wrong. Frankly, I don't understand your attitude."

"It is not an attitude, it is a rationale. You cannot mend what is not broken."

"I would never forgive myself, if I agreed with you, and then something happened, like it did with Billy. Don't ask me to go through that again." Tears filled Elizabeth's eyes.

Mocha softened. "All right. We'll see what the doctor says, but if I don't agree with the prescriptions or treatment, it is my body, my choice, my decision. And I believe the tests will reveal I am normal."

Elizabeth nodded her assent. Let the doctor deal with her obstinacy. She changed the subject. "What is the last thing you remember?"

"The last thing I remember is being in St. Croix. It stopped raining. I had fifteen minutes to get to the dock and board the ship."

"You were never in St. Croix. That was a dream."

"It wasn't a dream. I remember it vividly."

Elizabeth agonized and changed the subject. "Do you remember being in the cemetery?"

"Yes. But that was days ago."

"What do you remember of it?"

"I was lying asleep and there were fantastic colors, an amazing kaleidoscope of colors."

"What happened before the colors?"

"I don't know."

"You were attacked, Mocha, by Beach Comber. He forced you to have oral sex and then he panicked. He strangled you, and left you for dead. Do you remember when…?"

"Can we not discuss this? I have been waiting patiently for the doctor who has yet to come. And I would like my breakfast which, I fear, will never come. It must be three o'clock. Anyway, after breakfast, I will remember for you...mother." She had trouble getting the word out of her mouth. "Perhaps we can order out? The food isn't good here anyway, I imagine."

There was no arguing with her daughter. Even before the accident she could be recalcitrant. It seemed the concussion only exacerbated the character trait.

Dr. Delacroix appeared in the doorway, a huge smile on his face. "Ah, the patient has recovered from her long sleep, I see." He walked over to the bed taking his tiny flashlight and stethoscope out of his white lab coat pocket. "How are you feeling?"

"I'm famished. I would like eggs and toast and tea, but no one around here seems to be listening to my self-diagnosis or able to get me anything." Mocha frowned prettily, like a petulant doll.

Elizabeth thought to herself wryly, well, her flirting abilities, always in abundance, had remained intact.

He shined the flashlight in her eyes. "Your light response appears normal." He listened to her heart beat, and checked her lungs. He motioned for her to sit on the bed and checked her reflexes. "All seems to be in order. Now, make the strongest fist you can." Mocha curled her fingers under, turning her knuckles white with the pressure. Then, with both fists she jabbed a one two punch, aiming at his chest. He grabbed her hands and told her to pull. She drew him in a jerking motion toward her. He nearly fell on top of her onto the bed. He laughed, recovering himself. "Now when I press your fingers downward, resist me." Mocha resisted. The doctor was unable to bend forward the fingers of either hand.

"I work out three days a week, when I'm not in a coma," Mocha joked.

"There's no weakness which is an excellent sign." He gently touched underneath her neck and jaw. "How does it feel when you swallow?"

"Fine, much better after I had two glasses of water earlier."

"You were able to get the water down?"

"Easily. I was very thirsty."

A young, slight, male nurse's assistant entered the room, nodded to everyone and placed a glass of orange juice on the tray stand, then left.

The doctor bent down to Mocha's face. "Open." He checked her tongue and looked at the back of her throat. The lacerations had disappeared. Her throat glistened with the reflected light of the instrument. He went to the stand and retrieved the glass of orange juice. "Please drink." Mocha swallowed the liquid. Without hesitation, she drained the glass. Dr. Delacroix shook his head in amazement. "I would never have said it was possible."

"That was what I needed, delicious."

Elizabeth smiled broadly. "Didn't you say something about there being more things in heaven and earth, than are dreamt of in medical science, doctor?"

Dr. Delacroix grinned and nodded his head. "And she is one of those things, I guess."

"She is walking steadily."

"So I hear." The doctor laughed. "Though we expected you to come out of it sooner, I must say, you have surprised us all."

"So when can I be out of here? And where is my food?"

"I think we should proceed cautiously. Run a few more tests. Make sure your blood work is normal, and the MRI and CAT scan don't show any new developments."

"Doctor, I am fine. Isn't a sign of wellness the return of appetite? Well, indulge me." She laughed and looked at Elizabeth for encouragement.

Dr. Delacroix shook her hand. "Glad to see you back. Your food should be up shortly. Ms. Hamilton may I have a word?"

Mocha watched as they walked out of the room together, Dr. Delacroix's hand on her mother's shoulder. She resented being excluded from a conference that was solely about her. Once she got out of here, things were going to change. Like camera flashes, details of her life and significant events were returning. She pictured their house, her room, Billy's illness. He was in hospice, and she had been trying to get him well. That's how she landed here.

All of the facts were there in her resilient mind, but something had happened. She had changed. She had broken through to another self which she preferred to the old one. She felt confident, more autonomous. She felt strangely powerful after a lifetime of feeling unsure and off balance. She would no longer run after the good opinion of others, modeling their standards and their lifestyle as her own. That way was self-alienation, doubt, weakness. Now, she could discover the infinite boundaries of her identity and cast off the manipulations of those once close to her. Things were different and there was no going back. Elizabeth's little girl was no more. A perceptive, prescient and assertive black woman had taken her place.

Chapter Twenty-Four

Madeline played the quail as the relentless hunters roamed the cemetery grounds attempting to flush her out of the thickets near the family mausoleum. She was tired and hungry. The more desperate she grew, the more vulnerable she became. Her pursuers were ghouls to keep up this chase for hours. Because of her exhaustion, she assumed they eventually would tire and become bored. Then it occurred to her that they enjoyed terrorizing her, and kept up the pursuit for that purpose. She was the evening's entertainment, more intriguing than *Halo III*. At the end of the game she would be their reward. She wondered if they would have the energy.

Thank God the night was cool but not cold, otherwise she would have headed back to the family mausoleum, or broken into another mausoleum and been easily trapped. Earlier, near her first hiding place in the piney bushes on mausoleum row, they had tampered with the doors of each crypt, forced many of them open and walked into others, whose doors were not properly fastened. With the crashing of each break in, the giving way of the doors, her nerve endings electrified and stung her whole body. It took a superhuman effort not to panic run, to hold on with patience, as the execrable degenerates ransacked the mausoleum adjacent to her hiding place, and finding nothing, smashed the beautiful, old stained glass window, darkening it forever with their malice. At that point she had lost respect for them. She took back the power she had given them with her fear, and in her imagination, painted them wearing the pink cotton dress of the playground bully.

Resigned to the futility of their search at the mausoleums, the marauders walked to the other end of Old Calvary, Madeline thought, in the direction of the entrance. From her prickly hiding place, she watched their dark figures disappear behind a bank of trees. Crawling on her hands and knees, with eyes shut, she pulled herself out from her scratchy lair, and aching, stood up. She had crouched in that spot for at least two hours, and the shooting pains in her knees and legs so cramped and crippled her, she didn't think she could run or even walk. In the shadow of one of the smaller crypts, she had bent forward, stretched, and stomped her feet to shake out the pins and needles. Her rubbery legs limp, she nearly fell but she steadied herself against the outer crypt wall. Gradually, as the blood circulated, feeling came back, restoring solidity and strength to her limbs that had been like malleable reeds.

Madeline strained all her powers of hearing to listen for the men's voices or tramping sounds. The night had returned to silence. She breathed freely and reached in her pocket for her cell phone, the first chance she had gotten to use it with impunity. The battery was worn down. She phoned her attorney's cell, no answer. She texted a call back message with "emergency" in caps. Madeline looked at her watch incredulously. Was it 11:30 PM? The last time she looked at her watch had been when she was hiding near the mausoleum. She had been dodging these reprobates for over two hours. She shook her head in self-criticism. Soon it would be early Friday morning. Of course, her attorney wouldn't be in his office, and she didn't have his home landline number. She called her friend Esther.

After the eighth ring, Esther picked up, groggy with sleep. "Yeah?"

Madeline whispered, "It's me, I'm in trouble."

"Yeah?"

Her friend was still sleeping. "Esther, I am looking for Peregrine at Old Calvary Cemetery, and I'm being chased by grave robbers."

"Yeah?"

"Esther, are you listening to me?" Madeline scolded, raising her voice.

"What? Madeline? Where are you?"

She said faintly, "I'm at Old Calvary and I'm stuck here trying to hide from some gang members who want revenge because I kicked in their balls."

"What?"

Esther sounded awake. "Listen, call the police and send them here. Tell them your friend is in trouble and a gang is after her at Old Calvary cemetery in Queens." Then Madeline thought better of it. She would try without police involvement and the attendant publicity that would follow.

"No, I will try to handle this myself, but I need the help of some guys. Can you find Bill's landline number?"

"Yeah, I'll get it. I'll tell him to bring his PI friends. They're real thugs."

"Great. I don't want to involve law enforcement because I can't answer their questions. But I need protection and someone has to know where I am in case I don't return."

"In case you don't return? Sounds bad. I'm calling 911."

"Well, it's not good, but I've figured out what to do. Let's try my way first. Just get his number."

"Hold on."

Madeline waited for Esther. She would make a run for the parking lot as soon as she was off the phone. But what if the cretins were waiting for her? Esther returned and

Madeline gave her the Queens number.

"I thought he lived in Manhattan."

"He lives near you."

"Thanks. I'll call him, but just in case, you call him, too in about ten minutes to make sure. Tell him to bring his team and have them bring their guns. I don't know what I'll run into here." Madeline's voice trailed off.

"Will you be OK? I'm going to call the police anyway."

"No. There are too many issues that I can't deal with concerning my family. If the police know, then the press will know. I can't risk it. But if you don't hear from me or Bill by tomorrow morning, then call the police and send them here. OK?"

"Yeah. I would come out myself."

"There's only room for one crazy here, but thanks." Madeline clicked off the phone.

She pressed down on the menu for another number and secured it. She started to leave a text message but the battery died out with a beep. She pressed the numbers *3370# to recharge it when she saw a circular patch of bright white dripping off her body and diffusing into unnatural fragments that brought into focus a patch of grass here, a white marker there. She turned as if in slow motion to apprehend a loud crashing behind her and rushing sounds as bushes whipped to a chorus of heavy tramping. Precisely at the moment she lifted her leg to spring a running leap, she was slammed by the force of a man who had jumped on her and dragged her down. As both smashed into the ground, the momentum of their colliding bodies slid them from the gravel path to the grass. As they grappled to a halt, Madeline threw the phone away from her into a landscaping of box hedges, praying that the beast breathing into her ear was distracted by her behind twisting into his groin.

"Mindless distraction, technology; it will be the death of us all." A gruff voice intoned and followed up with deep throated laughter. Another higher voice added three short barks, which Madeline assumed was the equivalent of a laugh.

They had tracked her like blood hounds, and now the blond was on top of her. In one rapid movement he rolled off and raised himself to a kneeling position. The wind had been knocked out of her and she was in shock from her fall and their attack. As she attempted to normalize her breathing, the Aryan flipped her over easily with huge paw-like hands, then raised himself on one leg, and lifted the other to straddle her body. Then he sat on her abdomen with his legs bent and spread outward like a huge insect. The breath went out of her again, and she madly gasped for air. Grabbing her shirt, he pulled her toward him so her hair dangled backward. He inched slowly closer to her face, and she felt his hot breath upon her nose and cheeks.

"Who were you calling just now, the police?" In silent concert, the dark haired, short one shined the flashlight heavy into her eyes, initially startling her and making her look away to adjust to the brightness.

Panting more from the intensity and shock of the blow than fear, Madeline moved her mouth but nothing came out.

The blond shook her and screamed with deafening volume. "Who were you calling? The police?"

Madeline shivered and regained her breath but her voice came out like a wisp, faint, curiously Marilynesque. "No, my friend."

"So we're going to have company? Well, by the time the police come, we will all have left in your Mercedes. It will be one of those bogus 911 calls that end up in oblivion like you, if you give us any trouble."

"Ah, Messier X, women are nothing but trouble. Do her now." The dark haired one of shadows stood behind her, but she recognized his speech as completely American and parochial.

Madeline looked at the Aryan and studied his face in the diffusion of light. He had cold blue eyes and longish blond, yes, that was it, almost platinum blond straight hair. He looked Swedish, an Aryan master race type, with an angular jaw and sharp nose. He was gorgeous, photogenic. And Madeline would make sure his picture circulated all over the world, if she ever got out of there alive.

Monsieur X was staring into her eyes. She recoiled at his gaze. Was it admiration?

The Latin, Monsieur X referred to as Mauricio, saw the exchange between them and joined his friend standing by his side, shining the flashlight directly into her eyes. She turned her head away. X sized her up in the light of her profile. She imagined he was deciding what to do with her.

Madeline set her course to give them what they wanted. She turned her head and squinted into Monsieur X's ice blue eyes. "I have money, much more than you would get if you chopped up the Mercedes or me. I'll give it to you or have someone bring it, my attorney. Only let me up, I feel sick."

"Why are you here?" The Latin moved in closer but with the light in her eyes, he was a towering darkness. She was afraid he would kick her in the head and cave in her skull.

"I came looking for my daughter." She strained to look up at him while X pressed menacingly into her body. Madeline apprised Mauricio as the counterpart of his friend, a Mediterranean type, pick one of the above Spanish, Italian, Moroccan, Libyan, Grecian. He was more dynamic, younger than his friend; and frenetic, always moving, dancing like a boxer, while the other was circumspect and cautious, the brains of the crew. Together, the two couldn't be more stereotypical. If her situation were not so dire, she would be laughing until her stomach ached.

"You think we're dumb, you can play us?" The Latin motioned for the Aryan to lift her to her feet, which he did, hauling her up and ripping her blouse with the force of the pull. Mauricio screamed in her ear. "We're in charge now." He threw down the flashlight which hit a monument and dimmed and all three were equalized, thrown back into a tenebrous world of grey. Mauricio pulled her away from X, grabbing her blouse and arms. He shook her then slapped her so hard that she collapsed onto the grass on her hands and knees. She rebounded from the stinging welt of his handprint tattooed in red on her left cheek. He had done more than slap her, something was wrong. In the dimness of collapse, she felt herself fall forward like a rag doll and crumple to the ground. She smelled the earthiness of the grass and pretended she was unconscious so they would go away.

"Well, should we leave her? If we take her, trouble and more trouble. We travel light, remember? No questions, no hassles. Just take her car keys and the phone and disappear before the police arrive." X was matter-of-fact, rational. He picked up the flashlight and fiddled with it making it flicker brighter then dimmer then brighter again.

"Are you nuts? She's seen us."

"So what? She doesn't know what we look like." The blond man rollicked with laughter.

"Yeah," Mauricio gave out with his three short barks that sounded more like an animal's yelps than laughter. "No line ups for us."

Monsieur X held the light on her body as Mauricio's rough, crude hands searched her waist, her breasts then flipped her on her back to feel her front jeans pockets for the missing keys. She had thought to hide them in her underpants, and they had fallen in her crotch. In the seconds it took Mauricio to search her pockets, she had opened her eyes and closed them. Mauricio intuited the feint and squatted on the ground next to her, slapping her face and glancing another blow off her head. "You want me to give you something to remember before I do you?"

With full force and with a cat's stealth and faith in her uncertain strength, Madeline jabbed Mauricio in his right eye with her thumb, simultaneously raising her foot and kicking him in the groin. He screamed in pain and let go of his hold on her. Carried away from the momentum of her violence against Mauricio, who curled into a ball and rolled back and forth on the ground, whimpering, she jumped to her feet. But she was not ready for X who grabbed her around the arms and waist and struggled to wrestle her to the ground. He was stronger, and with his iron grip and muscular leverage, he lifted her up and threw her down. As she fell, she collided against a small headstone that broke into her flesh like a board breaking through glass. Madeline howled and flailed, kicking the grass with her heels and clawing the earth for a stone or rock to brain him. The

Aryan flung himself on top of her pressing into her body with his full weight. He locked her arms down with his hands. She gritted her teeth and spit in his face wriggling to free herself from his oppressive weight.

He laughed encouraged by her fight. "Can't you see it's useless? There are two of us, one of you." He pressed into her pelvis and dug his nails into the flesh of her arms as he brought his face inches away from hers.

"You don't want me. You want someone younger," Madeline panted turning her head from side to side, trying to bring up her right arm up to clobber him in the ear and distract him from feeling the keys with his groin.

He moved his face to hers and kissed her lips as if to penetrate inside her, possess her. Disgusted, Madeline couldn't hold the vomit down. The throw up came in a violent gagging motion that Monsieur X felt then tasted when a slime of bile trickled, then hurled out of her mouth. Horrified, he rolled back and away from her as she turned her head to the ground to cast up her riling stomach juices again.

"Uck. You bitch. I go to possess you and you throw up?" On all fours he scrabbled away from the stomach liquid, his lust overthrown by revulsion. In those precious moments, Madeline leaped to her feet and ran blind, jumping over grave markers and bumping against tall monuments that threw themselves in her path. She raced with exhilaration and freedom, extending a fifty yard distance between them by the time Monsieur X had recovered from his disgust to find the flashlight and run after her, with Mauricio limping behind in a forty-yard lag.

Madeline raced toward a dark clump of trees bordering a line of black monuments that were tall like obelisks with crosses at the very top. From the location of the men's cries and threats, she discerned they had confused her direction and had gone deeper into the graveyard when she had veered off into the tree-line. Taking advantage of the darkness, she stopped, perched herself behind a tree that was in back of the obelisks and knelt down on the ground, her hands on the rough trunk. She peeked out from its girth.

Monsieur X, who was forty feet to her right, was splaying the flashlight toward Mauricio who hobbled over and pointed in her direction. They would never give up the chase she thought in abject frustration, not until she had satisfied them. Though the phone was back there in the bushes by the small crypt, she still held the car keys. She slipped from the tree where she hid, to a tree next to it, then, with stealth crept to another, then another in a diagonal line down and away from them. In the shadowy darkness, she made out their figures. Heading toward her, they scanned the area in their path with the bright arc which led them like a dog straining on a leash. If they came into the grove, they would see her. She was twenty feet away. Madeline squatted down and quietly traced the leaves and earth with her hands, until she found a good sized rock. She stood up. The width of the tree blocked their vision of her. Still, they kept coming, their heavy, quick footsteps treading the ground.

"She's got to be here. Where else could she go?" Mauricio was convinced.

Still hidden, she ranged back from the tree and threw the rock to her right. It scraped and clattered, rebounding against a monument that was to the men's left.

"I told you! Over there." Monsieur X loped toward the diversion, and Mauricio trailed behind with deformed gait.

She must have done Mauricio more damage than she realized. Bad for her, good for him. He would have no compunctions about avenging himself. Moving deeper into the grove with each step backward, she obscured herself with the girth of this oak tree, and that maple, then another oak and another, slipping from tree to tree, as she peered out from their protection at the retreating figures. The darkness between them provided an invisible cloak. She hoped she would be able to work her way into the area of Old Calvary that was separated by a decline that ended in an abutment with a low stone wall.

While the predators blundered around the headstones, and pawed and stomped the bushes around the gravesites in the area where she had thrown the rock, they screamed epithets and threatened what they would do when they caught her. Clearly, their wounded egos groined them more roundly than she ever could. Smiling, Madeline managed to slink down to the ravine, then bracing herself, she left the security of the trees. In a crouching position, she scurried toward the low stone wall. Plunged in darkness, she couldn't see the hunters and their dim flashlight. But she was in danger of being sighted in the open field of gravestones, if they stood at the top of the hill and looked to the valley. She prayed they wouldn't see her scampering to the stone fence of the lower level graveyard. In her favor was the distance between them, which she increased by sprinting along the boundary wall that separated division A from division B. When she felt safe enough, she slowed her pace to a stop, then slithered on her stomach over the four foot high boundary of mortar and field stones into the next section.

Madeline wasn't familiar with this part of Old Calvary, which lay in a valley below the gentle sloping hills where her family crypt was situated. She flew along the serpentine paths, fearful Monsieur X's stalkers' intuition or Mauricio's wolf ears would apprehend her exertions across the city of the dead. With all her frantic racing, she had lost her bearings, not knowing whether she was nearer or farther away from the parking lot. She stopped to rest, inhaling deeply, amazed at her pluck and stamina. When her breathing was a normal rhythm, she picked up her jog, doubling back to the path where she believed she had made a wrong turn. Her shoe heel shied off a stone in the pathway, and she stumbled and fell hard on her chest onto a barren patch of unkempt ground, overlooked by the cemetery caretakers. Again her breath escaped and it took a minute of raspy hysterical panting for its return.

Now the accumulation of the evening's vicissitudes caved in her will. She panicked. They were coming. They would kill her; take her car. Peregrine would never be found. Tonight would be the sum total of her existence. She was stupid to come here without friends and stay so long. In anxiety, she glanced around, while she attempted to pull herself together. Looming above her head was a circle of dark monuments. From her supine position, she realized their configuration was like a miniature Stonehenge. If she had been running or standing upright, she easily would have missed the geometrical patterns because at eye level, the tombstone arrangement looked ordinary. Madeline imagined the monuments were situated in this fashion with great humor, so the deceased family would have easy conversational access to both the whole and the particular members, rather like Dorothy Parker's Algonquin round table, but probably less acerbic. She crawled within the stone circle and leaned her back against a monument that faced in the direction of the upper graveyard, Division A. She felt safe amongst the towering six foot monuments, grateful for the chance to renew her strength and cleanse her emotions with hope.

Madeline glanced at the luminous dial on her watch. Forty-five minutes had passed since she confronted her attackers. She wondered if Esther had contacted Bill, and if he was at the gates of Old Calvary, waiting for her with his friends. She was too frightened to make a run for it, sure that the grotesques, like Notre Dame Gargoyles, would swoop down and intercept her before she reached safety. In any case, if Mauricio and Monsieur X went to the parking lot, there would be a surprise for them. But, then they probably anticipated that and wouldn't go. No, they would look for her in the cemetery until dawn.

She prayed, that during the lull in the chase, they didn't go to her car and get her personal information for future use to make her life a misery. As it was, she wouldn't feel comfortable in her house with these cretins at large. Forced to hire a sleep-in body guard until circumstances quieted down and she felt safe, which might be never, she would be looking over her shoulder, haunted by Mauricio's menacing threats and Monsieur's flat-line kiss. Even if she knew their identities, pressed charges and took out court orders against them, what would the imperfect justice system do? Keep them in jail for a while, and then what? After their release, they could stalk her like avenging devils. They didn't seem the types to forgive and forget. Her mind backtracked. Of course, this was predicated on the assumption that she would live to see another day, and they wouldn't "do her" as Mauricio so charmingly suggested.

No, she decided. Staying until dawn was not an option. She had to get her car out of there. She would make a run for it in an hour. In an hour Bill and his friends were sure to be there. Maybe they would vault the gates and come with flashlights to rescue her with an adventurous flourish. An aggressive problem solver who never seemed to let anything daunt him, Bill was an intimidating litigator with political connections all over the city. No one ever dared take him on willingly, unless they were callow, suicidal or cavalier in warfare and supremely unlucky. He was the only one she could call, not law enforcement, which was oftentimes an ineffective means to a dead end.

Quietly, carefully, Madeline patted down the lumpy grass and crisscrossed her legs, tucking her feet under her knees in a partial lotus.

Again, she leaned her back against the obsidian stonework. In her heart, she thanked the family for their unusual circle of monuments, whose wide, smooth surface and unique geometrical arrangement provided a perfect, open hiding place. From her position, she could spy anyone approaching in front and in the periphery of her vision, and be completely invisible to their sight lines.

All was peaceful. The jackals had made no echoing calls and screamed no more taunts or threats. In weariness, Madeline drifted, shutting her eyelids, then she struggled to open them. She must stay awake, leave soon. She yawned, and minutes later nodded off. This time she did not awaken. Her head fell forward onto her chest, and her mouth opened, taking in and expelling air in noisy breaths.

The cemetery was bathed in darkness. Wispy cirrus clouds in horizontal streaks feathered the stark, dreary moon, gazing down coldly from its dimming perch in the heavens. Madeline slept, insensible to the forces and fates swirling around her. The despoilers, wearied by their search for the dark haired she-wolf, had returned to mausoleum row and with the broken flashlight pawed the ground for the cell phone. Not finding it, they headed back toward the Johnson mausoleum, where they entered into the swaddling clouds of evil that plumed out from the mausoleum's open door. Monsieur X sat with Mauricio on the top step of the portico. Like errant war-lords surveying their extensive domain, they drank from a bottle of magical elixir that Mauricio had stashed in the hedges. They passed the thick, purple liquid, poisonous to humans, back and forth between them. With each swig, they received renewed energy coursing through their veins. Bravado and brio fueled their laughter, which galloped into the night across the dry, fallow, stone fields, and played up the steps into the mausoleum's black maw. The more they guzzled, the stronger in spirit they became. Their human manifestations weakened and dimmed, until with the aid of the tonic, they had fully shape-shifted from matter to anti-matter, negative materiality, invisible substance of spiritual flesh and bone, shuffling off their mortal coils as Monsieur X and Mauricio, and returning to their demon states as Abracix and Oxelox.

The demons were off their intentions for the evening, distracted by their futile search for the woman and their excessive thirst for this forbidden nectar of the spiritual underworld, a distillate of henbane, Datura and monkshood. As they plied the thick, alchemical restorative down their invisible, but substantive throats, they swapped high flung stories of former conquests, further disarranging their apprehension of reality and stirring forgetfulness of the significance of their surroundings at this hour of the night. Exaggeration danced between the hard facts of attempted haunts and possessions, and their need to find new habitation until gradually, the sorcerous concoction enchanted them away from the gloom of the crypt's realities and their present enslavement to it.

After Abracix and Oxelox had drained the last drop of talismanic ambrosia, they readied themselves for the second phase of the potion's incantatory effects, hypnotic transcendence to a higher plane of power. They were oblivious to the time, 3:00 AM, the hour of destiny. At this specific hour, if a human soul is in extremis between life and death, time pounds an ever increasing crescendo that intensifies the turbulences between continuation and finality. During the ticking of each second of each minute, the moribund soul wrestles the spirit world. It hovers, vying between life dimensions and oblivion, until it fastens its hold on life, or relinquishes it to vaporizing death which inhabits the temple, declaiming its mortality. In the realm of spirit, the commensurate is the hour of infinity which ticks off three thousand six hundred seconds as time slows to naught. In infinity, the phantom soul struggles between freedom and tyranny. The battle waxes greater and greater until it climaxes at the last second of the last stroke, when the specter chooses, and its final impulse crashes down eternity. Then, the human hour of destiny and the spirit hour of infinity passes to return again for each soul traveler.

Abracix and Oxelox were ignorant of the metaphysics of human soul struggles not being of the pertinent species. And they had forgotten the significance of the hour of infinity on their spectral souls. They were spellbound, sprawled on the concrete steps, alchemized in a trance. They drifted and became the imagined rulers of deeply wicked realms; they consorted with shining principalities; they dreamed of a time when they would be elevated from the humiliation of their oppressed, lesser lot, to an exalted wicked state.

As the seconds progressed to encompass the first full minute of the hour, in the back of the crypt in the large room with no electrical wiring or any gadgets of modernity, the air became oppressive and unhealthily still, as it does before a cataclysmic event, an earthquake or volcanic eruption. All regular sound ceased, tamped down as if a great vacuum drained the living noises from the earth and distilled them into one soft, prolonged note, on a scale beyond the apprehension of human or animal hearing. The spiders ceased their spinning. The night watches in the wall halted their clicking, and even microscopic organisms became transfixed in their mediums. Everything in the room was suspended in a steady state.

But there was movement. A stone figure blacker than the surrounding blackness had lowered its outstretched arm with the crash of a thunderous rockslide. The noise lasted but a nanosecond. As the sound exploded into the nitrogen-oxygen rich atmosphere, the vacuum wave sealed it from animal hearing; and the echoing booms that resounded throughout the sixth realm of the spirit world, were the effervescent flutter of a moth wing in an alternate material reality. Slowly, with measured action, the blackly animate statue lifted its left leg and secured a step forward. Another explosion resounded and evanesced into a butterfly wing's flutter. Seconds ticked by. The figure only had the space of an hour to work its way to the mausoleum entrance and back to its place of permanence. With method and rapidity, it inched toward the door, laboring under the heaviness of atmosphere, moisture and gravity, and all the earthly elements that humans take for granted. In the realm of spirit, demons of Baal-peor and seducers of Jannes and Jambres howled as the thunderous explosions rolled and careened to the edges of their terrain of doom. A spiritual eternity of trespass and burning would come and go, before the holocaust of tumult ceased and the figure would seal its course back to material immobility in its quiet section of the Johnson mausoleum.

Abracix and Oxelox floated in the ethers, unaware of what was laboring through the crypt at this hour. If they had been aware, it would have been too late. Better for them the respite which was one starlight away from a longer spell, whose end, only God would be able to reconcile.

Madeline slept deeply and calmly. She dreamed she was a farmer who, under the stars of a night sky, guarded her fields of seeded corn from predatory crows, as she anticipated a good soaking rain to spark germination and initiate the growth cycle.

None of these slumbering unnaturally in the cemetery, members of different species who constantly warred against the other, would have believed that they had little to fear from their antipathy and that a more baleful and monstrous knave that now straddled the supernatural and material plane of existence was indeed one thousand times more dangerous. Even if they had been able to open their eyes and look upon this fantastic hell-born creature that crept inch by inch toward the open door of its prison, the crypt, they could not have imagined the extent of infernal malevolence that would reverberate throughout their existence as a result of this night, this hour.

It was 3:30 AM, the precise median of the hour. The stone figure stood towering in the lintel of the mausoleum entrance. It glared out at the stone city of the dead, then looked down at the two unclean ones on the steps in the ecstasy of a magical elixir blackout. Their time of evil authority on the earth was forfeited. They had broken the Law and punishment must be exacted. An explosion of nuclear magnitude went out into the supernatural ethers. Cerberus howled in terror and a look of horror paled Hades' features to a blinder shade of white. The stone creature saw the incorporeal and conned the demons' location. It whispered an ancient, spectral word, and the word became vapor and swirled around and about the hellions, anointing their heads, their arms, torsos and legs, shape-shifting them back into a hybrid phantasmal-corporeality.

Whoosh! Whirr, Whoosh! The stone scythe crackled electricity. It bit and crunched, easily slicing through Abracix's neck. The artery that vibrated energy in its vascular fragility burst open, rhythmically pulsating Abracix's black blood in a splattering, rushing river onto the concrete portico and over the stone figure's mammoth shoes. Abracix's eyes shocked open. His throat gurgled, sputtered and gushed, a spigot pouring ethereal essence. The scythe had chopped through phantasmal vertebrae. It snapped energy channels, severing the head from the body with a majestic sweep and swoosh. Abracix's open eyes stared inward. He watched his being fragment, and images of his past blur and disintegrate. The stone creation forcefully retracted the scythe. The dripping, matted head flew up, dislodged from Abracix's body that spasmodically shook and twitched. Then, it rolled to the portico edge and bumped and bounced down the concrete steps, smearing trails of thick, black, clotted gore in its wake.

Bleary in his trance, Mauricio/Oxelox awakened to crunching noises and the sight of Abracix's staring, blank eyes and dripping head twirling up, cresting, then plunging down in an arc. With shocked recognition, he heard splats of black liquid spirit and flesh-like mash thump and slap the concrete steps. Above him he saw the hungry sky's deep indigo curtain, and in the next instant, an immense black, stone scythe reeling toward him. In that twinkling of an eye, he spun to the edge of the third and fourth concrete risers where he had lain in a frozen stupor. He teetered precariously then fell off, flying and rolling in the air. He crashed and broke the bushes on the crypt's right side and slammed into the ground with a painful thud. In his last moments of sanity, Oxelox felt the indignity that comes with infernal demonic outrage. Then he crossed over the thin, black line into hell-spawn madness. He craned his neck toward the stone creation reigning on the top step and peeled out poisonous howls, virulent clamors that bridged and echoed through the corporeal and incorporeal realms with pestilential fury. He would awaken the heavens to this injustice that swarmed over him like a million bloodthirsty canker worms, lusting to parasite his energy.

Clump. Supernatural roarings, monstrous explosions in the sixth spirit realm. Clump, demoniacal torrents coursing and reverberating through the rings of the Inferno. Clump, the figure plodded the steps, coming, scythe raised to destroy for all time the condemned fiend that was Oxelox. Outrage that had been ignited with one blow would be dashed out with another.

Oxelox lay on his back, helpless, terrified at the incongruity of black, inert mobility. The figure tread toward him. With focused intention it stepped off the crypt's bottom riser. Crunch. Whish. The blade cleaved the air above him, gashed downward and grazed his shoulder, as Oxelox spun to the left. In that instant he looked into the creature's eyes. He saw a malevolence worse than death, worse than judgment, a malevolence that converted Apollyon into a fairy tale monster.

The stone creation lifted the scythe high in the air for the final renunciation. Oxelox jumped to his feet, leaped and waded through thick hedges and hurtled himself around the corner of the mausoleum. An elder magus of the Neri through an occult ceremony had fashioned the stone creation and appointed his destiny: guard the crypt after an Oblivion, and preside over the effects. Knowing this rule of the Law and using the creation's restriction to his advantage, Oxelox shuttled around the back of the crypt, booming his horror in thunderous shrieks. He ran because he knew there was a heaven and a hell, and he ran to fulfill this knowledge. In terror he would be running through one tortuous incorporeal realm after another, exceeding all the dimensions until he reached into eternity where he would race to the edge of time's gloom.

The stone creature grimaced and sneered as it conned the sounds of Oxelox's mortifications, his retreat and surrender, falling away into the distant tree grove. The Law of Powers was strict. The punishment adequate. The demons had forgotten the rule, floating in their intoxicating spell. One suffered the forfeit, a warning to the other. Now Oxelox must enact a human sacrifice for restoration, adhering to the conditions of the Law, or both would be slaves of the crypt with no respite of possession. The Master had acted. So be it!

The inanimate incarnation stomped back up the concrete risers. Gradually, the blasting reverberations throughout the planes of spirit softened their undulations and grew faint. As the creature stalked upward, the gore on the steps of the mausoleum portico dried up and withered away. The black bloody spirit mash, and Abracix's head and body particalized into elements visible only to the demon Oxelox. Abracix was, and was not, as his identity as Monsieur X, was and was not. To the naked human eye, his head and body were indistinguishable from the molecules of the landscape. His authority had evanesced. Had he ever existed? Certainly, he had not died. He had achieved oblivion, consigned to an absence of existence in the darkness of the vacuum, alone, and waiting for restoration, if the Law of Powers was obeyed.

It was 3:58 AM. The phenomenon entered the crypt and the door automatically shut behind it. In the sixth plane of spirit all was calm and bright. In the graveyard of corporeality, all was still once more. And then...

Startled, Madeline awakened. Blood curdling noises sounded in the area of dark trees. In the valley beyond the wall between divisions, the lost and damned howled. Someone was playing a tape from a lunatic asylum. They had turned it up to the highest volume and dotted speakers and amplifiers throughout the cemetery to drive her mad and flush her out into the open. The evil tumult intensified. Gruesome images cavorted and molested her peace. Bones cracked and splintered. Pectorals were excised. A man's heart was plucked from his fractured rib cage. Disembowelment, gutted entrails drawn out in thickened gore and feces on the ground in piles. Human abattoir. Macabre scenes flumed redundantly in her liquid imagination. She leaped to her feet and emerged from the circle of safety into the open lot of graves. The lunatic's braying augmented. It was coming her way.

Madeline, in high agitation and without thought for her direction, plunged into a wild gallop. Hours ago she raced to elude predatory hunters. Now she flew to outpace the tortures of the insane. The bedlam widened to a swelling din. It was thundering toward her. She must accelerate her flight. Through exhaustion and fear, she must cheetah fly, antelope dash, greyhound gallop, zigzag, hurtle, blast herself to warp velocity. She was hounded by a mash of flesh and bloodiness that evoked maniacal trumpeting. Escape, flee and warp to feral animal instincts to speed, speed away.

Fear of contagion, of the pestilential terror seeping into her soul, maddened her flight. She catapulted around stones, bolted over markers. She pitched in and out of serene plots with massive angelic monuments, her heartbeats skirting the edge of arrhythmia. The insane was scudding close behind her, ready to shoot out ahead so she would be the damned, the lost, like a specter flying in gloom. Yes, he was gaining on her. His baying uproar rose to booming pandemonium then in a crescendo it heightened in ferocious screeches until the shrieks became her own.

She trampled and galloped to free herself, to free him. She and he were one, and together they must whoop and surge, howling sirens of the night. Adrenalin spurt after adrenalin spurt jerked Madeline up and over granite hurdles, until her exertions rushed her into the lights of the parking lot one quarter mile away. She was going to make it. She was lightning fast.

Dreading the loneliness to come if she escaped him, the hellebore hallooed. The clangorous chords, like earsplitting bell tones, vibrated her soul and captured her mind. Madeline, demon oppressed rocketed an echoing, trumpeting call. His dreadful balefulness had penetrated her soul.

"Madeline, Madeline. It's OK. I'm here. It's OK." Bill quickened his steps down the rungs of the metal ladder that hung on both sides of the fence. He was helped down by a burly member of his security team who held the ladder firmly until Bill was on solid ground. Both men stood inside the cemetery gates and watched the panic engorged, dark-haired Lilith scramble and leap over headstones as she screamed, careening toward them.

Madeline was upon the gates. The whooping clangor was in and around her, entering her, encompassing her being. Without full cognizance of him, she slammed into Bills' chest, knocking him against the fence. As he recovered his balance, she collapsed in his arms, heaving and panting, unable to catch her breath. He hugged and comforted her like one would do for woman who has just witnessed the death of her child.

Watching the embrace from a distance, Oxelox infernally roared and after a final wretched wail was silent. Madeline threw back her head and opened her mouth, like a gaping cavern. She bayed in tumultuous commiseration, releasing all the misery of the world in her baneful cries.

"Banshee, hellion," Bill fretted as he smothered her face in his chest to still her aching shrieks. The woman he loved had gone mad.

Chapter Twenty-Five

Like her mother, Peregrine had spent most of the night escaping the terrors in Old Calvary. Unlike her, she had scrabbled through caverns and passageways below ground. If a cross section had been cut into the earth directly underneath the parking lot, it would have revealed that only fifteen feet of earthworks, stones and mortar separated the Randolfs. But it

might well have been the distance between The Milky Way and Andromeda Galaxy, such was the emotional and psychic distance between the two women, who each warred against her own realms of personal evil, and the desire to self-implode and renounce all that was resplendent and fruitful in their lives.

As a heavily sedated Madeline was chauffeured away by Bill and his security team, Peregrine sat in complete and irrevocable darkness. Though one quarter of the oil was left, her torch had eaten through her socks and a good portion of her right sneaker, the burning smell of which suffocated her in the close and stagnant air of the tunnel. She eventually put out the flames with her other sneaker, but had to inch ahead in the darkness nearly four thousand paces before she reached clean, pure air once more. As debilitating as the incident was, it spurred her on, for she realized there must be some way oxygen was filtering into the tunnels, perhaps through holes or a large entrance or exit. She knew she must persist to find it, and the realization gave her the hope that her exertions underground were not in vain.

Except for her thong and the scarf around her bosom, she was naked and her filthy, stinking body seemed a magnet for various insects that luxuriated in the blackness of the underground labyrinth, extending out from the Johnson mausoleum. On patches of her arms and legs she had scratched herself bloody with dirty fingernails. She itched all over and in the places where she scratched, the festering wounds oozed with infection. Desperate, she considered taking out the priest's robe, but hesitated, fearful that the wearing would produce a terrifying supernatural death. The clean robe was only used in sacred ceremonies on specific dates by the worthy. It was not to be abused for any other purpose. Wearing it, in disrespect of its holiness, was suicidal oblivion. Even the slimmest possibility that she could escape this prison, stopped her from imagining the silkiness of the robes which would be a balm against her fetid skin. Atheists and agnostics could afford the luxury of fear and unbelief. She could not. Faith demanded rigor, constancy and courage. If she fouled the robe, she would nullify the conditions necessary to inhabit the supernatural powers she, Mocha and Fen desired. Surviving the torments of the mausoleum, she had conquered death, and though he was stalking and lurking in every dark corner of the caverns, she would chance her escape without the robe. Her sufferings would not be in vain, even if she physically perished.

Peregrine's challenge to survive had been ratcheted up another level. Though the swelling in her ankle had decreased, her right knee still ached and galled. It slowed her progress in the tunnels and hampered her ability to bend, sit, lie down or squat, so she had difficulty relieving herself. As often as attempted, she begrimed herself with urine and feces which she cleaned off with the straps of her back pack with little success, especially after her recent bouts with diarrhea.

Peregrine recognized coolly that her physical and mental condition worsened by the minute. The countdown to coma was three quarters of the way wasted and she was no nearer discovering a tunnel exit. She hobbled forty paces or so, blundering against the tunnel walls then found she must collapse to the ground to rest. But her rest or sleep was never prolonged or sound, for spiders, bugs and the occasional mouse attracted by her noisome scent crawled over and about her body with impunity. Revolted by their audaciousness and imaginings of being bitten by rats, snakes and poisonous insects, she fell to itching, slapping and ripping her flesh, so self-mutilation accompanied sleep. She had not closed her eyes more than two hours at a stretch during her time underground. And she attributed her growing enervation and listlessness to her inability to bathe in the recuperative cessation of all thought, so her unconscious mind could untangle the day's labors and horrors.

In the tunnel, there was no day or night. She found the repressive sameness of her environs maddening, and coupled with her lack of sleep, hallucinogenic. Twice in the torchlight she had envisioned mundane objects, a water fountain and desk. She understood the association of the first was like a mirage, though not generated by the heat. When she visualized the desk, she realized it was a sign of utter madness caused by exhaustion. How much longer could she go on? The answer would be revealed soon enough.

She sustained all of these ills and torments and became inured to each devolution of her personal hygiene and dignity, but there was one she could not sustain, her thirst. With rabid and severe ferociousness greater than what she experienced in the crypt, Peregrine hungered for water with every molecule of her existence. More than to escape from her earthen dungeon, her need for water consumed her. She was an addict, obsessed with the cooling thoughts of anything liquid. Her lips cracked and bled for lack of moisture, her saliva and all the wetness of her tongue, throat and mouth had dried up or receded into her body to replenish her shrinking organs that were drying into prunes. She imagined the insides of her mouth were coated with white dust or ashes. That was the taste on her swollen tongue until she passed it over her teeth that like a serrated knife, cut the protruding member, releasing tiny molecules of thickened, metallic tasting blood. Cry to God for relief? She couldn't. Her tears had dried up.

This compulsion for water, infuriated all the more, when the watery diarrhea struck. The precious liquid she so desperately craved was delivered from the wrong end. Had she gotten dysentery from tasting the water in the large room in the tunnel days ago? Another worry was that she hadn't urinated in hours. Were her kidneys slowing their function, tolling the death knell of severe life threatening dehydration?

After the diarrhea and her failed attempt to clean up, she found she no longer had the energy or patience to favor her aching right knee and scrabble with the iron spike to stand. When she crawled on all fours, excruciating ice picks stabbed the joint. Even if she attempted to straighten her right leg and drag it behind her, slugging along on her left knee and stepping with the palms of her hands inside her left sneaker and what remained of the burned right one, she made slow progress down the black passageway, growing even more tired than when she hobbled upright. So, she slithered and soughed on her belly like a lizard, using her hands and left leg to claw the dirt and wriggle down the tunnel.

At each snaking she was more reptilian. She was a slug for sloughing, an asp consigned to eat the dust of the earth. Bitterly, she thought how humbled, how low she had been brought by this experience. But her right knee could sustain the reptilian movement, and she grew exhausted only when she raced in competition with herself. If she kept a steady wriggle, she could slide beyond what she imagined to be a thousand yards. When she tired, she continued her momentum by turning to her right and rolling, rolling, rolling on the ground, lifting her back pack over her head to increase her forward momentum and avoid colliding with the wall.

Rolling was enjoyable and the least stressful physically and psychically. It was a childhood game she had played with her friends. The object was to see how many turns she could make without stopping. As children, they got up to ten before they grew bored. Now she was able to multiply her spins to the round number of twenty-five, after which she stopped, panting with the effort. In shifting her mind back to childhood, she distracted herself from her thirst and the likelihood no one would come for her in this maze of stolen hopes.

She spun down the tunnel, yelling aloud each time she completed a circumlocution: "Eighteen, nineteen, twenty, twenty-one..." She lengthened the distance another four rounds before she stopped, strangely exhilarated by the maneuvers. She felt she could spiral into eternity, and laughed to think that might happen. It didn't matter, after all. Though she might physically die meandering in this unholy night with snarled passageways that went nowhere, emotionally and spiritually, she had mastered her fear of death. Let it come as fate would determine. She was at peace and would make a good end.

Peregrine comforted herself with those thoughts, and for the first time in days dozed off to sleep. She slept profoundly though the insects scurried over the obstacle in their path. And every now and then, a mouse would scamper to her, drawn by the smell of a particle of orange or molecule of pomegranate juice, then spiral away at the realization that this being was not the food it sought, but a huge creature alive and dangerous.

She woke some hours later to needles and pin pricks on the calves of her legs. At first, she had forgotten she was in the cave. Peregrine thought she was in her room. She cried out for her mother, then realized that the dungeon was home, and she had blundered into a nest of fiery ants, who punished her for the invasion. She sat up and brushed them off as best she could. She felt for her back pack and hauled it in front of her, then struggled to her hands and knees. Surprisingly, and without the impossible agony, she was able to crawl away from the area where the ants simmered. Her sleep had refreshed her, though her thirst had heightened. She plucked two stray ants tickling her arm and in one unthinking gulp swallowed them. Bitter taste, but their juices sidetracked her obsession with water, though she would not go back to their nest to nourish herself. They were too revolting and gruesome to prevent her from vomiting, if she crunched down any more.

Peregrine continued scrabbling in the darkness for a time, until saws hacked her limbs in vengeance, and grinding paroxysms seized her stomach, compelling her to stop. Cramping dehydration. What had she done before to beat this back? She stretched out first one arm then the other, then one leg and the other. The lancinating spasms accelerated. How to excise the cankerous tribulation that spiked her belly and manacled her limbs? How to redeploy her will? Before, her body could register only so much torture, replacing one bitter cup for another, which could be drained with a change in position or intellectual venue. Now, she realized this full bodied and horrific persecution would not siphon off with mere reaction. It was systemic. She tried anyway.

Peregrine slumped from her kneeling position onto her stomach, then rolled onto her back drawing her left knee up to her chin. The cramping broadened. She moaned the force of her misery out her lungs and into the air. The tension amplified, undulating in waves. She panted at each tormenting arc, attempting to ready herself as it peaked, but was shocked as the waves elevated their misery, refusing to crest and crash. Peregrine rolled sideways to the right and left, rocking herself like a baby. Had she ever known a time before this burning hell corkscrewed her limbs and stomach? Hadn't she always lived with this crucifixion? Or had she felt a general peaceful nothingness in her body? She couldn't remember. Emotionally overwrought she reviewed the question over and over: was there nothing she could do for relief except kill herself?

Action was better than inaction. She turned onto her stomach, attempting to smother the burning tyranny. Maybe she had been bitten by a poisonous spider and her immune system was warring against the nefarious distillate, stirring up her blood and kicking her nerve endings. No, it was dysentery and the beginnings of third stage dehydration. The loss of vital minerals and elements, potassium and magnesium were probably flushed out with the last of the diarrhea. The body signaled distress by persecuting its host to alert her to the need for reformation. So, her crushing ordeal would last until the signals were expended. Then would come the easy progression: paralysis, coma, organ shutdown, the cessation of all things.

Rolling back and forth seemed to lessen the stomach burning and convolutions. Maybe if she worked through the paroxysms in her limbs as well, their flagellation would subside. Peregrine raised her torso with her hands and arms, bent her left leg and lifted herself to a kneeling position, favoring her right knee, which she gingerly bent. She bore down her weight, which she equalized with her left knee. Peregrine snailed forward, moaning, then collapsed onto her belly and rolled back and forth. No way to work through this woe by crawling. Since rolling seemed to help her belly, she would roll. With her back pack over her head, Peregrine proceeded as before, spinning a progress of five revolutions, jarring her limbs and squashing the spasms in her nerves by applying pressure to the throbbing areas. It was the next best thing to a massage in this rat hole.

Peregrine propelled herself in quarter-inch turns. Though her torments had not subsided, emotionally she felt she was receding toward some finality. Pressing her right side into the ground, she imagined she was coating herself with fine particles of soil, like covering a piece of meat with flour to seal its flavor. She smothered her belly, abdomen and bosom with dirt, dragging her back pack on the ground as she turned slowly to her left side, coating that with soil and dragging her back pack over her head, making a scrunching sound in the dirt.

She stopped and listened. There was something else underneath her pale moans and the sounds she made. What was that noise that seemed just below the threshold of her hearing, a low rumbling sound, then humming, then rumbling again? She panicked, grabbed by fear. Was it a cave-in, somewhere in the maze that, like dominoes, was collapsing each section of the passageway, until all flattened to dust? No. The sound wasn't gaining in momentum and forcefulness like a cave-in would. It was steady and fairly regular, and it was coming from outside the tunnel. Peregrine shrieked with joy. She knew what it was. Traffic, the traffic of an expressway or highway.

A particularly obtuse muscle seizure clenched both her legs, and she writhed and moaned until the wave climaxed then modulated like a tolling bell its dread, dull sounding. Despite this crucifixion, she must continue. The passageway might run parallel to a street, and then exit up into a stairway and manhole cover. Why else would its creators extend it so far, but for an escape route to a road where a quick get-away was assured? Peregrine turned to her right side to begin the rolling motion. She felt dizzy, but thought if she stopped, she would lack the passion to act, would just squirm and writhe, burning like a worm in the noon sun, giving up all possibility of rescuing herself. So she spun and revolved, squeezing her eyes closed to press out the fierce assault on her body.

In the double darkness with eyes shut, Peregrine didn't perceive the wall looming up in her path. She crashed into the earth and stone with a thud and explosion of fire. Holding her stomach, and panting with submission to her complaining limbs, she slowly sat up and felt the rough sides of the passageway which seemed to be slanting in two different directions outward from the main tunnel like a Y. She was at a juncture. Not another crossroads! Did these tunnel branches lead to freedom or did they double back to the crypt? She looked down each in futility, her eyes useless in the blackness. She would have to be guided by her intuition which was occluded by the uninterrupted thrashing in her limbs and stomach. She said a silent prayer, and turned on her right side dragging her back pack that had grown heavier with her weakness. She rolled into the left passageway, finished one circumlocution massaging herself with the stones and earth, then rolled back to the left, and entered the right passageway where she resolved she would continue. It was her final decision, her last choice, and she would affirm it even to her physical death.

Peregrine flushed with heat. Her temperature was rising probably from the infection in her body and maybe from the dysentery and the ant stings or spider bites. Did it matter the cause, the result was obvious.

Slowly, she spun again, again, powdering herself with the earth which was finer and less compacted. This was the less traveled way. She reduced her thoughts to their purest form a sentence, a word, an erasure, then a monotone, and listened to the steady rumbling sounds which she believed were enlarging. She rolled down a gentle decline, which swung to the right. She rested for a moment, but the pain thumped and bounded through her body, bathing her mind in red heat. So, she spun her circumlocutions down the curving passage which wormed to the right in a huge semi-circle.

If Peregrine had been crawling on her hands and knees, she would not have been able to sense the change readily. Her rolling exertions sent her feet or back pack banging and careening into the walls. In her torment, she realized the walls accommodated this architectural curvature. Had she made a mistake at the crossroads? Was the tunnel doubling back from where she came? She let the blackness blot out such thoughts as useless. From the windings of the labyrinth, it was impossible to gauge whether any of the passages doubled back. She would not allow the anxiety to further weaken her dire condition. Eventually, the curvature of the tunnel straightened, for she no longer bumped into the walls. She revolved straightaway, until exhausted and panting.

Peregrine focused her mind on the traffic rumblings then rested every three spins, though the respite turned into a boxing match with her whopping aches. Whether she spun or reposed, she suffered. When she compelled herself beyond her body, she was able to turn to her right through two circumlocutions before being ejected into an unendurable torture returning her back into her body. It was useless to try to escape with her imagination. Physical anguish was never mind over matter. You succumbed to pain's tyranny. It was about cessation, relief. Purification through suffering was a noble joke. The religious and spiritual prophets and martyrs who lived to tell about it...how did they endure being boiled in oil, burned in heated metal chairs, gouged, broken? They didn't. Foxe's *Book of Martyrs* must be a lie.

She thought she had to urinate, but nothing happened. No. She wouldn't let herself think about kidney shut down or anything else. She must forge on. Rah, rah. Forge on, bullshit. She was enervated, drained by this wretchedness. The rolling was not a massage, it was like being belted with a bat. She had spun her last. That was it. This cavern would be the cathedral where she took her vows with Death.

Moaning, Peregrine lifted herself to a sitting position then pulled herself back to the wall. She reached for her back pack which she decided to keep near her for comfort. She ripped open the flaps and searched inside, taking out the cross she had used as a torch handle. It felt cool and smooth to the touch, for she had stripped all evidence of charred cloth from the cross pieces which she imagined had been blackened by the burning. She recalled the exhilaration she had felt when she found the back pack with the food, water, relics and implements. What joy at the discovery which had extended her life for days.

She should never have sought escape through the labyrinth. She could have stayed warm by the stair bottom ready to hear someone open the door of the mausoleum and run up to meet him or her. Surely, someone would have searched the mausoleum by now, Beach Comber or Fen. But if she hadn't gone underground and no one had come, without the food and water she would have been dead by now, "a consolation devoutly to be wished." Instead, she had prolonged her life of horror and agony, producing the same result. It was a bitter irony. Death had beat her after all. Who would search for her here in this series of man-made passages underneath Calvary Cemetery? Probably no one even knew these tunnels existed. During her lighted sojourn down the tunnels, it appeared they hadn't been used for many years. This would be the last place anyone would come. She could rely on no one, had to get out under her own power. But her power was finished. She had failed.

As much as Peregrine had made peace with herself, she didn't want to die. She knew she wouldn't die spiritually, but she didn't want to die physically, leastways not yet. She had so much to live for, was so young. She had planned to live a long time, like that blind French woman who had made a CD when she was one hundred twenty years old. Living long and well was the best revenge, for the sorrows one encountered in life. But for her, there would be no revenge. When she had found her pack she had had her second chance and she had wasted it.

Peregrine sighed and groaned as a wave of savage nerves lacerated her in rebellion, bringing her mind back to the task at hand: the cross which she had desperately clung to during her reverie, and her back pack which she would burn, using the last of the oil to anoint her for Death. As she scratched the handle into the ground to dig a hole to secure it, she listened for the rumbling traffic sounds. They had diminished soon after she had taken the right fork of the merging paths, evidence she had taken the passage back toward the crypt. She fixed the cross securely in the dirt, prayed silently and waited, enduring the pain waves which she hoped would dissolve, but didn't.

As a mindless diversion, she concentrated on one childhood event. When she was nine, against her mother's wishes, she had secretly gone to Bible class with a friend and lied about it. Together in class, they proudly memorized the names of God, but she never found out what they meant, because the lesson would be completed the following Saturday and that Saturday never came. Madeline had discovered her lie and had called up Beth's mother to discuss her own religious views, and discourage more invitations. Madeline was a rabid apostate who flirted with atheism. Her lifestyle had no room for the fantasy of an unjust and cruel God. Although Peregrine didn't fully understand why, the phone call ended her friendship with Beth. For months afterward, in passive aggression, Peregrine occasionally would say the names of God to irk her mother. The day Madeline caught on and asked her to chant the names quickly three times, Peregrine never repeated them after that. She laughed at the memory. Her mother had been such fun to annoy.

"Jehovah, Jehovah Jireh, Jehovah Nissi, Jehovah Rapha, Jehovah Shalom." Not bad considering she hadn't spoken them aloud for fourteen years. She wondered why her mother refused to discuss spirituality or mysticism when her aunt had encouraged her to believe and shared stories of the family's heritage which was steeped in mysticism, the dark arts and magic.

Peregrine's stomach contorted with ferocity, kinking the fury downward into her legs. She clutched her abdomen and doubled over to squeeze out the throes of hell and send them to her feet and into her toes and out into the ethers. Plop. She had knocked the cross over with her leg. Grabbing her belly with her right hand, with her left, Peregrine pushed the cross solidly in the earth and patted the soil around its base. As she forced the harrowing cramps from her body, bending and rocking forward and pummeling her legs with her fists, she chanced to look down the passageway to her right. In the far distance was a circular speck of white.

She knew she was hallucinating, a pre-coma symptom. Eventually, the speck would become rounder and brighter until it consumed her and she fused with an eternal tunnel of light. She blinked her eyes, turned away then looked again. The speck was still a speck. Nothing had changed. She was not hallucinating.

"Oh God, why now?" she whispered having lost her voice to the raging fires in her throat. She was ready to die. She had no energy or will to investigate. She moaned in frustration. Her curiosity would not allow her to die in peace, without knowing what the speck was. Peregrine considered that she should rest first. She would make it there faster. But her rests were equally if not more enervating. It was better if she moved, regardless of her slowness. If she left her back pack, she could make it to the speck more quickly. If it turned out to be nothing, she would crawl back to the cross, throw the back pack over it, light it and die gladly. But this was a canard. If the "speck" was nothing, it would cruelly destroy her peace, and she wouldn't have the heart to go back and light her funeral pyre. But by then it wouldn't matter where she died.

Peregrine slid her bottom away from the cross and shoved her pack next to it. Then she lowered her back and head to the ground and stretched out both legs. In this section, the width of the passage was only a few inches longer than she, so she lifted her hands above her head and touched the wall to prevent smacking her head as she rolled. Then she turned on her right side. Because all her hopes, like chips, were placed on this final bet, Peregrine found her movements to be most agonizing and restrictive. It took her a long time to make a complete circumlocution. When she did, she looked down the passage. The speck was the same size. She judged the distance was very far, maybe one thousand yards. How could she make that? With a heavy and fearful heart, Peregrine rolled again, slowly, then again. Without the pack to give her the momentum to use as a device to propel her body, she was forced to generate her own power. She considered going back for the pack, but she had gone too far to waste even an ounce of energy. It was energy she desperately needed to spin five revolutions, let alone the six hundred and five it would take.

Peregrine glanced down the tunnel. White in the gloom, the circle was now the size of a nickel. She was heartened, even though a nefarious spasm split her left side, stomping up and down from her torso to her calf. She raised herself to a sitting position and bent over touching her toes. She would slither on her back, propelling herself with her hands and legs. Enough of this spinning crap!

Peregrine slid and wormed and scooted, occasionally misjudging her closeness to the wall, careering into it sometimes on the left, sometimes on the right side. Without the pack she covered the ground at a more rapid pace, but she exhausted easily and lost time resting. When she looked in the far distance at her goal, she saw circular whiteness the size of a silver dollar. Could it be? Was she at the opposite end of a section of tunnel that exited out into miles and miles of Calvary Cemetery? This wisp of hope became an elixir that soothed and gave her strength.

As Peregrine scratched the ground with her palms, and dug with her feet to push herself forward, she noted a shifting in hues from whiteness to lighter then darker shades of gray. She must hurry. The situation was changing and she didn't understand how or why. In a final burst of energy and enjoying the receding tides of her body's excruciation, Peregrine sat up, tucked her left leg under her body and lifted herself so she was on all fours. Her right knee squeezed grief. Nevertheless, she put her weight on it. She had no time. She feared the exit hole was gradually closing. Placing most of her body weight on her bare hands, she palmed small stones and cool earth, scrabbling forward. She gave a little hop, each time she put her left knee down, favoring the right with as little weight as possible to increase her pace. The action was effective but agonizing. Still, she must hurry, despite the damage to her knee and the blaze of misery. She struggled and graveled twenty hand paces, panting loudly. Her mouth was a sand well rimmed by a thin, bloody, crevassed, shriveled line that was once plump lips.

The white silver dollar had turned dark gray. It was nearly impossible to see in the blackness of the passage. She could not clump along fast enough to reach it. The exit was closing. Would she be too late? She thought of other junctions she had blundered upon, maybe selecting the wrong one. How many exits had closed down before she could note they were exits? How many opportunities had she missed? She could not allow this to be another wasted chance.

She deplored the tribulation of spending one more hour dying of dehydration, the inevitable coma approaching with the ticking seconds. Hope drifting away, she increased her flopping pace, and intensified the wretchedness to her knees, her back, her abdomen. Then, she collapsed. Her knees had given out. Clawing the earth with her hands and digging with her toes, she groveled, a woman of dust and clay.

Worry racked her. Impending failure gnawed. She would arrive to discover nothing was there, and all was an illusion, a hallucination. She would be at the ultimate dead end. Worse, what if it indeed was an exit, and she escaped from her underground prison only to perish above ground, lost among the thousands of tombstones, less than a half a mile away from water? Pounding the earth with her anxiety, she clumped up a fine, dirt cloud of exquisite irony causing her to choke, gag and cough with fury. She had eaten nothing for days. The last drops of water had been squeezed out by her desiccating organs. So, no bile or hydrochloric acid refluxed to her throat. Foul air from her stomach's rebellion had belched up, and her mouth tasted like rotten meat.

Why continue? She was beyond exhaustion, mired by horrific aches in every member of her body. Even if she were lucky enough to be found, her mephitic smell and bestial appearance would drive away a rescuer. If she was supine, would they see life? If she was comatose, would they bury her? Deranging panic swamped logic. If she lay down to rest, her festering body layered with dirt, she couldn't be distinguished from the surrounding earth, or an exhumed corpse. She must remain on her feet or on all fours.

Overcome by this new dread, she halted and let her head fall face down in the earth. A bug frisked through her hair. She jolted up spooked. Distracted from her self-pity, she peered into the darkness, unable to clearly discern whether the circle, now graphite, had increased in size. If it was an exit, she was too depressed, too sucked dry to joy over her success. The probability of failing to be rescued, after she left the tunnels, was ninety percent. There was no reason for exuberance. Each movement brought her closer to death.

Peregrine rolled over on her back, moaning in her body's excoriation. The dust settled and she coughed. She craved sleep. Time speeded up and went backward. The earth spun faster and seconds dissolved and broke up into smaller and smaller units of infinity. She closed her eyes and imagined misery compressed into a feather and puffed it to the stars. Her deep, empty well of thirst flooded. The excruciating aches liquefied into sugar. Her hungers feasted on stones. Her desert throat and cracked, white, sand lips bloomed. She succumbed to the darkness and slept. The passage was filled with the sounds of her labored, heavy rasping, like the breaths of one who has entered the world of coma, the universe of the undead and nonliving.

A crash resounded in her mind. Peregrine shocked to wakefulness. She abruptly rose up like a ghost. She knew where she was. She knew what she must do. Though the fine earthen soot still clouded the air, she bleared fifty feet ahead of her, blinking and winking heavy eyelids as she waited for a clear perspective. Yes. There it was, a way out. She was peering into the night sky. And she could make out that the tunnel extended into a huge, circular, concrete pipe, which probably functioned as some sort of drain into the cemetery.

Peregrine compelled her last fiber of will. She could rest once she was through the drain. Lowering herself with a groaning thud onto her stomach, she snaked and slid the last yards of ground onto the cool, rough concrete. Superstitious, that some ill-fated circumstance would steal her happiness for finding her way out of the underground labyrinth, she concentrated her efforts. She could not slide like she had over the soft earth. As her filthy hands slapped the concrete, she was forced to lift herself on all fours and gingerly weigh her cut and bruised knees down on the hard surface, reopening wounds with new scrapings. She was a jangle of raw and exposed nerve endings, a shadow of the young woman who had exuberantly jogged down the path to the Johnson mausoleum weeks ago. But she breathed, panted, and was alive, if barely.

She had reached pipe's edge. It was the end of her underground hell and perhaps a new beginning. She made a whisper cry of joy through shriveled vocal chords, dry reeds in wind. She gripped the pipe rim and pulled herself up to its edge to survey the scene below. Its cover lay on the ground in a drop off of about seven feet. Obviously something had jarred it, or there was another explanation. She looked out onto fields of graves extending for miles in the dark indigo twilight. She saw that the drain extended out of a hillside which precipitously sheared off into the cemetery valley. Nothing looked familiar. She was not in Old Calvary. She didn't know where she was. There was no road nearby. She did see the pink diffusion of color in the cloudy sky indicating lights miles away. The hillside faced east, she guessed. So the passageway had doubled back into the cemetery, just like she thought.

It was a miracle that the drain cover was off. She shuddered at an image of her corpse roiling with creepy, gorging bugs, battling to keep their banquet seat against the onslaught of others who ferociously wiggled to feed at her fleshy trough. Ugh! Well, the same could happen outside the tunnel. Worse! The crows and ravens might start on her even before she was dead and peck out her eyeballs while she was in a coma. Despite her cravings for rest and horrible aches, this thought above all others drove her to action.

After the blackness of the tunnel, her eyes found the dim night comfortable, and her vision became acute like a cat's. The ground underneath the pipe looked soft and was overgrown with weeds and grasses indigenous to the area. She hoped she had the strength in her hands and arms to crawl backwards out of the pipe, dangle off the edge, then land and roll like stuntmen did in the movies. That way she would be falling about four feet, since she was five feet nine inches. If she misjudged the height of the pipe above the ground, she was screwed. She waited 5 minutes and pictured again and again the steps she would take. She would grip the edge of the pipe, let go and land, immediately dropping and rolling to break the fall's impact.

Despite the wretchedness in her knees and the aches throughout her entire body, she made herself ready. She panted in excitement taking in deep gulps of air. A paroxysm of cramping struck in a wave, and then subsided into its regular dull foreboding. Now! Peregrine slithered backward, until she felt her feet jut out in space. She continued wriggling until her legs up to her thighs swung over the edge. Whether out of stress or her dire state, the cramping in her legs and stomach intensified. Damn, damn, damn, she thought. How would she be able to do this and land safely? How could she support her body weight? She had no answers. Each day had been a tortuous precipice, where she had leaped into uncertainty at every turn. She knew if she stayed in the pipe and didn't try to jump, she would never be rescued. Even if she took this leap and broke bones, she could still slide, reptilian, and increase her minimal chances of rescue outside in the cemetery.

Peregrine panted through the fresh, suffering waves burning her limbs, as she rapidly took in and expelled dry air. She slid backwards, until she teetered half in and half out of the pipe. Now, for the tricky part. She must throw her weight forward with all her might, and precariously balance as her legs floated in air. The pipe was smooth. There was nothing to hold onto. With difficulty balancing, Peregrine continued to worm backwards. Elbows and palms flat against the concrete, her torso raised and thrust forward, she continued until her stomach draped over the edge. She felt gravity pulling her downward. She let it, and as the pull intensified, she kicked outward with her left leg bringing her bosom over the edge with her elbows and hands sliding and fumbling to grasp the edge of the pipe with her fingers. Now, her shoulders and head were overhanging the pipe edge. Her fingers worked furiously to grab, and she groaned as her left hand held for a few moments the slippery surface. But she never could reach up and grasp the pipe with the fingers of her right hand. Suspended above the drop, she clamped on with screaming fingers, until one by one, they weakened and gave way. She fell. Her left foot slammed into the ground with a thump. She bounced forward and heard a popping. She twisted, flexing to break her fall. Her right foot glanced the ground, as she somersaulted to her left side and rolled over on her back.

She couldn't breathe. She was suffocating. The wind had been knocked out of her. She gulped air and her body exploded in shock. She nearly went unconscious. Her left leg was a holocaust of pain. Swords pierced her heel and sliced into her calf. She had broken her foot, her leg. She couldn't move, didn't dare jostle anything.

Peregrine lay and looked up at the drifting grey clouds in the dark sky for two minutes, in shock. Death closed in with its morbid, broken and bony claws, and clasped her soul's life. No one would come for her. She was alone, and she was paralyzed.

A moment later, the revelation hit. The pain was shattering, screaming like blood fire. It signaled she couldn't be paralyzed. Hope flooded her soul. Maybe she was cramping. Maybe her leg and foot were not broken. Moaning, she struggled to lift herself to a sitting position. She could move. She breathed deeply and massaged her foot and calf. She smiled. The shooting undulations of agony were exactly that, waves, familiar, old friends, by now. She banged her legs to usher the ferocious peaks and valley of pain down to her feet and toes. These exertions forced her to take in breaths through her mouth, and she recovered her regular breathing, as the leg spasms subsided, like an ill formed tide, and droned into the usual sonorous excruciation.

She shook her head and thanked God. Checking herself, she manipulated and fingered her right leg for acute, stabbing pains. Nothing. Just infernal and ever present cramping, that reminded her she was dehydrating to death. She glanced around relieved. The night air was cool and pleasant, warmer than in the labyrinth. She still had a ten percent chance of crawling out of there under her own power.

Using her hands and feet, she moved forward, slipping her bottom on the grass, releasing its green fragrance in its smears. The contact with the fresh, life-filled blades brought on the urge to urinate. She opened her legs not to foul herself and straightening her arms, leaned back on her hands and lifted up her bottom, bending her left knee, while straightening out her right leg to use her right heel for leveraged support. The hot liquid soaked into the ground. She sighed in relief and momentary relaxation. Maybe her kidneys were functioning after all. Now she would try to stand, and maybe, if she could find a long stick or tree branch, though in this section of the cemetery there were few trees, she could hobble to a road and flag down a car.

When she finished urinating, she leaned to her stronger left side. Using her arm and favoring her left leg, she rose to a deep knee bend, wincing as she put pressure on her right knee. But she managed to stand, and if she held her right leg straight and tight, she was able to limp slowly. Now, for the first time, Peregrine turned one hundred and eighty degrees to survey her location. The Manhattan skyline, unmistakable in its magnificent radiance of lights against the darker profile of buildings shined, no, smiled back at her. It was a symbol that all things were possible to those that believed them to be so. A New Yorker, she had visited Manhattan countless times, but standing from this vantage point of Calvary Cemetery, having experienced the range of emotional heights and depths there, she was awestruck at the city's beauty and splendor. She felt she never before appreciated its perfection as a living application of humanity's greatness.

Peregrine looked up at the pipe mouth and sharp drop off. The tombstones dotted the hill and then extended on the level of ground where she stood. From the outside, nothing indicated that the concrete drain was part of an elaborate and complex series of passageways that formed a puzzling labyrinth, whose purpose she could not divine. Peregrine stared at the black hole yawning down at her, and memorized its position with the surrounding gravesites and fallen drain cover. If she lived through this perilous night, she would return for her back pack. If she didn't make it, her family's relics would be lost forever.

Peregrine turned away from the exit with renewed hope. The crucifixion pangs were seeping into her legs, into her feet and away from her body, down into the graveyard, an appropriate repository for suffering. She focused on direction and her knowledge of Calvary. She knew the LIE bounded different divisions of the cemetery, but she was far from the LIE and miles from the Johnson mausoleum. In fact, as she turned three hundred and sixty degrees, as far as sight lines permitted, there were no visible roads or crypts. There were only large monuments and headstones of varying sizes, and rows and rows of plots, sporting sliver paths between the graves. The daylight would yield a clear picture of her location, but by then, she might be comatose or dead. She had to act while she could hobble, slither, grovel.

Leaping into the abyss of uncertainty once more, she decided to head east, deeper into Queens, with her back to Manhattan. Perhaps she would run into Queens Boulevard and from there find her way to the southern entrance off Grace Road. Perhaps she would locate a bordering path. Anyway, she was aboveground for the first time in weeks. Ebullience and joy! Knowing the Manhattan skyline was behind her to the west, exhilarated her above her treacherous aches. She believed that she would drudge out of the stony fields before she collapsed and became the horrible repast of night creatures and insects.

In the immediate area, Peregrine scanned the ground for something to use as a cane. Finding nothing, she hopped on her left foot until she reached a headstone where she rested. Instead of using the paths, she decided to weave her way amongst the plots whose stone markers and monuments tightly abutted each other to save space. These would be her crutches.

She hobbled queerly among the blocks of granite. She leaned on some larger monuments, holding others with both hands when the graves were a few feet apart so she could limp and propel herself across the grass to the next plot. Unable to read the names of the deceased, she did see their oval or rectangular shaped, sepia toned photographs reflected by the dim, pinkish hue of the cloudy heavens. As she tottered past, she curiously scoped the women's hairstyles. Some were upswept, like in a Gibson girl portrait; others were curled shoulder length, others short cropped, depending upon the era. She wished she could read the carved inscriptions. These tombs held the social history of the unrecognized and uncelebrated mass of New Yorkers, who had rejoiced and sorrowed in their city; these were the insignificant rich, middle class and some lower classes, who at their time of living, experienced the incredible arrogance of believing their bones would never lie in such as place as this. Their numbers factored into the billions of dead that outnumbered the current living population on the planet, proving that life was a misnomer, mortality the reality.

"Life's a bitch and then you die?" Peregrine rasped in her desert throat to the deaf ones around her. Her thoughts rambled. "You stupid idiot. You're mortal, capable of dying, just not presently dead. There is no separation between the capability and the finality; it's all one continuum. The substance of existence verifies the fact that you're dying, but haven't yet achieved the steady state. What humans refer to as "life" is the dynamic state of death, the process of dying. If mortality is the reality, then why do we trouble so about life and think it what it isn't?"

Peregrine sighed. At twenty-four, she was realizing that the nature of existence, hers included, was impossible for any human to glean, regardless of their brilliance, intuition or natural splendor. That was probably the reason why there were so many depressives on the planet. Interesting, that after spending days and nights in a burial ground, she had gained a new perspective. The question remained how could she best apply it to her own dynamic state of dying?

Peregrine rested by a six foot tall, pale obelisk that resembled the Washington Monument. She was obsessed with these issues because her own mortality was the bitch grinning in her face. Exhausted by the peril of flesh, again her will was on a downhill race. Rest, and sleep, she craved sleep. There was a larger patch of grass to her right and behind it a mammoth, white, marble headstone striated with flecks of black and gray. Though the night seemed to be growing cooler, it was nothing like the freeze in the main chamber of the mausoleum. But it would be the first time she would be forced to sleep in the open, vulnerable to the elements and whatever else haunted the cemetery, including the gangs. Learning to cope with her aches and ongoing torments, she knew she could fall asleep on this soft earth mattress with its grass-bottom sheets. If she didn't wake up and went into a coma, so be it. She would take her chances. She wished she had a hat to cover her head from pecking ravens and scavenger birds. Well, she would cover her eyes with her arm. No, she would lie on her stomach and sleep with her face resting on folded arms.

Peregrine grasped the striated monument with her left hand to steady herself. She knelt on her left leg, then shifted down into a sitting position, quickly extending her right leg which tensed as knifing pulsations sliced through it. She growled. With her twisted fall and hobbled gait, she had reinjured her knee. She needed to stay off it until she received treatment, if she ever got to a hospital.

She stretched and lengthened her body on the grass lying face up to the night, then rolled over placing her forehead on her arms. It was an uncomfortable position. She turned sideways to the right and immediately fell asleep, despite the insect harpings, the macabre night sounds and her torments.

Fifteen minutes later Peregrine shifted gears into semi-consciousness. Her eyes blinked. She was blinded by wetness. Was it blood? Yes. Something was horribly wrong. She awoke. No something was utterly perfect, in fact, astonishing. Manna from heaven, the drops of rain pelted her with a bracing, soothing shower, cooling her parched lips, tinkling and paddling the grass, the headstones, her filthy body. It was liquid, limpid rapture. She sat up laughing and reached up in joyfulness to receive the great cleansing downpour. She closed her eyes and threw back her head, her mouth an open portal with gritty teeth, grinning like a child. She gulped the clouds' glory, sucking large droplets of rainwater with insatiable, ravenous longing. After days of deprivation, her imagination grew cavernous. If she could drink the entire cloud, it wouldn't be enough.

Rather than look for a container or cup her hands into a bowl, she stretched out on the ground, face heavenward, her mouth a catch basin, her arms and legs extended outward like the Da Vinci drawing, the Vitruvian Man. In this position she swallowed the liquid tonic with happiness, until she felt minimally sated then stopped herself because she did not want to vomit.

As the clouds opened with generosity, Peregrine sat up and scrubbed and sloughed the rainy spurts up and down her arms, washing off the soil, dust and crud as best she could. Yelping with pleasure, she cupped her hands to collect the rain, then massaged it onto her skin like a rich, thick emollient. She luxuriated in washing her legs and feet, removing her left sneaker and what remained of her right, clearing caked scruff between her toes. She turned over on her stomach and with her palms, from her backside, back and legs she scoured the earth and cleansed herself of the residues of waste and urine. As she showered, her finger tips felt the hundred ridges, scratches sores, bumps and insect bites. Some had crusted over. Others still oozed, open to the air. Her skin had taken a severe beating. But the watery, silk massage was like the Balm of Gilead. It reinvigorated and set to healing her sordid, moldering flesh.

For the first time in her eon of torture and hell, she relaxed. The pressure had lifted. The percentages had reversed their poles. She had a ninety percent chance of rescuing herself, a ten percent chance of failure. Like the demise of the Witch of the West, death's power against her had been melted by a bucket of rain. She would die, but not of dehydration.

By intermittently drinking the rainwater, she could easily make it through the next few hours until she found a road or the cemetery entrance. Then she realized her stupidity. The gates would probably be closed, and she didn't have the strength to climb over them and rip her skin apart on the barbed wire. She would be forced to stay until morning. To avoid a chill, if it continued to rain, she would have to take cover under a tree or break into a mausoleum. No matter. Whatever was expedient. She had many options, excepting one. She no longer had the option to die.

For the next half hour, Peregrine skidded over grassy plots and clumsily shunted and shuffled past marble pieces on the gravel path, as she dragged herself toward a dark clump of trees about four thousand yards from the concrete pipe exit. Periodically, she plopped on the soft bladed turf and lay on her back opening her mouth to capture the living water, grateful for the steady, quenching rain. The day would be hot and humid, if the clouds ever cleared. Another three thousand feet beyond the black two hundred year old pines to the east, Peregrine thought she saw spiraling barbed wire atop a metal fence. Was this the boundary to the road? The fluid atmosphere and devious night obscured her view. After she culled strength from a needed rest under the trees, she would investigate

Brushing aside the branches of one venerable pine, Peregrine sank to her left knee in an attempt to settle herself onto the blanket of soft, damp pine needles. As she tried to keep her right leg straight, she rolled to her left side, inadvertently bending her right knee backward. White lightning struck with the force of a shattering blow and cartoon-like, she saw stars. She screamed in pain and straightened her leg, holding it rigidly in front to halt the collision tearing the joint. She remained immobile on her side for long minutes, afraid any movement of her right leg would dislocate her knee cap and upend her peace. After a time, she sat up, keeping her leg stretched out. The generalized cramps caused by dehydration had stopped, only to be replaced by the pounding knee which desperately needed a brace and probably an operation. She knew she had exacerbated her original injury in the cavern. She moved from wheel to woe, valley to mountaintop, to valley. Where was the steady state, the harmony, the balance?

The question opened the floodgates of fear which blotted out her thankfulness for the miracle of rain. Panic slid up beside her. She could put no weight on her knee. She was immobilized. She was even more vulnerable than in the labyrinth. She couldn't run away from the gangs. If they found her they would torture and rape her, then kill her or leave her to die of her injuries. Peregrine moaned. Death's claws clutched her soul, and she fell through the fragile branches of happiness onto a nail bed of anxiety. There were no Good Samaritans in the world, only slaves and masters. Her condition made her the former. As her confidence deflated into self-pity, like a bad vein collapsing at a needle puncture, she devolved into complaint. All she wanted was a bed and clean sheets, a bubble bath and a thick, juicy cheeseburger with bacon and French fries, and a slice of pizza, and a shot of morphine. It was the resplendent opiate given in hospitals to ease terminal cases into Hades' arms.

"A self-administered morphine drip," she groaned aloud. "Bitch!" Her knee was an evil elf, menacing with searing, prodding tongs. She leaned back on her elbows, listening to the rain cascade off the dripping pine branches. Large droplets slid down her head, arms and legs, but the sheltering branches propelled a waterfall of rain outward and away from her. She started to inch backward against the trunk where the branches were darker, thicker, and more protective. But her movement sizzled and fired her knee. She decided to remain still. The miserable joint seared with a mere finger graze, and the tissues distended around the injury like troops in an armed camp, circling the wagons for attack.

If she could get a few hours of rest, perhaps the swelling would deflate. With care, Peregrine lowered her back to the ground trying not to jerk her knee. The dripping branches lightened their flow of droplets. She became inured to the drips that fell on her arms and legs until she was able to shut off the droning voices in her head and close her eyes. She dozed off to the soothing sounds of the rain lines on the outer branches that ticked the seconds like a pendulum clock. And her eyes shuttered to visuals of steak and mashed potatoes, ravioli, Thanksgiving turkey and pumpkin pie.

Peregrine awakened in a cold sweat of fear. It was quiet. The rain had stopped. The teaming water had sieved to a fine mist that rose off the ground, like fog sweeping through heath. There it was the sound that woke her. There were voices in the pine grove. Visible from her shelter amongst the feathery needles, were two powerful flashlight beams, grazing the ground and devouring the grass. They were closing the distance to the pine branches that scraped the ground, her pine branches. Within the pine cover Peregrine shivered. Gangs.

"Go over there. I'll go this way."

Footsteps tread heavily, slinging pebbles and gravel, crunching out sounds that amplified then stopped in front of the grove of pines where she hid. It was a perfect night for the marauders to traipse through the cemetery. During the downpour, no one would patrol the area, so they could get over or through the fence with impunity.

Peregrine cursed her misfortune. If she had her pack, she could brain them with the heavy metal cross or jab them with the spike. She had nothing to fight them with except one good leg. She held her breath afraid her rasps were audible. The footsteps had left the path and were trudging near her tree. Her limbs quivered and dripped fear. Bodies rustled and brushed the branches, creating a fresh shower of raindrops. She could hear shoes sloshing the wet grass, splashing through puddles created by rain water falling off the branches of the great pine. A flashlight halo was shining through the stiff, thick and prickly needles. The light eerily filtered into her haven in slivers, splaying the pine branches from black to green.

Peregrine felt faint. She didn't want to be sodomized, have her throat slashed and her bloated body fished out of that toxic sump of a lake in Flushing Meadow Park, like that young woman two months ago, who gang members had sexually assaulted and mutilated. A pentagram had been carved into the woman's stomach. Her navel had been burned and gouged out at the center of the pentagram.

Footsteps halted. Pine branches waved furiously pelting down water overflows. Peregrine urinated on the bed of needles. Rough hands plucked open the heaving pine barrier and a torch shined in her eyes like a blinding star. A man of darkness rushed forward with arms outstretched to grab her. She shrilled, "No, no," and slipped away into unconsciousness.

"Peregrine, Peregrine."

Her head was being moved from side to side. The gang member slapped her in the face. Outrage overtook her. She jerked her head forward and shook her shoulders free. "Stop. Leave me you bastard. Don't you touch me!" She tried to sound ferocious, but her voice was a mewling protest.

"Peregrine. It's me, Fen. Fen!" The deep, clear annunciation sounded familiar. Fen shined the flashlight on his face.

There in the eerie, fantastic and monstrous shadows created by the blast of white light against his cheek, were the chiseled jaw, aquiline nose, the handsome and gorgeous profile and beautiful white teeth smiling at her. When she believed it was truly Fen, she allowed herself to feel his loving grip on her shoulders.

"Oh Fen, Fen," she said, the tears streaming down her face. She hugged him and he held her tight, so tight she could barely whisper into his chest, "You came for me, you came for me."

THE ENTANGLING WEB

Chapter Twenty-Six

S hould she or shouldn't she get up? Madeline blinked her eyes three times and lifted her head from the sterile pillow. She turned 180 degrees from left to right. Her bedroom was at the top of a mountain in a snow-covered valley. The colors were bleak, like an icy, wind-swept day of steel. She knocked the pillow off the bed in frustration. Returning her head to its former position on the soft mattress, she looked above to the plastic headboard. The blinking, droning headlamp's glare, reflecting off the whiteness of the sheets and coverlet, neutralized the room's atmosphere into a bland, flat-line sameness. She thought of *Goldilocks and the Three Bears*. Not too hot, not too cold, but middling perfection, an artificial attempt to give off the appearance of just right, intoning gently the mantra of protection, "Everything is fine. All is well."

But all was not well. Her life sucked, and she somersaulted from heights to depths. Sometimes, she was in both places simultaneously, which meant she was nowhere. If she could just kindle the fires of imbalance and imperfection, she would be able to restore her emotional equilibrium of ever-present pain. Pain signified existence in time and place. Like an alcoholic drinking to correct brain function, she needed to feel the razor edge, not this numbing reassurance of nothingness that, like an embalming fluid, replaced the raw, messy, vibrant blood flow of anguish.

Her prayer was answered in the form of a Chanel linen suit, matching Jimmy Choo water-snake pumps and Kate Spade handbag sported by Sylvia Reynolds who burst open the door of the private hospital room, rushed to the side of the bed and looking down at Madeline, cooed in excitement.

"Madeline, fabulous news about Peregrine. Paul and Fen found her in Calvary Cemetery. She's an absolute mess, covered in sores, famished from hunger and thirst, and smelling like a corpse and looking like a concentration camp victim. But she's alive. I didn't see her, yet, but it's all over the news. They brought her to the same hospital as Deidre

Hamilton. And my son and Fen are heroes, heroes." Sylvia practically hugged herself in an orgasmic ecstasy of feeling. "I think the charges against Paul will be dropped." Out of breath, she was too ebullient to notice the effect of the great news on Madeline who sat up, an uncoiling spring.

Like a whirlwind descending on a trailer park and leveling it to sticks, Madeline took apart her friend splinter by splinter. "Is the world so beholden to you that you can feel free to barge in here without giving any notice or warning beforehand? Are you that pretentious, that egotistical? Do you imagine that I want to see you? That your news is so sacrosanct that it can't wait? That you are the anointed one to give me an exclusive?" Madeline lifted her hands in the air and mimed quotation marks around the media buzz word.

Distracted by her friend's appearance, Madeline's words flew past Sylvia like gnats on a summer wind. Madeline looked awful. Her complexion was pale. Her eyes glazed over with a haunted look created by the deep circles underneath. Emptiness rose to the surface of the skin, a portent of what cowered in her mind.

Sylvia added a dollop of sweetness and cajoled. "Oh, come off it, Madeline. It's time to celebrate. Your daughter's alive. And she'll be okay. And Paul will be vindicated. It's thrilling. I wanted to cheer you up." Sylvia sat sideways on the foot of the bed. She placed the Kate Spade on her lap, opened it and took out a Chris Botti CD waving it around. "Your favorite. Gorgeous, sexy, jazzy Chris."

Madeline's head was in her hands, and she spoke to the counterpane, knowing the impossibility of Sylvia, but trying to reason with her nevertheless. "I can't deal with you now, Sylvia. I have a crushing headache, and I'm on medication that has reduced me to a babbling, cranky idiot. How about I call you later?" She lifted up her head hopefully.

"You don't have the CD. It's his latest. Remember the time we saw him at the *Blue Note*?" Sylvia laughed. "And we tried to buy him a drink?"

"Yes!" Madeline screamed.

Startled, Sylvia began playback of her friend's behaviors, recognizing a vast difference from the past.

"Thanks for the CD, Sylvia. I feel like...there are no words to describe it. Please, please." She sighed. "Just go. I'll...call you when I'm feeling up to it." Madeline watched as Sylvia's smile froze in a grimace, watched as that freezing enveloped her body with paralysis. The glue of disbelief had fastened her to the foot of the hospital bed. Would this witch not take the hint?

"Sylvia. You can go now!" Madeline felt the darkness rise up in her voice to outrun civility and politeness. Screw Miss Manners. Madeline pointed to the door, as if to emphasize Sylvia's crime.

"What?" Sylvia's amazement lifted her eyebrows and parted her lips in the shape of a zero.

"You heard me. Get out. I don't want to talk to you now." Madeline's body was taut. Her tone vibrated rage.

"Madeline, what is wrong with you?" Sylvia moved closer to comfort her friend.

Madeline raised her hand to ward her off with a shaking motion. "Nothing that concerns you. Nothing that I can share with you."

Sylvia found herself. "I tell you that your daughter who went missing over ten days ago has been found, your daughter who you were practically delusional about, and you condemn me for barging in on you? You're not happy for Peregrine or Paul?" Sylvia jerked her friend's chain and dragged her back to reality since the doctors were obviously babying her and encouraging self-pity. "You're rusticating in a psychiatric ward, for Christ's sake, looking at four puke- colored walls. You need cheering up."

"How do you know what I need, you shallow, materialistic lunatic?" Madeline said in a soft refrain more to herself than Sylvia. Then she let the fury cascade, like a mountain spring in a thunderstorm. "If you don't leave under your own volition, I will make you leave." With more drama than force, Madeline threw back the covers, and swung her legs over the side and stood, towering strength over Sylvia.

Alarmed, Sylvia jumped up and faced Madeline. "All right, Madeline. I'll go, but you won't see me for a while, a long while."

Madeline menaced her, inching forward. Sylvia moved backward, bumping into a chair against the wall. "Fine. Anyway, visiting hours are over. Since when do they have unannounced visitors in a psych ward?" Madeline grabbed the remote and buzzed the nurse. "You just snuck up here to trouble me and be a snoop. Let's see. What could have happened to poor Madeline?" She mocked. "Well, had enough?" Madeline felt a compulsion to rush Sylvia, slam her, terrorize her as the woman cringed backward and deflated her body from its usual tall and erect posture.

The door opened, and a slight, young nurse entered the room. "Can I get anything for you, Ms. Randolf?" Like a brittle twig breaking, the interruption snapped the tension between Sylvia and Madeline.

"Could you please escort her out?" Her face an expressionless mask, Madeline gestured toward the door.

Despite her friend's need for sympathy against this newly acquired paranoid derangement, Sylvia sniffed disdainfully and stomped to the doorway, banging the door shut in the face of the nurse who was forced to reopen it and follow meekly behind her.

With uncomprehending fury, Madeline jumped out of the bed and ran to the chair where she had thrown her bathrobe earlier that morning. Dislodged by Sylvia's collision with the chair, the robe lay on the floor in a heap. *Similar to my emotional state*, Madeline thought ruefully. She picked up the black chenille and shook it out, then hurriedly slipped it on, tying the belt tightly. She bent over and reached under the bed for her fuzzy slippers that Bill had brought from home, along with a few changes of clothing. She had signed herself into the ward because she thought that the hospital followed a strict protocol about visitors. The place seemed the perfect haven from the media menagerie during a time when she needed to think about what to do next. Because she lived off her trust fund, a few days in the psychiatric ward wouldn't hurt her career; but such a stay was always a liability, though the records were supposed to be held in the strictest confidentiality.

Madeline left the room and headed straight for the nurse's station and waited until the young acolyte of caring, a Miss Racqett, looked up at her. Madeline was cold and curt. "What is the ward's policy on visitors? I thought the doctor left explicit instructions that I was to have no visitors or phone calls, except from my lawyer Bill and my daughter Peregrine?"

"Yes, I'm sorry, Ms. Randolf. Your friend just wouldn't take no for an answer." The nurse saw the dark clouds forming over Madeline's brow. "It won't happen again," she said in her most dutiful and innocent voice.

"Please. How is a person supposed to get the rest she needs if so-called friends sneak into my room? And how did she know where my private room was?" Madeline stared into the young woman's eyes to discern if she had colluded with Sylvia. Impossible to tell. She glared at her. "Someone on the staff tipped her off and let her up here. Who was it?" The nurse was silent. Madeline's bellicosity wavered, and then she was stalwart. "It won't happen again because your superiors will hear about this." She turned and stalked away in silence: Miss Madeline Manners gone forever.

At the desk, Miss Racqett rolled her eyes in the direction of Madeline's retreating figure and mouthed silently, "What a bitch," to her heavyset, retirement-age colleague who had just come in to relieve her for the evening shift. "I've been fielding calls from main reception." She raised her voice in irony and fluttered her eyelids. "They want to know if Ms. Randolf's representative is here yet. Reporters want to speak to him." She shook her head. "Can you believe it? Like we have nothing else to do."

Ponderous, Mrs. Honor sighed. "The visitor's parking lot at Main is a mess. Vans and print journalists have filled most of the spots. Family members are mad about it. A few made complaints. The media must be hanging around, waiting for action. Since I've been working here and I've been here a long time, I've never seen anything like it."

"Let the media come. She'll clear out the parking lot fast once she starts her banshee act. You know, when they brought her to the ER late Friday night, she was calm. Since she wasn't in pain and only had contusions, she was low priority. Being Friday, all the stations were full; there was a long wait time. Well, when the valium wore off, she flipped out. Nervous, combative, wouldn't sit still. Typical, right? But then she started with the shrieking and the hyena laughter. She screamed and screamed, and then she'd stop the screaming and laughed; you know, long, low laughter that would chill the marrow in your bones? Then all of a sudden after the laughter, the screaming, you know, high-pitched wails, again and again. And then she'd stop, and again comes that low laughter, rising up, higher and higher, then the screaming again. Like to make my blood run cold. The doctors couldn't figure out if she was hallucinating from the valium or doing it to get their attention because she was waiting so long, or just plain psycho. Her representative, the lawyer, said she was like that when he found her. She is one crazy, nutty bitch."

Mrs. Honor's eyes were round and bulged with the imagining as she spoke from experience. "Sounds like one of the patients from Pilgrim State Hospital, the locked ward in the 1960s."

The acolyte waved her hand dismissively. "Off her medication, she is bad. Well, her screams upset the patients in the ER. The normal chaos everyone is used to was ten times worse, and the nurses couldn't get it together until they sedated her. She set everybody off, like a full moon. That's when her friend suggested that she sign herself inpatient and get proper diagnosis and treatment. So, she's a private voluntary for now. She saw the doctors, and her charts say it all. She will probably go outpatient once things are on an even keel, except she's got some attitude. Here's the picture of her and her daughter in the *Post*." Miss Racqett threw the latest edition down on the desk in front of her colleague. "Very attractive, but you wouldn't know her from her picture. Hair's blonde. Probably taken last year."

Mrs. Honor was more forgiving. "Mother and daughter resemblance is strong. Her daughter is beautiful."

"Yeah, well, when they found her, she didn't look like this! I've got to run. Have fun with the Bridezilla of Frankenstein."

Mrs. Honor sighed. "Maybe she'll take to a round grandmotherly type like me. At the very least, she'll be here a few days. Once they stabilize her meds and establish group and individual treatment sessions, she'll be signing herself outpatient. They all do unless they've got insurance coverage and are looking to stay out of work for a while."

"Yeah. I'm glad I won't be here when they stabilize her. I can't take that low hyena laughter. She scares me."

"Just remember to be soothing and remain calm. Anyway, the media is going to be more trouble than she is. Think about it. They're looking to interview her now her daughter's been found. Everybody wants an exclusive. Security is going to be on special alert. They'll probably post men on either side of the stairwells to prevent anyone coming up the back way," Mrs. Honor said, as she reviewed the schedule. She smiled goodbye to the youngster. Judging from her experience at Pilgrim, this patient would be a cakewalk.

Outside in the parking lot, media staff was too busy to bother invading the hospital just yet. They had new fish to fry. There, Sylvia held court with a few reporters. She was determined to wipe out all memory of the negative press Paul had received after he achieved Olympian heights at Deidre's rescue to wallow in Icarian depths at his arrest and arraignment. Thanks to his latest rescue with Fen and Sylvia's heraldic spin, he would be wallowing no more!

She answered the young female reporter's question airily. "Well, Mrs. Randolf is very happy that my son Paul and Fennelly Girardo rescued Peregrine. No words can express it, really. What the young men did for their friend Peregrine is heroic." Sylvia emphasized the word heroic and smiled into the two lens caverns yawning black at her.

"Do you have any idea what made your son and Mr. Gerardo think that Peregrine was at Calvary Cemetery?" The young man was casually dressed and wearing a blue-tooth mike. He reminded her of a Vulcan.

"No, I don't." Sylvia changed the subject. "I do think that this will do a lot to prove that the allegations against my son are false and that the charges should be dropped. He is simply not the person the Queens District Attorney's office says he is. My son rescued Deidre Hamilton. She would have died if he didn't find her. Now he's helped to rescue Peregrine Randolf. He is a hero. That is his character, his nature. He has helped many people and is known for his charitable work for the Ocean Conservancy and other organizations. The circumstantial evidence the police found, in fact, proves his rescue of Deidre. How they can turn it around to say he harmed her speaks to the prosecution's rush to judgment. My son did not harm Deidre Hamilton. Now if you'll excuse me, I have appointments." Sylvia pushed passed the Vulcan and aimed for the direction of her car, the lead goose in the gaggle that followed close behind and on either side of her.

"Mrs. Reynolds, do you know why Ms. Randolf is in a psychiatric ward? Is it because of the stress related to her daughter?" A mike floated near her face.

"No, I don't really know. I'm sure the stress contributed to it." She didn't want to think about Madeline's reaction to her, or she would lose control and be punished for it later in newsprint or on TV. "I must be off."

"Did you know that your son tried to visit Deidre Hamilton at Parkland Hospital in contempt of the restraining order filed against him at the arraignment?" The question was from an attractive, casually dressed female who shoved the mike in Sylvia's face, like it was a sexual device she was supposed to willingly take up.

She took a step backward and grimaced at the mike, then confronted the smirking reporter, staring pointedly into the woman's brown eyes to scrub the smug expression from her blighted face. "Well, they are close friends, and I'm sure he wouldn't intentionally violate the restraining order. I think she asked to see him." Sylvia smiled, attempting to diminish her shock, ready to engage the reporter, who like a heat-seeking missile was hell-bent on striking her target, to gleefully record the devastation.

"You know your son has been arrested for violating the order?" Another female reporter standing back four feet shouted this above the murmurings of the two males and obtrusive female who were jostling outstretched mikes to vacuum the pearls that dropped from her lips. Well, they could stand there and suck dry rot. Sylvia broke away from the small crowd of reporters, camera operators and onlookers who had gathered. She speeded to her car with her reptilian train croaking out questions that her fury pulverized into garbled, choked-off phrases she refused to acknowledge. When she reached the door to her BMW convertible, she turned to stick it to them.

"You're investigative reporters. Why don't you investigate who pushed to have my son arrested on circumstantial evidence that does more to prove his heroism than anything else?"

"Why would anyone go after Paul Carver?" the washed-out blonde asked.

They would draw her out? Fine. Sylvia felt strangely calm gearing up for the inevitable battle that would come upon saying the culprit's name. If her lawyer was pissed, she would deal. With measured pauses between each word, she said, "You know, Detective Matthews is Deidre Hamilton's cousin. Ms. Hamilton is his aunt."

"What's the connection?"

Sylvia snorted inwardly. Were they just stupid or were they manipulating her to the edge before they pushed her off? "Matthews should be nowhere near this case. He's the one who incited the DA to press charges for assault and rape. This is a conflict of interest that involves blatant prosecutorial misconduct. I am sure that he influenced them to go after Paul for this court order violation. You want someone to interview? Interview the DA. Interview Matthews."

"What's your proof?"

"Young man." Sylvia was exasperated. "Maybe this is beyond your experience or your age. The media has reported numerous examples when wives or girlfriends have taken out court orders against their stalker ex-husbands or boyfriends. When those men continued to stalk them, the women had to move heaven and earth to get the police to arrest the bastards for court order violations." Sylvia could feel her voice rise and the blood pound in her temples. "Dammit. And when the police refused to take action or were slow about it, the women were killed. My son goes to visit his friend on her appeal, and they arrest him an hour later?"

"Well, for once the system worked," The Vulcan replied sarcastically. "What are you suggesting?"

"Bias. Unequal justice. Conflict of interest. Deidre and Paul used to date, then broke off. Maybe Matthews resents Paul or his life-style." Sylvia shrugged her shoulders and leveled her gaze as the three reporters snuggled nearer and the photographers nudged in behind them.

"There's no misconduct in detectives talking to each other across departments."

"Yeah. And police abuse is only white on black. Please! All I know is that ever since Paul found Deidre, Matthews has had a hard-on for my son, a hard-on to see him convicted." She smiled into the video camera. "Let's see you televise that!"

Sylvia got inside the car and slammed the door. She was about to lean forward, resting her head on the steering wheel as she breathed a sigh of relief, but she resisted. She knew the buzzards were scoping her every move, looking for signs of weakness. She remained dignified, and with head held high, she backed out of the parking space and drove away to her lawyer's office, leaving them to hunt other prey.

Upstairs in her private hospital room, Madeline finished her Diet Coke, placing it on the tray that held three dishes of her half-eaten, unappetizing dinner. She got up from the table cluttered with the tray and her laptop and assorted papers and books. She would answer the rest of her e-mails later. Bill would arrive any minute, and she wanted to look presentable. She drew off her robe and flung it on the bed, then went to the closet and dragged her frilly Donna Karen blouse off the hanger and quickly scrambled each arm into its sleeve, buttoning the bottom buttons, leaving the top open, revealing cleavage. She grabbed her jeans from the bed and slid them on, first one leg then the other, intermittently grabbing the back of the chair. The medications threw off her balance, and at times, she was unsteady on her feet. She reminded herself to discuss this with the doctor.

Gradually, she would wean herself off the potent dosages; but first, she must conquer her uncontrollable urges to become hysterical and siphon off the feelings of outrage that rose up in battalions, trampling her peace. Between the mountain and the valley was the precipice. With meds she was enervated, dead inside; without them, she was lunatic, hyper, terrorized, running from an unnamable something. The meds gave her a semblance of calm, but her life was a sham. With them, she was sacrificing body and mind to be lulled into a false sense of security, dangerous considering her European family's pragmatism.

In the bathroom, a stranger with deep set, large, brown eyes, appearing wan and haunted, stared back at her as she combed her hair, applied mascara and under eye make-up. She brushed her teeth and tried to refocus her thoughts on her mundane, physical maintenance. Megan, her hairdresser, always made her happy. She would call her again tomorrow to see if she could return in the evening to update her style and color. She needed to look in the mirror and see a different face grinning back at her. Attempting confidence, Madeline viewed herself once more. This time she primped, chin down, shoulders back, pursing her lips, expecting to see a dark-haired beauty beaming back. She smiled to make the vision true and broke down, collapsing forward into the sink, holding onto its sides with her head down and away from all reflection of a former self as she silently wept.

"What is the matter with me?" She hiccupped down her sorrow, swallowing the panic creeping up her throat, sucking in deep, regular breaths. She raised her tear-streaked face to look again. She was alienated from the woman who stared back. That woman's voice was silent for all time, a disembodied sylph, shut up in a disappearing chamber. Behind sad eyes, she stared back with miserable knowing. Madeleine turned away and dared not look again, frightened of the being that floated in the nether regions of her soul.

"Hey, anyone here?"

Bill sounded tentative, his cheerfulness forced as if he didn't want to upset her. She quickly used the white towel to dry any wetness from her cheeks, threw it on the floor and stepped out of the bathroom. She sauntered to Bill, kissing him on the cheek. "Hi." She attempted brightness, felt her mouth reverting to a slash, curving down.

"Hey, beautiful. You look better." He grabbed both her arms and kissed her on the mouth.

She pulled herself away and caught his hand steering him to the bed. "Yeah. I guess so." She motioned for him to sit as she forced an ugly, grey, plastic chair from the corner and sat opposite him.

"How do you feel?"

Madeline heard the concern in his voice but couldn't accept it. He was still dressed in his blue suit which strengthened his dark-haired good looks and transformed his light blue, heavily- lashed eyes into the steely Atlantic. Intermingled between the prowling male ego and the ambitious professional was the friend she used to tease. Now amiability was a chore, and she was in no mood for flirtation. "I don't know what I feel. Like, merde? Like my past is gone, and my future is black?"

"Well, this is the best place for you now. You'll have therapy sessions, individual and group, and you'll be able to work things out." He motioned to the window. "You don't want to be out there. Out there is the insane asylum. In here, it's safe, rational and peaceful."

"No one's gotten to Peregrine, have they?" Worried, Madeline stood up from the chair.

"No, no." He grabbed her hand and pulled her over to him. He grasped her other hand and looked up at her smiling. "Sit."

Madeline sat next to him on the bed. Their knees touched as Bill put his left arm around her shoulder to comfort her. "Visitors are strictly forbidden, and they've had to add security to prevent the media flitting up the stairwells. I have two of my team guarding exits on her floor. Peregrine is safe for now, but I am not relishing the day when she'll be released. The crush will be formidable. She'll be expected to say a few words in front of the cameras, as will you."

"No." Madeline jumped up. She turned with arms akimbo and faced Bill, an anxious, hysterical undercurrent in her voice. "You know I can't risk it. I can't have my European relatives see me on satellite or YouTube. To avoid publicity, I've got to stay here until she is discharged. We'll arrange a diversion and leave the country on an international charter."

Bill was silent, guilty. A picture of Madeline and Peregrine at her New York University graduation had been leaked by Peregrine's classmate to the *Post*. It was being used by some of the media outlets. He had tried to pull the photograph without success. "Don't worry. As spokesperson, I've kept the media at arm's length. As far as you and Peregrine are concerned, it's a blackout, the unkindest cut of all," he said, pleased with himself. He would wait until she was emotionally stable to tell her about the photo. Bill left the bed and went to the mini-refrigerator that doubled for a mini-bar minus the prohibited alcohol. He took out a Coke, tore off the metal plug and downed a few swigs then smiled.

Madeline sat back on the bed. Desensitized, she had confused the guilt on Bill's face with the desire for something to drink. She smiled. "So, what have you been telling the vultures?"

Bill picked up the black leather briefcase that he had dropped by the dresser. He swung it onto the bed, clicked it open and with a flourish, took out *The Daily News*, *U.S.A. Today* and *The New York Times,* dated Monday. "You can see for yourself. Very benign. Haven't you watched cable or followed online news clips?"

"I don't have the stomach for that kind of fiction masquerade." She waved away his proffered papers. "I don't want to read all the news that's fit to distort. Everybody knows that news stories are spun fantasy, peppered with grains of truth here and there. I prefer the internet. I get to pick and choose." Madeline got up from the bed and paced the floor, thinking.

"Substituting one adulteration for another?" Bill laughed. "Well, read the articles with a critical eye for my comments, and let me know if there's anything you would like me to say in the future."

Madeline ignored Bill who leaned against the wall sipping his Coke. "According to Gore Vidal's *Empire*, ever since the Hearst era, the news is confabulation. But at least William Randolph Hearst was honest about his prevarications: entertainment with no pretension to serious reportage. The current gang is besotted with themselves. They believe the dwindling market share craves the poisoned mushrooms they've passed off as truffles. Advertisers manipulated by market data that are manipulated. That, I understand. But when media people believe their own lies, they've obviated the necessity for truth." Madeleine sneered. "No surprise. Most of them are addicted to story-telling. Boomerang effect!"

Bill was irritated. Madeline didn't appreciate the subtly of his efforts. "So, what should I say next time? The problem with simply stating, 'No Comment,' is that their researchers are like pit-bulls. They bite down; your leg is gone. Talk about dishing the dirt, they examine your existence down to your DNA, re-sequence it, then bury you with your new Frankenstein image. Opaque facts, that's what I gave them."

Madeline sighed deeply and returned to sit on the bed. The unavoidable, the inevitable was coming. Even if she left the country, she would be looking over her shoulder, pursued by two monstrous enemies, her family and the media, who would probably work in concert to find her. Was there no escape route?

Bill placed the empty can on Madeline's food tray. He took off his jacket and put it on the back of the plastic chair, then joined her on the edge of the bed. He rationalized. "The more forth coming, the better. It's a traditional litigator's trick. Don't present them with any opportunity to perceive your actions or responses as covert. If we hide your past, it makes you look guilty. Then they can cast themselves as champions of truth and expose your horrible secrets. Since this is not a matter of national security, there is no way out. So…apologize for your existence and bore them to death with mundane facts, opaque truths. They'll go away, especially if you go on one of the afternoon shows. *Oprah*!"

Madeline stretched out on the bed and straightened her arms over her head. She could feel her anger rising, her anxiety increasing. Her thoughts fell over themselves. She had to convince Bill she couldn't go on TV, yet not tell him why. She began a rant.

"Celebrity is its own punishment. Fame kills autonomy, if there is such a thing. The irony is we can't ever really know what people are like. I mean we filter who we think people are through our own clogged debris. And those filters are the sum total of generations of historical filtering, inherited from our parents and grandparents and back. Talk about being far from the truth of things. And then we compound everything with veneers of pretense, convincing ourselves we're honest. Ha, ha."

She sat up and stared into Bill's eyes, which looked azure against the whiteness of his shirt, satisfied that he was paying attention. "Even if those in the media were sincere and moral and principled, they'd be foolish to presume they could even attempt such revelations. And since we know that the media outlets are neither moral nor principled, how can we trust their result?" Madeline mimed quotes in the air. "News as commodity." She continued with force a lesser ear would discern as passion. "They indulge our fantasies. They dupe us into believing that we can know what is unknowable. But all they present is illusions of illusions. And we've become intellectually malnourished by eating their trash. Dangerous stuff. Do I have to be caught up in the evil karmic rebound? I choose not to."

It was Bill's turn to lie down on the bed, his head propped up on his right hand as he bent his arm comfortably akimbo. "Why not capitalize on their game, Ms. Spider? Avenge thyself."

"What?"

"Weave your own myths. Let these predators become the prey that you spin into a cocoon, then suck their blood dry."

"I wish I could afford a spot-on PR firm." Madeline rubbed her hands together, grinning. "Have my own staff spin candy confections to palliate the sugar junkies." Madeline laughed. "Sorry, Bill, you're stuck being spokesperson." For the first time since Peregrine had gone missing and the media swarmed, Madeline felt hope. "But the spider thing has possibilities."

"Well, we have a few days to spin a candy web before Peregrine is released. By the way, after you called, five minutes later, she fell asleep in the middle of a sentence. On my way out, I spoke to the doctor. He's amazed she isn't in worse shape. But it's a crucial time for her. They've got to stabilize her electrolyte imbalance which can be tricky. And of course, work on the malnutrition, same thing he told you. Otherwise, she's fine. Her sprains, cuts and bruises are healing quickly. I'll visit her in the morning before I go to the office."

Madeline reclined on the bed and rolled over toward Bill. She pulled him toward her and gave him a long and penetrating kiss. "You have been so wonderful." She felt his arousal with her left knee as he put his arms around her.

Surprised, he held her for a moment, staring into her eyes and kissed her hungrily.

Abruptly, he stopped himself, pulling back. "Likewise. I'm glad I can be of help."

They snuggled against each other for comfort. Pressed against him, Madeline smelled Bill's scent, Polo, and the tell-tail aroma of a Cuban cigar, courtesy of clients who brought them in from the Caymans. She felt safe in his arms, felt her daughter was protected by Bill's tentacles of influence, his money and his law firm's status in the legal community. Though he was seven years younger than her forty-four years, his wisdom and professionalism aged him. She felt on equal footing.

"Do you feel the need to talk about what happened that night in the cemetery? You should you know."

Madeline reached up and nuzzled his neck, then brought her lips to his, opening her mouth. Their tongues were moist with desire and imagining. Bill breathed heavily in arousal and gave a low throated groan of enjoyment. He moved his hand to the front of her blouse and unbuttoned it. Madeline compelled all thoughts of that night in the cemetery to vanish, as she gave in to her cravings. "I do love you." Her voice was throaty, breathless with desire. Bill's eyes were half-closed in the sublime passion of needing her.

The door opened. Mrs. Honor saw the couple on the bed and lightly rapped the wall with her knuckles with an accompanying cough. Madeline and Bill disentangled their arms from around each other, annoyed at the interruption.

"It's late, Ms. Randolf. We try to keep a strict protocol about visitors." Mrs. Honor was wry with irony.

Bill kissed Madeline on her cheek and for a moment, held her chin and looked into her eyes, aware that Mrs. Honor hovered like a dragonfly over flowering mint in the burning sun. "I'll stop by tomorrow after work, but I'll text you during the day." He lifted himself easily from the bed, took his jacket from the chair and his briefcase, which had fallen to the floor. He waved goodbye and sauntered out the door, which Mrs. Honor smugly held open and smugly shut as she abruptly followed after him, leaving Madeline alone to black out her thoughts.

In this place, diversion was difficult unless there were visitors. Now she would be forced to occupy herself with internet searches and the last novel of Vidal's *Empire* series, which she had been reading before the fateful night in the cemetery. She might ask for more medication to stave off the subterranean terrors that grew like tangled and monstrous weeds in her unconscious. The meds subdued all eruptions from the sleeping volcano, the aural flashbacks of screaming and the sounds of racing, pounding footsteps and the voice, hers, in a long, lashing wail. When a flashback exploded into her consciousness, she suppressed her response, held it back to a proper oblivion. But occasionally, flashbacks of that night were accompanied by weird, male, high- pitched caterwauling. The cacophonous cries roared and blistered her tympanums, compelling her to relive her terror in the cemetery. This reenactment, like a destructive lava flow that consumed everything in its path, swept her into its super-heated fury until she could no longer suppress her urge to join in with her own shrieks and screams. Then came chaos, the flurry of nurses and attendants, the struggle, the ominous straightjacket, the hypodermic syringe, the doctor's furrowed brow and the invariable dosage increase. These wailing cries rising up from her soul's damnation were the only pleasurable release in her miserable life, except for the distraction of sex.

She missed Bill already, was happy their relationship had taken this unusual turn that she had avoided for over a year because she had felt no spark between them, though Bill had made his interest transparent. Well, if the medications and sex kept the wild and destructive forces suppressed, they were appropriate antidotes no one would question, least of all her psychiatrist, Dr. Poplar. Her only enemy now was herself, but she would be watchful. And if, like a sentinel, she guarded against it, memories of that night would never plague her again.

Chapter Twenty-Seven

F en gazed at Peregrine. As she slept, her light breathing belied the precariousness of her physical and mental condition, if the doctors on this shift were to be believed. There was a soft rap on the door. Fen got up from his chair and answered it. Mocha, dressed in slim jeans, a tight-fitting white GAP T- shirt and Skechers, bounded into the room feisty, ready for action. Guessing she had been discharged, though it was a day later than initially anticipated, Fen brought the index finger of his right hand to his lips, then motioned toward the bed indicating Peregrine swathed in sheets.

"But it's twelve o'clock in the afternoon. The day is half over," Mocha sang in a mellifluous soprano.

Fen tried to hide his chagrin. He still couldn't get used to her British accent, though he knew it was mysteriously anchored in her trauma at the crypt. Peregrine said it was Mocha's new identity born from amnesia and her desperation to forget

Mocha stood by the bed and bent down, hovering her face an inch from her friend's. They breathed the same air.

Waking up, Peregrine uplifted long lashes to cut through the mist of another reality and ground herself in the wake of Mocha's being as Fen moved to the hospital bed to greet her.

"Hey." Fen smiled.

Mocha leaped on top of Peregrine, then rolled to her left side next to her. "You have to be awake to celebrate my leaving. When I'm gone, you can go back to sleep." She effusively threw her arms around her friend and lobbed three smacking kisses on her cheek.

Peregrine laughed. Fen bent over and lightly kissed her on her mouth, then sat on the edge of the bed, lifting her from her reclining position and tenderly circling her in his arms. Mocha bear hugged both of them. The three friends were a tangle of arms and warmth for five strong seconds, then Fen broke their unity to speak while everyone settled into a comfortable position.

"You look like yourself again, even in that shabby hospital gown." Fen shook his head. "When I picked you up and held you in my arms, I thought I was holding a rotting corpse. Then you croaked out my name, and I knew it was you."

Peregrine laughed. "Poor Fen. Burn the clothes you wore when you and Beach Comber found me. I tried to wash myself in the rain. Like Pig Pen's dirt, the stench clings to my skin. I don't think I'll ever get it out of my nostrils. They gave me around three or four sponge baths until I was strong enough to be helped into the shower. I still smell the graveyard on me." Peregrine sniffed herself.

"The trauma of your experience takes a long time to move past. I still keep seeing fabulous sunsets and pinks, like the most beautiful heavenly place you can imagine, when I close my eyes before I go to sleep or just before I wake up." Mocha was thoughtful.

"That's not traumatic." Peregrine laughed easily.

"It is if you don't ever want to leave such a place and hate waking up to this."

Mocha gestured around her.

"Conventional wisdom be damned. You never get past the brutality of a traumatic experience. And time doesn't heal wounds. There's no peace," Fen said solemnly.

"Spoken like a man. You and Beach Comber feel the same way. I don't think he'll ever get over Rebecca's death. Speaking of Beach Comber, he should be here. Where is he?"

"In jail."

"Can we not talk about this? I feel guilty, and there's nothing I can do about it." Mocha glared at Fen.

"Spoken with conviction." Fen attempted irony, knew anything else he said would provoke Mocha to leave, and he needed to ply her for information to give Beach Comber and his attorney.

"Explain please. You forget, I've been away from seeing you guys for almost two weeks."

Her voice quivering, Mocha began her tirade. "It's my cousin. The situation is pulling me apart. I wake up from a coma to hear Beach Comber is my alleged rapist and see my mother and Reggie thick as thieves. He's the only family we are speaking to at the moment. It's a mess. And she feels alone and abandoned with no one to turn to, and he's the mortar that's filled in the breach. It'll take a concrete blaster to get him out of our lives. I'm going to move out of my house. Peregrine, we've always talked about it. Let's get an apartment together. I can't take him and my mother's happy conspiracies." She shifted her gaze to Fen. "And I don't agree with what they are doing to Beach Comber."

Fen let Peregrine ask the questions. He didn't trust himself. His rationality was too entangled with raw feeling and identification with Beach Comber.

"What are the charges?" Peregrine was grim.

"Well, the grand jury is convening now. And there is talk of attempted homicide. At the arraignment it was that, sexual assault, theft of Mocha's purse, whatever they could throw against the wall in the hope that some of it would stick." Fen couldn't help but respond.

"What? I can't believe it. What happened?"

"That's just it. I don't know. I can't remember."

"You still can't bring yourself to remember anything?"

"Duh? You know I have amnesia. The doctors still don't know why. Suffocation or being hit over the head."

"Beach Comber has it, too." Fen got off the bed and moved to the chair, which he dragged near the bed. Peregrine situated the pillow behind her, then scooted back to lean against it, keeping her braced right leg as straight as possible to avoid any twinges of pain in her knee.

Mocha moved to the foot of the bed and sat with her legs dangling over the side. She looked at Fen accusingly, a mountain of mistrust. "I shouldn't be talking to you. I know you are going to go back and tell him everything, which is a betrayal to me."

Fen leaned forward, his elbows on his thighs. He tried to be as calm and rational as his nerves allowed. "Look, Mocha. The grand jury has to find enough evidence to support an indictment. We have a window of about thirty-five days, but they could be out longer. If there is an indictment, the prosecution will have to turn over everything they have to Beach Comber's attorney, anyway. Discovery. The DA's office can't withhold anything from the defense. It would blow their case. So, what you say here will end up with his attorney anyway and with a little luck, if you talk about it, your memory may be jarred to recall."

Mocha sighed and looked at Peregrine. "The psychiatrist thinks that because of the trauma I went through, I have psychogenic amnesia. He put me on medication to calm me and see if my memory returns. So far, I only remember waking up in the hospital."

Fen was careful. "What's psychogenic amnesia?"

"They are still not sure if I received brain injuries when I was hit over the head, or even if I was hit over the head. Traumatic amnesia relates to a physical injury to my brain. But the doctors still don't know if the amnesia is physical as well as psychological. But they are fairly sure, it's psychogenic, related to a psychological cause. And if it is psychogenic, then it's dissociative. I won't be able to remember anything about the violent events with Beach Comber. It's like there's a black hole, and I can't remember anything about the attack or suffocation which happened after the rape which I can't remember either."

Fen piped up. "They have to do a DNA analysis to prove rape."

"Not according to my cousin. There didn't have to be ejaculation. He could have pulled out. But there was damage to my throat which is almost healed. But there are pictures, MRIs, X-rays, and clinical write-ups, the medical evidence which was turned over to the DA's office and sent to the grand jury. All I know is whatever happened to me during that time with Beach Comber sent me into a coma."

"You were in a coma?" Peregrine shook her head. "Poor Beach Comber, it doesn't look good for him."

"The problem is, Beach Comber has amnesia, too, but it's not psychological, it's physical. If he could remember, he would." Fen looked down not wanting to sound accusatory of Mocha, who had been influenced by her mother and cousin into a convenient forgetfulness. "He was hit in the head, and then, there was an impact injury when he crashed his car. That's twice. They were afraid his brain would swell, and he would die. I forget what it's called. Initially, there was no swelling. But he's still not back to normal. He blacked out in jail, and he is really irritable, which they say is a symptom of concussion. And because he was in jail, he wasn't able to get the proper follow-up treatment. And now he's in jail again, which means that he still isn't getting treatment and his life is being endangered by those bastards who think they have a real psycho on their hands." The words gushed out of Fen, hitting their mark.

Mocha leaped off the bed in anger and whirled around to confront her friend. "I can't do this. Don't put me in the middle, friends on one side, the only family I have on the other. I can't take this stress." She screamed. "It was not my fault. I didn't know. I couldn't believe he had done this to me. I wanted to talk to him, and he came to the hospital. I didn't know my mother took out an order of protection against him."

"Yeah, well, they arrested him for violating the order, and he's lucky." Fen dripped irony, trying to remain calm. "He only got thirty days because he has no priors, and he has a great attorney." Fen was sarcastic. "Oh, and you asked to see him."

Everyone was silent. Mocha looked at her hands instead of at Fen who sighed and continued pointedly. "Otherwise, he would be in jail until the grand jury indicted him. If they do indict him, then it's back to jail and maybe revoked bail because of the protective order violation and the seriousness of the charges. And meanwhile, the guy is hurting. He's injured. Doctors say you have to watch someone with a concussion because the symptoms can show up later. Well, if they show up during the next three weeks and something happens to him," Fen shook his head at Mocha, "Tell your mom to be prepared for a tremendous countersuit. I don't think he had the chance for doctors to prescribe the proper medication."

Mocha collected her purse from the floor and strode to the door. "That's not my fault. My mother said he left the hospital before he should have."

"Wait a minute, Mocha, please stay." Peregrine begged. "We're all friends here."

Hand on the doorknob, Mocha was silent, morosely uncomfortable, standing on the precipice of a symbolic decision to stay or leave. Spinning manipulations, Fen and Reggie weaved veiling webs, glistening sticky treachery, patient to catch the prize, her testimony.

"You are both going too fast." Peregrine attempted to divert the subject to one less explosive. "He crashed his car, his beautiful T-Bird?"

"Peregrine, he can't remember what happened. And no one knows whether he lost control of the car or if he was trying to break down the gates to rescue Mocha who was on the other side or...something else." Fen stopped and looked at Mocha. "Does any of this ring a bell?"

Mocha shook her head no but relaxed her grip on the doorknob and moved a step into the room. She leaned against the wall to alleviate the mental exhaustion, which seeped into her physical body.

"Anyway, they found Beach Comber slumped over the wheel, car totaled, unconscious. The car had smashed through the gates, which were on the ground. They just missed falling on Mocha who was unconscious nearby. Mocha had no identification. Later on, at the hospital, they found out she was one of the women who had been missing for five days." He stared into Mocha's coal brown eyes, attempting sympathy, pleading for Beach Comber. "You must remember something, Mocha. Lying on the grass? Beach Comber coming for you? Do you remember him carrying you? Do you remember being in the cemetery?"

"I can't remember any of it. Nothing." Mocha sat on the edge of the bed. She threw her purse down in disgust, then covered her hands with her eyes and wept. "Don't you think I want to remember? For God's sake, I love him. I've always loved him. We were together, and I left for college, then he was with Rebecca. And she died, and now he's with no one, and I'm with no one. And no one's with me. I should be the one comforting him. We should be together. And I can't even see him because of the civil lawsuit and the court order and the grand jury."

Fen spied an opportunity. "Mocha, Beach Comber loves you, will always love you and you may be together again, but not until he gets over Rebecca and now this. I'm afraid for his life physically. Is there any way you can prevail upon your mom to rescind the court order? He needs to be in a hospital, but the judge isn't seeing his way clear."

"No. She's not behind the order. It's standard procedure. Sexual offenses, rape charges, attempted homicide charges often have an order of protection tacked on, least that's what they told me."

"Who?"

"Reggie."

"Your cousin?"

"But Mocha, you know Beach Comber would never harm you."

Mocha raised her tear-streaked face and pleaded. "What do you want me to do, Fen? I can't have the charges removed. It's too late. They did that when I was in a coma. I can't make my mother stop the lawsuit. I can't stop the DA's office. What would you have me do?" Her voice vibrated with tension.

Fen stared past her, saw his friend lying on the cot in the jail cell, blacking out. "I don't know. I can't advise you. But I think there is a way to help him, and I think you have to find it. And Peregrine, I think you can help Mocha remember. There's a moral imperative here. And we don't have much time."

Mocha sighed. "I'll increase my sessions with the psychiatrist and group and ask him for other medication. God knows, I don't want Comber to be in jail. And even if he harmed me, he wouldn't have done it out of meanness. He would have had to be possessed, I mean, not himself, insane." She looked back at Peregrine who was thoughtful.

"Mocha, what do you remember of our time in the mausoleum?"

"Falling against the door, and the lights going out." Mocha hesitated.

"What else?"

"It's a blank."

"You were going to slap me silly because of the weird sound I was making, remember?"

Mocha shook her head, wide-eyed. "Peregrine. It's darkness, all manner of darkness. A blank. A void. What do I have to do to convince the two of you I have no memory of that night, or the following night or the following? I have lost almost two weeks of my life. I don't know what happened, where I was, what I did. Imagine what that feels like. I shouldn't have even been in a coma, the doctor said. And they still can't figure out if I was hit over the head or suffocated. But I did have marks on the inside of my throat, like it was stuffed with something. And it was weird. I had marks on my neck, but they came after I was in the hospital. The nurse thought my mother strangled me. Then the marks disappeared. And then this thing with the British accent. It comes so naturally to me, but everyone who knew me before the coma thinks I've gone bonkers, or I'm acting. The doctor says after a coma, he's seen worse changes happen to people. I should be glad it's just an accent. But I've been altered in some way, a different person, and I don't know who she is or what to expect next." Mocha's eyes bulged with fear. "Can't you see how frightened I am?"

Fen moved over to her on the bed and embraced her and held her, soothing and caressing her hair with his left hand. "Shhh. Shhh. Mocha, it's good that you tell us. We won't know otherwise. It's important to talk about it. Eventually, you'll remember." Mocha shook her head in despair. "You will." He removed his arms from the embrace and held her face between open palms and looked into her eyes. "Somewhere inside your unconscious, you'll remember everything. It has to come out. There's no time to waste. You'll be subpoenaed to go before the grand jury to testify. Saying you can't remember will go badly for Beach Comber. It will make him look guilty. You can't do that to him. He doesn't deserve that from you."

Mocha shook free from Fen's grip and broke into tears. "No. He's been through too much."

"Mocha, we're in this together." Peregrine encouraged her friend, fierce with recollections. "Always there for each other. Remember our vow? *In silence, security, in unity, safety, in agreement, warranty. Facing calamity or death, in strength we abide.* You came up with the idea to force the hand of destiny. The Ceremony of Powers. Remember? The miracle of faith, the ninth spiritual gift? Our lives would be changed: Billy's, Fen's, Beach Comber's, yours, mine."

Mocha wiped her face and smiled. "What an ass to make such a suggestion. Look where it got us, nearly killed, me in a coma, you in the hospital and Beach Comber in jail." Peregrine and Mocha snorted, chortling like dainty hyenas. Fen was quiet, a weird look on his face. Mocha pushed him in jest. "Except for Fen. Unscathed. So typical."

Peregrine extended the levity. "That's because he's Fennelly Girardo, supernova, ready for his close-up, Mr. Tarantino." Peregrine pretended seriousness. "Fen, just don't dump us when you're pulling down twenty million a picture with three babes on each arm at the Oscars."

Closed, solitary, with a grim expression on his face, Fen got off the bed walked to the door, opened it and walked out. Shocked, Peregrine motioned to Mocha. "Go after him. Apologize for me. I would, but my leg is aching, and you know how fast he is. I'd never catch up."

Mocha scrambled off the bed and quickly left the room. Peregrine leaned back on the pillow and straightened out her left leg, then stretched herself forward touching her toes. She had never known Fen to be so sensitive. Of the four friends, he was the bulwark, the shoulder to cry on. Older than Mocha and Peregrine, the same age as Beach Comber, whom he had known the longest, he was the wise one with all the answers. Hell, he had graduated from Yale on full scholarship and had finished his second semester at Yale Drama School. Bored, he dropped out to pursue his burgeoning career, probably because his agent cajoled him, or he lost a role to someone more famous, Peregrine surmised. Uninterested in anything but establishing himself as an acting phenome, out of all of them, Fen was the most focused, the most artistic, the most brilliant. Mocha referred to him as the horse with blinders since recently, he had spoken of nothing but his jobs, his agent and upcoming auditions.

Mocha banged open the door, a poker-faced Fen in tow behind her. Once in the room, Mocha stood behind him, placing both hands on his arms and pushed him to the bed. "Sit."

Fen turned around and sat. Peregrine pulled his left arm toward her.

"Just get comfortable." Fen moved back on the bed where he was discomfited, then he slid off and sat in the chair. Mocha went to the yellow plastic chair in the corner on the other side of the room and lifted it over her head, carrying it to where Fen was. She placed it on the floor in a right angle near him.

"There are Diet Cokes in the fridge. No alcohol, not even for medicinal purposes." Peregrine said with transparent lightness. "Too bad. What we all need is a good stiff drink. Ah, Mocha. Get us three Cokes, unless you want to share one. Please?"

Mocha got the cokes and handed them around as Peregrine moved to the edge of the bed closer to Fen. Carefully, she situated both of her legs over the side, the braced leg unbent but touching the floor. To the popping sound of the can tops, Peregrine initiated, "I'm sorry I upset you. What gives?"

Between swigs of Coke he told them the first story fragment about that night in Old Calvary. "Mocha, you're not the only one under tremendous stress here. Ever since we were supposed to meet that night, and I didn't make it, I've been in a living hell. Manny's dead."

"What? This is terrible. And you've been so concerned about us?" All judgment about Fen's solipsism flew out of Peregrine's mind, her stupidity chain jerked.

"Spill." Mocha shuffled in the yellow chair, leaned forward and put her hand on Fen's knee to comfort him.

"That night I brought Manny with me to the cemetery. My mother was away on a last minute business trip, and there was no one to take care of him. So I figured he could stay in the car while I went to the mausoleum to meet you. You know, he has his computer games to occupy him, and he really is cooperative and wonderful that way, not like others who suffer with his disability. It was on my way to the crypt when I remembered the ancient Greek oil lamp, you know, the only thing that connects me to my mother's family, and the oil. I had left them in the trunk. So I ran back to the parking lot. In the distance, I see Manny being pulled out of my car by two large men in suits. Then I see them push Manny into a black limousine, like a Lincoln Town Car. He wasn't screaming, and he didn't hear me when I shouted his name. That makes me think they drugged him before they got him out of my car. Then the limo raced out of there. I ran to my car and caught up with them on Queens Boulevard and followed them to the LIE where I lost them on Horace Harding, the service road. Five minutes later I located them again, on the LIE, heading past the Cross Island Expressway exit. I don't know how we weren't chased by police." Fen got up from the chair and paced back and forth. "We were going ninety and one hundred, especially out past Wading River."

"Out east?"

"Oh, yeah, way out east!" Fen's emphasis was dramatic. "I lost them again by the Seaford Oyster Bay Expressway. I thought they turned on it to go north, and I got off. But then I realized it was another car. I did a U-turn across the grass divider and barely avoided a collision with another car. Then I got back to the LIE where I caught up with them and followed them out to Southampton."

Mocha leaned back in her chair intently thinking. "Were you able to see if it was the same limo with Manny in the back?"

"Same year and make, same first couple of letters on the license plate. The windows were dark. Once I pulled right up next to them, but I couldn't see Manny." Interrupting his narrative, Fen tilted his head back to take a drink. He was pensive. "That's what the detectives asked."

"What detectives?"

"Some of the detectives in the same office as your cousin." Fen said wryly, looking at Mocha.

"You went to the Queens DA?"

"Yeah." He considered. "But it occurs to me now. Say, I made a mistake and followed the wrong car, and the guys were innocent. There would have been no need for a high-speed chase. They would have driven normally. Once they figured out that I was following them, they could have driven to a police station or called the police and reported me as a stalker. They didn't do any of that. They fled like they were guilty. I have to tell Dietz and Allan, remind them."

Mocha played the devil's advocate. "If they were scared you had a gun, they would flee."

Peregrine added, "Then why didn't they call the police or drive to a police station? Why not get the police involved? It's a high-speed chase. Something is not right."

All three nodded, and Mocha said, "You've convinced me."

"Thanks. I haven't discussed this with anyone but the detectives and they doubted everything I said, and that made me angry. And when I get angry, I forget blocks of detail, my train of thought gets thrown off, and I'm inarticulate."

Mocha laughed. "You're just a mess, Fen." They all laughed, grateful they were finally in agreement again.

"Well, they turned off by the Seven Eleven, Sunrise Highway in Southampton. Somehow, I knew they were going to the ocean, you know, the long, private, manicured driveways run up to those fabulous beachfront mansions, and the security is fatter than a Secret Service detail for the pope. Well, we raced through lights and went sixty through the town, and sure enough, I was right, raced up and around Agwam Reservoir on Ginn Lane, which fronts the Atlantic." Fen paused. "I still can't believe the cops didn't stop us; though by that point, it was around three o'clock in the morning."

"Maybe there was no one on duty. They're trying to save money." Mocha was coy.

Peregrine laughed. "Southampton? Right."

"It's something to think about; why no cop stopped us for speeding. It would be worth getting a speeding ticket to see if anyone is on duty around that time."

"Why not just call and ask?"

"Come on. If you were supposed to be on duty and were off somewhere, what would you say? Besides, I don't trust the officers I spoke with. Too tied in politically. I don't know. Maybe it was random, maybe not."

"What difference does it make?" Peregrine forced Fen to the logical conclusion.

"Well, if they stopped us, then I could have checked to see if Manny was in the back. And if he was, then there's the proof I needed that they kidnapped him." Fen's voice lowered. "Manny would have been saved." He got up and forcefully threw the can in the plastic bag lined waste basket and turned toward the women's expectant faces. "No. It was no coincidence that the police never showed up. It's likely that Manny was in the back seat, drugged. If he had seen my car pull up next to theirs, he would have moved to the window and pounded on it. Even though the windows were tinted, I would have seen movement in the back seat. There was nothing. Either he was tied up or drugged."

"What happened next?"

Fen turned the orange chair around and sat back to front. He told them about Liam's tour through the majestic estate, his nights on the beach and the helicopter explosion. In the retelling, Fen became more and more remote, winding down like an ancient timepiece, as remembrance of the brilliant exploding fireball scarring the black night sky jolted him into a profound silence.

The women were stunned.

"I'm so sorry, Fen." Mocha thought of her brother's terminal condition. "I know how much you loved him."

Peregrine murmured, "I can't believe Manny's gone." She shook off the depression. She had defied death in the labyrinth, had been empowered by serendipity and ingenuity to survive. Her experience had taught her well. Now, she rebutted his desolation with a curious thought. "Fen! You don't really know if that was Manny on the stretcher! You were far away."

Fen looked at her pointedly, as if to scold her for not listening carefully.

"I know you were looking through binoculars. Did you see his face?" Peregrine insisted.

Fen was distraught, his voice barely above a whisper. "It was his green jacket. I would recognize it anywhere."

"Did you see his face?"

"No."

"Did it look like his hair?"

"I don't know. It happened so fast. I had maybe ten seconds to see because they were running to the helicopter. In my sightlines, they were mostly in a vertical position. The man who held the handles of the stretcher closest to Manny's head blocked my view. So I couldn't clearly see his face or hair or most of his body. It looked like the back of his head, but his face was turned away from me. I had the best view when they ran around the front of the helicopter to the other side and lifted up the stretcher. It was Manny's jacket. His arm was hanging down, and I could see the stripes on the front. It was the one I gave him."

Mocha watched Peregrine and Fen in a death spiral of argument, amazed at Peregrine's ferociousness. She listened for pitfalls in her friend's logic.

Peregrine continued like a Jack Russell terrier after a scurrying rat. "Are you listening to yourself? You don't even know if the man in the jacket was Manny! You didn't see his face, didn't have a clear view of the body on the stretcher."

"Why would they dress someone else with Manny's jacket? It makes no sense."

He got up from the chair. "I need a cigarette."

Mocha laughed. "You stopped smoking."

"It's a good time to begin again." He pushed back the chair, got up, paced to the wall opposite the foot of the bed and leaned his back against it, crossing his arms, putting his right boot up on the wall. He looked at Peregrine who stared back, her blue eyes boring through his mind to ferret out the rat of doubt and destroy it.

"Don't leave me, Fen. Let's see. Why would they put Manny's jacket on someone else? To mislead you, obviously. How good is their security?"

"Millions of dollars good."

"Could security have seen you staked out on the beach?"

Fen was silent.

"Is it possible they knew you were scoping them out?"

Grudgingly, Fen nodded.

"To get you out of there, they brought in the helicopter, dressed someone in Manny's jacket, put him on the stretcher and MedEvac him away from there. My guess is that Manny is still at the estate, or was. Why go to all that trouble to take him around the other side of the helicopter?"

"Yeah, that's what confused me. Why go around the front of the helicopter to the other side. Was there an opening on the pilot's side?" Mocha looked at Fen encouragingly.

"Yes."

"Well, does it make sense they went around to the other side when they could cut off distance going to the nearest opening? They did that to obscure your view. You might have seen his face if they loaded him through the opening nearest you."

Fen didn't allow himself the hope of their logic. "First of all, it wasn't a MedEvac helicopter."

"Better. Nothing official is happening here, nothing that can be recorded. Private helicopter." Peregrine was fidgeting. "I want to pace. I think better when I'm on my feet."

"You mean limp…gimp. Relax, stay there. Keep on going." Mocha smiled. "You're doing great."

"Fen, just admit it's possible that they wanted to distract you into believing that Manny was on the helicopter. Admit it."

Fen squeaked the word out. "Yes. It is possible. But not likely."

"All you need to do is not be so conclusive about Manny's death. You don't even know if he was on the helicopter. Their behavior suggests the opposite."

"She's right." Mocha piped up, going over to Fen who was still leaning against the wall. "It's a testament to their power and money, the helicopter. It's in your face, like: "you want to follow us? Let's see you follow a helicopter." They must have known you were watching. Either security saw you, or there were spies on the beach."

Fen thought aloud. "No one from the estate came out on the beach after the explosion."

"What?"

"A crowd showed up after the explosion. We watched the burning refuse float on the water, and we looked for survivors." Fen shuddered. He considered that Manny exploded into burning debris. "But no one from the estate came out. I would have seen them, recognized them."

"What do you mean?"

"They didn't want to be connected with the accident. There were officers from the East Hampton police. They were cool. Well, I went to the estate with them to question Liam. He and the others denied the helicopter left from their helipad. Too bad my phone camera went dead. The video I took was blank. Since no one in the area saw the helicopter, it's my word against theirs. It's up to the FBI and NTSB to turn up clues, linking the helicopter with them. That night you could see they didn't want to answer any questions. That made me think Manny was in the helicopter, and they were afraid that they were guilty of the kidnapping and Manny's death...murder."

Peregrine got off the bed and limped to the white, faux wood bureau. "Guys, I'm going to get dressed. It's two o'clock." She opened the top drawer and pulled out a Ralph Lauren T-shirt with US Open Tennis logo that her mother had bought for her. She took off her robe and stood in her underwear, quickly pulling on the shirt. "What I don't understand, Fen, is why kidnap Manny? Have you or your mom received any phone calls asking for ransom money?" Peregrine limped to the closet where new jeans were hanging. She pulled them down, went to the chair Fen vacated. She sat in it, slipping on each pant leg.

"That's just it. If I hadn't followed them, then maybe we would have gotten the calls and could have arranged for the money drop, and Manny would be with us today. Instead, I had to be the big man and try to rescue my brother and totally screw things up. No. It's hopeless." Fen leaped onto the bed, landing on his stomach. Her turned over on his left side, leaned his head on his hand and watched Peregrine tying the shoelaces on her new NIKEs.

"Ransom is never that easy. Do you involve the police or not? Everybody's nervous at the transfer, money for victim, even if the police are not involved. Usually, the victim is killed because he can identify the kidnappers," said Mocha. "So, don't carry that weight around with you. You did what was needed. Anyway, you have no proof Manny's dead."

"No proof he's alive, either."

"It's a 50-50 chance either way. Those are pretty good odds. Do you concede?"

Fen gave a half-hearted smile. "Well, maybe."

"Let's go."

"You're not going anywhere." Mocha scolded her friend. "You have to rest."

"Let's get out of here. I have cabin fever. We'll go for a walk. We're missing something about Manny. If I limp," she looked at Mocha and smiled, "I'll think of it." Peregrine got up from the chair where she had been sitting and motioned to the door.

Fen sat up on the bed and laughed a belly laugh. "You're going to walk around the hospital? Do you have any idea what's out there? Didn't your mother tell you?"

"I have been sleeping for two and a half days. I spoke to her on the phone for like twenty seconds. She's in a hospital out on Long Island. And I saw Bill again this morning when they took out my IVs. Tell me what?"

Fen and Mocha looked at each other and smiled. "Peregrine, you're a celebrity. We're celebrities." Mocha got out of her chair and pranced "like an Egyptian" back and forth, then stopped to see the amazement on Peregrine's face.

Fen's mood perked up. "There's media on the prowl out there, right now. We came up the back stairway exit, but first we had to call Bill who made the arrangement for us to get passed his security team who are guarding you. Actually, I think this is going to jump start my career."

Peregrine slumped down into the orange chair as Mocha sat in the yellow one. "I don't understand."

"There's news coverage about Fen and Beach Comber rescuing you. When Beach Comber and I were brought in the ambulance to the hospital, we were flooded with calls and e-mails. Everyone wanted the story. They camped out at our door with cameras, followed my mom everywhere. The same happened to your mom and Sylvia. We all have spokespersons. Fen's agent is handling the media for him. When I leave later on, I'm supposed to call my mom, so our lawyer will be there if I speak before the cameras."

Fen was dry. "It started when Beach Comber rescued Mocha; and of course, you were still missing, so that created a shark effect. The media got the story and ran with it, maybe because Beach Comber's hands and torso were covered in lacerations, deep ones where the barbed wire…" Fen evoked the symbol because he knew Mocha's religious background. "The barbed wire crucified him. He was the martyred hero. Since you were in a coma, they couldn't speak to you, Mocha. Sylvia's spokesperson gave them information about his travels and his help during the 2004 tsunami; and the *Post, Daily News, People, Time* and *Newsweek* did this romantic surfer spread about him. But then the DA's office started sniffing around the conflicting medical evidence. And things got turned around. And soon the implication was that Beach Comber had sexually assaulted Mocha, and it went wrong, and it became an attempted homicide. And when he went back to the cemetery, it was interpreted as a return to the crime scene to destroy evidence."

"I didn't know any of this. After I woke up, my mom told me that the medical evidence could prove that Beach Comber assaulted me. I don't believe it, can't believe it. But she and Reggie think I'm protecting him."

"Well, the DA converted potential rescue evidence, the lacerations all over his torso and his hands, and his concussions, into evidence that they intend to use to prove his sexual assault. In their initial heroism version, the media said that Beach Comber climbed over the fence and used his car to smash through the gates to take Mocha to the hospital. But then they changed the story, probably influenced by the DA's office. Their suicide interpretation is that Comber and Mocha had arranged to meet and have lurid sex, but it went wrong; and she went unconscious. He panicked and left, then had guilt pangs and went back to her. In a depression, he tried to kill them both by driving his car into the gates, and of course, he failed." As Fen took a breath, Mocha and Peregrine took advantage of his silence to look at each other for support.

"For Christ's sake, I mean you were close friends, lovers at one point. There was no indication that any change in your relationship occurred. Sexually assault you and try to kill you? That's ridiculous." Fen avoided mentioning Reggie for fear it would chase Mocha back into her cocoon. "The homicide story is that Beach Comber climbed the fence to escape after he had sexually assaulted Mocha and tried to suffocate her, so she couldn't testify against him. Then he used his car as a weapon to smash the gates and finish the job on her, but his plan backfired." Fen saw Mocha sigh; he hoped with guilt. "What makes it worse is that Beach Comber can't remember much of anything except that he drove to the cemetery looking for you two."

Peregrine looked at Mocha. "Now that we know, we can poke holes in the DA's case to help Beach Comber."

Mocha nodded hesitantly. "But I thought the media was portraying Beach Comber as a hero with you?"

Fen didn't hold back. "We aren't sure, but we think that Reggie influenced a different spin. The media, hungry for controversy, is lapping up both versions."

Mocha was silent with guilt.

"After we rescued you, Peregrine, the media did more stories on Beach Comber, and interviewed me. Heroism stuff. But now that he's in jail, cable news segments are bringing on former prosecutors and defense lawyers as guests. They've talked up the controversy and discussed the possibilities of indictment, based on some of the evidence they obtained from public sources. For Beach Comber, it's been a nightmare."

"And I can't get near him to talk to him."

"We'll let him know how you feel," said Fen, then quickly changed the subject. "I guess I'm the only one who will benefit from the publicity. Funny, you think you want fame; but it's stressful, knowing you have to monitor everything you say and do, even your facial expressions because YouTube is watching. But it is a two-way street. You have to know how to manipulate the media to your side. And with a little luck, you find the whole world is in your corner. Well, at least my agent's happy. He's lining up auditions for me. Let's face it. We're going to have to think global coverage."

Anticipating cameras after Mocha's and Fen's rant, Peregrine limped to the door, opened it and looked out. No crowds adorned the hallway, but there was a well-built black man in jeans and a tailored short sleeve shirt, sitting outside the door and reading the newspaper. She waved at him when he looked up, then shut the door and went back inside. "This changes everything." She groaned. "I wonder how long it will take to get things back to normal."

"The saturation point. You should do interviews until the story is so well known it's boring, and then the media moves on. But if you make like J.D. Salinger, forget it. They'll track you like a bloodhound."

Fen thought of Manny. "Things will never be back to normal. Never."

Peregrine moved to the bed where Fen relaxed, sitting upright, his feet firmly on the floor. She sat next to him, favoring her right knee, placing the right heel on the floor to keep her leg straight, while she comfortably bent the left leg on the bed, all throbbing in the left ankle gone. "We've got to have a plan. Maybe we should do an interview together, but our stories have to be consistent."

"Beach Comber and I found you in a cemetery late at night, after twelve o'clock. Beach Comber and Mocha were found in a cemetery. Key question they want to know. Why were we there? Do you have a good answer for that?"

"Why tell them where you found me?"

"It slipped out when Beach Comber and I brought you to the ER. We had to tell the doctors something. They wanted to know where we found you to treat you. I thought I was helping to save your life. You were a mess."

"Oh God. What are the spokespersons saying when they ask why we, I, was there?"

"They don't know why we were there, and they want us to tell them." Mocha was vague.

"It's like chum to sharks. They want the story." Fen was cool. "Problem. Beach Comber and I are heroes. Our rescue helped his reputation with the grand jury. We don't want to do anything to destroy this image."

"When I'm discharged in a few days, if our representatives agree, we'll hold a news conference. And we'll tell them there are certain topics we won't discuss."

Fen shook his head. "If we don't want to talk about it, they'll try to find out. Since Beach Comber is involved, this might encourage the police to investigate. After all, we were trespassing. We were at the cemetery after hours. Some media outlets have mentioned that fact."

"I have to discuss this with my mom, but why not tell the truth? We went to pay respects to my family. Mocha and I were separated. I was locked inside. I found my way out through the labyrinth. I just won't tell them what time I went to visit my ancestors. I told you where I would be, and the rest is history. Beach Comber found Mocha; and later both of you found me. We can spin off our stories from that."

Fen nodded. "Makes sense. Speak to your mom about it."

Mocha's expression was one of doubt. "If you were locked inside and I was outside, then why didn't I go for help?"

"But you weren't locked out. You were with me inside the crypt, and then you disappeared. It was like you fell down the rabbit hole. I made myself hoarse crying your name. And it was dark. I crawled over every inch of that floor searching for you. You weren't there."

"I don't remember. It's a blank." Mocha was visibly upset and anxious. "But I do seem to remember the door shut on both of us."

"Yes. You said something about the wind slamming it."

Mocha's hands were shaking. She got up and paced back and forth. "And we got the crowbar out of the back-pack."

"No. I think I left it outside. We looked for it. We tried everything. Then you heard me shuffling toward you, and you told me to stop. Remember?"

Mocha screamed. "No, no. I don't want to remember. Can't remember, can't."

Fen rushed up from the bed and put his arms around Mocha, preventing her from sinking to the floor in a fit of hysterical crying. "It's going to be all right. Come on, Mocha." He walked her to the bed. She was still sobbing, so he sat her next to Peregrine who hugged her.

The door opened. The body-guard peeked into the room. "Is everything all right?"

Peregrine broke the hug, but kept her arm around Mocha who cried softly. "Yes. We're fine. Just trying to get it together. Everything's under control. I'm Peregrine. This is Mocha and Fen." Mocha didn't look up.

"I'm Michael."

Fen walked to the door and shook hands with Michael. "Hi."

"I'm your body-guard for as long as you need me."

"Thanks." There was an awkward silence. "Later, I might want to take a walk."

"Well, just let me know. I'll be ready. It's clear on this floor. But my colleague will have to check the lobby if you want to go downstairs. Reporters and camera people are waiting there."

"Maybe in an hour. Thanks."

Michael closed the door.

Fen nodded his head in approval. "You won't have to worry with him around." He sat in the yellow, plastic chair and faced the women on the bed.

Peregrine refocused her attention. "I'm sorry, Mocha. I didn't realize it was so upsetting, but you do remember some things. It's a first step."

"Something happened to her. Something horrible. It's like post-traumatic stress. All of us have it." Fen was curious. "Except you, Peregrine."

"I haven't had time to think. I've been so physically exhausted." She smiled brightly. "Don't worry. Maybe it will show up later."

"I'm not wishing it on you, Peregrine." Fen leaned over and reached for some tissues on the nightstand. "Feeling better?" He handed them to Mocha, who nodded, then blew her nose and dried her eyes.

"I have to face what happened. I'm petrified, but I will. You've helped me tremendously." She patted Peregrine's leg and smiled at Fen. "I'm counting on both of you to get me through this."

Again, Peregrine hugged her and kept her arm around her for reassurance. "Mocha, the way you reacted, like something happened when we were separated, and the door shut. We were in complete darkness. Don't think about it now, but later on, try to remember if your fear was mostly inside the crypt or outside."

Fen was excited. "It might help Beach Comber, if you can recall when you were most afraid. When they found you both, it was in broad daylight, not like when we found Peregrine."

"I am terrified of the darkness." Mocha's upper lip quivered. "Does that help?"

"Yes, Mocha." Peregrine hugged her again. "Anything that comes to your mind, write it down. That way your imagination will be grounded in your memory, and both will filter out the fear."

Mocha sighed and closed her eyes. She nodded. "I don't want to go home. My mom will be back really late. No one is there, except Billy and the nurse. He is struggling to get to the next day. I don't know if I can face him, going back there with no hope. Our ceremony was supposed to heal him. Everything is in a shambles."

"Why don't you stay with me tonight?" Peregrine removed her arm from Mocha's shoulder and turned to look at her. "You're officially discharged. I'll ask for a cot. We'll get takeout. Fen, you stay, too, at least for dinner. It'll be a great change from the disgusting hospital food, which I just pick at."

"OK. I'll call my mom. I'm sure she'll be happy if I'm happy. I'm afraid to go home. I don't want to be alone. I can't be alone."

"It's settled."

Peregrine and Mocha looked at Fen. "Whatdayasay, gorgeous?" Peregrine lifted her eyebrows and tilted her head toward Fen.

"I'll stay with you for dinner, but I have to get back to the city." Fen didn't mention that he intended to call Beach Comber. And if he couldn't get through to him at the lockup, he'd call Comber's lawyer to discuss the progress he'd made with Mocha. "I've let things slide, and tomorrow will be a busy day." Then thoughts flooded his consciousness and he made a heavy sighing sound. "I promised my mom I'd go out to the Island to see her." He put his head in his hands. "I haven't told her what I saw. She thinks Manny's alive, just missing." He lifted up his head to explain. "I didn't even tell her about the kidnapping. She thinks he's off wandering somewhere in Queens. I dread telling her. When you two were found, that gave her hope. She's convinced herself that he will turn up, that a nice, kind family who's been keeping him like a stray animal will eventually become bored with his endearing ways and contact the police."

"Before the detectives contact her with news of the investigation, you must tell her the truth." Mocha was direct.

"No. They know not to call her. I've warned them about it."

"Fen, you don't know that he's dead, conclusively. I don't know how to extricate you from your guilt about this. Look, you have a window of opportunity before you tell your mother what you think you saw. Wait until the investigation is concluded." Peregrine stood up in excitement. "I remember now what I was thinking. Is anyone watching the estate now?"

"No. There's no reason to."

"That's what they might want you to believe, Fen."

"Before the crash I thought of hiring a private detective to nose around, someone who networks with city and local law enforcement who would stake out the mansion since I couldn't do it."

"Fen, you need to get someone who is good, and that might be costly. Can you afford it?"

"What for?"

"To get more proof."

"The official investigation will give me the proof I need." Fen leaned back in the chair and nearly tipped it over. He righted it again, stood up and paced back and forth. Peregrine leaned against the bureau, giving him room to meander and think.

Mocha chided Fen. "Manny could still be at the estate. Maybe they're planning to take him somewhere else. I can't imagine why if he is alive, they haven't contacted you about a ransom."

"Maybe they were going to, but their plans backfired when you followed them and staked them out on the beach. Now they are so tangled in their own lies, they can't follow through with a ransom since they made it appear he was on the helicopter. That means either they're imprisoning Manny, or they'll get rid of him since he's lost his usefulness. He could still be alive. Maybe they're just waiting for the right time to dispose of him. You could be saving his life, Fen. Can you take the risk of letting things go? Not getting more proof to see if Manny's at the estate?" Peregrine could see the wind shift in Fen's attitude about his brother's death.

"I don't know." He stopped pacing and looked at Peregrine, shaking his head.

"I don't want to be mean, Fen, but death is a convenient finality for Manny. Alive means you have to save him. Alive means confronting Liam again and again. Ransoming your emotions to pay for Manny's death is a worse evil. It's resignation. Sustaining hope requires effort, more energy than nihilism. I know. That was my struggle in the labyrinth. Hope against resignation. I had to hope there would be an end, hope I would be alive to see it. I had to fight with every gram of my soul not to lay down and die. If I can do it, you can do it. You've done it. Acting is one of the toughest careers in the world. You have to have faith to keep going after hundreds of rejections."

Fen smiled. "Don't rub it in."

"Can't you see that Manny might still be alive?" Peregrine's eyes pooled with tears as she stared into his, penetrating his mind with the combustibility of hope.

Fen grabbed her and held her, his faith brightening, like a fireball in a night sky.

Mocha looked inward past her friends' close embrace. Peregrine's words ran through her like a sword. For Mocha, the trauma had made nihilism and denial easy. Fear caulked together the two negatives of existence, insuring the certainty that her rudderless ship floated on a sterile ocean toward death. She felt she understood Fen's destruction of hope. But this new Peregrine? Peregrine BC, before the crypt, had vanished in a strange reversal of attitude. Now, Peregrine was the one with the matchless faith. She smiled to herself. Was it true, the saying, "If it doesn't kill you, it makes you stronger?" Well, she was dying, her faith was dying, and nihilism was destroying her. And with her joy for life depleted, there wasn't a damn thing she could do about it.

As Peregrine and Fen gazed into each other's eyes, they recognized an extraordinary intimacy they had never experienced before.

"Don't mind me. I'll just sit here and watch." Mocha grinned.

Embarrassed, Peregrine was the first to move away and sit on the bed. "Promise me you will hire a private investigator?"

"Yes. Maybe Bill can recommend someone."

"I'll ask my mom."

"You do know you might be able to stake out the mansion without a PI, but it will involve a sacrifice," Mocha said to Fen, her eyelids widening in thoughtfulness.

"I'm listening." Fen went to the refrigerator and took out another Coke. "Would anyone like anything?"

"Could you get me an Evian?"

Mocha shook her head. "No thanks." She watched as Fen settled himself in the yellow chair and passed the Evian to Peregrine. As they drank, she continued. "Involve the media. Go on record about Manny's disappearance. Generate publicity about your filing a missing person's report and involving law enforcement. Connect the dots for the media. Seduce them into staking out the mansion to get the story. Let Liam confront the paparazzi. Think of the media outlets' resources. They're sure to turn up proof one way or another about Manny."

Fen shook his head in doubt. "My mother would have to know, then."

"Why is that an issue? Tell her that in all probability Manny was not in the helicopter and that he's still at the estate. And if Bill can recommend an investigator who works in concert with the media, then you'll have coverage of Liam's and the staff's activities."

"She's right. But first you must confront your mom's anger and desolation." Peregrine joked to lighten the truth. "So what if she openly loathes you and gives you the silent treatment and kicks you out of her life?" She shrugged her shoulders. "Worst case scenario, she never forgives you." She managed to get Fen to smile and then became serious. "It's not the easy route. For all of us in the weeks ahead, nothing will be easy or convenient. But you'll respect yourself and get your courage back. Besides, you're doing this for Manny, not yourself, not your mother...Manny."

Fen was silent. He thought of the misery he felt after the helicopter crash. He considered the possibility that Manny might still be alive. Logic, like an electric charge, prodded his mental somnolence. Without anyone watching the estate, the pressure was off. Liam could act against his brother with impunity, come and go as he pleased. Fen had no time to waste. He pushed back the chair and stood up. "I'm going to Long Island. I'll arrange media interviews with my mother present. They're interested in your rescue. I'll start with that." He saw Peregrine's disturbed look and cut her off with a raised hand before she could speak. "If it comes up, I know what to say. We were supposed to meet; you didn't show. And on a hunch, I figured something happened, and you were still at the cemetery. It won't come up. They'll be too interested in what I tell them about Manny."

Peregrine smiled. "If it gets rough, say that the three of us will do a press conference. When I talk to the doctor, I'll try for an earlier discharge. Maybe we can have the conference the day after my release."

Fen hugged Mocha and Peregrine and left with renewed purpose. Impatient, Peregrine waited for the doctor. After Michael had given the all clear signal, Mocha went to the ladies' room to call Elizabeth at work. When she couldn't get a clear signal on her cell, she moved to the exit stairwell, thinking about the strain and tension in their relationship. Mocha was a different woman, direct and authoritative. Elizabeth's assumptions about her daughter were being cut out from the foundation which she had built for her children and herself. But her mother didn't realize that the foundation, had cracks weakening its stability, and a minor shaking would crumble it to pieces. Let the earthquake come.

After briefly questioning Mocha on her scheduled doctor's appointments, Elizabeth listened anxiously to Mocha's proposal to stay overnight at the hospital with Peregrine. "Deidre, please go home and be with Billy. Watch and pray with him. We don't know how long he will be with us."

"You're coming home from work really late. I'm not ready to be alone with him and that nurse. You say there is no distance in Spirit. Well, I can pray for Billy here. It's for one night. Depending on Peregrine's blood tests and the doctor's examination, the doctor will probably discharge her late tomorrow afternoon. I'll be home then."

"Mocha, if you're afraid, maybe you should see the psychiatrist three times a week."

"No...I don't know."

"Although I don't agree, when he hears about this, maybe the doctor will feel the need to increase your medication."

Mocha was silent. She couldn't discern if her mother believed her.

"Deidre, please pray that the Lord gives you the strength to overcome your fears. Claim a sound mind and plead The Blood."

"Ummm." In the past, she would have accepted her mother's counsel. Now, it made her restless and uneasy.

"You are having this problem because you tampered with the occult, a seduction by the Powers. The door is open. Beyond are the principalities, the rulers of the darkness of this world and spiritual wickedness in high places. Extricate yourself from any dark practices you engaged in with Peregrine. End them. You don't want to become entangled in these other realms, which you can't control."

The last thing she wanted to think about were her failures of faith. "I'll call you tomorrow. Love you." She clicked off her phone. Her mother's interpretation of the dark arts was skewed. The Ceremony of Powers they had planned to enact in the crypt was a faith and healing ceremony, which she would have approved of if Mocha had been able to confide in her. But there was one thing her mother wouldn't sanction, the place where they had planned the ceremony. Elizabeth was accustomed to prayer or healing services being conducted in a church or synagogue or mosque. She was confused. The holy temple was the human being. Religious structures were a type of charnel house, even worse than a crypt. Oftentimes, religious leaders were whited sepulchers, dead inside, no power of love. Some hid behind religious forms and rituals. Others twisted holy writ to suit their political agendas. Corruptions and scandals exposed to the light revealed personal lives lacking in the faith they were supposed to be championing. No. She agreed with Peregrine. They had had enough of the isms…Protestantism, Catholicism, Judaism, Islamism, Buddhism, Mormonism, Bahá'í. All were short on God's glory and grace. She would seek the Spirit. Organized religion's laws were man-made, not God made. It was blasphemy to limit what was infinite and divine. She must regain the power of her faith for this new time in her life.

"Great news." Peregrine greeted Mocha's return to the room, beaming with happiness.

"The doctor is pleased with my recovery and says that I can be discharged, maybe tomorrow. I have to rest, of course, keep up fluid and nutritional intake. I'll see him in a week for a follow-up. He's amazed."

Mocha hugged her friend. She envied her power to heal quickly. "Things are moving. But that means we have to plan for the media conference, get our stories straight. Only I don't have much of a story."

"After dinner, we'll discuss it, as much as you can take. We'll be as truthful as you feel. You'll see. The truth will free you from fear."

Mocha's emotions were in a tumult. Peregrine was a child. In some circles, truth was blasphemy. But cynicism wouldn't work here. For her, nothing worked. She was wandering blind in the darkness, spinning round and round in the middle of a series of concentric circles. She didn't know how she got there, and she didn't know how to escape.

Chapter Twenty-Eight

B each Comber lay on the cot. His headache pounded like jack-hammers. When the guard, Mario, had asked whether he wanted to join the other prisoners in the common area, he had declined, exhausted. The concussion from the accident had searched him out, and he was its punching bag. Intermittent nausea and headaches interplayed with feelings of somnolence. Lethargy and torpor were the static that plagued his days and nights. Normally, Beach Comber despised sickness, refused to play handmaiden to pain. He had endured the climb over the barbed wire, once had surfed with a fractured wrist, refusing to give up on a spectacular series of swells that ended in a phenomenal tube ride.

This was different. He discovered his former resilience and stoicism had deserted him. Discomfit and frustration dogged his good nature, worsened by dulled wits, amnesia and inertia. What he wanted to remember, he couldn't, and what he had buried deep in his unconscious submerged. Sketches from the past, like invisible ink restored to visibility, made a long and protracted parade across his psyche, flashing muted pictures of his mother's former husband in the tyrannical state of heightened sexual arousal. As the despicable memories twisted around the nausea from the concussion, he vomited on the floor, barely clearing the cot.

The Borough of Queens lockup, understaffed and overcrowded, had more important details of operation, so there the mess stayed for three hours, stinking up his cell before anyone could get around to sopping it up. Beach Comber would have done it, but he was too dizzy to move, too groggy from waves of nausea to cry out for help. He imagined his mind becoming one with the gyrations of the Earth, its immense spinning so filling his brain that he couldn't stand upright unless he careened into the cell walls and bars. Immobilization was a gift. He lay as still as possible and rested as the first day of his incarceration melted into the second; the second faded into the third. And somewhere in-between, a block of hours had flown into oblivion, a blackout untouched by his imprint of being.

The medication prescribed by his attending physician when he was at the hospital seemed useless. The infirmary doctor in the lockup, where he was mandated to serve out his thirty days, was even more useless. He had to get out, felt sure that an MRI or CAT scan would reveal a gnarly patch, where the pummeling had taken up permanent residence in the once normal fissures and crevices of grey tissue. The boredom, the absence of stimulation, the depression and the amnesia escorted his already clouded judgment into a separate and inaccessible unit of personality. Irritably, Beach Comber sat and stared at the walls and bars or lay back on the rude bed, his mind a drill boring into the ceiling. He felt betrayed by life. Impassively, he gave his thoughts up to an impending apocalypse.

Sylvia, prompted by Don, who was Beach Comber's criminal defense attorney, petitioned the court to remand Beach Comber back to the hospital because of his concussion symptoms. But the judge stalled, and as the third day passed into the fourth and Beach Comber's condition remained status quo, Sylvia had grown frantic when he refused her visit and the lawyer's phone call. The only one he wanted to see was Fen who became the liaison to Sylvia and Don.

Unsteadily, Beach Comber had walked into the visitor's room where Fen waited at a table.

"How are you feeling since yesterday, bro?"

"Like crap. I blacked out again. Third time. My memory is still Jell-O."

"What's happening with your lawyer?"

"He's petitioned the court for sentence review on condition of extenuating medical circumstances. But the judge is hostile." Beach Comber imitated a typical hard-ass tone. "You fled the hospital to avoid speaking to the detective. Now you want back in to avoid serving your sentence? It shows a lack of cooperation with the court and law enforcement." Beach Comber sighed. "If this goes to trial, the DA will use the petition as evidence of my guilt with the added spin that I acted on my sense of entitlement because I'm rich. Did you know I have a privileged life style, and I think I'm above the law?"

"Even the wealthy get sick and need hospitalization. That should add humanity to your cause."

"Wealth is relative. Put my financial situation in perspective. You know, there's Hedge Fund founder wealthy, like my mom's second husband, and comfortable wealthy. We're comfortable. It's a matter of degree. I didn't go to Choate, Phillips Exeter or Andover. I went to St. Anthony's. I didn't finish Yale, where I met you. Yes, I travel whenever I want, but I live on the super cheap when I do, mooching off friends in a quid pro quo when they visit me. I don't work the classic job, but I do work. I write for online blogs and surfing magazines for which I receive a freelancer's wage. This idea of measuring wealth with the dipstick of a nine to five drudge is ridiculous."

"Your internet writing is not a slave. You don't work in an office, beholden to corporate. You don't live in fear of the Friday afternoon pink slip. You're beyond reorganization, downsizing and outsourcing."

"But I'm not wealthy. I'm middle upper class. The difference between the wealthy and middle to lower class is the alpha and omega…ambition and opportunity. Celebrated billionaires like Gates and Buffet achieve their visions and interface globally to advance their opportunities. They have elevated themselves beyond work and money, too busy manifesting their dreams. Driven by Volta, infused by the gods, they are change makers who have the power of choice.

"Volta?"

"The will, electric, forceful.

"The other classes, even the middle upper class are unjustly resentful. They lack the volta or power to manifest their dreams. They're too resigned, their major character failure."

"Perhaps. Certainly, the wealthy's financial independence and autonomy are resented. The rest of us slobs have no choice but to slave to pay off the mortgage on the vacation home in Lake George and make the payments on the second BMW. Meanwhile the middle class folds into the lower middle class, and their options are severely limited."

"Well, the DA's portrayal of me will cause the resentment he is looking to cause amongst the jurors, if this goes to trial. But Don's prepared his arguments. Inflation has obfuscated our concept of wealth. You can be a millionaire by owning two houses. That doesn't move you from your economic platform to the upper class. Inflationary tremors have gradually destabilized the system to the higher exponent. The scions of wealth have shifted in their spheres. Now, the divining rod measures the upper middle class as clotting a yearly salary of one million dollars."

"Prosecution's argument? You have a trust fund."

"But it's not one million dollars a year. And my lawyer will expose how I received the trust fund. I do not own property. The houses are in my mom's name. The property owners on Don's jury will have to reconsider the DA's twentieth century notions of wealth."

"Exposing how you received the trust fund? Will your mother's ex-husband permit it? I thought it was hush money that you would lose if his pederasty was vetted."

"If my trust fund comes with the price tag of a prison sentence, keep the money. I was an abused child whose mother took advantage of the legal system to vault her economic status. I never asked to be born to a gold digger and can't be held accountable for her actions. Rich kid characterization exploded!"

"You've got a point."

"My mom wanted to hire a private doctor, you know, bring him here to examine me. My lawyer said that would feed the DA's characterization." Beach Comber attempted irony. "I'm so entitled. But will I be entitled to a jury of my economic peers, in Queens?" He was bitter.

"During the voir dire of the jury, Don should select white male property owners or gays. Or nurse practitioners with Masters Degrees who understand the dangers of concussion symptoms." Fen smiled.

"In the immigrant capital of the world, Queens?"

"So, immigrants aren't gay?"

Beach Comber shook his head. He couldn't smile. His sense of humor was at the bottom of the Challenger Deep.

Fen saw his friend's despondency and changed the subject. "While Madeline is in South Oaks in a psych rehab, Mocha is staying with Peregrine to manage the house. Elizabeth is furious. She'll be even more upset when she finds out Mocha and Peregrine are getting a place together. In fact, today, they're looking at apartments at the Inn at Forest Hills. Madeline knows a few people interested in selling. It's a good investment for her, and she'll pay the mortgage and taxes until Mocha goes back to work and Peregrine finds a job."

"Well, they've been talking about getting a place. It only took life-threatening events for them to realize it was time."

"You know what that means. Mocha is being weaned off her mother's teats. Elizabeth's and Reggie's influence will end, and Mocha will shift her support to you. She could even destroy the DA's case. It's a breakthrough, the best chance you have. Without Mocha's cooperation, the DA will be spinning his wheels." Fen sounded hopeful. "That's why you have to try to remember. When you're resting, let your mind drift back to the cemetery. When you're in the twilight of sleep or wakefulness, that's when the revelations come."

Beach Comber was droll. "Where did you hear that bullshit?"

"Inventors, scientists, playwrights, artists. They get their ideas moments before awaking or falling asleep." Fen narrowed his eyelids. "Everybody knows that."

"Yeah? What about surfers?"

"Anyway, the three of us have scheduled a press conference tomorrow at Peregrine's lawyer's office to cool the heels of the media about Peregrine and Mocha. They should be fair with all of us. My interviews about Peregrine's rescue and Manny's kidnapping went well. Spokespersons were very sympathetic. The outlets have to take videos of the Southampton estate, so they're probably out there right now. At first, Detectives Dietz and Allan were upset that I tipped off the media, but then they were interviewed. That solidified my credibility."

"How did your mom react when you told her Manny was kidnapped?"

"Hyper-judgmental. But I was able to deal better than I imagined. And after she calmed down, she encouraged me to contact media outlets. She thinks the paparazzi are better at surveillance than law enforcement. We also hired a private detective, one of Bill's security team. One way or another, we'll get information about Manny, much faster than the police."

"You think he's still alive?"

"Peregrine convinced me he might be. I have no concrete proof otherwise."

"Did you hear anything from the NTSB?"

"No. Dietz said it will take months. The FBI is beginning to categorize the evidence, the bits and pieces of wreckage and other detritus. They're sifting through it for body parts, blood and offal. They still don't know who was flying the helicopter. There was no flight plan registered...not unusual. The copter left from a private heliport in the Hamptons, not a public air field. Don't forget to check the news for any coverage of the crash. Oh, while I remember, you can see our interviews tomorrow night on cable or on YouTube."

Beach Comber sighed. "There are a few computers in the common room, but I haven't been able to get there. I just rest in my cell. Dizzy, nauseous. I don't feel like eating, besides the fact that the food sucks. I've lost weight. Crackers and cokes. It's all I could keep down yesterday and today. I should do a fast like the yogis. Maybe it would help my frame of mind."

"You need vitamin B shots, bro, protein shakes and vitamins. I can bring you the shakes and supplements."

"No. That stuff destroys your liver. And stay off the human growth hormone."

Fen's look was sheepish. "You've got to have the edge in my line of work."

"Surfers aren't looking for diesel, bro. Like I said, that stuff throws off your body chemistry."

Fen looked at the clock above and to the right of Beach Comber. They had six minutes. The visits and phone calls were kept short, not as a punishment but because of the overcrowding. "I'll call you tonight again to fill you in. Peregrine says Mocha is writing a letter to the judge, emphasizing that she doesn't think you harmed her. She's declaring that she never wanted to pursue a case against you. It's her cousin's wet dream. Regarding the court order? She assumes responsibility for entrapping you. You came to see her because she asked, and you gallantly went despite the danger to your case. Your visit shows evidence of your true nature, not this trumped up, bestial rapist image that Reggie's sold to the DA."

"Yeah. But my lawyer says they'll reinterpret my visit to the hospital as an attempt to influence Mocha. She's the helpless amnesiac. I'm the evil Svengali. You should have seen Elizabeth's face when Mocha and I hugged. She went ballistic. She pulled me away from Mocha." Beach

Comber waved his hands in imitation. "'Stay away from her. Haven't you done enough?'" I nearly walked out. Should've. Minutes later the police were there, and I was taken out in handcuffs."

"They knew you were coming. Mocha told them. Elizabeth called Reggie who immediately had the warrant processed. Mocha knew nothing about the court order. They are keeping her in the dark. She thinks it's the DA's idea, but it could be Reggie's. The civil suit against you? Mocha doesn't think it is Elizabeth's idea. There's something more to this bond between Elizabeth and Reggie that Mocha can't figure out. Anyway, she's very bitter that they've tangled her in their legal snare. She wants no part of the civil suit either. There's going to be a big blow-up between them when Elizabeth discovers Mocha is moving out."

"Is that such a good idea? You know Elizabeth and Reggie will twist things, suggesting I've used you and Peregrine to pull Mocha's strings. Maybe it's better if she stays with Elizabeth."

"No. She can't resist Elizabeth and Reggie when she is with them. She's afraid her mother will force her into a psych ward, keep her drugged. I think the lawyer suggested it as a possibility if Mocha is uncooperative. So, it's war, bro. They're pushing; we're pushing. Influence? What about Reggie? He was never assigned to your case. He assigned himself to it and then worked it overtime, encouraging the DA and his colleagues not to investigate any other suspects. They railroaded you, man. Your lawyer filed a motion with the court and papers with the DA's office charging conflict of interest. He's trying to get Reggie suspended or transferred to another division in the city."

"I know. That's why I don't want to talk to my lawyer and my mom anymore. I'm not sure I agree. I think they're provoking him. Will it stop him from mining information from his family to spill to his buddies at the DA's office? No. If he's suspended, it will make him more antagonistic. If it is war, like you say, he'll stop at nothing until I'm convicted."

"He'll have less power once he's transferred."

"Well, it's probably too late, anyway. I told you what my lawyer said. The indictment is an inevitability. It's easy to get an indictment in Queens County. Yesterday, he told me why. The witnesses against me. Law enforcement, doctors, and the caretaker at the cemetery, most probably. We can only guess. Grand juries are secret. The witnesses will appear credible because they are obligated to make me responsible for the sexual assault. Then, I fled at the scene when I went back to supposedly destroy evidence that I left at the cemetery. For the police, it's a sure sign of guilt. My attorney can't cross-examine the witnesses, can't expose the holes in their testimony. Do you think the grand jurors have the ability to see the contradictions or notice slips in testimony? Not unless they are brilliant or psychic. Don can't make opening or closing statements, can't call witnesses on my behalf. I mean he is completely out of it. There is no judge to instruct the grand jurors. They'll subpoena Mocha. Even if she's a witness in my defense, they will ask her if she remembers what happened. She can't? It's enough that they've seen her to connect her with the other testimony and circumstantial evidence."

"Are you sure you have a good lawyer?"

"The best. He's a pragmatist. Years of experience as a criminal defense attorney. My mom is paying big bucks. You know the police haven't looked for anyone else, haven't questioned members of the suspected gang leaders. I'm their only suspect. To support the rightness of their cause, they've come up with charges upon charges, figuring some of it will stick. SOP. The Prosecution only has to convince the grand jurors that I could be responsible for her assault, even though that threshold of possibility is three to five percent. Could I have raped and tried to murder Mocha? Slight chance? Wham. Indictment."

"Can you testify?"

Beach Comber nodded his head. "I can make my case, protest my innocence in one long statement. But what I say will be used against me, if this goes to trial. How I appear to the grand jurors is crucial. My demeanor, my statements will cue the prosecution, help them decide how to spin their case. It'd be a huge risk. What if the jurors are not convinced? I'm indicted anyway. Worse, they have my testimony as the Petri dish to grow their case." Beach Comber shrugged his shoulders. "If I do testify, the statements would have to be very cleverly worded. To my credit, I have no priors except the court order violation." Beach Comber stared into Fen's eyes. "I'm innocent. Can I convince the grand jury? It depends. My lawyer thinks not. For an indictment to come down, the burden of proof of guilt needed is minimal. Don can't even find out the economic demographic of the grand jurors."

"Beach Comber, your memory must come back. Isn't the medication helping?"

"After I found Mocha, I was so concerned about leaving Peregrine behind that I left the hospital as soon as I could to rescue her. I didn't get the medication and then I couldn't because they arrested me at the crypt. When I was out on bail, I went with you to get Peregrine at the other crypt. I made an appointment to see the doctor, but we got caught up with the media. I'm glad we did the interviews. They're helping my case. But I never got the chance to see the doctor for the other tests and medication." Beach Comber nodded. "It's been two weeks. Like they said, the symptoms showed up. My mother is convinced if the doctor examines me in the hospital and I get this medication, my memory will come back. Then I can corroborate that my injuries on my chest and hands are from the fence when I tried to go for help. Our lawyer thinks that the last thing the DA wants is my memory to return. He thinks they'll prevent my release to the hospital before the sentence is up, then pull off the true bill."

"What's a true bill?"

"The grand jury's indictment. That publicity puts the DA in a positive light. My lawyer says he has political ambitions."

Standing near the doorway, the squat and heavy-set guard barked his announcement. "Time's up. Let's finish here, gentlemen."

"I'll call you tonight. Try to eat something if you can."

"Later." Beach Comber shook hands with Fen and gave him a thumb's- up sign. He joined the waiting guard and other men who lined up in single file, then walked out.

At six o'clock that evening, Fen called Beach Comber with the news. Mocha had FedEx-ed two letters to the DA and the court. They were a testimony of his innocence, but Fen could not overturn Beach Comber's cynicism about the impending indictment. As Fen ended the conversation with his friend, his thoughts unraveled, a flux of stale, dry winds. Then an hour later, the revelation spiked up from his unconscious spurred on by something Beach Comber had mentioned earlier in the day. Fen phoned the correction facility insisting it was an emergency, and he needed to speak to Beach Comber about his mother. It was ten minutes before evening lockdown.

"Sorry, Bro. I had to lie, the only way I could get through. You said something that's been bothering me, and I think it's important. You referred to there being different
crypts."

"What?" Beach Comber moved the receiver away from his ear and held it against his chest to speak to an inmate who, after tapping him on the shoulder, stood behind him menacingly. "I promise I won't be long," said Beach Comber. Sullen, the twenty-year-old backed off and leaned against the wall.

"What was that?"

"You said there was another crypt?"

Beach Comber tried to move his constipated mind.

"You referred to Peregrine's being at the other crypt?"

"Did I?"

"Bro, this afternoon, you implied there were two crypts."

"When we went to the cemetery to look for Peregrine, the mausoleum seemed different, weird, but I didn't say anything because I wasn't sure."

"Was Mocha at a crypt different from the one where we first looked for Peregrine at the Johnson Mausoleum?"

"Ummm."

"Was the stone material light marble?"

Beach Comber tried with all his heart to envision a mausoleum looming up before him. He pictured a huge black square mound of darkness. He trembled.

"Dark. Black."

"You were there in the dark, then?"

"I don't know. Maybe."

"They found you in the morning. So maybe you went to Calvary the night before."

"Trinity Hills."

"What?"

"Trinity Hills. I found Mocha at Trinity Hills. The police picked me up at Trinity Hills."

"It makes no sense. Peregrine and Mocha went to Calvary together, not Trinity Hills."

"Well, check the police record. Mocha was at Trinity Hills."

"How did she get there?"

"Bro, I can barely remember that I went to that cemetery. You want me to answer physics questions?"

"How did you know she was there and not at Calvary?"

"I think Peregrine said there are two family crypts. I went to the first and was going to check the second, but I never got there until I went with you days later. Beyond that, I don't remember."

"So Mocha was at the crypt in Trinity Hills and Peregrine was at the crypt in Calvary. Two different crypts. Peregrine said she and Mocha were separated. Someone or something separated them. This is getting weirder by the minute. When you went back to Trinity Hills the second time and the police arrested you, was it night?"

"No."

"When you went to Trinity the first time and found Mocha, was it at night?"

"No."

"Bro. do you remember being in the cemetery at night?"

Beach Comber shivered. He remembered darkness and a trembling fear. "Yeah. I remember being scared."

"What happened?"

Beach Comber paused and listened. He recalled the sounds of the night, the wind rustling through the trees; no, they were low-lying bushes, surrounding the building. Then the darkness. "I was hit over the head! Now I remember. Bam! Smashed in the back of my head."

"Evidence of your being knocked unconscious probably showed up on the MRI and CAT scan. You just haven't been able to confer with the doctor. You have to get Sylvia to review this with him. Now, think. When you woke up, was it dark? Were you on the ground? Did you feel the grass?"

There was a long pause. "No. Nothing."

The teenager who was pacing back and forth behind Beach Comber stopped and rushed him, grabbing his phone arm. "Man, you've had more than your minute"

Beach Comber was docile but wrenched his arm free as he looked at the wiry, short kid who was probably in for drug possession. "I'm almost done, here." To Fen he was abrupt. "Bro, I'll call you tomorrow."

"Wait, Comber. When you woke up after you were assaulted, was it night?"

"Screw you, man." The kid pushed Comber's face into the wall, attempting to wrest the phone away from him.

Dropping the phone, Beach Comber struggled with him, then used the judo technique of twisting his leg around the kid's ankle bringing him to the floor with a crash.

He heard Fen screaming in the dangling receiver.

"Comber. When you woke up from the assault, was it still night?"

Beach Comber grabbed the receiver and turned to watch the kid massage his behind. "I'm not sure."

"It couldn't have been because you said you found Mocha in daylight."

Beach Comber barely heard Fen. The kid and gotten to his feet and in a red-flushed rage, dusted himself off, glaring at Beach Comber. "Yeah, guess so."

"Chances are you were hit over the head at night and were unconscious until morning when you found Mocha. So, you weren't alone. And there's medical proof of the assault. So, someone else was there, hit you over the head and had all night to attack Mocha. And when you woke up in the morning, you found her unconscious. Is this how it went down?"

Distracted from the question, Beach Comber saw that the kid had inflated himself like a puffer fish. He was drawing back his right arm to lunge and pitch a side blow above Beach Comber's right ear. Comber yelled, "Yeah." He dropped the phone, grabbing the kid's arm with both hands, using his full weight to deflect the momentum of the punch. Fen's muffled, disembodied shouts, "It's proof, it's proof," became a humorous background chant for the struggle in the hall. Though Beach Comber was at least one foot taller, the kid used his brawn as a counterweight and pulled him down to the floor. They grappled with each other and rolled back and forth, seeking the final elusive blow that would compel defeat, while the black prize awaited, dangling limply from its silvery perch. Fen had hung up.

By this time, other inmates crowded the hallway, gorging their senses on the flesh struggle, grateful for the lapse in their eternity of boredom. Hearing the commotion, three guards came running from three different directions. Two pulled the snarling, feral flyweight off the torrid, rubicund-faced Beach Comber. Dazed, Beach Comber lay on his back momentarily, and then the third corrections office extended his right hand and helped him up.

"I hear you're goin' up for murder. Now you can add fightin' in jail to yer rap sheet." The kid spat out. He feigned lunging at Beach Comber as two grim officers dragged him cursing and swearing threats back to his cell.

Beach Comber was calm. "Sorry. I didn't get off the phone fast enough for him. He came after me."

The latte, hazel-eyed correction officer who had clinched his right arm and shoulder was sympathetic as he walked Beach Comber back to the cell he shared with an older man who allegedly beat his wife. "He was a juvie. But he's graduated to full-blown criminal, awaiting his trial for grand theft auto. He knows about rap sheets." The officer was wry.

Lying on his bunk readying himself to fall asleep, following Fen's advice, Beach Comber closed his eyes and opened his imagination. He pictured a vivid, cloud-clear, blue-sky morning. He remembered grass smells and sunshine beating on his head but wasn't sure if the memories were falsely induced from the logic of envisioning what it would be like to awaken, as Fen said, on a cemetery grass plot after a rough night of double darkness.

He thought about the importance of not being alone in the cemetery. Did it change anything? He tried to reason like his lawyer taught him, playing devil's advocate. He was assaulted. A man of lightening assaulted him. It was laughable. The DA would rip him apart, make him out to be a liar. Since he hadn't seen who assaulted him and he was not a witness to Mocha's assault, it was useless. Fen was wrong.

Evidence proved he was the only one in the cemetery with Mocha. He had produced the evidence against himself by driving into the gates. He was the witness for the prosecution, the prime suspect. He did remember the darkness, the pain of the crash to his head and his fear of the lightening man before the blow that knocked him unconscious. Whatever it was that had bludgeoned him, probably had assaulted Mocha, either before or after it knocked him out. But what was "it?" He thought he was rescuing Mocha when he went to Trinity Hills. Instead, he was destroying himself. Beach Comber drifted off to sleep, swathed in dreams where he carried Mocha in his arms through clouds of darkness.

Chapter Twenty-Nine

Mother and daughter sat on white wicker lounge chairs prettily situated in the wild-flower garden at Pine Forest Psychiatric Center in Bay Shore, Long Island. The lovely pathways were isolated and deserted, a perfect setting for the gentle sparring that Madeleine anticipated would inevitably follow, as she confronted her daughter about the theft, if she confronted her. She equivocated between judgment and forgiveness.

Both women had the same impression as they gazed at one another amidst the floral pageantry of pinks, lavenders, yellows and blues of primrose, purple sage, black-eyed Susans, honeysuckles, and blue flax. In each woman, there had been a transformation beyond which there was no turning. They considered the change warily, acknowledging that their relationship was on a foundation of shifting sands. Uncertainty and the unfathomability of recondite events, written by an unseen hand, swallowed up familiar borders beyond which they would not dare to venture a mere three weeks ago.

"I'll be here until Bill finalizes all the arrangements."

"How long will you stay in Europe?"

"I don't know."

"Will I know where you are?"

"I'll phone or email you or Bill will contact you. I can't let you know where I am. It's too risky. Not because I don't trust you. I don't trust those who'll try to use you to get to me." Madeline skidded around the parameters of logic, letting Peregrine's conscience do the rest.

"Mom, I'm so sorry the media became involved in this way. If Elizabeth hadn't been influenced by Reggie to make a case against Beach Comber, there would be much less interest in all of us."

"If you hadn't stolen the key to the mausoleum and the other artifacts but had confided in me, you never would have gotten into trouble there."

"You never would have let me go if I had told you my plans."

Madeline shape-shifted. She poured a few drops of acid into the brew she stirred. "I blame your Aunt Rachel. She was always the story-teller of the family. She would taste a small sample of reality, chew it and then spew outrageous fantasies. A walk in Central Park became a spiritual journey through the forests of Narnia." Madeline shook her head. "Urbane provincial. She had no sense of the risk she took with her ramblings about the world of Spirit. Of course, she fascinated with her discussions of the Old Way, luring you into her net. And like a happy, baby blue-bird, you flew straight in, trailing Mocha and Fen behind you."

Madeline looked inward past her daughter's attentive expression. "But then the supernatural always enthralls. *La Belle Dame Sans Merci.*" Madeline held out her palms to demonstrate, then bringing her right palm downward miming substance and weight, she intoned in a deep voice, "The supernatural, the occult and magic!" With her left palm, she held at waist height, mimicking the vapidity of the voice of the Jessica blonde, "Music, cars, clothes." She shifted to her right palm. "Angels, demons, supernatural power!" She shifted to the left palm. "Social alienation, powerlessness. Gee, which is more appealing?"

Peregrine laughed. "So, you understand."

Her daughter's remark was unnerving. Madeline understood Peregrine's impulse and was terrified of it. She got up and sauntered over to a trellis, covered with a vine of blooming Clematis, her back to Peregrine, who was stretched out against the white wicker, smoking a cigarette. "Our government has devolved its democratic principles and ceased to be one 'of the people, by the people, for the people.' As citizens, we have become powerless, vestigial." She turned to face her daughter. "Multiply this by the alienation we feel from consumerism. Then add our self-loathing and obsessions about enhancing our physical appearance and financial status. Identity and integrity are atomized. We no longer recognize what our values are, what our life means. Personal power is nullified. Young people, especially, rebel, search for new ways, destroy the old ones. As they seek meaning, the seeds of rebellion forged in powerlessness engender faith in a better world or another world."

Peregrine snuffed out the dead butt and reached for another cigarette. Her resolve to end smoking had been vacated in the stress of extricating Mocha from Reggie's tentacles to write letters of support for Beach

Comber. "Mom, you always skulk around using intellectual facades instead of confronting me face to face. Get to the point."

Madeline sighed. "It's all about belief. Muslim fanatics have illustrated this beautifully. Does it really matter what suicide bombers believe? Their belief has given them a readiness to take life. From that, they gain power, a power uplifted through fear and burnished by bloodshed. They strike whenever they please, wherever they please, like a whirlwind, terrorizing with the uncertainty they create. So what if they die losing a world where their life had no meaning? They have accessed another world where they have become heroes. In the transformation, there has been a transference of power. The powerful have been rendered powerless." Madeline shrugged her shoulders. "Faith has engined this power."

Peregrine was confused. Was her mother faulting her or validating her? "How can you equate me with them? Saying I believed in Aunt Rachel's stories because I craved power?"

Madeline took a step forward and lowered her voice. "I'm saying belief is power. Whoever believes with their whole heart has power. The efficacy of what is believed is irrelevant."

"My faith is not irrelevant."

Madeline was exasperated. "No. The subject of your faith is irrelevant." Madeline saw that finally, she had gotten through to Peregrine. She was determined to dilute her daughter's belief in Rachel's spurious stories. If Rachel had properly taught Peregrine the Old Way, Peregrine's attempts in the crypt would have succeeded, and they wouldn't be in this mess. Madeline wouldn't have to go to Europe to find answers explaining the mysteries that had been unearthed. Whatever had been resurrected in the Johnson mausoleum the night of Madeline's visit would have remained buried.

"You must understand that faith is the most dangerous commodity of all. Whoever controls the people's beliefs controls the people. Faith levels the playing field. It equalizes the economic classes, dilutes the strength of the power brokers. It restores personal power to the disenfranchised and alienated. Even great materialists know that without belief in something to bring substance to their lives, luxury and money are meaningless. That's why the lure of the supernatural, the spiritual, the occult appeals across the economic divide. Always did, always will. Every radical, revolutionary or liberation movement, every ism was sanctified with the belief of its followers. It didn't matter what they believed. What mattered was *that they believed*. Their belief gained an immortality of its own."

"Mom, you're wrong. Because I believed in Aunt Rachel's crazy stories, I stole the key, the Nard oil, the high priests' robe, the magic books, amulets and Tarot cards. But anyone who believed those relics had power would have done the same. And as I think about it now, maybe it's because of their power that I didn't die and join my ancestors in their resting place during the days I was lost and dying." From her reclining position, Peregrine looked at her mother who had moved back to the archway and had placed her right hand against a lacy rung, her beauty a complement to the twining purple Clematis. Peregrine sat up and spoke with fervency. "Admit it. If you were in my shoes, you would have done the same."

Inwardly, Madeline cursed the day she told Rachel of her theft of the relics twenty years ago. Now she was paying for it, as Rachel had paid for her deeds against the family with a premature death. "Someday, we will have a heart to heart about Aunt Rachel's stories of mysticism and the occult and how you came to be lost, imperiling your life and Mocha's."

Tweaked with guilt, Peregrine overlooked any further attempt to receive empathy from Madeline. Uncomfortable with her mother's reply, she energetically sucked smoke out of the cigarette. She had tried not to think about her experience in the mausoleum during her waking hours. Since her rescue, galling images of darkness and flames floated in her dreams; and her nerves were still raw from the seismic shift in her perspective that her decision not to swoon into Death's arms was largely happenstance, a coalition of mental, physical, emotional and spiritual energy, over which she had little or no control. Discussing this with her mother would further confound her sensibilities when all she wanted was distance and settlement in their relationship since Madeline was leaving. Philosophy and the supernatural were on hold until she was reconciled to her present reality.

Madeline allowed the silence between them to serve as a cul de sac to future conversation on the topic of the occult and Aunt Rachel, a divisive issue. She turned to walk through the archway. She didn't want to encourage her daughter to pursue the Old Way, but didn't want Peregrine to feel she prohibited her from seeking it either. She had to achieve a tenuous balance of playfulness and gravitas during this psychological fandango.

Peregrine put out the cigarette and got up to join her mother who was walking down the path past glorious fuchsia asters and pink peonies whose thick, outstretched blooms luxuriated in the sun's honey warm radiance. She was afraid to tell Madeline that the artifacts were still in the labyrinth. She planned to retrieve them tomorrow, taking Fen with her for support, hoping to return the relics to the safe before her mother came home to pack for Europe. She was compelled to fulfill Madeline's expectations that she had safeguarded the priceless items during her experiences in the tomb. If Madeline did not return to the house but left for JFK directly from Pine Forest to avoid the media, there would be no problem, and Peregrine could retrieve the artifacts at her leisure. Since she was loath to return to the cemetery so soon after the near cataclysm of losing her life, she was counting on the media outlets' rapacity to force Madeline's rapid departure.

Madeline stopped on the path and turned to Peregrine startling her. Peregrine halted in anticipation. Madeline took her time to speak the right words as she looked into her daughter's blue eyes, a remembrance of her husband. "I feel as if I understand you for the first time. What you did has made you visible to me. I don't think I ever really knew you until now." She smiled and touched Peregrine's right shoulder with affection. "I'm sorry we must postpone becoming closer until I return." Madeline saw the flood of hurt and shame on Peregrine's face and felt a tweak of vindication. "It's for the best, until this media storm blows out to sea."

Peregrine's actions had convinced Madeline to keep her own confidence about her horrifying experience at Calvary. In Italy and France, she would have to investigate the family's crypts to make sense of it. That meant risk and reconciliation, compromise and familial arrangements and deals to return the artifacts. But she must understand the arcane operations of the Johnson mausoleum or forever be oppressed by the powers of darkness that only were kept at bay by the strong medications she was taking. Madeline motioned to Peregrine to sit on a white wicker bench that was situated in front of a waterfall of honeysuckle, cascading over the whitewashed brick enclosure that surrounded the Pine Forest property. They had reached the farthest boundary of the flower garden.

Interpreting her mother's emotional outlay as absolution for her theft, Peregrine grasped Madeline's hands, looking deep into dark brown eyes, veiled by thick black lashes. "Don't go to Europe. I won't go to the news conference tomorrow. So, there'll be no need for you to leave. I'll call Mocha, and she won't appear either. Fen will field the questions alone. Anyway, the publicity is good for his career, and he's savvy with the media."

Madeline untangled herself from Peregrine's grasp. She moderated her tone to softness. "Peregrine, your decision has no bearing on mine. It's OK. By all means, go to the conference. Regardless, I have to leave."

Changing her mind, instead of sitting on the bench, Madeline walked past Peregrine who hesitated, a mash of contrition and confusion, then followed her mother's lead. They retraced their footsteps back down the path toward the sitting area at the entrance of the garden. "I've given Bill selective power of attorney for a few financial arrangements. If you need money, let him know, and he will contact me. I'll wire the money to your account. As usual, I'm conducting all business and bill paying online. You don't have to do anything. Bill will be handling the purchase of the apartment for you. If you prefer to look in Park Slope or at condos in DUMBO, Bill will help you with that also. I would rather you live nearby, so you can check on the house. But I suppose Bill could find a sitter to live there while I am gone, if you decide to move to Brooklyn."

Agitated, Peregrine reached the chairs and picked up the pack of cigarettes, took one and lit it hurriedly, then inhaled the pleasurable comfort and let the smoke out in a smooth stream. She vowed this would be her last pack. "I think leaving is premature. You don't really need to go." Peregrine paused then redirected her ploy, knowing argument with her mother was futile. "I'll miss you. We've never really been separated, except when I was away at camp. We've traveled together, lived together for all my life."

Madeline reclined on the lounge chair and shut her eyes, leaning her head back so her face was in full sun. "Yes. And it hasn't contributed to my understanding of you and your understanding of me." Madeline turned to squint up at Peregrine who was standing to the left of the chair, gazing at the brick buildings that resembled Ivy League dormitories. "Maybe we both need a break from each other to cement a new relationship."

A thought occurred to Peregrine who was desperate to assuage her guilt and dispel certain opaque fears about abandonment. She had been estranged from her father who was dead. Now she would be separated from her mother. Somehow, she felt responsible for both breaches between herself and her parents. What if Europe took her mother as it had taken her father? It was infantile to associate a place with loss, but there it was. The loss of her mother to another continent became associated with an eternal loss, probably because of the anxieties she felt about her father's death. What if she was orphaned before her children knew their grandmother? With a grey heaviness, Peregrine sat on the chair opposite Madeline who was sinking into the beaming sunshine with bliss. "I think the medication you're taking has influenced you to leave more than any wish to avoid the media."

"I no longer take any medication." Madeline snapped, jerking open her eyes and lifting her head away from comfort toward Peregrine. "Just some melatonin at night to sleep." She settled back into her luxuriant position. "I need to get away. You know how I loathe the media. It's a Catch-22. If you give the interviews to stop them from hounding you, then you are public property, their commodity, which increases their power and eliminates yours as a private citizen. You have given them a ticket to ride your reputation up and down their rollercoaster of abuse. You may be legally slandered, libeled and defamed because they know lawsuits increase publicity, enhancing their readership. Your personal life, what little of it exists with Big Brother watching over your shoulders, is Googlized. To sue, you must allow their sewage and swill to overflow the pipes of public decency and moral outrage to justify proof of pain and suffering. Litigation takes years. American slander and libel laws lack teeth. Say, you litigate and settle. The tabloids pay your lawyer to go away, so they can begin afresh. Cultural standards of decency decline during the interim, so now they can lie with egregious abandon."

"You make me feel sorry for celebrities."

"Don't. They sign on willingly and deserve what they get. For them, publicity knows no negative. If they're vilified by their wrongdoing, they just apologize and receive public absolution. But consider Beach Comber.

He has been maligned as a criminal. Will the media or the prosecution apologize to him for destroying his reputation when he is found innocent?"

Peregrine stubbed out her cigarette on the bottom of her shoe. She reached down for her Celene, which she had placed underneath the chaise where Madeline rested, and took out her sunglasses, cleaning them thoughtfully before putting them on. "I guess it's like opening a door into a world of trouble that doesn't end until someone jumps over the cliff." Turning the lattice wicker chair opposite the chaise into the sun, she dragged it next to her mother and sat.

"Usually, their prey does the jumping. Media outlets may investigate whomever, however and whatever they like, then distort their findings with impunity. This police state, abetted by a controlled press free to malign and invade one's privacy, extruded our civil liberties years ago. Since there is no recourse, I'll return like Rip Van Winkle when newspersons are distracted by other trivialities, and the media is coursing riper game." Madeline could no longer restrain herself. "And so should you. Come with me to Europe."

Peregrine hurriedly changed the subject. "So, you've become a civil libertarian!"

"All Vidalites are civil libertarians, not to be confused with supporters of the American Civil Liberties Union. Two different things." Madeline was casual, watching her daughter for any sign she would accept her offer.

"Gore Vidal? My professors thought him an irregular historian." Peregrine wagged her head and mimicked a high British tone. "Pretentiously controversial!"

"Anyone who rails against overarching power and group think is pretentiously controversial." Madeline laughed. "I'm pretentiously controversial."

"I thought the wealthy supported the status quo."

Madeline laughed. "It depends upon what status quo from what elitist quarter. There's the status quo and the status quo behind the status quo, which is quite the opposite of the stereotype. Power groups are always striving against one another to maintain a forward momentum. The status quo doesn't exist, except in the minds of reformers." Madeline sighed. "Back to my suggestion." She sat up and reached over to touch Peregrine's arm for emphasis. "Think about it. Europe. But you'd have to make up your mind soon. I leave in a few days."

"I would know where you are going."

"Yes, but would it matter? You would be away from here, where the most damage could be done, to you, me, to our family."

"What family?" We have no family here."

Madeline averred. "In Europe."

Peregrine whistled. "This is a sea change. When we went to the Amalfi Coast last year, you wished we had family there, so we could stay for six months. You said nothing about family. We both had dual citizenship passports. It would have been no problem staying with relatives. Remember?"

"We have no family in the South."

"Where are they?"

"In the North."

"Why didn't you say something?"

"You never seemed interested." Madeline used misdirection. "I haven't been in touch with them for a long time."

"Aunt Rachel said we had family in the US, in New York City, but that we didn't speak to them. Ancient grudges, recent wounds. She refused to tell me anything about them."

"Yes. We've disowned them, and they've disowned us."

"Why?"

"I thought it best at the time, as did they."

"Does the disowning extend to me? I would love to know them."

Madeline sat up. She moved her left, then right leg out from the chaise, placing her feet on the ground. Inwardly, she forced back the dark turmoil that threatened to rise up and overtake her tenuous control over flyaway emotions. Facing Peregrine, she leaned toward her conspiratorially, though no one was in the garden to overhear. "You will have to trust me about this. One branch of the family in America was against me marrying your father. They worked assiduously to estrange him from us. I cannot forgive them."

"How did they do it?"

"In business matters. They destroyed him, made it impossible for his company to thrive here. He went back to Europe; and though I don't know to this day because the truth was obscured by silence, I think they threatened him never to contact his wife and child again."

"You always said he left you."

"He did. After you were born."

"So, he divorced you from Europe?"

"I don't know."

"When he died, you were probably still married then, especially since the Catholic Church forbids divorce."

Madeline smiled. "The Church forbids it only for the masses. In special instances, they grant a dispensation for divorce. I was married in the Catholic Church for his sake, converted to please his family who was devout. But I am not Catholic, and the Church could have granted the divorce because of his family's influence. They may have even persuaded the Church to excommunicate me. I don't know."

"Could this have happened without your knowledge?"

"His family, old European blue bloods, might have arranged a quid pro quo with the Church, divorce or annulment granted in return for a large donation or other agreement. Maybe the deal was for free legal representation to offside a priest's pederastic peccadilloes." Madeline laughed emphasizing each word. "It's very likely."

"Would the Stewarts on our maternal grandmother's side have approved?"

"Not if the divorce happened sub rosa, they wouldn't. They do not easily suffer attacks against family. Surreption by his family would have been interpreted as a treacherous betrayal because both families had a monetary agreement. If we were divorced, it was to be publicized, and money was to exchange hands, a great deal of money." Madeline became thoughtful. "By the way, they are not Stewarts."

"The Americans aren't the Stewarts? Then Johnsons?"

"No. That is a branch of our family from Europe. First cousins." Madeline neglected to tell Peregrine the Johnsons were double first cousins, as close in kinship as siblings.

"Who are the Americans if not your dad's family?"

"You will never know their name or their kinship because I will never tell you. They do not deserve your grace." Madeline saw her daughter turn her head away in confusion, silent in the sun. She leaned over her daughter and gently grasped Peregrine's chin between her thumb and forefinger. Softly, she rocked her daughter's head side by side until Peregrine looked at her. Madeline peered intently into her blue-sky eyes. She measured each word. "Peregrine, I do not expect you to accept this. I do pray in the future you will understand. All I ask is that you trust that I always have your welfare at heart."

She released her hold on her daughter and stood up. With sidling steps, she edged herself between the chaise and the chair. She turned her back to Peregrine for dramatic effect, feeling Peregrine watching her as she wandered away into the nearest section of vibrant, multi-hued asters. She hunted for an exquisite specimen. "Here I was in another country. Family was systematically destroying the man for whom I had sacrificed everything."

Madeline stopped herself from her next sentence. Thoughtfully, she snapped a pink midway off its stem and twirled the pixie bloom, bringing it to her nose to tease out its aroma with a sniff. Chaos swirled about them in their present circumstances. She must resort to the expedient half-truth. She didn't trust Peregrine who would reconcile with the families despite Madeline's vociferous pleas not to. Peregrine was an innocent. Both families wielded tremendous power, were preternaturally wicked. Manipulated like a toy boat caught up in a maelstrom, her daughter would be thrown off course for the rest of her life. Obfuscation and omission were the operational law regarding family, and Madeline always used both in the parenting of her daughter. Unfortunately, Rachel had not.

As Peregrine watched her mother among the asters, she synthesized the bits and pieces of information. "The families made a deal that if you divorced, money changed hands. Then the Americans worked to make that happen, offering our lives as a sacrifice? I am beginning to understand why you disowned them."

"I had to. For some, money and power are drugs."

"Usually, money changes hands when a couple marries."

"That happened, too. Marriage is an economic union, a business arrangement, and divorce is its economic counterpart. About this, the law is absolute; and for European upper classes, its function is as clear as air, especially when it involves the sanctity of bloodlines." Madeline shook her head in frustration. "You must understand that with our marriage, a great deal was at stake: money, power, the reputation of ancestral names."

"You married for love. How can you be faulted?"

"Love is a recent development. You're immersed in American culture which places more value on progress than history and exalts youth not ancestry." There was so much her daughter didn't understand. Despite Madeline's efforts, Peregrine was hopelessly nouveaux American like the other well-off youth of her generation.

"I'm trying to understand."

"How can you? You are applying your life's experience to understanding an alien culture. I'll explain." Madeline stepped out into the path away from the flowers. "Though some claim the opposite, in America there really is no class system, only gradations of consumerism and economic groupings. The rags-to-riches myth has prevailed for three hundred years and has vitiated the need for class. It's the bedrock on which this nation has been founded. It's the prevailing popular iconography that engines the destinies of millions of Americans. Historically, the poor traveled to these shores to achieve wealth through discovery, first gold and precious metals, later coal, oil and other precious materials. Ingenious ones made canny investments as captains of industry. Others grew wealthy with their clever inventions or artistic endeavors. The majority prospered working opportunity and luck.

"When these immigrants gained wealth, an interesting phenomenon happened. They disavowed their European social and economic past, which had been wantonly carved out for them by the ruling blue bloods. With each nautical mile of ocean crossing, the theory of blue blood superiority evanesced, giving them the power to assert a transcendent identity. They atomized the cultural role that had voided their will and nullified their self-hood, namely that their tainted blood destined them to subordination. In effect, they genocided their ancestry to purify their tainted blood, eradicating all vestiges of the old blue blood system. Now the once captive underlings captivated by New World mythology believed that they ruled. No group understands this better than American Jewry. Blue bloods became extinct, like the dodo."

"That's not true. The dynastic upper class rules this country and American Jewry has kept its culture in America."

"First, do not confuse religion with culture. And second, in many instances, American culture and mythology have supplanted religious zeal by the third generation of immigrants. Only the enclaves have held out and embraced their culture by isolating themselves. Rule means to capture the beliefs of a people. Dynastic politicos? Nah. Blink, they're finished. They have no means to generationally perpetuate their ideologies with the fickle masses."

"What about the dynasties created during the Gilded Age?"

"You mean American robber barons, drug traffickers, slave traders, their piratical image alchemized by their charitable foundations? Nah. Their charities have made them marginally respectable, but not noble. There is always a historian or a biographer at the ready to cast them from their lofty perch to the abyss, the bleak opposite side of the rags to riches iconographic coin.

"In America, the economic grouping referred to as the middle class embraces the idea that wealth corrupts, destroys character and is a curse. This idea vaults the middle class onto a righteous ladder of grace. The more the wealthy behave amorally and with impunity, the more they sink into wickedness and a cursed moral state, the greater the sanctification of the middle class. Every example of moral degradation suffered by the wealthy is a rung lifting the middle class higher on the righteous ladder until they achieve a moral nobility, which old wealth, by dint of their riches, cannot attain. Old wealth may jeer at this transformation; but nevertheless, they are galled by their daily tarring as the wicked amoral. These concepts rule our culture's collective unconscious. Try as they might, old wealth's inexperienced attempts to govern are weakened by arrogance, undercut by insecurity and overthrown by faithlessness. They have a shallow understanding of power and stability, no comprehension of how to exalt blood lines. And their posterity, enamored of the American notion of love, frequently marry outside the social register. There is no blue blood aristocracy currently in America.

"In Europe, it is inescapable. Royal blood lines existed for millennia. They transcended borders and nation states as they do today. Blue bloods ruled and still rule Europe. How did they gain power then? They captured their underlings' hearts and souls, abetted by the church. Then they institutionalized the role of the serfs and merchants, the tainted bloods, ensuring that they never transgressed their destiny.

"Initially, blue bloods worked within the church. Securing members to key leadership positions, they retained their anointed status. In later times, expedience and the rising middle class forced blue bloods to strive against the church to capture middle class imagination and belief. This was not easy to do after Gutenberg democratized divinity with the concept that faith in Christ engrafted the common man into the blood line of Jesus as their blood brother. But the families managed to maintain their hold on the masses once they gained control of publishing houses and the seats of learning. They steered the common folk into opposition with their greatest power threat, the Church, by assisting surreptitiously with the Reformation, encouraging the Renaissance and leading the Enlightenment. In short, they ruled the masses against the Church under the guise of liberation and enlightenment, their form of liberation, their ideological enlightenment. Yet, for expedience sake some blue blood families remained aligned with the Church."

"Weren't the blue bloods overthrown by revolutions led by the masses? What of the American and French Revolutions?"

"The French Revolution was funded and provoked by the British and others in their revenge against the French for their help during the American. The American Revolution was instigated by warring European and English blue blood factions, the truth of which has not been revealed to this day. Was the American Revolution really won? The government of the City still holds the reins of power where their American puppet is concerned."

"What city?" Peregrine was stymied.

"It's the center of London, said to be the richest square mile in the world. It's like the Vatican, its own sovereign state."

"How do you know about this?"

"Not from reading standard European and American history books on university reading lists. Not from reading historians connected with universities which receive huge endowments with numerous stipulations attached."

Peregrine whistled. "You wasted your money on my degree."

"We had to start somewhere, even if you spend the rest of your life unlearning some of the information you picked up in your college history classes. The point is today, the Black Nobility, the Neri still exercise power as a divine right." Madeline was droll. "And they are liberals in their use of power, though you won't be reading about this in *The New York Times*."

"What do you mean the Black Nobility?"

"The ruthless nobility with their secret, unfathomable blood lines. They are bound by arcane, mystical knowledge and practice that has been passed down for twenty-five generations. To usurp and endow their power to the next generation, they regularly enact rituals and occult ceremonies steeped in the ancient mystery religions. They're serious about the duty of ancestry and maintaining their global power. They do this primarily by controlling the financial institutions of the world and the money supply. Over the centuries to influence and rule governments, they've encouraged wars and revolutions; they've murdered, raped, kidnapped, assassinated and robbed. They eviscerate any threat which would overthrow the purity of the hereditary line, to them, divine. Even blue bloods with no money have power, the power of the bloodline."

"I've never lived anywhere but here. I have no concept of a class system, thought the rise of the middle class wiped it out. Doesn't globalization eradicate the notion of blue blood rule?"

Madeline laughed. "No. It intensifies it. Despite this age of the internet's hyped egalitarianism, ideological websites demonstrate their agendas to capture the beliefs of the populace. This is the same modus operandi that royal blood lines used historically with the technology of the current time. They are in the forefront of globalization and their intentions to continue world domination have become more surreptitious than ever, like I said, through financial institutions and the money supply."

Peregrine stood up and stretched. "It's depressing. It's like the Black Nobility and blue bloods control and manipulate the nations, and our lives are worthless."

"That may be what they believe. That is not what I or you believe. Remember it is the ability to believe, not what is believed, that creates power. Anyway, eventually, one is victimized by one's beliefs, unless they inhabit the truth. And this will happen to them."

"Mom. You are confusing me."

"Your beliefs can destroy you, unless they are grounded in truth."

"How can you tell if they are?"

"What?"

"If your beliefs are grounded in truth. That sounds absolutist."

"You can't, except by trial and error. And for that, you must believe consistently, or you will be at sea in what's known as the Kali-Ma syndrome." Madeline laughed.

"I don't understand."

Madeline left the flowers and rejoined her daughter who propped her hands on the back of her chair and listened. "Your husband is dying of some disease. To save him, you sacrifice your child to Kali-Ma, a goddess who requires a blood sacrifice."

"Mom, you are using an example from *Indiana Jones and the Temple of Doom*!"

"Kali-Ma is a Hindu goddess, good or ill depending upon whom you speak to. Back to our example. After the sacrifice, your husband lives. Success! But failure would have been better. Anyway, your faith in Kali-Ma is strengthened. You overlook your child's death, and you worship Kali-Ma for restoring your husband. Time passes. Your husband contracts another disease. You sacrifice another child to Kali-Ma to save him. He dies. Now comes the whirlwind of confusion, error, doubt. You destroyed a second child and your husband's dead? Why didn't Kali-Ma come through for you this time? What did you do wrong? Despair, hopelessness, shattering doubts and questions. Do you continue believing in Kali- Ma? Do you continue to sacrifice your children, ending their lives and your self-respect? You think for what? A capricious goddess? Do you switch loyalties and pray to Ganesha a kinder god, perhaps equally ineffectual? Will Kali-Ma avenge your disloyalty to her if you switch to Ganesha? Do you become an atheist which is much easier than sustaining the trials of your faith? This cycle of hope and despair of hope is the Kali-Ma syndrome."

"Why Kali-Ma?"

"She is female. If you like, plug in Buddha, Krishna the Bahá'í Faith. Any ineffectual god will do. Back to our illustration. When the crisis of faith diminishes and it will because change is inevitable, despair becomes a dull, disembodied ache that gnaws at your soul; for without firm belief, life is pain and questions with no answers. Time passes. You gradually peek out from under your rock and resume routine living until the next disaster. Now, you have a long memory of the Kali-Ma syndrome. What to do? If you are smart, you are consistent. You pray to Kali-Ma and sacrifice another child. If Kali-Ma fails you, you will free yourself and break the Kali-Ma syndrome. Failure brings you toward the truth. With failure, you despair, lose hope. By degrees, you think Kali-Ma is a lie. You are brought to an end of your belief in her. When you stop believing in her, you come to the end of yourself. It is there, that the truth strikes. Kali-Ma is an illusion."

"What is the syndrome?"

"Ah. If you succeed and disaster is averted, you prolong the inevitable crisis of faith, which will come when Kali-Ma inevitably fails you; and she will, for she is an illusion. On the other hand, if you pray to Ganesha or another god and fail, you become more entangled in the Kali-Ma syndrome. Did you fail because you didn't sacrifice to Kali-Ma? Did she avenge your disloyalty? How could you be so faithless, so cowardly? If another disaster comes, the battle of inconstancy which breeds uncertainty, doubt and confusion intensifies. Regardless of whom you choose to believe, Ganesha or Kali-Ma, the confusion deepens because you betrayed yourself and your faith in Kali-Ma."

"Back and forth the cycle continues. After each success and failure, failure and success you become addicted to second guessing yourself. You drown in doubt. You become more and more unstable, until eventually, you are unable to believe you believe. Randomness grips your life. And in the end the void creeps into your soul and resides there, governing all your actions and interpretations of actions, all your results and interpretations of results. In the void, there is no power because there is no belief. In the void, you never reach the end of yourself! And never reaching the end of yourself, you never know the truth."

"Better to believe foolishly and fervently."

"Blindly, ignoring the circumstances you see in front of you. Eventually, the truth will smack you over the head. Your belief, like gold in fire, will be purified into faith through truth, an unstoppable power, or you will see that the idea or god you've been believing in is a worthless lie."

"Believing without seeing." Peregrine felt the hairs on the back of her neck thrill with cold electricity. She knew she had the integrity of belief, knew she would never lose it. Her experience in the crypt had burned her belief into faith, and truth had made it an unstoppable power. She considered. "If you choose not to believe in Kali-Ma and become an atheist, then you never fail or succeed. It's like never trying at all."

"The integrity of faith. It takes genius and courage to overthrow, continually, the seasons of doubt. The irrational hope of atheism is that under the guise of logic, nonbelief eliminates the despair of hope and the crisis of faith. But it is crisis that eventually brings you to truth. In life, atheism is prosaic, the easy lie. Then Death comes, and the atheist discovers that cowardice and fear are useless when confronting eternity."

"You said that blue bloods are eventually victimized by their own beliefs."

"Yes. Blue bloods are constantly blindsided by the truth. Most inconvenient." Madeline chuckled as if at some private joke.

"That means they are fervent and consistent in their belief." Peregrine was confused.

"Yes."

"But I thought you implied they would destroy themselves."

"Peregrine, the truth always destroys the self-destruction continually."

"As the self destructs, more truth inhabits the soul. Ok, I get it." Peregrine left the seating area and joined her mother on the path. "You always win these discussions, proving either you're more intelligent, or your European education prepared you for argument."

"The latter."

"My family is pretty wild, then."

"Ravening and outrageous. Welcome to my world."

"Aunt Rachel was so off the mark. Listening to her, I imagined a family out of a febrile soap opera. She neglected the discussion of blue bloods."

Madeline shrugged her shoulders. Inwardly, she vowed that the half-truths would continue if Peregrine stayed in America. If she came with her to Europe, she'd stop the lies of omission.

"Where does that leave us?" Peregrine joined her mother, who was trailing the nearby path into the larkspur, having already clipped four additional red aster heads, during her philosophy and sociology lesson, to make a bouquet.

Madeline shifted her gaze from the mess of blue larkspur to their complement, Peregrine's eyes. She had achieved a slim, temporary success with her daughter for the time being. "That leaves us where Catholicism has consigned us, limbo, and none dare follow." Madeline laughed. "And I intend it to stay that way." Madeline handed the bouquet of the four reds and the singular pink to Peregrine. She broke off four larkspur stalks and kept them for herself as she followed her daughter back to the chairs. "I have protected you from family machinations, saved you from deceitful entanglements. Both families are like one-celled creatures, devouring, dividing, sub-dividing their loves for the sake of expedience. Do you really want to be a part of that?"

Examining the asters for any imperfection, Peregrine noticed the ragged thumbnail of her right hand. Her nails had been breaking, and she had taken to biting the cuticles. "No." She searched Madeline's eyes for truth. "I know you haven't told me everything. But at some point, I expect you will when the dust has settled."

Madeline was a bit unnerved at her daughter's perceptiveness. "I'm curious. What did Aunt Rachel tell you?"

"Very little. She said my father left because family made it impossible for him here. She said he was killed in a car accident while driving on the Amalfi Coast."

Madeline laughed. "So, that's why your graduation present had to be a trip to Amalfi, Italy. You thought you would visit the place where your father died. You never mentioned any of this to me. Let me guess. Aunt Rachel swore you to secrecy?"

"Yes."

"I wondered why you selected Amalfi instead of the Italian Riviera."

"Was she telling me the truth?"

Madeline sighed and closed her eyes. "Did his family circulate the story to Rachel to prevent my search for him? I don't know. Right after he left, I'm sure his mother feared I would attempt reconciliation."

"Why?"

"My heart was broken by love, shattered into pieces. Like the John Donne poem, 'My rags of heart can like, wish and adore, but after one such love, can love no more.'"

"Sentimentalist."

"Realist. You didn't know your father."

Peregrine's heart did cartwheels. "So, you are going to Europe to verify the truth? I'm tempted to come with you."

"Peregrine," Madeline paused. "I'm sure he's dead. Aunt Rachel who was in Paris at the time received the news of his death through friends two months after he was buried. The accident was a terrible shock, and his family was in seclusion. When I phoned to speak to him, not knowing what happened, I was told by servants that the family was away. Apparently, his mother had a nervous breakdown and never recovered. They withheld the truth from me because they were concerned I would commit suicide. I had a young child. Whether they influenced Aunt Rachel or she them, they both agreed I shouldn't be told until you were at least two years old. By then, Rachel, was back from Europe. That's when she moved in and helped me take care of you and helped me through that horrible time. And that's when Nanny Elizabeth came to live with us. I was on medication, went to therapy and a grieving group. I was a mess, but at least I knew why he never answered my calls and mail.

"Months later, I sent condolences to his family. I received a wonderful phone call from his father. That's when I found out about his mother's breakdown. But time dissolved the correspondence which was too painful to keep up. Anyway, by the time you were old enough for me to take you to Europe to get know your grandparents, they were dead. Your grandmother died two years after your dad, and her husband two years after that. They were the glue that could have held us together. Then when my parents died in the accident, I became estranged from all family, especially the Americans.

"Why didn't Aunt Rachel fill in the rest of the story?"

Madeline shrugged her shoulders in resignation. "I guess she felt it was my place to tell you. Well, now you know. It is pointless to hunt for ghosts in Europe." Madeline felt the vibration against her hip. She put the larkspur on the chaise and took the phone out of her jeans pocket and read the crystal display. Bill. She texted a call back in ten minutes. From her peripheral vision, she glanced at Peregrine, all hope blasted away from her daughter's face. The charade was complete.

Peregrine was numb. It was true, what she had believed her entire life while yearning in hopeful expectation that there was a mistake that her father would eventually show up. Her birthdays and graduations had been the worst. She had come to accept the reality by high school and was glad she never knew her father. If he was alive and had ignored her throughout her childhood and young adulthood, she would be furious at him. Better he was dead. She could love her idol in serenity. Peregrine lit the last cigarette in the pack and waited for her mother to finish messaging.

With her right hand, Madeline made a motion with the phone. "It was Bill. I'll call him back in five. I have to take the call."

Peregrine glanced at her watch. She was supposed to meet Mocha at the house by 4:00 PM and it was now 3:00 PM. Traffic would begin piling up on the Southern State and LIE. "I have to go anyway." She got up and walked with her mother across the great green backyard lawn of the Pine Forest grounds.

Madeline linked her arm in Peregrine's as they sauntered slowly. "I would love for you to come to Italy and France. But I've been disappointed enough for the two of us. I'm not going there to search for a lost dream. And if you come with me, you must promise that you will not be disappointed when your father doesn't float down the steps in front of the Winged Victory at the Louvre." Madeline was sober. "Anyway, we'll both think about it, especially since you are not working."

"Do you have any pictures of Dad? I never found any."

"The night he left he confiscated all of them."

"Why?"

Madeline shrugged her shoulders. "I don't know. I didn't know he had done it until I was looking for some bank records in the study, and I came across the scrapbooks of our elopement and our travels to Vancouver to visit distant relatives. We had been arguing, bitterly for a week. He was adamant, wanted a clean break. Now, I believe he did not want me to be haunted, did not want you to be haunted." A small tear welled up in Madeline's right eye. "But you see, it's no good. I am still haunted by an unfulfilled past and my daughter's blue eyes." Madeline sighed.

"I'm glad we talked about Dad. You used to be shut up against him."

"Let the dead bury the dead. Discussion will never substitute for substance. He was right. Better to leave before you knew him, or he knew you. He never would have left afterwards. If the rumors were true, you wouldn't have lived, nor would I. Let the dead bury the dead."

Peregrine stopped, one foot on the brick patio, the other on the grass edging. She turned to face Madeline, who stood near some patients sitting around a table, having snacks. "You can't believe those rumors."

A nurse was administering medication to patients who were seated on the patio in plush loungers, facing out toward the wildflower garden. Madeline whispered, "Was my lesson on blue blood aristocracy lost on you?"

"So, by leaving he may have saved our lives?" Peregrine continued in low tones.

"That is one mystery I would like to solve."

"But who threatened him?"

"They must be dead by now. The dead have buried the dead. The rest is left to the living."

"Some family you will not deign to acknowledge!"

Madeline walked across the patio to the walkway, leading off to the left side of the main building, which was landscaped with bushes and was secluded. Peregrine followed closely behind her. There, they could talk quietly without anyone eavesdropping.

"Do you think that your values and theirs are the same? Open your eyes."

"The Europeans?" Both women stood by a six-foot hedgerow and faced one another.

"To you an alien culture."

"I'm very adaptable."

Madeline smiled. "Hmmm. If you come with me, we will see how adaptable."

"You'll see the family?"

"Perhaps." Madeline smiled at the pleasure she saw on her daughter's face.

"Then perhaps I will come with you." Peregrine was ecstatic.

"You may come on one condition. If I decide not to see family, you will not pout about it and will abide by my decision cheerfully. I will not suffer your disappointment."

"I don't know if I will be able to contain myself. I would love to meet my cousins and other relatives. If we don't see family, I can't tell you I won't be disappointed." Peregrine looked down at the aster bouquet. She arranged the pink bloom in the center of the reds. The bouquet looked like a macabre, expressionistic eye.

"The situation is complicated. I haven't spoken to them in years. They have tried to find me. I haven't acknowledged them. I do not know what kind of strain that has placed on the relationships."

"Shouldn't they be thrilled to see you and meet me?" Peregrine searched her mother's face for any weakening of argument.

"It depends on circumstances. I am not privy to their current machinations and don't know what happened with your father's family…if there was a divorce dispensation, if agreements were kept, if there was litigation. Perhaps my cousins and any remaining family elders will look favorably upon my return." Madeline paused unnaturally. "That is if there was no loss of power, if there were a series of quid pro quos that resolved any differences. And then, there are the Americans. I don't know how they may have influenced the Europeans against me, though the American branch was never respected."

Madeline studied her phone for other messages, using her free hand; her left held the drooping larkspur. "If time has done its work, I think the Europeans would be thrilled to meet you. But Peregrine." Madeline looked into Peregrine's eyes. She held her daughter's stare and was serious. "If I sense any intrigue during our visit, I'm out of there, and so are you." Madeline was grim. "Do I have your consent you will leave with me?"

Peregrine hesitated. "Let me think about it. I'll let you know tomorrow, whether I can give you my word of agreement. If I can't, I won't go."

"Fair enough. Now, shall I tell Bill that he will continue to represent you to the media? Or are you going to the conference tomorrow?"

Peregrine looked at her Santos 100 Cartier, another graduation present. "I'm meeting Mocha, and I'm running late. I'll call Bill after I discuss the media conference with her and Fen, after I make my decision. Whatever I do, Mocha will do."

"Call me before you call Bill. That way I will be able to prepare for the feral beasts if they come sniffing around to satisfy their ravening appetite for interviews. And don't leave here until you are sure there is no one waiting to follow you."

Peregrine rolled her eyes. "Mom, please. I don't think they know where you are."

"I left the other hospital because someone tipped them off. So much for confidentiality. If I knew who did it, I would have his or her job."

"You are safe here. As usual, Bill's advice was spot on."

"I would like to come home in two days to pack, but I dread the thought of having to run the gauntlet up my walkway thick with photographers and interviewers. I need a diversion. If you don't go to Europe, maybe you could be my diversion?"

"Who's going to be my diversion?"

Madeline laughed. "What about Fen or Elizabeth!"

"I think Reggie has taken over as her media representative."

Madeline groaned. "Does he need to become any more puffed up than he is? I'm sure he'll use his media platform to smack down Beach Comber."

"And Sylvia will use the tapes of his loudmouthed rantings on TV. She's bringing a whopping lawsuit against Elizabeth, Reggie and the DA's office."

"Am I surprised?" Madeline hugged Peregrine and watched her leave, tracing the path through a break in the hedgerows, which fanned the border of the parking lot. It would be so much easier if Peregrine didn't go with her. She was almost sorry she invited her daughter. How could she explain her family history to Peregrine? Outrageous and wild were benign characterizations that didn't even begin to tell the story. On the other hand, through her daughter's veins, ran the same blood. Sooner or later those generational energies, which had roiled for millennia, would threaten to boil over in Peregrine. And she was the one anointed to explain to her daughter what flowed in her veins, as it had been explained to her. What better place than in Europe, after meeting the family!

Madeline sighed. She had a headache. She wished Rachel was with her. Her sister had been her comfort. When Rachel died, she was left with no confidante, no one to trust, no one but herself. And now in her present state, she didn't even appear to have that.

Chapter Thirty

When Peregrine arrived in Forest Hills Gardens, she spied reporters and photographers parked in front of her house in vans, trucks and cars with large white permits conspicuously showing inside their windshields. Other vehicles swarmed up and down Greenway North, the nearby cross street. Peregrine said a curse under her breath. Despite her warning to an oblivious Mocha, they probably had followed her friend right to the house. When Peregrine left for Bay Shore earlier that morning, she had been careful to take a circuitous, lengthy route to Pine Forest, avoiding the LIE and major parkways that crisscrossed Long Island. Her intention of losing any media person to Merrick Road's annoying succession of off-timed red lights and glutting traffic succeeded. As a result, no one knew where she had gone and no one had followed her back. Mocha wasn't herself, wasn't thinking, unless Reggie or Elizabeth, upset that Mocha had moved in with her, tipped off the media.

Peregrine considered speeding past her house, then decided to front them, so she pulled into the driveway. On cue, a group of news people, like servers at a wedding, simultaneously opened car and van doors, adjusting Blue-tooth mikes and other gadgets. As they sprinted across the sidewalk and lawn, attempting to head her off before she raced by them unmolested to the back door, she grabbed her Celine, choked in a deep breath and flung open the car door, bashing a camera person who hovered next to the car pointing a huge lens at her, a big black vacuum hose poised ready to suck up her image and rearrange it in pixels. "Sorry," she yelled as he fell into a backward sprawl onto the concrete. Whirrings and metallic hummings peppered the air. Thirty buttons closed down the moment, rendering her brutalization of the chapfallen photographer in digital eternity and capturing her rude escape as she raced up the driveway. Peregrine barreled past Mocha who held open the door, then shut it in the expectant faces of the gathering infestation of media personnel.

In the newly renovated kitchen with arms and body bent forward on the granite topped center island, Peregrine panted. "Damn it. I'm out of shape. I haven't played tennis or jogged in a month."

"You're in shape, but your nutrition isn't back to normal yet which makes a difference in your speed. You need to take soy protein to regain lost muscle mass. You're still too thin."

"Like you." Peregrine smiled, regaining her normal breath. "What happened here?"

"I don't know. About fifteen minutes before you came, I looked out the window and saw this crowd had showed up. I thought that Bill might have notified the media to hold a conference here."

"No. That's not his style. He usually has conferences at his office. Do you think someone spotted me on the Southern State, figured I was coming home and notified the others, hoping to get an exclusive?"

"Maybe." Mocha sounded puzzled, sauntering into the dining room where she peeked under a slat of the custom made paisley blinds and peered out the window looking down the street. "What's my mother doing out there?" The blind snapped and banged against the window, as she let it go, stepping backward in horror. "Reggie's with her."

"What?" Peregrine brushed past Mocha and stood at the same window, peeking between the vibrant colors. "Your mom and Reggie are coming this way. Everybody's following them. Quick. Turn on New York One."

"Are you crazy?" Mocha chided. She scampered in the kitchen to the portable combo HDTV/DVD and switched on the channel, pausing to watch. "You must be paranoid. News about a fire in Brooklyn."

"Well, then they're taping it. All the major New York media outlets are here." Peregrine left the window and looked across the room at Mocha who stared back at her in amazement.

"Let's go downstairs to the den. I don't want to deal with her."

There was a knock on the back door. Peregrine froze. Mocha whispered, "Don't answer it. Don't answer it."

Elizabeth's voice was unmistakable, though muffled through the thick hardwood. "Mocha, please open up. I need to speak to you."

Rooted to the spot where she stood, Peregrine looked down, intently listening to the cacophony of noise outside. She thought she heard

Reggie's voice polarizing and contentious in the background. She motioned for Mocha to be quiet and ran through the dining room and living room to the front foyer and up the stairs. Again, there was a knock and Elizabeth's faint and plaintive call for her daughter to let her in. Peregrine hoped that Mocha wouldn't cave. She jetted across the landing and opened the door to her mother's huge bedroom, which extended the length of the house to peer out the left south window. Below, Reggie swaggered in the driveway, holding court, waving his right hand toward the house. Clumped around him, spilling up the driveway, onto the lawn and down the sidewalk were the media acolytes sponging up the wisdom that streamed from his lips. Peregrine heard Elizabeth knocking below. She ran out of the bedroom, across the landing and nearly fell, skipping a step on the way down. She raced back into the kitchen, panting. Mocha was at the door, hand on the knob, ready to let her mother in. "Wait." Peregrine hushed.

Mocha spun around. "I can't let her stay out there with those rats taping this."

"I have a mind to call the police on him and them for trespassing. Reggie is using this to his advantage to embarrass us and weaken Beach Comber's position. I can just imagine what he's saying, that you're under my influence. You're going to throw the DA's case. Blah, blah." She saw Mocha's confusion. Peregrine was being forced to think like a hostage negotiator. "I have an idea."

"Mocha, please let me in. Don't make me beg." Elizabeth knocked again. "Mocha. Mocha. You're not well. You have amnesia."

"God. What am I going to do?" Mocha's hands held each cheek, as if her head would explode; her eyes pleaded with Peregrine to take control.

"On one condition, we let your mom in. Reggie and the media leave. No quid without the quo. I don't care if they stay out there until the apocalypse. She comes in alone. Reggie and his puppets must be swept from the area first." Peregrine reached into her jeans pocket for her phone. "Here." She tossed the phone to Mocha. "Tell her."

"Mocha, Mocha."

Peregrine shook her head, watching Mocha's trembling fingers press the number. Reggie's idea was brilliant but humiliating for Elizabeth. She couldn't believe the woman wouldn't let her daughter go. What had

Reggie said to make her so desperate? What had Mocha and she argued about? Mocha had refused to tell Peregrine.

Peregrine and Mocha heard the distinctive ring of her mom's phone go off beyond the door. Elizabeth answered. Peregrine could hear unintelligible fussing pour into Mocha's ear.

Mocha fumed. "How could you do this? Can you imagine what you look like on nationwide TV? What is your boss going to say? Your dignity is at carbon freezing."

Elizabeth snarled.

"My welfare at heart? Reggie? What are you thinking?"

Elizabeth's reply was a fulmination of hisses.

"That's ridiculous. Beach Comber has nothing to do with it. Reggie is the canker sore!" Mocha spat out the venomous words.

They were acting like caged animals. Mocha was forgetting the quid pro quo. Peregrine whispered, "Get her to call off the wolves. Then she can come in and argue as much as she likes."

Mocha rolled her eyes. "Mom, I'll open the door if Reggie and the media leave."

Elizabeth wrangled with her daughter, vaulting her position.

"If Reggie doesn't leave, we don't talk." Mocha's voice ruptured with anger.

Peregrine watched for signs of weakness on her friend's face. She could hear Elizabeth's harangue, but couldn't make out the words. Peregrine imagined the council she would give Elizabeth: Wrong, Elizabeth. Wrong. Don't you know how to manipulate your own daughter? Don't push her away, or what you fear most will come upon you.

Silence on the other end of the line. Mocha was quiet, waiting. Elizabeth started up again, Peregrine felt uncomfortable. She wanted to leave the room but stopped herself, knowing Mocha needed her. She felt like an eavesdropping interloper. Then she remembered that Reggie had engineered the scene to embarrass and pressure Mocha. Peregrine stared into her friend's eyes. Mocha turned from her with her head down as Elizabeth hammered away.

Finally, Mocha interrupted, "Mom. This is pointless. I'm hanging up. Now, you can continue to pound on the door, but I'm telling Peregrine to call the police and have you and those leeches arrested for trespassing on her property. I'm not a little girl anymore. Don't treat me like one." Mocha clicked off the phone. She handed it to Peregrine. "Call the police."

"Are you sure?"

"If you don't, your neighbors will. I'm furious. I think I'm beginning to despise her more than Reggie. He has her so wound up that, she could unravel around the sun twice with room to spare. She is not even relying on her faith, so unlike her. She used to be iron-willed. Now she's jellyfish." Mocha muttered under her breath. "That's what she gets for listening to an atheist."

Peregrine cocked her head. The crowd noises continued outside but Elizabeth's knocking had stopped. "All she has is you and your brother."

"Well, she's lost me. This has opened my eyes." Mocha pounded her right fist in her left palm. "The moment I express my independence, she's Hitler."

"Don't be hard on her. The last weeks have been a smack down. First Billy, then you.

"This is a woman who goes head to head with reality and comes out victorious. It's Reggie's influence. He's an evil bastard."

With boldness, Peregrine peeked beneath the vertical tiers of the cream-colored blinds at the kitchen window. "Progress. She's talking to him."

"Peregrine, if I let her in, then what? More push and shove? I'm sick of it. I can't deal with her now."

Peregrine stepped away from the window and sat down on a stool at the counter and motioned for Mocha to sit opposite her. "At least we'll be rid of the media. I've decided. Fen is not going with me to Old Calvary."

"But you have to get the stuff and return it to the safe before your mom gets back."

"I need a diversion. While Fen is conferencing with media people, you and I will go to Old Calvary and get the stuff. The media won't find out we're not showing up until Bill arrives to represent us. We won't tip our hand. That will free us from the stalker paparazzi. Since they've royally screwed us today with Reggie's showdown, we'll screw them tomorrow."

"I think I'll stay here. I don't ever want to go back to the crypt."

"I'm not going to the crypt. The stuff is not in the crypt. It's in a drainage pipe that connects to this huge labyrinth under the cemetery. That's where I nearly died, well, one of the places."

"I don't know."

"Well, if you stay here and media people show up, you could always give an interview." Peregrine laughed.

Mocha gave her a hard look. The land line rang, startling both women. Peregrine jumped up to answer it, thinking it was Fen returning her call. It was Elizabeth.

"Look out the window." Her voice was glacial.

Peregrine stepped to the window and pulled back the blinds to look up and down the street. Many of the cars parked on both sides were leaving. Crews were stowing equipment in their vans. The crowd had dwindled to a few newspersons speaking with Reggie who was standing by his car. The scene was one of movement away to another place. Peregrine wondered where Reggie was taking them.

"OK, Mrs. Hamilton. Do I have your word everyone is leaving, no stragglers and no paparazzi hiding around the block?"

"Yes. If you like, I'll wait until every car, every van has left before I come in."

Peregrine sensed trouble, knew Mocha was in for a slanging match. "Well, you won't have privacy. It's my house, and I'm not leaving."

"I thought that's why you wanted the media to leave. You had somewhere to go and didn't want to be followed."

Peregrine thought the woman was canny. "No, but I will be privy to everything you say to Mocha."

"Well, I have nothing to hide. But this is between Mocha and me. Please stay out of our affairs, and don't interject your opinions. If Mocha is going to make a decision, it should be free from your influence."

"And yours. She is over the age of majority. If she had gone away to college, she would have been making autonomous decisions at eighteen."

"I will not be lectured by you."

Peregrine was hibernal. "Likewise. And I will speak if I like. You were willing to make this a public affair by dragging the media here. You can't have it both ways. Video clips of you and Reggie will be uploaded on YouTube in a few hours, and all sorts of folks will be giving their opinions. You'll have mine within seconds. If I tape your battle with Mocha and put it on YouTube, it will probably exceed regular hits." Peregrine realized she didn't want Elizabeth in the house. But it was too late.

Elizabeth sensed Peregrine's hesitation. "You can't drive me away with your unpleasantness. Everyone has gone. I'm coming in."

Peregrine sighed into the silent receiver and then clicked the off button. "Ironsides is back. No spineless jellyfish there." She watched as Mocha moved back the stool and got up. Her friend was shaking.

"Let me get you something to drink. Water? Diet Coke? Iced tea?" Peregrine went to the fridge.

"Water. I'm glad you're not leaving. I can't do this alone."

Elizabeth rang the front doorbell. Mocha went to the door and let her mother in while Peregrine got a glass from the overhead walnut cabinetry and pressed it under the refrigerator tap to release the fresh, icy water. Mocha entered the kitchen a queer expression on her face. Elizabeth followed, her mouth a red slit. She was dressed in her office clothes. Peregrine handed the glass of water to Mocha who stood uncomfortably, still shaking with fury.

"Would you like something to drink?"

"No thank you, Peregrine." The chill in the air vibrated electricity. "I hold you accountable for what has happened to Mocha. Whatever you two were doing in that dead house was not only illegal, it was against the laws of God."

"How would you know that? You weren't there with us. You don't know what the ceremony was."

Mocha's words dripped bile. "Reggie has played you like an accordion. I can't believe you gave up trusting me to believe that atheist! We went there to save Billy. That's how much you know."

"Calling on the dead to save your brother? That's rich. Don't you know why this has happened? It has nothing to do with Reggie. You have been tampering with the dark arts, the powers of darkness. Do you know what happens when a family of faith does that?"

"These were the healing arts. You don't know the difference."

"From what source?"

"There is only one source of power that heals." Peregrine jumped in.

Elizabeth stood placing her hands on her hips, shoulders back in attack pose. Only her slim shoulder bag dangling on her forearm belied her underlying insecurity. She shook her head in wonder. "Peregrine, you are so naïve. Haven't you heard of the beautiful side of evil? The seductive side?"

Peregrine opened her eyes wide and said with force. "Who controls? Satan? Is Satan greater than God? Or does God have him on a long chain in His service? You don't believe that Satan is the master of God, do you?"

"And if you toss the dice using your only throw to prove Satan is on a long leash, and find out that he is roaming free, you've lost everything on your bet. But you won't know you've lost. You'll believe that lie for eternity. Up is down. Black is white. Left is right. Good is evil. You'll never know the difference."

"You can't convert me." Peregrine smiled at Elizabeth.

"Is this who you want as a friend?" Elizabeth directed this to Mocha who was still shaking as she put the half empty glass of water on the counter and confronted her mother.

"You betrayed me. You went against my back and supported Reggie against Beach Comber. You profess to be so good. But you are willing to send someone to prison on a pack of lies. You are willing to milk his family in a lawsuit because they have the money, and you see it as a God given opportunity to become wealthy. You slime. And you call yourself a Christian? You are a Pharisee. A synagogue of Satan. A hypocrite."

"Beach Comber must be held accountable for his actions. He must learn there are consequences. You are blinded by your love for him. He tried to kill you. He was the only one who could have done it, the only one there. You say you have amnesia. You don't want to remember. Because when you do, you will see his face bending over you, strangling you to get a rush from his sexual climax. Remember why you broke it off?" Elizabeth held Mocha in a powerful look then whispered and nodded her head. "Perverse. Perverse."

The disclosure shocked Peregrine who looked at Mocha. Her friend looked sick, the color draining from her face. Mocha reached for the counter-top to steady herself and nearly went down in a faint but for Elizabeth who rushed to her and grabbed her around the waist. She placed Mocha, groggy with lowered blood pressure on the stool.

"Put your head between your legs." Elizabeth swiveled Mocha around in the stool and gently pushed her forward, holding her head downward. "You'll be OK in a moment."

Peregrine and Elizabeth were voyeurs until Mocha straightened herself, lifted her head and breathed deeply. Mocha finished the water then held out the glass to Peregrine. "Refill?"

While Peregrine got the water, Elizabeth reached for a stool, placed it next to her daughter and sat down. "I do not want to upset you with the past, just remind you that Beach Comber's actions show probable cause at the very least for sexual abuse. There is no other explanation for your injuries. I feel one reason why you are here is because you are escaping a truth you don't want to face. What better place to hide than at Peregrine's, where you are enabled in self-delusion."

Peregrine handed Mocha the refill, stood at the end of the counter and watched mother and daughter. The granite counter-top between them might well have been a mountain. Elizabeth, sensing an advantage, restrained herself from further argument. She let the silent screen save their thoughts.

Finally, as the last resort of negotiation, Peregrine attempted empathy. "Ms. Hamilton, I am not a parent, but I have imagination. I know these last weeks have been very hard for you. You have no one you can turn to, but your nephew. He has come through for you like no one else, not even your friends. I don't want to get into whether his actions are ethical. That will be for a judge, maybe even the Attorney General to decide. The point is Mocha needs to work this out for herself, on her own. I didn't persuade her to stay with me. She came of her own volition. She woke up from the coma. She couldn't remember. Her world was in shambles; her friend in jail, suffering, and she was responsible. You can't expect her to agree with you outright without some understanding of her position. She feels utterly guilty. She is on medication for night terrors. She is going to group and individual therapy sessions. Even the doctors are encouraging her to be out on her own. They think it will help her recall. Now, you were not willing to give her the money to get her own apartment, so she broached the subject with me. And you know we always talked about living together after I got my master's degree. This is not some plot to kidnap your daughter and derail the justice system. As for Beach Comber?"

Peregrine couldn't believe she brought herself to say it: "Let the chips fall where they may."

"I'm not sure the therapy she is receiving is effective. I don't agree with the doctors. The medication isn't working like it should. Mocha, you should face the night terrors, confront your fears. I will help you. Together, we will bring back your memory." Elizabeth was gentle.

"Mom, you're outrageous. Do you know what you are saying? Do you want to torture me? Do you want me to face those dreams, night after night?" Mocha's voice shrilled. "You want me to be afraid! Are you listening to yourself?" Mocha regained control and directed her attention to the present. "Isn't it enough you've embarrassed me by bringing the media here? And Reggie trying to put Beach Comber in jail for life! You've lost all sense of proportion. You never would have suggested this. Reggie put you up to it. He's driven a wedge between us." Mocha shook her head. "I don't understand what his motive is. Money, power? Is my happiness supposed to be the sacrifice for his ambition?"

Peregrine breathed an inner sigh of relief, grateful that Mocha had recovered herself. Elizabeth deflated, a tennis court bubble in a category five hurricane. Peregrine soothed her into accepting failure. "Mrs. Hamilton, at least you and Mocha are on speaking terms. The future will brighten. Her memory may return with therapy. She may move back in with you. Maybe you'll decide to give her the money to be on her own until she goes back to work. Whatever you decide, it should involve only you two and Mocha should not have to feel that you and Reggie are deciding her future. I think you can agree that when you were her age, you were in possession of your own soul. That is as it should be. Parents can't decide the eternal fate of their children. They can only guide them to make the best decisions. You've given her all the weapons. Let her decide. Trust her to do the right thing. You don't want your actions or Reggie's to compel her to the worst decision out of rebellion. Do you honestly think that your lack of trust hasn't influenced Mocha?"

Elizabeth was unresponsive. She got up from the stool and placed it back under the bar. "Peregrine, there are so many variables, so many forces swirling about us. I am not sure to what extent any or all of this is out of our control because we let in chaos by opening the door to those powers." She looked at Peregrine and Mocha pointedly.

"Then pray that the door be closed if that is what you believe." Peregrine encouraged.

"I will continue to pray."

Mocha was clever. "Why don't you ask Reggie to pray with you?"

"C.S. Lewis was an atheist before he became a Christian apologist. Some of the most ethical, moral individuals are atheists. I have never known of any atheists who've supported war." Elizabeth was matter-of-fact.

"Considering how many religious adherents have used God's coattails to ride into battle, as a believer you are truly damned." Peregrine laughed. "Why talk absolutism? There is not enough storage to hold the lives of all the atheists in the balance to measure whether at one point in time their non-belief wavered into belief. It's a spurious argument."

"You're both giving me a headache. All I meant was, Mom, please exercise your faith. What do you call it? Get alone in your prayer closet? I really believe that was why I came out of the coma. Your prayers, your faith. Don't give up on me just because I'm not living with you. I'll never leave you in spirit. You always say that. Don't you believe it?"

Elizabeth sighed. She had lost. Reggie would be angry. How to handle him? But Mocha was right about exercising her faith. Elizabeth felt more alone now than she did when her daughter's life was held in the balance. There was only one reason for it. Uncertainty. Doubt had insinuated itself. But from where? "I'm going." Elizabeth was morose. "I'll call you. I won't argue with you about coming home anymore. I'll keep you informed about Billy. Thank God he is holding on. He's iron-willed like me. I'm thinking of taking him out of hospice."

"Mom, whatever. Anything is possible."

"Except my daughter moving back in with me." Elizabeth felt sorry for herself.

Peregrine interjected. "It's not forever."

Mocha hugged her mom. "I'll call you later." Peregrine and Mocha escorted Elizabeth to the front door, and Peregrine pushed open the strong, heavy hardwood.

"Good luck tomorrow with the interviews."

Peregrine and Mocha nodded in reply and from the threshold, watched as Elizabeth walked down the landscaped path to Greenway North, where her car was parked. Peregrine glanced down the street then gestured to Mocha to look right. Five hundred yards away, Reggie leaned against his car, smoking a cigarette. Behind him were a thinned-out media crew of about four camera persons, focusing Elizabeth, Mocha and Peregrine in their viewfinders. A few spokespersons, obviously Reggie's hand-picked pigeons, cooed and clucked nearby. Reggie waved to Elizabeth who waved back, got in her car, and then drove to the location. She stopped and got out of her car to talk to Reggie and the others. Disgusted, Mocha turned and went into the house. She sat in the living room, waiting for Peregrine. Peregrine watched Elizabeth comfortably chat with Reggie and the others for some minutes, then Elizabeth got in her car and Reggie got in his, and both left Forest Hills Gardens. The two media vans parked on Greenway North remained parked. Peregrine cursed under her breath and slammed the door with a bang.

She yelled to Mocha from the foyer. "They're still out there."

"You see what I'm up against? She reneged on her promise because Reggie's word is crap. He has no integrity. And that slime is influencing my mother!"

Peregrine walked into the living room and stood on the Oriental rug's elaborate pattern. "Mocha, the paparazzi will probably stay there all night to get an exclusive tomorrow morning, as we leave for the conference."

"Only we're not going to the conference."

Peregrine collapsed on the newly upholstered Eastlake loveseat and leaned her head back, her hair brushing the intricate walnut woodwork. She spread her legs out in front of her and rubbed her eyes with both hands. "Let me think. Let me think."

Mocha was sitting opposite her friend in the mahogany barrel chair. "Call Fen."

"He's not picking up his messages. I don't know where he is."

"Do you want me to give an interview here to distract them? I'll do it if you think it will work. I'll hate you for it. But I'll do it."

"That means I go alone to Calvary."

"You'll be there in daylight." Mocha noted the look of unsettlement on Peregrine's face. "You see what I mean about returning there? It's scary, weird. I can't do it. I'd rather let them interview me."

Peregrine sighed. "I would have taken the stuff, but I just didn't have the strength to drag it around with me, so I left it there. It's a good thing because it would have been ruined in the rain. My backpack isn't waterproof."

"When is your mom coming back?"

"Tomorrow night. I know she'll check the safe before she leaves for Europe. I think she wants to take the Tarot cards and the robe with her, so the stuff has to be back in the safe."

"Worst case. She checks the safe and finds the stuff missing; and together, you go to Calvary."

"She'll never trust me again. I mean these artifacts are priceless. Museum pieces. Aunt Rachel told me that they are stolen, and my mother risked her life to get them. They're our inheritance from our family, the inheritance we were denied."

"She knows you took them."

"She thought Fen kept the stuff for me when he took me to the ER, and then returned it to me when he took me home from the hospital." Peregrine groaned. "No. There's no way out of it. As much as I hate to, I'll go tomorrow. If we can divert the paparazzi to follow you instead of me, then Bill and Fen will busy the rest of them for about an hour. I have to get to Calvary without being followed. No one must know I'm going there. Afterward, they can be my permanent escort." Peregrine thought afterward they wouldn't be following her anywhere. She would be out of the country and luxuriating incognito in some Italian hill town.

"If I have to talk to them, I'll do it on the condition they ask me no questions about Beach Comber and no questions about my being at the cemetery."

A pang of guilt struck Peregrine about whether to tell Mocha she might be leaving the country. "Then what will you discuss with them?"

"Being in the coma and remembering nothing. And if I can't remember, then I can't answer any of their questions. Like I said, I'll do it to help you out, but I'll hate you for it. God, how I wish I could get away!"

"It's too much to process, the media, Beach Comber in jail, Manny's disappearance, recovering from the crypt. Actually, I was thinking about going to Europe with my mom."

"I thought we were going to look for a place together, this week, as soon as your mom left. If you go, it changes everything. I might as well move back home." Mocha was livid.

"Of course not. Your getting away is not the same as mine. You'll be leaving your mom and Reggie, so you can make decisions on your own. You can't do that at your house with her breathing down your neck and Reggie popping over every day. This will be your seclusion home. You can get back on your feet in solitude. Then you'll be back at work, seeing our city friends. Of course, Fen will stop by. Mom will be grateful. Otherwise, she'd have to get a house sitter."

"I won't feel comfortable without you, especially at night."

"I thought the medication was helping."

Mocha hesitated. "It's at strange moments. I see things. Like just before I go to sleep."

"What things?"

"Darkness coming to strangle me. Long black fingers squeezing my throat harder and harder until I pass out. Then usually I wake up, and I can't get back to sleep."

"Then you lied to your mom. The medication isn't helping."

"I forgot to take the meds one day. That's when it happened."

"Just one day?"

"Well, sometimes I felt that I didn't need any meds. But I noticed when I didn't take them, the compulsion to speak with the accent was strong, and the accent sounded strange. I was another person. And then the recurring dreams and daytime terrors and depression frightened me. So I started to take them more regularly. The diazepam lets me sleep through the night. And the anti-depressants take a while to kick in, and then I just feel numb. I hate taking drugs. Side effects. Addictive pharmakia."

"What?"

"A spiritual word, pharmakia. Physical drug addiction leads to emotional addiction. You need the drugs like you need air. If you try to wean yourself off them, horrible things happen. You can't live with the terrors. You overcompensate and take more drugs, maybe accidentally overdose. Or you're so emotionally weakened, you hate yourself and want to end it. Fearful of suicidal urges off meds, you keep on using. After a certain point, you never get better. You stay on them the rest of your life, living with the dependency and loathing yourself for it. Pharmakia, spiritual oppression caused by drugs."

"Doctor prescribed."

"Of course. Middle and upper class drug addicts are users of controlled substances prescribed by doctors. After a certain period, I'm supposed to be off certain ones, but he'll just redesign the cocktails and give me something else and something else and something else. I won't be addicted to any of them. Only I'll be addicted to taking meds; my liver and immune system compromised. Mom is right. Better to deal with the terrors and depression without the medication. But I'm not ready. It's too soon after the trauma." Mocha paused in thoughtfulness. "Reggie offered to help me. Can you imagine?"

"A wolf in sheep's clothing guarding the sheep. How Twenty-third Psalm."

"Mom thinks I can gradually get off the medication if I pray. I can't. I can't even be alone. I'm terrified. That's why I need you to be around, especially at night. I can't be alone." Mocha's voice rose to a high-pitched squeal. "I can't be alone."

"All right, calm down. It's OK." Peregrine got up from the loveseat and threw her arms around Mocha's neck and patted her back. She sat down on the carpet's black background, which emphasized the intricate geometric borders.

"I haven't made up my mind yet. I'm just considering it. I might even join her after a few months, after you and I find a place together. I would be able to help you get through the nights if you want to gradually get off the medication. And by then, you will be back at work."

"After a few months? OK. But what if Beach Comber is indicted? I don't know if

I have the strength to resist my mother and Reggie who will force me to testify. I don't want to be the DA's stooge, putting away a man I believe is innocent."

"Do you believe it? Your mom said something about the intimate details of your sexual relationship with Beach Comber? What was that about?"

"I don't want to discuss it, Peregrine. Please drop it."

"If he is indicted and the case goes to trial, any detail like that would sink any chances of his being proved innocent."

"I said I don't want to talk about it!"

Peregrine was hurt. "This is me, Mocha. We confide in each other."

"Not always. There are private matters in my life that I haven't shared with you."

"Well, of course. But they're not private where Beach Comber's concerned. They're public. And you'll be called to share them on the witness stand. And if you don't, you could go to jail for contempt of court."

Mocha screamed. "I am standing on a cliff. Why are you forcing me to jump?" She got up from the chair and stood towering over Peregrine who sat cross-legged on the carpet, looking up at her. "It was ridiculous to think you could help me." She stalked into the kitchen to get her handbag.

Quickly, Peregrine jumped up and went after her. "You have to understand. I'm at sea with you ever since your coma, the British accent and your emotionalism. You are so different from your usual self. Please forgive me. In the past, you would have told me everything."

Mocha stood at the granite counter where she had placed her handbag and turned to face her friend. She was matter-of-fact. "Well, the past is gone. I'm gone. Don't expect Mocha to return." She considered for a moment and then spoke. "And your interpretation of reality is really off because I didn't tell you everything. I certainly didn't tell you about my intimacies with Beach Comber." She turned to her bag and rummaged in the bottom for her car keys.

Peregrine was dumbfounded. She choked on her next words. "Can you bring yourself to forgive me?"

Mocha glared at Peregrine, the atmosphere between them an ice storm. "Forgiveness means you never hurt the person in that way again. I don't know if you are capable."

"Mocha, friendship allows that at times people hurt one another, but there is the will to forgive, the acceptance of forgiveness and change, as incomplete and flawed as that may be. You hurt me just now, but I'm willing to forgive you. Though you'll probably hurt me again, you are worth that risk. If I am not worth the same in return, then go and live with your mother and be influenced by Reggie and ruin Beach Comber's life. Be happy if you can. But I will not be silent while you do something so utterly destructive to someone you love and destroy yourself in the process. It would mean you are beyond self-forgiveness. And if you are so arrogant to believe yourself beyond forgiveness, then you should kill yourself. You are not fit for life."

"Thanks for the comforting words," Mocha said, empty of bitterness.

Peregrine flushed with fire, regretting her harshness. She watched her friend, car keys in hand, let herself out. As the door clicked shut, Peregrine's rationality collapsed in on itself. She had allowed Mocha to dismantle her peace, thread by thread. Stupid, stupid, stupid. Was she discussing Mocha or herself? Regardless, both used manipulation, a bad beginning. Their friendship had shifted its paradigm and the rules set by Mocha, the game's master, would be altered at whim, until this long fit was over. And Peregrine could guarantee her own response would be as insecure, mean and belittling as her friend's. She had peeked behind the veil of her own character and was dismantled by the ugliness she saw. God. They were both full of crap.

Peregrine felt drained. She realized she hadn't eaten anything all day. She went to the refrigerator and took out half of the turkey, mayo, lettuce, tomato and bacon sandwich wrapped in white paper from Ben's Deli, poured herself a glass of iced-tea and standing at the counter, hungrily devoured the sandwich and drank the tea. She thought about Elizabeth's comment. Beach Comber was in much worse shape than Fen and Sylvia's lawyer realized. Sexual practices out of an S and M manual? Reggie probably filled in the DA about the prurient details of Comber's sexual relationship with Mocha. Such scintillating testimony would titillate the public and gain a 15 share on Court TV. The DA couldn't lose. Men and Sex. Screw the truth. Anything sounded believable when the subject was perversion.

After she wiped the counter-top of crumbs, threw away the remains of the sandwich and washed the glass, she opened the door to the finished basement den-library, skipped down the eleven plush brown carpeted steps and slipped over to the cream-colored leather sofa. Sinking into the soft cushions, she relaxed for a few moments with groans of pleasure and took off her new purple rimmed Nikes and her white matching socks. She reclined her head on the huge rust and gold paisley pillow that they used as a head rest and swung her legs onto the sofa. Exhausted, she closed her eyes and immediately fell asleep.

The jarring ring of the land line awakened Peregrine. Dislocated by her sleepiness, she realized the phone was in front of her on the coffee table and picked up the receiver on the third ring. She yawned, "Hello?"

"It's me. There's no one in front of the house because they've followed me to my mom's. Now would be a good time to go to Calvary."

"What time is it?"

"Six o'clock. Did you hear from Fen?"

"No. Are you coming back later?"

"I don't know. No one is here, except Billy and the nurse and the media. I'm in my car in front of the house."

"Just took a nap." Peregrine left the sofa and gracefully mounted the stairs two at a time and opened the door into the kitchen. She proceeded to the window and peered out. No vans. She opened the front door and checked right and left. "I don't see anyone. Strange."

"They're here, waiting for me to get out of my car. It's a standoff. If they get out before I get out, I'll drive away. So here we sit playing chicken. Ridiculous."

"I don't know when I'll hear from Fen. He got my message, so he knows we won't be there, unless you changed your mind?"

"I don't want to deal with news people. It's bad enough I can't get out of my car in peace. I'm not going to do any interviews tomorrow. Go to Calvary now when you have the chance before they close the gates. Call if you need my help. I'll bring my news entourage. They'll scare all the ghouls."

From the utility drawer in the kitchen pantry, Peregrine removed a flashlight, which she stuffed in her Louis Vuitton bag. "The gangs only show up at night. I'll be long gone with my back-pack in tow." She took a bottle of Evian out of the refrigerator and dropped it in the bag with the flashlight. "Call you later. I've got to make all the green lights on Queens Boulevard." She went to the hall closet for her belly pack, which she located and grabbed.

"Be careful. I'm sorry I was a maniac. I'll see you back at your house in a few hours to discuss an idea I think you'll be interested in."

"Ciao." Peregrine put down the phone. She secured the belly pack, slung the bag over her shoulder and opened the kitchen door, scanning the driveway for paparazzi. So far, so good. She locked the kitchen door, quickly walked to the car and got in expecting a reporter to jump up from his hiding place by the right wheel on the passenger side. But there was no one.

Peregrine sighed and turned the ignition key, wishing there had been media persons there to stop her. In the last sixteen days, she had spent thirteen of them in places where death stalked or presided. Maybe the word life was a misnomer. Maybe it was the other way around in similitude.

As she drove down Queens Boulevard and headed for Old Calvary, she thought philosophically to comfort herself. Perhaps what was viewed as "death," since it was irrevocable and eternal, was actually "life." It seemed unreasonable to be "dead" forever. One moment you were getting the hang of how to deal with the ups and downs of the "life" process and the next moment you had to prepare yourself to die. Not much time between the two and plenty of time to get used to death. And after having been "dead" for millennia, she could see how one might think about "life" experiences not really existing at all, especially as time and change eradicated all matter that supported memories. But if death was non-existence, and time and change eradicated what was once alive, making it non-existent, then a case could be made that life and death were different sides of the coin of non-existence. Either way, at time's end, no one's existence could be proved, meaning no one existed. If one didn't exist, then one's fears, hurts, joys and sorrows were liquefied, dissolved into a blessed state of immateriality, and all of the struggles of the wealthy, middle class and the poor were ultimately non-existent.

However, if death and life were the reverse of their meaning, then non-existence was eradicated. From now on in her mind, she would reverse the meaning of the words. Her present existence was death, over in the twinkling of an eye when she would live forever. That way she wouldn't mind terribly going back into the maw of the Johnson tomb and its environs. After all, the people there lived forever; and there, she would be staring into her not too distant, if one considered all the millennia in the human history of time, future. As a denouement to her thought, Peregrine turned right and drove between the black iron gates of Old Calvary.

Chapter Thirty-One

Fen couldn't believe what Jackson, one of Bill's security team, was telling him. He stared up at the striking, iron jawed face of the thirty-five year old, the tendons of his massive neck stretched taut against an Izod collar. The six-foot, eight-inch bulk dwarfed the actor. Fen looked for duplicity in Jackson's grey eyes. Sincerity stared back. Was he reading the light-skinned black man correctly? The private investigator and Fen sat across each other drinking iced coffees at the Southampton Starbucks, Fen's choice of location. Still sickened by the tragic events of the helicopter accident, he couldn't bear to meet anywhere near the multimillion dollar compound overlooking the steely Atlantic.

"Man, I'm telling you, the place is deserted. Don and I vaulted the fence on the ocean side, between the motion detectors, where there's always a blind spot. Went at sundown, took flashlights. We were able to front the windows along the first floor. No one's there. The place is closed. Sheets on the furniture. Kitchen undisturbed."

"Maintain surveillance a few more days according to our plan. They know they're being watched."

"Well, remember it's been five days since you arranged the twenty-four seven with Bill. After the third day, no one went in or came out. Bro, only ghosts walk those halls."

"But you and your guys saw no one leave. How is it possible then?"

"Maybe there's things we don't know about the place. Like passageways between the mansions or tunnels leading out to the beach, exits hidden amongst ticks and dune grass and beach plums bushes. Centuries ago, Long Island was the playground of pirates and later, eccentric millionaires and bootleggers."

"Jackson, those are legends. It would have been tough to build tunnels in this type of terrain, with the unstable, shifting sands."

"Did you ever hear of concrete, mortar and brick?"

Fen shrugged. "So? The building materials would be exposed, and we'd see the remnants."

"Did the house have a basement?"

"Not one that Liam showed us."

"So, you don't know."

"No."

"And you're not an engineer. You don't know about reinforced tunnel bunkers, and water tables, and pressure pumps and storm drains."

"No."

"And you aren't familiar with the history of this area, the previous owners, or the mansion's blueprints."

"No."

"The idea isn't ridiculous. We just need more information. Isn't there a huge storm drain half a mile down the beach?"

"I can just imagine snobby Liam and his craven boys crawling through the muck of a storm drain."

"It hasn't rained in over a week."

"Did you check the upper floors?"

"We climbed onto the roof of the conservatory and looked into the second floor windows. Same as downstairs. Dust covers."

"You could only see into one room."

"And down the long hallway vista. No activity and no signs of activity. Two simple explanations. They're there, hiding, in which case eventually, we'll see them. Or they've left, probably at night, using underground tunnels, camouflage, something else."

"You and the others might have missed them. They could have walked out onto the beach."

"Not likely. No, there's another exit, maybe on the eastern side of the helipad in the dense brush and hedges."

Fen was silent. He was running out of ideas, upset he was losing control over the situation which was proving to be impossible.

"We'll check blueprints, construction permits filed at town hall; but even then, the possibility exists that only the owner and the private engineering and construction firms knew about such additions. Maybe at the time the tunnel was built, there were no permits required. If it was built in the beginning of the last century, maybe money changed hands, so permits didn't have to be filed. An absence of documentation at town hall means nothing. You know Long Island is thick with such practices. Southampton could be awash in it."

"All right, all right. Say there is a tunnel. Why didn't they take Manny out in it? Why the production number?"

"What better way to get you and the detectives off on a wild goose chase, while they head in another direction with Manny. Maybe they didn't count on the explosion. Maybe Manny wasn't on the helicopter, and they removed him two days ago prior"

Both men sipped their iced drinks in silence. Fen was heartbroken. Though he was getting a discount, the thousands he was spending on the private investigators, would severely distress his finances by the time the official investigation was complete in a few weeks. Without a shred of proof, the FBI and DA's office would unofficially discontinue their search, distracted by recent crimes and missing person's cases.

His only hope was the media. They had stationed a few reporters outside the mansion, waiting to hound the servants with more questions inspired by their first day on the prowl when they had caught Liam unawares, his befuddled comments just skirting guiltiness.

Fen had given the media open access. They were gracious and kept their promise of sticking to topics he preferred to discuss, contingent upon his securing Mocha and Peregrine for the media conference tomorrow. He hadn't let his reporter friends know the women were ditching. If the media turned on him, he was ready to take the heat and woo them with additional interviews.

"Anyway, my guys will continue their twenty-four-seven shifts and will turn up one of the two possibilities: they're there or they're not. Either way something's amiss. If Liam and his men have nothing to hide, then why are they hiding? If they left, why not in broad daylight? Even if they wanted to avoid the media, they could have just driven the limo out the gates. The point is they didn't want anyone to follow them to an airport, train station or safe house. God knows, they weren't going to use another helicopter." Jackson swirled the ice around in the glass, tilted the glass to his lips and drank the residue, then put the glass down, looking at Fen with confidence. "All we need is a few more days. The longer their absence, the greater the suspicion. Innocents don't behave this way."

Fen sat back in his chair and glanced at his watch.

"Do you want to go down to the mansion and talk to Don and the reporters?"

"Nah. I have to be back in the city for an eight-thirty business dinner with my agent and a producer. Media recognition is everything. I'm getting offers I never would have dreamed of getting. It will multiply exponentially after tomorrow's news conference."

"My guys have the place covered. Tomorrow, I'll head over to town hall and see what I can dig up. I also have friends who work for a title insurance company. I'll ask them to check documents for the former owners of the mansion and the adjoining properties to the immediate right and left."

Fen and Jackson stood up. Fen shook Jackson's hand. "Thanks." He felt the phone vibrate in his jeans pocket. He took it out and read the display, then motioned to Jackson to wait. "I have to take the call. I'll want to talk to you afterward. It's Dietz, Queens DA's office."

Jackson went to the counter and ordered an iced chai latte while Fen spoke to the homicide detective. When he returned with his drink, Fen was seated and off the phone.

"It's a break through, good news and bad." Fen was deep in thought.

Jackson raised his eyebrows. "Do you want one of these? I'll get it for you."

Fen shook his head. "Liam left the country on a private international charter."

Jackson whispered a whistle. "So that's why we've seen no one at the estate. But it doesn't explain what happened to the other servants. Wasn't he supposed to notify Dietz and Allan if he was leaving the country? It's standard procedure when there's an investigation. Weren't they checking for proof that the helicopter didn't take off from the estate?"

Fen gave a wry smile. "Yeah. Liam lied and said the helicopter never landed there or took off. So investigators and police were checking through eyewitness testimony and other leads and waiting to see if the examination of the wreckage indicated any clues linking the helicopter to the estate's heliport."

"Not notifying the detectives puts Liam under further suspicion. He's running from a crime scene. Unless there's another reason, or he had special clearance."

"They're checking into that."

"Clearance would have been given by the State Department. They're the only ones who have the power to override the orders of federal investigators. But that would mean he's a spook, or connected to individuals in high places, or has diplomatic immunity. Any of those circumstances would make tracking his whereabouts impossible. Much easier to score, if he's on the lam. How did Dietz find out he left?"

"Serendipity. A charter pilot tipped off a friend of his who is also a pilot and who flies for a few different private charter companies. The pilot said the guy was paranoid, didn't want anyone to trace the arrangements he was making, all last minute, destination, flight plan, number of passengers."

"Is that normal?"

"Think elite. Don't think commercial airlines. You can charter an international flight four hours before take-off, only not at Travelocity prices."

"Are they sure it was Liam?"

"His friend recognized Liam from news programs reporting on the helicopter crash when Liam was interviewed saying he knew nothing about it. The pilot was sure it was the man connected with the Southampton mansion under investigation with the helicopter incident. That's what he said."

"Did the pilot return?"

"Dietz is trying to find out. There are a lot of questions he intends to ask him"

"Yeah, like who was with him."

"Dietz doesn't know whether Liam was the only one on the flight. The arrangement was that if anyone else was to fly with him, they would bring their documents and money on departure."

"So what does that mean?"

"It means the son of a bitch has left the contiguous United States. He could be in downtown Dubai or Dublin for all we know."

"This changes everything.

"Dietz thinks this goes a long way to prove Liam lied, doubly so if it turns out he had special clearance to leave the country on a chartered jet. There are so many hypotheticals."

"Like what?"

"What if the helicopter accident wasn't an accident? What if Manny's kidnapping wasn't a kidnapping?"

"Abduction not for ransom, for something else?"

There was urgency in Fen's voice. "We never got the money call." He caught himself and shook his head. "Then again, I was the X factor. I foiled their plans, followed them, staked them out, and confronted them with the police before they could set up any deal-making. If they continued with the ransom after the police visit, search warrants and arrests would have followed. As it was, Liam pulled out his charm and his employer's status to get us off the property without allowing the detectives to search upstairs or in the basement."

"No chance for ransom? They cut their losses. Manny was expendable. They disposed of him, destroying the evidence in a neat helicopter crash."

"That was no simple crash I witnessed. The helicopter exploded in a fireball. Could have been a bomb on board. Say it was a bomb. Terrorism falls under the Patriot Act."

"That would explain why Liam was in a big hurry to leave. He wasn't taking a chance on being linked to the explosion."

"If the explosion was intentional, then I don't get it. The penalties are much worse for acts of terrorism than for kidnapping. Why risk involving the police or Feds? Just take Manny out to Montauk and drop him on the street. By the time he finds his way back home, they're out of the country. No one would have pursued them because Manny would have been returned, and we would have been utterly grateful."

"It's a null set. What is, isn't and what isn't, is. No logic applies. Maybe it's dominoes. They make mistake after mistake, bad decision after bad decision, complicating their position. When they try to extricate themselves, they become entangled so deeply, they can't find a way out. Maybe the abduction, cover up, explosion, cover up and flight are just panic moves."

"It doesn't explain the initial kidnapping."

"Sure it does. It was a way to get a lot of money. A stupid way, but that's from our perspective. Criminals don't think about credit ratings. Maybe they dried up all their financial resources with gambling, loan sharks or robberies. Maybe they were desperate. All criminals are desperate. They saw an opportunity and they grabbed it, the beginning of the chain. What followed was negative serendipity."

"Random circumstance, confused."

"Nothing premeditated about it. The premeditation came later when they tried to get out of their own web and couldn't. Anyway, the crash investigation and Dietz's questioning of the charter pilot will fill in some of the gaps in our information. Maybe not. Maybe we'll never know what Liam and his crew were up to. In light of this information, should we keep up the surveillance?"

Fen sighed. "Yeah. Have the guys on site leak to the reporters about Liam's skipping the country. See if they can use their contacts to do some more digging about the flight plan and other passengers. And follow through with your documents search and your friend at the title company. Anything we find is grist for Dietz and Allan."

"I have to tell you, buddy, things are bleak. Manny's gone, and so is Liam. Regardless of whether the investigation proves Manny was or wasn't on board, Liam is probably beyond US law enforcement. The case isn't high priority. You better pray that the NTSB and FBI investigators find the helicopter was sabotaged or primed with C-4."

"Cellulose bomb, anything."

"If Liam flies to a country without extradition treaties with the US, he's under the radar. What then?"

"I'll never stop, Jackson. Never. Maybe Manny wasn't on board that helicopter. Maybe they brought him on board the international charter. Maybe they killed him later and incinerated him or dropped his body over the Atlantic. I don't know. But if evidence indicates any possibility that he's alive, I'll keep on looking until I find him. If evidence links Liam with the crash, I'll force the FBI and Queens detectives to keep the investigation open and keep the media involved. If Manny's bones wash up on Southampton Beach three years from now, I won't stop until I find Liam and bring him to justice."

"Thousands of people go missing every year, and the families never stop looking and wondering what happened to their loved ones. You can never give up. You just never know when enough evidence leads to something."

"I won't have peace in my life until Manny is found, alive or dead."

"I hear ya, bro." Jackson and Fen both stood up and shook hands. "You can count on my help."

"You'll call me later with the information you uncovered at town hall?"

"You got it."

"I'll pass it on to Dietz. The man's okay. He's become a friend."

"You need friends in circumstances like this. People complain about law enforcement and the media. But they can target information through a vast network of resources like no one else."

"Yeah. I just have to keep the steady state with them, and my professional website updated. I've added a section about Manny, the crash and the investigation, and I've received lots of hits. My interviews have been on YouTube. Now I've got Dietz's information to post. A friend of mine has mocked up some great "'Wanted'" pictures of Liam which I'll upload to the site this evening. After tonight, the search for the bastard will be global." Fen was solemn as he followed Jackson out the door.

Chapter Thirty-Two

S ection B, Avenue H. How is anyone supposed to locate anybody? This place is huge,"

Peregrine grumbled to herself. She had been wandering lost for an hour near the border of Old Calvary and a newer division of the cemetery, scouring the stony terrain for hills and a cliff that housed the huge drainage pipe which abruptly jutted out above a field of tombstones. Using the New York City skyline to relate to her position that fateful, rainy night, she had navigated in ever widening circles doubling back on herself in uncertainty. She trudged angular paths dumbfounded, recognizing none of the gravesites. All was a vast, boring sameness of pyramids, angels, obelisks, monuments and marble slabs.

Memory was fogged in by the passage of time and the oppression of daylight and clear weather upon her senses. She stood and looked up in the distance. Was the Empire State Building and Chrysler Building to the left of the new mausoleums and perpendicular to the bank of trees behind her? Or was that the view after her crawl away from the drainage pipe to the pines where Fen and Beach Comber found her? She turned one hundred and eighty degrees. There were no pine trees, only spreading oaks behind her.

Peregrine glanced at her watch, growing more and more panicky, a panic instigated by Mocha who, moments before, had mobiled her with the warning to leave the cemetery and quit her search before nightfall. She had about twenty-five minutes before the gates closed at sunset. It would take every minute to get back to the Old Calvary entrance, unless she traveled through Section B into another division, Section C, that looked to be hillier. She thought that might be the division that spilled its borders onto Queens Boulevard where another entrance lay. If she didn't make it before the gates closed, at least she could be easily located adjacent to Queens Boulevard with its attendant businesses and identifiable cross streets. She would phone Mocha to bring help, and if necessary, they could contact the fire department. But she'd have to lie elegantly about getting lost, which could cause even more of a stir if one of the firemen tipped off the media. Better have Mocha come alone, bringing the retractable ladder and four blankets from home. With those, she could get over the barbed wire with little harm.

Peregrine stood still and thought. Keep on going or give up? How much would her mother be disappointed in her? Horribly. Could she come back in the morning, eluding the media? Not likely. The conference was at 9:00 AM. They would be waiting in front of her house to escort her to Bill's office. The cemetery gates opened at 9:00 AM. She was here now. Might as well get it over with.

Peregrine decided to forge ahead into Section C, heading west toward the sun's diffusion of spun gold slipping behind the city's jagged, adamantine profile. One mile away and behind her was the family mausoleum. Pointless to visit it since the labyrinth spiked in an unfathomable dark limbo underground, and she had no concept of its coinciding direction or length above ground, only that one of its interminable branches bled into a huge drainage pipe.

After her mother returned from Europe, she would share her experiences in the dark passageways, and then maybe her mother would feel freer to share the mausoleum's secrets, if Madeline knew them. There had been no maps or clues of any kind in the safe or the strong box where the artifacts were kept. Since her Aunt Rachel had never mentioned the vast underground network, Peregrine figured she probably didn't know it existed. Strange how suppressed family secrets, like diseased roots, stunted the entire family tree and twisted the viability of the current generation. She felt certain that the revealed knowledge would have increased her wisdom and acumen for circumventing the wheel and woe of her life's magnifying tribulations.

Peregrine had been walking with her head down. A shadow movement and noise caught her attention so that she looked up to locate the cause unsettling her peace. Shocked, she rasped an intake of air and stopped. In the distance, about one hundred yards away, was a very odd looking deformed man in tattered and filthy clothing, leaning against a pyramid gravestone. He was staring at his fingers, counting and muttering to himself.

Peregrine thought; homeless man has made a shelter out of a nearby mausoleum. She gave up all plans of continuing to look for Division C and quietly turned around to walk back toward Old Calvary. A rushing movement compelled her to turn around and look in the direction of the creepy, homeless man. He was racing toward her now, his mouth wide open to reveal a black abyss, his jaws growing wider and wider like the maw of a voracious sinkhole eating away the bordering earth and anything in its path. Peregrine became transfixed, rooted to the ground. In horror, she watched as the creature threw back its head and screamed hideously, like a panicked animal in severe distress, like a demon about to lose his head.

In answering duality, Peregrine peeled out a bloodcurdling scream, turned left and raced forward, not toward Old Calvary, but in an arc that headed north, deeper into Section G and away from the Queens Boulevard entrance, away from the racing demon, away from the light of the setting sun, away from herself. Oxelox accelerated his flight, crossing the spot where Peregrine had stood, brushing past alternate universes and realities, bumping against time platforms and dimensions, peeling back high blown waves of reverberating noise to pierce the world of spirit and place it in high alert, signaling that an untold horror now broke into the realms of heaven. The man who was not human but of spirit dimension raced through the material realm, carrying his baneful, dread evil toward Old Calvary, toward the place where his demon friend groveled headless and tortured, unable to holler or lament.

Peregrine wailed out the soul's torment, possessed by a horror that made her fears in the labyrinth seem like a baby's. She threw her head back and pierced the sky with the sounds of her agony, her bones ready to break with the pain. Peregrine caterwauled because she was racing like she had never raced before. She shrieked because her nerves were shattering any hold on the dimension she thought was reality. She roared because of what she was, alive and tortured and vulnerable. And she hallooed because he hallooed. He had nothing else to do but bring pandemonium with him in a unity of horror and pain.

As the woman and demon fled from each other in opposite directions, they were distinct but unified. And the light of the setting sun leaked out of the cemetery, and the shadows leapt up to revel in the malevolent horrors of Peregrine and her unhoused companion.

Oxelox galloped to the Johnson mausoleum. He frantically searched the area for the decapitated, vivid body of his companion and finding it, tucked under the hedge rows where he had stowed it, gathered the twitching form of Abracix into his tremoring arms. He enfolded the hulking mass, pressing the gored stump of neck against his chest and rocked for comfort until his lamentations ended, supplanted by low moans. He dragged his throbbing friend over to his head which Oxelox had perched on the top of a nearby monument to reconcile it with the impossible, lonely and agonized body.

Abracix's authority and power over the natural elements of materialism had been broken. If a blood sacrifice could be offered, the demoniac could be made whole again. Oxelox didn't know exactly how he would effect the sacrifice at the precise hour, only that that was required in the other dimension where the power could be loosed if the conditions were right. If they were not, his friend would be eternally severed from authority, a slave of the mausoleum. And he, the feeble second, would be doomed to wander alone without Abracix and his power. So Oxelox grieved and moved Abracix's body and head to safety before daylight and brought them out from under cover at the setting sun and mourned and moaned Abracix's fate. For he could do nothing without his companion until a blood sacrifice released them to prowl the earth and possess hapless souls that they hunted between the dimensions of the vestigial and forgotten realities of humankind.

Two miles away, blindly, Peregrine raced and leaped among the tombstones as her mother had done one week before. Only Madeline had raced toward an end, the parking lot and Bill's waiting arms. Peregrine ran until exhaustion from yelling and running outran her, and with her voice in tatters, only the whisper of faded screeches blistered out from her mouth. Hasping and choking, she stumbled into a large circle of headstones. She threw herself gratefully upon the soft-looking grass that ran its border up against the circular marble arrangement, and there she rested, squeezed out anxiety and conformed her breathing to familiar rhythms. By degrees, she forced her mind into an opaque stillness and eventual steady state of emptiness and non-thought. A recuperative metaphysical curtain rolled across memory and emotion, blotting out the creature's cavernous, gaping mouth and despairing cries. Her self-possession grasped, she counted backwards from one hundred, vowing that when she reached "one," activity would be hers again. Fifteen minutes passed. As Peregrine drifted into semi-consciousness, the cemetery shifted into nightfall.

Awakening, Peregrine rolled from her left side to a recumbent position, feeling the sweet earth pillow her head and cushion her torso. She gazed back at the interested, pale stars and slothful, cream moon and moderated her breathing to a dull normal. She felt safe and calm in her sanctuary of encircling monuments. There was no urge to scream or cry out; but in her consciousness, she was aware that her emotions would never again know the peace she had felt one hour ago. All innocence had fled, and there was a growing alarm that for the first time in her life, for her special viewing, reality had vomited up a bottomless evil capable of ravaging the depths of her eternity.

Peregrine shuddered and sat up. Too bad she couldn't stay here where it was soft, and she was made invisible to any onlookers outside the circular shield of marble. But logic was returning. The goal of her journey to find her backpack loomed over her and blotted out the horror of that foul, yelling, raggedy man. She had to find the concrete drain. She must hurry. Where was she? Was she anywhere near the exit? She had brought the flashlight and water and left her purse locked in the trunk of her car, which, she thought ruefully, was parked in the Old Calvary parking lot, probably a couple of miles away. She took the flashlight out of her belly pack and turned it on then off. She would use it in the drain-pipe. Here, it was unnecessary. The full moon provided ample light.

Peregrine listened for any night sounds. She listened beyond the silence of the grave. In anxiety, she got to her feet and moved outside the circle of high monuments to familiarize herself with her surroundings. She had run into the deepest part of this cemetery division. In the distance, she noted two groves of trees that appeared to follow a sloped decline. Was that the embankment and the cliff drop off to the valley? A brooding anxiousness supplanted vague fears. She did not want to be here overnight. She must keep moving.

Able to identify rough tombstones yards away and the leafy shadows of trees and bushes, she understood how Indian tribes didn't move but under cover of a new moon and under a full moon, at their peril. The skyline was for her bearings. But where was it? She turned. There it was, west. Then the grove of trees was north. Strange. She looked again at the uneven jeweled skyline. Now the anchor buildings looked nearly the same as they did a week ago in the rain. She was probably closer to the drainage pipe than she had imagined. If that homeless man had not terrified her into running helter-skelter into this division, she never would have recognized these surroundings. Now, if she could manage to stay calm and make for the grove of trees, maybe she would find the pipe. The flashlight would lead her through the tunnel to her backpack which was maybe one hundred yards from the end of the drain's drop-off. The only problem would be how to get into the pipe again. Maybe she could climb on top of it from the cliff and ease her way inside.

With renewed hope, determined to stave off any fearful pangs or urges to hiss out raspy yells, Peregrine slowly jogged down the jigsaw puzzle paths through the gravesites. Soon she stood gazing at the shadowy trees that, like sentinels ranked in importance by height, devolved into diminutive clumps in a valley below. One hundred yards in the distance, the slope gradually declined and then abruptly banked. She surmised this was an earthen overhang, resembling the terrain of what she had thought almost two weeks ago was the cliff out of which the pipe protruded. Beyond were the fields of headstones that extended for miles. In the distance, Peregrine thought she could make out strings of car headlights. Was that the LIE or was she disoriented? Peregrine turned to look at her North Star, the Manhattan skyline. Her position lined up, spot on with memory.

Peregrine said a silent prayer that she would locate the drainage pipe by the earthen overhang and headed in the direction of the declivity adjacent to the grove of trees. Here everything seemed familiar. Soon she was on top of a ridge, looking into the stone valley below, the moonlight faintly glimmering on the whites and light grays of the highly polished stones. In the multihued graded shadows of blue-black, graphite, cinder, slate and mouse-gray, seraphim perched atop impassive monuments. They blew trumpets, posed prettily or fanned and outstretched their huge wings like ribbed sails.

In this division, the poorer cousin of Old Calvary, there were no mausoleums, just thousands upon thousands of adamantine markers, crowded against one another, not the thickness of a blade of grass between two-foot square plots. Marble traffic jam. The final parking lot. Here was the real New York City, the repository of dried up dreams, moldering memories, desiccated lives. So many dead. The coffins had been placed vertically in the ground to yield more space; the dead forced to watchfully stand throughout eternity, no sleep or rest there. Or maybe the coffins were stacked one upon the other, like inverted skyscrapers plunging deep into the earth's crust. Peregrine mused, *"The numbers of global dead accumulated from every age probably exceeded the planet's current life-obsessed, solipsistic population for whom the dead never lived."* She sighed heavily. The living were delusional, arrogant. She vowed that she would raise her children with humility of heart, nurtured by a healthy dose of the reality of cemeteries.

Peregrine loped toward the ridge and cliff overhang that accentuated the economic disparity revealed in the spaciousness or lack of it within the distinct cemetery sections. In the valley were the lower and middle class, the teeming masses tripping over each other. On the hill in the elevated, rarefied terrain, outstretched the gracious, moneyed plots dotted with lushly landscaped, exclusively appointed mausoleums or monolithic monuments. The contrast intended to remind one of the undemocratic social economies of scale and hinted that Death wasn't such an equalizer after all. As she traversed this divide, Peregrine saw in the distance a mound of earth creating an irregular rise in the cliff's form, a rise that ran away from the cliff embankment in the opposite direction and gradually assimilated with the hilly section of the moneyed gravesites. Was this the pipe? As she moved closer, she scoped the valley and the hillside. Yes. Now all was quiet familiarity. It must be from that ridge in the distance that she had hung from the pipe and jumped to the valley below risking broken bones. From this height looking downward, she was amazed at her courage, stymied by her strength to escape from the darkness and Death's gaping maw. Desperate circumstances brought out the best of individual achievement, only if one did not seek out such circumstances for that purpose.

As she closed the distance between herself and the pipe, Peregrine fumbled in her belly pack for the flashlight. Grasping the yellow plastic case, she pulled it out and closed the flap of the taupe pack, then felt for the black button and clicked on the torch. The moon, playing hide and seek beneath a bank of clouds. It had plunged the graveyard into a pale darkness, and she had lost patience waiting for it to tire of the game. Peregrine splayed the light, illuminating a path down which she tread in anticipation, carefully picking her way around the lumpy upheavals in the earth and the occasional small outcropping of rock along the edge of the cliff. Luckily, the drop-off appeared as a line of pitch to her left. The valley of stone was as black as an abyss; otherwise, she might have slipped and accidentally fallen the seven feet to the valley floor, breaking the bones she had managed to salvage in her rescue jump nearly two weeks prior.

Ahead, the thin stream of light particles diffused and melded into the darkness as she skirted the black rim two feet to her left. The petulant, shy moon refused to emerge from the billowing, overblown cumulus clouds; and the ray of light emanating from the torch was too weak to shine past five feet, so she imagined the mound of terrain that covered the pipe to be just ahead where she remembered it to be ten minutes before in the full moonlight. Without the moon to panorama the rise in the earth, she stumbled along, looking at patches of ground in the wan torchlight, trying to locate the rounded incline with her feet since her eyes and the lack of light betrayed her purpose. She found if she swept the flashlight like a pendulum to her left, beyond the cliff and in front of her, and to her right while inching her way forward, she gleaned a notion of the general turf. Finally, she noticed a rise upward in front of her leading into the mausoleum section. When she focused the torch, she gave a cry of delight. There, not ten feet ahead in the disappearing light looked to be the massive gray pipe, leaping into the darkness of the overhanging cliff and beyond.

Peregrine quickened her pace continuing the swinging motion with the flashlight until she reached the huge mound of earth covering the pipe. Thankful that her knee was wrapped in an ace bandage, and she was on anti-inflammatories for any pain, she dropped on all fours. Holding the flashlight with her right hand, she crawled along the top of the grassy mound until she reached the cliff edge of earthen bank. She swept the torch to her right, left and front. The leaden concrete protruded into the blackness of space. The valley floor was there, but she could see nothing in the cloud shrouding moonlessness. Peregrine regretted not bringing a flashlight that she could have hitched to the belt of her jeans, which would have guided her along the pipe quickly. Now she would be dragging the flashlight, then stopping and sweeping it carefully every few inches, crawling like a caterpillar with a slow irregular movement along the top of the pipe until she reached its cavernous opening. Too bad there wasn't a wind to breeze the clouds from the occult moon. She was desperate to return to the blue-black shimmering fullness of moonlight. But there wasn't breath or stir in the still night. Peregrine guessed that the oppressive clouds holding in the heat of the day and voiding the full cheeked moon were now growing heavy with moisture. She didn't want to be caught slipping on the edge of the pipe in the rain to lose her grip and fall, so she must move quickly.

Placing her left hand on the thick pipe, with her right dragging the flashlight scraping against the concrete, Peregrine advanced forward. She was away from the earthen cliff, out in the darkness of space with nothing but the pipe to keep her up. Four feet to go until she reached the opening. Peregrine directed her energies and concentration to the careful placement of her hands and knees between the thick, concrete ribs, which dug into her palms and her knees. Between movements, she flashed the torch ahead of her, making sure not to shine it to the left or right. She was nervous that a stray light beam might illumine the gravestones on the valley floor, and the flash, telescoping the drop off, would spin her dizzy with vertigo and plunge her into a cartwheel, spinning and slamming her into a marble slab, splitting open her head.

Now she was hyper aware that all manner of night creatures sounded. There were buzzings and chirps echoed by the hoot of the predatory owl, nudging out the terrified vole and the piercing sporadic cry of the night hawk on the wing. The dark time welcomed her nocturnal children; and Peregrine, a child of the day, began to tremble in her groveling state, alienated by her displacement and the desperate acknowledgement of her dangerous position. Her acute mind took an omniscient overhead view of herself. There she was, her head down, her back in an arc, crouching and kneeling, two feet away from the edge of a massive drain pipe with only a thin wand of light to keep her from falling into the abyss of blackness. Why didn't she leave well enough alone? If she fell and broke her back or neck, she would paralyze herself, a quadriplegic, unable to move, unable to reach inside her belly pack for her phone. Now the terror of her own imagination assaulted her. "Hold on," she cried aloud. "Hold on to logic. You're fine. You're fine."

But the tendril of fear thickened like a vine irradiated by an electrical storm, and Peregrine's imagination sprouted a ganglia of alarm and dread. She stopped inching forward, fright-filled, immobile. She must call for help. She couldn't. She lost her phone. Her phone wasn't in the belly pack. And if she called, what if Mocha wasn't home? Call Fen. She couldn't. He was at his mother's preparing for the conference tomorrow. Was her phone there? She had to check. She couldn't. She was terrified. "Hold on. You're OK," she cried aloud, again.

A nighthawk flew overhead and screamed a demented hunting cry. Peregrine felt like the little mouse quaking in the bushes waiting for the talons to plunge into its quivering back. *Breathe. Breathe. Hold, Hold.*

Peregrine inhaled deeply. She felt with her flashlight hand for the phone in the pack. She exhaled sharply. Relief. She must stop this insanity of terrifying herself. The phone was where it should be. But the hawk's searing cry pierced the shadows as the punctured mouse was dragged writhing into space and death. A new anxiety crept forward into her mind from a vision the length of a nanosecond. A wayward band of light from her awkward movements holding the torch had crazily flashed something weird, something she wished it had not. Movement down there in the black valley. Something was bumbling and grappling, like a huge beetle mired in the pitch of the valley floor.

Her imagination ran riot, consumed by curiosity. What was it? Nothing. Or was it? She must know. She was not imagining this. The light rays illumined two feet to the end of the pipe. She could flash the beam down and to the right, where she saw the rolling movement. The ray would tell all. But she didn't want to know. Then Peregrine realized. She couldn't see it; but whatever it was could see her up there, the pale halo from the flashlight like a beacon. She must see who was looking up at her. Inexorably, impulsively, she directed the light downward to the crowded monuments directly below. The light crisscrossed the marble headstones, which reflected back the emptiness. Nothing. She flashed the light to the left. Nothing. She beamed the short ray in the distance ahead of her. Still nothing. *God, but I am stupid,* Peregrine thought. *Now, let's get this over with.*

As the woman slagged her way across the pipe in the heights of the overhang, Oxelox slinked back among the gravestones quietly, congratulating himself on his spiritual ability to conform his shape to the shadows and the tall dark monument behind where he had stood. He laughed the hooting cry of the predator owl. Indeed, humans were stupid. They refused to note the realms and the powers. They trusted their natural senses to distinguish one reality, confounding the truth that there were multitudes of realities. They couldn't see; they never heard; they were blind to the truth and believers of falsehood. They were so easy to deceive. He trotted back across the valley floor, his dead-on visual acuity in the darkness leading him gracefully past the city of graves. His curiosity had been satisfied once he had seen who it was. In the daylight, she had frightened him. Now, under the blanket of darkness, he could comfortably skulk at will, haunting the haunted with impunity, fearful of no one except Him.

Strange, his confusion. He thought it was the others that came at odd moments, the ones he and Abracix had targeted. Usually, he was never confused. He attributed it to his earlier scare and the nature of the one who had scared him. Regrettable, it had not been that other bunch. Those fools' houses were empty and ripe for the plucking. If the opportunity arose, he might pull a possession. But it was not them; it was her. And despite her stupidity, despite her confusion, her house was spiritually whole. Even oppression of her soul was impossible. So, he would have to wait, until the time. The other vulgars would eventually return to enact their mischief, and then he would pick and choose amongst them. He must find habitation.

Oxelox set his sights dead reckoning back to the crypt and willed himself through spirit realms. This setback was not even a blip in eternity. There was so much to do. In three seconds, he rejoined Abracix at the Johnson mausoleum. He encircled his headless friend in his arms, obscured by shadows and darkness.

Chapter Thirty-Three

How long was she outside waiting in her car?"

"Maryanne said maybe about an hour. She left with the media trailing her. I think she went back to Peregrine's."

"It's nine forty-five. Is there any way you can leave work and go back there?"

"No. I'll be here late because I met you at Peregrine's this afternoon. I got in around five, and I'll work until twelve. A limo will take me home."

Reggie sighed. "Corporate perks. Well, anyway, good news. I hear through channels that Paul Carver will be indicted. The indictment is easy. The case will be tough. There's too much reasonable doubt. The logical divide must be breached, and that means Deidre must come in as a witness against him. And not a hostile one. She's really our case."

"Well, as I said, we left on speaking terms; but if she is going to come back home, I have to give her space to make her own decisions. She's as sensitive as a tick to flame, and she will dig in and close herself off with any heat we send her way. Wait a minute. I have to take this call."

Reggie heard the land line click to dead silence. He shuffled through papers on his desk that he had arranged in piles and placed one set in a folder that he planned to take with him. Elizabeth clicked on. "You aren't going to cave on me are you?" said Reggie.

"Oh, please. You have to learn to trust God and be patient."

"Aunt Elizabeth, I trust myself first. God helps those that help themselves. Do I have your full support?"

"Reggie, I support what you are doing. But this has to be my way. I know my daughter better than you do. If you want to alienate her, by all means, go ahead and call her, visit her, do what you please. You cannot control human beings. You above all should know that."

"Well, I'm feeling pressure from the DA. You know with Carver's lawsuit? Today, I received the transfer out of Queens to the Bronx."

"You knew that was coming. It actually gives justification to the DA and helps our case."

"But you can't expect me to be happy with the results."

"Can I do anything?"

"No. Just that it's hard for me not to want to speak to Deidre about her relationship with Carver, the abuse, you know. That's the linchpin of the case against him. It will go a long way with a jury."

"She won't speak to me about it. How will she speak to you? I don't even think Peregrine knows about the situation. She looked dumbfounded when I confronted Deidre about their sexual relationship."

"Too bad we don't have hard evidence, like a diary or letter or phone conversation with Carver."

"I looked in every part of her room, the bureaus, closets, stray boxes. Unless she has secret hiding places, there's nothing."

"Too bad you didn't hack into the delete files of her laptop like I told you. That's where the stuff is."

"Well, she has her laptop with her. Unless I go over to Peregrine's and somehow get it from her, I'll never gain access to those files."

"Not a bad idea. Maybe we can arrange something. At some point, you'll visit for a chat. I'll come over and distract her, and then you can review them. I know she must have deleted emails to him."

"I'm sure you're right. Only, I don't agree with your methods. At some point, we must respect an individual's latitude of privacy."

"How can you say that Aunt Elizabeth, when you know that Deidre isn't in her right mind? She has to be protected from herself. Abused women protect their abusers."

"Yes, I know. No need to remind me of my own past."

"The sooner Deidre is back with you, the sooner we can gain access. The case will be made, and Deidre doesn't even have to go on the stand against Carver. We have experts who will testify about abused women's syndrome. The emails are hard evidence against him. Voila."

"It's because of you we separated. There it is. Your pressure. Your rush, rush, rush. It's a delicate matter. The two of them still love each other. She is still waiting for him to get over Rebecca. Remember, he broke up with her because of what happened after Rebecca died."

"The break-up is an admission of his abusive behavior."

"The defense could use it to his credit. There is only one incident of abuse, and it was an accident that I discovered anything about it."

"An overheard conversation."

"You said in a court of law, it's hearsay."

"Yes, without hard evidence, inadmissible, but there are ways we can get it in, objections afterward, but we can get it in."

Elizabeth sighed. "I don't know. We'll have to wait and see how Deidre and Peregrine and her mother get along. This will be the first time she is away from me. I miss her. I don't know if she will miss me."

"You are very close."

"Not now, not after her coma and the amnesia. She is a different woman. I don't recognize her, and it frightens me. There were so many things I wanted to tell her about herself and family, and now, it's as if I will never have the chance. Sometimes I think my faith is faltering."

"Nonsense. You are completely yourself." Reggie shifted the topic matter-of-factly. "Well, it's quiet here, no interruptions. I'm packing up my desk." Reggie was sour. "Tonight will be the last of Queens, for a while." He paused to let his words gain their target, then he maneuvered. "So, you've convinced me that doing nothing is best. In the next few days, we'll see how she is getting along at Peregrine's. And who knows? With all the media attention, she may decide to return home, splitting the media between your house and Peregrine's. Both of them may tire of that entourage."

"When is the indictment coming down?"

"We're not sure. Probably by the end of the week."

"Well, when it comes down, we've lost her."

"So, we have between now and maybe Friday to get to her laptop."

"I guess so. I just don't know how we are going to do it."

"Let me think of something."

"Like today? No, Reggie. If we are to have that information, then somehow it will find its way into our hands."

"Aunt Elizabeth, are you suggesting that God is going to come down, sneak into Peregrine's house unnoticed, take the laptop and fly it to your office?" Reggie could no longer contain his anger at his aunt's stupidity.

"No, Reggie, I am asking that patience have its perfect work."

"Whatever that means," Reggie growled. "Patience is not a person, and no work is perfect. Nothing is perfect."

"Yes." Elizabeth's tone was level. "You see the problem? We don't agree because fundamentally, our values are different. How do you expect to succeed in your lawsuit and in this case? Your ego is constantly getting in the way. Your need to control things is mucking up our outcomes. It's what caused Mocha to become estranged. And if you continue, this situation will blow up in your face. I am not telling you what to do. But if you allow things to unfold as they will, then the results you want may follow. It's the Tao or Zen of cause and effect."

Reggie only knew the Zen of results. The only results were ones he effected. If his actions produced reactions he didn't like, he got around them. There were billions of permutations. One only had to think of them. There was no one he couldn't manipulate; no situation he couldn't change to suit his needs. His aunt was stuck in fantasy. He didn't know how she progressed as far in life as she did. "OK. Fine. But how will you feel if Carver is not held accountable for impacting your daughter's ability to have healthy and normal relationships for the rest of her life? Will you be okay with that? Is there no accountability for abusers and molesters of women?"

"No. Sometimes, not in this life."

"So, you are saying that Deidre must suffer the same fate that you suffer?"

"No. But if we push and force and prod for a result, my experience has been that you get the opposite, and sometimes, much worse."

Reggie whispered his hope to Elizabeth. "And my experience has been that my actions bring results; and if they are not the results I want, eventually, I get them. Aunt Elizabeth, let's compromise. We'll agree. Tonight, we do nothing. Tomorrow, we do nothing overt, but we plan. By Thursday, if Deidre is still at Peregrine's, then we'll make an arrangement so that you go in with friends of hers, maybe from work. You'll call and elicit their help. You just say you're having a little surprise pick-me-up party for Deidre, and can they come? While she is distracted with them, you locate the laptop and access the deleted files. You know how, right?"

"Please."

"Well?"

Elizabeth shook her head. "I don't know. It's deceitful."

"Hasn't she deceived you, countless times? Wasn't her relationship with Paul Carver one of those times? Aren't the chickens coming home to roost, as Malcolm X would say? You are fighting to give your daughter a chance that you weren't offered. Do the means justify the ends? Yes. You're freeing yourself from the past. Exorcising demons. Making sure the sins of the mothers are not repeated on the daughters."

"I hope you are right. We'll know in a week."

"We'll know before that, Aunt Elizabeth. This is the only way to get her to testify against him. There is no other way after the indictment."

"I just don't want her to be lost to me forever. That's what I am risking here. Losing her. If this doesn't come from her own free will, then I will lose her. She will hate me, and this will push her into Paul Carver's arms."

"Not if he's in jail, it won't. I don't think you have a choice, do you? If you do nothing and he is indicted, and she doesn't testify and there is no hard evidence to destroy reasonable doubt, he goes free. Where does that leave her? Eventually, she will go back to him, and that will be the last you will see of her. This way, she may be estranged from you, but your daughter will be alive. Eventually, she will understand. Believe me. She will know you did this to save her from herself." Reggie had convinced himself of his own goodness and rightness. And convincing himself, he had convinced Elizabeth.

"By tomorrow afternoon, the party will be arranged; the friends invited."

"It's set then."

"And if Deidre wiped out her deleted emails, then we've failed."

"Why would she? She has no reason to suspect her mother would sweep them for evidence."

"No. But she might suspect her cousin of it."

"How would I get her laptop? You don't even have access to her laptop. That would mean she's canny. She doesn't even realize Carter will be indicted so soon. His own lawyer doesn't even suspect it. Besides, she has amnesia. She doesn't remember what's on the emails to consider they are evidence to wipe them out.

Elizabeth had exhausted all argument. "OK. The only problem is that Peregrine and Deidre will suspect something is amiss once she sees me and her friends. Too bad we didn't think of this before you brought the media to the house. My credibility with Deidre and Peregrine is zero."

"You could elicit Peregrine's help with the party."

"Better as a surprise. No chance for them to say no. Deidre would never shut the door to work colleagues who have come to cheer her up. She'll let us in, but they'll suspect us. I have to gain their trust, which means I can't look for the laptop until the party has been going on for a while."

Reggie was pleased. Elizabeth was engaged. "Good idea. You know the DA was planning to call her in as a hostile witness. A nasty business. Possible contempt of court if she perjures herself. Now, just her emails will be used. You are saving her. You won't regret it. There is no other way."

After they said their goodbyes and Elizabeth hung up, she thought about Reggie's arguments. Was she so desperate for her daughter's love it impaired her judgment? Should she let her daughter find her own way, absolving herself of all responsibility, ignoring the knowledge that Deidre was at sea and might be on medication for the rest of her life, the truth disappearing deeper and deeper inside of her? Then it would be too late. She would never recover. Reggie was right. Before the situation repeated itself when Carver got out of jail, prevent. In the prevention was Deidre's safety. In the prevention was Elizabeth's unhappiness. Both children would be lost to her. Her boy was already in Death's clutches. But there was the chance that one, in due season, would be alive for reconciliation. She would take that chance.

Chapter Thirty-Four

Peregrine laid face up, staring into the darkness, the pipe's ridges digging the muscles of her upper back. She had just completed a forward somersault into the cavernous mouth, holding on to the edge of the rim and letting go at the last possible second to land with a banging thump on her back with her torso inside the great curve of cement and her legs hanging outside in space with gravity tugging, pulling, dragging her to plummet, until she managed to wriggle backwards and save herself.

Peregrine grappled for her belly pack, which was still strapped around her waist, the zipper and flaps fastened securely. It had taken her a full half hour to come up with the tumbling plan, and she had chickened out three times before she firmed her resolve and did it. Thank God her plan had worked. It was going to be so much easier to climb out. Now, all she had to do was retrieve the pack, check in with Mocha for the last time, climb out of the pipe, then make her way back through this cemetery division to one of the adjacent roads. She was not looking forward to traipsing through the darkness, enduring creepy night sounds and brushing up against crawly things. It was nearing midnight. The witching hour brought out all manner of evil. But she had no other options. Wait until sunrise, spending the night in the pipe, reliving horrible nightmare realities? No way!

Peregrine unzipped the belly pack, reached for the flashlight, pulled it out and pressed the on button. Light! The batteries were holding, but for how long? She had better hurry. She sat up and sprayed the light up and around the sides of the enclosure. There were at least three feet between her head and top of the pipe, and it was about six feet wide. No wonder she was able to see the light from a distance inside the labyrinth. Huge pipe, letting the sunshine leak in, though it had been a grayish day. She bent her body forward and raised herself up, bending over, careful not to graze her head against the curving roof. She was five feet nine inches. The pipe was a little less than her height, but she was comfortable and could move quickly, though she must bend forward. Peregrine shuddered, remembering her pain and desperation and hope, as she neared the gray light of the opening. She must be insane to be going in the opposite direction back into the abyss, back into the horror of a network of traps and dead ends. Only for the priceless artifacts that she must put into the safe would she come back to this hole.

With each step Peregrine returned to the past, the terrors, the longings for freedom, the implacable knowledge that she was going to die. Hurry, hurry, she told herself. You cannot bare much more of this. Just get the pack, get the pack, get the pack and go. But how far in did she leave it? There was no way of knowing. She wished she had left a scratch mark, a huge X, or signs along the way, indicating that she was getting closer. But she had been dying, dehydrated, in hellish agony. Returning was the last thing on her mind, and taking the time to make scratch marks would have sapped what little strength she had. It was a miracle she had lived. Thus far, she had shared the details of her adventures with no one.

Peregrine hunted the concentrated beam as her sneakers scraped and scratched the rough floor. Get the pack, get the pack, her steps became a regular rhythm as she whispered the command to herself. Periodically, she felt a scream rise up to fill her mouth and swallow her. She pushed it down, gulped air and belched. The *brruuup* echoed off the walls, and she laughed which settled her nerves and intensified her determination.

Get the pack, the pack, the pack. Get the pack, the pack, the pack. She stopped. Silence. She was heading deeper into the earth. As she tread, she sensed the pipe gently sloping downward. A most unusual drain-pipe. Then Peregrine realized. This wasn't a drain pipe. It was something else, with another purpose. But what? She didn't care. All she wanted was the pack, the pack, the pack. The rays of light projected eerie shadows along the curvature of darkness and played and bounced, melding the contours of her black figure into the darkness ahead. Peregrine listened for sounds and looked for sights other than her own and was comforted by the stillness and her aloneness. She was beginning to grow calm from the familiarity and regularity of her movements.

She noticed the difference first when her sneaker sounded with a dull thud, not a scraping slash. And she found she had to bend way over to avoid bumping her head. Shining the flashlight upward, she saw the rock and earth and stone of the labyrinth. She was out of the pipe and into one of the tunnels spiraling out from the vast subterranean network, snaking underneath and past the mausoleum. Peregrine halted and looked at the construction of the tunnel walls. The earth was packed solid and glazed over with niter, salt deposits that were whitish like web work that a huge spider had spun and spun and left to catch her prey. She struggled against the nightmare terrors, a remembrance of things past that now mingled with present fright. Peregrine expected to see a hissing gigantic tarantula drop from a thick web right in her face, murdering her with fright.

"You ass," she screamed.

"Ass, sss, ssss," the walls echoed and chided her. She felt better screaming and resumed her hunchback of Notre Dame gait down the tunnel. If she had held it in, that shriek, she eventually would have collapsed into a shuddering, moaning blob on the bug-ridden floor of the cave. She had to control her imagination.

"Have to control yourself, dearie," she cackled like the old witch in *Snow White and the Seven Dwarfs*. The cartoon had terrified her when she was six. The transformation of the witch from beautiful to ugly repelled and fascinated her to this day. "Beauty and ugliness, one in the same. One is the truth and the other a game." She posed the nonsense rhyme in a sing-song childish voice.

What was happening to her? She was like another person. *"God, where is the damn back pack?* Where are you, you fucker?" Peregrine cried out loudly. Then she remembered something. She stopped and shined the beam of light behind her at the opening of the pipe. There were only turgid graphite hues, the light particles eaten away by the powerful blackness. She had traveled bent over, her back was now killing her, for about one hundred yards past the cement of the pipe. Wasn't this about where she first looked in the distance to see the pinhole of light? Peregrine blazed the light against the walls. Niter, earth, white rock, masonry. Clearly, the tunnel had been constructed intentionally, but for what purpose, and whose? It seemed a mammoth job to fashion such a place underground. And there was enough air in the passageway to breathe comfortably; though in parts, she remembered the odor was rather musty. But she had smelled so bad; she was probably the cause of the rankness. Peregrine inhaled. The air seemed fresh. There must be vents somewhere, blowing in the fresh air. But how? Probably in the walls of the ceiling. It was a mystery that would have to be solved another day with a stronger flashlight and better equipment. She had to hurry. She didn't want dead batteries to leave her unsettled in darkness. She had had enough of darkness for a lifetime, thank you.

Peregrine beamed the light back on the ground, moving carefully as she penetrated deeper into the cavern. The earthen floor appeared to be undisturbed, but then it was packed firm and solid, though damp to the touch. Had she dragged herself through this portion? Did she miss a turn off? Or had she mistaken one drain-pipe for another? No. The position of the Manhattan skyline as backdrop located her in the right place. The problem was she miscalculated how far into the tunnel she had left the pack. Because of her condition then and her impatience now, she realized she must have dropped it much deeper inside the tunnel. Now, she had to back-peddle maybe a mile to hit pay dirt. Too bad it was dark outside. She had no referent, no pinpoint of light to judge her distance. She must continue, as distasteful as it was, deeper into the labyrinth, if she was to retrieve the artifacts. Maybe she should just give up and return in a couple of days with the proper equipment, three halogen lamps and batteries, along with some water and food. But that would provoke problems. She would be forced to cleverly dissuade her mother from coming home to pack. Once Madeline was back in the house, she would check the safe before she left for Europe.

Bent over nearly double as the cavern walls narrowed to three feet and the ceiling closed down on her, Peregrine reluctantly sloughed forward. She had slowed her pace and scoured the ground for any scrapings or minute indications of her previous journey through the passage. The solidly tamped earth yielded few signs. At one point, she thought she could make out ill-formed footprints, but her mind couldn't grasp what they might be doing there. After all, she had slid and wriggled on her stomach, rolled and crawled on all fours a good part of the distance down this section of the labyrinth before she sighted the exit's light. Footprints and shoe treads were anomalous. To offside her disbelief, she had knelt down; and placing the flashlight above the ground to shine directly over the marks, she had lowered her face three inches above the earth and closely eyeballed the faint five circled indentations that looked like sneaker treads. Perhaps she had errantly rested her foot on the ground at one point. No matter. The back-pack was not there. It was not twenty feet ahead where she fastened the light rays to the tunnel floor, watching them fade to darkness. Once more a decision. Turn back or continue? Flicking the light to her wrist, the watch hands on her Cartier read five to midnight. She had been so overwhelmed by her obsession with finding the pack, that she hadn't realized her phone had been inactive for four hours since Mocha had mobiled her.

Peregrine collapsed from her crawl position to sit with her back against the cavern wall with the exit to her right, anxieties volcanically erupting. Why hadn't Mocha phoned or texted her? Was her mobile damaged by her somersault into the pipe? Had it fallen during her amble and crawl down the tunnel? Peregrine felt around her waist for the belly pack and zeroed in on the zipper. It was halfway open.

"Damn!" Peregrine shouted. She would have to retrace her steps immediately to get her phone. She tore into the cloth pouch. No. The phone was there. She pulled it out and fumbled with the flashlight shining it on the phone. The screen was not cracked, but it was black. What the hell? She pressed the green button. Nothing. Dead battery.

After a few dodgy seconds of frantic pressing, Peregrine realized the phone had been switched off. She turned it on. Twelve midnight. Would it work in the tunnel? Comforting half tonal beeps as she pressed Mocha's number. The screen registered "no signal available." No surprise there. She checked her messages, two frantic ones from Mocha registered at 10:30 PM and 11:00 PM. In the second one, Mocha threatened to call the police and send them after her if she didn't message back immediately. Worse. There was a message from her mother registered at 11:05 PM. When she played it back on speaker, her mother's hysterical voice rose and fell, like a wretched mouse's high-pitched squeaks. Then she became imperious, demanding a call back. Great. Mocha had told her where she went and why, and the police were probably searching for her this very moment. Now she was screwed, and all hell would rain its fury upon her. The police, the press and worst of all her mother. Damn Mocha's cowardice! But then she couldn't blame her friend who was maniacal as a result of her injuries. The damn phone had conspired against them both.

Peregrine groaned aloud. Why didn't she think to check her phone? She knew why. Her powers of concentration and stubborn persistence to reach a goal, any goal, had become a situational liability. Coupled with her general lack of discipline and guilt and desperation, the foul ingredients mingled into a witches' brew of chaos.

For a minute, Peregrine hacked away at her soul in self-mutilation, then stepped away from her brutal flagellation to back track her movements with rationality. After Mocha's call, she had not switched off the phone. She had kept it on. She must have pressed the off button during her gyrations, running from that weird man or angling herself into the tunnel.

Unlikely. The phone was protected in the pack. It had received worse jolts in her purse, clacking around with sharp pens and eyeliner pencils and various other junk, which should have pierced the on button off, but never did. It took hard pressing to do that. No. There was another explanation. And that explanation had no sentient way to be articulated. No language existed for it because it was in the realm of metaphysics. There was a gap between concrete reality and the ethers of twilight. And somewhere in that gap, the phone had been switched off, and no physical pressing of the button had caused it.

She hadn't had a mad cow moment or lapse of memory. She never switched off her phone. She had told Mocha she would phone when she was ready to enter the pipe. Something had disrupted her train of thought, and now she remembered what she had felt when she was creeping out to the edge of the pipe's mouth. Someone was watching her, gloating at her. That's what it was, and she had felt it before in the haunted cemetery. Peregrine pressed the off switch to save the batteries since the phone was useless underground. She considered her circumstances.

In this cemetery, in the mausoleum, in the labyrinth where anything was possible and the unexpected must be anticipated, there was a crazy quilt Murphy's Law for the spiritual realms that acted upon human thought and emotion. Just under the radar of consciousness, there, down in the tunnels, she intuited that she was in a different world, that time morphed, depending upon some arbitrary factor. When she had entered the labyrinth weeks before, time had speeded up, and she had believed that she had been lost one month when she had been gone ten days. This evening, time had slowed. In what she had assumed was the passage of an hour, was the flight of three. Obviously, the tunnels were not subject to the natural order of earthly things. But she would never find out what the order was because she must leave immediately.

Pragmatism spoke, and she heard, though she refused to accept. From all appearances, her search had been in vain, worse, malignant for what it had spawned, her mother's wrath, an arrest, bad publicity. Posing another possibility, she considered. What if the pack had been stolen? What if that weird man who lived amongst the tombs had found his way into the tunnels and had taken the pack and the artifacts, thinking they were something other than what they were? If it had to be anyone, she hoped it was he, for he looked harmless, terrified and confused, like he wouldn't know the significance of the articles any more than the average person on the street.

In her anxiety, she thought of a worse problem. What if he destroyed the articles or threw them away, and the ancient arcane magic fell into the wrong hands by chance? What further evils might be unleashed on the already dismal future of the planet? Then again, maybe he still had the pack. She had to find him and question him, offer him food, money, anything in exchange. But first, she would count one hundred more paces into the blackness before she turned around. She must discipline herself to leave the passageway after these final yards. Soon, the long-lasting batteries would be dead, and she was terrified to think she could be in the same position she had been in a week ago.

Peregrine jumped to her feet and cracked her head on the ceiling, jarring loose some earth and pebbles that showered her with dust and dirt, and whose pointy edges stung her arms. That's all she needed, a cave in. She said aloud, "Jesus Christ of Nazareth!" The words punctuated her bent postured steps, as she moved deeper into the passageway. Peregrine stopped after twenty paces, unhooked the penknife that was attached to the belly pack, swung out the small blade and made a huge X and arrow pointing toward the exit of the tunnel. Then she wrote the word "Exit," in large block letters. If she ever returned, she would have an indication how far underground she had traversed to reach this portion of the tunnel. She decided on her way back out in a few minutes that she would carve the walls with signs every twenty paces. Marking off the direction in this way comforted her and drove back the tiny insect terrors that nibbled her soul. As Peregrine stuffed the blade back into the penknife holder, she averred she would never visit this place again, especially if she located the back-pack in the cemetery near where the homeless man had terrorized himself and her with his frenzied running. Just twenty more paces, she reminded herself, and she would quit this place.

At the sixteenth step, Peregrine noted a shiny object in the distance and a big lump of earth near it. Her heart raced. Maybe whoever had come into this section of the cave had dumped out the back-pack and left the contents on the ground. She quickened her pace as best she could in her doubled-up position, taking an extra fifteen steps to reach the area. There was her back pack, turned inside out, its guts, the brownish pile of earth, she had seen in the distance. She picked it up in her right hand, feeling its emptiness in weight. Putting the flashlight between her knees, she ran her right hand in and all around the sides of the pack. "No. No. No," she moaned. The high priest's outfit and the book translations of arcane, mystical secrets and the Randolf journal of magical spells were gone. The Book of the Tarot was gone along with the three- hundred-year old cards. Priceless, or so said her Aunt Rachel. Holding the flashlight under her armpit, she futilely felt around inside each of the side pockets after ripping open their flaps.

"Hell, hell, hell!" Peregrine screamed. Then she hushed her frustration and anger. What if the thief who had stolen the books was still in the tunnel, only deeper inside? She must be quiet. If it was the creepy, crawly man, she was taller than he and would bash him down if he attacked her. She would yell and terrorize him, pray in tongues, if necessary, if she remembered how. Mocha had once anointed her for it, but she never had prayed like that, feeling embarrassed and ridiculous. Well, now she would frighten him by her babble. She remained still and listened for an echoing cry or sound. There was none. She relaxed her tight grip on the pack and realized the flashlight was digging into her side; she was so tense. She took the torch from under her arm and put it between her knees directing the beam upward into her face. She must hold in her fury and think rationally. She did not want a confrontation with anyone during the witching hours in this claustrophobic space.

Peregrine returned her concentration upon her pack. She had exhausted her search through all the flaps except one. She pulled it open. Deep inside in the bottom of the section was an overlay of material that folded into a false crease where the cloth pack had been stitched together. Her fingers nimbly pushed into the fold and parted the cloth, feeling along the seam of the stitching. A few months ago, her pearl earrings had fallen into this crevice, and she had found them happily a week after they had gone missing. Another time, Mocha's friendship ring had slipped inside the folds only to be breathlessly retrieved.

She expected to find something there; she anticipated it beyond wanting. When her fingers touched cold metal, she was not surprised. Simultaneously, pulling out the amulet with her right hand and dropping the pack with her left, she grabbed the flashlight with her free hand from between her knees and shined it on the cold metal, bringing it to life. The platinum and diamond unicorn gleamed with brilliant radiance, happy on its chain. For one split second, she thought she saw the magical beast smile at her a tiny, winking, surreal smile. No. It was just the way the ray of light hit the creature's face. This was an antique.

"Thank God, thank God, thank God," she whispered under her breath. She was upset that the other three amulets were not in the pack, but at least this one was safe. Placing the flashlight between her knees again, she unhooked the clasp and held it with her index finger and thumb. With her left index finger and thumb, she grasped the other end of the necklace. She bent her head down and hooked the ancient clasp and checked the necklace, pulling down on it in the front. The unicorn sat snugly and solidly against her heart.

With renewed hope, Peregrine picked up the flashlight and slowly circled the rays of white light carefully on the ground directly in front of her and up each inch of gnarled earth, old brick and stone walls of the tunnel. Everywhere within a five-foot radius of where she stood in the center, she beamed the light. A shiny object at the border of the growing darkness! Peregrine hurriedly hunched over to it.

The bottle of Nard oil! That was something. She picked it up and placed in her jeans pocket. What else would she find discarded deeper along the tunnel? Did she dare to continue, braving Mocha's and her mother's wrath? Or should she move back to the tunnel entrance where she could get a signal and text them, then return to check for the other items? She shined the flashlight on her watch. It was 1:00 AM. Five more minutes, she promised herself, addicted to the discovery of the hunt.

If she had been aware of the dangers that lurked farther along the tunnel in a connecting underground artery which ran underneath a line of crypts in the wealthy section of the cemetery division and continued hundreds of yards, intersecting the vast underground labyrinth, she would have fled, bumbling in panic to the exit. But an innocent, Peregrine progressed deeper into the labyrinth back-tracking along her former path, convinced there were more discarded artifacts to be found.

Chapter Thirty-Five

Aboveground, inside an abandoned and neglected crypt whose entrance had been neatly blocked off with an iron grate, a heated parry of wits peppered with smatterings of stray gypsy accented English boiled thickly.

"I say go into the worm guts and cap her, early. Milkshake's luka. And her's milkshake." The jaunty cap pulled down low over thick black curls bobbed with each plunge of the head up and down, as the tall fellow haughtily dueled, using his slanging skills like a sword against his two British countrymen standing directly across from him.

"Oi, Mouly. Youse craze, always, always craze. Contrare. Ditch the leaves and treasure at Tiny's. No fuzz, no nappin', too done fo slavin'." A half-head shorter, Spoon had to look up at Mouly, but he emphasized each point with his gold ringed finger jabbing Mouly's chest. Crippled in his word weaponry, he made up for it with gestures.

As both men sharpened the knives of intellect and ratcheted up the stakes to outword the other, Fiker attempted a direct hit. The same height as Spoon, he grasped Spoon's right arm, dislodging his finger from Mouly's chest, and spun him away while thrusting his slang toward the smaller man. "Pig's bum. We's fo. Her's one. No speed bumps. Bing, bang, bam. Pancake's flappin, and we's eatin'."

During the stir, Battery, the most conservatively dressed of the lot, had whipped out his lighter and gold cigarette case and lit a cigarette, then spoke with it between his teeth, exasperatedly. "No, you sops! Pancake's not flappin'" When he spoke, the men shut up like infantrymen on point. "Easy translation. There's no time for jazzin'."

As he smoked, Battery sauntered around the men in the dank, dark, musty crypt that they had lighted with flashlights and ionized wands. He was lanky, taller than Mouly with cropped red hair and a whisper of freckles bridging his nose and cheeks. Though he thought he downplayed his style, he reflexively worked to appear more refined than his buddies.

Battery gestured with the lit cigarette between the bejeweled index and middle fingers of his right hand. "Gents, need I remind you why we came here tonight?" The three men, dressed alike in Gap jeans and T-shirts that glorified their muscular bodies, looked at him and each other sheepishly. "This is not a night to slave women. Besides, she's notorious, a media skank, not ripe for plucking. Useless in pieces. If she gets in our way, you can have her, but not for luka. But after you're done, then we have to crash one of the other crypts and dump her." With his thumb and forefinger, Battery pitched the cigarette stub to the floor, tipped his head down, stopped pacing and eyed the men between hooded pale brows for agreement.

"Pipe it!"

"Cheers!"

"Steamin'."

In the half light, the men in their thirties appeared to be regular fellows with angular good looks. If they had not been standing in a crypt, but had been transported to a ballgame amongst thousands of fans, it would have been impossible to discern that they were wicked and selfish with few natural qualities to redeem them. Battery continued over the multi-pitched tonal chorus, acknowledging his buds' agreement, but not grateful for it. They were his. He owned them, and being property, he did not appreciate them. He took them for granted. "Seals gave me the print- out of the locations we'll work tomorrow. The Hallows are planning an event, so in the next few weeks we'll be busy. The equipment is already on site. Use the east tunnel passageway. Bring the cargo to Old Calvary this time."

"That's a haul." Mouly's expression was sullen.

"There are three of you for two trips. Alternate your carrying. Is it a problem?"

The three were quiet, and Battery interpreted this as consent.

"I'll meet you by the safe house in Old Calvary at 4:00 AM. That should give you enough time."

"Fuck." Spoon was annoyed. "There's something about that Johnson hole that creeps me. It's fucked up shit is what."

Mouly laughed. "Right. Ghouls are floating around in there."

"Why can't we go to one of the other safe houses nearby, arrange the stash, then haul?" Spoon insisted.

"You want to haul further? That's the closest." Fiker always supported Battery.

"Yeah, but last time, I swear someone was pushin' me from behind, and all of you was standing in front of me." Spoon felt the back of his neck grow cold with sweat.

"Your imagination tiggered you." Fiker added for good measure, not totally disbelieving Spoon.

"Ya saffron craybob! When it's chompin' on yer bleedin' eyeballs, don't expect this Spiderman to rescue ya." Spoon threatened, pointing to himself.

Battery shined the flashlight on his watch. "The place stays. It's the closest. We go at 1:30 AM to get the cargo, and I get the wheels. That's in ten. Synchronize."

While the three men checked their watches, Fiker pointed to the neat stack of books and artifacts against the wall behind the men. "So how much we get for the leaves and the rest of this stuff?"

"I have to put my contacts on it. Too dense for Tiny Tim." Battery strode over confidently to the pile and picked up a plastic zippered pouch and unzipped it to find a richly ornate red and black beaded brocade drawstring purse. He wedged his hand in the puckered mouth of the purse, felt inside, then pulled out half-way a thin card which, upon examination, looked to be a combination of some light material, perhaps papier-mâché and wood. The entire back of the card was embossed with gold leaf and studded with tiny stones which Battery suspected were jewels, though he didn't tell or show the others. He glanced at the top half of the card intricately painted with a full moon and crescent and two pillars, the Moon card of the Tarot deck.

Battery quickly put it back inside the purse and drew the drawstring, then zipped up the plastic holding pouch and placed it next to the priest's outfit, also sealed in plastic. He knew the artifacts were related to the arcane mysteries, and he gauged that they had been stolen from blue bloods that practiced mysticism and magic. Battery decided not to chance the information with his workhorses in case a double cross was necessary later on. He was obscure. "I think this stuff is antique. Could bring some fine luka from the right blokes who go fienin' for this stuff. My boys at the big NYC houses will nose around, see if the stuff is serialized by Interpol. If so, auction'd have to be secret, invitation only."

"Makes no sense milkshake's draggin' this blight through the tunnels. Ain't it? I mean less she's doing the devil's work like us." Spoon laughed.

Fiker growled. "But there ain't enough to go around. She's the alien, and we dogg her if she messes."

"What about this?" Mouly grabbed the plastic that contained the high priest's robe and other effects. He pulled out the garment. "This bleedin' thing's got hooks on the bottom and bells. This can't be worth nothing."

Battery sidled over to Mouly who was trying on the long robe to the laughter of Spoon and Fiker. He drew what appeared to be a scarf around his neck and put on the crazy big hat. As Mouly paraded around making the sign of the cross absolving his buddies, Battery recognized that the red and purple letterings on the bottom of the white robe and down the front in a thick strip were in Hebrew.

Fiker collapsed to his knees in front of Mouly. With his head down in a penitent position and a high-pitched voice, he wailed, "Help me father, help me. I like little boys."

Amidst Spoon's and Mouly's laughter, Battery quickly pushed Fiker over so that he sprawled face forward on the concrete. "You don't play with this shit! Don't you know where you are? What yer wearin'?"

Fiker, normally docile, leaped up and lunged at Battery who in a quick judo move sidestepped him. Hooking Fiker's ankle, Battery tangled his legs, so once more Fiker crashed in a heap face forward on the cold, concrete floor. Battery rolled him over with his foot and glared. "Does God have a sense of humor, you blasphemer? Just pray that He does, and you're his little joke in Hell."

Fiker was silent. It was Mouly who spoke in anger. "You hypocrite. Who are you to be preaching about God, and you doin' whatcha doin'!"

Battery smoked. His voice was a febrile, raging whisper. "Be ye hot or be ye cold. You do my bidding. If ye are lukewarm, I will spit you out of my mouth. Mouly, consider yourself spit."

"Come, old sons." Spoon was pacific. "We have to leave in three. Come, Fiker."

Spoon held out his hand to raise Fiker to his feet. He lifted the shoulders of the robe off Mouly and pulled his arms out of each sleeve, then folded the robe and put it back in the plastic. He took the scarf from Mouly's neck and the headpiece. He folded the scarf and placed it and the headpiece in the container, which he returned to the corner with the books and journal.

Battery and Mouly smoldered in a stare down. Fiker watched the two men, open-mouthed in amazement, and Spoon sighed at the tragedy of the human condition, fearful their plans would end right there in a thesis antithesis of physical viewpoints.

Mouly shook his head at Battery. "I don't get you." War in his voice.

"Who I am is none of your concern. Look to yourself."

Mouly dropped all pretense of slang. His muscles tensed ready for action. "I can't, bro. Your hypocrisy is as wide and bottomless as the universe, and it's crowding my breathing space."

Spoon stepped between them reasoning. "Are we going to do this? Or are we going to have it bloody and end our fortunes now?" He slapped his hands together and shrugged his shoulders. "OK. Whatever you want."

On some unrehearsed, intuitively silent note that only Mouly and Battery could hear, both men jumped away from each other at the same time, like cats after a spitting fit. It was a draw.

Mouly thought to himself. *"One day, bro, you and I are going to have a serious metaphysical discussion."*

Battery envisioned himself towering over Mouly, lifting his leg and urinating on him. The mental picture played a small smile on his lips. "Let's do, gents. Remember, if you run into media skank, you know where to take her when it's over."

"Word." Fiker was the only one who responded. None of the three felt much like sexually entertaining themselves at this late hour and especially after the morbid tension between Battery and Mouly. In fact, they secretly hoped they wouldn't run into her. If they did, they would be performing for each other more than for themselves, the pleasure perfunctory. It would be a tiresome, competitive business with blood-letting and no paycheck afterward. Who needed it!

With their flashlights shining the way, the men moved over to the area of the crypt where the ancient bodies were interred in the wall in three rows, one above the other. Battery went to the middle row, the middle square where the name of the deceased was carved from one end of the square to the other. He pressed the first letter of the first name and the last letter of the last name with force, until he heard the click, and the drawer ejected automatically and moved out from the wall. The drawer was empty. Battery leaped in and maneuvered himself, so he was sitting inside the drawer with his legs dangling over the left side. He looked at each of the men, then lifted both legs into the drawer where he lay down. He wriggled forward until he hit cold metal. Casually, he snaked down the slide ten feet, slowing himself when he got to its end, where he placed both feet on the earthen floor of the tunnel and perched for a moment, shining the flashlight and gleaning his surroundings.

The vast labyrinth of stone, brick and earth spread out in darkness before him, an isolated underworld only traversed by the few who knew of its existence and used it for malevolent purposes. Battery was familiar with some of the tunnels' arteries, especially those under the newest cemetery divisions. Other sections had eluded him because of their intricacy of doubling back in circles and crazy right angles, like the maze at the fun house which he always hated as a kid. Then there was an entire network under Old Calvary which no one used because of the legends that swirled about the Johnson mausoleum, the epicenter of the catacombs. Supposedly, one could travel through every division of Old and New Calvary from one end of the mammoth burial grounds to the other via the tunnel network. No one he knew had ever done it. Legend had it that whoever tried would die before he reached the other side. And somehow this death would be related to the tunnels under the Johnson crypt which the traveler would have to pass through to reach any of the four compass points of the cemetery: north, south, east and west. No one knew the original purpose of the tunnels or who had them built, only that they existed. A few thought they were built as part of New York's Underground Railroad for escaping slaves; the organization of men and materials and the cost required to build the vast labyrinth exacted in the name of charity. For others, like Mouly, the labyrinth existed for one reason only, to exercise human ambition in the name of greed. For them, the idea that altruistic charity motivated the tunnel's construction was not only anathema, it was childish.

Luckily, there were many entrances and exits into the vast network, usually in the bowels of crypts, and only those amongst their immediate business acquaintance knew of a few of these. All three of the black work cartels suspected there were many more entrances, but they feared to look for them, afraid that any unfamiliar tunnels they navigated would lead to the tunnel epicenter where Death lurked. Through criminal underground connections, maps of the entrances and tunnel arteries had been passed along to Battery for a hefty commission. It was a tradition that would pass to the next generation of cemetery moles. Battery had paid the huge fee willingly, as he willingly paid his tribute to Quinn each time he and his fellows hauled cargo out of Calvary. They alternated their business arrangements with two other cartels, adhering to a rigid schedule that Quinn and Seals laid out during the lush summer months. Wintertime was the slower season because no one liked the inconveniences of the cold, the frozen ground and the dreary weather despite the increase in wintertime cargo.

Battery stood up. He had to bend his body forward to accommodate himself to the five foot height of the tunnel ceiling. He went to the right wall adjacent to the slide and squeezed himself beneath the slide's high arch, where there was a metal storage box which each cartel used that was filled with supplies: packages of batteries of every size, three spare flashlights, ionized wands, energy bars in sealed plastic bags, bottled water, a hammer and crowbar. Whatever he took out of the box must be replaced before the next cartel had scheduled access. So it was with the storage boxes sprinkled in various areas of the tunnel network and none near the Johnson passageways.

Battery took quick inventory and mentally noted that they were running low on wands. One of the cartels was not living up to the arrangement. He would tell Quinn. He took out four, leaving four, and then opened the plastic bag of energy bars and took four and took out four eight-ounce bottles of water. He slammed the metal lid shut, then squeezed himself out from underneath the slide, and moved outward into the tunnel a few feet, calling up to the others to come down. Checking his watch, Battery realized the argument with Mouly put them back ten minutes. They would have to make up the time once they surfaced from the tunnels.

Spoon came down the slide next and joined Battery out in the tunnel to make room for the others. After Mouly and Fiker joined their colleagues in the passageway, they moved to the left of the slide, where a lever that protruded from the ceiling controlled the opening and closing of the drawer in the crypt wall from this underground level. Facing each other with both hands, they grasped the large, circular handle of the resistant metal lever and groaning with the effort, pulled down. As the scraping, grinding cries of the closing drawer echoed through the farthest reaches of this tunnel section, the mortuary wall leveled once more. Viewing the names on the marble slabs, it was impossible to detect the difference between this drawer, which was an entrance to the tunnel network, and the others which held the moldering occupants of the last century.

"We're running late, so cover the ground with the cargo as fast as you possibly can, then head over to the J, where I'll meet you for the pickup." Battery raised his eyebrows, waiting for acknowledgement.

"Savvy."

"Word."

"Amen," Mouly said, dripping sarcasm.

After distributing the wands, energy bars and water, Battery, at the front of the line of dark figures, waved his flashlight, signaling the go-ahead. Each man, bending forward with a distorted and gruesome gait, shuffled off to do the loathsome and dirty business for which they would be richly paid.

Chapter Thirty-Six

F rom her awkward, bent over position in the passage, Peregrine heard the first grating sounds of the drawer that Battery clicked open. The noises were like the muffled groans of a machine waking from a deep sleep. It was evidence that she was not alone and she intuited that it was not the weird little man who made a home amongst the graves, but something else, equally wicked and horrible. Spurred to leave, she counted the items that she had found after putting the Nard Oil in her jeans pocket: the beloved metal cross, her torch in the darkness, and the stake, her makeshift crutch. She had found the Templar ring in the same fold she had found the unicorn amulet. But the third amulet she had not found. She put on the ring and secured the other items in her pack. The high priest's garments, the Book of the Tarot, the Tarot Cards and the other books were missing. She was particularly upset about the magic books and the spells in translation. The books were in King James English like the Bible. According to Aunt Rachel, they had been banned by James I who had ordered the confiscation of occult material and the burning of arcane books and immolation of their owners on charges of witchcraft. The subversive materials were extremely rare, virtually priceless. Not only was the loss upsetting because of their value, even more upsetting was Peregrine's belief that in the wrong hands, great damage could be done with the occult knowledge, especially the magic spells. As for the high priest's outfit, she couldn't believe it was gone. There was no way the Ceremony of Powers could be conducted without it. If there ever was to be a ceremony, she would have to get another robe, and she had no idea if that was possible.

Peregrine was convinced that the books, robe and amulets had been picked up by the same individuals responsible for the strange sounds at the other end of the tunnel. Maybe her presence had scared them away, and that was why the other items had been left. What other explanation was there? Too bad she had taken one-half hour to decide how to get into the drainage pipe. If she had gotten to the pack sooner, then she might have recouped all the items. As she struggled to thread the straps over her arms and shoulders and the pack against her back, Peregrine cursed her rotten timing, then stopped herself. Maybe she was really fortunate not to have gotten there earlier. In an encounter with whomever was in the tunnel, she might not have lived to retrieve any of the artifacts. *Let events unfold as they will, and do not regret. The alternatives could be much worse,* she thought to herself as she moved through the tunnel toward the exit, guided by the flashlight and a firm resolve not to wish for anything other than what happened.

She would explain the truth to her mother when she saw her. She would tell her what she had done and why. She would even tell her about her confrontations with Death. What was she thinking? She would do all that, but first, she had to get out of the labyrinth alive and then out of the cemetery. Regardless of what she hoped to tell her mom, as long as she was in the tunnel with whomever was there with her, she was in danger. She must call Mocha as soon as she was at the mouth of the drainpipe.

Peregrine moved quickly, though her back was killing her and her knee ached from the strain of running. She had taken two Advil soft-gels before she left for the cemetery and had popped two more into her mouth with a swig of water before she entered the drain. When she got home, she would have to wear the brace on her leg for a few days and consume anti-inflammatories like candy, repeating the process she had used to nullify the burning in her knee after leaving the hospital. The long-lasting batteries in the flashlight were holding out, thank God. She prayed they would light her wanderings through the other cemetery divisions or that the full moon would finally peek out from the clouds.

Peregrine had reached her arrowed exit markings when the groaning metallic echoes of the closing of the drawer sounded in the section where she was moving slug-like through the shadowed passage. She halted for a moment, listening after the perverse metallic scrapings, and imagined that she heard garbled voices from within the bowels of the cavern. It couldn't be. They were coming her way. She must move fast. No more ambling. Despite her complaining back and knee, she intensified her pace, reminding herself that once she reached the pipe she could stand and race in comfort, if she could straighten herself up. It would take her creaking back a few minutes before she would be able to smooth out the kinks. The only problem was she had no minutes to spare to stay ahead of the men. She had to increase her distance between them and herself, so she could speed away.

Peregrine's thoughts raced, though her body swam in slow motion, like in a nightmare, where you had to outrun the monster and couldn't because your limbs were paralyzed. Peregrine retooled her plans. Once she reached the mouth of the pipe, she couldn't take the time to call Mocha. She would have to climb out and find a place to hide from the thieves. She couldn't count on their exiting the tunnel another way. She had to assume they were using the same exit.

Peregrine shuffled quickly and listened for more garbled voices. She didn't hear any, but that didn't mean the men weren't behind her. She could not assume what was easy, could not anticipate a smooth landing. If they were in the vast labyrinth, then what were they doing at this hour? If they were filled with goodness, they would have left her back-pack closed and not scattered the contents and stolen the rest, a footprint of their dark intentions.

She moaned under her breath. She would never ever see the relics again, never find out how to use them and never know her family's history and traditions. A confluence of feelings flooded her soul, mixing regret with sadness, frustration with boldness. The faster she sloughed through the brick, stone and earth, the more indignant she became. Who were these criminals to take her family's treasures, her own inheritance? How dare they deprive her of an opportunity to see into realms that for centuries were hidden to all but a select few? They were not privileged; and now by virtue of their own wickedness, they had usurped her rights. This was not to be tolerated!

Halting her clumsy steps, Peregrine boiled over with rage. "No way. Screw it. I'm going back," she said aloud. She felt strong and powerful, felt she could face them and with a supernatural force in her heart, disarm them into giving the stuff back. She would offer a reward, dissuade them from thinking the antiquities were worth their time. Books were, after all, useless. Guys didn't read. And from their low muffled voices, she intuited the thieves were men.

Peregrine turned around. With determination, she paced a few steps in the opposite direction. She would confront them. When she looked into the dark passage and shined the flashlight, she saw something in the distance. She concentrated her gaze. She couldn't believe what she was seeing. She blinked, two, three, four times. There it was. Unmistakable. She closed her eyes, then opened them slowly. Embarrassment and shame filled her. She was going mental, manic, nuts, wacko. She turned from the path, and pressing her back into the wall, she straightened as far as she could without banging her head against the ceiling. She talked aloud to herself. "Well, now that you've lost your mind, you think you can convince those thugs to give up your stuff? You are one demented chick." She shook her head, then turned to her right, looking into the depths of the cavern. It was still there, shining brilliantly in the dark 300 yards away, a white unicorn staring at her. It was smiling.

Peregrine turned toward the exit and nodded her head. "OK, that's it. I'm leaving." She walked, skipped. Somehow, it was easier. Her back didn't ache, and her knee didn't burn because she was laughing hysterically, silent laughter, joy at her own foolishness. Of all things to hallucinate, a unicorn. Christ, get the meds, remove the sharp objects. She hadn't had sleep, and it was late; and her mind was stressed, and it had created a unicorn to save her from herself. Unbelievable.

Despite the silly ridiculousness, she felt impending danger. Peregrine sped like a well-oiled machine, gears racing, covering ground quickly. The stones in the wall and the bricks and the earth fell away, as her feet skimmed over them, right foot, left, foot, right foot, left, rapidly, rapidly in a rhythm that forced her to concentrate all her energies in the ever-present moments of time.

Ahead, she saw the bulging of the pipe meeting the tunnel construction, and the expansion of the tunnel and the curvature of the great drain. Thank God, she had made it. She stopped and listened. There was only silence. She was afraid to shine the light behind her, afraid the unicorn would be there, afraid that she was now certifiable and would have to be put in Pine Forest. No, she would forget about what she saw. And at some point when she had the courage, she would select a juicy rationalization to explain to herself the embarrassing hallucination.

Peregrine clomped through the enlarging pipe and when the ceiling was high enough, straightened, slowly making sure to swivel her waist and move her neck in a right and then left side stretch. She lifted her arms and placed her palms flat on the rough cement ceiling. Relief. As she lowered her arms, she listened again for sounds or voices. There were none. In defiance of herself, she turned and splayed the flashlight beam behind her. Darkness swallowed up the light ray once more. No smiling unicorn. More relief. Exhilarated, Peregrine turned and ran through the pipe. Maybe the voices she had heard and the clanging sounds were her imagination playing tricks, like the unicorn. Perhaps she should call Mocha as she sat on the edge of the great pipe. No, she would rather be safe and look for a hiding place, perhaps behind a crypt. She didn't want to be too optimistic. Besides, her belongings had been stolen. Chances were high that the thieves were still in the area. She was alone and defenseless, despite her courage. Wisdom dictated she should hide, call Mocha, then find her way out of the cemetery without being detected. Maybe she should devise a signal with Mocha to alert the police in case of an emergency. She was impatient to mobile her friend.

The blue-black exit loomed ahead of her. She must be extra careful not to draw attention to herself. She shined the flashlight down on the ground and away from the pipe mouth. Peregrine decided to flip the backpack up on top of the pipe, then use her arm strength to pull herself up. The pack would weigh her down, and she thought she could aim the pack in the center of the large pipe, so it wouldn't fall off.

Time to work her plan quickly. The thieves might be lurking, waiting to pounce. She slipped out of the familiar, worn pack, an old friend, and lengthening one of the straps to a singleton, wrapped it twice around her wrist. With her back to the exit and holding on with her left hand, she was strong enough with her right to throw the pack and its contents on top of the pipe, while still holding on to the strap. That way, she would ensure that if it fell, she would still be holding it, in which case all she had to do was haul it up and try again. She had no intention of allowing the pack to fall to the stone valley below, where she would be forced to repeat another leap, risking broken bones.

Peregrine practiced her motion of throwing the pack, but was distracted from sounds from inside the tunnel. "Crap," she whispered under her breath. The thieves were creeping toward her and had just given themselves away. She had to work fast. She clicked off the flashlight. She would work in the dark since there was no moon. She carefully positioned herself with her back facing the stone valley and her front facing the tunnel. She held on to the top rim of the pipe with her left hand. With her right, she dangled the pack heavily by her side and swung it like a pendulum forward and back, forward and back in larger arcs until at once in the backward motion, she flipped it up to the top of the pipe.

Success! It had landed with a thud while she still held the strap wrapped around her wrist. Hurry, hurry, she said to herself. She must not fail. She thought she heard a shoe hit the cement edge, where the pipe and tunnel construction merged. They were coming faster now, and soon might be running. She could hold back no longer. Fast, fast, haul yourself up. Peregrine's left grip was sweaty. She wiped her left hand against her jeans. She unwrapped the strap from her right wrist and let it dangle. She couldn't be encumbered by the pack, had to have all her strength in her hands. She heard muffled sounds like shoe treads clomping upward. They were reaching the slight incline and would soon shine their flashlights on her. Now, haul, haul.

Peregrine gripped the pipe with both her hands and pulled, pulled herself upward, her legs kicking and swinging to the sides of the pipe for any toehold of leverage. Slowly, painfully she grappled, her arm muscles twitching with exertion. She put her left hand palm down and kicked up to the side of the pipe with her right leg. She found she could place her right foot on the pipe rim with enough force to leverage herself upward so that now she was able to place both hands flat and strain and tug, lifting upward her head, then arms, elbows and the upper part of her torso to the top of the arced concrete. She was nearly there. She wriggled and kicked her legs propelling her body forward just barely missing dislodging the pack to the valley below. She dangled, hanging half in space, her buttocks and legs swinging outward. She pushed the pack out of the way, giving herself more room to lift herself up, straining her arm strength until her stomach slipped across the cement drain.

At that moment, the clomping footsteps intensified their pace amplifying their scraping against the concrete. Time had run out. She thrust the pack ahead, wriggling and kicking until only her legs dangled in space. She squirmed and kicked and pulled her body another inch forward. Below her the footfalls were running, running through the concrete. She split her legs, straddling the pipe so her legs and feet couldn't be seen hanging, and held her breath, preventing her muscles from tensing, her nerves from twitching, lest animal intuition sensed she was above them.

Light beams blared into the darkness and faded outward toward the stone valley.

Peregrine closed her eyes and prayed they wouldn't think to go to the edge and shine the light upward. Her buttocks and legs were near the very edge of the mouth. If they scoped her, she would be forced to scramble to gain her footing on the curved surface then flee and she couldn't outrun them in her tiredness and panic.

"Told ya you were imagining things, ya bleedin' tripe." Mouly said with venom from the bowels of the drain pipe. "Now we've gotta head back to the crossroads where we parted company with Battery which'll take fifteen minutes, ya fecal cephalic. Ya know, we can't be late."

"We're late? I'm blamin' you." Fiker yelled.

There was a banging and tussling sound. Peregrine took advantage of the chaos to slide farther out of sight of the opening.

"Quit, quit it." Spoon got between Mouly and Fiker, blocking Mouly's punch with his arm and knocking Fiker's flashlight down. The men stopped and watched distracted as it rolled near the edge of the pipe opening.

"Hey get it, get it. Don't let it fall!" Fiker said, annoyed.

"I got it." Mouly grabbed the torch and handed it to Fiker. "There was something there, moving in the dark. When I shined the flashlight, it vanished."

"I saw it. We have to tell Battery when we see him. He'll want to know. No use takin' it out on each other," Fiker mumbled.

"You started with me."

"I didn't make us late."

"Enough of this, ya bleedin' sheep." Spoon sounded annoyed. "I know what we can do to save time. Instead of going back through the tunnel, we'll drop down easy like and cut through the valley here, over to section D. Faster that way."

Peregrine could barely hear the garbled men's voices that were muffled by the concrete. But she thought they said something about going back through the tunnel. She breathed a sigh of relief and waited for the clomping sounds of their boots against concrete to sound their departure.

"Fiker'll shine the light on the ground. Mouly, you hold my hands while I hang and drop easy to the ground."

"Don't break yer ankle."

"Runnin' from women I done worse. Don't worry, ya craybob. I'm inchin' it."

While Fiker shined the flashlight on the valley floor, Spoon lay down on his stomach facing the tunnel's interior and slid his body backwards, as Mouly held his hands and waited for Spoon to get over the edge, waited for the pressure to build when his strength would be required.

Below, Peregrine heard banging stray movements, not the steady stomping rhythm of departing steps that she expected. She turned to look behind her to discover what was happening. There was a light beam spraying from inside the pipe to the valley. She shrank back in horror. The men were going to jump and take a shortcut instead of going back through the tunnel. She cursed her bad luck, lowering her cheek to the pipe. Even if the men jumped clear, she must not be seen. They could give each other a boost and climb up after her. Though she would have a head start, they would pursue and catch her. She must certainly not be seen while any of them were still in the pipe. With their arm strength, climbing up would be easy. They would be on her in seconds.

Peregrine closed her eyes and made the scene evaporate. She was glad she faced the opposite direction, away from the valley, so she couldn't see what the men were doing. And then she realized that with her back to them, she was completely vulnerable. She shivered in panic; her imagination rioted. One of them was climbing up. A ghoulish face poked over the side. He was leering at her bottom. He was reaching to grab her legs and drag her shrieking to the edge and over the side crashing to the stone valley. As life leaked from her dashed out brains and gored body, impaled on the black obelisk monument whose needle spire had pierced her guts, he frolicked in a witches' circle, then set her body aflame, a torch lighting the stone city.

Her arms weakened. She had to pee. She was losing her grip. Soon, she would be slipping over the side, rolling in space to the concrete valley. On crashing impact she would crack open her skull, leaking blood and brains, as mortality flooded her tissues. Peregrine softly moaned and opened her eyes to stare into reality. Dark shadowy trees towered in the distance. She was going to collapse with the tension of being discovered.

Thump. Spoon had landed on his feet. Mouly threw two flashlights down to Spoon who caught them and placed one on a nearby headstone. He shined the other on the unencumbered patch of grass where Fiker was to land. Mouly helped Fiker maneuver himself over the drain's rim and held his hands tightly as Fiker's body floated in space but for Mouly's grip.

"Maybe I should throw you over," said Mouly menacingly as he swung Fiker back and forth like a pendulum.

"Let me go, you sonofabitch."

"Easy, Mouly. Don't swing him over that pointy monument."

"Let me go, ya wanker."

"Say pretty please."

"Mouly. Lay off. We got no time for this." Spoon was impatient.

"Say, I suck turtle dick."

"Fuck you."

"Say it, or I'll throw you on that slab and break ya head. I wonder how much we'll get for ya?"

"Mouly. I'm leavin'. You're on your own." Spoon took the flashlight off the monument. With the one in his hand, he shined both in the opposite direction, forging a path of light to guide him amongst the graves.

"All right, mate. Come back. Put the lights back." Mouly was pliant.

Spoon shined both torches toward the pipe and on Mouly's leering face. In the shadows created by the diffusing beams, he saw a bulge on top of the pipe. He shone each of the rays upward, but he was too close to the pipe and at the wrong angle to see clearly. Even though there were two torches, the light was eaten up by the surrounding darkness. To gain a better angle of vision, he would have to pace out thirty feet into the valley.

"What are ya doing? I'm gettin' tired. Shine it on the landing pad. I'm droppin' him."

Spoon played the lights on the bare patch of grass, and Mouly let Fiker go with a flourish. Fiker landed hard on his feet, then fell forward.

"Stupid twit," said Fiker, rolling on his back, looking up at the pipe and shaking his fist at Mouly. "My ankle's tiggered."

Spoon rushed over and groaned. "Bollocks. You're jokin', old son. Can you stand on it?"

"Ha, ha, like I'm jokin'. It ain't funny, ya mouse. It pains me."

Peregrine chortled silently, then stopped herself. The guys were Brits, from the gypsy lands of Britain's wild interior or London wharf rats. She could barely make out what they were saying, but she got the message from their tone. Though she loved Brits, she did not want to meet these men face-to-face. She had a bad feeling about them; like not only were they up to no good, they were no good.

"Hey, ya crabs, turn up the lights. I'm coming down." Mouly yelled from inside the pipe.

"Shine the light yaself, ya clown fucker. Now ya set us back with ma bleedin' ankle."

"Christ! Ya landed wrong. Ya supposed to tuck and roll like I told ya, turtle dick. Here. The flashlight. Come on, Spoon, old son. Catch it." Mouly twirled the flashlight up higher than the pipe, and it fell somersaulting like a lit baton down to Spoon.

Before he caught it, one of the spiraling beams bounced to an irregular spot on the pipe, illuminating it. Spoon was convinced someone or something was up there, but it was too late to check. They had to let it go, but he would have to tell the others to can the conversation. Spoon placed the three flashlights on the monument, illuminating the landing pad more brightly. "Can ya handle it by yaself?"

"That's why I went last, ya twit. I'm taller and got the strength fer it."

"So I won't spot ya, then. Yer on yer own. I'll help Fiker."

Peregrine cowered on the pipe. The moment the belligerent Brit jumped, she would move. She prayed that the men would be too distracted by the guy with the ankle problem to hear or see her. Had she been already detected? Twice, one of the men had sprayed a ray of light at her while she held still and tried to look like a clump of earth.

As Mouly maneuvered into position for his leap, Spoon lightly massaged Fiker's ankle and helped him to his feet. Fiker was able to put weight on his ankle, though he hobbled. Both men slowly moved toward the grassy spot over which Mouly now dangled, clinging to the rough bottom rim about four and a half feet from the ground. Readying himself, the six footer jumped and landed, tucking his knees under him to absorb the fall as he rolled on his side. Dusting himself off, he leaped to his feet, clapping his hands.

"Nothing to it. Parkour makes it easy! Drink?" Mouly joined the others and each of the men took out the water bottles from the waists of their jeans. They took long gulps, halfway emptying the bottles, then put them back. Mouly signaled the men to pick up their flashlights from the monument.

On top of the pipe, anxious and fearful, Peregrine could wait no longer. She began slithering toward the embankment, pushing the pack in front of her.

The sloughing sound ruffled the men. "What's that?" Spoon asked.

Busy with negotiating the throbbing ache in his ankle, Fiker said, "What? I didn't hear nothing."

"I heard it." Mouly said. "Where?"

"Pipe." Spoon was knowing.

Mouly flashed his torch. "Don't see nothing."

Peregrine figured she had moved just outside the sight lines from where the men stood.

"Me either," said Spoon, jumping up and shining his torch rays to get the light over the top of the pipe. He pointed the light to his face and put his finger in front of his lips, the universal sign for quiet. He pointed in the direction away from the pipe, the direction in which they were headed anyway, and he nodded his head, mouthing the words, "Someone's there." Aloud, he said, "OK, blokes, let's out." Spoon grabbed Fiker underneath his arm. "Get the other side, and we'll fly across them stones," he said to Mouly who complied, wanting to know more about "the someone" and figuring Spoon wanted to get out of earshot of the drain.

Grateful for the help, Fiker hobbled, allowing Spoon and Mouly to drag him into the valley which appeared to be lightening as the clouds diffused away from the moon. "Yeah, I can do this," he said. "I think I can go it alone."

"Faster this way," Spoon said loudly for the alien hearer's benefit.

Their voices fading, Peregrine snaked her body, wriggling along the pipe, making sure the pack was centered. Explosive relief flooded her, and she exhaled deeply. She had made it without detection from those horrible men whom, she didn't doubt, would rape her and leave her for dead in one of the abandoned mausoleums. She squirmed and panted. Three feet, and she would be over land. It wouldn't matter if she or the pack fell onto the grass, surrounding and swallowing the pipe, as it wormed underground six feet ahead.

The men had proceeded twenty feet into the stone valley when the clouds fled away from the moon, and once more, the plump-faced princess of the night heralded the vast expansion of the dead city. Each man could see the other's features shaded in dark blue, the shadows of blackness vanishing.

Spoon motioned for the threesome to stop and whispered, "Wait here." He unshouldered Fiker to Mouly and stepped three feet ahead of the men, then turned to shine his flashlight on the top of the pipe. He didn't need to. There, in the high standing moonlight was media skank in all her glory, slugging atop the pipe toward the cliff where the pipe protruded. Fiker and Mouly turned to see what caused Spoon to gape open-mouthed in recognition. Wriggling on the pipe was the same woman they had seen before wearing the jeans and light T-shirt.

Concentrating intently on reaching the solid ground beneath her, Peregrine was at first unaware of the moonlight's gradual brightening. She had one foot to go to be free from space and danger. Psychically, she felt eyes staring at her twisting behind. The lightening connection of minds blew in the revelation that she could see much more clearly in front of her. She turned to the left to see the grinning moon announcing its awakening.

Mouly gulped in the greatest breath he could muster, then expelled it in a voluminous, deep, ear-splitting plea. "Oi, girlie."

His dark baritone traveled with force and upended each fiber of nerve coiling in Peregrine's body. She found herself losing tight grasp of the pipe and felt herself sliding in a free fall toward the moon. She grappled with the pipe, flailing hands and knees for stability, and for a moment, was hanging in the balance with her onlookers maliciously praying for her to fall. Aided by grabbing the back-pack strap which anchored her mind and centered her focus, she regained her equilibrium, disappointing the men. She closed her eyes and panted, "Hold your nerve, hold your nerve. They can't get at you. It's too late, too late."

Ferocious, Mouly called out more loudly than before. "Oi, whore. Next time we'll have a date with destiny. Savvy?"

Peregrine was immobilized.

Mouly thundered. "I said, Savvy?"

Incapable of even a weak, "Fuck you," under her breath, Peregrine melted into the concrete pipe. She was stiff and cold. She willed herself invisibility, a cloak of brown, grey- flecked, rust camouflage covering her.

The men looked at the pipe, astonished.

"What the fuck?" said Spoon under his breath.

"Where did she go?" said Fiker.

Mouly countered with pragmatism. "Hold tight to ya dicks, ya sorry sods. She just stopped movin' and those clouds there," he pointed up where the feathery striations of dim wisps webbed the moon's face, "make it hard to see her in the dark. I say we go for her. She'll rat us as sure as she's a twat."

"No cargo, no luka. If we make headway now, maybe we'll be ten minutes after Battery. We do her, and we'll be an hour. There's no time." Spoon took the leadership.

"Ya want her, you get her. Tiggered." Fiker lifted his ankle. "I'm out."

Mouly had soldiered his image and now could back down with his machismo intact. "Too bad. She looks tight."

Spoon sighed. "Yeah, yeah. Later. We got her stuff. She'll be back. The date's set, and we'll be ready for her." Spoon motioned for Mouly to grab Fiker underneath the arm. Begrudgingly, Mouly did so. Then the two walked Fiker quickly on the bare patches of ground, cutting a diagonal short-cut across the dead city.

Peregrine waited in the dimming moonlight. She had to turn around, had to see what the men looked like, had to see where they were going. No. She must first crawl off the pipe, then look. Panting, so she wouldn't faint, Peregrine slithered the last foot, lifted the pack that had saved her from falling and shoved it three feet ahead, where the pipe was sinking underground. She lifted herself up from her prone position and with both legs straddling the cement, lunged her body three feet forward.

She was in safety, a foot from the cliff's ledge. She sighed, turned around and faced the valley. The men had vanished. She didn't see their flashlights or prancing shadows. She saw nothing creeping in the hollow of darkness. Had they come back for her? Were they hiding? Were they underneath the pipe where she couldn't see them? Peregrine knew she shouldn't wait to find out. She leaped up on her feet, grabbed her pack and quickly threw the straps over each shoulder. She jogged out along the serpentine path from which she came. As the torchlight beams directed her secure pathway, she prayed that the men were not this very second excitedly lifting each other into the pipe to pursue the whore.

Chapter Thirty-Seven

On the leather sofa at Peregrine's, Mocha tossed fitfully. Mr. Witherspoon sat on a settee and watched as she unbuttoned the yellow, silk Robe a l'Anglaise and daintily stepped out of the filmy material. It was as if he had a right to watch her undress, even though minutes before, she demurred and commanded him from her lush and exquisitely appointed bed chamber. She stood before him now, in her flaring petticoats, pocket hoops and stays, embarrassed. He motioned for her to continue undressing; but instead, she reached for the dark blue caraco jacket flung over the back of the brocade slipper chair and hurriedly drew it over her arms in defiance of the gentleman who was clearly disappointed. The atmosphere was hot and muggy, unusually tropical like in an island paradise.

She was comfortable in her surroundings, except for Mr. Witherspoon who greatly disturbed her. She didn't know why he didn't leave, why she had to suffer his presence. Mocha walked to the other side of the bed chamber and sat at the vanity and arranged herself in front of the mirror in an attempt to avoid the older man who was dressed like a colonial gentleman. Distracted by her appearance, she forgot about his aggressive stares. Her hair was a different color than her usual brown. It was fawn colored, upswept and curled high on her head. Ringlets framed her face. She realized she wore a wig. No wonder why her neck seemed inordinately stiff and upright, like she was balancing a tray holding fine china teacups on her head.

Mr. Witherspoon clapped his hands as if to say, "Well, let's get going!" Her mind intruded in confusion. Who was he? How arrogant and cold he seemed. She could avoid him no longer. He had gotten up from the settee. With a fixed and determined look in his black eyes, he marched toward her, fists clenched.

A brash, loud ringing interrupted. Mocha was startled to wakefulness. She sat up on the second jarring ring expecting to see Mr. Witherspoon reaching for her shoulders. She was dislocated for a moment, then she remembered she was at Peregrine's. The blaring phone was in the kitchen. She looked at her watch. It was 2:38 AM. Fully awake, she realized it must either be Madeline or Peregrine. Fourth ring. She jumped off the sofa and ran through the dining room. Fifth ring. The answering machine clicked in. She looked at the caller ID screen and recognized Peregrine's number and picked up, overriding the answering machine.

"Christ, it's about time! Where are you? Are you OK?"

"I'm at Calvary. I'm OK. Did you tell the police to come after me?"

"No. You texted me twice everything was OK."

"Pity. I could use them about now."

"You can't get out on your own?"

"Scare tactics."

For the first time, Mocha realized Peregrine was whispering into the phone. "Who are you scaring?"

"I think I know who's been marauding the cemetery and who knocked you over the head."

"You mean strangled me."

"Yeah."

"Who?"

"I'll tell you when I see you."

"Should I phone the police?"

"Nah. Too much to explain to them. Anyway, I'm on my way out of here. I was lost at first and went to the wrong division, D instead of C. I was exhausted, still am. I rested for a bit, and then I must have wandered around for about half an hour. My flashlight went dead, and then I realized where I was when the moon was bright again."

"Are those marauders still there?"

"I don't know."

"Well, get the hell out of there. Do you know the way out?"

"I'm heading toward Old Calvary. Can you overcome your fear to meet me?"

"As promised, I took my meds. I'll bring the chain ladder and some blankets, like we said, and Fen."

"Laurel Hill Road entrance. That's where I left the car. Are you sure you want to bring Fen? Don't you think he needs his sleep for the news conference? It's going on 3:00 AM. Anyone else before we call Fen?"

"Jake."

Peregrine considered. Jake knew what they had planned, and they had counted him out over Fen. He was a joker and never took anything seriously. But he would be perfect for a rescue. "It's late. You think he'll come?"

"Wouldn't miss it."

"Text me in fifteen if everything's OK. Call right away if there's a problem."

"Gottcha. Ciao."

"Don't forget flashlights, just in case, and really thick blankets for the barbed wire."

"Of course."

Peregrine clicked off the phone. She shifted the back-pack and tightened the straps, then crossed the boundary line of Division D to move deeper into Division C, toward the Johnson mausoleum. She knew Calvary was the largest cemetery in Queens, but viscerally, she never realized how huge until this night of walking miles through the maze of paths above ground. In the labyrinth, she couldn't tell her direction and assumed she had doubled back and had gone in circles in the network of caverns. Perhaps, the labyrinth extended the length and breadth of Calvary. But how could that make sense? Peregrine found she was unable to think cogently, and after treading over gravel and sand paths for another half hour, she no longer tried. All she wanted was to see the entrance gates of Old Calvary and the nearby parking lot and Mocha and Jake waving at her.

Peregrine was not the only one who wanted to be at the entrance gates of Old Calvary. Mouly was tired from having to haul cargo with only the help of Spoon since Fiker hopped along, like a wounded insect, carrying the shovel, pickax and borer. For their latest haul, Mouly and Spoon had lugged two hundred pounds of dead weight, but it was Fiker who complained and moaned every time his foot hit the ground. Mouly doubted his ankle was as wrecked as Fiker said it was. He thought of him as a lazy shirker who looked for any excuse to avoid the scut work, while being the first to stick out his hand, as Battery palmed the cash pay to each man.

Mouly was sick of him and ready to haul him out as cargo, along with the three bags piled up inside the Johnson mausoleum. But Battery and Spoon would loudly protest and come after him, so he had no recourse but to shut up and wait for an opportunity.

Mouly and Spoon dumped their treasure to the right of the crypt steps, next to their other haul of the early morning hours.

"Let's go through the bleedin' tunnel last haul." Mouly groused to Spoon.

"No way. The place is skulls. We'll never get out alive."

"Fairy tales, fairy tales." Mouly grumbled but didn't press the issue with Spoon.

"I'm stayin' and waitin' for Bats. No use me comin'."

Mouly was sour. "Yeah, you do that, ya lump of fish bait." Mouly alluded to unsuspecting Fiker's future fate at his hands. "Les go. Last haul. Maybe we can make it before Battery." Mouly directed Spoon. Together, the men loped off to the treasure trove while Fiker sat on the mausoleum steps and watched their shadows grow smaller in the distance against the blue-black colors of the night.

The cemetery was solemn and spiritual, like one would imagine a typical cemetery might be. The small, white, full moon high in the sky cheerfully broadcast sufficient light for Peregrine to pick her way between the benign headstones. And after her second call to Mocha verifying that Jake was coming and everything was okay, Peregrine settled back into a staid, sleepy rhythmic routine of loping and walking, covering ground at a moderate pace. She anticipated that she would arrive at the gates around 3:45 AM, if she didn't stop to rest and if she was right about the Johnson mausoleum being just beyond the grove of trees. She was too exhausted to be disturbed by nocturnal cries of night hawks and owls and the scurrying rustlings of other creatures; her mind deadened to any thought but her goal.

That was why Peregrine missed the shadowy figures of Mouly and Spoon who were walking with their backs to her across the northern end of Division C to where it bordered with Division D. Likewise, Mouly and Spoon didn't see Peregrine coming up from the southern end of the graveyard division, for they hurriedly paced with their heads down, intent on delivering the luka to Battery at the Johnson tomb by 4:00 AM.

But there was one who spied the movement of all of these blue figures in the white moonlight, including the one sitting on the mausoleum steps. And he was happy, very, very happy. The injured one nursing his ankle and carelessly resting on the steps, leaning back on his elbows, was one of the vulgarians, the black workers of darkness whose souls were as empty and cavernous as space.

From the far side of the mausoleum, where he had dragged his headless companion and hid him away in the bushes, the demon laughed quietly and congratulated himself on his good fortune. Tonight would be the beginning of the end to their miseries and would pave the way for the great release. It was just a matter of mesmerizing the brutal simian into sleep and then taking possession.

Peregrine tramped through the grove of trees and up the incline. In the distance was the Johnson crypt. She shuddered. The place seemed haunted in the paling light. A cloud was obscuring the moon again, and a breeze startled the leaves, rustling them and sending shivers through her spine. She vowed not to go near the mausoleum but would launch a wide arc around it, keeping a safe distance of about two hundred yards. She felt a strangeness overtake her. She was an alien walking in a foreign land, and some great evil was in the area watching and waiting for her to leave. Peregrine quickened her pace and then began jogging her great arc to the left. She knew this would extend her time to the gates but didn't care. Fear was growing in her heart and mind, an uncertain, nameless fear that she couldn't shake off. It reminded her of the vapors of darkness descending in the mausoleum when Mocha was lost to her. Peregrine didn't look to her right. She ran across gravel paths, across gravesites, regardless of her disrespect for the dead. She was going to gratify whatever wanted her out of the area. *With pleasure*, she thought. *I'm going as fast as I can*, she said to the shapeless fear that stalked her with its eyes.

Oxelox willed the woman away from the mausoleum, for he had work to do. Psychically, he had projected his mind into hers. She understood, for she was running, running, far away from him, and she was too afraid to look back and see him emerge from the bushes, salivating at the prey that dozed before him on the steps. The vulgarian was drifting in the twilight between consciousness and sleep, the vulnerable time when the mind was least occupied and most open. Now, the demon mesmerized

Fiker's will, exerted his seduction and eased himself into the realm of fairy ethereal. He transformed into a wistful, pale sylvan nymph, lingering in the shadows, a wondrous, phantasmagorical beauty beckoning him sprite-like toward her, toward her. The vulgarian's mind was overcome. He was confounded in the depths of his being. His soul lifted and came to the stunning damsel whose outstretched glittering arms enfolded him with a gossamer embrace. They caressed, and he was hers. The possession was complete. Oxelox had captivated his soul, and Fiker, bedeviled, fell into a deep, deep sleep.

Peregrine was running hard now. She scarcely breathed nor did she turn her head. Onward, straight. She leaped over small grave-stones and dodged large ones, putting out her hand to leverage herself and shove her way forward. When she felt out of range of whatever glowered at her evilly, she slowed to a jog and then to a lope. Now she was conscious of her rasping breath. She halted after two large steps, bent over and took deep breaths in and out. She straightened up and was calm again.

God. What a night this had been. If she hadn't been in such a weird malaise, she never would have stayed in the cemetery so long. She reconsidered. Not so. She stayed because it was who she was. Her stubbornness and perseverance could be a liability. And they could be a salvation. The circumstances determined the effect. Peregrine walked at a brisk pace, and soon in the distance, she saw the gates. And there were Jake and Mocha who waved their flashlights. The beams danced a shining path to her through the darkness.

They couldn't hold their flashlights and lug cargo, and they needed the light to see. Mouly and Spoon cursed the darkness. The clouds hovered over the moon like dark billows, and the air felt close like a storm was on the wing. They crept slowly with the dead weight and had to take periodic rests. In the lead, Mouly stumbled on level headstones and bumped into large monuments, upsetting Spoon's balance and his own. Twice, they dropped the cargo; but since Death had already finished his work, there was no damage done. The men reached the rise where the Johnson mausoleum loomed black in the distance. Both were relieved yet frightened, believing that Battery had gotten there before them. It was after 4:00 AM.

On they trudged in the blue-blackness. As they drew nearer to the towering, frightful crypt, terror struck a minor chord in Spoon's heart, like a maniacal dirge. "Christ, this place gives me the creeps."

"Shut up and haul. We're nearly there."

"Where's Battery? Is that him?"

The darkness masked his features which had not changed. It was not Battery; it was Fiker, and he was asleep. Mouly became enraged. He was enervated to the bone and this craybob was relaxing and enjoying his beauty's rest? He dumped his end of the body bag, startling Spoon. He lunged forward, foaming at the mouth and gnashing his teeth at the sweetly sleeping Fiker. Mouly covered the one hundred feet to the somnambulant man in about three seconds of steam-boiling fury. He grabbed Fiker's shirt, ripped it and shook the sleeper until his shaking, slack jaw rattled him awake.

"You lousy, fuck. You bleedin' lout."

Fiker came alive like Mouly had never seen before. He leaped up on his bad ankle which was miraculously whole and burst through Mouly's grip, shooting both hands outward, shoving Mouly backwards. "Don't you touch me. You never, ever touch me again. Don't you ever swear at me again. You're through, do you hear? Through."

Spoon and Mouly were shocked at Fiker's transformation. Spoon thought he saw fire leap from Fiker's eyes.

Fiker took advantage of Mouly's amazement. Spying the pick-axe that had been promiscuously strewn with the other implements at the bottom of the steps, he lunged for the axe, grabbed it with both hands and stood up swiftly in one flowing movement. With a swooping, crashing blow, he rammed the point into Mouly's skull, splitting his head in two pieces, exposing gnarled grey matter beneath the gaping bloody crevice and lop siding Mouly's eyes and expression. The body twitched its nerve endings and stood for a full three seconds, then accepting death, collapsed in a heap. Blood and brains gushed like a fountain onto the steps and splattered Fiker and Spoon, who fell to the ground in a faint.

Fiker seethed at an unhearing Mouly. "Just remember, I killed you in self-defense. You were planning to do me for a long time. Well, how's this for a reversal of fortune? Ha, ha, ha." He threw down the pick axe and watched the dark fluid seep from the huge crevice in Mouly's head. He watched in the moonlight as Mouly's life soaked the grass from shadowed-green to black-red, searing the brown earth in deep rust.

"Spoon." Fiker stood over the yellow craybob who had crumpled like a pussy. He thought of taking the axe and braining him, but Spoon had always stuck up for Fiker, been nice to him. Spoon would be glad he did in the bastard. Mouly was hated by everyone. He had done the world a big favor, even had increased their take for the evening's haul. More for all of them. How could Spoon object?

As the wind kicked up and blew the clouds away from the moon, the light penetrated the darkness, and Fiker regained his senses and surveyed his handiwork. He was confused. Softly, he called to Spoon who didn't appear to be breathing. He was terrified of himself, didn't want to be alone, while Spoon lay still on the ground. Fiker thought maybe Spoon died of a heart attack, died of fright. Moaning in upset, Fiker kicked Spoon in his right side, then kneeled on the ground and shook him. He wouldn't wake up. Something was wrong. Something was very wrong.

Near the entrance gates, standing on the ground with both hands on the sides of the shaky ladder, Peregrine found it impossible to climb the chains, though Mocha and Jake held it from the other side. "Something is wrong here. Maybe one of you should come over and hold it from this side, and then I'll be able to climb without it swinging and folding like this," Peregrine said, exasperated.

"Right. Then the ghoul will hold it for the person who is holding it for you." Jake laughed.

"Laugh if you want to. There is a ghoul in this place, and I saw him."

"All right, all right. You're safe now. We're here."

"You can say that. You're on the other side. I'm over here." Peregrine saw Jake's eyes widening like a bug's. He gasped and babbled and pointed in the distance. Terrified, Peregrine jerked her head around, expecting to see the weird, homeless man reaching out his bony fingers for her neck. The monuments and trees and bushes looked back at her against the backdrop of a dark-blue late-night sky. Jake's rollicking laughter pealed out in waves.

"Gottcha."

Peregrine looked at Mocha. "Why did we call him?"

"Cause I'm a parkour monkey." Jake leaped onto the fence, grasping the metal with both hands and feet and climbed up to the thick blankets which they had thrown over the barbed wire coil.

"Impressive."

"Show off. Anyone can do that." Mocha jeered.

Jake felt for barbs. Finding that none had come through the layers of heavy quilting, he swung his right leg over and sat astride the wire, balanced for a moment, then rolled on his stomach while his foot jabbed in space for the nearest rung of the ladder. The ladder swung crazily, and he almost careened to the ground; but Peregrine guided his foot to the top bar, then stabilized his position by standing on the bottom rung and grasping the ladder firmly on both sides. Jake bounded down the wooden slats and playfully collided into her and hugged her as both tumbled to the ground, laughing.

Mocha heard the howling first, deep, long and penetrating whoops. Jake stopped laughing and looked in the direction of the trees. Peregrine scrambled to her feet and grabbed Jake's arm tugging him to his feet.

"Hurry up. Hurry up." Mocha said fiercely, shaking the fence for emphasis. "It's coming this way."

"Go. Go." Jake shoved Peregrine to the ladder and held it steady, as she began her climb. "Hurry. Hurry."

Peregrine pressed down on the blankets and vaulted one leg over to straddle the fence as Jake swung crazily on the ladder making little progress.

"Oh my God." Mocha pointed in the distance. Beams of light were flashing crazily, and dark figures were running. The wailing intensified; another man's voice screeched and hollered in terrible cacophony.

Motivated by his survival instinct and panic, a rush of adrenalin electrified Jake up the ladder, steadying it with pressure from his torso. He leaped to the top rung and swung his leg over to join Peregrine straddling the quilting. In his haste, he knocked her crazily forward then caught her from plunging to the ground on her head. There was only room for one on the blankets.

"Swing your other leg over and perch. Then jump. Can't you jump from there?" Jake's panic was furious with urgency.

"I'm afraid."

"Hurry, they're coming. Hurry." Mocha was terrorized.

"Forget the ladder. Grab onto the blankets. The barbed wire will hold them. Turn around, roll on your stomach, hold onto the blankets and jump free."

Peregrine listened to Jake's instructions while Mocha watched in the distance for the running figures. The screeching had stopped as had the crazy crisscrossing light beams. The cemetery was quiet once more. But that meant nothing. The monstrous lamenting might begin at any moment to terrify her. She thought she must go crazy or join the men crying in their dreadful release. She had kept still, but she heard their pandemonium in her mind.

Peregrine grabbed the blankets fastened to the wire coil by the barbs. She let gravity pull her down while she held on, and then jumped the remaining four feet to the ground as Mocha spotted her.

Now Jake straddled the blanket atop the barbed wire. He was beginning to roll forward on his stomach when something caught the corner of his eye. At that moment, Mocha who was facing the cemetery saw the shadowy figure racing up to the fence. It was holding a pick-axe.

"Jake, leap. Jump!" Mocha shrilled.

Jake rolled over the wire and dropped just as he heard the dull sound of metal on metal scraping the fence. He grabbed the blanket on the way down to soften his fall. Mocha and Peregrine tried to catch him, but he crashed to the ground with a painful thud, landing on his right side. As Peregrine helped him up, Mocha wailed. Peregrine and Jake looked at her. Mocha edged the fence, too paralyzed to move. She shrieked dread, mesmerized as she watched the shadow slam the pick-axe through the fence holes, plunging the point nearer and nearer to her face. Peregrine dragged Mocha away and slapped her to stop her animal cries. The wild figure whose face remained in shadow plunged the axe into the chain links with clanging danger until finally, he ripped a long gash in the metal mesh. Mocha shrieked and hallooed with increasing intensity. Her dread encouraged the snarling madman who banged and tore the metal, widening the gash with violent strokes intending to plunge through it and axe them all.

Something had gotten into Peregrine, something she didn't understand. Fury? Anger? Righteous anger. She picked up Mocha's flashlight from the ground, marshaled her determination and stalked to the fence. She shined the light beam directly at the shadowy, dark- haired maniac. He halted, axe raised in the air, as the light slammed into his face, brightening it. Eyes, sad and plaintive stared back at her. They looked vaguely familiar. They looked like the weird, homeless man's eyes, the eerie man she had run into hours ago.

"In the Name of everything that's Holy, I command you to leave." Peregrine was adamant.

Startled, the creature-man demoniac glared into her eyes and dropped the upraised pick- axe to the ground. He bowed his head, and his body seemed to wither and shrink. Without a word or even a grunt, he turned abruptly and trotted off toward the depths of Division C, his dark figure evanescing against the black trees and monuments, indistinguishable in the graveyard panorama.

Peregrine realized she was trembling. She shined the flashlight back to Jake whose arms were around Mocha; her head buried in his chest.

"Who or what was he?" Jake panted, grateful to hold on to Mocha to comfort her and himself.

"I don't know."

"He was a ghoul. A devil. There are such things, you know." Jake was serious, suddenly a believer. "Funny, when you commanded him, like you really believed what you were saying, all panic left me. And I was furious but felt bad for him. He's crazy. He probably hangs out at cemeteries and bays at the full moon. Scary!"

Mocha lifted her head up, still clinging to Jake. "I couldn't move. I would have stood there, and he would have brained me and split open my skull."

Peregrine was inarticulate, unable to define the wellspring of calm she felt confronting the maniac. "I... my reaction to him... just... happened... like swerving a car to avoid an accident."

"I'd say it was a supernatural reaction! A sort of spiritual parkour of the soul." Jake's humor was back.

The three friends laughed. But Peregrine turned once more and shined a beam of light through the iron rungs of the entrance gates of Old Calvary. All was silent and grave. Even the nocturnal animals, birds and insects had been stilled. She breathed a sigh of relief as she joined Jake and Mocha and walked to the car.

Jake stopped and turned to Peregrine. "What about the blankets and ladder?"

Peregrine shifted her back-pack. "Leave them. I have a hunch the madman will make use of them. Let's get out of here before he returns. He's not alone." Peregrine shuddered. A skeleton reached in his bony, claw fingers and squeezed her heart.

As they neared the car, Jake's jokes drew Mocha away from her terrors, while Peregrine retreated into herself. This would be the last time she would visit Old Calvary. Madeline would have to understand about the missing artifacts. She would make her understand. She would never return. She had learned her lesson. Let the dead bury the dead. She wanted to live.

Twenty minutes after Peregrine in her Mercedes followed Mocha and Jake in his Camaro, winding around Laurel Road away from Old Calvary, the dead, indeed, were burying the dead. In the grove of trees below the rise of the Johnson crypt, an exhausted, emotionally deadened Battery slammed his shovel in the soft ground underneath a huge oak tree. As he tapped it with his right foot deeper into the rich dark grains and lifted up a portion of earth slinging it to the left of the hole he was carving, he nearly broke down. To the right of the hole, twin halves of Mouly's head were cradled together in a pile of blood-soaked leaves.

Upon his return to the crypt, from a distance of ten yards away, Battery knew something had gone wrong. Fiker and Spoon were missing. Mouly lay on the ground, his face clotted with gore, gazing up at the black, tangled web-work of thick tree branches above his head. Upon closer inspection, Battery was shocked to see that Mouly's right eye had been knocked out from the impact of a blow which had split his skull open, seeped thick, dark blood and lighter brain matter into the indigo light. Battery shuddered at Mouly's grisly, misaligned expression: the empty eye socket on one side of the bloody chasm was higher than the right eye which glazed death, as it traversed the vacuum of eternal oblivion. Who had done this? Battery thought of the other recent death at the Johnson crypt. This place was malignant, foul. He never should have insisted the others meet him here.

As he dug, Battery refused to glance in the direction of the mangled mess. He was frightened and upset. Next to Mouly's head, Battery had placed his right eye which he had eventually found after a fifteen-minute search. Alongside the small, slippery globe, he nestled Mouly's hands and his feet with the boots still laced. He had hacked them off along with the head. A razor sharp machete carried in the motorized cart had made the job easy. The evidence of Mouly's identity must be destroyed, but he had no time to burn it or dump it in the river. Burial would have to do.

As he dug, he looked over his shoulder, trying to shake the impression that something or someone watched him. He hated being alone with his thoughts, normally. Now, his nerves twigged and jangled if an insect stirred or a mouse scampered. He felt he would explode with panic, wanted to throw down and run far away, where his dark deeds would never find him out. Instead, he whimpered and fumed, a captive of chaos, anarchy's clown. If he could get through Mouly's burial, he could recoup and conduct the business of the evening as planned, load the cart with the other cargo, haul it off to the parking lot where it would be transported to the final drop-off and receive payment. Others were waiting. As much as he felt to ditch and save himself like Spoon and Fiker had done, he must finish the job alone. He must redirect his panic. Then he could make decisions about whether to continue in this line of work which was growing more dangerous by the second.

As the night wound down toward close, Battery cursed a string of foul epithets in accompaniment with the sounds of the shovel biting into the earth. His mind had shifted from fear to anger and the shock and horror of Mouly's mutilation gave way to rationality. As the sun stretched her fingers toward the east, an idea pulled Battery's consciousness into calculating calm. Mouly had been slaughtered not by a ghoul or supernatural monster. He had been destroyed by the beast that enjoyed killing, and it came in human form. He remembered the bloodied pick-axe behind the hedges. Obviously, there had been a fight. Between whom? Spoon was a peacemaker. He recalled former fights and tensions between Mouly and Fiker. And Mouly hated that Fiker was Battery's loyal second. So, the pieces fit together. What had occurred was a natural outgrowth of their animosity and the macabre work of the cemetery. Probably Fiker had brained Mouly, and Spoon tried to stop him. Frightened, they had run like cowards, leaving Battery to clean the mess.

Clever, the perfect crime, Mouly murdered with impunity. He wouldn't turn in Spoon and Fiker. What questions could be answered without incrimination? It would mean an end to the three teams' illegal, covert business. Take the body and dump it elsewhere, leaving evidence to incriminate Fiker and Spoon? Not an option. Body remains were always a problem, though investigators were notoriously lame despite the advances of forensic science in criminology. He knew from friends in law enforcement that investigations weren't as simple and conclusive as they appeared to be on *CSI*. Fiker and Spoon knew he wouldn't risk all betting on a criminalist's incompetence.

No. Fiker and Spoon anticipated that Battery would deal with Mouly's killing as if it never happened. Mouly would have gone missing from this night onward, his identity scuppered, his remains scattered. Missing persons must stay missing, so no evidence merged with cold case files, which always had the potential of becoming hot. This was especially true where Mouly was concerned; his prints, scars, DNA could be traced, since he had served six months at Rikers for larceny. No gore could remain to be connected with Mouly. The hole had to be deep enough so hungry animals wouldn't dig up the head, hands and feet. To make sure there would be no problems, he would come back to the cemetery next week to dig up the identifying parts and cover them with lime to dissolve them. Then he would bury them in a safer location or encase them in quick-drying cement and scuttle them off a boat in the Atlantic Ocean.

Battery stopped to rest. His back ached and burned. He wasn't used to black work. He measured the depth of the excavation with the length of the shovel. More digging. It still wasn't deep enough! He was meticulous about preparation, obsessive about organization, a professor of Murphy's Law. He worked out the hundred ways to screw up, running them through his mind like a statistical program. Afterward, he made adjustments. He minimized the monstrous threat of randomness like a researcher, holding for variables in a science experiment. Randomness brought hurried, bad decisions which brought on errors, which often were impossible to amend. In the realm of error, one had to rely on luck not to get jammed. And luck trended like the weather, unpredictably. There was no way to gauge when it would turn. The signs deceived. And when luck turned, you were left to the mercy of the elements. In this line of work, the mercy of the elements was even more unreliable than luck and the weather's unpredictability. It propelled you into the rough seas of karma and justice which were synonymous with anarchy and chaos. Battery felt sick. He would be forced to live in the shadow of uncertainty and the anarchy of the night's events for which he did not and could not prepare. All this brought on by the foul weather created by Fiker, Mouly and Spoon who wanked up the job, betrayed him like a pussy and flung him to the whirlwinds. Murphy's Law proved true. The something that could go wrong did.

Plotting revenge, Battery tried to soothe himself. He would turn over Fiker and Spoon, spreading the word that they were hot-headed wild cards and double crossers. But maybe he shouldn't involve the other teams. It heightened the risk of exponentially multiplying mistakes. And regardless, the fallout would rain down on him. Yet, unchecked, Spoon and Fiker were very dangerous. They must be dealt with. And soon. He would call upon efficient expediters outside the three teams' sphere of influence.

With sighing resolve, he switched to the present task. One half hour to bury the gore, get a container for Mouly's remains and deal with the cargo. It was nearing 5:00 AM. The sky was lightening, the greater the likelihood of being seen leaving the cemetery. He would be late for the drop-off. Quinn would be steaming because the operation was an hour behind. More mistakes and cover-ups and an ever-widening spiral of chaos. Would it never end?

"Bleedin', craybobs! No one does this to Battery. No one!" he muttered under his breath as he excavated the hole deeper and deeper, down, down, to the other side of the world, away from the sour, foul stench of anarchy.

After ten more minutes of digging, Battery judged the hole to be about five feet deep. Separately, he picked up Mouly's head, hands, eyeball and feet and dumped each in the pit. He scraped portions of the mound of earth back into the cavity, gradually covering the bloody refuse that had been his colleague. After he had filled in the excavation, he tamped down the earth so that it was level with the surrounding area. He picked up handfuls of leaves and twigs and carelessly scattered them over Mouly's grave until the spot looked undisturbed. Then he trudged back toward the mausoleum in the dawn to haul the cargo to the parking lot in the motorized cart and through the gates of Old Calvary, gates which he would open with a duplicate of the caretaker's keys.

Battery grumbled with his exertions, infuriated with himself that things were so bad. He must think positively, glass half-full, not half-empty. He would reap the rewards and glam the full share of the profits. After Fiker and Spoon went missing, he would receive a finder's fee for their cargo. But he didn't need the extra money. He needed peace of mind. Anarchy and error were lurking, waiting to do him in. Worst of all, he had to find and train a new team. It could take months, another setback that could threaten the whole operation. In mental torment, Battery zipped up Mouly's torso in the body bag and lifted it into the cart. His life was a misery.

From two hundred yards away, the demon in Fiker watched Battery drive the cart toward the cemetery entrance. He gloated and chortled over Battery's inner hell and his success in derailing Battery's plans. He wouldn't go after him now when the diffusion of light was spreading across the eastern sky. He didn't have full power in the daylight. When he lured Battery to the graveyard in a month when the time was ripe, the Powers would be active for sacrifice and rebirth. Then his colleague would be whole for a short season of the moon's cycle. During that time, they must quickly locate another vulgarian for possession, or Abracix would become a slave of the Johnson mausoleum, consigned to do its bidding.

Fiker had lost an opportunity to gain Spoon's trust after Spoon had regained consciousness. The cretin had become hysterical and anticipating doom had scuttled away. He had run after, coaxing him to wait, assuring him that he wouldn't be harmed, but Spoon was paranoid. When the time was right, Spoon would have to be enticed and lured to the cemetery. This wouldn't be easy. He didn't have Spoon's address or even know his last name. As a protection in case someone from their crew was caught, nicknames were used to keep each of them anonymous from the others since they all lived respectable lives in the daytime. Battery was their contact. Only Battery knew their personal information to make the arrangements for a haul. It was he they got in touch with when there was a problem. He would get Spoon's or another's address from Battery, another empty, pitiless vulgar, whose soul was hollow to the core. The possession would be easy, and Abracix would have secured a human habitation, adhering to the requirements of the Law of Powers.

Oxelox smiled to himself. He could read Battery's thoughts, could pull information from his mind psychically. He knew what Battery had planned for him. It would be poetic justice for Battery to be the sacrifice, beat the fool at his own game. Until then, he, in his new habitat would act as Fiker by day and Oxelox at dusk, haunting the tombs by night, tormenting whatever prey he could, like those at the fence. He would save Battery as the prize to be offered up at 3:00 AM.

Upon this resolve, the demon settled into the nether regions of Fiker's soul and allowed Fiker's consciousness to emerge and take control. Fiker awakened as if from a dream sleep. He found himself resting on the ground, leaning against a monument with a brightening sky illuminating the graveyard in pale hues. He couldn't remember anything after he fell asleep on the mausoleum steps, couldn't recall how he ended up in this strange section of a different cemetery division. Spoon and Mouly had vanished, and he was alone. He couldn't even remember if he had helped the others with the haul. All he knew was that he was depressed and utterly exhausted. He felt lost and alone. And he hated his life, like he had never hated it before.

Fiker walked with his head down, his soul a witches' stew of noxious feelings. He instinctively navigated through Division C, away from Old Calvary's gates, back to the lot where he and Spoon had parked their cars by Division B. It was a long, tiresome journey, and he felt he was traveling across a separate universe that he couldn't navigate or become accustomed to. He could barely wait to arrive home to his apartment in Long Island City and Maryanne, his girlfriend. Only she had the power to soothe him and staunch the fires of his emotional inferno.

Six miles away in the peace and beauty of Forest Hills Gardens, Peregrine unlocked the back door and entered the kitchen with Mocha following close behind. They had said goodbye to Jake after breakfasting at the T-Bone Diner on Queens Boulevard, one half-mile from Peregrine's home. It was now six o'clock in the morning and Peregrine had been without sleep for twenty-four hours. She was getting used to living with exhaustion. Mocha, having napped before Peregrine messaged her, was wide awake.

"Well, what do you think?"

Peregrine yawned a huge gaping yawn and stretched her arms upward to stay focused on Mocha's idea, then released them to drop in a slap at her side. "You would sacrifice your relationship with your mother and Reggie?"

"A relationship built on deceit and manipulation is no relationship."

"You've just negated about three-quarters of the human relationships on the planet." Peregrine threw the door keys in the utility drawer of the center island and plopped herself on a stool at the granite topped counter.

Mocha pulled out the stool next to hers and sat looking at her friend with confidence. "My mother will come around after a time, once she's free from Reggie's web."

"Do you have enough money to bring with you?"

"I can always get a job with my skills after my savings runs out. I did take Italian and Spanish in college, you know."

"My mom can help, if you're in a squeeze. And I bet Sylvia would bankroll you, too."

"It would have to be done in such a way that it's not traceable. Otherwise it would look like she bribed the key witness for the prosecution to disappear."

"Well, if they are stupid enough to push through an indictment in the next few days, the prosecution will look like fools. What case will they have without you? If the indictment is still pending and they find out you've left, they'll have to vacate."

"Unless they attempt extradition. But they won't know where I am. I'll be lost in Italy. I have to deal in cash transactions. Before we arrive in Italy, maybe we should take a circuitous route through all the countries that don't have extradition treaties with the US."

"You mean like Iran, Afghanistan, Libya and the Sudan?"

"Ha, Ha. Wait. What are we thinking? They don't extradite witnesses, only criminals. You see what Reggie and my mother have done to me? They've made me think that I'm criminal for defying them and the prosecution. I've been oppressed not to think and act for myself." Mocha slapped her hand on the counter for emphasis. "Peregrine, my decision is firm. I want to go with you and your mom. It'll be a statement to Reggie and my mom. I won't do your bidding. You're on your own."

"Well, we have a lot to do if we're leaving day after tomorrow. Let's rest for a few hours. After, I'll call my mom. She'll be thrilled." Peregrine slipped off the kitchen stool and pushed it under the counter. "I've got to crash."

"Me too. The strain is going to be overwhelming. I need all the rest I can get."

Mocha lifted herself from the stool to join Peregrine who slowly moved up the stairs, her every muscle aching for sleep.

Chapter Thirty-Eight

The digital alarm blared with intransigence in the shade darkened bedroom. Taut muscles rippled under cool, silk sheets, and a firm, wiry arm shot out from underneath their softness to smash down the snooze button of the clock-radio, whose luminescent green dial fogged 4:45 AM. Once, just once, he agonized, I would like to be awakened by natural sunlight or a day already in full bloom. But such were the hazards of an early makeup call, the price of fame and the compulsion to hustle every waking moment to feed the wheel of destiny threshing out his soul. This frenzy would cease when he achieved the American equivalent of British knighthood for actors: establishing a profitable non-profit organization, having his life and career memorialized on Turner Classic Movies or AME.

Fen groaned into his abdomen and stretched his arms in a ninety-degree angle to his body. He tightened his hands into a fist, then lit out a lightning fast left upper cut, undergirded by two right jabs, blows to the chest of an imaginary opponent. He continued to shadow box with the atmosphere above his bed for another minute, fully awakening himself, then drew away the silky sheets, bent his legs and jumped out of bed. He dropped to the floor and finished forty push- ups in rapid succession, clapping in between each press into the Oriental rug, as the schedule of his day's events paraded through his consciousness.

During lunch, there was an on-set interview and publicity shoot for *GQ*. Dinner was at 6:45 PM with his agent and an up-and-coming producer. Then there was a sit-down with Bob, his acting coach at 9:00 PM for the next day's scene. He would work out in his trailer between takes and set ups, and maybe Bob could come to the location in Brooklyn and work with him there. He'd message him before he left for work.

Events in his career had snowballed after the news conference at Madeline's lawyer's office one month ago. According to his agent, any free publicity was like a multi-million dollar account in the Caymans, and this advice proved to be true. The offers for TV, films and commercials had increased, as had his work schedule once he finished his then current job. On the advice of his agent, two days ago, he had hired a manager to read scripts and handle publicity, and an assistant, to read and answer his emails and update his websites and Social Media. Two weeks before, he had hired a personal manager, an old college buddy, to handle the intimate affairs of his life, his apartment, bills, laundry, dry cleaning, groceries and daily schedule. Most importantly, Sam had kept abreast of the investigation and was a liaison to Detectives Dietz and Allan. Fen didn't know what he would do without Sam to shore up the breaches in his personal life.

After his shower, Fen toweled off, brushed his teeth and quickly blew dry his hair. Back in his bedroom, he plucked his cell phone from the nightstand and messaged Bob and Sam, who had a key to his apartment, and would be arriving there about 9:00 AM to do odds and ends. He quick checked his emails without reading them. There was one from Beach Comber and another from Jane, an actress in LA. Two months ago, before the convergence of the spheres of fortune and destiny, he would have read and answered both immediately, but he was out of time. He would have Sam phone Beach Comber and maybe bring him to Brooklyn in the afternoon. At least, he would be able to see his friend and catch him up, maybe even get him a job. After all notoriety, regardless of the extent of infamy, was the coin of the realm in America.

Fen pulled on his jeans and selected a simple white shirt to show off his tan, dark hair and blue eyes. He tucked in the shirt, zipped up the pants and buttoned the waist, then the shirt front. His life had taken off like a space shuttle flight to Mars, while his friends' lives were like a snail's sledging forward across a sun-beaten, concrete highway. But appearances might be deceiving. While he rode the jet stream, his inner life was at a standstill, fogbound in the shallows. Only his brother's disappearance connected him with his inner self which had become a dull agony of regret gnawing away the faith that something, any day now, would turn up about Liam, the investigation or Manny's disappearance.

On the other hand, Beach Comber, released yesterday after serving his sentence for violating the court order, had languished in prison with only the deepest determination and inner strength to keep him from shattering into a mental and emotional collapse. His inner life was flourishing from the ordeal that had made him stronger. Each time Fen had talked to him, Comber was peaceful, uplifted. Occasionally, he would have blackouts, and he still couldn't remember the events surrounding the incident at the cemetery, but he was in excellent emotional health and planning his next surfing trek and articles about being a virtual surfer jailbird.

Fen imagined Comber had been heartened by the news of Mocha's loyalty, though her disappearance hadn't inspired the DA to send home the grand jury. The key witness had left the US and would never allow herself to be used in a trial against Beach Comber. However, his attorney said the grand jury was still accepting testimony, and the DA continued the investigation, in a vain attempt to manipulate the results, making it appear that there was enough evidence to indict him on an attempted manslaughter charge or at the very least, sexual assault. Through his connections in the DA's office, Comber's attorney heard that there had been a flurry of activity to rush through an indictment against him until the prosecution discovered that their hostile witness had vanished. Elizabeth had received a letter from Mocha who was vacationing in Tangier, Morocco.

Fen chuckled. Through her connections, Madeline probably had worked out the postmark. At present, no one really knew if they were in Europe or Africa, though Fen knew Peregrine would eventually call him from a public phone in Tangier or Paris when he least expected it. If the prosecution was desperate enough, perhaps they would try to use the assistance of the FBI and INTERPOL to locate Peregrine, Madeline and Mocha; and that was why he had not heard from them after Peregrine messaged him from Kennedy before they left. Regardless, Mocha was beyond the reach of the DA's office and her family's influence. Once the grand jury discovered that they were waiting for a phantom witness, they would return a No True Bill, and Beach Comber's horrors would be over, except for Elizabeth's civil suit. But the Comber was confident he would be exonerated, as he was confident that heads would roll as a consequence of his lawsuit against Reggie and the DA. Though the money didn't matter to Comber, his reputation had been ruined, and Sylvia was gunning for four pounds of flesh.

Fen looked at himself in the mirror and brushed his hair. He preferred it long, but this suited the character, a redeemed Madison Avenue type. Grabbing the script and his briefcase that held his laptop and phone, he let himself out of his apartment and locked both dead bolts. He didn't have time to eat anything and would get an iced chai latte at the Starbucks on the corner before he caught the train to Brooklyn.

As he rode down the elevator of his West End Avenue apartment building, Fen made a mental note to have Sam call Dietz and Allan to check the latest information they had received, if any, from INTERPOL. Ironically, like Peregrine, Madeline and Mocha who left the US, the villain of the Southampton mansion had submerged either in Europe or Asia. His disappearance, since he was wanted for questioning, gave credence to Fen's story. Would an innocent man flee the country? Upon further investigation after contacting the Johnstone family, Dietz and Allan had discovered that the head servant identified as "Liam" was not the same man the Johnstones had hired to oversee their household while they were vacationing in Europe. From photographs and Mr. Johnstone's description, detectives discovered that the real Liam was an older gentleman with an Irish accent and thinning red hair.

After the detectives had notified Mr. Johnstone of their concerns that the man he had hired was not at the estate and others, perhaps thieves, squatted there, Mr. Johnstone had sent his Manhattan attorney to investigate. The attorney had found the place locked and deserted and had discovered that family heirlooms, the silver tea set, the silver cutlery, the silver coffee urn and trays were missing. The detectives surmised those items easily could be fenced. Fen had gone out to the estate with the detectives to search for any signs of Manny. They found none. If he had been there, all traces of his presence had been wiped away.

Over the past month, Fen, Dietz and Allan pieced together the situation with "Liam." Since no one from the Southampton police knew the original Liam, they wouldn't be able to identify the masquerader as a fraud. The detectives and police had been duped by a clever scam artist who was confident that they wouldn't confirm his physical identity with Mr. Johnstone. The irony that the Southampton police legitimized and supported the deceiver's false identity was not lost on the detectives or Fen. However, the media proved to be "Liam's" undoing. With various digital photographers and reporters on the doorstep producing streaming video clips, there were those amongst the viewing public who would know the original servant from the fake. Fearing that he and his cronies were about to be exposed, "Liam" fled the country. Traveling under his real name or with a false passport and visa would make it difficult to find any records of his transit out of the country. Only his sub rosa international chartering of a jet, if that individual indeed was "Liam," a fact as yet unconfirmed, held a clue to his real identity and his and Manny's whereabouts, if Manny had not perished in the explosion.

As Fen cleared the building and headed toward Broadway and Starbucks, he considered the initial angst and frustration of being doubted by the police and detectives. So much time and effort had been wasted trying to get them to listen. Finally, he had been vindicated and his testimony believed, and as a result, Fen had grown very close to the two detectives who trusted the accuracy of his testimony. He or Sam spoke with the men at least three times a week, rehashing and evaluating events in the hope of turning up something any of them might have overlooked.

But the wheels of the investigation had been stalled, and Fen always seemed to be wading through postponements and cancellations and rescheduling. The detectives had to reschedule the questioning of the Johnstone's attorney three times after their second search of the estate. And they were still waiting for the international charter pilot to contact them. To add to the delay, the results of the NTSB's investigation of the helicopter crash were inconclusive. Since there was no record of the flight plan, it was unknown who was piloting the copter. But they believed there were three victims who had been incinerated by the explosion, their identities unconfirmed. This was consistent with Fen's eyewitness account. Though there was suspicion the crash was not an accident, federal investigators theorized that a spark from a faulty wire had ignited fuel from a leaking fuel tank. There was a probability that other incendiaries were involved since the fireball was particularly intense. The investigation had been reassigned to the FBI's special explosives unit.

Despite the lack of evidence to the contrary, the detectives now agreed with Fen that there was a fifty percent likelihood that Manny was not on board, a speculation which left more questions unanswered. Had Manny been killed and his body dumped elsewhere? Or was he still alive and being held by "Liam" or others to be trafficked in the black market human slave trade? Had Liam taken him to Europe or Asia? Was he in the United States? Or had Manny been abducted by someone else entirely? Underlying the mystery of Manny's disappearance was Fen's and the detectives' growing trepidation that Manny was alive and had been trafficked for his strength and child-like mind. Someone like Manny would never try to escape; he was an innocent who would do as he was told.

In an attempt to continue building a case against the imposter, Dietz had come up with the plan to circulate Manny's and "Liam's" photos at ports of entry in countries with reciprocal treaties with the US and their law enforcement agencies. Mr. Johnstone had filed grand larceny charges against "Liam," and he was officially wanted for questioning in Manny's kidnapping/murder. Law enforcement was hampered since they didn't know "Liam's" true identity, but the FBI notified INTERPOL. All the material information, including Manny's physical records and the photos of both men had been sent. Allan countered that there were black market ports all over the world that were not monitored, ports through which humans, drugs and weapons were trafficked. The likelihood that "Liam," his crew and a pliant Manny slipped through one of these to weave like invisible flotsam and jetsam amongst the world's teaming masses explained why the photos and information yielded few leads.

Fen sighed as he entered Starbucks. Too little too late. His only hope was that through the media and internet, someone would recognize Manny if he was alive, and they would contact him. This most of all spurred on his ambition to accelerate his career ascendancy to become a household name. As his fame increased, so would his global media campaign to find his brother.

Hell, if he discovered that Manny had been trafficked, he'd use his celebrity to intensify international efforts against the human slave trade. He had to increase the pressure through his website, YouTube postings, Social Media and his blogs.

Thus far, he had some international online leads which he turned over to the detectives who turned them over to INTERPOL, though some of the tipsters were crackpots. A few had sighted Manny in England. All they needed was confirmation from Dietz's pilot friend that England was the destination and "Liam" was his passenger, and they would be on their way;

that, and an official determination that C-4 or some incendiary, caused the helicopter's massive explosion. The gravitas of the latter finding would elevate the crash to the level of terrorism, and the powers of the Patriot Act would be invoked. Then INTERPOL would issue a Red Notice, and internationally, the search would be stepped up. Ironically, Fen had been opposed to the curtailing of civil liberties the Patriot Act authorized. He objected to the way its passage had been rammed through Congress with three quarters of the House and Senate not even reading the legislation. But now he would be grateful if it could be used to help him find his brother. For Fen, as for most, expediency spoke louder than principle.

Fen grabbed his latte from the counter and sipped it as he walked toward the entrance. He glanced at his watch. He was running late. Plopping *The Times* under his arm, he smacked the door open. He turned right and ran half a block down the empty street toward the subway. He skipped down the steps leaping them two at a time and entered the complex, cavernous New York City underground. Furious at himself for allowing his thoughts to overwhelm him and turn him into a sloth, he raced to the turnstile as he heard the squeal of the train breaking in the station. Dammit! This latest film project was crucial to his plan to accelerate his career for one purpose: to discover where Manny was. He must not screw it up.

Chapter Thirty-Nine

Darkness was upon the face of the deep, but no voice proclaimed, "Let there be light!" Hope drained from Battery who lay on the ground by the bushes on the far side of the Johnson mausoleum. It leaked from his vast and essential network of vessels, like the dribble from a crack in the wall of a levee which seeps slowly at first but with each accumulated drop of fluid, builds force and broadens its flow, then augments in a gushing current which has no turning, but pools in an ever-widening circle of destruction, until the entire structure gives way and crumbles. Battery lay quiet, willing his mind to bring cessation, to initiate a massive clotting of blood from the veins of both arms that had been slashed at the wrist, to stem the seepage at his throat which had been lacerated sufficiently to produce a dependable, prolonged, nerve-racking ooze. He was human after all, and he did not want to die. But he had no choice. Fiker had chosen for him. And his own body, over which he had lost control, had become his master. Like a slave, he must bend to its commands to ebb into eternity or oblivion, whichever would be the reality for him.

In his last moments, Battery saw all. He saw the futility of his life. He saw the chances he had been given and had squandered. Grace stood before him and chastened him with a multitude of love he had despised and the opportunities he had wasted to apply his energy to make a difference. He had tossed his chances into a sea of detritus, made salty with the tears now flowing from his eyes. Waste, for there was no turning back! He had had his final chance and blew it when he had arranged for a disposal unit to clean up Fiker. His naturally suspicious and meticulous nature had been thwarted, and his plan had collapsed in on him. Now, he was the mess being cleaned-up. The double-crosser had been spectacularly double-crossed, and it was Fiker who looked down upon him, gloating, victorious. If he could pray to God for absolution, if he could touch the heavens with his regret, grasp a filament of faith, be redeemed, but he could not. His mind was as soundless as his throat, and all he could muster was a dumb mouthing as he wept, Fiker's fool.

With the curious objectivity of the lab technician, dispassionately investigating and recording the signs of humanity's waning toward death, the demon in Fiker waited, and watched, pleased with his cleverness. The ebbing blood tide soon would cease, and he and his companion would use the proceeds to improve their spiritual lifestyle. Fiker's body was as good as any other house of inhabitation, though he found Fiker's mind occasionally trundled into goodness with his mother, sister and girlfriend. To compensate, the demon had to torment Fiker into a heroin addiction to mask its inherently wicked and cruel attitudes. His war of attrition against Fiker's loving family ground the women into impatient and frustrated shrikes enslaved to Fiker's bottomless needs. Aggression storms repeatedly broke the peace of the household, and Fiker, with increasing guilt and depression, distanced himself from them, which was perfect for the demon. Fiker's long absences into the unconsciousness of addiction and clinical depression and his increasing alienation from family vacated his logic and made his body a lethargic, insensate heap. At these times, the demon returned to the cemetery, where he kept his partner company through his terrible despair of being without the power and the authority of his head. But according to the Law of the Powers, this evening would ensure that his companion would be made whole again as the last drop of Battery's blood flooded the mausoleum steps.

Battery's eyelids fluttered. He focused all his strength to open his mouth and beg Fiker for help. But he was afraid to speak, knowing any stir would thrust his blood outward in a rush, while death crept in, filling the vacuum created by the pouring onslaught. Battery's eyes, roaming upward and around in desperation, locked with Fiker's for a second. He saw it was no use to beg or plead. A vast ice storm had frozen his being beyond human compassion. Fiker was in the abyss of darkness, moving toward its outer canyons.

In a last effort of despair, Battery's mind became lucid. He found his heart soften like an opening bud. In earnest, he prayed silent words Fiker could not hear, words he himself did not fathom, words that extended out to the universe, out beyond all life and consciousness, out to the realm of Eternal Spirit. He prayed with surprising eloquence in his aloneness as

Death entered, the inertia of Battery's body no longer willed by his mind but by the organs screaming for the oxygen denied to them. At these last few seconds of life, his words reached up and touched the heart of God. This amoralist, this cruel and brutish beast, wept for the frailty of humanity. And as his tears watered his parched soul, returning him to the compassion of his own human need, Battery died.

As if on signal at the curtain closing his life, Battery's essence, piping through the blood that drenched the steps and soaked into the earth of the mausoleum threshold, vanished. Then his blood vanished. Then Battery vanished.

Oxelox gave a little scream of pure delight to see Abracix, headless no more, step from the shadowed hedges, where he had atrophied in his bondage but was now restored by Battery's blood. The two partners whispered in their dark spirit language and embraced. They leered up at their tormentor, Luna. The transit of the moon's eight phases was their timepiece. They must labor within twenty-eight days to obey the Law of Powers or suffer the twice cruel forfeit, this time with no escape.

The rest of this night they would plot and plan how they might entice Spoon to the graveyard, where he would be possessed. After the possession, they would lure another to the sacrifice. Again, blood would flow over the mausoleum threshold. Then they would recover the books in the crypt and the journal that held the magic spells and arcane secrets of ancient civilizations. The secrets would give them knowledge to upgrade their status and spiritual living quarters and possess and control finer minds, like the girl and woman who had overcome them and made them cower in fear. But for now, they would exult and celebrate their good fortune. They were together once more in power and authority.

Chapter Forty

Peregrine stood on the iron balcony of the two-hundred-year-old villa snuggled amidst the native Mediterranean shrubbery, Datura bushes and pines on top of the steep limestone cliff, that dropped 500 yards to the water below. Alone, she gazed out into the darkness of the Ionian Sea, watching two lights, one white, one red, at the bow and starboard of the small boat which cruised past, the faint hum of the motor barely audible. It was 5:00 AM, and she was thinking of the cemetery, the Johnson mausoleum, the horror of the labyrinth and her fight to escape death. It had been the most alive time of her life, straining every second against uncertainty and peril, wandering in the darkness, in the mud, in the filth of excrement and urine, freezing, thirsting, starving, and relying on her instincts and intuition to survive. Could she do it again? She had heard that one had the strength and courage to undergo such an ordeal once and could not do it a second time and survive.

A chill ran up her spine. When Death finally came for her, as she willed it, in old age, would she confront it with honor and succumb with dignity? Or would she go to war, and like in the Dylan Thomas poem, "Rage against the dying of the light?"

Peregrine stopped herself. This was not the cold, dark crypt. Why such morbid thoughts in this paradise retreat of sublime beauty? She was safe, in seclusion, far from the media, the mausoleum's ordeals, the labyrinth's oppression, the cemetery's ghouls and those weirdly accented men! Stony emotions shattered, and her soul fused with the electricity of life. God! She was bored beyond belief! That was it! The life of leisure and relaxation was not for her. She craved adventure and excitement. Maybe her mom and Mocha were happy to recuperate on their psychotropic meds, indulge their fantasies, meet young men and forget the past in this land of the Lotus eaters. She was not.

In the month after her last night at the cemetery, she had become edgier. Discontented with lounging at their pool and dining with new friends or chatting up guys they met at cappuccino bars, she spent her days investigating the historic sites and her nights wandering alone. Enough. At breakfast, she would encourage her mother to plan the itinerary for their journey up north. If she didn't inspire Madeline soon, they would be here forever in this padded cell oblivion. The money would never run out.

Thrilled with the anticipation of a new journey, Peregrine was in control once more. She had discovered an interesting element of her character, the necessity to discover, explore and challenge her life's alternate realities. Perhaps it was an inherent trait, this restless, wandering spirit. She recalled the dinner conversation about her name. Only this evening her mother had revealed that she was named by her maternal grandmother after a bohemian female ancestor from the fourteenth century, who had traveled the world, when women, like slaves, lived a narrow life, imprisoned in their homes. Her ancestor had wandered in caravans and on trade ships, facing perils disguised as a young boy. She had stayed true to the substance of her namesake, the Peregrine Falcon, the wanderer.

The blue-black darkness extended in an uninterrupted blanket across the sea. Peregrine glanced at the sparse, pink-hued lights on the cliff below her. Most of the populace had ended their partying and had gone to bed. She gripped the iron railing. People were their names. Selecting the right name for a child was an ancient folkway of humanity. Probably, her soul had ached to wander her entire life. But caught up in her mother's manipulation to provide her the comfortable security of privilege, a private school education, college, a lucrative career, her true nature had not emerged until she entered the mausoleum. Scales lifted from the eyes of her inner spirit, and she saw that her life was more imperiled than when she was physically dying in the labyrinth. She must take authority over her destiny, achieve fulfillment, the manifestation of Peregrine, wander like her namesake ancestor or rot away on the treacherous shoals of la dolce vita, living in a lassitude of lies. Hadn't she and the others tried to evoke the Law of Powers in the ceremony at the mausoleum to change their lives and embrace a new destiny? Her mother and the random events after her rescue had derailed her. And Mocha was completely lost. She could only save herself. Her inertia would end this night. She was worthy of a noble destiny. Her soul would not perish, succumbing to the boredom of inconsequential materialism, *measuring out her life with coffee spoons.*

She had been reborn in the labyrinth. She would continue to embrace all that the world and spirit in their colossal antagonism offered. In the next week, she would head to Torino, Italy, alone. She would locate the family with or without Madeline's help. And she would discover the truth of who she was. She would find out why Madeline was an emotional cripple who lived in fear of her ancestors, a fear so oppressive that it smothered the very essence of her life. She would bring reconciliation and restore her mother. But first, she would discover the significance of her family's history of blood and darkness.

Chapter Forty-One

In the blackest part of the mausoleum, deep in the room of statues, Battery stood impassively, a sad expression carved on his face, marble tears carved in the corners of his eyes. Immobilized, a stone figure amongst the stone figures populating the large, otherwise vacant wing of the Johnson crypt, Battery confronted the cruelty and barbarity of eternity. He was in a state of non-existence, oblivion's hell. Unable to weep, wail in torment or gnash his teeth, for emotional release is the foundation of one's identity in the world, he was no place: his being, understanding of himself, his perception of his own goodness, vacated. Without awareness of his condition, he would have experienced peace and forgetfulness, like the somnolence delivered by an opiate or the forgetfulness of Lethe Warf. But poor Battery had no peace. He was tormented by consciousness. His awareness of time's slow pace agonized him. The static emptiness of his condition horrified. Disengaged from the power of action, frozen in misery, moment by moment, he was forced to acknowledge his isolation in a cold, vacant universe. This was timelessness in time, absence in vacancy, his portion until the Judgment arrived to sweep him into the outer darkness.

The Master, a punisher who could move upon condition and strike as he had struck nearly two months before against the demon, oversaw his latest arrival with pleasure. His retinue of stone figures was growing, fueled by the rituals of the mausoleum. Their numbers would continue to increase until it was sufficient for him to move against the world of flesh. At that still point, the paradigm would shift, and the battle would begin. The struggle between the spiritual and material realms would fuse and become manifest. The rough beast was rising up, and he knew that the outcome was not fated, as had been foretold in the books. The books were written by false prophets. So, he would wait. Again, the blood would flow over the steps, onto the threshold, transmogrifying into a solid, stone warrior, one of many warriors who would exact a fitting oblivion for the human race…when the principalities, the powers, the rulers of the darkness of this world and the high-placed spiritually wicked would converge and come to the fullness of their time.

The Master gloated to think of it, and as his cruel grin curled wider into a grimace of irony, he gave the release to the wanderer of the skies. Upon the signal, there was a click, the faintest shuffle of movement, and the flutter of wings. Perched on the small turret to the right side of the mausoleum's cupola and camouflaged by an angel, guarding that side of the mausoleum, a large, marble Peregrine Falcon shuddered and shook off its somber and gruesome stony stance. It stretched each leg in a shattering and crumbling, and transformed into living, breathing flesh.

Strutting in the sublime joy of beauty and power, the falcon screamed a piercing cry of predation, fanned its great wings and lifted off into the indigo-black sky, jettisoning its home perch on the turret. It was hungry, and it craved the taste of warm, rich blood. Swiftly, round and round, upward and upward, it circled and hovered over the mausoleum, reveling in the strength of its wing beats and the coolness of the air, moving through its flight feathers. Unlike the mortal falcon, this Peregrine Falcon, the mascot of the mausoleum, was a predator of faith, its prey those humans filled with supernatural faith, the kind of faith that produced impossible results. Unlike its mortal counterpart, this Peregrine Falcon could dive, strike and explode its prey at the speed of lightening and carry it with an ease borne of ancient evil to far flung corners of the world.

Upward and upward, the Peregrine sped, hurtling over the cemetery as it fixed its course for the brilliant jeweled lights, shining from the dark towering structures of the vast stone city whose occupants were filled with the faith to do exploits. Intuitively, it flew across the river and headed for the two tall and graceful buildings with needle spires. There, the Peregrine knew it would find other falcons like itself and amongst them, it would stay for a season learning the language of flesh in spirit. If they were not exactly of its kind in purpose, they were in similitude of its outer form.

On the ledge of the building which bore the falcon profile, it would wait in the warm night for the signal to kill and bring the Master the richest, most savory spirit blood in all the world. The Master was hungry. The new stone warrior must be sanctified. Then following ritual, it would return to its home on the turret of the mausoleum to rest in stony sleep, until the next awakening of the Powers. Then once more, it would shatter its stone prison and wander the skies for Faith, delivered by The Blood.

AUTHOR'S NOTE

Though some of the names of the cemetery locales, sites, Long Island locations and streets referenced or described exist, their association or relation to actual persons or events as related here is coincidental. This is a work of fiction. There is no vast labyrinth underneath any of the cemeteries or mausoleums referenced. The history of the New York City Borough of Queens cemeteries may be found online or in pertinent reference books on the subject.

With one exception, nobody in this story, and no outfit or organizational entity, public or private is based upon an actual person, outfit or organizational entity in the real world. The exception is William Hamilton. I first became acquainted with the knowledge of the existence of William Hamilton (1773-1836) reading Ron Chernow's biography of *Alexander Hamilton*. In his "Acknowledgements" (735) Chernow states that "William Hamilton, a free black carpenter and a noted journalist and abolitionist before the Civil War, claimed to be Hamilton's son." Chernow investigated this prospect with a number of qualified individuals. After his exploration he remained dubious about William Hamilton's claims and stated "the paucity of evidence makes it impossible to deliver a final verdict" (735).

This tenuous and unproven claim of William Hamilton to be Alexander Hamilton's son was the inspiration for the characterizations of the Hamilton family in this novel. There is no truth to the assertions of ancestry by the characters: the "senile" great grandmother or her great granddaughter Elizabeth. Both characters are fictional and their relationship to William Hamilton and Alexander Hamilton is imagined.

C.M. Di Tosti

www.ingramcontent.com/pod-product-compliance
Lightning Source LLC
Chambersburg PA
CBHW030754260626
47169CB00001B/43